THE E.M. FORSTER FILM OMNIBUS

A ROOM WITH A VIEW

A PASSAGE TO INDIA

MAURICE

Other novels by the same author

Where Angels Fear to Tread
The Longest Journey
Howards End

THE E.M. FORSTER FILM OMNIBUS

A ROOM WITH A VIEW

A PASSAGE TO INDIA

MAURICE

HUTCHINSON
London Melbourne Auckland Johannesburg

This edition first published in 1987 by Hutchinson, an imprint of Century Hutchinson Ltd, Brookmount House, 62-65 Chandos Place, London WC2N 4NW

Century Hutchinson Australia Pty Ltd
PO Box 496, 16–22 Church Street, Hawthorn, Victoria 3122, Australia

Century Hutchinson New Zealand Limited
PO Box 40–086, Glenfield, Auckland 10, New Zealand

Century Hutchinson South Africa (Pty) Ltd
PO Box 337, Berglvei, 2012 South Africa

ISBN 0 09 173728 1

Printed and bound in Great Britain by Mackays of Chatham

CONTENTS

A ROOM WITH A VIEW

Part One

Chapter 1
The Bertolini

"The Signora had no business to do it," said Miss Bartlett, "no business at all. She promised us south rooms with a view, close together, instead of which here are north rooms, here are north rooms, looking into a courtyard, and a long way apart. Oh, Lucy!"

"And a Cockney, besides!" said Lucy, who had been further saddened by the Signora's unexpected accent. "It might be London." She looked at the two rows of English people who were sitting at the table; at the row of white bottles of water and red bottles of wine that ran between the English people; at the portraits of the late Queen and the late Poet Laureate that hung behind the English people, heavily framed; at the notice of the English church (Rev. Cuthbert Eager, M.A. Oxon.), that was the only other decoration of the wall. "Charlotte, don't you feel, too, that we might be in London? I can hardly believe that all kinds of other things are just outside. I suppose it is one's being so tired."

"This meat has surely been used for soup," said Miss Bartlett, laying down her fork.

"I wanted so to see the Arno. The rooms the Signora promised us in her letter would have looked over the Arno. The Signora had no business to do it at all. Oh, it is a shame!"

"Any nook does for me," Miss Bartlett continued; "but it does seem hard that you shouldn't have a view."

Lucy felt that she had been selfish. "Charlotte, you mustn't spoil me: of course, you must look over the Arno, too. I meant that. The first vacant room in the front—"

"You must have it," said Miss Bartlett, part of whose travelling expenses were paid by Lucy's mother—a piece of generosity to which she made many a tactful allusion.

"No, no. You must have it."

"I insist on it. Your mother would never forgive me, Lucy."

"She would never forgive *me*."

The ladies' voices grew animated, and—if the sad truth be owned—a little peevish. They were tired, and under the guise of unselfishness they wrangled. Some of their neighbours interchanged glances, and one of them—one of the ill-bred people whom one does meet abroad—leant forward over the table and actually intruded into their argument. He said:

"I have a view, I have a view."

Miss Bartlett was startled. Generally at a pension people looked them over for a day or two before speaking, and often did not find out that they would "do" till they had gone. She knew that the intruder was ill-bred, even before she glanced at him. He was an old man, of heavy build, with a fair, shaven face and large eyes. There was something childish in those eyes, though it was not the childishness of senility. What exactly it was Miss Bartlett did not stop to consider, for her glance passed on to his clothes. These did not attract her. He was probably trying to become acquainted with them before they got into the swim. So she assumed a dazed expression when he spoke to her, and then said: "A view? Oh, a view! How delightful a view is!"

"This is my son," said the old man; "his name's George. He has a view, too."

"Ah," said Miss Bartlett, repressing Lucy, who was about to speak.

"What I mean," he continued, "is that you can have our rooms, and we'll have yours. We'll change."

The better class of tourist was shocked at this, and sympathized with the newcomers. Miss Bartlett, in reply, opened her mouth as little as possible, and said:

"Thank you very much indeed; that is out of the question."

"Why?" said the old man, with both fists on the table.

"Because it is quite out of the question, thank you."

"You see, we don't like to take—" began Lucy.

Her cousin again repressed her.

"But why?" he persisted. "Women like looking at a view; men don't." And he thumped with his fists like a naughty child, and turned to his son, saying, "George, persuade them!"

"It's so obvious they should have the rooms," said the son. "There's nothing else to say."

He did not look at the ladies as he spoke, but his voice was perplexed and sorrowful. Lucy, too, was perplexed; but she saw that they were in for what is known as "quite a scene", and she had an odd feeling that whenever these ill-bred tourists spoke the contest widened and deepened till it dealt, not with rooms and views, but with—well, with something quite different, whose existence she had not realized before. Now the old man attacked Miss Bartlett almost violently: Why should she not change? What possible objection had she? They would clear out in half an hour.

Miss Bartlett, though skilled in the delicacies of conversation, was powerless in the presence of brutality. It was impossible to snub anyone so gross. Her face reddened with displeasure. She looked around as much as to say, "Are you all like this?" And two little old ladies, who were sitting further up the table, with shawls hanging over the backs of the chairs, looked back, clearly indicating, "We are not; we are genteel."

"Eat your dinner, dear," she said to Lucy, and began to toy again with the meat that she had once censured.

Lucy mumbled that those seemed very odd people opposite.

"Eat your dinner, dear. This pension is a failure. Tomorrow we will make a change."

Hardly had she announced this fell decision when she reversed it. The curtains at the end of the room parted, and revealed a clergyman, stout but attractive, who hurried forward to take his place at the table, cheerfully apologizing for his lateness. Lucy, who had not yet acquired decency, at once rose to her feet, exclaiming: "Oh, oh! Why, it's Mr

Beebe! Oh, how perfectly lovely! Oh, Charlotte, we must stop now, however bad the rooms are. Oh!"

Miss Bartlett said, with more restraint:

"How do you do, Mr Beebe? I expect that you have forgotten us: Miss Bartlett and Miss Honeychurch, who were at Tunbridge Wells when you helped the vicar of St Peter's that very cold Easter."

The clergyman, who had the air of one on a holiday, did not remember the ladies quite as clearly as they remembered him. But he came forward pleasantly enough and accepted the chair into which he was beckoned by Lucy.

"I *am* so glad to see you," said the girl, who was in a state of spiritual starvation, and would have been glad to see the waiter if her cousin had permitted it. "Just fancy how small the world is. Summer Street, too, makes it so specially funny."

"Miss Honeychurch lives in the parish of Summer Street," said Miss Bartlett, filling up the gap, "and she happened to tell me in the course of conversation that you have just accepted the living—"

"Yes, I heard from mother so last week. She didn't know that I knew you at Tunbridge Wells; but I wrote back at once, and I said: 'Mr Beebe is—' "

"Quite right," said the clergyman. "I move into the rectory at Summer Street next June. I am lucky to be appointed to such a charming neighbourhood."

"Oh, how glad I am! The name of our house is Windy Corner."

Mr Beebe bowed.

"There is mother and me generally, and my brother, though it's not often we get him to ch—the church is rather far off, I mean."

"Lucy dearest, let Mr Beebe eat his dinner."

"I am eating it, thank you, and enjoying it."

He preferred to talk to Lucy, whose playing he remembered, rather than to Miss Bartlett, who probably remembered his sermons. He asked the girl whether she knew Florence well, and was informed at some length that she had never been there before. It is delightful to advise a newcomer, and he was first in the field.

"Don't neglect the country round," his advice concluded. "The first fine afternoon drive up to Fiesole, and round by Settignano, or something of that sort."

"No!" cried a voice from the top of the table. "Mr Beebe, you are wrong. The first fine afternoon your ladies must go to Prato."

"That lady looks so clever," whispered Miss Bartlett to her cousin. "We are in luck."

And, indeed, a perfect torrent of information burst on them. People told them what to see, when to see it, how to stop the electric trams, how to get rid of the beggars, how much to give for a vellum blotter, how much the place would grow upon them. The Pension Bertolini had decided, almost enthusiastically, that they would do. Whichever way they looked, kind ladies smiled and shouted at them. And above all rose the voice of the clever lady, crying: "Prato! They must go to Prato. That place is too sweetly squalid for words. I love it; I revel in shaking off the trammels of respectability, as you know."

The young man named George glanced at the clever lady, and then returned moodily to his plate. Obviously he and his father did not do. Lucy, in the midst of her success, found time to wish they did. It gave her no extra pleasure that anyone should be left in the cold; and when she rose to go she turned back and gave the two outsiders a nervous little bow.

The father did not see it; the son acknowledged it, not by another bow, but by raising his eyebrows and smiling; he seemed to be smiling across something.

She hastened after her cousin, who had already disappeared through the curtains—curtains which smote one in the face, and seemed heavy with more than cloth. Beyond them stood the unreliable Signora, bowing good-evening to her guests, and supported by 'Enery, her little boy, and Victorier, her daughter. It made a curious little scene, this attempt of the Cockney to convey the grace and geniality of the South. And even more curious was the drawing-room, which attempted to rival the solid comfort of a Bloomsbury boarding-house. Was this really Italy?

Miss Bartlett was already seated on a tightly stuffed armchair, which had the colour and the contours of a tomato. She was talking to Mr Beebe, and as she spoke her long narrow head drove backwards and forwards, slowly, regularly, as though she were demolishing some invisible obstacle. "We are most grateful to you," she was saying. "The first evening means so much. When you arrived we were in for a peculiarly *mauvais quart d'heure.*"

He expressed his regret.

"Do you, by any chance, know the name of an old man who sat opposite us at dinner?"

"Emerson."

"Is he a friend of yours?"

"We are friendly—as one is in pensions."

"Then I will say no more."

He pressed her very slightly, and she said more.

"I am, as it were," she concluded, "the chaperon of my young cousin, Lucy, and it would be a serious thing if I put her under an obligation to people of whom we knew nothing. His manner was somewhat unfortunate. I hope I acted for the best."

"You acted very naturally," said he. He seemed thoughtful, and after a few moments added: "All the same, I don't think much harm would have come of accepting."

"No *harm*, of course. But we could not be under an obligation."

"He is rather a peculiar man." Again he hesitated, and then said gently: "I think he would not take advantage of your acceptance, nor expect you to show gratitude. He has the merit—if it is one—of saying exactly what he means. He has rooms he does not value, and he thinks you would value them. He no more thought of putting you under an obligation than he thought of being polite. It is so difficult—at least, I find it difficult—to understand people who speak the truth."

Lucy was pleased, and said: "I was hoping that he was nice; I do so always hope that people will be nice."

"I think he is; nice and tiresome. I differ from him on almost every point of any importance, and so, I expect—I may say I hope—you will differ. But his is a type one disagrees with rather than deplores. When he first came here he not unnaturally put people's backs up. He has no tact and no manners—I don't mean by that that he has bad manners—and he will not keep his opinions to himself. We nearly complained about him to our depressing Signora, but I am glad to say we thought better of it."

"Am I to conclude," said Miss Bartlett, "that he is a Socialist?"

Mr Beebe accepted the convenient word, not without a slight twitching of the lips.

"And presumably he has brought up his son to be a Socialist, too?"

"I hardly know George, for he hasn't learned to talk yet. He seems a nice creature, and I think he has brains. Of course, he has all his father's mannerisms, and it is quite possible that he, too, may be a Socialist."

"Oh, you relieve me," said Miss Bartlett. "So you think I ought to have accepted their offer? You feel I have been narrow-minded and suspicious?"

"Not at all," he answered; "I never suggested that."

"But ought I not to apologize, at all events, for my apparent rudeness?"

He replied, with some irritation, that it would be quite unnecessary, and got up from his seat to go to the smoking-room.

"Was I a bore?" said Miss Bartlett, as soon as he had disappeared. "Why didn't you talk, Lucy? He prefers young people, I'm sure. I do hope I haven't monopolized him. I hoped you would have him all the evening, as well as all dinner-time."

"He is nice," exclaimed Lucy. "Just what I remember. He seems to see good in everyone. No one would take him for a clergyman."

"My dear Lucia—"

"Well, you know what I mean. And you know how

clergymen generally laugh; Mr Beebe laughs just like an ordinary man."

"Funny girl! How you do remind me of your mother. I wonder if she will approve of Mr Beebe."

"I'm sure she will; and so will Freddy."

"I think everyone at Windy Corner will approve; it is the fashionable world. I am used to Tunbridge Wells, where we are all hopelessly behind the times."

"Yes," said Lucy despondently.

There was a haze of disapproval in the air, but whether the disapproval was of herself, or of Mr Beebe, or of the fashionable world at Windy Corner, or of the narrow world at Tunbridge Wells, she could not determine. She tried to locate it, but as usual she blundered. Miss Bartlett sedulously denied disapproving of anyone, and added: "I am afraid you are finding me a very depressing companion."

And the girl again thought: "I must have been selfish or unkind; I must be more careful. It is so dreadful for Charlotte, being poor."

Fortunately one of the little old ladies, who for some time had been smiling very benignly, now approached and asked if she might be allowed to sit where Mr Beebe had sat. Permission granted, she began to chatter gently about Italy, the plunge it had been to come there, the gratifying success of the plunge, the improvement in her sister's health, the necessity of closing the bedroom windows at night, and of thoroughly emptying the water-bottles in the morning. She handled her subjects agreeably, and they were, perhaps, more worthy of attention than the high discourse upon Guelfs and Ghibellines which was proceeding tempestuously at the other end of the room. It was a real catastrophe, not a mere episode, that evening of hers at Venice, when she had found in her bedroom something that is one worse than a flea, though one better than something else.

"But here you are as safe as in England; Signora Bertolini is so English."

"Yet our rooms smell," said poor Lucy. "We dread going to bed."

"Ah, then you look into the court." She sighed. "If only Mr Emerson was more tactful! We were so sorry for you at dinner."

"I think he was meaning to be kind."

"Undoubtedly he was," said Miss Bartlett. "Mr Beebe has just been scolding me for my suspicious nature. Of course, I was holding back on my cousin's account."

"Of course," said the little old lady; and they murmured that one could not be too careful with a young girl.

Lucy tried to look demure, but could not help feeling a great fool. No one was careful with her at home; or, at all events, she had not noticed it.

"About old Mr Emerson—I hardly know. No, he is not tactful; yet, have you ever noticed that there are people who do things which are most indelicate, and yet at the same time—beautiful?'

"Beautiful?" said Miss Bartlett, puzzled at the word. "Are not beauty and delicacy the same?"

"So one would have thought," said the other helplessly. "But things are so difficult, I sometimes think."

She proceeded no further into things, for Mr Beebe reappeared, looking extremely pleasant.

"Miss Bartlett," he cried, "it's all right about the rooms. I'm so glad. Mr Emerson was talking about it in the smoking-room, and, knowing what I did, I encouraged him to make the offer again. He has let me come and ask you. He would be so pleased."

"Oh, Charlotte," cried Lucy to her cousin, "we must have the rooms now. The old man is just as nice and kind as he can be."

Miss Bartlett was silent.

"I fear," said Mr Beebe, after a pause, "that I have been officious. I must apologize for my interference."

Gravely displeased, he turned to go. Not till then did Miss Bartlett reply: "My own wishes, dearest Lucy, are unimportant in comparison with yours. It would be hard indeed if I stopped you doing as you liked at Florence, when I am only here through your kindness. If you wish me to turn these gentlemen out of their rooms, I will do it. Would you then, Mr Beebe, kindly tell Mr Emerson that I accept his kind offer, and then conduct him to me, in order that I may thank him personally?"

She raised her voice as she spoke; it was heard all over the drawing-room, and silenced the Guelfs and the Ghibellines. The clergyman, inwardly cursing the female sex, bowed and departed with her message.

"Remember, Lucy, I alone am implicated in this. I do not wish the acceptance to come from you. Grant me that, at all events."

Mr Beebe was back, saying rather nervously:

"Mr Emerson is engaged, but here is his son instead."

The young man gazed down on the three ladies, who felt seated on the floor, so low were their chairs.

"My father," he said, "is in his bath, so you cannot thank him personally. But any message given by you to me will be given by me to him as soon as he comes out."

Miss Bartlett was unequal to the bath. All her barbed civilities came forth wrong end first. Young Mr Emerson scored a notable triumph, to the delight of Mr Beebe and to the secret delight of Lucy.

"Poor young man!" said Miss Bartlett, as soon as he had gone. "How angry he is with his father about the rooms! It is all he can do to keep polite."

"In half an hour or so your rooms will be ready," said Mr Beebe. Then, looking rather thoughtfully at the two cousins, he retired to his own room, to write up his philosophic diary.

"Oh dear!" breathed the little old lady, and shuddered as if all the winds of heaven had entered the apartment. "Gentlemen sometimes do not realize—" Her voice faded away, but Miss Bartlett seemed to understand, and a conversation developed, in which gentlemen who did not thoroughly realize played a principal part. Lucy, not realizing either, was reduced to literature. Taking up Baedeker's *Handbook to Northern Italy*, she committed to memory the most important dates of Florentine history. For she was determined to enjoy herself on the morrow. Thus the half-hour crept profitably away, and at last Miss Bartlett rose with a sigh, and said:

"I think one might venture now. No, Lucy, do not stir. I will superintend the move."

"How you do do everything," said Lucy.

"Naturally, dear. It is my affair."

"But I would like to help you."

"No, dear."

Charlotte's energy! And her unselfishness! She had been thus all her life, but really, on this Italian tour, she was surpassing herself. So Lucy felt, or strove to feel. And yet—there was a rebellious spirit in her which wondered whether the acceptance might not have been less delicate and more beautiful. At all events, she entered her own room without any feeling of joy.

"I want to explain," said Miss Bartlett, "why it is that I have taken the largest room. Naturally, of course, I should have given it to you; but I happen to know that it belongs to the young man, and I was sure your mother would not like it."

Lucy was bewildered.

"If you are to accept a favour, it is more suitable you should be under an obligation to his father than to him. I am a woman of the world, in my small way, and I know where things lead to. However, Mr Beebe is a guarantee of a sort that they will not presume on this."

"Mother wouldn't mind, I'm sure," said Lucy, but again had the sense of larger and unsuspected issues.

Miss Bartlett only sighed, and enveloped her in a protecting embrace as she wished her goodnight. It gave Lucy the sensation of a fog, and when she reached her own room she opened the window and breathed the clean night air, thinking of the kind old man who had enabled her to see the lights dancing in the Arno, and the cypresses of San Miniato, and the foothills of the Apennines, black against the rising moon.

Miss Bartlett, in her room, fastened the window-shutters

and locked the door, and then made a tour of the apartment to see where the cupboards led, and whether there were any oubliettes or secret entrances. It was then that she saw, pinned up over the wash-stand, a sheet of paper on which was scrawled an enormous note of interrogation. Nothing more.

"What does it mean?" she thought, and she examined it carefully by the light of a candle. Meaningless at first, it gradually became menacing, obnoxious, portentous with evil. She was seized with an impulse to destroy it, but fortunately remembered that she had no right to do so, since it must be the property of young Mr Emerson. So she unpinned it carefully, and put it between two pieces of blotting-paper to keep it clean for him. Then she completed her inspection of the room, sighed heavily according to her habit, and went to bed.

Chapter 2
In Santa Croce with no Baedeker

It was pleasant to wake up in Florence, to open the eyes upon a bright bare room, with a floor of red tiles which look clean though they are not; with a painted ceiling whereon pink griffins and blue amorini sport in a forest of yellow violins and bassoons. It was pleasant, too, to fling wide the windows, pinching the fingers in unfamiliar fastenings, to lean out into sunshine with beautiful hills and trees and marble churches opposite, and, close below, the Arno, gurgling against the embankment of the road.

Over the river men were at work with spades and sieves on the sandy foreshore, and on the river was a boat, also diligently employed for some mysterious end. An electric tram came rushing underneath the window. No one was inside it, except one tourist; but its platforms were overflowing with Italians, who preferred to stand. Children tried to hang on behind, and the conductor, with no malice, spat in their faces to make them let go. Then soldiers appeared—good-looking, undersized men—wearing each a knapsack covered with mangy fur, and a greatcoat which had been cut for some larger soldier. Beside them walked officers, looking foolish and fierce, and before them went little boys, turning somersaults in time with the band. The tram-car became entangled in their ranks, and moved on painfully, like a caterpillar in a swarm of ants. One of the little boys fell down, and some white bullocks came out of an archway. Indeed, if it had not been for the good advice of an old man who was selling buttonhooks, the road might never have got clear.

Over such trivialities as these many a valuable hour may slip away, and the traveller who has gone to Italy to study the tactile values of Giotto, or the corruption of the Papacy, may return remembering nothing but the blue sky and the men and women who live under it. So it was as well that Miss Bartlett should tap and come in, and having commented on Lucy's leaving the door unlocked, and on her leaning out of the window before she was fully dressed, should urge her to hasten herself, or the best of the day would be gone. By the time Lucy was ready her cousin had done her breakfast, and was listening to the clever lady among the crumbs.

A conversation then ensued, on not unfamiliar lines. Miss Bartlett was, after all, a wee bit tired, and thought they had better spend the morning settling in; unless Lucy would at all like to go out? Lucy would rather like to go out, as it was her first day in Florence, but, of course, she could go alone. Miss Bartlett could not allow this. Of course she would accompany Lucy everywhere. Oh, certainly not; Lucy would stop with her cousin. Oh no! That would never do! Oh yes!

At this point the clever lady broke in.

"If it is Mrs Grundy who is troubling you, I do assure you that you can neglect the good person. Being English, Miss Honeychurch will be perfectly safe. Italians understand. A dear friend of mine, Contessa Baroncelli, has two daughters, and when she cannot send a maid to school with them she lets them go in sailor-hats instead. Everyone takes them for English, you see, especially if their hair is strained tightly behind."

Miss Bartlett was unconvinced by the safety of Contessa Baroncelli's daughters. She was determined to take Lucy herself, her head not being so very bad. The clever lady then said that she was going to spend a long morning in Santa Croce, and if Lucy would come too she would be delighted.

"I will take you by a dear dirty back way, Miss Honeychurch, and if you bring me luck we shall have an adventure."

Lucy said that this was most kind, and at once opened the Baedeker, to see where Santa Croce was.

"Tut, tut! Miss Lucy! I hope we shall soon emancipate you from Baedeker. He does but touch the surface of things.

As to the true Italy—he does not even dream of it. The true Italy is only to be found by patient observation."

This sounded very interesting, and Lucy hurried over her breakfast, and started with her new friend in high spirits. Italy was coming at last. The Cockney Signora and her works had vanished like a bad dream.

Miss Lavish—for that was the clever lady's name—turned to the right along the sunny Lungarno. How delightfully warm! But a wind down the side-streets that cut like a knife, didn't it? Ponte alle Grazie—particularly interesting, mentioned by Dante. San Miniato—beautiful as well as interesting; the crucifix that kissed a murderer—Miss Honeychurch would remember the story. The men on the river were fishing. (Untrue; but then so is most information.) Then Miss Lavish darted under the archway of the white bullocks, and she stopped, and she cried:

"A smell! A true Florentine smell! Every city, let me teach you, has its own smell."

"Is it a very nice smell?" said Lucy, who had inherited from her mother a distaste to dirt.

"One doesn't come to Italy for niceness," was the retort; "one comes for life. Buon giorno! Buon giorno!" bowing right and left. "Look at that adorable wine-cart! How the driver stares at us, dear, simple soul!"

So Miss Lavish proceeded through the streets of the city of Florence, short, fidgety, and playful as a kitten, though without a kitten's grace. It was a treat for the girl to be with anyone so clever and so cheerful; and a blue military cloak, such as an Italian officer wears, only increased the sense of festivity.

"Buon giorno! Take the word of an old woman, Miss Lucy: you will never repent of a little civility to your inferiors. *That* is the true democracy. Though I am a real Radical as well. There, now you're shocked."

"Indeed, I'm not!" exclaimed Lucy. "We are Radicals, too, out and out. My father always voted for Mr Gladstone, until he was so dreadful about Ireland."

"I see, I see. And now you have gone over to the enemy."

"Oh, please—! If my father was alive, I am sure he would vote Radical again now that Ireland is all right. And as it is, the glass over our front door was broken last election, and Freddy is sure it was the Tories; but mother says nonsense, a tramp."

"Shameful! A manufacturing district, I suppose?"

"No—in the Surrey hills. About five miles from Dorking, looking over the Weald."

Miss Lavish seemed interested, and slackened her trot.

"What a delightful part; I know it so well. It is full of the very nicest people. Do you know Sir Harry Otway—a Radical if ever there was?"

"Very well indeed."

"And old Mrs Butterworth the philanthropist?"

"Why, she rents a field of us! How funny!"

Miss Lavish looked at the narrow ribbon of sky, and murmured:

"Oh, you have property in Surrey?"

"Hardly any," said Lucy, fearful of being thought a snob. "Only thirty acres—just the garden, all downhill, and some fields."

Miss Lavish was not disgusted, and said it was just the size of her aunt's Suffolk estate. Italy receded. They tried to remember the last name of Lady Louisa someone, who had taken a house near Summer Street the other year, but she had not liked it, which was odd of her. And just as Miss Lavish had got the name she broke off and exclaimed:

"Bless us! Bless us and save us! We've lost the way."

Certainly they had seemed a long time in reaching Santa Croce, the tower of which had been plainly visible from the landing window. But Miss Lavish had said so much about knowing her Florence by heart, that Lucy had followed her with no misgivings.

"Lost! Lost! My dear Miss Lucy, during our political diatribes we have taken a wrong turning. How those horrid Conservatives would jeer at us! What are we to do? Two lone females in an unknown town. Now, this is what *I* call an adventure."

Lucy, who wanted to see Santa Croce, suggested, as a possible solution, that they should ask the way there.

"Oh, but that is the word of a craven! And no, you are not, not, *not* to look at your Baedeker. Give it to me; I shan't let you carry it. We will simply drift."

Accordingly they drifted through a series of those gray-brown streets, neither commodious nor picturesque, in which the eastern quarter of the city abounds. Lucy soon lost interest in the discontent of Lady Louisa, and became discontented herself. For one ravishing moment Italy appeared. She stood in the Square of the Annunziata and saw in the living terracotta those divine babies whom no cheap reproduction can ever stale. There they stood, with their shining limbs bursting from the garments of charity, and their strong white arms extended against circlets of heaven. Lucy thought she had never seen anything more beautiful; but Miss Lavish, with a shriek of dismay, dragged her forward, declaring that they were out of their path now by at least a mile.

The hour was approaching at which the continental breakfast begins, or rather ceases, to tell, and the ladies bought some hot chestnut paste out of a little shop, because it looked so typical. It tasted partly of the paper in which it was wrapped, partly of hair-oil, partly of the great unknown. But it gave them strength to drift into another piazza, large and dusty, on the further side of which rose a black-and-white façade of surpassing ugliness. Miss Lavish spoke to it dramatically. It was Santa Croce. The adventure was over.

"Stop a minute; let those two people go on, or I shall have to speak to them. I do detest conventional intercourse. Nasty! They are going into the church, too. Oh, the Britisher abroad!'

"We sat opposite them at dinner last night. They have given us their rooms. They were so very kind."

"Look at their figures!" laughed Miss Lavish. "They walk through my Italy like a pair of cows. It's very naughty of me, but I would like to set an examination paper at Dover, and turn back every tourist who couldn't pass it."

"What would you ask us?"

Miss Lavish laid her hand pleasantly on Lucy's arm, as if to suggest that she, at all events, would get full marks. In this exalted mood they reached the steps of the great church, and were about to enter it when Miss Lavish stopped, squeaked, flung up her arms, and cried:

"There goes my local-colour box! I must have a word with him!"

And in a moment she was away over the Piazza, her military cloak flapping in the wind; nor did she slacken speed till she caught up an old man with white whiskers, and nipped him playfully upon the arm.

Lucy waited for nearly ten minutes. Then she began to get tired. The beggars worried her, the dust blew in her eyes, and she remembered that a young girl ought not to loiter in public places. She descended slowly into the Piazza with the intention of rejoining Miss Lavish, who was really almost too original. But at that moment Miss Lavish and her local-colour box moved also, and disappeared down a side-street, both gesticulating largely.

Tears of indignation came to Lucy's eyes—partly because Miss Lavish had jilted her, partly because she had taken her Baedeker. How could she find her way home? How could she find her way about in Santa Croce? Her first morning was ruined, and she might never be in Florence again. A few minutes ago she had been all high spirits, talking as a woman of culture, and half-persuading herself that she was full of originality. Now she entered the church depressed and humiliated, not even able to remember whether it was built by the Franciscans or the Dominicans.

Of course, it must be a wonderful building. But how like a barn! And how very cold! Of course, it contained frescoes by Giotto, in the presence of whose tactile values she was capable of feeling what was proper. But who was to tell her which they were? She walked about disdainfully, unwilling to be enthusiastic over monuments of uncertain authorship or date. There was no one even to tell her which, of all the sepulchral slabs that paved the nave and transepts, was the one that was really beautiful, the one that had been most praised by Mr Ruskin.

Then the pernicious charm of Italy worked on her, and, instead of acquiring information, she began to be happy. She puzzled out the Italian notices—the notice that forbade people to introduce dogs into the church—the notice that prayed people, in the interests of health and out of respect to the sacred edifice in which they found themselves, not to spit. She watched the tourists: their noses were as red as their Baedekers, so cold was Santa Croce. She beheld the horrible fate that overtook three Papists—two he-babies and a she-baby—who began their career by sousing each other with the Holy Water, and then proceeded to the Machiavelli memorial, dripping, but hallowed. Advancing towards it very slowly and from immense distances, they touched the stone with their fingers, with their handkerchiefs, with their heads, and then retreated. What could this mean? They did it again and again. Then Lucy realized that they had mistaken Machiavelli for some saint, and by continual contact with his shrine were hoping to acquire virtue. Punishment followed quickly. The smallest he-baby stumbled over one of the sepulchral slabs so much admired by Mr Ruskin, and entangled his feet in the features of a recumbent bishop. Protestant as she was, Lucy darted forward. She was too late. He fell heavily upon the prelate's upturned toes.

"Hateful bishop!" exclaimed the voice of old Mr Emerson, who had darted forward also. "Hard in life, hard in death. Go out into the sunshine, little boy, and kiss your hand to the sun, for that is where you ought to be. Intolerable bishop!"

The child screamed frantically at these words, and at these dreadful people who picked him up, dusted him, rubbed his bruises, and told him not to be superstitious.

"Look at him!" said Mr Emerson to Lucy. "Here's a mess: a baby hurt, cold and frightened! But what else can you expect from a church?"

The child's legs had become as melting wax. Each time that old Mr Emerson and Lucy set it erect it collapsed with a roar. Fortunately an Italian lady, who ought to have been saying her prayers, came to the rescue. By some mysterious virtue, which mothers alone possess, she stiffened the little boy's backbone and imparted strength to his knees. He stood. Still gibbering with agitation, he walked away.

"You are a clever woman," said Mr Emerson. "You have done more than all the relics in the world. I am not of your creed, but I do believe in those who make their fellow creatures happy. There is no scheme of the universe—"

He paused for a phrase.

"Niente," said the Italian lady, and returned to her prayers.

"I'm not sure she understands English," suggested Lucy.

In her chastened mood she no longer despised the Emersons. She was determined to be gracious to them, beautiful rather than delicate, and, if possible, to erase Miss Bartlett's civility by some gracious reference to the pleasant rooms.

"That woman understands everything," was Mr Emerson's reply. "But what are you doing here? Are you doing the church? Are you through with the church?"

"No," cried Lucy, remembering her grievance. "I came here with Miss Lavish, who was to explain everything; and just by the door—it is too bad!—she simply ran away, and after waiting quite a time I had to come in by myself."

"Why shouldn't you?" said Mr Emerson.

"Yes, why shouldn't you come by yourself?" said the son, addressing the young lady for the first time.

"But Miss Lavish has even taken away Baedeker."

"Baedeker?" said Mr Emerson. "I'm glad it's *that* that you minded. It's worth minding, the loss of a Baedeker. *That*'s worth minding."

Lucy was puzzled. She was again conscious of some new idea, and was not sure whither it would lead her.

"If you've no Baedeker," said the son, "you'd better join us."

Was this where the idea would lead? She took refuge in her dignity.

"Thank you very much, but I could not think of that. I hope you do not suppose that I came to join on to you. I really came to help with the child, and to thank you for so kindly giving us your rooms last night. I hope that you have not been put to any great inconvenience."

"My dear," said the old man gently, "I think that you are repeating what you have heard older people say. You are pretending to be touchy; but you are not really. Stop being so tiresome, and tell me instead what part of the church you want to see. To take you to it will be a real pleasure."

Now, this was abominably impertinent, and she ought to have been furious. But it is sometimes as difficult to lose one's temper as it is difficult at other times to keep it. Lucy could not get cross. Mr Emerson was an old man, and surely a girl might humour him. On the other hand, his son was a young man, and she felt that a girl ought to be offended with him, or at all events be offended before him. It was at him that she gazed before replying.

"I am not touchy, I hope. It is the Giottos that I want to see, if you will kindly tell me which they are."

The son nodded. With a look of sombre satisfaction, he led the way to the Peruzzi Chapel. There was a hint of the teacher about him. She felt like a child in school who had answered a question rightly.

The chapel was already filled with an earnest congregation, and out of them rose the voice of a lecturer, directing them how to worship Giotto, not by tactile valuations, but by the standards of the spirit.

"Remember," he was saying, "the facts about this church of Santa Croce; how it was built by faith in the full fervour of medievalism, before any taint of the Renaissance had appeared. Observe how Giotto in these frescoes—now, unhappily, ruined by restoration—is untroubled by the snares of anatomy and perspective. Could anything be more majestic, more pathetic, beautiful, true? How little, we feel, avails knowledge and technical cleverness against a man who truly feels!"

"No!" exclaimed Mr Emerson, in much too loud a voice

for church. "Remember nothing of the sort! Built by faith indeed! That simply means the workmen weren't paid properly. And as for the frescoes, I see no truth in them. Look at that fat man in blue! He must weigh as much as I do, and he is shooting into the sky like an air-balloon."

He was referring to the fresco of the Ascension of St John. Inside, the lecturer's voice faltered, as well it might. The audience shifted uneasily, and so did Lucy. She was sure that she ought not to be with these men; but they had cast a spell over her. They were so serious and so strange that she could not remember how to behave.

"Now, did this happen, or didn't it? Yes or no?"

George replied:

"It happened like this, if it happened at all. I would rather go up to heaven by myself than be pushed by cherubs; and if I got there I should like my friends to lean out of it, just as they do here."

"You will never go up," said his father. "You and I, dear boy, will lie at peace in the earth that bore us, and our names will disappear as surely as our work survives."

"Some of the people can only see the empty grave, not the saint, whoever he is, going up. It did happen like that, if it happened at all."

"Pardon me," said a frigid voice. "The chapel is somewhat small for two parties. We will incommode you no longer."

The lecturer was a clergyman, and his audience must be also his flock, for they held prayerbooks as well as guidebooks in their hands. They filed out of the chapel in silence. Amongst them were the two little old ladies of the Pension Bertolini—Miss Teresa and Miss Catharine Alan.

"Stop!" cried Mr Emerson. "There's plenty of room for us all. Stop!"

The procession disappeared without a word. Soon the lecturer could be heard in the next chapel, describing the life of St Francis.

"George, I do believe that clergyman is the Brixton curate."

George went into the next chapel and returned, saying: "Perhaps he is. I don't remember."

"Then I had better speak to him and remind him who I am. It's that Mr Eager. Why did he go? Did we talk too loud? How vexatious! I shall go and say we are sorry. Hadn't I better? Then perhaps he will come back."

"He will not come back," said George.

But Mr Emerson, contrite and unhappy, hurried away to apologize to the Rev. Cuthbert Eager. Lucy, apparently absorbed in a lunette, could hear the lecture again interrupted, the anxious, aggressive voice of the old man, the curt, injured replies of his opponent. The son, who took every little contretemps as if it were a tragedy, was listening also.

"My father has that effect on nearly everyone," he informed her. "He will try to be kind."

"I hope we all try," said she, smiling nervously.

"Because we think it improves our characters. But he is kind to people because he loves them; and they find him out, and are offended, or frightened."

"How silly of them!" said Lucy, though in her heart she sympathized; "I think that a kind action done tactfully—"

"Tact!"

He threw up his head in disdain. Apparently she had given the wrong answer. She watched the singular creature pace up and down the chapel. For a young man his face was rugged, and—until the shadows fell upon it—hard. Enshadowed, it sprang into tenderness. She saw him once again at Rome, on the ceiling of the Sistine Chapel, carrying a burden of acorns. Healthy and muscular, he yet gave her the feeling of grayness, of tragedy that might only find solution in the night. The feeling soon passed; it was unlike her to have entertained anything so subtle. Born of silence and of unknown emotion, it passed when Mr Emerson returned, and she could re-enter the world of rapid talk, which was alone familiar to her.

"Were you snubbed?" asked his son tranquilly.

"But we have spoilt the pleasure of I don't know how many people. They won't come back."

". . . full of innate sympathy . . . quickness to perceive good in others . . . vision of the brotherhood of man. . . ." Scraps of the lecture on St Francis came floating round the partition wall.

"Don't let us spoil yours," he continued to Lucy. "Have you looked at those saints?"

"Yes," said Lucy. "They are lovely. Do you know which is the tombstone that is praised in Ruskin?"

He did not know, and suggested that they should try to guess it. George, rather to her relief, refused to move, and she and the old man wandered not unpleasantly about Santa Croce, which, though it is like a barn, has harvested many beautiful things inside its walls. There were also beggars to avoid, and guides to dodge round the pillars, and an old lady with her dog, and here and there was a priest modestly edging to his Mass through the groups of tourists. But Mr Emerson was only half-interested. He watched the lecturer, whose success he believed that he had impaired, and then he anxiously watched his son.

"Why will he look at that fresco?" he said uneasily. "I saw nothing in it."

"I like Giotto," she replied. "It is so wonderful what they say about his tactile values. Though I like things like the Della Robbia babies better."

"So you ought. A baby is worth a dozen saints. And my baby's worth the whole of Paradise, and as far as I can see he lives in Hell."

Lucy again felt that this did not do.

"In Hell," he repeated. "He's unhappy."

"Oh dear!" said Lucy.

"How can he be unhappy when he is strong and alive? What more is one to give him? And think how he has been brought up—free from all the superstition and ignorance that lead men to hate one another in the name of God. With such an education as that, I thought he was bound to grow up happy."

She was no theologian, but she felt that here was a very foolish old man, as well as a very irreligious one. She also felt that her mother might not like her talking to that kind of person, and that Charlotte would object most strongly.

"What are we to do with him?" he asked. "He comes out for his holiday to Italy, and behaves—like that; like the little child who ought to have been playing, and who hurt himself upon the tombstone. Eh? What did you say?"

Lucy had made no suggestion. Suddenly he said:

"Now, don't be stupid over this. I don't require you to fall in love with my boy, but I do think you might try and understand him. You are nearer his age, and if you let yourself go I am sure you are sensible. You might help me. He has known so few women, and you have the time. You stop here several weeks, I suppose? But let yourself go. You are inclined to get muddled, if I may judge from last night. Let yourself go. Pull out from the depths those thoughts that you do not understand, and spread them out in the sunlight and know the meaning of them. By understanding George you may learn to understand yourself. It will be good for both of you."

To this extraordinary speech Lucy found no answer.

"I only know what it is that's wrong with him; not why it is."

"And what is it?" asked Lucy fearfully, expecting some harrowing tale.

"The old trouble: things won't fit."

"What things?"

"The things of the universe. It is quite true. They don't."

"Oh, Mr Emerson, what ever do you mean?"

In his ordinary voice, so that she scarcely realized he was quoting poetry, he said:

"From far, from eve and morning
And yon twelve-winded sky,
The stuff of life to knit me
Blew hither: here am I.

George and I both know this, but why does it distress him? We know that we come from the winds, and that we shall return to them; that all life is perhaps a knot, a tangle, a blemish in the eternal smoothness. But why should this make us unhappy? Let us rather love one another, and work and rejoice. I don't believe in this world-sorrow."

Miss Honeychurch assented.

"Then make my boy think like us. Make him realize that by the side of the everlasting Why there is a Yes—a transitory Yes if you like, but a Yes."

Suddenly she laughed; surely one ought to laugh. A young man melancholy because the universe wouldn't fit, because life was a tangle or a wind, or a Yes, or something!

"I'm very sorry," she cried. "You'll think me unfeeling, but—but—" Then she became matronly. "Oh, but your son wants employment. Has he no particular hobby? Why, I myself have worries, but I can generally forget them at the piano; and collecting stamps did no end of good for my brother. Perhaps Italy bores him; you ought to try the Alps or the Lakes."

The old man's face saddened, and he touched her gently with his hand. This did not alarm her; she thought that her advice had impressed him, and that he was thanking her for it. Indeed, he no longer alarmed her at all; she regarded him as a kind thing, but quite silly. Her feelings were as inflated spiritually as they had been an hour ago aesthetically, before she lost Baedeker. The dear George, now striding towards them over the tombstones, seemed both pitiable and absurd. He approached, his face in the shadow. He said:

"Miss Bartlett."

"Oh, good gracious me!" said Lucy, suddenly collapsing and again seeing the whole of life in a new perspective. "Where? Where?"

"In the nave."

"I see. Those gossiping little old Miss Alans must have—" She checked herself.

"Poor girl!" exploded old Mr Emerson. "Poor girl!"

She could not let this pass, for it was just what she was feeling herself.

"Poor girl? I fail to understand the point of that remark. I think myself a very fortunate girl, I assure you. I'm thoroughly happy, and having a splendid time. Pray don't waste time mourning over *me*. There's enough sorrow in the world, isn't there, without trying to invent it. Goodbye. Thank you both so much for all your kindness. Ah yes! There does come my cousin. A delightful morning! Santa Croce is a wonderful church."

She rejoined her cousin.

Chapter 3
Music, Violets and the Letter S

It so happened that Lucy, who found daily life rather chaotic, entered a more solid world when she opened the piano. She was then no longer either deferential or patronizing; no longer either a rebel or a slave. The kingdom of music is not the kingdom of this world; it will accept those whom breeding and intellect and culture have alike rejected. The commonplace person begins to play, and shoots into the empyrean without effort, whilst we look up, marvelling how he has escaped us, and thinking how we could worship him and love him, would he but translate his visions into human words, and his experiences into human actions. Perhaps he cannot; certainly he does not, or does so very seldom. Lucy had done so never.

She was no dazzling *exécutante*; her runs were not at all like strings of pearls, and she struck no more right notes than was suitable for one of her age and situation. Nor was she the passionate young lady, who performs so tragically on a summer's evening with the window open. Passion was there, but it could not be easily labelled; it slipped between love and hatred and jealousy, and all the furniture of the pictorial style. And she was tragical only in the sense that she was great, for she loved to play on the side of Victory. Victory of what and over what—that is more than the words of daily life can tell us. But that some sonatas of Beethoven are written tragic no one can gainsay; yet they can triumph or despair as the player decides, and Lucy had decided that they should triumph.

A very wet afternoon at the Bertolini permitted her to do the thing she really liked, and after lunch she opened the little draped piano. A few people lingered round and praised her playing, but, finding that she made no reply, dispersed to their rooms to write up their diaries or to sleep. She took no notice of Mr Emerson looking for his son, nor of Miss Bartlett looking for Miss Lavish, nor of Miss Lavish looking for her cigarette-case. Like every true performer, she was intoxicated by the mere feel of the notes: they were fingers caressing her own; and by touch, not by sound alone, did she come to her desire.

Mr Beebe, sitting unnoticed in the window, pondered over this illogical element in Miss Honeychurch, and recalled the occasion at Tunbridge Wells when he had discovered it. It was at one of those entertainments where the upper classes entertain the lower. The seats were filled with a respectful audience, and the ladies and gentlemen of the parish, under the auspices of their vicar, sang, or recited, or imitated the drawing of a champagne-cork. Among the promised items was "Miss Honeychurch. Piano. Beethoven", and Mr Beebe was wondering whether it would be *Adelaide* or the march of *The Ruins of Athens*, when his composure was disturbed by the opening bars of Opus 111. He was in suspense all through the introduction, for not until the pace quickens does one know what the performer intends. With the roar of the opening theme he knew that things were going extraordinarily; in the chords that herald the conclusion he heard the hammer-strokes of victory. He was glad that she only played the first movement, for he could have paid no attention to the winding intricacies of the measure of nine-sixteen. The audience clapped, no less respectful. It was Mr Beebe who started the stamping; it was all that one could do.

"Who is she?" he asked the vicar afterwards.

"Cousin of one of my parishioners. I do not consider her choice of a piece happy. Beethoven is usually so simple and direct in his appeal that it is sheer perversity to choose a thing like that, which, if anything, disturbs."

"Introduce me."

"She will be delighted. She and Miss Bartlett are full of the praises of your sermon."

"My sermon?" cried Mr Beebe. "Why ever did she listen to it?"

When he was introduced he understood why, for Miss Honeychurch, disjoined from her music-stool, was only a young lady with a quantity of dark hair and a very pretty, pale, undeveloped face. She loved going to concerts, she loved stopping with her cousin, she loved iced coffee and meringues. He did not doubt that she loved his sermon also. But before he left Tunbridge Wells he made a remark to the vicar, which he now made to Lucy herself when she closed the little piano and moved dreamily towards him.

"If Miss Honeychurch ever takes to live as she plays, it will be very exciting—both for us and for her."

Lucy at once re-entered daily life.

"Oh, what a funny thing! Someone said just the same to mother, and she said she trusted I should never live a duet."

"Doesn't Mrs Honeychurch like music?"

"She doesn't mind it. But she doesn't like one to get excited over anything; she thinks I am silly about it. She thinks—I can't make out. Once, you know, I said that I liked my own playing better than anyone's. She has never got over it. Of course, I didn't mean that I played well; I only meant—"

"Of course," said he, wondering why she bothered to explain.

"Music—" said Lucy, as if attempting some generality. She could not complete it, and looked out absently upon Italy in the wet. The whole life of the South was disorganized, and the most graceful nation in Europe had turned into formless lumps of clothes. The street and the river were dirty yellow, the bridge was dirty gray, and the hills were dirty purple. Somewhere in their folds were concealed Miss Lavish and Miss Bartlett, who had chosen this afternoon to visit the Torre del Gallo.

"What about music?" said Mr Beebe.

"Poor Charlotte will be sopped," was Lucy's reply.

The expedition was typical of Miss Bartlett, who would return cold, tired, hungry and angelic, with a ruined skirt, a pulpy Baedeker, and a tickling cough in her throat. On another day, when the whole world was singing and the air ran into the mouth like wine, she would refuse to stir from the drawing-room, saying that she was an old thing, and no fit companion for a hearty girl.

"Miss Lavish has led your cousin astray. She hopes to find the true Italy in the wet, I believe."

"Miss Lavish is so original," murmured Lucy. This was the stock remark, the supreme achievement of the Pension Bertolini in the way of definition. Miss Lavish was so original. Mr Beebe had his doubts, but they would have been put down to clerical narrowness. For that and for other reasons, he held his peace.

"Is it true," continued Lucy in awestruck tones, "that Miss Lavish is writing a book?"

"They do say so."

"What is it about?"

"It will be a novel," replied Mr Beebe, "dealing with modern Italy. Let me refer you for an account to Miss Catharine Alan, who uses words herself more admirably than anyone I know."

"I wish Miss Lavish would tell me herself. We started such friends. But I don't think she ought to have run away with Baedeker that morning in Santa Croce. Charlotte was most annoyed at finding me practically alone, and so I couldn't help being a little annoyed with Miss Lavish."

"The two ladies, at all events, have made it up."

He was interested in the sudden friendship between women so apparently dissimilar as Miss Bartlett and Miss Lavish. They were always in each other's company, with Lucy a slighted third. Miss Lavish he believed he understood, but Miss Bartlett might reveal unknown depths of strangeness, though not, perhaps, of meaning. Was Italy deflecting her from the path of prim chaperon, which he had assigned to her at Tunbridge Wells? All his life he had loved to study maiden ladies; they were his speciality, and his profession had provided him with ample opportunities for the work. Girls like Lucy were charming to look at, but Mr Beebe was, from rather profound reasons, somewhat chilly in his attitude towards the other sex, and preferred to be interested rather than enthralled.

Lucy, for the third time, said that poor Charlotte would be sopped. The Arno was rising in flood, washing away the traces of the little carts upon the foreshore. But in the south-west there had appeared a dull haze of yellow, which might mean better weather if it did not mean worse. She opened the window to inspect, and a cold blast entered the room, drawing a plaintive cry from Miss Catharine Alan, who entered at the same moment by the door.

"Oh, dear Miss Honeychurch, you will catch a chill! And Mr Beebe here besides. Who would suppose this is Italy? There is my sister actually nursing the hot-water can; no comforts or proper provisions."

She sidled towards them and sat down, self-conscious as she always was on entering a room which contained one man, or a man and one woman.

"I could hear your beautiful playing, Miss Honeychurch, though I was in my room with the door shut. Doors shut; indeed, most necessary. No one has the least idea of privacy in this country. And one person catches it from another."

Lucy answered suitably. Mr Beebe was not able to tell the ladies of his adventure at Modena, where the chambermaid burst in upon him in his bath, exclaiming cheerfully, "Fa niente, sono vecchia." He contented himself with saying: "I quite agree with you, Miss Alan. The Italians are a most unpleasant people. They pry everywhere, they see everything, and they know what we want before we know it ourselves. We are at their mercy. They read our thoughts, they foretell our desires. From the cab-driver down to—to Giotto, they turn us inside out, and I resent it. Yet in their heart of hearts they are—how superficial! They have no conception of the intellectual life. How right is Signora Bertolini, who exclaimed to me the other day: 'Ho, Mr Beebe, if you knew what I suffer over the children's edjucaishion! *Hi* won't 'ave my little Victorier taught by a hignorant Italian what can't explain nothink!" '

Miss Alan did not follow, but gathered that she was being mocked in an agreeable way. Her sister was a little disappointed in Mr Beebe, having expected better things from a clergyman whose head was bald and who wore a pair of russet whiskers. Indeed, who would have supposed that tolerance, sympathy and a sense of humour would inhabit that militant form?

In the midst of her satisfaction she continued to sidle, and at last the cause was disclosed. From the chair beneath her she extracted a gun-metal cigarette-case, on which were powdered in turquoise the initials E. L.

"That belongs to Lavish," said the clergyman. "A good fellow, Lavish, but I wish she'd start a pipe."

"Oh, Mr Beebe," said Miss Alan, divided between awe and mirth. "Indeed, though it is dreadful of her to smoke, it is not quite as dreadful as you suppose. She took to it, practically in despair, after her life's work was carried away in a landslip. Surely that makes it more excusable."

"What was that?" asked Lucy.

Mr Beebe sat back complacently, and Miss Alan began as follows:

"It was a novel—and I am afraid, from what I can gather, not a very nice novel. It is so sad when people who have abilities misuse them, and I must say they nearly always do. Anyhow, she left it almost finished in the Grotto of the Calvary at the Cappuccini Hotel at Amalfi while she went for a little ink. She said: 'Can I have a little ink, please?' But you know what Italians are, and meanwhile the Grotto fell roaring onto the beach, and the saddest thing of all is that she cannot remember what she has written. The poor thing was very ill after it, and so got tempted into cigarettes. It is a great secret, but I am glad to say that she is writing another novel. She told Teresa and Miss Pole the other day that she had got up all the local colour—this novel is to be about modern Italy; the other was historical—but that she could not start till she had an idea. First she tried Perugia for an inspiration, then she came here—this must on no account get round. And so cheerful through it all! I cannot help thinking that there is something to admire in everyone, even if you do not approve of them."

Miss Alan was always thus being charitable against her

better judgement. A delicate pathos perfumed her disconnected remarks, giving them unexpected beauty, just as in the decaying autumn woods there sometimes rise odours reminiscent of spring. She felt she had made almost too many allowances, and apologized hurriedly for her toleration.

"All the same, she is a little too—I hardly like to say unwomanly, but she behaved most strangely when the Emersons arrived."

Mr Beebe smiled as Miss Alan plunged into an anecdote which he knew she would be unable to finish in the presence of a gentleman.

"I don't know, Miss Honeychurch, if you have noticed that Miss Pole, the lady who has so much rather yellow hair, takes lemonade. That old Mr Emerson, who puts things very strangely—"

Her jaw dropped. She was silent. Mr Beebe, whose social resources were endless, went out to order some tea, and she continued to Lucy in a hasty whisper:

"Stomach. He warned Miss Pole of her stomach—acidity, he called it—and he may have meant to be kind. I must say I forgot myself and laughed; it was so sudden. As Teresa truly said, it was no laughing-matter. But the point is that Miss Lavish was positively *attracted* by his mentioning S., and said that she liked plain speaking, and meeting different grades of thought. She thought they were commercial travellers—'drummers' was the word she used—and all through dinner she tried to prove that England, our great and beloved country, rests on nothing but commerce. Teresa was very much annoyed and left the table before the cheese, saying as she did so: 'There, Miss Lavish, is one who can confute you better than I,' and pointed to that beautiful picture of Lord Tennyson. Then Miss Lavish said: 'Tut! The early Victorians.' Just imagine! 'Tut! The early Victorians.' My sister had gone, and I felt bound to speak. I said: 'Miss Lavish, *I* am an early Victorian; at least, that is to say, I will hear no breath of censure against our dear Queen.' It was horrible speaking. I reminded her how the Queen had been to Ireland when she did not want to go, and I must say she was dumbfoundered, and made no reply. But, unluckily, Mr Emerson overheard this part, and called in his deep voice: 'Quite so, quite so! I honour the woman for her Irish visit.' The woman! I tell things so badly; but you see what a tangle we were in by this time, all on account of S. having been mentioned in the first place. But that was not all. After dinner Miss Lavish actually came up and said: 'Miss Alan, I am going into the smoking-room to talk to those two nice men. Come too.' Needless to say, I refused such an unsuitable invitation, and she had the impertinence to tell me that it would broaden my ideas, and said that she had four brothers, all university men, except one who was in the Army, who always made a point of talking to commercial travellers."

"Let me finish the story," said Mr Beebe, who had returned. "Miss Lavish tried Miss Pole, myself, everyone, and finally said: 'I shall go alone.' She went. At the end of five minutes she returned unobtrusively with a green baize board, and began playing patience."

"What ever happened?" cried Lucy.

"No one knows. No one will ever know. Miss Lavish will never dare to tell, and Mr Emerson does not think it worth telling."

"Mr Beebe—old Mr Emerson, is he nice or not nice? I do so want to know."

Mr Beebe laughed and suggested that she should settle the question for herself.

"No; but it is so difficult. Sometimes he is so silly, and then I do not mind him. Miss Alan, what do you think? Is he nice?"

The little old lady shook her head, and sighed disapprovingly. Mr Beebe, whom the conversation amused, stirred her up by saying:

"I consider that you are bound to class him as nice, Miss Alan, after that business of the violets."

"Violets? Oh dear! Who told you about the violets? How do things get round? A pension is a sad place for gossips. No, I cannot forget how they behaved at Mr Eager's lecture at

Santa Croce. Oh, poor Miss Honeychurch! It really was too bad! No, I have quite changed. I do *not* like the Emersons. They are *not* nice."

Mr Beebe smiled nonchalantly. He had made a gentle effort to introduce the Emersons into Bertolini society, and the effort had failed. He was almost the only person who remained friendly to them. Miss Lavish, who represented intellect, was avowedly hostile, and now the Miss Alans, who stood for good breeding, were following her. Miss Bartlett, smarting under an obligation, would scarcely be civil. The case of Lucy was different. She had given him a hazy account of her adventures in Santa Croce, and he gathered that the two men had made a curious and possibly concerted attempt to annex her, to show her the world from their own strange standpoint, to interest her in their private sorrows and joys. This was impertinent; he did not wish their cause to be championed by a young girl; he would rather it should fail. After all, he knew nothing about them, and pension joys, pension sorrows, are flimsy things; whereas Lucy would be his parishioner.

Lucy, with one eye upon the weather, finally said that she thought the Emersons were nice; not that she saw anything of them now. Even their seats at dinner had been moved.

"But aren't they always waylaying you to go out with them, dear?" said the little lady inquisitively.

"Only once. Charlotte didn't like it, and said something —quite politely, of course."

"Most right of her. They don't understand our ways. They must find their level."

Mr Beebe rather felt that they had gone under. They had given up their attempt—if it was one—to conquer society, and now the father was almost as silent as the son. He wondered whether he would not plan a pleasant day for these folk before they left—some expedition, perhaps, with Lucy well chaperoned to be nice to them. It was one of Mr Beebe's chief pleasures to provide people with happy memories.

Evening approached while they chatted; the air became brighter; the colours on the trees and hills were purified, and the Arno lost its muddy solidity and began to twinkle. There were a few streaks of bluish-green among the clouds, a few patches of watery light upon the earth, and then the dripping façade of San Miniato shone brilliantly in the declining sun.

"Too late to go out," said Miss Alan in a voice of relief. "All the galleries are shut."

"I think I shall go out," said Lucy. "I want to go round the town in the circular tram—on the platform by the driver."

Her two companions looked grave. Mr Beebe, who felt responsible for her in the absence of Miss Bartlett, ventured to say:

"I wish we could. Unluckily I have letters. If you do want to go out alone, won't you be better on your feet?"

"Italians, dear, you know," said Miss Alan.

"Perhaps I shall meet someone who reads me through and through!"

But they still looked disapproval, and she so far conceded to Mr Beebe as to say that she would only go for a little walk, and keep to the streets frequented by tourists.

"She oughtn't really to go at all," said Mr Beebe, as they watched her from the window, "and she knows it. I put it down to too much Beethoven."

Chapter 4
Fourth Chapter

Mr Beebe was right. Lucy never knew her desires so clearly as after music. She had not really appreciated the clergyman's wit, nor the suggestive twitterings of Miss Alan. Conversation was tedious; she wanted something big, and she believed that it would have come to her on the wind-swept platform of an electric tram.

This she might not attempt. It was unladylike. Why? Why were most big things unladylike? Charlotte had once explained to her why. It was not that ladies were inferior to men; it was that they were different. Their mission was to inspire others to achievement rather than to achieve themselves. Indirectly, by means of tact and a spotless name, a lady could accomplish much. But if she rushed into the fray herself she would be first censured, then despised, and finally ignored. Poems had been written to illustrate this point.

There is much that is immortal in this medieval lady. The dragons have gone, and so have the knights, but still she lingers in our midst. She reigned in many an early Victorian castle, and was queen of much early Victorian song. It is sweet to protect her in the intervals of business, sweet to pay her honour when she has cooked our dinner well. But alas! the creature grows degenerate. In her heart also there are springing up strange desires. She too is enamoured of heavy winds, and vast panoramas, and green expanses of the sea. She has marked the kingdom of this world, how full it is of wealth, and beauty, and war—a radiant crust, built around the central fires, spinning towards the receding heavens. Men, declaring that she inspires them to it, move joyfully over the surface, having the most delightful meetings with other men, happy, not because they are masculine, but because they are alive.

Before the show breaks up she would like to drop the august title of the Eternal Woman, and go there as her transitory self.

Lucy does not stand for the medieval lady, who was rather an ideal to which she was bidden to lift her eyes when feeling serious. Nor has she any system of revolt. Here and there a restriction annoyed her particularly, and she would transgress it, and perhaps be sorry that she had done so. This afternoon she was peculiarly restive. She would really like to do something of which her well-wishers disapproved. As she might not go on the electric tram, she went to Alinari's shop.

There she bought a photograph of Botticelli's *Birth of Venus*. Venus, being a pity, spoiled the picture, otherwise so charming, and Miss Bartlett had persuaded her to do without it. (A pity in art of course signified the nude.) Giorgione's *Tempesta*, the *Idolino*, some of the Sistine frescoes and the Apoxyomenos were added to it. She felt a little calmer then, and bought Fra Angelico's *Coronation*, Giotto's *Ascension of St John*, some Della Robbia babies, and some Guido Reni Madonnas. For her taste was catholic, and she extended uncritical approval to every well-known name.

But though she spent nearly seven lire the gates of liberty seemed still unopened. She was conscious of her discontent; it was new to her to be conscious of it. "The world," she thought, "is certainly full of beautiful things, if only I could come across them." It was not surprising that Mrs Honeychurch disapproved of music, declaring that it always left her daughter peevish, unpractical and touchy.

"Nothing ever happens to me," she reflected, as she entered the Piazza Signoria and looked nonchalantly at its marvels, now fairly familiar to her. The great square was in shadow; the sunshine had come too late to strike it. Neptune was already unsubstantial in the twilight, half god, half ghost, and his fountain plashed dreamily to the men and satyrs who idled together on its marge. The Loggia showed as the triple entrance of a cave, wherein dwelt many a deity, shadowy but immortal, looking forth upon the arrivals and departures of mankind. It was the hour of unreality—the hour, that is, when unfamiliar things are real. An older person at such an hour and in such a place might think that sufficient was happening to him, and rest content. Lucy desired more.

She fixed her eyes wistfully on the tower of the palace, which rose out of the lower darkness like a pillar of roughened gold. It seemed no longer a tower, no longer supported by earth, but some unattainable treasure throbbing in the tranquil sky. Its brightness mesmerized her, still dancing before her eyes when she bent them to the ground and started towards home.

Then something did happen.

Two Italians by the Loggia had been bickering about a debt. "Cinque lire," they had cried, "cinque lire!" They sparred at each other, and one of them was hit lightly upon the chest. He frowned; he bent towards Lucy with a look of interest, as if he had an important message for her. He opened his lips to deliver it, and a stream of red came out between them and trickled down his unshaven chin.

That was all. A crowd rose out of the dusk. It hid this extraordinary man from her, and bore him away to the fountain. Mr George Emerson happened to be a few paces away, looking at her across the spot where the man had been. How very odd! Across something. Even as she caught sight of him he grew dim; the palace itself grew dim, swayed above her, fell onto her softly, slowly, noiselessly, and the sky fell with it.

She thought: "Oh, what have I done?"

"Oh, what have I done?" she murmured, and opened her eyes.

George Emerson still looked at her, but not across anything. She had complained of dullness, and lo! one man was stabbed, and another held her in his arms.

They were sitting on some steps in the Uffizi Arcade. He must have carried her. He rose when she spoke, and began to dust his knees. She repeated:

"Oh, what have I done?"

"You fainted."

"I—I am very sorry."

"How are you now?"

"Perfectly well—absolutely well." And she began to nod and smile.

"Then let us come home. There's no point in our stopping."

He held out his hand to pull her up. She pretended not to see it. The cries from the fountain—they had never ceased—rang emptily. The whole world seemed pale and void of its original meaning.

"How very kind you have been! I might have hurt myself falling. But now I am well. I can go alone, thank you."

His hand was still extended.

"Oh, my photographs!" she exclaimed suddenly.

"What photographs?"

"I bought some photographs at Alinari's. I must have dropped them out there in the square." She looked at him cautiously. "Would you add to your kindness by fetching them?"

He added to his kindness. As soon as he had turned his back, Lucy arose with the cunning of a maniac and stole down the arcade towards the Arno.

"Miss Honeychurch!"

She stopped with her hand on her heart.

"You sit still; you aren't fit to go home alone."

"Yes, I am, thank you so very much."

"No, you aren't. You'd go openly if you were."

"But I had rather—"

"Then I don't fetch your photographs."

"I had rather be alone."

He said imperiously: "The man is dead—the man is probably dead; sit down till you are rested." She was bewildered, and obeyed him. "And don't move till I come back."

In the distance she saw creatures with black hoods, such as appear in dreams. The palace tower had lost the reflection of the declining day, and joined itself to earth. How should she talk to Mr Emerson when he returned from the shadowy square? Again the thought occurred to her, "Oh, what have I done?"—the thought that she, as well as the dying man, had crossed some spiritual boundary.

He returned, and she talked of the murder. Oddly enough, it was an easy topic. She spoke of the Italian character; she became almost garrulous over the incident that had made her faint five minutes before. Being strong physically, she soon overcame the horror of blood. She rose without his assistance, and though wings seemed to flutter inside her she walked firmly enough towards the Arno. There a cabman signalled to them; they refused him.

"And the murderer tried to kiss him, you say—how very odd Italians are!—and gave himself up to the police! Mr Beebe was saying that Italians know everything, but I think they are rather childish. When my cousin and I were at the Pitti yesterday—what was that?"

He had thrown something into the stream.

"What did you throw in?"

"Things I didn't want," he said crossly.

"Mr Emerson!"

"Well?"

"Where are the photographs?"

He was silent.

"I believe it was my photographs that you threw away."

"I didn't know what to do with them," he cried, and his voice was that of an anxious boy. Her heart warmed towards him for the first time. "They were covered with blood. There! I'm glad I've told you; and all the time we were making conversation I was wondering what to do with them." He pointed downstream. "They've gone." The river swirled under the bridge. "I did mind them so, and one is so foolish, it seemed better that they should go out to the sea—I don't know; I may just mean that they frightened me." Then the boy verged into a man. "For something tremendous has happened; I must face it without getting muddled. It isn't exactly that a man has died."

Something warned Lucy that she must stop him.

"It has happened," he repeated, "and I mean to find out what it is."

"Mr Emerson—"

He turned towards her frowning, as if she had disturbed him in some abstract quest.

"I want to ask you something before we go in."

They were close to their pension. She stopped and leant her elbows against the parapet of the embankment. He did likewise. There is at times a magic in identity of position; it is one of the things that have suggested to us eternal comradeship. She moved her elbows before saying:

"I have behaved ridiculously."

He was following his own thoughts.

"I was never so much ashamed of myself in my life; I cannot think what came over me."

"I nearly fainted myself," he said; but she felt that her attitude repelled him.

"Well, I owe you a thousand apologies."

"Oh, all right."

"And—this is the real point—you know how silly people are gossiping—ladies especially, I am afraid—you understand what I mean?"

"I'm afraid I don't."

"I mean, would you not mention it to anyone, my foolish behaviour?"

"Your behaviour? Oh yes, all right—all right."

"Thank you so much. And would you—"

She could not carry her request any further. The river was gushing below them, almost black in the advancing night. He had thrown her photographs into it, and then he had told her the reason. It struck her that it was hopeless to look for chivalry in such a man. He would do her no harm by idle gossip; he was trustworthy, intelligent, and even kind; he might even have a high opinion of her. But he lacked chivalry; his thoughts, like his behaviour, would not be modified by awe. It was useless to say to him, "And would you—" and hope that he would complete the sentence for himself, averting his eyes from her nakedness like the knight in that beautiful picture. She had been in his arms, and he remembered it, just as he remembered the blood on the photographs that she had bought in Alinari's shop. It was not exactly that a man had died; something had happened to the living: they had come to a situation where character tells, and where Childhood enters upon the branching paths of Youth.

"Well, thank you so much," she repeated. "How quickly these accidents do happen, and then one returns to the old life!"

"I don't."

Anxiety moved her to question him.

His answer was puzzling: "I shall probably want to live."

"But why, Mr Emerson? What do you mean?"

"I shall want to live, I say."

Leaning her elbows on the parapet, she contemplated the River Arno, whose roar was suggesting some unexpected melody to her ears.

Chapter 5
Possibilities of a Pleasant Outing

It was a family saying that "you never knew which way Charlotte Bartlett would turn". She was perfectly pleasant and sensible over Lucy's adventure, found the abridged account of it quite adequate, and paid suitable tribute to the courtesy of Mr George Emerson. She and Miss Lavish had had an adventure also. They had been stopped at the *dazio* coming back, and the young officials there, who seemed impudent and *désœuvré*, had tried to search their reticules for provisions. It might have been most unpleasant. Fortunately, Miss Lavish was a match for anyone.

For good or for evil, Lucy was left to face her problem alone. None of her friends had seen her, either in the Piazza or, later on, by the embankment. Mr Beebe, indeed, noticing her startled eyes at dinner-time, had again passed to himself the remark of "Too much Beethoven". But he only supposed that she was ready for an adventure, not that she had encountered it. This solitude oppressed her; she was accustomed to have her thoughts confirmed by others or, at all events, contradicted; it was too dreadful not to know whether she was thinking right or wrong.

At breakfast next morning she took decisive action. There were two plans between which she had to choose. Mr Beebe was walking up to the Torre del Gallo with the Emersons and some American ladies. Would Miss Bartlett and Miss Honeychurch join the party? Charlotte declined for herself; she had been there in the rain the previous afternoon. But she thought it an admirable idea for Lucy, who hated shopping, changing money, fetching letters, and other irksome duties—all of which Miss Bartlett must accomplish this morning, and could easily accomplish alone.

"No, Charlotte!" cried the girl, with real warmth. "It's

very kind of Mr Beebe, but I am certainly coming with you. I had much rather."

"Very well, dear," said Miss Bartlett, with a faint flush of pleasure that called forth a deep flush of shame on the cheeks of Lucy. How abominably she behaved to Charlotte, now as always! But now she should alter. All the morning she would be really nice to her.

She slipped her arm into her cousin's, and they started off along the Lungarno. The river was a lion that morning in strength, voice and colour. Miss Bartlett insisted on leaning over the parapet to look at it. She then made her usual remark, which was:

"How I do wish Freddy and your mother could see this, too!"

Lucy fidgeted; it was tiresome of Charlotte to have stopped exactly where she did.

"Look, Lucia! Oh, you are watching for the Torre del Gallo party. I feared you would repent you of your choice."

Serious as the choice had been, Lucy did not repent. Yesterday had been a muddle—queer and odd, the kind of thing one could not write down easily on paper—but she had a feeling that Charlotte and her shopping were preferable to George Emerson and the summit of the Torre del Gallo. Since she could not unravel the tangle, she must take care not to re-enter it. She could protest sincerely against Miss Bartlett's insinuations.

But, though she had avoided the chief actor, the scenery unfortunately remained. Charlotte, with the complacency of fate, led her from the river to the Piazza Signoria. She could not have believed that stones, a loggia, a fountain, a palace tower, would have such significance. For a moment she understood the nature of ghosts.

The exact site of the murder was occupied, not by a ghost, but by Miss Lavish, who had the morning newspaper in her hand. She hailed them briskly. The dreadful catastrophe of the previous day had given her an idea which she thought would work up into a book.

"Oh, let me congratulate you!" said Miss Bartlett. "After your despair of yesterday! What a fortunate thing!"

"Aha! Miss Honeychurch, come you here! I am in luck. Now, you are to tell me absolutely everything that you saw from the beginning."

Lucy poked at the ground with her parasol.

"But perhaps you would rather not?"

"I'm sorry—if you could manage without it, I think I would rather not."

The elder ladies exchanged glances, not of disapproval; it is suitable that a girl should feel deeply.

"It is I who am sorry," said Miss Lavish. "We literary hacks are shameless creatures. I believe there's no secret of the human heart into which we wouldn't pry."

She marched cheerfully to the fountain and back, and did a few calculations in realism. Then she said that she had been in the Piazza since eight o'clock collecting material. A good deal of it was unsuitable, but of course one always had to adapt. The two men had quarrelled over a five-franc note. For the five-franc note she should substitute a young lady, which would raise the tone of the tragedy, and at the same time furnish an excellent plot.

"What is the heroine's name?" asked Miss Bartlett.

"Leonora," said Miss Lavish; her own name was Eleanor.

"I do hope she's nice."

That desideratum would not be omitted.

"And what is the plot?"

Love, murder, abduction, revenge, was the plot. Out it all came while the fountain plashed to the satyrs in the morning sun.

"I hope you will excuse me for boring on like this," Miss Lavish concluded. "It is so tempting to talk to really sympathetic people. Of course, this is the barest outline. There will be a deal of local colouring, descriptions of Florence and the neighbourhood, and I shall also introduce some humorous characters. And let me give you all fair warning: I intend to be unmerciful to the British tourist."

"Oh, you wicked woman!" cried Miss Bartlett. "I am sure you are thinking of the Emersons."

Miss Lavish gave a Machiavellian smile.

"I confess that in Italy my sympathies are not with my own countrymen. It is the neglected Italians who attract me, and whose lives I am going to paint so far as I can. For I repeat and I insist, and I have always held most strongly, that a tragedy such as yesterday's is not the less tragic because it happened in humble life."

There was a fitting silence when Miss Lavish had concluded. Then the cousins wished success to her labours, and walked slowly away across the square.

"She is my idea of a really clever woman," said Miss Bartlett. "That last remark struck me as so particularly true. It should be a most pathetic novel."

Lucy assented. At present her great aim was not to get put into it. Her perceptions this morning were curiously keen, and she believed that Miss Lavish had her on trial for an *ingénue*.

"She is emancipated, but only in the very best sense of the word," continued Miss Bartlett slowly. "None but the superficial would be shocked at her. We had a long talk yesterday. She believes in justice and truth and human interest. She told me also that she has a high opinion of the destiny of woman—Mr Eager! Why, how nice! What a pleasant surprise!"

"Ah, not for me," said the chaplain blandly, "for I have been watching you and Miss Honeychurch for quite a little time."

"We were chatting to Miss Lavish."

His brow contracted.

"So I saw. Were you indeed? Andate via! Sono occupato!" The last remark was made to a vendor of panoramic photographs who was approaching with a courteous smile. "I am about to venture a suggestion. Would you and Miss Honeychurch be disposed to join me in a drive some day this week—a drive in the hills? We might go up by Fiesole and back by Settignano. There is a point on that road where we could get down and have an hour's ramble on the hillside. The view thence of Florence is most beautiful—far better than the hackneyed view from Fiesole. It is the view that Alessio Baldovinetti is fond of introducing into his pictures. That man had a decided feeling for landscape. Decidedly. But who looks at it today? Ah, the world is too much with us."

Miss Bartlett had not heard of Alessio Baldovinetti, but she knew that Mr Eager was no commonplace chaplain. He was a member of the residential colony who had made Florence their home. He knew the people who never walked about with Baedekers, who had learned to take a siesta after lunch, who took drives the pension tourists had never heard of, and saw by private influence galleries which were closed to them. Living in delicate seclusion, some in furnished flats, others in Renaissance villas on Fiesole's slope, they read, wrote, studied and exchanged ideas, thus attaining to that intimate knowledge, or rather perception, of Florence which is denied to all who carry in their pockets the coupons of Cook.

Therefore an invitation from the chaplain was something to be proud of. Between the two sections of his flock he was often the only link, and it was his avowed custom to select those of his migratory sheep who seemed worthy, and give them a few hours in the pastures of the permanent. Tea at a Renaissance villa? Nothing had been said about it yet. But if it did come to that—how Lucy would enjoy it!

A few days ago and Lucy would have felt the same. But the joys of life were grouping themselves anew. A drive in the hills with Mr Eager and Miss Bartlett—even if culminating in a residential tea-party—was no longer the greatest of them. She echoed the raptures of Charlotte somewhat faintly. Only when she heard that Mr Beebe was also coming did her thanks become more sincere.

"So we shall be a *partie carrée*," said the chaplain. "In these days of toil and tumult one has great need of the country and its message of purity. Andate via! Andate presto, presto! Ah, the town! Beautiful as it is, it is the town."

They assented.

"This very square—so I am told—witnessed yesterday the most sordid of tragedies. To one who loves the Florence of Dante and Savonarola there is something portentous in such desecration—portentous and humiliating."

"Humiliating indeed," said Miss Bartlett. "Miss Honeychurch happened to be passing through as it happened. She can hardly bear to speak of it." She glanced at Lucy proudly.

"And how came we to have you here?" asked the chaplain paternally.

Miss Bartlett's recent liberalism oozed away at the question. "Do not blame her, please, Mr Eager. The fault is mine: I left her unchaperoned."

"So you were here alone, Miss Honeychurch?" His voice suggested sympathetic reproof, but at the same time indicated that a few harrowing details would not be unacceptable. His dark, handsome face drooped mournfully towards her to catch her reply.

"Practically."

"One of our pension acquaintances kindly brought her home," said Miss Bartlett, adroitly concealing the sex of the preserver.

"For her also it must have been a terrible experience. I trust that neither of you were at all—that it was not in your immediate proximity."

Of the many things Lucy was noticing today, not the least remarkable was this: the ghoulish fashion in which respectable people will nibble after blood. George Emerson had kept the subject strangely pure.

"He died by the fountain, I believe," was her reply.

"And you and your friend—"

"Were over at the Loggia."

"That must have saved you much. You have not, of course, seen the disgraceful illustrations which the gutter press— This man is a public nuisance; he knows that I am a resident perfectly well, and yet he goes on worrying me to buy his vulgar views."

Surely the vendor of photographs was in league with Lucy—in the eternal league of Italy with youth. He had suddenly extended his book before Miss Bartlett and Mr Eager, binding their hands together by a long glossy ribbon of churches, pictures and views.

"This is too much!" cried the chaplain, striking petulantly at one of Fra Angelico's angels. She tore. A shrill cry arose from the vendor. The book, it seemed, was more valuable than one would have supposed.

"Willingly would I purchase—" began Miss Bartlett.

"Ignore him," said Mr Eager sharply, and they all walked rapidly away from the square.

But an Italian can never be ignored, least of all when he has a grievance. His mysterious persecution of Mr Eager became relentless; the air rang with his threats and lamentations. He appealed to Lucy; would not she intercede? He was poor—he sheltered a family—the tax on bread. He waited, he gibbered, he was recompensed, he was dissatisfied, he did not leave them until he had swept their minds clean of all thoughts, whether pleasant or unpleasant.

Shopping was the topic that now ensued. Under the chaplain's guidance they selected many hideous presents and mementoes—florid little picture-frames that seemed fashioned in gilded pastry; other little frames, more severe, that stood on little easels, and were carven out of oak; a blotting book of vellum; a Dante of the same material; cheap mosaic brooches, which the maids, next Christmas, would never tell from real; pins, pots, heraldic saucers, brown art-photographs; Eros and Psyche in alabaster; St Peter to match—all of which would have cost less in London.

This successful morning left no pleasant impressions on Lucy. She had been a little frightened, both by Miss Lavish and by Mr Eager, she knew not why. And as they frightened her she had, strangely enough, ceased to respect them. She doubted that Miss Lavish was a great artist. She doubted that Mr Eager was as full of spirituality and culture as she had been led to suppose. They were tried by some new test, and they were found wanting. As for Charlotte—as for Charlotte, she was exactly the same. It might be possible to be nice to her; it was impossible to love her.

"The son of a labourer; I happen to know it for a fact. A mechanic of some sort himself when he was young; then he took to writing for the Socialistic press. I came across him at Brixton."

They were talking about the Emersons.

"How wonderfully people rise in these days!" sighed Miss Bartlett, fingering a model of the leaning Tower of Pisa.

"Generally," replied Mr Eager, "one has only sympathy with their success. The desire for education and for social advance—in these things there is something not wholly vile. There are some working men whom one would be very willing to see out here in Florence—little as they would make of it."

"Is he a journalist now?" Miss Bartlett asked.

"He is not; he made an advantageous marriage."

He uttered this remark with a voice full of meaning, and ended it with a sigh.

"Oh, so he has a wife."

"Dead, Miss Bartlett, dead. I wonder—yes, I wonder how he has the effrontery to look me in the face, to dare to claim acquaintance with me. He was in my London parish long ago. The other day in Santa Croce, when he was with Miss Honeychurch, I snubbed him. Let him beware that he does not get more than a snub."

"What?" cried Lucy, flushing.

"Exposure!" hissed Mr Eager.

He tried to change the subject; but in scoring a dramatic point he had interested his audience more than he had intended. Miss Bartlett was full of very natural curiosity. Lucy, though she wished never to see the Emersons again, was not disposed to condemn them on a single word.

"Do you mean," she asked, "that he is an irreligious man? We know that already."

"Lucy dear—" said Miss Bartlett, gently reproving her cousin's penetration.

"I should be astonished if you knew all. The boy—an innocent child at the time—I will exclude. God knows what his education and his inherited qualities may have made him."

"Perhaps," said Miss Bartlett, "it is something that we had better not hear."

"To speak plainly," said Mr Eager, "it is. I will say no more."

For the first time Lucy's rebellious thoughts swept out in words—for the first time in her life.

"You have said very little."

"It was my intention to say very little," was his frigid reply. He gazed indignantly at the girl, who met him with equal indignation. She turned towards him from the shop counter; her breast heaved quickly. He observed her brow, and the sudden strength of her lips. It was intolerable that she should disbelieve him.

"Murder, if you want to know," he cried angrily. "That man murdered his wife!"

"How?" she retorted.

"To all intents and purposes he murdered her. That day in Santa Croce—did they say anything against me?"

"Not a word, Mr Eager—not a single word."

"Oh, I thought they had been libelling me to you. But I suppose it is only their personal charms that makes you defend them."

"I'm not defending them," said Lucy, losing her courage, and relapsing into the old chaotic methods. "They're nothing to me."

"How could you think she was defending them?" said Miss Bartlett, much discomfited by the unpleasant scene. The shop-man was possibly listening.

"She will find it difficult. For that man has murdered his wife in the sight of God."

The addition of God was striking. But the chaplain was really trying to qualify a rash remark. A silence followed which might have been impressive, but was merely awkward. Then Miss Bartlett hastily purchased the Leaning Tower, and led the way into the street.

"I must be going," said he, shutting his eyes and taking out his watch.

Miss Bartlett thanked him for his kindness, and spoke with enthusiasm of the approaching drive.

"Drive? Oh, is our drive to come off?"

Lucy was recalled to her manners, and after a little exertion the complacency of Mr Eager was restored.

"Bother the drive!" exclaimed the girl, as soon as he had departed. "It is just the drive we had arranged with Mr Beebe without any fuss at all. Why should he invite us in that absurd manner? We might as well invite him. We are each paying for ourselves."

Miss Bartlett, who had intended to lament over the Emersons, was launched by this remark into unexpected thoughts.

"If that is so, dear—if the drive we and Mr Beebe are going with Mr Eager is really the same as the one we were going with Mr Beebe, then I foresee a sad kettle of fish."

"How?"

"Because Mr Beebe has asked Eleanor Lavish to come, too."

"That will mean another carriage."

"Far worse. Mr Eager does not like Eleanor. She knows it herself. The truth must be told: she is too unconventional for him."

They were now in the newspaper-room at the English bank. Lucy stood by the central table, heedless of *Punch* and the *Graphic*, trying to answer, or at all events to formulate, the questions rioting in her brain. The well-known world had broken up, and there emerged Florence, a magic city where people thought and did the most extraordinary things. Murder, accusations of murder, a lady clinging to one man and being rude to another—were these the daily incidents of her streets? Was there more in her frank beauty than met the eye—the power, perhaps, to evoke passions, good and bad, and to bring them speedily to a fulfilment?

Happy Charlotte, who, though greatly troubled over things that did not matter, seemed oblivious to things that did; who could conjecture with admirable delicacy "where things might lead to", but apparently lost sight of the goal as she approached it! Now she was crouching in the corner trying to extract a circular note from a kind of linen nosebag which hung in chaste concealment round her neck. She had been told that this was the only safe way to carry money in Italy; it must only be broached within the walls of the

English bank. As she groped she murmured: "Whether it is Mr Beebe who forgot to tell Mr Eager, or Mr Eager who forgot when he told us, or whether they have decided to leave Eleanor out altogether—which they could scarcely do—but in any case we must be prepared. It is you they really want; I am only asked for appearances. You shall go with the two gentlemen, and I and Eleanor will follow behind. A one-horse carriage would do for us. Yet how difficult it is!"

"It is indeed," replied the girl, with a gravity that sounded sympathetic.

"What do you think about it?" asked Miss Bartlett, flushed from the struggle, and buttoning up her dress.

"I don't know what I think, nor what I want."

"Oh dear, Lucy! I do hope Florence isn't boring you. Speak the word, and, as you know, I would take you to the ends of the earth tomorrow."

"Thank you, Charlotte," said Lucy, and pondered over the offer.

There were letters for her at the bureau—one from her brother, full of athletics and biology; one from her mother, delightful as only her mother's letters could be. She read in it of the crocuses which had been bought for yellow and were coming up puce, of the new parlourmaid, who had watered the ferns with essence of lemonade, of the semi-detached cottages which were ruining Summer Street, and breaking the heart of Sir Harry Otway. She recalled the free, pleasant life of her home, where she was allowed to do everything, and where nothing ever happened to her. The road up through the pine-woods, the clean drawing-room, the view over the Sussex Weald—all hung before her bright and distinct, but pathetic as the pictures in a gallery to which, after much experience, a traveller returns.

"And the news?" asked Miss Bartlett.

"Mrs Vyse and her son have gone to Rome," said Lucy, giving the news that interested her least. "Do you know the Vyses?"

"Oh, not that way back. We can never have too much of the dear Piazza Signoria."

"They're nice people, the Vyses. So clever—my idea of what's really clever. Don't you long to be in Rome?"

"I die for it!"

The Piazza Signoria is too stony to be brilliant. It has no grass, no flowers, no frescoes, no glittering walls of marble or comforting patches of ruddy brick. By an odd chance—unless we believe in a presiding genius of place—the statues that relieve its severity suggest, not the innocence of childhood nor the glorious bewilderment of youth, but the conscious achievements of maturity. Perseus and Judith, Hercules and Thusnelda, they have done or suffered something, and, though they are immortal, immortality has come to them after experience, not before. Here, not only in the solitude of Nature, might a hero meet a goddess, or a heroine a god.

"Charlotte!" cried the girl suddenly. "Here's an idea. What if we popped off to Rome tomorrow—straight—to the Vyses' hotel? For I do know what I want. I'm sick of Florence. Now, you said you'd go to the ends of the earth! Do! Do!"

Miss Bartlett, with equal vivacity, replied:

"Oh, you droll person! Pray, what would become of your drive in the hills?"

They passed together through the gaunt beauty of the square, laughing over the unpractical suggestion.

Chapter 6

The Reverend Arthur Beebe, the Reverend Cuthbert Eager, Mr Emerson, Mr George Emerson, Miss Eleanor Lavish, Miss Charlotte Bartlett, and Miss Lucy Honeychurch Drive out in Carriages to See a View; Italians Drive them

It was Phaethon who drove them to Fiesole that memorable day, a youth all irresponsibility and fire, recklessly urging his master's horses up the stony hill. Mr Beebe recognized him at once. Neither the Ages of Faith nor the Age of Doubt had touched him; he was Phaethon in Tuscany driving a cab. And it was Persephone whom he asked leave to pick up on the way, saying that she was his sister—Persephone, tall and slender and pale, returning with the spring to her mother's cottage, and still shading her eyes from the unaccustomed light. To her Mr Eager objected, saying that here was the thin edge of the wedge, and one must guard against imposition. But the ladies interceded, and, when it had been made clear that it was a very great favour, the goddess was allowed to mount beside the god.

Phaethon at once slipped the left rein over her head, thus enabling himself to drive with his arm round her waist. She did not mind. Mr Eager, who sat with his back to the horses, saw nothing of the indecorous proceeding, and continued his conversation with Lucy. The other two occupants of the carriage were old Mr Emerson and Miss Lavish. For a dreadful thing had happened: Mr Beebe, without consulting Mr Eager, had doubled the size of the party. And, though Miss Bartlett and Miss Lavish had planned all the morning how people were to sit, at the critical moment when the carriages came round they lost their heads, and Miss Lavish got in with Lucy, while Miss Bartlett, with George Emerson and Mr Beebe, followed on behind.

It was hard on the poor chaplain to have his *partie carrée* thus transformed. Tea at a Renaissance villa, if he had ever meditated it, was now impossible. Lucy and Miss Bartlett had a certain style about them, and Mr Beebe, though unreliable, was a man of parts. But a shoddy lady writer and a journalist who had murdered his wife in the sight of God—they should enter no villa at his introduction.

Lucy, elegantly dressed in white, sat erect and nervous amid these explosive ingredients, attentive to Mr Eager, repressive towards Miss Lavish, watchful of old Mr Emerson—hitherto fortunately asleep, thanks to a heavy lunch and the drowsy atmosphere of spring. She looked on the expedition as the work of Fate. But for it she would have avoided George Emerson successfully. In an open manner he had shown that he wished to continue their intimacy. She had refused, not because she disliked him, but because she did not know what had happened, and suspected that he did know. And this frightened her.

For the real event—whatever it was—had taken place, not in the Loggia, but by the river. To behave wildly at the sight of death is pardonable. But to discuss it afterwards, to pass from discussion into silence, and through silence into sympathy, that is an error, not of a startled emotion, but of the whole fabric. There was really something blameworthy (she thought) in their joint contemplation of the shadowy stream, in the common impulse which had turned them to the house without the passing of a look or word. This sense of wickedness had been slight at first. She had nearly joined the party to the Torre del Gallo. But each time that she avoided George it became more imperative that she should avoid him again. And now celestial irony, working through her cousin and two clergymen, did not suffer her to leave Florence till she had made this expedition with him through the hills.

Meanwhile Mr Eager held her in civil converse; their little tiff was over.

"So, Miss Honeychurch, you are travelling? As a student of art?"

"Oh, dear me, no—oh no!"

"Perhaps as a student of human nature," interposed Miss Lavish, "like myself?"

"Oh no. I am here as a tourist."

"Oh, indeed," said Mr Eager. "Are you indeed? If you will not think me rude, we residents sometimes pity you poor tourists not a little—handed about like a parcel of goods from Venice to Florence, from Florence to Rome, living herded together in pensions or hotels, quite unconscious of anything that is outside Baedeker, their one anxiety to get 'done' or 'through' and go on somewhere else. The result is, they mix up towns, rivers, palaces in one inextricable whirl. You know the American girl in *Punch* who says: 'Say, poppa, what did we see at Rome?' And the father replies: 'Why, guess Rome was the place where we saw the yaller dog.' There's travelling for you. Ha! ha! ha!"

"I quite agree," said Miss Lavish, who had several times tried to interrupt his mordant wit. "The narrowness and superficiality of the Anglo-Saxon tourist is nothing less than a menace."

"Quite so. Now, the English colony at Florence, Miss Honeychurch—and it is of considerable size, though, of course, not all equally—a few are here for trade, for example. But the greater part are students. Lady Helen Laverstock is at present busy over Fra Angelico. I mention her name because we are passing her villa on the left. No, you can only see it if you stand—no, do not stand; you will fall. She is very proud of that thick hedge. Inside, perfect seclusion. One might have gone back six hundred years. Some critics believe that her garden was the scene of *The Decameron*, which lends it an additional interest, does it not?"

"It does indeed!" cried Miss Lavish. "Tell me, where do they place the scene of that wonderful seventh day?"

But Mr Eager proceeded to tell Miss Honeychurch that on the right lived Mr Someone Something, an American of the best type—so rare!—and that the Somebody Elses were further down the hill. "Doubtless you know her monographs in the series of 'Mediaeval Byways'? He is working at

'Gemistus Pletho'. Sometimes as I take tea in their beautiful grounds I hear, over the wall, the electric tram squealing up the new road with its load of hot, dusty, unintelligent tourists who are going to 'do' Fiesole in an hour in order that they may say they have been there, and I think—I think—I think how little they think what lies so near them."

During this speech the two figures on the box were sporting with each other disgracefully. Lucy had a spasm of envy. Granted that they wished to misbehave, it was pleasant for them to be able to do so. They were probably the only people enjoying the expedition. The carriage swept with agonizing jolts up through the Piazza of Fiesole and into the Settignano road.

"Piano! Piano!" said Mr Eager, elegantly waving his hand over his head.

"Va bene, signore, va bene, va bene," crooned the driver, and whipped his horses up again.

Now Mr Eager and Miss Lavish began to talk against each other on the subject of Alessio Baldovinetti. Was he a cause of the Renaissance, or was he one of its manifestations? The other carriage was left behind. As the pace increased to a gallop the large, slumbering form of Mr Emerson was thrown against the chaplain with the regularity of a machine.

"Piano! Piano!" said he, with a martyred look at Lucy.

An extra lurch made him turn angrily in his seat. Phaethon, who for some time had been endeavouring to kiss Persephone, had just succeeded.

A little scene ensued, which, as Miss Bartlett said afterwards, was most unpleasant. The horses were stopped, the lovers were ordered to disentangle themselves, the boy was to lose his *pourboire*, the girl was immediately to get down.

"She is my sister," said he, turning round on them with piteous eyes.

Mr Eager took the trouble to tell him that he was a liar. Phaethon hung down his head, not at the matter of the accusation, but at its manner. At this point Mr Emerson, whom the shock of stopping had awoken, declared that the lovers must on no account be separated, and patted them on the back to signify his approval. And Miss Lavish, though unwilling to ally with him, felt bound to support the cause of bohemianism.

"Most certainly I would let them be," she cried. "But I dare say I shall receive scant support. I have always flown in the face of the conventions all my life. This is what *I* call an adventure."

"We must not submit," said Mr Eager. "I knew he was trying it on. He is treating us as if we were a party of Cook's tourists."

"Surely no!" said Miss Lavish, her ardour visibly decreasing.

The other carriage had drawn up behind, and sensible Mr Beebe called out that after this warning the couple would be sure to behave themselves properly.

"Leave them alone," Mr Emerson begged the chaplain, of whom he stood in no awe. "Do we find happiness so often that we should turn it off the box when it happens to sit there? To be driven by lovers—a king might envy us, and if we part them it's more like sacrilege than anything I know."

Here the voice of Miss Bartlett was heard saying that a crowd had begun to collect.

Mr Eager, who suffered from an over-fluent tongue rather than a resolute will, was determined to make himself heard. He addressed the driver again. Italian in the mouth of Italians is a deep-voiced stream, with unexpected cataracts and boulders to preserve it from monotony. In Mr Eager's mouth it resembled nothing so much as an acid whistling fountain which played ever higher and higher, and quicker and quicker, and more and more shrilly, till abruptly it was turned off with a click.

"Signorina!" said the man to Lucy, when the display had ceased. Why should he appeal to Lucy?

"Signorina!" echoed Persephone in her glorious contralto. She pointed at the other carriage. Why?

For a moment the two girls looked at each other. Then Persephone got down from the box.

"Victory at last!" said Mr Eager, smiting his hands together as the carriages started again.

"It is not victory," said Mr Emerson. "It is defeat. You have parted two people who were happy."

Mr Eager shut his eyes. He was obliged to sit next to Mr Emerson, but he would not speak to him. The old man was refreshed by sleep, and took up the matter warmly. He commanded Lucy to agree with him; he shouted for support to his son.

"We have tried to buy what cannot be bought with money. He has bargained to drive us, and he is doing it. We have no rights over his soul."

Miss Lavish frowned. It is hard when a person you have classed as typically British speaks out of his character.

"He was not driving us well," she said. "He jolted us."

"That I deny. It was as restful as sleeping. Aha! He is jolting us now. Can you wonder? He would like to throw us out, and most certainly he is justified. And if I were superstitious I'd be frightened of the girl, too. It doesn't do to injure young people. Have you ever heard of Lorenzo de' Medici?"

Miss Lavish bristled.

"Most certainly I have. Do you refer to Lorenzo il Magnifico, or to Lorenzo, Duke of Urbino, or to Lorenzo surnamed Lorenzino on account of his diminutive stature?"

"The Lord knows. Possibly he does know, for I refer to Lorenzo the poet. He wrote a line—so I heard yesterday—which runs like this: 'Don't go fighting against the spring.' "

Mr Eager could not resist the opportunity for erudition.

"Non fate guerra al Maggio," he murmured. " 'War not with the May' would render a correct meaning."

"The point is, we have warred with it. Look." He pointed to the Val d' Arno, which was visible far below them, through the budding trees. "Fifty miles of spring, and we've come up to admire them. Do you suppose there's any difference between spring in nature and spring in man? But there we go, praising the one and condemning the other as improper, ashamed that the same laws work eternally through both."

No one encouraged him to talk. Presently Mr Eager gave a signal for the carriages to stop, and marshalled the party for their ramble on the hill. A hollow like a great amphitheatre, full of terraced steps and misty olives, now lay between them and the heights of Fiesole, and the road, still following its curve, was about to sweep on to a promontory which stood out into the plain. It was this promontory, uncultivated, wet, covered with bushes and occasional trees, which had caught the fancy of Alessio Baldovinetti nearly five hundred years before. He had ascended it, that diligent and rather obscure master, possibly with an eye to business, possibly for the joy of ascending. Standing there, he had seen that view of the Val d' Arno and distant Florence, which he afterwards had introduced not very effectively into his work. But where exactly had he stood? That was the question which Mr Eager hoped to solve now. And Miss Lavish, whose nature was attracted by anything problematical, had become equally enthusiastic.

But it is not easy to carry the pictures of Alessio Baldovinetti in your head, even if you have remembered to look at them before starting. And the haze in the valley increased the difficulty of the quest. The party sprang about from tuft to tuft of grass, their anxiety to keep together being only equalled by their desire to go in different directions. Finally they split into groups. Lucy clung to Miss Bartlett and Miss Lavish; the Emersons returned to hold laborious converse with the drivers; while the two clergymen, who were expected to have topics in common, were left to each other.

The two elder ladies soon threw off the mask. In the audible whisper that was now so familiar to Lucy they began to discuss, not Alessio Baldovinetti, but the drive. Miss Bartlett had asked Mr George Emerson what his profession was, and he had answered "the railway". She was very sorry that she had asked him. She had no idea that it would be such a dreadful answer, or she would not have asked him. Mr Beebe had turned the conversation so cleverly, and she hoped that the young man was not very much hurt at her asking him.

"The railway!" gasped Miss Lavish. "Oh, but I shall die! Of course it was the railway!" She could not control her mirth. "He is the image of a porter—on, on the South-Eastern."

"Eleanor, be quiet," plucking at her vivacious companion. "Hush! They'll hear—the Emersons—"

"I can't stop. Let me go my wicked way. A porter—"

"Eleanor!"

"I'm sure it's all right," put in Lucy. "The Emersons won't hear, and they wouldn't mind if they did."

Miss Lavish did not seem pleased at this.

"Miss Honeychurch listening!" she said rather crossly. "Pouf! Wouf! You naughty girl! Go away!"

"Oh, Lucy, you ought to be with Mr Eager, I'm sure."

"I can't find them now, and I don't want to either."

"Mr Eager will be offended. It is your party."

"Please, I'd rather stop here with you."

"No, I agree," said Miss Lavish. "It's like a school feast; the boys have got separated from the girls. Miss Lucy, you are to go. We wish to converse on high topics unsuited for your ear."

The girl was stubborn. As her time at Florence drew to its close she was only at ease amongst those to whom she felt indifferent. Such a one was Miss Lavish, and such for the moment was Charlotte. She wished she had not called attention to herself; they were both annoyed at her remark and seemed determined to get rid of her.

"How tired one gets," said Miss Bartlett. "Oh, I do wish Freddy and your mother could be here."

Unselfishness with Miss Bartlett had entirely usurped the functions of enthusiasm. Lucy did not look at the view either. She would not enjoy anything till she was safe at Rome.

"Then sit you down," said Miss Lavish. "Observe my foresight."

With many a smile she produced two of those mackintosh squares that protect the frame of the tourist from damp grass or cold marble steps. She sat on one; who was to sit on the other?

"Lucy; without a moment's doubt, Lucy. The ground will do for me. Really I have not had rheumatism for years. If I do feel it coming on I shall stand. Imagine your mother's feelings if I let you sit in the wet in your white linen." She sat down heavily where the ground looked particularly moist. "Here we are, all settled delightfully. Even if my dress is thinner it will not show so much, being brown. Sit down, dear; you are too unselfish; you don't assert yourself enough." She cleared her throat. "Now don't be alarmed; this isn't a cold. It's the tiniest cough, and I have had it three days. It's nothing to do with sitting here at all."

There was only one way of treating the situation. At the end of five minutes Lucy departed in search of Mr Beebe and Mr Eager, vanquished by the mackintosh square.

She addressed herself to the drivers, who were sprawling in the carriages, perfuming the cushions with cigars. The miscreant, a bony young man scorched black by the sun, rose to greet her with the courtesy of a host and the assurance of a relative.

"*Dove?*" said Lucy, after much anxious thought.

His face lit up. Of course he knew where. Not so far either. His arm swept three-fourths of the horizon. He should just think he did know where. He pressed his finger-tips to his forehead and then pushed them towards her, as if oozing with visible extract of knowledge.

More seemed necessary. What was the Italian for "clergymen"?

"Dove buoni uomini?" said she at last.

Good? Scarcely the adjective for those noble beings! He showed her his cigar.

"Uno—piu—piccolo," was her next remark, implying "Has the cigar been given to you by Mr Beebe, the smaller of the two good men?"

She was correct as usual. He tied the horse to a tree, kicked it to make it stay quiet, dusted the carriage, arranged his hair, remoulded his hat, encouraged his moustache, and in rather less than a quarter of a minute was ready to conduct her. Italians are born knowing the way. It would seem that the whole earth lay before them, not as a map, but as a chess-board, whereon they continually behold the changing pieces as well as the squares. Anyone can find places, but the finding of people is a gift from God.

He only stopped once, to pick her some great blue violets. She thanked him with real pleasure. In the company of this common man the world was beautiful and direct. For the first time she felt the influence of spring. His arm swept the horizon gracefully; violets, like other things, existed in great profusion there; would she like to see them?

"Ma buoni uomini."

He bowed. Certainly. Good men first, violets afterwards. They proceeded briskly through the undergrowth, which became thicker and thicker. They were nearing the edge of the promontory, and the view was stealing round them, but the brown network of the bushes shattered it into countless pieces. He was occupied in his cigar, and in holding back the pliant boughs. She was rejoicing in her escape from dullness. Not a step, not a twig, was unimportant to her.

"What is that?"

There was a voice in the wood, in the distance behind them. The voice of Mr Eager? He shrugged his shoulders. An Italian's ignorance is sometimes more remarkable than his knowledge. She could not make him understand that perhaps they had missed the clergymen. The view was forming at last; she could discern the river, the golden plain, other hills.

"Eccolo!" he exclaimed.

At the same moment the ground gave way, and with a cry she fell out of the wood. Light and beauty enveloped her. She had fallen onto a little open terrace, which was covered with violets from end to end.

"Courage!" cried her companion, now standing some six feet above. "Courage and love."

She did not answer. From her feet the ground sloped sharply into the view, and violets ran down in rivulets and streams and cataracts, irrigating the hillside with blue, eddying round the tree stems, collecting into pools in the hollows, covering the grass with spots of azure foam. But never again were they in such profusion; this terrace was the well-head, the primal source whence beauty gushed out to water the earth.

Standing at its brink, like a swimmer who prepares, was the good man. But he was not the good man that she had expected, and he was alone.

George had turned at the sound of her arrival. For a moment he contemplated her, as one who had fallen out of heaven. He saw radiant joy in her face, he saw the flowers beat against her dress in blue waves. The bushes above them closed. He stepped quickly forward and kissed her.

Before she could speak, almost before she could feel, a voice called, "Lucy! Lucy! Lucy!" The silence of life had been broken by Miss Bartlett, who stood brown against the view.

Chapter 7
They Return

Some complicated game had been playing up and down the hillside all the afternoon. What it was and exactly how the players had sided, Lucy was slow to discover. Mr Eager had met them with a questioning eye. Charlotte had repulsed him with much small-talk. Mr Emerson, seeking his son, was told whereabouts to find him. Mr Beebe, who wore the heated aspect of a neutral, was bidden to collect the factions for the return home. There was a general sense of groping and bewilderment. Pan had been amongst them—not the great god Pan, who has been buried these two thousand years, but the little god Pan, who presides over social contretemps and unsuccessful picnics. Mr Beebe had lost everyone, and had consumed in solitude the tea-basket which he had brought up as a pleasant surprise. Miss Lavish had lost Miss Bartlett. Lucy had lost Mr Eager. Mr Emerson had lost George. Miss Bartlett had lost a mackintosh square. Phaethon had lost the game.

That last fact was undeniable. He climbed onto the box shivering, with his collar up, prophesying the swift approach of bad weather.

"Let us go immediately," he told them. "The signorino will walk."

"All the way? He will be hours," said Mr Beebe.

"Apparently. I told him it was unwise." He would look no one in the face; perhaps defeat was particularly mortifying for him. He alone had played skilfully, using the whole of his instinct, while the others had used scraps of their intelligence. He alone had divined what things were, and what he wished them to be. He alone had interpreted the message that Lucy had received five days before from the lips of a dying man. Persephone, who spends half her life in the grave—she could interpret it also. Not so these English. They gain knowledge slowly, and perhaps too late.

The thoughts of a cab-driver, however just, seldom affect the lives of his employers. He was the most competent of Miss Bartlett's opponents, but infinitely the least dangerous. Once back in the town, he and his insight and his knowledge would trouble English ladies no more. Of course, it was most unpleasant; she had seen his black head in the bushes; he might make a tavern story out of it. But, after all, what have we to do with taverns? Real menace belongs to the drawing-room. It was of drawing-room people that Miss Bartlett thought as she journeyed downwards towards the fading sun. Lucy sat beside her; Mr Eager sat opposite, trying to catch her eye; he was vaguely suspicious. They spoke of Alessio Baldovinetti.

Rain and darkness came on together. The two ladies huddled together under an inadequate parasol. There was a lightning flash, and Miss Lavish, who was nervous, screamed from the carriage in front. At the next flash, Lucy screamed also. Mr Eager addressed her professionally.

"Courage, Miss Honeychurch, courage and faith. If I might say so, there is something almost blasphemous in this horror of the elements. Are we seriously to suppose that all these clouds, all this immense electrical display, is simply called into existence to extinguish you or me?"

"No—of course—"

"Even from the scientific standpoint the chances against our being struck are enormous. The steel knives, the only articles which might attract the current, are in the other carriage. And, in any case, we are infinitely safer than if we were walking. Courage—courage and faith."

Under the rug, Lucy felt the kindly pressure of her cousin's hand. At times our need for a sympathetic gesture is so great that we care not what exactly it signifies or how much we may have to pay for it afterwards. Miss Bartlett, by this timely exercise of her muscles, gained more than she would have got in hours of preaching or cross-examination.

She renewed it when the two carriages stopped, half into Florence.

"Mr Eager!" called Mr Beebe. "We want your assistance. Will you interpret for us?"

"George!" cried Mr Emerson. "Ask your driver which way George went. The boy may lose his way. He may be killed."

"Go, Mr Eager," said Miss Bartlett. "No, don't ask our driver; our driver is no help. Go and support poor Mr Beebe; he is nearly demented."

"He may be killed!" cried the old man. "He may be killed!"

"Typical behaviour," said the chaplain, as he quitted the carriage. "In the presence of reality that kind of person invariably breaks down."

"What does he know?" whispered Lucy as soon as they were alone. "Charlotte, how much does Mr Eager know?"

"Nothing, dearest; he knows nothing. But"—she pointed at the driver—"*he* knows everything. Dearest, had we better? Shall I?" She took out her purse. "It is dreadful to be entangled with low-class people. He saw it all." Tapping Phaethon's back with her guidebook, she said, "Silenzio!" and offered him a franc.

"Va bene," he replied, and accepted it. As well this ending to his day as any. But Lucy, a mortal maid, was disappointed in him.

There was an explosion up the road. The storm had struck the overhead wire of the tramline, and one of the great supports had fallen. If they had not stopped perhaps they might have been hurt. They chose to regard it as a miraculous preservation, and the floods of love and sincerity, which might fructify every hour of life, burst forth in tumult. They descended from the carriages; they embraced each other. It was as joyful to be forgiven past unworthinesses as to forgive them. For a moment they realized vast possibilities of good.

The older people recovered quickly. In the very height of their emotion they knew it to be unmanly or unladylike. Miss Lavish calculated that, even if they had continued, they would not have been caught in the accident. Mr Eager mumbled a temperate prayer. But the drivers, through miles of dark squalid road, poured out their souls to the dryads and the saints, and Lucy poured out hers to her cousin.

"Charlotte, dear Charlotte, kiss me. Kiss me again. Only you can understand me. You warned me to be careful. And I —I thought I was developing."

"Do not cry, dearest. Take your time."

"I have been obstinate and silly—worse than you know, far worse. Once by the river—oh, but he isn't killed—he wouldn't be killed, would he?"

The thought disturbed her repentance. As a matter of fact, the storm was worst along the road; but she had been near danger, and so she thought it must be near to everyone.

"I trust not. One would always pray against that."

"He is really—I think he was taken by surprise, just as I was before. But this time I'm not to blame; I do want you to believe that. I simply slipped into those violets. No, I want to be really truthful. I am a little to blame. I had silly thoughts. The sky, you know, was gold, and the ground all blue, and for a moment he looked like someone in a book."

"In a book?"

"Heroes—gods—the nonsense of schoolgirls."

"And then?"

"But, Charlotte, you know what happened then."

Miss Bartlett was silent. Indeed, she had little more to learn. With a certain amount of insight she drew her young cousin affectionately to her. All the way back Lucy's body was shaken by deep sighs, which nothing could repress.

"I want to be truthful," she whispered. "It is so hard to be absolutely truthful."

"Don't be troubled, dearest. Wait till you are calmer. We will talk it over before bed-time in my room."

So they re-entered the city with hands clasped. It was a shock to the girl to find how far emotion had ebbed in others. The storm had ceased, and Mr Emerson was easier about his son. Mr Beebe had regained good humour, and Mr

Eager was already snubbing Miss Lavish. Charlotte alone she was sure of—Charlotte, whose exterior concealed so much insight and love.

The luxury of self-exposure kept her almost happy through the long evening. She thought not so much of what had happened as of how she should describe it. All her sensations, her spasms of courage, her moments of unreasonable joy, her mysterious discontent, should be carefully laid before her cousin. And together in divine confidence they would disentangle and interpret them all.

"At last," thought she, "I shall understand myself. I shan't again be troubled by things that come out of nothing, and mean I don't know what."

Miss Alan asked her to play. She refused vehemently. Music seemed to her the employment of a child. She sat close to her cousin, who, with commendable patience, was listening to a long story about lost luggage. When it was over she capped it by a story of her own. Lucy became rather hysterical with the delay. In vain she tried to check, or at all events to accelerate, the tale. It was not till a late hour that Miss Bartlett had recovered her luggage and could say in her usual tone of gentle reproach: "Well, dear, I at all events am ready for Bedfordshire. Come into my room, and I will give a good brush to your hair."

With some solemnity the door was shut, and a cane chair placed for the girl. Then Miss Bartlett said:

"So what is to be done?"

She was unprepared for the question. It had not occurred to her that she would have to do anything. A detailed exhibition of her emotions was all that she had counted upon.

"What is to be done? A point, dearest, which you alone can settle."

The rain was streaming down the black windows, and the great room felt damp and chilly. One candle burned trembling on the chest of drawers close to Miss Bartlett's toque, which cast monstrous and fantastic shadows on the bolted door. A tram roared by in the dark, and Lucy felt unaccountably sad, though she had long since dried her eyes. She lifted them to the ceiling, where the griffins and bassoons were colourless and vague, the very ghosts of joy.

"It has been raining for nearly four hours," she said at last.

Miss Bartlett ignored the remark.

"How do you propose to silence him?"

"The driver?"

"My dear girl, no; Mr George Emerson."

Lucy began to pace up and down the room.

"I don't understand," she said at last.

She understood very well, but she no longer wished to be absolutely truthful.

"How are you going to stop him talking about it?"

"I have a feeling that talk is a thing he will never do."

"I, too, intend to judge him charitably. But unfortunately I have met the type before. They seldom keep their exploits to themselves."

"Exploits?" cried Lucy, wincing under the horrible plural.

"My poor dear, did you suppose that this was his first? Come here and listen to me. I am only gathering it from his own remarks. Do you remember that day at lunch when he argued with Miss Alan that liking one person is an extra reason for liking another?"

"Yes," said Lucy, whom at the time the argument had pleased.

"Well, I am no prude. There is no need to call him a wicked young man, but obviously he is thoroughly unrefined. Let us put it down to his deplorable antecedents and education, if you wish. But we are no further on with our question. What do you propose to do?"

An idea rushed across Lucy's brain, which, had she thought of it sooner and made it part of her, might have proved victorious.

"I propose to speak to him," said she.

Miss Bartlett uttered a cry of genuine alarm.

"You see, Charlotte, your kindness—I shall never forget it. But—as you said—it is my affair. Mine and his."

"And you are going to *implore* him, to *beg* him to keep silence?"

"Certainly not. There would be no difficulty. Whatever you ask him he answers, yes or no; then it is over. I have been frightened of him. But now I am not one little bit."

"But we fear him for you, dear. You are so young and inexperienced, you have lived among such nice people, that you cannot realize what men can be—how they can take a brutal pleasure in insulting a woman whom her sex does not protect and rally round. This afternoon, for example, if I had not arrived, what would have happened?"

"I can't think," said Lucy gravely.

Something in her voice made Miss Bartlett repeat her question, intoning it more vigorously.

"What would have happened if I hadn't arrived?"

"I can't think," said Lucy again.

"When he insulted you, how would you have replied?"

"I hadn't time to think. You came."

"Yes, but won't you tell me now what you would have done?"

"I should have—" She checked herself, and broke the sentence off. She went up to the dripping window and strained her eyes into the darkness. She could not think what she would have done.

"Come away from the window, dear," said Miss Bartlett. "You will be seen from the road."

Lucy obeyed. She was in her cousin's power. She could not modulate out of the key of self-abasement in which she had started. Neither of them referred again to her suggestion that she should speak to George and settle the matter, whatever it was, with him.

Miss Bartlett became plaintive.

"O for a real man! We are only two women, you and I. Mr Beebe is hopeless. There is Mr Eager, but you do not trust him. O for your brother! He is young, but I know that his sister's insult would rouse in him a very lion. Thank God, chivalry is not yet dead. There are still left some men who can reverence woman."

As she spoke, she pulled off her rings, of which she wore several, and ranged them upon the pin-cushion. Then she blew into her gloves and said:

"It will be a push to catch the morning train, but we must try."

"What train?"

"The train to Rome." She looked at her gloves critically.

The girl received the announcement as easily as it had been given.

"When does the train to Rome go?"

"At eight."

"Signora Bertolini would be upset."

"We must face that," said Miss Bartlett, not liking to say that she had given notice already.

"She will make us pay for a whole week's pension."

"I expect she will. However, we shall be much more comfortable at the Vyses' hotel. Isn't afternoon tea given there for nothing?"

"Yes, but they pay extra for wine."

After this remark she remained motionless and silent. To her tired eyes Charlotte throbbed and swelled like a ghostly figure in a dream.

They began to sort their clothes for packing, for there was no time to lose, if they were to catch the train to Rome. Lucy, when admonished, began to move to and fro between the rooms, more conscious of the discomforts of packing by candlelight than of a subtler ill. Charlotte, who was practical without ability, knelt by the side of an empty trunk, vainly endeavouring to pave it with books of varying thickness and size. She gave two or three sighs, for the stooping posture hurt her back, and, for all her diplomacy, she felt that she was growing old. The girl heard her as she entered the room, and was seized with one of those emotional impulses to which she could never attribute a cause. She only felt that the candle would burn better, the packing go easier, the world be happier, if she could give and receive some human love. The impulse had come before today, but never so strongly. She knelt down by her cousin's side and took her in her arms.

Miss Bartlett returned the embrace with tenderness and warmth. But she was not a stupid woman, and she knew perfectly well that Lucy did not love her, but needed her to love. For it was in ominous tones that she said, after a long pause:

"Dearest Lucy, how will you ever forgive me?"

Lucy was on her guard at once, knowing by bitter experience what forgiving Miss Bartlett meant. Her emotion relaxed; she modified her embrace a little, and she said:

"Charlotte dear, what do you mean? As if I have anything to forgive!"

"You have a great deal, and I have a very great deal to forgive myself, too. I know well how much I vex you at every turn."

"But no—"

Miss Bartlett assumed her favourite role, that of the prematurely aged martyr.

"Ah, but yes! I feel that our tour together is hardly the success I had hoped. I might have known it would not do. You want someone younger and stronger and more in sympathy with you. I am too uninteresting and old-fashioned—only fit to pack and unpack your things."

"Please—"

"My only consolation was that you found people more to your taste, and were often able to leave me at home. I had my own poor ideas of what a lady ought to do, but I hope I did not inflict them on you more than was necessary. You had your own way about these rooms, at all events."

"You mustn't say these things," said Lucy softly.

She still clung to the hope that she and Charlotte loved each other, heart and soul. They continued to pack in silence.

"I have been a failure," said Miss Bartlett, as she struggled with the straps of Lucy's trunk instead of strapping her own. "Failed to make you happy; failed in my duty to your mother. She has been so generous to me; I shall never face her again after this disaster."

"But mother will understand. It is not your fault, this trouble, and it isn't a disaster either."

"It is my fault, it is a disaster. She will never forgive me, and rightly. For instance, what right had I to make friends with Miss Lavish?"

"Every right."

"When I was here for your sake? If I have vexed you it is equally true that I have neglected you. Your mother will see this as clearly as I do, when you tell her."

Lucy, from a cowardly wish to improve the situation, said:

"Why need mother hear of it?"

"But you tell her everything?"

"I suppose I do generally."

"I dare not break your confidence. There is something sacred in it. Unless you feel that it is a thing you could not tell her."

The girl would not be degraded to this.

"Naturally I should have told her. But in case she should blame you in any way, I promise I will not. I am very willing not to. I will never speak of it either to her or to anyone."

Her promise brought the long-drawn interview to a sudden close. Miss Bartlett pecked her smartly on both cheeks, wished her goodnight, and sent her to her own room.

For a moment the original trouble was in the background. George would seem to have behaved like a cad throughout; perhaps that was the view which one would take eventually. At present she neither acquitted nor condemned him; she did not pass judgement. At the moment when she was about to judge him her cousin's voice had intervened, and, ever since, it was Miss Bartlett who had dominated; Miss Bartlett who, even now, could be heard sighing into a crack in the partition wall; Miss Bartlett who had really been neither pliable nor humble nor inconsistent. She had worked like a great artist; for a time—indeed, for years—she had been meaningless, but at the end there was presented to the girl the complete picture of a cheerless, loveless world in which the young rush to destruction until they learn better—a shamefaced world of precautions and barriers which may avert evil, but which do not seem to bring good, if we may judge from those who have used them most.

Lucy was suffering from the most grievous wrong which this world has yet discovered: diplomatic advantage had been taken of her sincerity, of her craving for sympathy and love. Such a wrong is not easily forgotten. Never again did she expose herself without due consideration and precaution against rebuff. And such a wrong may react disastrously upon the soul.

The doorbell rang, and she started to the shutters. Before she reached them she hesitated, turned, and blew out the candle. Thus it was that, though she saw someone standing in the wet below, he, though he looked up, did not see her.

To reach his room he had to go by hers. She was still dressed. It struck her that she might slip into the passage and just say that she would be gone before he was up, and that their extraordinary intercourse was over.

Whether she would have dared to do this was never proved. At the critical moment Miss Bartlett opened her own door, and her voice said:

"I wish one word with you in the drawing-room, Mr Emerson, please."

Soon their footsteps returned, and Miss Bartlett said: "Good night, Mr Emerson."

His heavy, tired breathing was the only reply; the chaperon had done her work.

Lucy cried aloud: "It isn't true. It can't all be true. I want not to be muddled. I want to grow older quickly."

Miss Bartlett tapped on the wall.

"Go to bed at once, dear. You need all the rest you can get."

In the morning they left for Rome.

Part Two

Chapter 8
Medieval

The drawing-room curtains at Windy Corner had been pulled to meet, for the carpet was new and deserved protection from the August sun. They were heavy curtains, reaching almost to the ground, and the light that filtered through them was subdued and varied. A poet—none was present—might have quoted, "Life like a dome of many-coloured glass", or might have compared the curtains to sluice-gates, lowered against the intolerable tides of heaven. Without was poured a sea of radiance; within, the glory, though visible, was tempered to the capacities of man.

Two pleasant people sat in the room. One—a boy of nineteen—was studying a small manual of anatomy, and peering occasionally at a bone which lay upon the piano. From time to time he bounced in his chair and puffed and groaned, for the day was hot and the print small, and the human frame fearfully made; and his mother, who was writing a letter, did continually read out to him what she had written. And continually did she rise from her seat and part the curtains so that a rivulet of light fell across the carpet, and make the remark that they were still there.

"Where aren't they?" said the boy, who was Freddy, Lucy's brother. "I tell you I'm getting fairly sick."

"For goodness' sake go out of my drawing-room, then!" cried Mrs Honeychurch, who hoped to cure her children of slang by taking it literally.

Freddy did not move or reply.

"I think things are coming to a head," she observed, rather wanting her son's opinion on the situation if she could obtain it without undue supplication.

"Time they did."

"I am glad that Cecil is asking her this once more."

"It's his third go, isn't it?"

"Freddy, I do call the way you talk unkind."

"I didn't mean to be unkind." Then he added: "But I do think Lucy might have got this off her chest in Italy. I don't know how girls manage things, but she can't have said 'No' properly before, or she wouldn't have to say it again now. Over the whole thing—I can't explain—I do feel so uncomfortable."

"Do you indeed, dear? How interesting!"

"I feel—never mind."

He returned to his work.

"Just listen to what I have written to Mrs Vyse. I said: 'Dear Mrs Vyse—'"

"Yes, mother, you told me. A jolly good letter."

"I said: 'Dear Mrs Vyse, Cecil has just asked my permission about it, and I should be delighted, if Lucy wishes it. But—'" She stopped reading. "I was rather amused at Cecil asking my permission at all. He has always gone in for unconventionality, and parents nowhere, and so forth. When it comes to the point, he can't get on without me."

"Nor me."

"You?"

Freddy nodded.

"What do you mean?"

"He asked me for my permission also."

She exclaimed: "How very odd of him!"

"Why so?" asked the son and heir. "Why shouldn't my permission be asked?"

"What do you know about Lucy or girls or anything? What ever did you say?"

"I said to Cecil, 'Take her or leave her; it's no business of mine!'"

"What a helpful answer!" But her own answer, though more normal in its wording, had been to the same effect.

"The bother is this," began Freddy.

Then he took up his work again, too shy to say what the bother was. Mrs Honeychurch went back to the window.

"Freddy, you must come. There they still are!"

"I don't see you ought to go peeping like that."

"Peeping like that! Can't I look out of my own window?"

But she returned to the writing-table, observing, as she passed her son, "Still page 322?" Freddy snorted, and turned over two leaves. For a brief space they were silent. Close by, beyond the curtains, the gentle murmur of a long conversation had never ceased.

"The bother is this: I have put my foot in it with Cecil most awfully." He gave a nervous gulp. "Not content with 'permission', which I did give—that is to say, I said, 'I don't mind'—well, not content with that, he wanted to know whether I wasn't off my head with joy. He practically put it like this: Wasn't it a splendid thing for Lucy and for Windy Corner generally if he married her? And he would have an answer—he said it would strengthen his hand."

"I hope you gave a careful answer, dear."

"I answered 'No'," said the boy, grinding his teeth. "There! Fly into a stew! I can't help it—I had to say it. I had to say no. He ought never to have asked me."

"Ridiculous child!" cried his mother. "You think you're so holy and truthful, but really it's only abominable conceit. Do you suppose that a man like Cecil would take the slightest notice of anything you say? I hope he boxed your ears. How dare you say no?"

"Oh, do keep quiet, mother! I had to say no when I couldn't say yes. I tried to laugh as if I didn't mean what I said, and, as Cecil laughed too, and went away, it may be all right. But I feel my foot's in it. Oh, do keep quiet, though, and let a man do some work."

"No," said Mrs Honeychurch, with the air of one who had considered the subject, "I shall not keep quiet. You know all that has passed between them in Rome; you know why he is down here, and yet you deliberately insult him, and try to turn him out of my house."

"Not a bit!" he pleaded. "I only let out I didn't like him. I don't hate him, but I don't like him. What I mind is that he'll tell Lucy."

He glanced at the curtains dismally.

"Well, *I* like him," said Mrs Honeychurch. "I know his mother; he's good, he's clever, he's rich, he's well connected—oh, you needn't kick the piano! He's well connected—I'll say it again if you like: he's well connected." She paused, as if rehearsing her eulogy, but her face remained dissatisfied. She added: "And he has beautiful manners."

"I liked him till just now. I suppose it's having him spoiling Lucy's first week at home; and it's also something that Mr Beebe said, not knowing."

"Mr Beebe?" said his mother, trying to conceal her interest. "I don't see how Mr Beebe comes in."

"You know Mr Beebe's funny way, when you never quite know what he means. He said: 'Mr Vyse is an ideal bachelor.' I was very cute. I asked him what he meant. He said: 'Oh, he's like me—better detached.' I couldn't make him say any more, but it set me thinking. Since Cecil has come after Lucy he hasn't been so pleasant, at least—I can't explain."

"You never can, dear. But I can. You are jealous of Cecil because he may stop Lucy knitting you silk ties."

The explanation seemed plausible, and Freddy tried to accept it. But at the back of his brain there lurked a dim mistrust. Cecil praised one too much for being athletic. Was that it? Cecil made one talk in his way, instead of letting one talk in one's own way. This tired one. Was that it? And Cecil was the kind of fellow who would never wear another fellow's cap. Unaware of his own profundity, Freddy checked himself. He must be jealous, or he would not dislike a man for such foolish reasons.

"Will this do?" called his mother. " 'Dear Mrs Vyse, Cecil has just asked my permission about it, and I should be delighted if Lucy wishes it.' Then I put in at the top, 'and I have told Lucy so.' I must write the letter out again—'and I have told Lucy so. But Lucy seems very uncertain, and in these days young people must decide for themselves.' I said that because I didn't want Mrs Vyse to think us old-fashioned. She goes in for lectures and improving her mind, and all the time a thick layer of flue under the beds, and the maids' dirty thumb-marks where you turn on the electric light. She keeps that flat abominably—"

"Suppose Lucy marries Cecil, would she live in a flat, or in the country?"

"Don't interrupt so foolishly. Where was I? Oh yes—'Young people must decide for themselves. I know that Lucy likes your son, because she tells me everything, and she wrote to me from Rome when he asked her first.' No, I'll cross that last bit out—it looks patronizing. I'll stop at 'because she tells me everything'. Or shall I cross that out, too?"

"Cross it out, too," said Freddy.

Mrs Honeychurch left it in.

"Then the whole thing runs: 'Dear Mrs Vyse, Cecil has just asked my permission about it, and I should be delighted if Lucy wishes it, and I have told Lucy so. But Lucy seems very uncertain, and in these days young people must decide for themselves. I know that Lucy likes your son, because she tells me everything. But I do not know—' "

"Look out!" cried Freddy.

The curtains parted.

Cecil's first movement was one of irritation. He couldn't bear the Honeychurch habit of sitting in the dark to save the furniture. Instinctively he gave the curtains a twitch, and sent them swinging down their poles. Light entered. There was revealed a terrace, such as is owned by many villas, with trees each side of it, and on it a little rustic seat, and two flower-beds. But it was transfigured by the view beyond, for Windy Corner was built on the range that overlooks the Sussex Weald. Lucy, who was in the little seat, seemed on the edge of a green magic carpet which hovered in the air above the tremulous world.

Cecil entered.

Appearing thus late in the story, Cecil must be at once described. He was medieval. Like a Gothic statue. Tall and refined, with shoulders that seemed braced square by an effort of the will, and a head that was tilted a little higher than the usual level of vision, he resembled those fastidious saints who guard the portals of a French cathedral. Well educated, well endowed, and not deficient physically, he remained in the grip of a certain devil whom the modern world knows as self-consciousness, and whom the medieval, with dimmer vision, worshipped as asceticism. A Gothic statue implies celibacy, just as a Greek statue implies fruition, and perhaps this was what Mr Beebe meant. And Freddy, who ignored history and art, perhaps meant the same when he failed to imagine Cecil wearing another fellow's cap.

Mrs Honeychurch left her letter on the writing-table and moved towards her young acquaintance.

"Oh, Cecil!" she exclaimed—"oh, Cecil, do tell me!"

"I promessi sposi," said he.

They stared at him anxiously.

"She has accepted me," he said, and the sound of the thing in English made him flush and smile with pleasure, and look more human.

"I am so glad," said Mrs Honeychurch, while Freddy proffered a hand that was yellow with chemicals. They wished that they also knew Italian, for our phrases of approval and of amazement are so connected with little occasions that we fear to use them on great ones. We are obliged to become vaguely poetic, or to take refuge in Scriptural reminiscence.

"Welcome as one of the family!" said Mrs Honeychurch, waving her hand at the furniture. "This is indeed a joyous day! I feel sure that you will make dear Lucy happy."

"I hope so," replied the young man, shifting his eyes to the ceiling.

"We mothers—" simpered Mrs Honeychurch, and then realized that she was affected, sentimental, bombastic—all the things she hated most. Why could she not be as Freddy, who stood stiff in the middle of the room, looking very cross and almost handsome?

"I say, Lucy!" called Cecil, for conversation seemed to flag.

Lucy rose from the seat. She moved across the lawn and smiled in at them, just as if she was going to ask them to play tennis. Then she saw her brother's face. Her lips parted, and she took him in her arms. He said, "Steady on!"

"Not a kiss for me?" asked her mother.

Lucy kissed her also.

"Would you take them into the garden and tell Mrs Honeychurch all about it?" Cecil suggested. "And I'd stop here and tell my mother."

"We go with Lucy?" said Freddy, as if taking orders.

"Yes, you go with Lucy."

They passed into the sunlight. Cecil watched them cross the terrace, and descend out of sight by the steps. They would descend—he knew their ways—past the shrubbery, and past the tennis lawn and the dahlia-bed, until they reached the kitchen-garden, and there, in the presence of the potatoes and the peas, the great event would be discussed.

Smiling indulgently, he lit a cigarette, and rehearsed the events that had led to such a happy conclusion.

He had known Lucy for several years, but only as a commonplace girl who happened to be musical. He could still remember his depression that afternoon at Rome, when she and her terrible cousin fell on him out of the blue, and demanded to be taken to St Peter's. That day she had seemed a typical tourist—shrill, crude, and gaunt with travel. But Italy worked some marvel in her. It gave her light, and—which he held more precious—it gave her shadow. Soon he detected in her a wonderful reticence. She was like a woman of Leonardo da Vinci's, whom we love not so much for herself as for the things that she will not tell us. The things are assuredly not of this life; no woman of Leonardo's could have anything so vulgar as a 'story'. She did develop most wonderfully day by day.

So it happened that from patronizing civility he had slowly passed, if not to passion, at least to a profound uneasiness. Already at Rome he had hinted to her that they might be suitable for each other. It had touched him greatly that she had not broken away at the suggestion. Her refusal had been clear and gentle; after it—as the horrid phrase went—she had been exactly the same to him as before. Three months later, on the margin of Italy, among the flower-clad Alps, he had asked her again in bald, traditional language. She reminded him of a Leonardo more than ever; her sunburnt features were shadowed by fantastic rocks; at his words she had turned and stood between him and the light with immeasurable plains behind her. He walked home with her unashamed, feeling not at all like a rejected suitor. The things that really mattered were unshaken.

So now he had asked her once more, and, clear and gentle as ever, she had accepted him, giving no coy reasons for her delay, but simply saying that she loved him and would do her best to make him happy. His mother, too, would be pleased; she had counselled the step; he must write her a long account.

Glancing at his hand, in case any of Freddy's chemicals had come off on it, he moved to the writing-table. There he saw "Dear Mrs Vyse", followed by many erasures. He recoiled without reading any more, and after a little hesitation sat down elsewhere, and pencilled a note on his knee.

Then he lit another cigarette, which did not seem quite as divine as the first, and considered what might be done to make the Windy Corner drawing-room more distinctive. With that outlook it should have been a successful room, but the trail of Tottenham Court Road was upon it; he could almost visualize the motor-vans of Messrs Shoolbred and Messrs Maple arriving at the door and depositing this chair, those varnished book-cases, that writing-table. The table recalled Mrs Honeychurch's letter. He did not want to read that letter—his temptations never lay in that direction; but he worried about it none the less. It was his own fault that she was discussing him with his mother; he had wanted her support in his third attempt to win Lucy; he wanted to feel that others, no matter who they were, agreed with him, and so he had asked their permission. Mrs Honeychurch had been civil, but obtuse in essentials, while as for Freddy—

"He is only a boy," he reflected. "I represent all that he despises. Why should he want me for a brother-in-law?"

The Honeychurches were a worthy family, but he began to realize that Lucy was of another clay; and perhaps—he did not put it very definitely—he ought to introduce her into more congenial circles as soon as possible.

"Mr Beebe!" said the maid, and the new rector of Summer Street was shown in; he had at once started on friendly relations, owing to Lucy's praise of him in her letters from Florence.

Cecil greeted him rather critically.

"I've come for tea, Mr Vyse. Do you suppose that I shall get it?"

"I should say so. Food is the thing one does get here—don't sit in that chair; young Honeychurch has left a bone in it."

"Pfui!"

"I know," said Cecil, "I know. I can't think why Mrs Honeychurch allows it."

For Cecil considered the bone and the Maple's furniture separately; he did not realize that, taken together, they kindled the room into the life that he desired.

"I've come for tea and for gossip. Isn't this news?"

"News? I don't understand you," said Cecil. "News?"

Mr Beebe, whose news was of a very different nature, prattled forward.

"I met Sir Harry Otway as I came up; I have every reason to hope that I am first in the field. He has bought Cissie and Albert from Mr Flack!"

"Has he indeed?" said Cecil, trying to recover himself. Into what a grotesque mistake had he fallen! Was it likely that a clergyman and a gentleman would refer to his engagement in a manner so flippant? But his stiffness remained, and, though he asked who Cissie and Albert might be, he still thought Mr Beebe rather a bounder.

"Unpardonable question! To have stopped a week at Windy Corner and not to have met Cissie and Albert, the semi-detached villas that have been run up opposite the church! I'll set Mrs Honeychurch after you."

"I'm shockingly stupid over local affairs," said the young

man languidly. "I can't even remember the difference between a Parish Council and a Local Government Board. Perhaps there is no difference, or perhaps those aren't the right names. I only go into the country to see my friends and to enjoy the scenery. It is very remiss of me. Italy and London are the only places where I don't feel to exist on sufferance."

Mr Beebe, distressed at this heavy reception of Cissie and Albert, determined to shift the subject.

"Let me see, Mr Vyse—I forget—what is your profession?"

"I have no profession," said Cecil. "It is another example of my decadence. My attitude—quite an indefensible one—is that so long as I am no trouble to anyone I have a right to do as I like. I know I ought to be getting money out of people, or devoting myself to things I don't care a straw about, but somehow I've not been able to begin."

"You are very fortunate," said Mr Beebe. "It is a wonderful opportunity, the possession of leisure."

His voice was rather parochial, but he did not quite see his way to answering naturally. He felt, as all who have regular occupation must feel, that others should have it also.

"I am glad that you approve. I daren't face the healthy person—for example, Freddy Honeychurch."

"Oh, Freddy's a good sort, isn't he?"

"Admirable. The sort who has made England what she is."

Cecil wondered at himself. Why, on this day of all others, was he so hopelessly contrary? He tried to get right by inquiring effusively after Mr Beebe's mother, an old lady for whom he had no particular regard. Then he flattered the clergyman, praised his liberal-mindedness, his enlightened attitude towards philosophy and science.

"Where are the others?" said Mr Beebe at last. "I insist on extracting tea before evening service."

"I suppose Anne never told them you were here. In this house one is so coached in the servants the day one arrives. The fault of Anne is that she begs your pardon when she hears you perfectly, and kicks the chair-legs with her feet.

The faults of Mary—I forget the faults of Mary, but they are very grave. Shall we look in the garden?"

"I know the faults of Mary. She leaves the dustpans standing on the stairs."

"The fault of Euphemia is that she will not, simply will not, chop the suet sufficiently small."

They both laughed, and things began to go better.

"The faults of Freddy—" Cecil continued.

"Ah, he has too many. No one but his mother can remember the faults of Freddy. Try the faults of Miss Honeychurch; they are not innumerable."

"She has none," said the young man, with grave sincerity.

"I quite agree. At present she has none."

"At present?"

"I'm not cynical. I'm only thinking of my pet theory about Miss Honeychurch. Does it seem reasonable that she should play so wonderfully, and live so quietly? I suspect that one day she will be wonderful in both. The watertight compartments in her will break down, and music and life will mingle. Then we shall have her heroically good, heroically bad—too heroic, perhaps, to be good or bad."

Cecil found his companion interesting.

"And at present you think her not wonderful as far as life goes?"

"Well, I must say I've only seen her at Tunbridge Wells, where she was not wonderful, and at Florence. Since I came to Summer Street she has been away. You saw her, didn't you, at Rome and in the Alps. Oh, I forgot; of course, you knew her before. No, she wasn't wonderful in Florence either, but I kept on expecting that she would be."

"In what way?"

Conversation had become agreeable to them, and they were pacing up and down the terrace.

"I could as easily tell you what tune she'll play next. There was simply the sense that she had found wings, and meant to use them. I can show you a beautiful picture in my Italian diary: Miss Honeychurch as a kite, Miss Bartlett holding the string. Picture number two: the string breaks."

The sketch was in his diary, but it had been made afterwards, when he viewed things artistically. At the time he had given surreptitious tugs to the string himself.

"But the string never broke?"

"No. I mightn't have seen Miss Honeychurch rise, but I should certainly have heard Miss Bartlett fall."

"It has broken now," said the young man in low, vibrating tones.

Immediately he realized that of all the conceited, ludicrous, contemptible ways of announcing an engagement this was the worst. He cursed his love of metaphor; had he suggested that he was a star and that Lucy was soaring up to reach him?

"Broken? What do you mean?"

"I meant," said Cecil stiffly, "that she is going to marry me."

The clergyman was conscious of some bitter disappointment which he could not keep out of his voice.

"I am sorry; I must apologize. I had no idea you were intimate with her, or I should never have talked in this flippant, superficial way. Mr Vyse, you ought to have stopped me." And down the garden he saw Lucy herself; yes, he was disappointed.

Cecil, who naturally preferred congratulations to apologies, drew down his mouth at the corners. Was this the reception his action would get from the world? Of course, he despised the world as a whole; every thoughtful man should; it is almost a test of refinement. But he was sensitive to the successive particles of it which he encountered.

Occasionally he could be quite crude.

"I am sorry I have given you a shock," he said dryly. "I fear that Lucy's choice does not meet with your approval."

"Not that. But you ought to have stopped me. I know Miss Honeychurch only a little as time goes. Perhaps I oughtn't to have discussed her so freely with anyone; certainly not with you."

"You are conscious of having said something indiscreet?"

Mr Beebe pulled himself together. Really, Mr Vyse had

the art of placing one in the most tiresome positions. He was driven to use the prerogatives of his profession.

"No, I have said nothing indiscreet. I foresaw at Florence that her quiet, uneventful childhood must end, and it has ended. I realized dimly enough that she might take some momentous step. She has taken it. She has learned—you will let me talk freely, as I have begun freely—she has learned what it is to love: the greatest lesson, some people will tell you, that our earthly life provides." It was now time for him to wave his hat at the approaching trio. He did not omit to do so. "She has learned through you," and if his voice was still clerical it was now also sincere; "let it be your care that her knowledge is profitable to her."

"Grazie tante!" said Cecil, who did not like parsons.

"Have you heard?" shouted Mrs Honeychurch as she toiled up the sloping garden. "Oh, Mr Beebe, have you heard the news?"

Freddy, now full of geniality, whistled the wedding march. Youth seldom criticizes the accomplished fact.

"Indeed I have!" he cried. He looked at Lucy. In her presence he could not act the parson any longer—at all events not without apology. "Mrs Honeychurch, I'm going to do what I am always supposed to do, but generally I'm too shy. I want to invoke every kind of blessing on them, grave and gay, great and small. I want them all their lives to be supremely good and supremely happy as husband and wife, as father and mother. And now I want my tea."

"You only asked for it just in time," the lady retorted. "How dare you be serious at Windy Corner?"

He took his tone from her. There was no more heavy beneficence, no more attempts to dignify the situation with poetry or the Scriptures. None of them dared or was able to be serious any more.

An engagement is so potent a thing that sooner or later it reduces all who speak of it to this state of cheerful awe. Away from it, in the solitude of their rooms, Mr Beebe, and even Freddy, might again be critical. But in its presence and in the presence of each other they were sincerely hilarious. It has a strange power, for it compels not only the lips, but the very heart. The chief parallel—to compare one great thing with another—is the power over us of a temple of some alien creed. Standing outside, we deride or oppose it, or at the most feel sentimental. Inside, though the saints and gods are not ours, we become true believers, in case any true believer should be present.

So it was that after the gropings and the misgivings of the afternoon they pulled themselves together and settled down to a very pleasant tea-party. If they were hypocrites they did not know it, and their hypocrisy had every chance of setting and of becoming true. Anne, putting down each plate as if it were a wedding present, stimulated them greatly. They could not lag behind that smile of hers which she gave them ere she kicked the drawing-room door. Mr Beebe chirruped. Freddy was at his wittiest, referring to Cecil as the "Fiasco"—family-honoured pun on fiancé. Mrs Honeychurch, amusing and portly, promised well as a mother-in-law. As for Lucy and Cecil, for whom the temple had been built, they also joined in the merry ritual, but waited, as earnest worshippers should, for the disclosure of some holier shrine of joy.

Chapter 9
Lucy as a Work of Art

A few days after the engagement was announced Mrs Honeychurch made Lucy and her Fiasco come to a little garden party in the neighbourhood, for naturally she wanted to show people that her daughter was marrying a presentable man.

Cecil was more than presentable; he looked distinguished, and it was very pleasant to see his slim figure keeping step with Lucy, and his long, fair face responding when Lucy spoke to him. People congratulated Mrs Honeychurch, which is, I believe, a social blunder, but it pleased her, and she introduced Cecil rather indiscriminately to some stuffy dowagers.

At tea a misfortune took place: a cup of coffee was upset over Lucy's figured silk, and though Lucy feigned indifference her mother feigned nothing of the sort, but dragged her indoors to have the frock treated by a sympathetic maid. They were gone some time, and Cecil was left with the dowagers. When they returned he was not as pleasant as he had been.

"Do you go to much of this sort of thing?" he asked when they were driving home.

"Oh, now and then," said Lucy, who had rather enjoyed herself.

"Is it typical of county society?"

"I suppose so. Mother, would it be?"

"Plenty of society," said Mrs Honeychurch, who was trying to remember the hang of one of the dresses.

Seeing that her thoughts were elsewhere, Cecil bent towards Lucy and said:

"To me it seemed perfectly appalling, disastrous, portentous."

"I am so sorry that you were stranded."

"Not that, but the congratulations. It is so disgusting, the way an engagement is regarded as public property—a kind of waste place where every outsider may shoot his vulgar sentiment. All those old women smirking!"

"One has to go through it, I suppose. They won't notice us so much next time."

"But my point is that their whole attitude is wrong. An engagement—horrid word in the first place—is a private matter, and should be treated as such."

Yet the smirking old women, however wrong individually, were racially correct. The spirit of the generations had smiled through them, rejoicing in the engagement of Cecil and Lucy because it promised the continuance of life on earth. To Cecil and Lucy it promised something quite different—personal love. Hence Cecil's irritation and Lucy's belief that his irritation was just.

"How tiresome!" she said. "Couldn't you have escaped to tennis?"

"I don't play tennis—at least, not in public. The neighbourhood is deprived of the romance of me being athletic. Such romance as I have is that of the Inglese Italianato."

"Inglese Italianato?"

"È un diavolo incarnato! You know the proverb?"

She did not. Nor did it seem applicable to a young man who had spent a quiet winter in Rome with his mother. But Cecil, since his engagement, had taken to affect a cosmopolitan naughtiness which he was far from possessing.

"Well," said he, "I cannot help it if they do disapprove of me. There are certain irremovable barriers between myself and them, and I must accept them."

"We all have our limitations, I suppose," said wise Lucy.

"Sometimes they are forced on us, though," said Cecil, who saw from her remark that she did not quite understand his position.

"How?"

"It makes a difference, doesn't it, whether we fence ourselves in, or whether we are fenced out by the barriers of others?"

She thought a moment, and agreed that it did make a difference.

"Difference?" cried Mrs Honeychurch, suddenly alert. "I don't see any difference. Fences are fences, especially when they are in the same place."

"We were speaking of motives," said Cecil, on whom the interruption jarred.

"My dear Cecil, look here." She spread out her knees and perched her card-case on her lap. "This is me. That's Windy Corner. The rest of the pattern is the other people. Motives are all very well, but the fence comes here."

"We weren't talking of real fences," said Lucy, laughing.

"Oh, I see, dear—poetry."

She leant placidly back. Cecil wondered why Lucy had been amused.

"I tell you who has no 'fences', as you call them," she said, "and that's Mr Beebe."

"A parson fenceless would mean a parson defenceless."

Lucy was slow to follow what people said, but quick enough to detect what they meant. She missed Cecil's epigram, but grasped the feeling that prompted it.

"Don't you like Mr Beebe?" she asked thoughtfully.

"I never said so!" he cried. "I consider him far above the average. I only denied—" And he swept off on the subject of fences again, and was brilliant.

"Now, a clergyman that I do hate," said she, wanting to say something sympathetic, "a clergyman that does have fences, and the most dreadful ones, is Mr Eager, the English chaplain at Florence. He was truly insincere—not merely the manner unfortunate. He was a snob, and so conceited, and he did say such unkind things."

"What sort of things?"

"There was an old man at the Bertolini whom he said had murdered his wife."

"Perhaps he had."

"Why, no."

"Why 'no'?"

"He was such a nice old man, I'm sure."

Cecil laughed at her feminine inconsequence.

"Well, I did try to sift the thing. Mr Eager would never come to the point. He prefers it vague—said the old man had 'practically' murdered his wife—had murdered her in the sight of God."

"Hush, dear!" said Mrs Honeychurch absently.

"But isn't it intolerable that a person whom we're told to imitate should go round spreading slander? It was, I believe, chiefly owing to him that the old man was dropped. People pretended he was vulgar, but he certainly wasn't that."

"Poor old man! What was his name?"

"Harris," said Lucy glibly.

"Let's hope that Mrs Harris there warn't no sich person," said her mother.

Cecil nodded intelligently.

"Isn't Mr Eager a parson of the cultured type?" he asked.

"I don't know. I hate him. I've heard him lecture on Giotto. I hate him. Nothing can hide a petty nature. I *hate* him!"

"My goodness gracious me, child!" said Mrs Honeychurch. "You'll blow my head off! What ever is there to shout over? I forbid you and Cecil to hate any more clergymen."

He smiled. There was indeed something rather incongruous in Lucy's moral outburst over Mr Eager. It was as if one should see the Leonardo on the ceiling of the Sistine. He longed to hint to her that not here lay her vocation; that a woman's power and charm reside in mystery, not in muscular rant. But possibly rant is a sign of vitality: it mars the beautiful creature, but shows that she is alive. After a moment, he contemplated her flushed face and excited gestures with a certain approval. He forbore to repress the sources of youth.

Nature—simplest of topics, he thought—lay around them. He praised the pine-woods, the deep lakes of bracken, the crimson leaves that spotted the hurt-bushes, the serviceable beauty of the turnpike road. The outdoor world was not very familiar to him, and occasionally he went wrong in a question of fact. Mrs Honeychurch's mouth twitched when he spoke of the perpetual green of the larch.

"I count myself a lucky person," he concluded. "When I'm in London I feel I could never live out of it. When I'm in the country I feel the same about the country. After all, I do believe that birds and trees and the sky are the most wonderful things in life, and that the people who live amongst them must be the best. It's true that in nine cases out of ten they don't seem to notice anything. The country gentleman and the country labourer are each in their way the most depressing of companions. Yet they may have a tacit sympathy with the workings of Nature which is denied to us of the town. Do you feel that, Mrs Honeychurch?"

Mrs Honeychurch started and smiled. She had not been attending. Cecil, who was rather crushed on the front seat of the victoria, felt irritable, and determined not to say anything interesting again.

Lucy had not attended either. Her brow was wrinkled, and she still looked furiously cross—the result, he concluded, of too much moral gymnastics. It was sad to see her thus blind to the beauties of an August wood.

" 'Come down, O maid, from yonder mountain height,' " he quoted, and touched her knee with his own.

She flushed again and said: "What height?"

"Come down, O maid, from yonder mountain height:
What pleasure lives in height (the shepherd sang),
In height and in the splendour of the hills?

Let us take Mrs Honeychurch's advice and hate clergymen no more. What's this place?"

"Summer Street, of course," said Lucy, and roused herself.

The woods had opened to leave space for a sloping triangular meadow. Pretty cottages lined it on two sides, and the upper and third side was occupied by a new stone church, expensively simple, with a charming shingled spire. Mr Beebe's house was near the church. In height it scarcely exceeded the cottages. Some great mansions were at hand, but they were hidden in the trees. The scene suggested a Swiss alp rather than the shrine and centre of a leisured world, and was only marred by two ugly little villas—the villas that had competed with Cecil's engagement, having been acquired by Sir Harry Otway the very afternoon that Lucy had been acquired by him.

"Cissie" was the name of one of these villas, "Albert" of the other. These titles were not only picked out in shaded Gothic on the garden gates, but appeared a second time on the porches, where they followed the semicircular curve of the entrance arch in block capitals. Albert was inhabited. His tortured garden was bright with geraniums and lobelias and polished shells. His little windows were chastely swathed in Nottingham lace. Cissie was to let. Three noticeboards, belonging to Dorking agents, lolled on her fence and announced the not surprising fact. Her paths were already weedy; her pocket-handkerchief of a lawn was yellow with dandelions.

"The place is ruined!" said the ladies mechanically. "Summer Street will never be the same again."

As the carriage passed, Cissie's door opened, and a gentleman came out of her.

"Stop!" cried Mrs Honeychurch, touching the coachman with her parasol. "Here's Sir Harry. Now we shall know. Sir Harry, pull those things down at once!"

Sir Harry Otway—who need not be described—came to the carriage and said:

"Mrs Honeychurch, I meant to. I can't, I really can't turn out Miss Flack."

"Am I not always right? She ought to have gone before the contract was signed. Does she still live rent-free, as she did in her nephew's time?"

"But what can I do?" He lowered his voice. "An old lady, so very vulgar, and almost bedridden."

"Turn her out," said Cecil bravely.

Sir Harry sighed, and looked at the villas mournfully. He had had full warning of Mr Flack's intentions, and might have bought the plot before building commenced; but he was apathetic and dilatory. He had known Summer Street for so many years that he could not imagine it being spoilt. Not till Mrs Flack had laid the foundation stone, and the apparition of red and cream brick began to rise, did he take alarm. He called on Mr Flack, the local builder—a most reasonable and respectful man—who agreed that tiles would have made a more artistic roof, but pointed out that slates were cheaper. He ventured to differ, however, about the Corinthian columns which were to cling like leeches to the frames of the bow-windows, saying that, for his part, he liked to relieve the façade by a bit of decoration. Sir Harry hinted that a column, if possible, should be structural as well as decorative. Mr Flack replied that all the columns had been ordered, adding, "and all the capitals different—one with dragons in the foliage, another approaching to the Ionian style, another introducing Mrs Flack's initials—every one different." For he had read his Ruskin. He built his villas according to his desire; and not till he had inserted an immovable aunt into one of them did Sir Harry buy.

This futile and unprofitable transaction filled the knight with sadness as he leant on Mrs Honeychurch's carriage. He had failed in his duties to the countryside, and the countryside was laughing at him as well. He had spent money, and yet Summer Street was spoilt as much as ever. All he could do now was to find a desirable tenant for Cissie—someone really desirable.

"The rent is absurdly low," he told them, "and perhaps I am an easy landlord. But it is such an awkward size. It is too large for the peasant class, and too small for anyone the least like ourselves."

Cecil had been hesitating whether he should despise the villas or despise Sir Harry for despising them. The latter impulse seemed the more fruitful.

"You ought to find a tenant at once," he said maliciously. "It would be a perfect paradise for a bank-clerk."

"Exactly!" said Sir Harry excitedly. "That is exactly what I fear, Mr Vyse. It will attract the wrong type of people. The train service has improved—a fatal improvement, to my mind. And what are five miles from a station in these days of bicycles?"

"Rather a strenuous clerk it would be," said Lucy.

Cecil, who had his full share of medieval mischievousness, replied that the physique of the lower middle classes was improving at a most appalling rate. She saw that he was laughing at their harmless neighbour, and roused herself to stop him.

"Sir Harry!" she exclaimed, "I have an idea. How would you like spinsters?"

"My dear Lucy, it would be splendid. Do you know any such?"

"Yes; I met them abroad."

"Gentlewomen?" he asked tentatively.

"Yes, indeed, and at the present moment homeless. I heard from them last week. Miss Teresa and Miss Catharine Alan. I'm really not joking. They are quite the right people. Mr Beebe knows them, too. May I tell them to write to you?"

"Indeed you may!" he cried. "Here we are with the difficulty solved already. How delightful it is! Extra facilities—please tell them they shall have extra facilities, for I shall have no agents' fees. Oh, the agents! The appalling people they have sent me! One woman, when I wrote—a tactful letter, you know—asking her to explain her social position to me, replied that she would pay the rent in advance. As if one cares about that! And several references I took up were most unsatisfactory—people swindlers, or not respectable. And oh, the deceit! I have seen a good deal of the seamy side this last week. The deceit of the most promising people! My dear Lucy, the deceit!"

She nodded.

"My advice," put in Mrs Honeychurch, "is to have nothing to do with Lucy and her decayed gentlewomen at all. I know the type. Preserve me from people who have seen better days, and bring heirlooms with them that make the house smell stuffy. It's a sad thing, but I'd far rather let to someone who is going up in the world than to someone who has come down."

"I think I follow you," said Sir Harry; "but it is, as you say, a very sad thing."

"The Miss Alans aren't that!" cried Lucy.

"Yes, they are!" said Cecil. "I haven't met them, but I should say they were a highly unsuitable addition to the neighbourhood."

"Don't listen to him, Sir Harry—he's tiresome."

"It's I who am tiresome," he replied. "I oughtn't to come with my troubles to young people. But really I am so worried, and Lady Otway will only say that I cannot be too careful, which is quite true, but no real help."

"Then may I write to my Miss Alans?"

"Please!" he cried.

But his eye wavered when Mrs Honeychurch exclaimed:

"Beware! They are certain to have canaries. Sir Harry, beware of canaries: they spit the seed out through the bars of the cages, and then the mice come. Beware of women altogether. Only let to a man."

"Really—" he murmured gallantly, though he saw the wisdom of her remark.

"Men don't gossip over teacups. If they get drunk, there's an end of them—they lie down comfortably, and sleep it off. If they're vulgar, they somehow keep it to themselves. It doesn't spread so. Give me a man—of course, provided he's clean."

Sir Harry blushed. Neither he nor Cecil enjoyed these open compliments to their sex. Even the exclusion of the dirty did not leave them much distinction. He suggested that Mrs Honeychurch, if she had time, should descend from the carriage and inspect Cissie for herself. She was delighted. Nature had intended her to be poor and to live in such a house. Domestic arrangements always attracted her, especially when they were on a small scale.

Cecil pulled Lucy back as she followed her mother.

"Mrs Honeychurch," he said, "what if we two walk home and leave you?"

"Certainly!" was her cordial reply.

Sir Harry likewise seemed almost too glad to get rid of them. He beamed at them knowingly, said, "Aha! Young people, young people, young people!" and then hastened to unlock the house.

"Hopeless vulgarian!" exclaimed Cecil, almost before they were out of earshot.

"Oh, Cecil!"

"I can't help it. It would be wrong not to loathe that man."

"He isn't clever, but really he is nice."

"No, Lucy; he stands for all that is bad in country life. In London he would keep his place. He would belong to a brainless club, and his wife would give brainless dinner-parties. But down here he acts the little god with his gentility, and his patronage, and his sham aesthetics, and everyone—even your mother—is taken in."

"All that you say is quite true," said Lucy, though she felt discouraged. "I wonder whether—whether it matters so very much."

"It matters supremely. Sir Harry is the essence of that garden party. Oh, goodness, how cross I feel! How I do hope he'll get some vulgar tenant in that villa—some woman so really vulgar that he'll notice it. *Gentlefolks*! Ugh! With his bald head and retreating chin! But let's forget him."

This Lucy was glad enough to do. If Cecil disliked Sir Harry Otway and Mr Beebe, what guarantee was there that the people who really mattered to her would escape? For instance, Freddy. Freddy was neither clever nor subtle nor beautiful, and what prevented Cecil from saying, any minute, "It would be wrong not to loathe Freddy"? And what would she reply? Further than Freddy she did not go, but he gave her anxiety enough. She could only assure herself that Cecil had known Freddy some time, and that they had always got on pleasantly, except, perhaps, during the last few days, which was an accident, perhaps.

"Which way shall we go?" she asked him.

Nature—simplest of topics, she thought—was around them. Summer Street lay deep in the woods, and she had stopped where a footpath diverged from the highroad.

"Are there two ways?"

"Perhaps the road is more sensible, as we're got up smart."

"I'd rather go through the wood," said Cecil, with that subdued irritation that she had noticed in him all the afternoon. "Why is it, Lucy, that you always say the road? Do you know that you have never once been with me in the fields or the wood since we were engaged?"

"Haven't I? The wood, then," said Lucy, startled at his queerness, but pretty sure that he would explain later; it was not his habit to leave her in doubt as to his meaning.

She led the way into the whispering pines, and sure enough he did explain before they had gone a dozen yards.

"I had got an idea—I dare say wrongly—that you feel more at home with me in a room."

"A room?" she echoed, hopelessly bewildered.

"Yes. Or, at the most, in a garden, or on a road. Never in the real country like this."

"Oh, Cecil, what ever do you mean? I have never felt anything of the sort. You talk as if I was a kind of poetess sort of person."

"I don't know that you aren't. I connect you with a view—a certain type of view. Why shouldn't you connect me with a room?"

She reflected a moment, and then said, laughing:

"Do you know that you're right? I do. I must be a poetess after all. When I think of you it's always as in a room. How funny!"

To her surprise, he seemed annoyed.

"A drawing-room, pray? With no view?"

"Yes, with no view, I fancy. Why not?"

"I'd rather," he said reproachfully, "that you connected me with the open air."

She said again, "Oh, Cecil, what ever do you mean?"

As no explanation was forthcoming, she shook off the subject as too difficult for a girl, and led him further into the wood, pausing every now and then at some particularly beautiful or familiar combination of the trees. She had known the wood between Summer Street and Windy Corner ever since she could walk alone; she had played at losing Freddy in it, when Freddy was a purple-faced baby; and though she had now been to Italy it had lost none of its charm.

Presently they came to a little clearing among the pines—

another tiny green alp, solitary this time, and holding in its bosom a shallow pool.

She exclaimed, "The Sacred Lake!"

"Why do you call it that?"

"I can't remember why. I suppose it comes out of some book. It's only a puddle now, but you see that stream going through it? Well, a good deal of water comes down after heavy rains, and can't get away at once, and the pool becomes quite large and beautiful. Then Freddy used to bathe there. He is very fond of it."

"And you?"

He meant, "Are you fond of it?" But she answered dreamily: "I bathed here, too, till I was found out. Then there was a row."

At another time he might have been shocked, for he had depths of prudishness within him. But now, with his momentary cult of the fresh air, he was delighted at her admirable simplicity. He looked at her as she stood by the pool's edge. She was got up smart, as she phrased it, and she reminded him of some brilliant flower that has no leaves of its own, but blooms abruptly out of a world of green.

"Who found you out?"

"Charlotte," she murmured. "She was stopping with us. Charlotte—Charlotte."

"Poor girl!"

She smiled gravely. A certain scheme, from which hitherto he had shrunk, now appeared practical.

"Lucy!"

"Yes, I suppose we ought to be going," was her reply.

"Lucy, I want to ask something of you that I have never asked before."

At the serious note in his voice she stepped frankly and kindly towards him.

"What, Cecil?"

"Hitherto never—not even that day on the lawn when you agreed to marry me—"

He became self-conscious and kept glancing round to see if they were observed. His courage had gone.

"Yes?"

"Up to now I have never kissed you."

She was as scarlet as if he had put the thing most indelicately.

"No—more you have," she stammered.

"Then I ask you—may I now?"

"Of course you may, Cecil. You might before. I can't run at you, you know."

At that supreme moment he was conscious of nothing but absurdities. Her reply was inadequate. She gave such a businesslike lift to her veil. As he approached her he found time to wish that he could recoil. As he touched her, his gold pince-nez became dislodged and was flattened between them.

Such was the embrace. He considered, with truth, that it had been a failure. Passion should believe itself irresistible. It should forget civility and consideration and all the other curses of a refined nature. Above all, it should never ask for leave where there is a right of way. Why could he not do as any labourer or navvy—nay, as any young man behind the counter would have done? He recast the scene. Lucy was standing flower-like by the water; he rushed up and took her in his arms; she rebuked him, permitted him, and revered him ever after for his manliness. For he believed that women revere men for their manliness.

They left the pool in silence, after this one salutation. He waited for her to make some remark which should show him her inmost thoughts. At last she spoke, and with fitting gravity.

"Emerson the name was, not Harris."

"What name?"

"The old man's."

"What old man?"

"That old man I told you about. The one Mr Eager was so unkind to."

He could not know that this was the most intimate conversation they had ever had.

Chapter 10
Cecil as a Humorist

The society out of which Cecil proposed to rescue Lucy was perhaps no very splendid affair, yet it was more splendid than her antecedents entitled her to. Her father, a prosperous local solicitor, had built Windy Corner as a speculation at the time the district was opening up, and, falling in love with his own creation, had ended by living there himself. Soon after his marriage, the social atmosphere began to alter. Other houses were built on the brow of that steep southern slope, and others, again, among the pine trees behind, and northward on the chalk barrier of the downs. Most of these houses were larger than Windy Corner, and were filled by people who came, not from the district, but from London, and who mistook the Honeychurches for the remnants of an indigenous aristocracy. He was inclined to be frightened, but his wife accepted the situation without either pride or humility. "I cannot think what people are doing," she would say, "but it is extremely fortunate for the children." She called everywhere; her calls were returned with enthusiasm, and by the time people found out that she was not exactly of their milieu they liked her, and it did not seem to matter. When Mr Honeychurch died, he had the satisfaction—which few honest solicitors despise—of leaving his family rooted in the best society obtainable.

The best obtainable. Certainly many of the immigrants were rather dull, and Lucy realized this more vividly since her return from Italy. Hitherto she had accepted their ideals without questioning—their kindly affluence, their inexplosive religion, their dislike of paper bags, orange-peel and broken bottles. A Radical out and out, she learned to speak with horror of Suburbia. Life, so far as she troubled to conceive it, was a circle of rich, pleasant people, with identical interests and identical foes. In this circle one thought, married and died. Outside it were poverty and vulgarity, for ever trying to enter, just as the London fog tries to enter the pinewoods, pouring through the gaps in the northern hills. But in Italy, where anyone who chooses may warm himself in equality, as in the sun, this conception of life vanished. Her senses expanded; she felt that there was no one whom she might not get to like, that social barriers were irremovable, doubtless, but not particularly high. You jump over them just as you jump into a peasant's olive-yard in the Apennines, and he is glad to see you. She returned with new eyes.

So did Cecil; but Italy had quickened Cecil, not to tolerance, but to irritation. He saw that the local society was narrow, but instead of saying, "Does this very much matter?" he rebelled, and tried to substitute for it the society he called broad. He did not realize that Lucy had consecrated her environment by the thousand little civilities that create a tenderness in time, and that though her eyes saw its defects her heart refused to despise it entirely. Nor did he realize a more important point—that if she was too great for this society she was too great for all society, and had reached the stage where personal intercourse would alone satisfy her. A rebel she was, but not of the kind he understood—a rebel who desired, not a wider dwelling-room, but equality beside the man she loved. For Italy was offering her the most priceless of all possessions—her own soul.

Playing bumble-puppy with Minnie Beebe, niece to the rector, and aged thirteen—an ancient and most honourable game, which consists in striking tennis-balls high into the air, so that they fall over the net and immoderately bounce; some hit Mrs Honeychurch; others are lost. The sentence is confused, but the better illustrates Lucy's state of mind, for she was trying to talk to Mr Beebe at the same time.

"Oh, it has been such a nuisance—first he, then they—no one knowing what they wanted, and everyone so tiresome."

"But they really are coming now," said Mr Beebe. "I wrote to Miss Teresa a few days ago—she was wondering how often the butcher called, and my reply of once a month must have impressed her favourably. They are coming. I heard from them this morning."

"I shall hate those Miss Alans!" Mrs Honeychurch cried. "Just because they're old and silly one's expected to say, 'How sweet!' I hate their 'if'-ing and 'but'-ing and 'and'-ing. And poor Lucy—serve her right—worn to a shadow."

Mr Beebe watched the shadow springing and shouting over the tennis court. Cecil was absent—one did not play bumble-puppy when he was there.

"Well, if they are coming—no, Minnie, not Saturn." Saturn was a tennis-ball whose skin was partially unsewn. When in motion his orb was encircled by a ring. "If they are coming, Sir Harry will let them move in before the twenty-ninth, and he will cross out the clause about whitewashing the ceilings, because it made them nervous, and put in the fair-wear-and-tear one.—That doesn't count. I told you not Saturn."

"Saturn's all right for bumble-puppy," cried Freddy, joining them. "Minnie, don't you listen to her."

"Saturn doesn't bounce."

"Saturn bounces enough."

"No, he doesn't."

"Well, he bounces better than the Beautiful White Devil."

"Hush, dear," said Mrs Honeychurch.

"But look at Lucy—complaining of Saturn, and all the time's got the Beautiful White Devil in her hand, ready to plug it in. That's right, Minnie, go for her—get her over the shins with the racquet—get her over the shins!"

Lucy fell; the Beautiful White Devil rolled from her hand.

Mr Beebe picked it up, and said: "The name of this ball is Vittoria Corombona, please." But his correction passed unheeded.

Freddy possessed to a high degree the power of lashing little girls to fury, and in half a minute he had transformed Minnie from a well-mannered child into a howling wilderness. Up in the house Cecil heard them, and, though he was full of entertaining news, he did not come down to impart it, in case he got hurt. He was not a coward, and bore necessary pain as well as any man. But he hated the physical violence of the young. How right he was! Sure enough it ended in a cry.

"I wish the Miss Alans could see this," observed Mr Beebe, just as Lucy, who was nursing the injured Minnie, was in turn lifted off her feet by her brother.

"Who are the Miss Alans?" Freddy panted.

"They have taken Cissie Villa."

"That wasn't the name—"

Here his foot slipped, and they all fell most agreeably onto the grass. An interval elapses.

"Wasn't what name?" asked Lucy, with her brother's head in her lap.

"Alan wasn't. The name of the people Sir Harry's let to."

"Nonsense, Freddy! You know nothing about it."

"Nonsense yourself! I've this minute seen him. He said to me: 'Ahem! Honeychurch' "—Freddy was an indifferent mimic—" 'Ahem! Ahem! I have at last procured really dee-sire-rebel tenants.' I said, 'Hooray, old boy!' and slapped him on the back."

"Exactly. The Miss Alans?"

"Rather not. More like Anderson."

"Oh, good gracious, there isn't going to be another muddle!" Mrs Honeychurch exclaimed. "Do you notice, Lucy, I'm always right? I *said* don't interfere with Cissie Villa. I'm always right. I'm quite uneasy at being always right so often."

"It's only another muddle of Freddy's. Freddy doesn't even know the name of the people he pretends have taken it instead."

"Yes, I do. I've got it. Emerson."

"What name?"

"Emerson. I'll bet you anything you like."

"What a weathercock Sir Harry is," said Lucy quietly. "I wish I had never bothered over it at all."

Then she lay on her back and gazed at the cloudless sky. Mr Beebe, whose opinion of her rose daily, whispered to his niece that *that* was the proper way to behave if any little thing went wrong.

Meanwhile the name of the new tenants had diverted Mrs Honeychurch from the contemplation of her own abilities.

"Emerson, Freddy? Do you know what Emersons they are?"

"I don't know whether they're any Emersons," retorted Freddy, who was democratic. Like his sister, and like most young people, he was naturally attracted by the idea of equality, and the undeniable fact that there are different kinds of Emersons annoyed him beyond due measure.

"I trust they are the right sort of person. All right, Lucy"—she was sitting up again—"I see you looking down your nose and thinking your mother's a snob. But there *is* a right sort and a wrong sort, and it's affectation to pretend there isn't."

"Emerson's a common enough name," Lucy remarked.

She was gazing sideways. Seated on a promontory herself, she could see the pine-clad promontories descending one beyond another into the Weald. The further one descended the garden, the more glorious was this lateral view.

"I was merely going to remark, Freddy, that I trusted they were no relations of Emerson the philosopher, a most trying man. Pray, does that satisfy you?"

"Oh yes," he grumbled. "And you will be satisfied, too, for they're friends of Cecil; so"—with elaborate irony—"you and the other county families will be able to call in perfect safety."

"*Cecil?*" exclaimed Lucy.

"Don't be rude, dear," said his mother placidly. "Lucy, don't screech. It's a new bad habit you're getting into."

"But has Cecil—"

"Friends of Cecil's," he repeated, " 'and so really dee-sire-rebel. Ahem! Honeychurch, I have just telegraphed to them.' "

She got up from the grass.

It was hard on Lucy. Mr Beebe sympathized with her very much. While she believed that her snub about the Miss Alans came from Sir Harry Otway, she had borne it like a good girl. She might well "screech" when she heard that it came partly from her lover. Mr Vyse was a tease—something worse than a tease: he took a malicious pleasure in thwarting people. The clergyman, knowing this, looked at Miss Honeychurch with more than his usual kindness.

When she exclaimed, "But Cecil's Emersons—they can't possibly be the same ones—there is that—" he did not consider that the exclamation was strange, but saw in it an opportunity of diverting the conversation while she recovered her composure. He diverted it as follows:

"The Emersons who were at Florence, do you mean? No, I don't suppose it will prove to be them. It is probably a long cry from them to friends of Mr Vyse's. Oh, Mrs Honeychurch, the oddest people! The queerest people! For our part we liked them, didn't we?" He appealed to Lucy. "There was a great scene over some violets. They picked violets and filled all the vases in the room of these very Miss Alans who have failed to come to Cissie Villa. Poor little ladies! So shocked and so pleased. It used to be one of Miss Catharine's great stories. 'My dear sister loves flowers,' it began. They found the whole room a mass of blue—vases and jugs—and the story ends with 'So ungentlemanly and yet so beautiful. It is all very difficult.' Yes, I always connect those Florentine Emersons with violets."

"Fiasco's done you this time," remarked Freddy, not seeing that his sister's face was very red. She could not recover herself. Mr Beebe saw it, and continued to divert the conversation.

"These particular Emersons consisted of a father and a son—the son a goodly, if not a good young man; not a fool, I fancy, but very immature—pessimism, et cetera. Our special joy was the father—such a sentimental darling, and people declared he had murdered his wife."

In his normal state Mr Beebe would never have repeated such gossip, but he was trying to shelter Lucy in her little trouble. He repeated any rubbish that came into his head.

"Murdered his wife?" said Mrs Honeychurch. "Lucy, don't desert us—go on playing bumble-puppy. Really, the Pension Bertolini must have been the oddest place. That's the second murderer I've heard of as being there. What ever was Charlotte doing to stop? By the by, we really must ask Charlotte here some time."

Mr Beebe could recall no second murderer. He suggested that his hostess was mistaken. At the hint of opposition she warmed. She was perfectly sure that there had been a second tourist of whom the same story had been told. The name escaped her. What was the name? Oh, what was the name? She clasped her knees for the name. Something in Thackeray. She struck her matronly forehead.

Lucy asked her brother whether Cecil was in.

"Oh, don't go!" he cried, and tried to catch her by the ankles.

"I must go," she said gravely. "Don't be silly. You always overdo it when you play."

As she left them her mother's shout of "Harris!" shivered the tranquil air, and reminded her that she had told a lie and had never put it right. Such a senseless lie, too, yet it shattered her nerves, and made her connect these Emersons, friends of Cecil's, with a pair of nondescript tourists. Hitherto truth had come to her naturally. She saw that for the future she must be more vigilant, and be—absolutely truthful? Well, at all events, she must not tell lies. She hurried up the garden, still flushed with shame. A word from Cecil would soothe her, she was sure.

"Cecil!"

"Hullo!" he called, and leant out of the smoking-room window. He seemed in high spirits. "I was hoping you'd come. I heard you all bear-gardening, but there's better fun up here. I, even I, have won a great victory for the Comic Muse. George Meredith's right—the cause of Comedy and the cause of Truth are really the same; and I, even I, have found tenants for the distressful Cissie Villa. Don't be angry! Don't be angry! You'll forgive me when you hear it all."

He looked very attractive when his face was bright, and he dispelled her ridiculous forebodings at once.

"I have heard," she said. "Freddy has told us. Naughty Cecil! I suppose I must forgive you. Just think of all the trouble I took for nothing! Certainly the Miss Alans are a little tiresome, and I'd rather have nice friends of yours. But you oughtn't to tease one so."

"Friends of mine?" he laughed. "But, Lucy, the whole joke is to come! Come here." But she remained standing where she was. "Do you know where I met these desirable tenants? In the National Gallery, when I was up to see my mother last week."

"What an odd place to meet people!" she said nervously. "I don't quite understand."

"In the Umbrian Room. Absolute strangers. They were admiring Luca Signorelli—of course, quite stupidly. However, we got talking, and they refreshed me not a little. They had been to Italy."

"But, Cecil—"

He proceeded hilariously.

"In the course of conversation they said that they wanted a country cottage—the father to live there, the son to run down for weekends. I thought, 'What a chance of scoring off Sir Harry!' and I took their address and a London reference, found they weren't actual blackguards—it was great sport—and wrote to him, making out—"

"Cecil! No, it's not fair. I've probably met them before—"

He bore her down.

"Perfectly fair. Anything is fair that punishes a snob. That old man will do the neighbourhood a world of good. Sir Harry is too disgusting with his 'decayed gentlewomen'. I meant to read him a lesson some time. No, Lucy, the classes ought to mix, and before long you'll agree with me. There ought to be intermarriage—all sorts of things. I believe in democracy—"

"No, you don't," she snapped. "You don't know what the word means."

He stared at her, and felt again that she had failed to be Leonardesque. "No, you don't!" Her face was inartistic—that of a peevish virago.

"It isn't fair, Cecil. I blame you—I blame you very much indeed. You had no business to undo my work about the Miss Alans, and make me look ridiculous. You call it scoring off Sir Harry, but do you realize that it is all at my expense? I consider it most disloyal of you."

She left him.

"Temper!" he thought, raising his eyebrows.

No, it was worse than temper—snobbishness. As long as Lucy thought that his own smart friends were supplanting the Miss Alans, she had not minded. He perceived that these new tenants might be of value educationally. He would tolerate the father and draw out the son, who was silent. In the interests of the Comic Muse and of Truth, he would bring them to Windy Corner.

Chapter 11
In Mrs Vyse's Well-Appointed Flat

The Comic Muse, though able to look after her own interests, did not disdain the assistance of Mr Vyse. His idea of bringing the Emersons to Windy Corner struck her as decidedly good, and she carried through the negotiations without a hitch. Sir Harry Otway signed the agreement, met Mr Emerson, and was duly disillusioned. The Miss Alans were duly offended, and wrote a dignified letter to Lucy, whom they held responsible for the failure. Mr Beebe planned pleasant moments for the newcomers, and told Mrs Honeychurch that Freddy must call on them as soon as they arrived. Indeed, so ample was the Muse's equipment that she permitted Mr Harris, never a very robust criminal, to droop his head, to be forgotten, and to die.

Lucy—to descend from bright heaven to earth, whereon there are shadows because there are hills—Lucy was at first plunged into despair, but settled after a little thought that it did not matter in the very least. Now that she was engaged, the Emersons would scarcely insult her, and were welcome to come into the neighbourhood. And Cecil was welcome to bring whom he would into the neighbourhood. Therefore Cecil was welcome to bring the Emersons into the neighbourhood. But, as I say, this took a little thinking, and—so illogical are girls—the event remained rather greater and rather more dreadful than it should have done. She was glad that a visit to Mrs Vyse now fell due; the tenants moved into Cissie Villa while she was safe in the London flat.

"Cecil—Cecil darling," she whispered the evening she arrived, and crept into his arms.

Cecil, too, became demonstrative. He saw that the needful fire had been kindled in Lucy. At last she longed for attention, as a woman should, and looked up to him because he was a man.

"So you do love me, little thing?" he murmured.

"Oh, Cecil, I do, I do! I don't know what I should do without you."

Several days passed. Then she had a letter from Miss Bartlett.

A coolness had sprung up between the two cousins, and they had not corresponded since they parted in August. The coolness dated from what Charlotte would call "the flight to Rome", and in Rome it had increased amazingly. For the companion who is merely uncongenial in the medieval world becomes exasperating in the classical. Charlotte, unselfish in the Forum, would have tried a sweeter temper than Lucy's, and once, in the Baths of Caracalla, they had doubted whether they could continue their tour. Lucy had said she would join the Vyses—Mrs Vyse was an acquaintance of her mother, so there was no impropriety in the plan—and Miss Bartlett had replied that she was quite used to being abandoned suddenly. Finally nothing happened; but the coolness remained, and, for Lucy, was even increased when she opened the letter and read as follows. It had been forwarded from Windy Corner.

Tunbridge Wells,
September.

Dearest Lucia,

I have news of you at last! Miss Lavish has been bicycling in your parts, but was not sure whether a call would be welcome. Puncturing her tyre near Summer Street, and it being mended while she sat very woebegone in that pretty churchyard, she saw, to her astonishment, a door open opposite and the younger Emerson man come out. He said his father had just taken the house. He *said* he did not know that you lived in the neighbourhood (?). He never suggested giving Eleanor a cup of tea. Dear Lucy, I am much worried, and I advise you to make a clean breast of his past behaviour to your mother, Freddy and Mr Vyse, who will forbid him to enter the house, etc. That was a great misfortune, and I dare say you have told them already. Mr Vyse is so sensitive. I remember how I used to get on his nerves at Rome.

I am very sorry about it all, and should not feel easy unless I warned you.

Believe me,
Your anxious and loving cousin,
Charlotte.

Lucy was much annoyed, and replied as follows:

Beauchamp Mansions, S.W.

Dear Charlotte,

Many thanks for your warning. When Mr Emerson forgot himself on the mountain, you made me promise not to tell mother, because you said she would blame you for not being always with me. I have kept that promise, and cannot possibly tell her now. I have said both to her and to Cecil that I met the Emersons at Florence, and that they are respectable people—which I *do* think—and the reason that he offered Miss Lavish no tea was probably that he had none himself. She should have tried at the Rectory. I cannot begin making a fuss at this stage. You must see that it would be too absurd. If the Emersons heard I had complained of them, they would think themselves of importance, which is exactly what they are not. I like the old father, and look forward to seeing him again. As for the son, I am sorry for *him* when we meet, rather than for myself. They are known to Cecil, who is very well, and spoke of you the other day. We expect to be married in January.

Miss Lavish cannot have told you much about me, for I am not at Windy Corner at all, but here. Please do not put "Private" outside your envelope again. No one opens my letters.

Yours affectionately,
L. M. Honeychurch.

Secrecy has this disadvantage: we lose the sense of proportion; we cannot tell whether our secret is important or not. Were Lucy and her cousin closeted with a great thing which would destroy Cecil's life if he discovered it, or with a little thing which he would laugh at? Miss Bartlett suggested the former. Perhaps she was right. It had become a great thing now. Left to herself, Lucy would have told her mother and her lover ingenuously, and it would have remained a little thing. "Emerson, not Harris": it was only that a few weeks ago. She tried to tell Cecil even now when they were laughing about some beautiful lady who had smitten his heart at school. But her body behaved so ridiculously that she stopped.

She and her secret stayed ten days longer in the deserted metropolis visiting the scenes they were to know so well later on. It did her no harm, Cecil thought, to learn the framework of society, while society itself was absent on the golf-links or the moors. The weather was cool, and it did her no harm. In spite of the season, Mrs Vyse managed to scrape together a dinner-party consisting entirely of the grandchildren of famous people. The food was poor, but the talk had a witty weariness that impressed the girl. One was tired of everything, it seemed. One launched into enthusiasms only to collapse gracefully, and pick oneself up amid sympathetic laughter. In this atmosphere the Pension Bertolini and Windy Corner appeared equally crude, and Lucy saw that her London career would estrange her a little from all that she had loved in the past.

The grandchildren asked her to play the piano. She played Schumann. "Now some Beethoven," called Cecil, when the querulous beauty of the music had died. She shook her head and played Schumann again. The melody rose, unprofitably magical. It broke; it was resumed broken, not marching once from the cradle to the grave. The sadness of the incomplete—the sadness that is often Life, but should never be Art—throbbed in its disjected phrases, and made the nerves of the audience throb. Not thus had she played on the little draped piano at the Bertolini, and "Too much Schumann" was not the remark that Mr Beebe had passed to himself when she returned.

When the guests were gone, and Lucy had gone to bed, Mrs Vyse paced up and down the drawing-room, discussing her little party with her son. Mrs Vyse was a nice woman, but her personality, like many another's, had been swamped by London, for it needs a strong head to live among many people. The too vast orb of her fate had crushed her; she had seen too many seasons, too many cities, too many men for her abilities, and even with Cecil she was mechanical, and behaved as if he was not one son, but, so to speak, a filial crowd.

"Make Lucy one of us," she said, looking round intelligently at the end of each sentence, and straining her lips apart until she spoke again. "Lucy is becoming wonderful—wonderful."

"Her music always was wonderful."

"Yes, but she is purging off the Honeychurch taint—most excellent Honeychurches, but you know what I mean. She is not always quoting servants, or asking one how the pudding is made."

"Italy has done it."

"Perhaps," she murmured, thinking of the museum that represented Italy to her. "It is just possible. Cecil, mind you marry her next January. She is one of us already."

"But her music!" he exclaimed. "The style of her! How she kept to Schumann when, like an idiot, I wanted Beethoven. Schumann was right for this evening. Schumann was the thing. Do you know, mother, I shall have our children educated just like Lucy. Bring them up among honest country folk for freshness, send them to Italy for subtlety, and then—not till then—let them come to London. I don't believe in these London educations—" He broke off, remembering that he had had one himself, and concluded, "At all events, not for women."

"Make her one of us," repeated Mrs Vyse, and processed to bed.

As she was dozing off, a cry—the cry of nightmare—rang from Lucy's room. Lucy could ring for the maid if she liked, but Mrs Vyse thought it kind to go herself. She found the girl sitting upright with her hand on her cheek.

"I am so sorry, Mrs Vyse—it is these dreams."

"Bad dreams?"

"Just dreams."

The elder lady smiled and kissed her, saying very distinctly: "You should have heard us talking about you, dear. He admires you more than ever. Dream of that."

Lucy returned the kiss, still covering one cheek with her hand. Mrs Vyse recessed to bed. Cecil, whom the cry had not awoke, snored. Darkness enveloped the flat.

Chapter 12
Twelfth Chapter

It was a Saturday afternoon, gay and brilliant after abundant rains, and the spirit of youth dwelt in it, though the season was now autumn. All that was gracious triumphed. As the motor-cars passed through Summer Street they raised only a little dust, and their stench was soon dispersed by the wind and replaced by the scent of the wet birches or of the pines. Mr Beebe, at leisure for life's amenities, leant over his rectory gate. Freddy leant by him, smoking a pendant pipe.

"Suppose we go and hinder those new people opposite for a little."

"M'm."

"They might amuse you."

Freddy, whom his fellow creatures never amused, suggested that the new pecple might be feeling a bit busy, and so on, since they had only just moved in.

"I suggested we should hinder them," said Mr Beebe. "They are worth it." Unlatching the gate, he sauntered over the triangular green to Cissie Villa. "Hullo!" he called, shouting in at the open door, through which much squalor was visible.

A grave voice replied, "Hullo!"

"I've brought someone to see you."

"I'll be down in a minute."

The passage was blocked by a wardrobe, which the removal men had failed to carry up the stairs. Mr Beebe edged round it with difficulty. The sitting-room itself was blocked with books.

"Are these people great readers?" Freddy whispered. "Are they that sort?"

"I fancy they know how to read—a rare accomplishment.

What have they got? Byron. Exactly. *A Shropshire Lad.* Never heard of it. *The Way of All Flesh.* Never heard of it. Gibbon. Hullo! Dear George reads German. Um—um—Schopenhauer, Nietzsche, and so we go on. Well, I suppose your generation knows its own business, Honeychurch."

"Mr Beebe, look at that," said Freddy in awestruck tones.

On the cornice of the wardrobe the hand of an amateur had painted this inscription: "Mistrust all enterprises that require new clothes."

"I know. Isn't it jolly? I like that. I'm certain that's the old man's doing."

"How very odd of him!"

"Surely you agree?"

But Freddy was his mother's son and felt that one ought not to go spoiling the furniture.

"Pictures!" the clergyman continued, scrambling about the room. "Giotto—they got that at Florence, I'll be bound."

"The same as Lucy's got."

"Oh, by the by, did Miss Honeychurch enjoy London?"

"She came back yesterday."

"I suppose she had a good time?"

"Yes, very," said Freddy, taking up a book. "She and Cecil are thicker than ever."

"That's good hearing."

"I wish I wasn't such a fool, Mr Beebe."

Mr Beebe ignored the remark.

"Lucy used to be nearly as stupid as I am, but it'll be very different now, mother thinks. She will read all kinds of books."

"So will you."

"Only medical books. Not books that you can talk about afterwards. Cecil is teaching Lucy Italian, and he says her playing is wonderful. There are all kinds of things in it that we have never noticed. Cecil says—"

"What on earth are those people doing upstairs? Emerson —we think we'll come another time."

George ran downstairs and pushed them into the room without speaking.

"Let me introduce Mr Honeychurch, a neighbour."

Then Freddy hurled one of the thunderbolts of youth. Perhaps he was shy, perhaps he was friendly, or perhaps he thought that George's face wanted washing. At all events, he greeted him with: "How d'ye do? Come and have a bathe."

"Oh, all right," said George, impassive.

Mr Beebe was highly entertained.

" 'How d'ye do? How d'ye do? Come and have a bathe,' " he chuckled. "That's the best conversational opening I've ever heard. But I'm afraid it will only act between men. Can you picture a lady who has been introduced to another lady by a third lady opening civilities with 'How do you do? Come and have a bathe'? And yet you will tell me that the sexes are equal."

"I tell you that they shall be," said Mr Emerson, who had been slowly descending the stairs. "Good afternoon, Mr Beebe. I tell you they shall be comrades, and George thinks the same."

"We are to raise ladies to our level?" the clergyman inquired.

"The Garden of Eden," pursued Mr Emerson, still descending, "which you place in the past, is really yet to come. We shall enter it when we no longer despise our bodies."

Mr Beebe disclaimed placing the Garden of Eden anywhere.

"In this—not in other things—we men are ahead. We despise the body less than women do. But not until we are comrades shall we enter the Garden."

"I say, what about this bathe?" murmured Freddy, appalled at the mass of philosophy that was approaching him.

"I believed in a return to Nature once. But how can we return to Nature when we have never been with her? Today, I believe that we must discover Nature. After many conquests we shall attain simplicity. It is our heritage."

"Let me introduce Mr Honeychurch, whose sister you will remember at Florence."

"How do you do? Very glad to see you, and that you are

taking George for a bathe. Very glad to hear that your sister is going to marry. Marriage is a duty. I am sure that she will be happy, for we know Mr Vyse, too. He has been most kind. He met us by chance in the National Gallery, and arranged everything about this delightful house. Though I hope I have not vexed Sir Harry Otway. I have met so few Liberal landowners, and I was anxious to compare his attitude towards the game laws with the Conservative attitude. Ah, this wind! You do well to bathe. Yours is a glorious country, Honeychurch!"

"Not a bit!" mumbled Freddy. "I must—that is to say, I have to—have the pleasure of calling on you later on, my mother says, I hope."

"*Call*, my lad? Who taught us that drawing-room twaddle? Call on your grandmother! Listen to the wind among the pines! Yours is a glorious country."

Mr Beebe came to the rescue.

"Mr Emerson, he will call, I shall call; you or your son will return our calls before ten days have elapsed. I trust that you have realized about the ten days' interval. It does not count that I helped you with the stair-eyes yesterday. It does not count that they are going to bathe this afternoon."

"Yes, go and bathe, George. Why do you dawdle talking? Bring them back to tea. Bring back some milk, cakes, honey. The change will do you good. George has been working very hard at his office. I can't believe he's well."

George bowed his head, dusty and sombre, exhaling the peculiar smell of one who has handled furniture.

"Do you really want this bathe?" Freddy asked him. "It is only a pond, don't you know. I dare say you are used to something much better."

"Yes—I have said 'Yes' already."

Mr Beebe felt bound to assist his young friend, and led the way out of the house and into the pine-woods. How glorious it was! For a little time the voice of old Mr Emerson pursued them, dispensing good wishes and philosophy. It ceased, and they only heard the fair wind blowing the bracken and the trees.

Mr Beebe, who could be silent, but who could not bear silence, was compelled to chatter, since the expedition looked like a failure, and neither of his companions would utter a word. He spoke of Florence. George attended gravely, assenting or dissenting with slight but determined gestures that were as inexplicable as the motions of the tree-tops above their heads.

"And what a coincidence that you should meet Mr Vyse! Did you realize that you would find all the Pension Bertolini down here?"

"I did not. Miss Lavish told me."

"When I was a young man I always meant to write a 'History of Coincidence'."

No enthusiasm.

"Though, as a matter of fact, coincidences are much rarer than we suppose. For example, it isn't pure coincidentality that you are here now, when one comes to reflect."

To his relief, George began to talk.

"It is. I have reflected. It is Fate. Everything is Fate. We are flung together by Fate, drawn apart by Fate—flung together, drawn apart. The twelve winds blow us—we settle nothing—"

"You have not reflected at all," rapped the clergyman. "Let me give you a useful tip, Emerson: attribute nothing to Fate. Don't say, 'I didn't do this,' for you did it, ten to one. Now I'll cross-question you. Where did you first meet Miss Honeychurch and myself?"

"Italy."

"And where did you meet Mr Vyse, who is going to marry Miss Honeychurch?"

"National Gallery."

"Looking at Italian art. There you are, and yet you talk of coincidence and Fate! You naturally seek out things Italian, and so do we and our friends. This narrows the field immeasurably, and we meet again in it."

"It is Fate that I am here," persisted George. "But you can call it Italy if it makes you less unhappy."

Mr Beebe slid away from such heavy treatment of the

subject. But he was infinitely tolerant of the young, and had no desire to snub George.

"And so for this and for other reasons my 'History of Coincidence' is still to write."

Silence.

Wishing to round off the episode, he added:

"We are all so glad that you have come."

Silence.

"Here we are!" called Freddy.

"Oh, good!" exclaimed Mr Beebe, mopping his brow.

"In there's the pond. I wish it was bigger," he added apologetically.

They climbed down a slippery bank of pine-needles. There lay the pond, set in its little alp of green—only a pond, but large enough to contain the human body, and pure enough to reflect the sky. On account of the rains, the waters had flooded the surrounding grass, which showed like a beautiful emerald path, tempting the feet towards the central pool.

"It's distinctly successful, as ponds go," said Mr Beebe. "No apologies are necessary for the pond."

George sat down where the ground was dry, and drearily unlaced his boots.

"Aren't those masses of willow-herb splendid? I love willow-herb in seed. What's the name of this aromatic plant?"

No one knew or seemed to care.

"These abrupt changes of vegetation—this little spongeous tract of water-plants, and on either side of it all the growths are tough or brittle—heather, bracken, hurts, pines. Very charming, very charming."

"Mr Beebe, aren't you bathing?" called Freddy, as he stripped himself.

Mr Beebe thought he was not.

"Water's wonderful!" cried Freddy, prancing in.

"Water's water," murmured George. Wetting his hair first—a sure sign of apathy—he followed Freddy into the divine, as indifferent as if he were a statue and the pond a pail of soapsuds. It was necessary to use his muscles. It was necessary to keep clean. Mr Beebe watched them, and watched the seeds of the willow-herb dance chorically above their heads.

"Apooshoo, apooshoo, apooshoo," went Freddy, swimming for two strokes in either direction, and then becoming involved in reeds or mud.

"Is it worth it?" asked the other, Michelangelesque on the flooded margin.

The bank broke away, and he fell into the pool before he had weighed the question properly.

"Hee—poof—I've swallowed a polly-wog. Mr Beebe, water's wonderful, water's simply ripping."

"Water's not so bad," said George, reappearing from his plunge, and sputtering at the sun.

"Water's wonderful. Mr Beebe, do."

"Apooshoo, kouf."

Mr Beebe, who was hot, and who always acquiesced where possible, looked around him. He could detect no parishioners except the pine trees, rising up steeply on all sides, and gesturing to each other against the blue. How glorious it was! The world of motor-cars and Rural Deans receded illimitably. Water, sky, evergreens, a wind—these things not even the seasons can touch, and surely they lie beyond the intrusion of man?

"I may as well wash too"; and soon his garments made a third little pile on the sward, and he too asserted the wonder of the water.

It was ordinary water, nor was there very much of it, and, as Freddy said, it reminded one of swimming in a salad. The three gentlemen rotated in the pool breast high, after the fashion of the nymphs in *Götterdämmerung*. But either because the rains had given a freshness, or because the sun was shedding a most glorious heat, or because two of the gentlemen were young in years and the third young in the spirit—for some reason or other a change came over them, and they forgot Italy and Botany and Fate. They began to play. Mr Beebe and Freddy splashed each other. A little deferentially, they splashed George. He was quiet; they feared they had offended him. Then all the forces of youth burst out. He smiled, flung himself at them, splashed them, ducked them, kicked them, muddied them, and drove them out of the pool.

"Race you round it, then," cried Freddy, and they raced in the sunshine, and George took a short cut and dirtied his shins, and had to bathe a second time. Then Mr Beebe consented to run—a memorable sight.

They ran to get dry, they bathed to get cool, they played at being Indians in the willow-herbs and in the bracken, they bathed to get clean. And all the time three little bundles lay discreetly on the sward, proclaiming:

"No. We are what matters. Without us shall no enterprise begin. To us shall all flesh turn in the end."

"A try! A try!" yelled Freddy, snatching up George's bundle and placing it beside an imaginary goalpost.

"Soccer rules," George retorted, scattering Freddy's bundle with a kick.

"Goal!"

"Goal!"

"Pass!"

"Take care my watch!" cried Mr Beebe.

Clothes flew in all directions.

"Take care my hat! No, that's enough, Freddy. Dress now. No, I say!"

But the two young men were delirious. Away they twinkled into the trees, Freddy with a clerical waistcoat under his arm, George with a wide-awake hat on his dripping hair.

"That'll do!" shouted Mr Beebe, remembering that after all he was in his own parish. Then his voice changed as if every pine tree was a Rural Dean. "Hi! Steady on! I see people coming, you fellows!"

Yells, and widening circles over the dappled earth.

"Hi! Hi! *Ladies*!"

Neither George nor Freddy was truly refined. Still, they did not hear Mr Beebe's last warning, or they would have avoided Mrs Honeychurch, Cecil and Lucy, who were walking down to call on old Mrs Butterworth. Freddy dropped the waistcoat at their feet, and dashed into some bracken. George whooped in their faces, turned, and scudded away down the path to the pond, still clad in Mr Beebe's hat.

"Gracious alive!" cried Mrs Honeychurch. "Who ever were those unfortunate people? Oh, dears, look away! And poor Mr Beebe, too! What ever has happened?"

"Come this way immediately," commanded Cecil, who always felt that he must lead women, though he knew not whither, and protect them, though he knew not against what. He led them now towards the bracken where Freddy sat concealed.

"Oh, poor Mr Beebe! Was that his waistcoat we left in the path? Cecil, Mr Beebe's waistcoat—"

"No business of ours," said Cecil, glancing at Lucy, who was all parasol and evidently "minded".

"I fancy Mr Beebe jumped back into the pond."

"This way, please, Mrs Honeychurch, this way."

They followed him up the bank, attempting the tense yet nonchalant expression that is suitable for ladies on such occasions.

"Well, *I* can't help it," said a voice close ahead, and Freddy reared a freckled face and a pair of snowy shoulders out of the fronds. "I can't be trodden on, can I?"

"Good gracious me, dear; so it's you! What miserable management! Why not have a comfortable bath at home, with hot and cold laid on?"

"Look here, mother: a fellow must wash, and a fellow's got to dry, and if another fellow—"

"Dear, no doubt you're right as usual, but you are in no position to argue. Come, Lucy." They turned. "Oh, look—don't look! Oh, poor Mr Beebe! How unfortunate again—"

For Mr Beebe was just crawling out of the pond, on whose surface garments of an intimate nature did float; while George, the world-weary George, shouted to Freddy that he had hooked a fish.

"And me, I've swallowed one," answered he of the

bracken. "I've swallowed a polly-wog. It wriggleth in my tummy. I shall die—Emerson, you beast, you've got on my bags."

"Hush, dears," said Mrs Honeychurch, who found it impossible to remain shocked. "And do be sure you dry yourselves thoroughly first. All these colds come of not drying thoroughly."

"Mother, do come away," said Lucy. "Oh, for goodness' sake, do come."

"Hullo!" cried George, so that again the ladies stopped.

He regarded himself as dressed. Barefoot, bare-chested, radiant and personable against the shadowy woods, he called:

"Hullo, Miss Honeychurch! Hullo!"

"Bow, Lucy; better bow. Who ever is it? I shall bow."

Miss Honeychurch bowed.

That evening and all that night the water ran away. On the morrow the pool had shrunk to its old size and lost its glory. It had been a call to the blood and to the relaxed will, a passing benediction whose influence did not pass, a holiness, a spell, a momentary chalice for youth.

Chapter 13
How Miss Bartlett's Boiler was so Tiresome

How often had Lucy rehearsed this bow, this interview! But she had always rehearsed them indoors, and with certain accessories, which surely we have a right to assume. Who could foretell that she and George would meet in the rout of a civilization, amidst an army of coats and collars and boots that lay wounded over the sunlit earth? She had imagined a young Mr Emerson, who might be shy or morbid or indifferent or furtively impudent. She was prepared for all of these. But she had never imagined one who would be happy and greet her with the shout of the morning star.

Indoors herself, partaking of tea with old Mrs Butterworth, she reflected that it is impossible to foretell the future with any degree of accuracy, that it is impossible to rehearse life. A fault in the scenery, a face in the audience, an irruption of the audience onto the stage, and all our carefully planned gestures mean nothing, or mean too much. "I will bow," she had thought. "I will not shake hands with him. That will be just the proper thing." She had bowed—but to whom? To gods, to heroes, to the nonsense of schoolgirls! She had bowed across the rubbish that cumbers the world.

So ran her thoughts, while her faculties were busy with Cecil. It was another of those dreadful engagement calls. Mrs Butterworth had wanted to see him, and he did not want to be seen. He did not want to hear about hydrangeas, why they change their colour at the seaside. He did not want to join the C.O.S. When cross he was always elaborate, and made long, clever answers where "Yes" or "No" would have done. Lucy soothed him and tinkered at the conversation in a way that promised well for their married peace. No one is perfect, and surely it is wiser to discover the imperfections before wedlock. Miss Bartlett, in deed, though not in word, had taught the girl that this our life contains nothing satisfactory. Lucy, though she disliked the teacher, regarded the teaching as profound, and applied it to her lover.

"Lucy," said her mother, when they got home, "is anything the matter with Cecil?"

The question was ominous: up till now Mrs Honeychurch had behaved with charity and restraint.

"No, I don't think so, mother; Cecil's all right."

"Perhaps he's tired."

Lucy compromised: perhaps Cecil was a little tired.

"Because otherwise"—she pulled out her bonnet-pins with gathering displeasure—"because otherwise I cannot account for him."

"I do think Mrs Butterworth is rather tiresome, if you mean that."

"Cecil has told you to think so. You were devoted to her as a little girl, and nothing will describe her goodness to you through the typhoid fever. No—it is just the same thing everywhere."

"Let me just put your bonnet away, may I?"

"Surely he could answer her civilly for one half-hour?"

"Cecil has a very high standard for people," faltered Lucy, seeing trouble ahead. "It's part of his ideals—it is really that that makes him sometimes seem—"

"Oh, rubbish! If high ideals make a young man rude, the sooner he gets rid of them the better," said Mrs Honeychurch, handing her the bonnet.

"Now mother! I've seen you cross with Mrs Butterworth yourself!"

"Not in that way. At times I could wring her neck. But not in that way. No. It is the same with Cecil all over."

"By the by—I never told you. I had a letter from Charlotte while I was away in London."

This attempt to divert the conversation was too puerile, and Mrs Honeychurch resented it.

"Since Cecil came back from London, nothing appears to please him. Whenever I speak he winces—I see him, Lucy; it is useless to contradict me. No doubt I am neither artistic nor literary nor intellectual nor musical, but I cannot help the drawing-room furniture: your father bought it and we must put up with it, will Cecil kindly remember."

"I—I see what you mean, and certainly Cecil oughtn't to. But he does not mean to be uncivil—he once explained—it is the *things* that upset him—he is easily upset by ugly things—he is not uncivil to *people*."

"Is it a thing or a person when Freddy sings?"

"You can't expect a really musical person to enjoy comic songs as we do."

"Then why didn't he leave the room? Why sit wriggling and sneering and spoiling everyone's pleasure?"

"We mustn't be unjust to people," faltered Lucy. Something had enfeebled her, and the case for Cecil, which she had mastered so perfectly in London, would not come forth in an effective form. The two civilizations had clashed—Cecil had hinted that they might—and she was dazzled and bewildered, as though the radiance that lies behind all civilization had blinded her eyes. Good taste and bad taste were only catchwords, garments of diverse cut; and music itself dissolved to a whisper through pine trees, where the song is not distinguishable from the comic song.

She remained in much embarrassment, while Mrs Honeychurch changed her frock for dinner; and every now and then she said a word, and made things no better. There was no concealing the fact—Cecil had meant to be supercilious, and he had succeeded. And Lucy—she knew not why—wished that the trouble could have come at any other time.

"Go and dress, dear; you'll be late."

"All right, mother—"

"Don't say 'All right' and stop. Go."

She obeyed, but loitered disconsolately at the landing window. It faced north, so there was little view, and no view of the sky. Now, as in the winter, the pine trees hung close to her eyes. One connected the landing window with depression. No definite problem menaced her, but she sighed to herself,

"Oh dear, what shall I do, what shall I do?" It seemed to her that everyone else was behaving very badly. And she ought not to have mentioned Miss Bartlett's letter. She must be more careful: her mother was rather inquisitive, and might have asked what it was about. Oh dear, what should she do?—and then Freddy came bounding upstairs, and joined the ranks of the ill-behaved.

"I say, those are topping people."

"My dear baby, how tiresome you've been! You had no business to take them bathing in the Sacred Lake; it's much too public. It was all right for you, but most awkward for everyone else. Do be more careful. You forget the place is growing half suburban."

"I say, is anything on tomorrow week?"

"Not that I know of."

"Then I want to ask the Emersons up to Sunday tennis."

"Oh, I wouldn't do that, Freddy, I wouldn't do that with all this muddle."

"What's wrong with the court? They won't mind a bump or two, and I've ordered new balls."

"I meant *it's* better not. I really mean it."

He seized her by the elbows and humorously danced her up and down the passage. She pretended not to mind, but she could have screamed with temper. Cecil glanced at them as he proceeded to his toilet and they impeded Mary with her brood of hot-water cans. Then Mrs Honeychurch opened her door and said: "Lucy, what a noise you're making! I have something to say to you. Did you say you had had a letter from Charlotte?" and Freddy ran away.

"Yes. I really can't stop. I must dress too."

"How's Charlotte?"

"All right."

"Lucy!"

The unfortunate girl returned.

"You've a bad habit of hurrying away in the middle of one's sentences. Did Charlotte mention her boiler?"

"Her *what*?"

"Don't you remember that her boiler was to be had out

in October, and her bath cistern cleaned out, and all kinds of terrible to-doing?"

"I can't remember all Charlotte's worries," said Lucy bitterly. "I shall have enough of my own, now that you are not pleased with Cecil."

Mrs Honeychurch might have flamed out. She did not. She said: "Come here, old lady—thank you for putting away my bonnet—kiss me." And, though nothing is perfect, Lucy felt for the moment that her mother and Windy Corner and the Weald in the declining sun were perfect.

So the grittiness went out of life. It generally did at Windy Corner. At the last minute, when the social machine was clogged hopelessly, one member or other of the family poured in a drop of oil. Cecil despised their methods—perhaps rightly. At all events, they were not his own.

Dinner was at half past seven. Freddy gabbled a grace, and they drew up their heavy chairs and fell to. Fortunately, the men were hungry. Nothing untoward occurred until the pudding. Then Freddy said:

"Lucy, what's Emerson like?"

"I saw him in Florence," said Lucy, hoping that this would pass for a reply.

"Is he the clever sort, or is he a decent chap?"

"Ask Cecil; it is Cecil who brought him here."

"He is the clever sort, like myself," said Cecil.

Freddy looked at him doubtfully.

"How well did you know them at the Bertolini?" asked Mrs Honeychurch.

"Oh, very slightly. I mean, Charlotte knew them even less than I did."

"Oh, that reminds me—you never told me what Charlotte said in her letter."

"One thing and another," said Lucy, wondering whether she would get through the meal without a lie. "Among other things, that an awful friend of hers had been bicycling through Summer Street, wondered if she'd come up and see us, and mercifully didn't."

"Lucy, I do call the way you talk unkind."

"She was a novelist," said Lucy craftily. The remark was a happy one, for nothing roused Mrs Honeychurch so much as literature in the hands of females. She would abandon every topic to inveigh against those women who (instead of minding their houses and their children) seek notoriety by print. Her attitude was: "If books must be written, let them be written by men"; and she developed it at great length, while Cecil yawned and Freddy played at "This year, next year, now, never" with his plum-stones, and Lucy artfully fed the flames of her mother's wrath. But soon the conflagration died down, and the ghosts began to gather in the darkness. There were too many ghosts about. The original ghost—that touch of lips on her cheek—had surely been laid long ago; it could be nothing to her that a man had kissed her on a mountain once. But it had begotten a spectral family—Mr Harris, Miss Bartlett's letter, Mr Beebe's memories of violets—and one or other of these was bound to haunt her before Cecil's very eyes. It was Miss Bartlett who returned now, and with appalling vividness.

"I have been thinking, Lucy, of that letter of Charlotte's. How is she?"

"I tore the thing up."

"Didn't she say how she was? How does she sound? Cheerful?"

"Oh yes, I suppose so—no—not very cheerful, I suppose."

"Then, depend upon it, it *is* the boiler. I know myself how water preys upon one's mind. I would rather anything else—even a misfortune with the Meat."

Cecil laid his hand over his eyes.

"So would I," asserted Freddy, backing his mother up—backing up the spirit of her remark rather than its substance.

"And I have been thinking," she added rather nervously, "surely we could squeeze Charlotte in here next week, and give her a nice holiday while the plumbers at Tunbridge Wells finish. I have not seen poor Charlotte for so long."

It was more than her nerves could stand. And yet she could not protest violently after her mother's goodness to her upstairs.

"Mother, no!" she pleaded. "It's impossible. We can't have Charlotte on the top of the other things; we're squeezed to death as it is. Freddy's got a friend coming Tuesday, there's Cecil, and you've promised to take in Minnie Beebe because of the diphtheria scare. It simply can't be done."

"Nonsense! It can."

"If Minnie sleeps in the bath. Not otherwise."

"Minnie can sleep with you."

"I won't have her."

"Then, if you're so selfish, Mr Floyd must share a room with Freddy."

"Miss Bartlett, Miss Bartlett, Miss Bartlett," moaned Cecil, again laying his hand over his eyes.

"It's impossible," repeated Lucy. "I don't want to make difficulties, but it really isn't fair on the maids to fill up the house so."

Alas!

"The truth is, dear, you don't like Charlotte."

"No, I don't. And no more does Cecil. She gets on our nerves. You haven't seen her lately, and don't realize how tiresome she can be, though so good. So please, mother, don't worry us this last summer; but spoil us by not asking her to come."

"Hear, hear!" said Cecil.

Mrs Honeychurch, with more gravity than usual, and with more feeling than she usually permitted herself, replied: "This isn't very kind of you two. You have each other and all these woods to walk in, so full of beautiful things; and poor Charlotte has only the water turned off and plumbers. You are young, dears, and however clever young people are, and however many books they read, they will never guess what it feels like to grow old."

Cecil crumbled his bread.

"I must say Cousin Charlotte was very kind to me that year I called on my bike," put in Freddy. "She thanked me for coming till I felt like such a fool, and fussed round no end to get an egg boiled for my tea just right."

"I know, dear. She is kind to everyone, and yet Lucy

makes this difficulty when we try to give her some little return."

But Lucy hardened her heart. It was no good being kind to Miss Bartlett. She had tried herself too often and too recently. One might lay up treasure in heaven by the attempt, but one enriched neither Miss Bartlett nor anyone else upon earth. She was reduced to saying: "I can't help it, mother. I don't like Charlotte. I admit it's horrid of me."

"From your own account, you told her as much."

"Well, she would leave Florence so stupidly. She flurried—"

The ghosts were returning; they filled Italy, they were even usurping the places she had known as a child. The Sacred Lake would never be the same again, and, on Sunday week, something would even happen to Windy Corner. How would she fight against ghosts? For a moment the visible world faded away, and memories and emotions alone seemed real.

"I suppose Miss Bartlett must come, since she boils eggs so well," said Cecil, who was in rather a happier frame of mind, thanks to the admirable cooking.

"I didn't mean the egg was *well* boiled," corrected Freddy, "because in point of fact she forgot to take it off, and as a matter of fact I don't care for eggs. I only meant how jolly kind she seemed."

Cecil frowned again. Oh, these Honeychurches! Eggs, boilers, hydrangeas, maids—of such were their lives compact. "May me and Lucy get down from our chairs?" he asked, with scarcely veiled insolence. "We don't want no dessert."

Chapter 14
How Lucy Faced the External Situation Bravely

Of course Miss Bartlett accepted. And, equally of course, she felt sure that she would prove a nuisance, and begged to be given an inferior spare room—something with no view, anything. Her love to Lucy. And, equally of course, George Emerson could come to tennis on the Sunday week.

Lucy faced the situation bravely, though, like most of us, she only faced the situation that encompassed her. She never gazed inwards. If at times strange images rose from the depths, she put them down to nerves. When Cecil brought the Emersons to Summer Street, it had upset her nerves. Charlotte would burnish up past foolishness, and this might upset her nerves. She was nervous at night. When she talked to George—they met again almost immediately at the rectory—his voice moved her deeply, and she wished to remain near him. How dreadful if she really wished to remain near him! Of course, the wish was due to nerves, which love to play such perverse tricks upon us. Once she had suffered from "things that came out of nothing and meant she didn't know what". Now Cecil had explained psychology to her one wet afternoon, and all the troubles of youth in an unknown world could be dismissed.

It is obvious enough for the reader to conclude, "She loves young Emerson." A reader in Lucy's place would not find it obvious. Life is easy to chronicle, but bewildering to practise, and we welcome "nerves" or any other shibboleth that will cloak our personal desire. She loved Cecil; George made her nervous; will the reader explain to her that the phrases should have been reversed?

But the external situation—she will face that bravely.

The meeting at the rectory had passed off well enough.

Standing between Mr Beebe and Cecil, she had made a few temperate allusions to Italy, and George had replied. She was anxious to show that she was not shy, and was glad that he did not seem shy either.

"A nice fellow," said Mr Beebe afterwards. "He will work off his crudities in time. I rather mistrust young men who slip into life gracefully."

Lucy said: "He seems in better spirits. He laughs more."

"Yes," replied the clergyman. "He is waking up."

That was all. But, as the week wore on, more of her defences fell, and she entertained an image that had physical beauty.

In spite of the clearest directions, Miss Bartlett contrived to bungle her arrival. She was due at the South-Eastern station at Dorking, whither Mrs Honeychurch drove to meet her. She arrived at the London and Brighton station, and had to hire a cab up. No one was at home except Freddy and his friend, who had to stop their tennis and to entertain her for a solid hour. Cecil and Lucy turned up at four o'clock, and these, with little Minnie Beebe, made a somewhat lugubrious sextet upon the upper lawn for tea.

"I shall never forgive myself," said Miss Bartlett, who kept on rising from her seat, and had to be begged by the united company to remain. "I have upset everything. Bursting in on young people! But I insist on paying for my cab up. Grant me that, at any rate."

"Our visitors never do such a dreadful thing," said Lucy, while her brother, in whose memory the boiled egg had already grown unsubstantial, exclaimed in irritable tones: "Just what I've been trying to convince Cousin Charlotte of, Lucy, for the last half-hour."

"I do not feel myself an ordinary visitor," said Miss Bartlett, and looked at her frayed gloves.

"All right, if you'd really rather. Five shillings, and I gave a bob to the driver."

Miss Bartlett looked in her purse. Only sovereigns and pennies. Could anyone give her change? Freddy had half a quid and his friend had four half-crowns. Miss Bartlett accepted their moneys and then said: "But who am I to give the sovereign to?"

"Let's leave it all till mother comes back," suggested Lucy.

"No, dear; your mother may take quite a long drive now that she is not hampered with me. We all have our little foibles, and mine is the promptly settling of accounts."

Here Freddy's friend, Mr Floyd, made the one remark of his that need be quoted: he offered to toss Freddy for Miss Bartlett's quid. A solution seemed in sight, and even Cecil, who had been ostentatiously drinking his tea at the view, felt the eternal attraction of Chance, and turned round.

But this did not do, either.

"Please—please—I know I am a sad spoil-sport, but it would make me wretched. I should practically be robbing the one who lost."

"Freddy owes me fifteen shillings," interposed Cecil. "So it will work out right if you give the pound to me."

"Fifteen shillings," said Miss Bartlett dubiously. "How is that, Mr Vyse?"

"Because, don't you see, Freddy paid your cab. Give me the pound, and we shall avoid this deplorable gambling."

Miss Bartlett, who was poor at figures, became bewildered and rendered up the sovereign, amidst the suppressed gurgles of the other youths. For a moment Cecil was happy. He was playing at nonsense among his peers. Then he glanced at Lucy, in whose face petty anxieties had marred the smiles. In January he would rescue his Leonardo from this stupefying twaddle.

"But I don't see that!" exclaimed Minnie Beebe, who had narrowly watched the iniquitous transaction. "I don't see why Mr Vyse is to have the quid."

"Because of the fifteen shillings and the five," they said solemnly. "Fifteen shillings and five shillings make one pound, you see."

"But I don't see—"

They tried to stifle her with cake.

"No, thank you. I'm done. I don't see why—Freddy, don't poke me. Miss Honeychurch, your brother's hurting me. Ow! What about Mr Floyd's ten shillings? Ow! No, I don't see and I never shall see why Miss What's-her-name shouldn't pay that bob for the driver."

"I had forgotten the driver," said Miss Bartlett, reddening. "Thank you, dear, for reminding me. A shilling, was it? Can anyone give me change for half a crown?"

"I'll get it," said the young hostess, rising with decision. "Cecil, give me that sovereign. No—give me up that sovereign. I'll get Euphemia to change it, and we'll start the whole thing again from the beginning."

"Lucy—Lucy—what a nuisance I am!" protested Miss Bartlett, and followed her across the lawn. Lucy tripped ahead, simulating hilarity. When they were out of earshot, Miss Bartlett stopped her wails and said quite briskly: "Have you told him about him yet?"

"No, I haven't," replied Lucy, and then could have bitten her tongue for understanding so quickly what her cousin meant. "Let me see—a sovereign's worth of silver."

She escaped into the kitchen. Miss Bartlett's sudden transitions were too uncanny. It sometimes seemed as if she planned every word she spoke or caused to be spoken; as if all this worry about cabs and change had been a ruse to surprise the soul.

"No, I haven't told Cecil or anyone," she remarked, when she returned. "I promised you I shouldn't. Here is your money—all shillings, except two half-crowns. Would you count it? You can settle your debt nicely now."

Miss Bartlett was in the drawing-room, gazing at the photograph of St John ascending, who had been framed.

"How dreadful!" she murmured, "how more than dreadful, if Mr Vyse should come to hear of it from some other source."

"Oh no, Charlotte," said the girl, entering the battle, "George Emerson is all right, and what other source is there?"

Miss Bartlett considered. "For instance, the driver. I saw

him looking through the bushes at you. I remember he had a violet between his teeth."

Lucy shuddered a little. "We shall get the silly affair on our nerves if we aren't careful. How could a Florentine cab-driver ever get hold of Cecil?"

"We must think of every possibility."

"Oh, it's all right."

"Or perhaps old Mr Emerson knows. In fact, he is certain to know."

"I don't care if he does. I was grateful to you for your letter, but even if the news does get round, I think I can trust Cecil to laugh at it."

"To contradict it?"

"No, to laugh at it." But she knew in her heart that she could not trust him, for he desired her untouched.

"Very well, dear, you know best. Perhaps gentlemen are different to what they were when I was young. Ladies are certainly different."

"Now, Charlotte!" She struck at her playfully. "You kind, anxious thing! What *would* you have me do? First you say, 'Don't tell'; and then you say, 'Tell.' Which is it to be? Quick!"

Miss Bartlett sighed. "I am no match for you in conversation, dearest. I blush when I think how I interfered at Florence, and you so well able to look after yourself, and so much cleverer in all ways than I am. You will never forgive me."

"Shall we go out, then? They will smash all the china if we don't."

For the air rang with the shrieks of Minnie, who was being scalped with a teaspoon.

"Dear, one moment—we may not have this chance for a chat again. Have you seen the young one yet?"

"Yes, I have."

"What happened?"

"We met at the rectory."

"What line is he taking up?"

"No line. He talked about Italy, like any other person. It

is really all right. What advantage would he get from being a cad, to put it bluntly? I do wish I could make you see it my way. He really won't be any nuisance, Charlotte."

"Once a cad, always a cad. That is my poor opinion."

Lucy paused. "Cecil said one day—and I thought it so profound—that there are two kinds of cads—the conscious and the subsconcious." She paused again, to be sure of doing justice to Cecil's profundity. Through the window she saw Cecil himself, turning over the pages of a novel. It was a new one from Smith's library. Her mother must have returned from the station.

"Once a cad, always a cad," droned Miss Bartlett.

"What I mean by subconscious is that Mr Emerson lost his head. I fell into all those violets, and he was silly and surprised. I don't think we ought to blame him very much. It makes such a difference when you see a person with beautiful things behind him unexpectedly. It really does; it makes an enormous difference, and he lost his head; he doesn't admire me, or any of that nonsense, one straw. Freddy rather likes him, and has asked him up here on Sunday, so you can judge for yourself. He has improved: he doesn't always look as if he is going to burst into tears. He is a clerk in the General Manager's office at one of the big railways—not a porter!—and runs down to his father for week-ends. Papa was to do with journalism, but is rheumatic and has retired. There! Now for the garden." She took hold of her guest by the arm. "Suppose we don't talk about this silly Italian business any more. We want you to have a nice restful visit at Windy Corner, with no worriting."

Lucy thought this rather a good speech. The reader may have detected an unfortunate slip in it. Whether Miss Bartlett detected the slip one cannot say, for it is impossible to penetrate into the minds of elderly people. She might have spoken further, but they were interrupted by the entrance of her hostess. Explanations took place, and in the midst of them Lucy escaped, the images throbbing a little more vividly in her brain.

Chapter 15
The Disaster Within

The Sunday after Miss Bartlett's arrival was a glorious day, like most of the days of that year. In the Weald, autumn approached, breaking up the green monotony of summer, touching the parks with the gray bloom of mist, the beech trees with russet, the oak trees with gold. Up on the heights, battalions of black pines witnessed the change, themselves unchangeable. Either country was spanned by a cloudless sky, and in either arose the tinkle of church bells.

The garden of Windy Corner was deserted except for a red book, which lay sunning itself upon the gravel path. From the house came incoherent sounds, as of females preparing for worship. "The men say they won't go"—"Well, I don't blame them"—"Minnie says, need she go?"—"Tell her, no nonsense"—"Anne! Mary! Hook me behind!"—"Dearest Lucia, may I trespass upon you for a pin?" For Miss Bartlett had announced that she at all events was one for church.

The sun rose higher on its journey, guided, not by Phaethon, but by Apollo, competent, unswerving, divine. Its rays fell on the ladies whenever they advanced towards the bedroom windows; on Mr Beebe down at Summer Street as he smiled over a letter from Miss Catharine Alan; on George Emerson cleaning his father's boots; and lastly, to complete the catalogue of memorable things, on the red book mentioned above. The ladies move, Mr Beebe moves, George moves, and movement may engender shadow. But this book lies motionless, to be caressed all the morning by the sun and to raise its covers slightly, as though acknowledging the caress.

Presently Lucy steps out of the drawing-room window. Her new cerise dress has been a failure, and makes her look tawdry and wan. At her throat is a garnet brooch, on her finger a ring set with rubies—an engagement-ring. Her eyes are bent to the Weald. She frowns a little—not in anger, but as a brave child frowns when he is trying not to cry. In all that expanse no human eye is looking at her, and she may frown unrebuked and measure the spaces that yet survive between Apollo and the western hills.

"Lucy! Lucy! What's that book? Who's been taking a book out of the shelf and leaving it about to spoil?"

"It's only the library book that Cecil's been reading."

"But pick it up, and don't stand idling there like a flamingo."

Lucy picked up the book and glanced at the title listlessly: *Under a Loggia*. She no longer read novels herself, devoting all her spare time to solid literature in the hope of catching Cecil up. It was dreadful how little she knew, and even when she thought she knew a thing, like the Italian painters, she found she had forgotten it. Only this morning she had confused Francesco Francia with Piero della Francesca, and Cecil had said, "What! You aren't forgetting your Italy already?" And this too had lent anxiety to her eyes when she saluted the dear view and the dear garden in the foreground, and above them, scarce conceivable elsewhere, the dear sun.

"Lucy—have you a sixpence for Minnie and a shilling for yourself?"

She hastened in to her mother, who was rapidly working herself into a Sunday fluster.

"It's a special collection—I forget what for. I do beg, no vulgar clinking in the plate with halfpennies; see that Minnie has a nice bright sixpence. Where is the child? Minnie! That book's all warped. (Gracious, how plain you look!) Put it under the atlas to press. Minnie!"

"Oh, Mrs Honeychurch—" from the upper regions.

"Minnie, don't be late. Here comes the horse"—it was always the horse, never the carriage. "Where's Charlotte? Run up and hurry her. Why is she so long? She had nothing to do. She never brings anything but blouses. Poor Charlotte—how I do detest blouses! Minnie!"

Paganism is infectious—more infectious than diphtheria

or piety—and the Rector's niece was taken to church protesting. As usual, she didn't see why. Why shouldn't she sit in the sun with the young men? The young men, who had now appeared, mocked her with ungenerous words. Mrs Honeychurch defended orthodoxy, and in the midst of the confusion Miss Bartlett, dressed in the very height of the fashion, came strolling down the stairs.

"Dear Marian, I am very sorry, but I have no small change—nothing but sovereigns and half-crowns. Could anyone give me—"

"Yes, easily. Jump in. Gracious me, how smart you look. What a lovely frock! You put us all to shame."

"If I did not wear my best rags and tatters now, when should I wear them?" said Miss Bartlett reproachfully. She got into the victoria and placed herself with her back to the horse. The necessary uproar ensued, and then they drove off.

"Goodbye! Be good!" called out Cecil.

Lucy bit her lip, for the tone was sneering. On the subject of "church and so on" they had had rather an unsatisfactory conversation. He had said that people ought to overhaul themselves, and she did not want to overhaul herself; she did not know how it was done. Honest orthodoxy Cecil respected, but he always assumed that honesty is the result of a spiritual crisis; he could not imagine it as a natural birthright, that might grow heavenward like the flowers. All that he said on this subject pained her, though he exuded tolerance from every pore; somehow the Emersons were different.

She saw the Emersons after church. There was a line of carriages down the road, and the Honeychurch vehicle happened to be opposite Cissie Villa. To save time, they walked over the green to it, and found father and son smoking in the garden.

"Introduce me," said her mother. "Unless the young man considers that he knows me already."

He probably did; but Lucy ignored the Sacred Lake and introduced them formally. Old Mr Emerson claimed her with much warmth, and said how glad he was that she was going to be married. She said yes, she was glad too; and then, as Miss Bartlett and Minnie were lingering behind with Mr Beebe, she turned the conversation to a less disturbing topic, and asked him how he liked his new house.

"Very much," he replied, but there was a note of offence in his voice; she had never known him offended before. He added: "We find, though, that the Miss Alans were coming, and that we have turned them out. Women mind such a thing. I am very much upset about it."

"I believe that there was some misunderstanding," said Mrs Honeychurch uneasily.

"Our landlord was told that we should be a different type of person," said George, who seemed disposed to carry the matter further. "He thought we should be artistic. He is disappointed."

"And I wonder whether we ought to write to the Miss Alans and offer to give it up. What do you think?" He appealed to Lucy.

"Oh, stop now you have come," said Lucy lightly. She must avoid censuring Cecil. For it was on Cecil that the little episode turned, though his name was never mentioned.

"So George says. He says that the Miss Alans must go to the wall. Yet it does seem so unkind."

"There is only a certain amount of kindness in the world," said George, watching the sunlight flash on the panels of the passing carriages.

"Yes!" exclaimed Mrs Honeychurch. "That's exactly what I say. Why all this twiddling and twaddling over two Miss Alans?"

"There is a certain amount of kindness, just as there is a certain amount of light," he continued in measured tones. "We cast a shadow on something wherever we stand, and it is no good moving from place to place to save things; because the shadow always follows. Choose a place where you won't do harm—yes, choose a place where you won't do very much harm, and stand in it for all you are worth, facing the sunshine."

"Oh, Mr Emerson, I see you're clever!"

"Eh—?"

"I see you're going to be clever. I hope you didn't go behaving like that to poor Freddy."

George's eyes laughed, and Lucy suspected that he and her mother would get on rather well.

"No, I didn't," he said. "He behaved that way to me. It is his philosophy. Only he starts life with it; and I have tried the Note of Interrogation first."

"What *do* you mean? No, never mind what you mean. Don't explain. He looks forward to seeing you this afternoon. Do you play tennis? Do you mind tennis on Sunday—?"

"George mind tennis on Sunday! George, after his education, distinguish between Sunday—"

"Very well, George doesn't mind tennis on Sunday. No more do I. That's settled. Mr Emerson, if you could come with your son we should be so pleased."

He thanked her, but the walk sounded rather far: he could only potter about in these days.

She turned to George: "And then he wants to give up his house to the Miss Alans."

"I know," said George, and put his arm round his father's neck. The kindness that Mr Beebe and Lucy had always known to exist in him came out suddenly, like sunlight touching a vast landscape—a touch of the morning sun? She remembered that in all his perversities he had never spoken against affection.

Miss Bartlett approached.

"You know our cousin, Miss Bartlett," said Mrs Honeychurch pleasantly. "You met her with my daughter in Florence."

"Yes, indeed!" said the old man, and made as if he would come out of the garden to greet the lady. Miss Bartlett promptly got into the victoria. Thus entrenched, she emitted a formal bow. It was the Pension Bertolini again, the dining-table with the decanters of water and wine. It was the old, old battle of the room with the view.

George did not respond to the bow. Like any boy, he blushed and was ashamed; he knew that the chaperon remembered. He said: "I—I'll come up to tennis if I can manage it," and went into the house. Perhaps anything that he did would have pleased Lucy, but his awkwardness went straight to her heart: men were not gods after all, but as human and as clumsy as girls; even men might suffer from unexplained desires, and need help. To one of her upbringing, and of her destination, the weakness of men was a truth unfamiliar, but she had surmised it at Florence, when George threw her photographs into the river Arno.

"George, don't go," cried his father, who thought it a great treat for people if his son would talk to them. "George has been in such good spirits today, and I am sure he will end by coming up this afternoon."

Lucy caught her cousin's eye. Something in its mute appeal made her reckless. "Yes," she said, raising her voice, "I do hope he will." Then she went to the carriage and murmured, "The old man hasn't been told; I knew it was all right." Mrs Honeychurch followed her, and they drove away.

Satisfactory that Mr Emerson had not been told of the Florence escapade; yet Lucy's spirits should not have leapt up as if she had sighted the ramparts of heaven. Satisfactory; yet surely she greeted it with disproportionate joy. All the way home the horses' hoofs sang a tune to her: "He has not told, he has not told." Her brain expanded the melody: "He has not told his father—to whom he tells all things. It was not an exploit. He did not laugh at me when I had gone." She raised her hand to her cheek. "He does not love me. No. How terrible if he did! But he has not told. He will not tell."

She longed to shout the words: "It is all right. It's a secret between us two for ever. Cecil will never hear." She was even glad that Miss Bartlett had made her promise secrecy, that last dark evening at Florence, when they had knelt packing in his room. The secret, big or little, was guarded. Only three English people knew of it in the world.

Thus she interpreted her joy. She greeted Cecil with unusual radiance, because she felt so safe. As he helped her out of the carriage, she said:

"The Emersons have been so nice. George Emerson has improved enormously."

"Oh, how are my protégés?" asked Cecil, who took no real interest in them, and had long since forgotten his resolution to bring them to Windy Corner for educational purposes.

"Protégés!" she exclaimed with some warmth.

For the only relationship which Cecil conceived was feudal: that of protector and protected. He had no glimpse of the comradeship after which the girl's soul yearned.

"You shall see for yourself how your protégés are. George Emerson is coming up this afternoon. He is a most interesting man to talk to. Only don't—" She nearly said, "Don't protect him." But the bell was ringing for lunch, and, as often happened, Cecil had paid no great attention to her remarks. Charm, not argument, was to be her forte.

Lunch was a cheerful meal. Generally Lucy was depressed at meals. Someone had to be soothed—either Cecil or Miss Bartlett or a Being not visible to the mortal eye—a Being who whispered to her soul: "It will not last, this cheerfulness. In January you must go to London to entertain the grandchildren of celebrated men." But today she felt she had received a guarantee. Her mother would always sit there, her brother here. The sun, though it had moved a little since the morning, would never be hidden behind the western hills. After luncheon they asked her to play. She had seen Gluck's *Armide* that year, and played from memory the music of the enchanted garden—the music to which Renaud approaches, beneath the light of an eternal dawn, the music that never gains, never wanes, but ripples for ever like the tideless seas of fairyland. Such music is not for the piano, and her audience began to get restive, and Cecil, sharing the discontent, called out: "Now play us the other garden—the one in *Parsifal*."

She closed the instrument.

"Not very dutiful," said her mother's voice.

Fearing that she had offended Cecil, she turned quickly round. There George was. He had crept in without interrupting her.

"Oh, I had no idea!" she exclaimed, getting very red; and

then, without a word of greeting, she reopened the piano. Cecil should have the *Parsifal*, and anything else that he liked.

"Our performer has changed her mind," said Miss Bartlett, perhaps implying, "She will play the music to Mr Emerson." Lucy did not know what to do, nor even what she wanted to do. She played a few bars of the Flower Maidens' song very badly, and then she stopped.

"I vote tennis," said Freddy, disgusted at the scrappy entertainment.

"Yes, so do I." Once more she closed the unfortunate piano. "I vote you have a men's four."

"All right."

"Not for me, thank you," said Cecil. "I will not spoil the set." He never realized that it may be an act of kindness in a bad player to make up a fourth.

"Oh, come along, Cecil. I'm bad, Floyd's rotten, and so I dare say's Emerson."

George corrected him: "I am not bad."

One looked down one's nose at this. "Then certainly I won't play," said Cecil, while Miss Bartlett, under the impression that she was snubbing George, added: "I agree with you, Mr Vyse. You had much better not play. Much better not."

Minnie, rushing in where Cecil feared to tread, announced that she would play. "I shall miss every ball anyway, so what does it matter?" But Sunday intervened and stamped heavily upon the kind suggestion.

"Then it will have to be Lucy," said Mrs Honeychurch; "you must fall back on Lucy. There is no other way out of it. Lucy, go and change your frock."

Lucy's Sabbath was generally of this amphibious nature. She kept it without hypocrisy in the morning, and broke it without reluctance in the afternoon. As she changed her frock, she wondered whether Cecil was sneering at her; really she must overhaul herself and settle everything up before she married him.

Mr Floyd was her partner. She liked music, but how

much better tennis seemed. How much better to run about in comfortable clothes than to sit at the piano and feel girt under the arms. Once more music appeared to her the employment of a child. George served, and surprised her by his anxiety to win. She remembered how he had sighed among the tombs at Santa Croce because things wouldn't fit; how after the death of that obscure Italian he had leant over the parapet by the Arno and said to her: "I shall want to live, I tell you." He wanted to live now, to win at tennis, to stand for all he was worth in the sun—in the sun which had begun to decline and was shining in her eyes; and he did win.

Ah, how beautiful the Weald looked! The hills stood out above its radiance, as Fiesole stands above the Tuscan plain, and the South Downs, if one chose, were the mountains of Carrara. She might be forgetting her Italy, but she was noticing more things in her England. One could play a new game with the view, and try to find in its innumerable folds some town or village that would do for Florence. Ah, how beautiful the Weald looked!

But now Cecil claimed her. He chanced to be in a lucid critical mood, and would not sympathize with exaltation. He had been rather a nuisance all through the tennis, for the novel that he was reading was so bad that he was obliged to read it aloud to others. He would stroll round the precincts of the court and call out: "I say, listen to this, Lucy. Three split infinitives." "Dreadful!" said Lucy, and missed her stroke. When they had finished their set, he still went on reading; there was some murder scene, and really everyone must listen to it. Freddy and Mr Floyd were obliged to hunt for a lost ball in the laurels, but the other two acquiesced.

"The scene is laid in Florence."

"What fun, Cecil! Read away. Come, Mr Emerson, sit down after all your energy." She had "forgiven" George, as she put it, and she made a point of being pleasant to him.

He jumped over the net and sat down at her feet, asking: "You—and are you tired?"

"Of course I'm not!"

"Do you mind being beaten?"

She was going to answer "No" when it struck her that she did mind, so she answered "Yes". She added merrily: "I don't see *you're* such a splendid player, though. The light was behind you, and it was in my eyes."

"I never said I was."

"Why, you did!"

"You didn't attend."

"You said—oh, don't go in for accuracy at this house. We all exaggerate, and we get very angry with people who don't."

"The scene is laid in Florence," repeated Cecil, with an upward note.

Lucy recollected herself.

" 'Sunset. Leonora was speeding—' "

Lucy interrupted. "Leonora? Is Leonora the heroine? Who's the book by?"

"Joseph Emery Prank. 'Sunset. Leonora was speeding across the square. Pray the saints she might not arrive too late. Sunset—the sunset of Italy. Under Orcagna's Loggia—the Loggia de' Lanzi, as we sometimes call it now—' "

Lucy burst into laughter. " 'Joseph Emery Prank' indeed! Why, it's Miss Lavish! It's Miss Lavish's novel, and she's publishing it under somebody else's name."

"Who may Miss Lavish be?"

"Oh, a dreadful person—Mr Emerson, you remember Miss Lavish?" Excited by her pleasant afternoon, she clapped her hands.

George looked up. "Of course I do. I saw her the day I arrived at Summer Street. It was she who told me that you lived here."

"Weren't you pleased?" She meant—"to see Miss Lavish," but when he bent down to the grass without replying it struck her that she could mean something else. She watched his head, which was almost resting against her knee, and she thought that the ears were reddening. "No wonder the novel's bad," she added. "I never liked Miss Lavish. But I suppose one ought to read it as one's met her."

"All modern books are bad," said Cecil, who was annoyed

at her inattention, and vented his annoyance on literature. "Everyone writes for money in these days."

"Oh, Cecil—!"

"It is so. I will inflict Joseph Emery Prank on you no longer."

Cecil, this afternoon, seemed such a twittering sparrow. The ups and downs in his voice were noticeable, but they did not affect her. She had dwelt amongst melody and movement, and her nerves refused to answer to the clang of his. Leaving him to be annoyed, she gazed at the black head again. She did not want to stroke it, but she saw herself wanting to stroke it; the sensation was curious.

"How do you like this view of ours, Mr Emerson?"

"I never notice much difference in views."

"What do you mean?"

"Because they are all alike. Because all that matters in them is distance and air."

"H'm!" said Cecil, uncertain whether the remark was striking or not.

"My father"—he looked up at her (and he was a little flushed)—"says that there is only one perfect view—the view of the sky straight over our heads, and that all these views on earth are but bungled copies of it."

"I expect your father has been reading Dante," said Cecil, fingering the novel, which alone permitted him to lead the conversation.

"He told us another day that views are really crowds—crowds of trees and houses and hills—and are bound to resemble each other, like human crowds—and that the power they have over us is something supernatural, for the same reason."

Lucy's lips parted.

"For a crowd is more than the people who make it up. Something gets added to it—no one knows how—just as something has got added to those hills."

He pointed with his racquet to the South Downs.

"What a splendid idea!" she murmured. "I shall enjoy hearing your father talk again. I'm so sorry he's not so well."

"No, he isn't well."

"There's an absurd account of a view in this book," said Cecil.

"Also that men fall into two classes—those who forget views and those who remember them, even in small rooms."

"Mr Emerson, have you any brothers or sisters?"

"None. Why?"

"You spoke of 'us'."

"My mother, I was meaning."

Cecil closed the novel with a bang.

"Oh, Cecil—how you make me jump!"

"I will inflict Joseph Emery Prank on you no longer."

"I can just remember us all three going into the country for the day and seeing as far as Hindhead. It is the first thing that I remember."

Cecil got up: the man was ill-bred—he hadn't put on his coat after tennis—he didn't do. He would have strolled away if Lucy had not stopped him.

"Cecil, do read the thing about the view."

"Not while Mr Emerson is here to entertain us."

"No—read away. I think nothing's funnier than to hear silly things read out loud. If Mr Emerson thinks us frivolous, he can go."

This struck Cecil as subtle, and pleased him. It put their visitor in the position of a prig. Somewhat mollified, he sat down again.

"Mr Emerson, go and find tennis balls." She opened the book. Cecil must have his reading and anything else that he liked. But her attention wandered to George's mother, who—according to Mr Eager—had been murdered in the sight of God and—according to her son—had seen as far as Hindhead.

"Am I really to go?" asked George.

"No, of course not really," she answered.

"Chapter two," said Cecil, yawning. "Find me chapter two, if it isn't bothering you."

Chapter two was found, and she glanced at its opening sentences.

She thought she had gone mad.

"Here—hand me the book."

She heard her voice saying: "It isn't worth reading—it's too silly to read—I never saw such rubbish—it oughtn't to be allowed to be printed."

He took the book from her.

" 'Leonora,' " he read, " 'sat pensive and alone. Before her lay the rich champaign of Tuscany, dotted over with many a smiling village. The season was spring.' "

Miss Lavish knew, somehow, and had printed the past in draggled prose, for Cecil to read and for George to hear.

" 'A golden haze,' " he read. He read: " 'Afar off the towers of Florence, while the bank on which she sat was carpeted with violets. All unobserved, Antonio stole up behind her—' "

Lest Cecil should see her face she turned to George, and she saw his face.

He read: " 'There came from his lips no wordy protestation such as formal lovers use. No eloquence was his, nor did he suffer from the lack of it. He simply enfolded her in his manly arms.' "

There was a silence.

"This isn't the passage I wanted," he informed them. "There is another much funnier, further on." He turned over the leaves.

"Should we go in to tea?" said Lucy, whose voice remained steady.

She led the way up the garden, Cecil following her, George last. She thought a disaster was averted. But when they entered the shrubbery it came. The book, as if it had not worked mischief enough, had been forgotten, and Cecil must go back for it; and George, who loved passionately, must blunder against her in the narrow path.

"No—" she gasped, and, for the second time, was kissed by him.

As if no more was possible, he slipped back; Cecil rejoined her; they reached the upper lawn alone.

Chapter 16
Lying to George

But Lucy had developed since the spring. That is to say, she was now better able to stifle the emotions of which the conventions and the world disapprove. Though the danger was greater, she was not shaken by deep sobs. She said to Cecil, "I am not coming in to tea—tell mother—I must write some letters," and went up to her room. There she prepared for action. Love felt and returned, love which our bodies exact and our hearts have transfigured, love which is the most real thing that we shall ever meet, reappeared now as the world's enemy, and she must stifle it.

She sent for Miss Bartlett.

The contest lay not between love and duty. Perhaps there never is such a contest. It lay between the real and the pretended, and Lucy's first aim was to defeat herself. As her brain clouded over, as the memory of the views grew dim and the words of the book died away, she returned to her old shibboleth of nerves. She "conquered her breakdown". Tampering with the truth, she forgot that the truth had ever been. Remembering that she was engaged to Cecil, she compelled herself to confused remembrances of George: he was nothing to her; he never had been anything; he had behaved abominably; she had never encouraged him. The armour of falsehood is subtly wrought out of darkness, and hides a man not only from others, but from his own soul. In a few moments Lucy was equipped for battle.

"Something too awful has happened," she began, as soon as her cousin arrived. "Do you know anything about Miss Lavish's novel?"

Miss Bartlett looked surprised, and said that she had not read the book, nor known that it was published; Eleanor was a reticent woman at heart.

"There is a scene in it. The hero and heroine make love. Do you know about that?"

"Dear—?"

"Do you know about it, please?" she repeated. "They are on a hillside, and Florence is in the distance."

"My good Lucia, I am all at sea. I know nothing about it whatever."

"There are violets. I cannot believe it is a coincidence. Charlotte, Charlotte, how *could* you have told her? I have thought before speaking: it *must* be you."

"Told her what?" she asked, with growing agitation.

"About that dreadful afternoon in February."

Miss Bartlett was genuinely moved. "Oh, Lucy, dearest girl—she hasn't put that in her book?"

Lucy nodded.

"Not so that one could recognize it?"

"Yes."

"Then never—never—never more shall Eleanor Lavish be friend of mine."

"So you did tell?"

"I did just happen—when I had tea with her at Rome—in the course of conversation—"

"But, Charlotte—what about the promise you gave me when we were packing? Why did you tell Miss Lavish, when you wouldn't even let me tell mother?"

"I will never forgive Eleanor. She has betrayed my confidence."

"Why did you tell her, though? This is a most serious thing."

Why does anyone tell anything? The question is eternal, and it was not surprising that Miss Bartlett should only sigh faintly in response. She had done wrong—she admitted it; she only hoped that she had not done harm; she had told Eleanor in the strictest confidence.

Lucy stamped with irritation.

"Cecil happened to read out the passage aloud to me and to Mr Emerson; it upset Mr Emerson, and he insulted me again. Behind Cecil's back. Ugh! Is it possible that men are such brutes? Behind Cecil's back as we were walking up the garden."

Miss Bartlett burst into self-accusations and regrets.

"What is to be done now? Can you tell me?"

"Oh, Lucy—I shall never forgive myself, never to my dying day. Fancy if your prospects—"

"I know," said Lucy, wincing at the word. "I see now why you wanted me to tell Cecil, and what you meant by 'some other source'. You knew that you had told Miss Lavish, and that she was not reliable."

It was Miss Bartlett's turn to wince.

"However," said the girl, despising her cousin's shiftiness, "what's done's done. You have put me in a most awkward position. How am I to get out of it?"

Miss Bartlett could not think. The days of her energy were over. She was a visitor, not a chaperon, and a discredited visitor at that. She stood with clasped hands while the girl worked herself into the necessary rage.

"He must—that man must have such a setting down that he won't forget. And who's to give it him? I can't tell mother now—owing to you. Nor Cecil, Charlotte, owing to you. I am caught up every way. I think I shall go mad. I have no one to help me. That's why I've sent for you. What's wanted is a man with a whip."

Miss Bartlett agreed: one wanted a man with a whip.

"Yes—but it's no good agreeing. What's to be *done*? We women go maundering on. What *does* a girl do when she comes across a cad?"

"I always said he was a cad, dear. Give me credit for that, at all events. From the very first moment—when he said his father was having a bath."

"Oh, bother the credit and who's been right or wrong! We've both made a muddle of it. George Emerson is still down the garden there, and is he to be left unpunished, or isn't he? I want to know."

Miss Bartlett was absolutely helpless. Her own exposure had unnerved her, and thoughts were colliding painfully in her brain. She moved feebly to the window, and tried to detect the cad's white flannels among the laurels.

"You were ready enough at the Bertolini when you rushed me off to Rome. Can't you speak again to him now?"

"Willingly would I move heaven and earth—"

"I want something more definite," said Lucy contemptuously. "Will you speak to him? It is the least you can do, surely, considering it all happened because you broke your word."

"Never again shall Eleanor Lavish be friend of mine."

Really, Charlotte was outdoing herself.

"Yes or no, please; yes or no."

"It is the kind of thing that only a gentleman can settle."

George Emerson was coming up the garden with a tennis-ball in his hand.

"Very well," said Lucy, with an angry gesture. "No one will help me. I will speak to him myself." And immediately she realized that this was what her cousin had intended all along.

"Hullo, Emerson!" called Freddy from below. "Found the lost ball? Good man! Want any tea?" And there was an irruption from the house onto the terrace.

"Oh, Lucy, but that is brave of you! I admire you—"

They had gathered round George, who beckoned, she felt, over the rubbish, the sloppy thoughts, the furtive yearnings that were beginning to cumber her soul. Her anger faded at the sight of him. Ah! The Emersons were fine people in their way. She had to subdue a rush in her blood before saying:

"Freddy has taken him into the dining-room. The others are going down the garden. Come. Let us get this over quickly. Come. I want you in the room, of course."

"Lucy, do you mind doing it?"

"How can you ask such a ridiculous question?"

"Poor Lucy—" She stretched out her hand. "I seem to bring nothing but misfortune wherever I go." Lucy nodded. She remembered their last evening at Florence—the packing, the candle, the shadow of Miss Bartlett's toque on the door.

She was not to be trapped by pathos a second time. Eluding her cousin's caress, she led the way downstairs.

"Try the jam," Freddy was saying. "The jam's jolly good."

George, looking big and dishevelled, was pacing up and down the dining-room. As she entered he stopped, and said:

"No—nothing to eat."

"You go down to the others," said Lucy; "Charlotte and I will give Mr Emerson all he wants. Where's mother?"

"She's started on her Sunday writing. She's in the drawing-room."

"That's all right. You go away."

He went off singing.

Lucy sat down at the table. Miss Bartlett, who was thoroughly frightened, took up a book and pretended to read.

She would not be drawn into an elaborate speech. She just said: "I can't have it, Mr Emerson. I cannot even talk to you. Go out of this house, and never come into it again as long as I live here"—flushing as she spoke, and pointing to the door. "I hate a row. Go, please."

"What—"

"No discussion."

"But I can't—"

She shook her head. "Go, please. I do not want to call in Mr Vyse."

"You don't mean," he said, absolutely ignoring Miss Bartlett—"you don't mean that you are going to marry that man?"

The line was unexpected.

She shrugged her shoulders, as if his vulgarity wearied her. "You are merely ridiculous," she said quietly.

Then his words rose gravely over hers: "You cannot live with Vyse. He's only for an acquaintance. He is for society and cultivated talk. He should know no one intimately, least of all a woman."

It was a new light on Cecil's character.

"Have you ever talked to Vyse without feeling tired?"

"I can scarcely discuss—"

"No, but have you ever? He is the sort who are all right so long as they keep to things—books, pictures—but kill when they come to people. That's why I'll speak out through all this muddle even now. It's shocking enough to lose you in any case, but generally a man must deny himself joy, and I would have held back if your Cecil had been a different person. I would never have let myself go. But I saw him first in the National Gallery, when he winced because my father mispronounced the names of great painters. Then he brings us here, and we find it is to play some silly trick on a kind neighbour. That is the man all over—playing tricks on people, on the most sacred form of life that he can find. Next, I meet you together, and find him protecting and teaching you and your mother to be shocked, when it was for *you* to settle whether you were shocked or no. Cecil all over again. He daren't let a woman decide. He's the type who's kept Europe back for a thousand years. Every moment of his life he's forming you, telling you what's charming or amusing or ladylike, telling you what a man thinks womanly; and you, you of all women, listen to his voice instead of to your own. So it was at the rectory, when I met you both again; so it has been the whole of this afternoon. Therefore—not 'therefore I kissed you', because the book made me do that, and I wish to goodness I had more self-control. I'm not ashamed. I don't apologize. But it has frightened you, and you may not have noticed that I love you. Or would you have told me to go, and dealt with a tremendous thing so lightly? But therefore—therefore I settled to fight him."

Lucy thought of a very good remark.

"You say Mr Vyse wants me to listen to him, Mr Emerson. Pardon me for suggesting that you have caught the habit."

And he took the shoddy reproof and touched it into immortality. He said:

"Yes, I have," and sank down as if suddenly weary. "I'm the same kind of brute at bottom. This desire to govern a woman—it lies very deep, and men and women must fight it together before they shall enter the Garden. But I do love you—surely in a better way than he does." He thought. "Yes

—really in a better way. I want you to have your own thoughts even when I hold you in my arms." He stretched them towards her. "Lucy, be quick—there's no time for us to talk now—come to me as you came in the spring, and afterwards I will be gentle and explain. I have cared for you since that man died. I cannot live without you. 'No good,' I thought: 'she is marrying someone else'; but I meet you again when all the world is glorious water and sun. As you came through the wood I saw that nothing else mattered. I called. I wanted to live and have my chance of joy."

"And Mr Vyse?" said Lucy, who kept commendably calm. "Does he not matter? That I love Cecil and shall be his wife shortly? A detail of no importance, I suppose?"

But he stretched his arms over the table towards her.

"May I ask what you intend to gain by this exhibition?"

He said: "It is our last chance. I shall do all that I can." And, as if he had done all else, he turned to Miss Bartlett, who sat like some portent against the skies of evening. "You wouldn't stop us this second time if you understood," he said. "I have been into the dark, and I am going back into it, unless you will try to understand."

Her long, narrow head drove backwards and forwards, as though demolishing some invisible obstacle. She did not answer.

"It is being young," he said quietly, picking up his racquet from the floor and preparing to go. "It is being certain that Lucy cares for me really. It is that love and youth matter intellectually."

In silence the two women watched him. His last remark, they knew, was nonsense, but was he going after it or not? Would not he, the cad, the charlatan, attempt a more dramatic finish? No. He was apparently content. He left them, carefully closing the front door; and when they looked through the hall window they saw him go up the drive and begin to climb the slopes of withered fern behind the house. Their tongues were loosed, and they burst into stealthy rejoicings.

"Oh, Lucia—come back here—oh, what an awful man!"

Lucy had no reaction—at least, not yet. "Well, he amuses me," she said. "Either I'm mad, or else he is, and I'm inclined to think it's the latter. One more fuss through with you, Charlotte. Many thanks. I think, though, that this is the last. My admirer will hardly trouble me again."

And Miss Bartlett, too, essayed the roguish:

"Well, it isn't everyone who could boast such a conquest, dearest, is it? Oh, one oughtn't to laugh, really. It might have been very serious. But you were so sensible and brave—so unlike the girls of my day."

"Let's go down to them."

But, once in the open air, she paused. Some emotion—pity, terror, love, but the emotion was strong—seized her, and she was aware of autumn. Summer was ending, and the evening brought her odours of decay, the more pathetic because they were reminiscent of spring. That something or other mattered intellectually? A leaf, violently agitated, danced past her, while other leaves lay motionless. That the earth was hastening to re-enter darkness, and the shadows of those trees to creep over Windy Corner?

"Hullo, Lucy! There's still light enough for another set, if you two'll hurry."

"Mr Emerson has had to go."

"What a nuisance! That spoils the four. I say, Cecil, do play, do, there's a good chap. It's Floyd's last day. Do play tennis with us, just this once."

Cecil's voice came: "My dear Freddy, I am no athlete. As you well remarked this very morning, 'There are some chaps who are no good for anything but books'; I plead guilty to being such a chap, and will not inflict myself on you."

The scales fell from Lucy's eyes. How had she stood Cecil for a moment? He was absolutely intolerable, and the same evening she broke her engagement off.

Chapter 17
Lying to Cecil

He was bewildered. He had nothing to say. He was not even angry, but stood, with a glass of whiskey between his hands, trying to think what had led her to such a conclusion.

She had chosen the moment before bed, when, in accordance with their bourgeois habit, she always dispensed drinks to the men. Freddy and Mr Floyd were sure to retire with their glasses, while Cecil invariably lingered, sipping at his while she locked up the sideboard.

"I am very sorry about it," she said; "I have carefully thought things over. We are too different. I must ask you to release me, and try to forget that there ever was such a foolish girl."

It was a suitable speech, but she was more angry than sorry, and her voice showed it.

"Different—how—how—"

"I haven't had a really good education, for one thing," she continued, still on her knees by the sideboard. "My Italian trip came too late, and I am forgetting all that I learned there. I shall never be able to talk to your friends, or behave as a wife of yours should."

"I don't understand you. You aren't like yourself. You're tired, Lucy."

"Tired!" she retorted, kindling at once. "That is exactly like you. You always think women don't mean what they say."

"Well, you sound tired, as if something has worried you."

"What if I do? It doesn't prevent me from realizing the truth. I can't marry you, and you will thank me for saying so some day."

"You had that bad headache yesterday—all right"—for she had exclaimed indignantly—"I see it's much more than headaches. But give me a moment's time." He closed his eyes. "You must excuse me if I say stupid things, but my brain has gone to pieces. Part of it lives three minutes back, when I was sure that you loved me, and the other part—I find it difficult—I am likely to say the wrong thing."

It struck her that he was not behaving so badly, and her irritation increased. She again desired a struggle, not a discussion. To bring on the crisis, she said:

"There are days when one sees clearly, and this is one of them. Things must come to a breaking-point some time, and it happens to be today. If you want to know, quite a little thing decided me to speak to you—when you wouldn't play tennis with Freddy."

"I never do play tennis," said Cecil, painfully bewildered; "I never could play. I don't understand a word you say."

"You can play well enough to make up a four. I thought it abominably selfish of you."

"No, I can't—well, never mind the tennis. Why couldn't you—couldn't you have warned me if you felt anything wrong? You talked of our wedding at lunch—at least, you let me talk."

"I knew you wouldn't understand," said Lucy quite crossly. "I might have known there would have been these dreadful explanations. Of course, it isn't the tennis—that was only the last straw to all I have been feeling for weeks. Surely it was better not to speak till I felt certain." She developed this position. "Often before, I have wondered if I was fitted for your wife—for instance, in London; and are you fitted to be my husband? I don't think so. You don't like Freddy, nor my mother. There was always a lot against our engagement, Cecil, but all our relations seemed pleased, and we met so often, and it was no good mentioning it until—well, until all things came to a point. They have today. I see clearly. I must speak. That's all."

"I cannot think you were right," said Cecil gently. "I cannot tell why, but though all that you say sounds true, I feel that you are not treating me fairly. It's all too horrible."

"What's the good of a scene?"

"No good. But surely I have a right to hear a little more."

He put down his glass and opened the window. From where she knelt, jangling her keys, she could see a slit of darkness, and, peering into it, as if it would tell him that "little more", his long, thoughtful face.

"Don't open the window; and you'd better draw the curtain, too; Freddy or anyone might be outside." He obeyed. "I really think we had better go to bed, if you don't mind. I shall only say things that will make me unhappy afterwards. As you say, it is all too horrible, and it is no good talking."

But to Cecil, now that he was about to lose her, she seemed each moment more desirable. He looked at her, instead of through her, for the first time since they were engaged. From a Leonardo she had become a living woman, with mysteries and forces of her own, with qualities that even eluded art. His brain recovered from the shock, and, in a burst of genuine devotion, he cried: "But I love you, and I did think you loved me!"

"I did not," she said. "I thought I did at first. I am sorry, and ought to have refused you this last time, too."

He began to walk up and down the room, and she grew more and more vexed at his dignified behaviour. She had counted on his being petty. It would have made things easier for her. By a cruel irony she was drawing out all that was finest in his disposition.

"You don't love me, evidently. I dare say you are right not to. But it would hurt a little less if I knew why."

"Because"—a phrase came to her, and she accepted it—"you're the sort who can't know anyone intimately."

A horrified look came into his eyes.

"I don't mean exactly that. But you will question me, though I beg you not to, and I must say something. It is that, more or less. When we were only acquaintances, you let me be myself, but now you're always protecting me." Her voice swelled. "I won't be protected. I will choose for myself what is ladylike and right. To shield me is an insult. Can't I be trusted to face the truth but I must get it second-hand through you? A woman's place! You despise my mother—I know you do—because she's conventional and bothers over puddings; but, oh goodness!"—she rose to her feet—"conventional, Cecil, you're that, for you may understand beautiful things, but you don't know how to use them; and you wrap yourself up in art and books and music, and would try to wrap up me. I won't be stifled, not by the most glorious music, for people are more glorious, and you hide them from me. That's why I break off my engagement. You were all right as long as you kept to things, but when you came to people—" She stopped.

There was a pause. Then Cecil said with great emotion:

"It is true."

"True on the whole," she corrected, full of some vague shame.

"True, every word. It is a revelation. It is—I."

"Anyhow, those are my reasons for not being your wife."

He repeated: " 'The sort that can know no one intimately.' It is true. I fell to pieces the very first day we were engaged. I behaved like a cad to Beebe and to your brother. You are even greater than I thought." She withdrew a step. "I'm not going to worry you. You are far too good to me. I shall never forget your insight; and, dear, I only blame you for this: you might have warned me in the early stages, before you felt you wouldn't marry me, and so have given me a chance to improve. I have never known you till this evening. I have just used you as a peg for my silly notions of what a woman should be. But this evening you are a different person: new thoughts—even a new voice—"

"What do you mean by a new voice?" she asked, seized with incontrollable anger.

"I mean that a new person seems speaking through you," said he.

Then she lost her balance. She cried: "If you think I am in love with someone else, you are very much mistaken."

"Of course I don't think that. You are not that kind, Lucy."

"Oh yes, you do think it. It's your old idea, the idea that has kept Europe back—I mean the idea that women are always thinking of men. If a girl breaks off her engagement, everyone says: 'Oh, she had someone else in her mind; she hopes to get someone else.' It's disgusting, brutal! As if a girl can't break it off for the sake of freedom."

He answered reverently: "I may have said that in the past. I shall never say it again. You have taught me better."

She began to redden, and pretended to examine the windows again.

"Of course, there is no question of 'someone else' in this, no 'jilting' or any such nauseous stupidity. I beg your pardon most humbly if my words suggested that there was. I only meant that there was a force in you that I hadn't known of up till now."

"All right, Cecil, that will do. Don't apologize to me. It was my mistake."

"It is a question between ideals, yours and mine—pure abstract ideals, and yours are the nobler. I was bound up in the old vicious notions, and all the time you were splendid and new." His voice broke. "I must actually thank you for what you have done—for showing me what I really am. Solemnly, I thank you for showing me a true woman. Will you shake hands?"

"Of course I will," said Lucy, twisting up her other hand in the curtains. "Good night, Cecil. Goodbye. That's all right. I'm sorry about it. Thank you very much for your gentleness."

"Let me light your candle, shall I?"

They went into the hall.

"Thank you. Good night again. God bless you, Lucy!"

"Goodbye, Cecil."

She watched him steal upstairs, while the shadows from the banisters passed over his face like the beat of wings. On the landing he paused, strong in his renunciation, and gave her a look of memorable beauty. For all his culture, Cecil was an ascetic at heart, and nothing in his love became him like the leaving of it.

She could never marry. In the tumult of her soul, that

stood firm. Cecil believed in her; she must some day believe in herself. She must be one of the women whom she had praised so eloquently, who care for liberty and not for men; she must forget that George loved her, that George had been thinking through her and gained her this honourable release, that George had gone away into—what was it?—the darkness.

She put out the lamp.

It did not do to think, nor, for the matter of that, to feel. She gave up trying to understand herself, and joined the vast armies of the benighted, who follow neither the heart nor the brain, and march to their destiny by catchwords. The armies are full of pleasant and pious folk. But they have yielded to the only enemy that matters—the enemy within. They have sinned against passion and truth, and vain will be their strife after virtue. As the years pass, they are censured. Their pleasantry and their piety show cracks, their wit becomes cynicism, their unselfishness hypocrisy; they feel and produce discomfort wherever they go. They have sinned against Eros and against Pallas Athene, and not by any heavenly intervention, but by the ordinary course of nature, those allied deities will be avenged.

Lucy entered this army when she pretended to George that she did not love him, and pretended to Cecil that she loved no one. The night received her, as it had received Miss Bartlett thirty years before.

Chapter 18
Lying to Mr Beebe, Mrs Honeychurch, Freddy and the Servants

Windy Corner lay, not on the summit of the ridge, but a few hundred feet down the southern slope, at the springing of one of the great buttresses that supported the hill. On either side of it was a shallow ravine, filled with ferns and pine trees, and down the ravine on the left ran the highway into the Weald.

Whenever Mr Beebe crossed the ridge and caught sight of these noble dispositions of the earth, and, poised in the middle of them, Windy Corner—he laughed. The situation was so glorious, the house so commonplace, not to say impertinent. The late Mr Honeychurch had affected the cube, because it gave him the most accommodation for his money, and the only addition made by his widow had been a small turret, shaped like a rhinoceros' horn, where she could sit in wet weather and watch the carts going up and down the road. So impertinent—and yet the house "did", for it was the home of people who loved their surroundings honestly. Other houses in the neighbourhood had been built by expensive architects, over others their inmates had fidgeted sedulously, yet all these suggested the accidental, the temporary; while Windy Corner seemed as inevitable as an ugliness of Nature's own creation. One might laugh at the house, but one never shuddered.

Mr Beebe was bicycling over this Monday afternoon with a little piece of gossip. He had heard from the Miss Alans. These admirable ladies, since they could not go to Cissie Villa, had changed their plans. They were going to Greece instead.

"Since Florence did my poor sister so much good," wrote Miss Catharine, "we do not see why we should not try Athens this winter. Of course, Athens is a plunge, and the doctor has ordered her special digestive bread; but, after all, we can take that with us, and it is only getting first into a steamer and then into a train. But is there an English Church?" And the letter went on to say: "I do not expect we shall go any further than Athens, but if you knew of a really comfortable pension at Constantinople, we should be so grateful."

Lucy would enjoy this letter, and the smile with which Mr Beebe greeted Windy Corner was partly for her. She would see the fun of it, and some of its beauty, for she must see some beauty. Though she was hopeless about pictures, and though she dressed so unevenly—oh, that cerise frock yesterday at church!—she must see some beauty in life, or she could not play the piano as she did. He had a theory that musicians are incredibly complex, and know far less than other artists what they want and what they are; that they puzzle themselves as well as their friends; that their psychology is a modern development, and has not yet been understood. This theory, had he known it, had possibly just been illustrated by facts. Ignorant of the events of yesterday, he was only riding over to get some tea, to see his niece, and to observe whether Miss Honeychurch saw anything beautiful in the desire of two old ladies to visit Athens.

A carriage was drawn up outside Windy Corner, and just as he caught sight of the house it started, bowled up the drive, and stopped abruptly when it reached the main road. Therefore it must be the horse, who always expected people to walk up the hill in case they tired him. The door opened obediently, and two men emerged, whom Mr Beebe recognized as Cecil and Freddy. They were an odd couple to go driving; but he saw a trunk beside the coachman's legs. Cecil, who wore a bowler, must be going away, while Freddy—a cap—was seeing him to the station. They walked rapidly, taking the short cuts, and reached the summit while the carriage was still pursuing the windings of the road.

They shook hands with the clergyman, but did not speak.

"So you're off for a minute, Mr Vyse?" he asked.

Cecil said, "Yes," while Freddy edged away.

"I was coming to show you this delightful letter from those

friends of Miss Honeychurch's." He quoted from it. "Isn't it wonderful? Isn't it Romance? Most certainly they will go to Constantinople. They are taken in a snare that cannot fail. They will end by going round the world."

Cecil listened civilly, and said he was sure that Lucy would be amused and interested.

"Isn't Romance capricious! I never notice it in you young people; you do nothing but play lawn-tennis, and say that Romance is dead, while the Miss Alans are struggling with all the weapons of propriety against the terrible thing. 'A really comfortable pension at Constantinople!' So they call it out of decency, but in their hearts they want a pension with magic windows opening on the foam of perilous seas in fairylands forlorn! No ordinary view will content the Miss Alans. They want the Pension Keats."

"I'm awfully sorry to interrupt, Mr Beebe," said Freddy, "but have you any matches?"

"I have," said Cecil, and it did not escape Mr Beebe's notice that he spoke to the boy more kindly.

"You have never met these Miss Alans, have you, Mr Vyse?"

"Never."

"Then you don't see the wonder of this Greek visit. I haven't been to Greece myself, and don't mean to go, and I can't imagine any of my friends going. It is altogether too big for our little lot. Don't you think so? Italy is just about as much as we can manage. Italy is heroic, but Greece is godlike or devilish—I am not sure which, and in either case absolutely out of our suburban focus. All right, Freddy—I am not being clever, upon my word I am not—I took the idea from another fellow; and give me those matches when you've done with them." He lit a cigarette, and went on talking to the two young men. "I was saying, if our poor little Cockney lives must have a background, let it be Italian. Big enough in all conscience. The ceiling of the Sistine Chapel for me. There the contrast is just as much as I can realize. But not the Parthenon, not the frieze of Phidias at any price; and here comes the victoria."

"You're quite right," said Cecil. "Greece is not for our

little lot"; and he got in. Freddy followed, nodding to the clergyman, whom he trusted not to be pulling one's leg, really. And before they had gone a dozen yards he jumped out, and came running back for Vyse's matchbox, which had not been returned. As he took it, he said: "I am so glad you only talked about books. Cecil's hard hit. Lucy won't marry him. If you'd gone on about her, as you did about them, he might have broken down."

"But when—"

"Late last night. I must go."

"Perhaps they won't want me down there."

"No—go on. Goodbye."

"Thank goodness!" exclaimed Mr Beebe to himself, and struck the saddle of his bicycle approvingly. "It was the one foolish thing she ever did. Oh, what a glorious riddance!" And, after a little thought, he negotiated the slope into Windy Corner, light of heart. The house was again as it ought to be —cut off for ever from Cecil's pretentious world.

He would find Miss Minnie down the garden.

In the drawing-room Lucy was tinkling at a Mozart sonata. He hesitated a moment, but went down the garden as requested. There he found a mournful company. It was a blustering day, and the wind had taken and broken the dahlias. Mrs Honeychurch, who looked cross, was tying them up, while Miss Bartlett, unsuitably dressed, impeded her with offers of assistance. At a little distance stood Minnie and the "garden child", a minute importation, each holding either end of a long piece of bass.

"Oh, how do you do, Mr Beebe? Gracious, what a mess everything is! Look at my scarlet pompoms, and the wind blowing your skirts about, and the ground so hard that not a prop will stick in, and then the carriage having to go out, when I had counted on having Powell, who—give everyone their due—does tie up dahlias properly."

Evidently Mrs Honeychurch was shattered.

"How do you do?" said Miss Bartlett, with a meaning glance, as though conveying that more than dahlias had been broken off by the autumn gales.

"Here, Lennie, the bass," cried Mrs Honeychurch. The garden child, who did not know what bass was, stood rooted to the path with horror. Minnie slipped to her uncle and whispered that everyone was very disagreeable today, and that it was not her fault if dahlia-strings would tear longways instead of across.

"Come for a walk with me," he told her. "You have worried them as much as they can stand. Mrs Honeychurch, I only called in aimlessly. I shall take her up to tea at the Beehive Tavern, if I may."

"Oh, must you? Yes, do.—Not the scissors, thank you, Charlotte, when both my hands are full already—I'm perfectly certain that the orange cactus will go before I can get to it."

Mr Beebe, who was an adept at relieving situations, invited Miss Bartlett to accompany them to this mild festivity.

"Yes, Charlotte, I don't want you—do go; there's nothing to stop about for, either in the house or out of it."

Miss Bartlett said that her duty lay in the dahlia-bed, but, when she had exasperated everyone, except Minnie, by a refusal, she turned round and exasperated Minnie by an acceptance. As they walked up the garden, the orange cactus fell, and Mr Beebe's last vision was of the garden child clasping it like a lover, his dark head buried in a wealth of blossom.

"It is terrible, this havoc among the flowers," he remarked.

"It is always terrible when the promise of months is destroyed in a moment," enunciated Miss Bartlett.

"Perhaps we ought to send Miss Honeychurch down to her mother. Or will she come with us?"

"I think we had better leave Lucy to herself, and to her own pursuits."

"They're angry with Miss Honeychurch, because she was late for breakfast," whispered Minnie, "and Mr Floyd has gone, and Mr Vyse has gone, and Freddy won't play with me. In fact, Uncle Arthur, the house is not *at all* what it was yesterday."

"Don't be a prig," said her Uncle Arthur. "Go and put on your boots."

He stepped into the drawing-room, where Lucy was still attentively pursuing the sonatas of Mozart. She stopped when he entered.

"How do you do? Miss Bartlett and Minnie are coming with me to tea at the Beehive. Would you come too?"

"I don't think I will, thank you."

"No, I didn't suppose you would care to much."

Lucy turned to the piano and struck a few chords.

"How delicate those sonatas are!" said Mr Beebe, though, at the bottom of his heart, he thought them silly little things.

Lucy passed into Schumann.

"Miss Honeychurch!"

"Yes."

"I met them on the hill. Your brother told me."

"Oh, did he?" She sounded annoyed. Mr Beebe felt hurt, for he had thought that she would like him to be told.

"I needn't say that it will go no further."

"Mother, Charlotte, Cecil, Freddy, you," said Lucy, playing a note for each person who knew, and then playing a sixth note.

"If you'll let me say so, I am very glad, and I am certain that you have done the right thing."

"So I hoped other people would think, but they don't seem to."

"I could see that Miss Bartlett thought it unwise."

"So does mother. Mother minds dreadfully."

"I am very sorry for that," said Mr Beebe with feeling.

Mrs Honeychurch, who hated all changes, did mind, but not nearly as much as her daughter pretended, and only for the minute. It was really a ruse of Lucy's to justify her despondency—a ruse of which she was not herself conscious, for she was marching in the armies of darkness.

"And Freddy minds."

"Still, Freddy never hit it off with Vyse much, did he? I gathered that he disliked the engagement, and felt it might separate him from you."

"Boys are so odd."

Minnie could be heard arguing with Miss Bartlett through the floor. Tea at the Beehive apparently involved a complete change of apparel. Mr Beebe saw that Lucy—very properly—did not wish to discuss her action, so after a sincere expression of sympathy he said: "I have had an absurd letter from Miss Alan. That was really what brought me over. I thought it might amuse you all."

"How delightful!" said Lucy, in a dull voice.

For the sake of something to do, he began to read her the letter. After a few words her eyes grew alert, and soon she interrupted him with—"Going abroad? When do they start?"

"Next week, I gather."

"Did Freddy say whether he was driving straight back?"

"No, he didn't."

"Because I do hope he won't go gossiping."

So she did want to talk about her broken engagement. Always complaisant, he put the letter away. But she at once exclaimed in a high voice: "Oh, do tell me more about the Miss Alans! How perfectly splendid of them to go abroad!"

"I want them to start from Venice, and go in a cargo steamer down the Illyrian coast!"

She laughed heartily. "Oh, delightful! I wish they'd take me."

"Has Italy filled you with the fever of travel? Perhaps George Emerson is right. He says that Italy is only an euphemism for Fate."

"Oh, not Italy, but Constantinople. I have always longed to go to Constantinople. Constantinople is practically Asia, isn't it?"

Mr Beebe reminded her that Constantinople was still unlikely, and that the Miss Alans only aimed at Athens, "with Delphi, perhaps, if the roads are safe". But this made no difference to her enthusiasm. She had always longed to go to Greece even more, it seemed. He saw, to his surprise, that she was apparently serious.

"I didn't realize that you and the Miss Alans were still such friends, after Cissie Villa."

"Oh, that's nothing; I assure you Cissie Villa's nothing to me; I would give anything to go with them."

"Would your mother spare you again so soon? You have scarcely been home three months."

"She *must* spare me!" cried Lucy, in growing excitement. "I simply *must* go away. I have to." She ran her fingers hysterically through her hair. "Don't you see that I *have* to go away? I didn't realize at the time— and of course I want to see Constantinople so particularly."

"You mean that since you have broken off your engagement you feel—"

"Yes, yes. I knew you would understand."

Mr Beebe did not quite understand. Why could not Miss Honeychurch repose in the bosom of her family? Cecil had evidently taken up the dignified line, and was not going to annoy her. Then it struck him that her family itself might be annoying. He hinted this to her, and she accepted the hint eagerly.

"Yes, of course; to go to Constantinople until they are used to the idea and everything has calmed down."

"I am afraid it has been a bothersome business," he said gently.

"No, not at all. Cecil was very kind indeed; only—I had better tell you the whole truth, since you have heard a little—it was that he is so masterful. I found that he wouldn't let me go my own way. He would improve me in places where I can't be improved. Cecil won't let a woman decide for herself—in fact, he daren't. What nonsense I do talk! But that is the kind of thing."

"It is what I gathered from my own observation of Mr Vyse; it is what I gather from all that I have known of you. I do sympathize and agree most profoundly. I agree so much that you must let me make one little criticism: is it worth while rushing off to Greece?"

"But I must go somewhere!" she cried. "I have been worrying all the morning, and here comes the very thing." She struck her knees with clenched fists, and repeated: "I must! And the time I shall have with mother, and all the money she spent on me last spring. You all think much too highly of me. I wish you weren't so kind." At this moment Miss Bartlett entered, and her nervousness increased. "I must get away, ever so far. I must know my own mind and where I want to go."

"Come along; tea, tea, tea," said Mr Beebe, and hustled his guests out of the front door. He hustled them so quickly that he forgot his hat. When he returned for it he heard, to his relief and surprise, the tinkling of a Mozart sonata.

"She is playing again," he said to Miss Bartlett.

"Lucy can always play," was the acid reply.

"One is very thankful that she has such a resource. She is evidently much worried, as, of course, she ought to be. I know all about it. The marriage was so near that it must have been a hard struggle before she could wind herself up to speak."

Miss Bartlett gave a kind of wriggle, and he prepared for a discussion. He had never fathomed Miss Bartlett. As he had put it to himself at Florence, "she might yet reveal depths of strangeness, if not of meaning." But she was so unsympathetic that she must be reliable. He assumed that much, and he had no hesitation in discussing Lucy with her. Minnie was fortunately collecting ferns.

She opened the discussion with: "We had much better let the matter drop."

"I wonder."

"It is of the highest importance that there should be no gossip in Summer Street. It would be *death* to gossip about Mr Vyse's dismissal at the present moment."

Mr Beebe raised his eyebrows. Death is a strong word—surely too strong. There was no question of tragedy. He said: "Of course, Miss Honeychurch will make the fact public in her own way, and when she chooses. Freddy only told me because he knew she would not mind."

"I know," said Miss Bartlett civilly. "Yet Freddy ought not to have told even you. One cannot be too careful."

"Quite so."

"I do implore absolute secrecy. A chance word to a chattering friend, and—"

"Exactly." He was used to these nervous old maids and to the exaggerated importance that they attach to words. A rector lives in a web of petty secrets, and confidences, and warnings, and the wiser he is the less he will regard them. He will change the subject, as did Mr Beebe, saying cheerfully: "Have you heard from any Bertolini people lately? I believe you keep up with Miss Lavish. It is odd how we of that pension, who seemed such a fortuitous collection, have been working into one another's lives. Two, three, four, six of us—no, eight; I had forgotten the Emersons—have kept more or less in touch. We must really give the Signora a testimonial."

And, Miss Bartlett not favouring the scheme, they walked up the hill in a silence which was only broken by the rector naming some fern. On the summit they paused. The sky had grown wilder since he stood there last hour, giving to the land a tragic greatness that is rare in Surrey. Gray clouds were charging across tissues of white, which stretched and shredded and tore slowly, until through their final layers there gleamed a hint of the disappearing blue. Summer was retreating. The wind roared, the trees groaned, yet the noise seemed insufficient for those vast operations in heaven. The weather was breaking up, breaking, broken, and it is a sense of the fit rather than of the supernatural that equips such crises with the salvos of angelic artillery. Mr Beebe's eyes rested on Windy Corner, where Lucy sat, practising Mozart. No smile came to his lips, and, changing the subject again, he said: "We shan't have rain, but we shall have darkness, so let us hurry on. The darkness last night was appalling."

They reached the Beehive Tavern at about five o'clock. That amiable hostelry possesses a veranda, in which the young and the unwise do dearly love to sit, while guests of more mature years seek a pleasant sanded room, and have tea at a table comfortably. Mr Beebe saw that Miss Bartlett would be cold if she sat out, and that Minnie would be dull if she sat in, so he proposed a division of forces. They would hand the child her food through the window. Thus he was incidentally enabled to discuss the fortunes of Lucy.

"I have been thinking, Miss Bartlett," he said, "and, unless you very much object, I would like to reopen that discussion." She bowed. "Nothing about the past. I know little and care less about that; I am absolutely certain that it is to your cousin's credit. She has acted loftily and rightly, and it is like her gentle modesty to say that we think too highly of her. But the future. Seriously, what do you think of this Greek plan?" He pulled out the letter again. "I don't know whether you overheard, but she wants to join the Miss Alans in their mad career. It's all—I can't explain—it's wrong."

Miss Bartlett read the letter in silence, laid it down, seemed to hesitate, and then read it again.

"I can't see the point of it myself."

To his astonishment, she replied: "There I cannot agree with you. In it I spy Lucy's salvation."

"Really. Now, why?"

"She wanted to leave Windy Corner."

"I know—but it seems so odd, so unlike her, so—I was going to say—selfish."

"It is natural, surely—after such painful scenes—that she should desire a change."

Here, apparently, was one of those points that the male intellect misses. Mr Beebe exclaimed: "So she says herself, and since another lady agrees with her, I must own that I am partially convinced. Perhaps she must have a change. I have no sisters or—and I don't understand these things. But why need she go as far as Greece?"

"You may well ask that," replied Miss Bartlett, who was evidently interested, and had almost dropped her evasive manner. "Why Greece? (What is it, Minnie dear—jam?) Why not Tunbridge Wells? Oh, Mr Beebe! I had a long and most unsatisfactory interview with dear Lucy this morning. I cannot help her. I will say no more. Perhaps I have already said too much. I am not to talk—a point on which she is almost bitter. I am not to talk. I wanted her to spend six months with me at Tunbridge Wells, and she refused."

Mr Beebe poked at a crumb with his knife.

"But my feelings are of no importance. I know too well that I get on Lucy's nerves. Our tour was a failure. She wanted to leave Florence, and when we got to Rome she did not want to be in Rome, and all the time I felt that I was spending her mother's money—"

"Let us keep to the future, though," interrupted Mr Beebe. "I want your advice."

"Very well," said Charlotte, with a choky abruptness that was new to him, though familiar to Lucy. "I for one will help her to go to Greece. Will you?"

Mr Beebe considered.

"It is absolutely necessary," she continued, lowering her veil and whispering through it with a passion, an intensity, that surprised him. "I know—I *know*." The darkness was coming on, and he felt that this odd woman really did know. "She must not stop here a moment, and we must keep quiet till she goes. I trust that the servants know nothing. Afterwards—but I may have said too much already. Only, Lucy and I are helpless against Mrs Honeychurch alone. If you help, we may succeed. Otherwise—"

"Otherwise—?"

"Otherwise," she repeated, as if the word held finality.

"Yes, I will help her," said the clergyman, setting his jaw firm. "Come, let us go back now, and settle the whole thing up."

Miss Bartlett burst into florid gratitude. The tavern sign—a beehive trimmed evenly with bees—creaked in the wind outside as she thanked him. Mr Beebe did not quite understand the situation; but then, he did not desire to understand it, nor to jump to the conclusion of "another man" that would have attracted a grosser mind. He only felt that Miss Bartlett knew of some vague influence from which the girl desired to be delivered, and which might well be clothed in the fleshly form. Its very vagueness spurred him into knight-errantry. His belief in celibacy, so reticent, so carefully concealed beneath his tolerance and culture, now came to the surface and expanded like some delicate flower. "They that marry do well, but they that refrain do better."

So ran his belief, and he never heard that an engagement was broken off but with a slight feeling of pleasure. In the case of Lucy, the feeling was intensified through dislike of Cecil; and he was willing to go further—to place her out of danger until she could confirm her resolution of virginity. The feeling was very subtle and quite undogmatic, and he never imparted it to any other of the characters in this entanglement. Yet it existed, and it alone explains his action subsequently, and his influence on the action of others. The compact that he made with Miss Bartlett in the tavern was to help not only Lucy, but religion also.

They hurried home through a world of black and gray. He conversed on indifferent topics: the Emersons' need of a housekeeper; servants; Italian servants; novels about Italy; novels with a purpose; could literature influence life? Windy Corner glimmered. In the garden, Mrs Honeychurch, now helped by Freddy, still wrestled with the lives of her flowers.

"It gets too dark," she said hopelessly. "This comes of putting off. We might have known the weather would break up soon; and now Lucy wants to go to Greece. I don't know what the world's coming to."

"Mrs Honeychurch," he said, "go to Greece she must. Come up to the house and let's talk it over. Do you, in the first place, mind her breaking with Vyse?"

"Mr Beebe, I'm thankful—simply thankful."

"So am I," said Freddy.

"Good. Now come up to the house."

They conferred in the dining-room for half an hour.

Lucy would never have carried the Greek scheme alone. It was expensive and dramatic—both qualities that her mother loathed. Nor would Charlotte have succeeded. The honours of the day rested with Mr Beebe. By his tact and common sense, and by his influence as a clergyman—for a clergyman who was not a fool influenced Mrs Honeychurch greatly—he bent her to their purpose.

"I don't see why Greece is necessary," she said; "but as you do, I suppose it is all right. It must be something I can't understand. Lucy! Let's tell her. Lucy!"

"She is playing the piano," Mr Beebe said. He opened the door, and heard the words of a song:

"Look not thou on beauty's charming—"

"I didn't know that Miss Honeychurch sang, too."

"Sit thou still when kings are arming,
Taste not when the wine-cup glistens—"

"It's a song that Cecil gave her. How odd girls are!"

"What's that?" called Lucy, stopping short.

"All right, dear," said Mrs Honeychurch kindly. She went into the drawing-room, and Mr Beebe heard her kiss Lucy and say: "I am sorry I was so cross about Greece, but it came on the top of the dahlias."

Rather a hard voice said: "Thank you, mother; that doesn't matter a bit."

"And you are right, too—Greece will be all right; you can go if the Miss Alans will have you."

"Oh, splendid! Oh, thank you!"

Mr Beebe followed. Lucy still sat at the piano with her hands over the keys. She was glad, but he had expected greater gladness. Her mother bent over her. Freddy, to whom she had been singing, reclined on the floor with his head against her, and an unlit pipe between his lips. Oddly enough, the group was beautiful. Mr Beebe, who loved the art of the past, was reminded of a favourite theme, the *Santa Conversazione*, in which people who care for one another are painted chatting together about noble things—a theme neither sensual nor sensational, and therefore ignored by the art of today. Why should Lucy want either to marry or to travel when she had such friends at home?

"Taste not when the wine-cup glistens,
Speak not when the people listens,"

she continued.

"Here's Mr Beebe."

"Mr Beebe knows my rude ways."

"It's a beautiful song and a wise one," said he. "Go on."

"It isn't very good," she said listlessly. "I forget why—harmony or something."

"I suspected it was unscholarly. It's so beautiful."

"The tune's right enough," said Freddy, "but the words are rotten. Why throw up the sponge?"

"How stupidly you talk!" said his sister. The *Santa Conversazione* was broken up. After all, there was no reason that Lucy should talk about Greece or thank him for persuading her mother, so he said goodbye.

Freddy lit his bicycle-lamp for him in the porch, and, with his usual felicity of phrase, said: "This has been a day and a half."

> "Stop thine ear against the singer—"

"Wait a minute; she is finishing."

> "From the red gold keep thy finger;
> Vacant heart, and hand, and eye,
> Easy live and quiet die."

"I love weather like this," said Freddy.

Mr Beebe passed into it.

The two main facts were clear. She had behaved splendidly, and he had helped her. He could not expect to master the details of so big a change in a girl's life. If here and there he was dissatisfied or puzzled, he must acquiesce; she was choosing the better part.

> "Vacant heart, and hand, and eye—"

Perhaps the song stated "the better part" rather too strongly. He half fancied that the soaring accompaniment—which he did not lose in the shout of the gale—really agreed with Freddy, and was gently criticizing the words that it adorned:

> "Vacant heart, and hand, and eye,
> Easy live and quiet die."

However. For the fourth time Windy Corner lay poised below him—now as a beacon in the roaring tides of darkness.

Chapter 19
Lying to Mr Emerson

The Miss Alans were found in their beloved temperance hotel near Bloomsbury—a clean, airless establishment much patronized by provincial England. They always perched there before crossing the great seas, and for a week or two would fidget gently over clothes, guidebooks, mackintosh squares, digestive bread, and other continental necessaries. That there are shops abroad, even in Athens, never occurred to them, for they regarded travel as a species of warfare, only to be undertaken by those who have been fully armed at the Haymarket Stores. Miss Honeychurch, they trusted, would take care to equip herself duly. Quinine could now be obtained in tabloids; paper soap was a great help towards freshening up one's face in the train. Lucy promised, a little depressed.

"But, of course, you know all about these things, and you have Mr Vyse to help you. A gentleman is such a stand-by."

Mrs Honeychurch, who had come up to town with her daughter, began to drum nervously upon her card-case.

"We think it so good of Mr Vyse to spare you," Miss Catharine continued. "It is not every young man who would be so unselfish. But perhaps he will come out and join you later on."

"Or does his work keep him in London?" said Miss Teresa, the more acute and less kindly of the two sisters. "However, we shall see him when he sees you off. I do so long to see him."

"No one will see Lucy off," interposed Mrs Honeychurch. "She doesn't like it."

"No, I hate seeings-off," said Lucy.

"Really? How funny! I should have thought that in this case—"

"Oh, Mrs Honeychurch, you aren't going? It is such a pleasure to have met you!"

They escaped, and Lucy said with relief: "That's all right. We just got through that time."

But her mother was annoyed. "I shall be told, dear, that I am unsympathetic. But I cannot see why you didn't tell your friends about Cecil and be done with it. There all the time we had to sit fencing, and almost telling lies, and be seen through, too, I dare say, which is most unpleasant."

Lucy had plenty to say in reply. She described the Miss Alans' character: they were such gossips, and, if one told them, the news would be everywhere in no time.

"But why shouldn't it be everywhere in no time?"

"Because I settled with Cecil not to announce it until I left England. I shall tell them then. It's much pleasanter. How wet it is! Let's turn in here."

"Here" was the British Museum. Mrs Honeychurch refused. If they must take shelter, let it be in a shop. Lucy felt contemptuous, for she was on the tack of caring for Greek sculpture, and had already borrowed a mythological dictionary from Mr Beebe to get up the names of the goddesses and gods.

"Oh, well, let it be a shop, then. Let's go to Mudie's. I'll buy a guidebook."

"You know, Lucy, you and Charlotte and Mr Beebe all tell me I'm so stupid, so I suppose I am, but I shall never understand this hole-and-corner work. You've got rid of Cecil—well and good, and I'm thankful he's gone, though I did feel angry for the minute. But why not announce it? Why this hushing up and tiptoeing?"

"It's only for a few days."

"But why at all?"

Lucy was silent. She was drifting away from her mother. It was quite easy to say, "Because George Emerson has been bothering me, and if he hears I've given up Cecil may begin again"—quite easy, and it had the incidental advantage of being true. But she could not say it. She disliked confidences, for they might lead to self-knowledge and to that king of terrors—Light. Ever since that last evening at Florence she had deemed it unwise to reveal her soul.

Mrs Honeychurch, too, was silent. She was thinking: "My daughter won't answer me; she would rather be with those inquisitive old maids than with Freddy and me. Any rag, tag and bobtail apparently does if she can leave her home." And, as in her case thoughts never remained unspoken long, she burst out with: "You're tired of Windy Corner."

This was perfectly true. Lucy had hoped to return to Windy Corner when she escaped from Cecil, but she discovered that her home existed no longer. It might exist for Freddy, who still lived and thought straight, but not for one who had deliberately warped the brain. She did not acknowledge that her brain was warped, for the brain itself must assist in that acknowledgement, and she was disordering the very instruments of life. She only felt: "I do not love George; I broke off my engagement because I did not love George; I must go to Greece because I do not love George; it is more important that I should look up gods in the dictionary than that I should help my mother; everyone else is behaving very badly." She only felt irritable and petulant, and anxious to do what she was not expected to do, and in this spirit she proceeded with the conversation.

"Oh, mother, what rubbish you talk! Of course I'm not tired of Windy Corner."

"Then why not say so at once, instead of considering half an hour first?"

She laughed faintly. "Half a *minute* would be nearer."

"Perhaps you would like to stay away from your home altogether?"

"Hush, mother! People will hear you"; for they had entered Mudie's. She bought Baedeker, and then continued: "Of course I want to live at home; but as we are talking about it, I may as well say that I shall want to be away in the future more than I have been. You see, I come into my money next year."

Tears came into her mother's eyes.

Driven by nameless bewilderment, by what is in older

people termed "eccentricity", Lucy determined to make this point clear. "I've seen the world so little—I felt so out of things in Italy. I have seen so little of life; one ought to come up to London more—not a cheap ticket like today, but to stop. I might even share a flat for a little with some other girl."

"And mess with typewriters and latchkeys," exploded Mrs Honeychurch. "And agitate and scream, and be carried off kicking by the police. And call it a Mission—when no one wants you! And call it Duty—when it means that you can't stand your own home! And call it Work—when thousands of men are starving with the competition as it is! And then to prepare yourself, find two doddering old ladies, and go abroad with them."

"I want more independence," said Lucy lamely; she knew that she wanted something, and independence is a useful cry; we can always say that we have not got it. She tried to remember her emotions in Florence: those had been sincere and passionate, and had suggested beauty rather than short skirts and latchkeys. But independence was certainly her cue.

"Very well. Take your independence and be gone. Rush up and down and round the world, and come back as thin as a lath with the bad food. Despise the house that your father built and the garden that he planted, and our dear view—and then share a flat with another girl."

Lucy screwed up her mouth and said: "Perhaps I spoke hastily."

"Oh, goodness!" her mother flashed. "How you do remind me of Charlotte Bartlett!"

"*Charlotte*?" flashed Lucy in her turn, pierced at last by a vivid pain.

"More every moment."

"I don't know what you mean, mother; Charlotte and I are not the very least alike."

"Well, I see the likeness. The same eternal worrying, the same taking back of words. You and Charlotte trying to divide two apples among three people last night might be sisters."

"What rubbish! And if you dislike Charlotte so, it's rather a pity you asked her to stop. I warned you about her;

I begged you, implored you not to, but of course I was not listened to."

"There you go."

"I beg your pardon?"

"Charlotte again, my dear; that's all; her very words."

Lucy clenched her teeth. "My point is that you oughtn't to have asked Charlotte to stop. I wish you would keep to the point." And the conversation dies off into a wrangle.

She and her mother shopped in silence, spoke little in the train, little again in the carriage, which met them at Dorking station. It had poured all day, and as they ascended through the deep Surrey lanes showers of water fell from the overhanging beech trees and rattled on the hood. Lucy complained that the hood was stuffy. Leaning forward, she looked out into the steaming dusk, and watched the carriage-lamp pass like a searchlight over mud and leaves, and reveal nothing beautiful. "The crush when Charlotte gets in will be abominable," she remarked. For they were to pick up Miss Bartlett at Summer Street, where she had been dropped as the carriage went down, to pay a call on Mr Beebe's old mother. "We shall have to sit three a side, because the trees drop, and yet it isn't raining. O for a little air!" Then she listened to the horse's hoofs—"He has not told—he has not told." That melody was blurred by the soft road. "*Can't* we have the hood down?" she demanded, and her mother, with sudden tenderness, said: "Very well, old lady, stop the horse." And the horse was stopped, and Lucy and Powell wrestled with the hood, and squirted water down Mrs Honeychurch's neck. But now that the hood was down she did see something that she would have missed—there were no lights in the windows of Cissie Villa, and round the garden gate she fancied she saw a padlock.

"Is that house to let again, Powell?" she called.

"Yes, miss," he replied.

"Have they gone?"

"It is too far out of town for the young gentleman, and his father's rheumatism has come on, so he can't stop on alone, so they are trying to let furnished," was the answer.

"They have gone, then?"

"Yes, miss, they have gone."

Lucy sank back. The carriage stopped at the rectory. She got out to call for Miss Bartlett. So the Emersons had gone, and all this bother about Greece had been unnecessary. Waste! That word seemed to sum up the whole of life. Wasted plans, wasted money, wasted love, and she had wounded her mother. Was it possible that she had muddled things away? Quite possible. Other people had. When the maid opened the door, she was unable to speak, and stared stupidly into the hall.

Miss Bartlett at once came forward, and after a long preamble asked a great favour: might she go to church? Mr Beebe and his mother had already gone, but she had refused to start until she obtained her hostess's full sanction, for it would mean keeping the horse waiting a good ten minutes more.

"Certainly," said the hostess wearily. "I forgot it was Friday. Let's all go. Powell can go round to the stables."

"Lucy dearest—"

"No church for me, thank you."

A sigh, and they departed. The church was invisible, but up in the darkness to the left there was a hint of colour. This was a stained window, through which some feeble light was shining, and when the door opened Lucy heard Mr Beebe's voice running through the litany to a minute congregation. Even their church, built upon the slope of the hill so artfully, with its beautiful raised transept and its spire of silvery shingle—even their church had lost its charm; and the thing one never talked about—religion—was fading like all the other things.

She followed the maid into the rectory.

Would she object to sitting in Mr Beebe's study? There was only that one fire.

She would not object.

Someone was there already, for Lucy heard the words: "A lady to wait, sir."

Old Mr Emerson was sitting by the fire, with his foot upon a gout-stool.

"Oh, Miss Honeychurch, that you should come!" he quavered; and Lucy saw an alteration in him since last Sunday.

Not a word would come to her lips. George she had faced, and could have faced again, but she had forgotten how to treat his father.

"Miss Honeychurch, dear, we are so sorry! George is so sorry! He thought he had a right to try. I cannot blame my boy, and yet I wish he had told me first. He ought not to have tried. I knew nothing about it at all."

If only she could remember how to behave!

He held up his hand. "But you must not scold him."

Lucy turned her back, and began to look at Mr Beebe's books.

"I taught him," he quavered, "to trust in love. I said: 'When love comes, that is reality.' I said: 'Passion does not blind. No. Passion is sanity, and the woman you love, she is the only person you will ever really understand.' " He sighed: "True, everlastingly true, though my day is over, and though there is the result. Poor boy! He is so sorry! He said he knew it was madness when you brought your cousin in; that whatever you felt you did not mean. Yet"—his voice gathered strength; he spoke out to make certain—"Miss Honeychurch, do you remember Italy?"

Lucy selected a book—a volume of Old Testament commentaries. Holding it up to her eyes, she said: "I have no wish to discuss Italy or any subject connected with your son."

"But you do remember it?"

"He has misbehaved himself from the first."

"I only was told that he loved you last Sunday. I never could judge behaviour. I—I—suppose he has."

Feeling a little steadier, she put the book back and turned round to him. His face was drooping and swollen, but his eyes, though they were sunken deep, gleamed with a child's courage.

"Why, he has behaved abominably," she said. "I am glad he is sorry. Do you know what he did?"

"Not 'abominably'," was the gentle correction. "He only tried when he should not have tried. You have all you want, Miss Honeychurch: you are going to marry the man you love. Do not go out of George's life saying he is abominable."

"No, of course," said Lucy, ashamed at the reference to Cecil. " 'Abominable' is much too strong. I am sorry I used it about your son. I think I will go to church, after all. My mother and my cousin have gone. I shall not be so very late—"

"Especially as he has gone under," he said quietly.

"What was that?"

"Gone under naturally." He beat his palms together in silence; his head fell on his chest.

"I don't understand."

"As his mother did."

"But, Mr Emerson—*Mr Emerson*—what are you talking about?"

"When I wouldn't have George baptized," said he.

Lucy was frightened.

"And she agreed that baptism was nothing, but he caught that fever when he was twelve, and she turned round. She thought it a judgement." He shuddered. "Oh, horrible, when we had given up that sort of thing and broken away from her parents. Oh, horrible—worst of all—worse than death, when you have made a little clearing in the wilderness, planted your little garden, let in your sunlight, and then the weeds creep in again! A judgement! And our boy had typhoid because no clergyman had dropped water on him in church! Is it possible, Miss Honeychurch? Shall we slip back into the darkness for ever?"

"I don't know," gasped Lucy. "I don't understand this sort of thing. I was not meant to understand it."

"But Mr Eager—he came when I was out, and acted according to his principles. I don't blame him or anyone . . . but by the time George was well she was ill. He made her think about sin, and she went under thinking about it."

It was thus that Mr Emerson had murdered his wife in the sight of God.

"Oh, how terrible!" said Lucy, forgetting her own affairs at last.

"He was not baptized," said the old man. "I did hold firm." And he looked with unwavering eyes at the rows of books, as if—at what cost!—he had won a victory over them. "My boy shall go back to the earth untouched."

She asked whether young Mr Emerson was ill.

"Oh—last Sunday." He started into the present. "George last Sunday—no, not ill; just gone under. He is never ill. But he is his mother's son. Her eyes were his, and she had that forehead that I think so beautiful, and he will not think it worth while to live. It was always touch and go. He will live; but he will not think it worth while to live. He will never think anything worth while. You remember that church at Florence?"

Lucy did remember, and how she had suggested that George should collect postage-stamps.

"After you left Florence—horrible. Then we take the house here, and he goes bathing with your brother, and became better. You saw him bathing?"

"I am so sorry, but it is no good discussing this affair. I am really deeply sorry about it."

"Then there came something about a novel. I didn't follow it all; I had to hear so much, and he minded telling me; he finds me too old. Ah, well, one must have failures. George comes down tomorrow, and takes me up to his London rooms. He can't bear to be about here, and I must be where he is."

"Mr Emerson," cried the girl, "don't leave—at least, not on my account. I am going to Greece. Don't leave your comfortable house."

It was the first time her voice had been kind, and he smiled. "How good everyone is! And look at Mr Beebe housing me—came over this morning and heard I was going! Here I am so comfortable with a fire."

"Yes, but you won't go back to London. It's absurd."

"I must be with George; I must make him care to live, and down here he can't. He says the thought of seeing you and of hearing about you—I am not justifying him; I am only saying what has happened."

"Oh, Mr Emerson"—she took hold of his hand— "you mustn't. I've been bother enough to the world by now. I can't have you moving out of your house when you like it, and perhaps losing money through it—all on my account. You must stop! I am just going to Greece."

"All the way to Greece?"

Her manner altered.

"To Greece?"

"So you must stop. You won't talk about this business, I know. I can trust you both."

"Certainly you can. We either have you in our lives, or leave you to the life that you have chosen."

"I shouldn't want—"

"I suppose Mr Vyse is very angry with George? No, it was wrong of George to try. We have pushed our beliefs too far. I fancy that we deserve sorrow."

She looked at the books again—black, brown, and that acrid, theological blue. They surrounded the visitors on every side; they were piled on the tables, they pressed against the very ceiling. To Lucy—who could not see that Mr Emerson was profoundly religious, and differed from Mr Beebe chiefly by his acknowledgement of passion—it seemed dreadful that the old man should crawl into such a sanctum, when he was unhappy, and be dependent on the bounty of a clergyman.

More certain than ever that she was tired, he offered her his chair.

"No, please sit still. I think I will sit in the carriage."

"Miss Honeychurch, you do sound tired."

"Not a bit," said Lucy, with trembling lips.

"But you are, and there's a look of George about you. And what were you saying about going abroad?"

She was silent.

"Greece"—and she saw that he was thinking the word over—"Greece; but you were to be married this year, I thought."

"Not till January, it wasn't," said Lucy, clasping her hands. Would she tell an actual lie when it came to the point?

"I suppose that Mr Vyse is going with you. I hope—it isn't because George spoke that you are both going?"

"No."

"I hope that you will enjoy Greece with Mr Vyse."

"Thank you."

At that moment Mr Beebe came back from church. His cassock was covered with rain. "That's all right," he said kindly. "I counted on you two keeping each other company. It's pouring again. The entire congregation, which consists of your cousin, your mother and my mother, stands waiting in the church till the carriage fetches it. Did Powell go round?"

"I think so; I'll see."

"No—of course, I'll see. How are the Miss Alans?"

"Very well, thank you."

"Did you tell Mr Emerson about Greece?"

"I—I did."

"Don't you think it very plucky of her, Mr Emerson, to undertake the two Miss Alans? Now, Miss Honeychurch, go back—keep warm. I think three is such a courageous number to go travelling." And he hurried off to the stables.

"He is not going," she said hoarsely. "I made a slip. Mr Vyse does stop behind in England." Somehow it was impossible to cheat this old man. To George, to Cecil, she would have lied again; but he seemed so near the end of things, so dignified in his approach to the gulf, of which he gave one account, and the books that surrounded him another, so mild to the rough paths that he had traversed, that the true chivalry—not the worn-out chivalry of sex, but the true chivalry that all the young may show to all the old—awoke in her, and, at whatever risk, she told him that Cecil was not her companion to Greece. And she spoke so seriously that the risk became a certainty and he, lifting his eyes, said: "You are leaving him? You are leaving the man you love?"

"I—I had to."

"Why, Miss Honeychurch, why?"

Terror came over her, and she lied again. She made the long, convincing speech that she had made to Mr Beebe, and intended to make to the world when she announced that her engagement was no more. He heard her in silence, and then said: "My dear, I am worried about you. It seems to me"—dreamily; she was not alarmed—"that you are in a muddle."

She shook her head.

"Take an old man's word: there's nothing worse than a muddle in all the world. It is easy to face Death and Fate, and the things that sound so dreadful. It is on my muddles that I look back with horror—on the things that I might have avoided. We can help one another but little. I used to think I could teach young people the whole of life, but I know better now, and all my teaching of George has come down to this: beware of muddle. Do you remember in that church, when you pretended to be annoyed with me and weren't? Do you remember before, when you refused the room with the view? Those were muddles—little, but ominous—and I am fearing that you are in one now." She was silent. "Do trust me, Miss Honeychurch. Though life is very glorious, it is difficult." She was still silent. " 'Life,' wrote a friend of mine, 'is a public performance on the violin, in which you must learn the instrument as you go along.' I think he puts it well. Man has to pick up the use of his functions as he goes along—especially the function of Love." Then he burst out excitedly: "That's it; that's what I mean. You love George!" And after his long preamble the three words burst against Lucy like waves from the open sea.

"But you do," he went on, not waiting for contradiction. "You love the boy body and soul, plainly, directly, as he loves you, and no other word expresses it. You won't marry the other man for his sake."

"How dare you!" gasped Lucy, with the roaring of waters in her ears. "Oh, how like a man!—I mean, to suppose that a woman is always thinking about a man."

"But you are."

She summoned physical disgust.

"You're shocked, but I mean to shock you. It's the only hope at times. I can reach you no other way. You must marry, or your life will be wasted. You have gone too far to retreat. I have no time for the tenderness, and the comradeship, and the poetry, and the things that really matter, and *for which* you marry. I know that, with George, you will find them, and that you love him. Then be his wife. He is already part of you. Though you fly to Greece, and never see him again, or forget his very name, George will work in your thoughts till you die. It isn't possible to love and to part. You will wish that it was. You can transmute love, ignore it, muddle it, but you can never pull it out of you. I know by experience that the poets are right: love is eternal."

Lucy began to cry with anger, and, though her anger passed away soon, her tears remained.

"I only wish poets would say this, too: that love is of the body; not the body, but of the body. Ah! the misery that would be saved if we confessed that! Ah for a little directness to liberate the soul! Your soul, dear Lucy! I hate the word now, because of all the cant with which superstition has wrapped it round. But we have souls. I cannot say how they came nor whither they go, but we have them, and I see you ruining yours. I cannot bear it. It is again the darkness creeping in; it is hell." Then he checked himself. "What nonsense I have talked—how abstract and remote! And I have made you cry! Dear girl, forgive my prosiness; marry my boy. When I think what life is, and how seldom love is answered by love—marry him; it is one of the moments for which the world was made."

She could not understand him; the words were indeed remote. Yet as he spoke the darkness was withdrawn, veil after veil, and she saw to the bottom of her soul.

"Then, Lucy—"

"You've frightened me," she moaned. "Cecil—Mr Beebe—the ticket's bought—everything." She fell sobbing into the chair. "I'm caught in the tangle. I must suffer and grow old away from him. I cannot break the whole of life for his sake. They trusted me."

A carriage drew up at the front door.

"Give George my love—once only. Tell him, 'Muddle.' " Then she arranged her veil, while the tears poured over her cheeks inside.

"Lucy—"

"No—they are in the hall—oh, please not, Mr Emerson—they trust me—"

"But why should they, when you have deceived them?"

Mr Beebe opened the door saying: "Here's my mother."

"You're not worthy of their trust."

"What's that?" said Mr Beebe sharply.

"I was saying, why should you trust her when she deceived you?"

"One minute, mother." He came in and shut the door.

"I don't follow you, Mr Emerson. To whom do you refer? Trust whom?"

"I mean, she has pretended to you that she did not love George. They have loved one another all along."

Mr Beebe looked at the sobbing girl. He was very quiet, and his white face, with its ruddy whiskers, seemed suddenly inhuman. A long black column, he stood and awaited her reply.

"I shall never marry him," quavered Lucy.

A look of contempt came over him, and he said, "Why not?"

"Mr Beebe—I have misled you—I have misled myself—"

"Oh, rubbish, Miss Honeychurch!"

"It is not rubbish!" said the old man hotly. "It's the part of people that you don't understand."

Mr Beebe laid his hand on his shoulder pleasantly.

"Lucy! Lucy!" called voices from the carriage.

"Mr Beebe, could you help me?"

He looked amazed at the request, and said in a low, stern voice: "I am more grieved than I can possibly express. It is lamentable, lamentable—incredible."

"What's wrong with the boy?" fired up the other again.

"Nothing, Mr Emerson, except that he no longer interests me. Marry George, Miss Honeychurch. He will do admirably."

He walked out and left them. They heard him guiding his mother upstairs.

"Lucy!" the voices called.

She turned to Mr Emerson in despair. But his face revived her. It was the face of a saint who understood.

"Now it is all dark. Now Beauty and Passion seem never to have existed. I know. But remember the mountains over Florence and the view. Ah, dear, if I were George, and gave you one kiss, it would make you brave. You have to go cold into a battle that needs warmth, out into the muddle that you have made yourself; and your mother and all your friends will despise you, oh my darling, and rightly, if it is ever right to despise. George still dark, all the tussle and the misery without a word from him. Am I justified?" Into his own eyes tears came. "Yes, for we fight for more than Love or Pleasure: there is Truth. Truth counts, Truth does count."

"You kiss me," said the girl. "You kiss me. I will try."

He gave her a sense of deities reconciled, a feeling that, in gaining the man she loved, she would gain something for the whole world. Throughout the squalor of her homeward drive—she spoke at once—his salutation remained. He had robbed the body of its taint, the world's taunts of their sting; he had shown her the holiness of direct desire. She "never exactly understood," she would say in after years, "how he managed to strengthen her. It was as if he had made her see the whole of everything at once."

Chapter 20
The End of the Middle Ages

The Miss Alans did go to Greece, but they went by themselves. They alone of this little company will double Malea and plough the waters of the Saronic gulf. They alone will visit Athens and Delphi, and either shrine of intellectual song—that upon the Acropolis, encircled by blue seas; that under Parnassus, where the eagles build and the bronze charioteer drives undismayed towards infinity. Trembling, anxious, cumbered with much digestive bread, they did proceed to Constantinople, they did go round the world. The rest of us must be contented with a fair, but a less arduous, goal. *Italiam petimus*: we return to the Pension Bertolini.

George said it was his old room.

"No, it isn't," said Lucy; "because it is the room I had, and I had your father's room. I forget why; Charlotte made me, for some reason."

He knelt on the tiled floor, and laid his face in her lap.

"George, you baby, get up."

"Why shouldn't I be a baby?" murmured George.

Unable to answer this question, she put down his sock, which she was trying to mend, and gazed out through the window. It was evening and again the spring.

"Oh, bother Charlotte," she said thoughtfully. "What can such people be made of?"

"Same stuff as parsons are made of."

"Nonsense!"

"Quite right. It is nonsense."

"Now you get up off the cold floor, or you'll be starting rheumatism next, and you stop laughing and being so silly."

"Why shouldn't I laugh?" he asked, pinning her with

his elbows, and advancing his face to hers. "What's there to cry at? Kiss me here." He indicated the spot where a kiss would be welcome.

He was a boy, after all. When it came to the point, it was she who remembered the past, she into whose soul the iron had entered, she who knew whose this room had been last year. It endeared him to her strangely that he should be sometimes wrong.

"Any letters?" he asked.

"Just a line from Freddy."

"Now kiss me here; then here."

Then, threatened again with rheumatism, he strolled to the window, opened it (as the English will), and leant out. There was the parapet, there the river, there to the left the beginnings of the hills. The cab-driver, who at once saluted him with the hiss of a serpent, might be that very Phaethon who had set this happiness in motion twelve months ago. A passion of gratitude—all feelings grow to passions in the South—came over the husband, and he blessed the people and the things who had taken so much trouble about a young fool. He had helped himself, it is true, but how stupidly! All the fighting that mattered had been done by others—by Italy, by his father, by his wife.

"Lucy, you come and look at the cypresses; and the church, whatever its name is, still shows."

"San Miniato. I'll just finish your sock."

"Signorino, domani faremo un giro," called the cabman, with engaging certainty.

George told him that he was mistaken; they had no money to throw away on driving.

And the people who had not meant to help—the Miss Lavishes, the Cecils, the Miss Bartletts! Ever prone to magnify Fate, George counted up the forces that had swept him into this contentment.

"Anything good in Freddy's letter?"

"Not yet."

His own content was absolute, but hers held bitterness: the Honeychurches had not forgiven them; they were disgusted at her past hypocrisy; she had alienated Windy Corner, perhaps for ever.

"What does he say?"

"Silly boy! He thinks he's being dignified. He knew we should go off in the spring—he has known it for six months—that if mother wouldn't give her consent we should take the thing into our own hands. They had fair warning, and now he calls it an elopement. Ridiculous boy—"

"Signorino, domani faremo un giro—"

"But it will all come right in the end. He has to build us both up from the beginning again. I wish, though, that Cecil had not turned so cynical about women. He has, for the second time, quite altered. Why will men have theories about women? I haven't any about men. I wish, too, that Mr Beebe—"

"You may well wish that."

"He will never forgive us—I mean, he will never be interested in us again. I wish that he did not influence them so much at Windy Corner. I wish he hadn't—but if we act the truth, the people who really love us are sure to come back to us in the long run."

"Perhaps." Then he said more gently: "Well, I acted the truth—the only thing I did do—and you came back to me. So possibly you know." He turned back into the room. "Nonsense with that sock." He carried her to the window, so that she, too, saw all the view. They sank upon their knees invisible from the road, they hoped, and began to whisper one another's names. Ah! it was worth while; it was the great joy that they had expected, and countless little joys of which they had never dreamt. They were silent.

"Signorino, domani faremo—"

"Oh, bother that man!"

But Lucy remembered the vendor of photographs and said, "No, don't be rude to him." Then, with a catching of her breath, she murmured: "Mr Eager and Charlotte, dreadful frozen Charlotte! How cruel she would be to a man like that!"

"Look at the lights going over the bridge."

"But this room reminds me of Charlotte. How horrible to grow old in Charlotte's way! To think that evening at the rectory that she shouldn't have heard your father was in the house. For she would have stopped me going in, and he was the only person alive who could have made me see sense. You couldn't have made me. When I am very happy"—she kissed him—"I remember on how little it all hangs. If Charlotte had only known, she would have stopped me going in, and I should have gone to silly Greece, and become different for ever."

"But she did know," said George; "she did see my father, surely. He said so."

"Oh no, she didn't see him. She was upstairs with old Mrs Beebe, don't you remember, and then went straight to the church. She said so."

George was obstinate again. "My father," said he, "saw her, and I prefer his word. He was dozing by the study fire, and he opened his eyes, and there was Miss Bartlett. A few minutes before you came in. She was turning to go as he woke up. He didn't speak to her."

Then they spoke of other things—the desultory talk of those who have been fighting to reach one another, and whose reward is to rest quietly in each other's arms. It was long ere they returned to Miss Bartlett, but when they did her behaviour seemed more interesting. George, who disliked any darkness, said: "It's clear that she knew. Then, why did she risk the meeting? She knew he was there, and yet she went to church."

They tried to piece the thing together.

As they talked, an incredible solution came into Lucy's mind. She rejected it, and said: "How like Charlotte to undo her work by a feeble muddle at the last moment." But something in the dying evening, in the roar of the river, in their very embrace, warned them that her words fell short of life, and George whispered: "Or did she mean it?"

"Mean what?"

"Signorino, domani faremo un giro—"

Lucy bent forward and said with gentleness: "Lascia, prego, lascia. Siamo sposati."

"Scusi tanto, signora," he replied, in tones as gentle, and whipped up his horse.

"Buona sera—e grazie."

"Niente."

The cabman drove away singing.

"Mean what, George?"

He whispered: "Is it this? Is this possible? I'll put a marvel to you. That your cousin has always hoped. That from the very first moment we met, she hoped, far down in her mind, that we should be like this—of course, very far down. That she fought us on the surface, and yet she hoped. I can't explain her any other way. Can you? Look how she kept me alive in you all the summer; how she gave you no peace; how month after month she became more eccentric and unreliable. The sight of us haunted her—or she couldn't have described us as she did to her friend. There are details—it burned. I read the book afterwards. She is not frozen, Lucy, she is not withered up all through. She tore us apart twice, but in the rectory that evening she was given one more chance to make us happy. We can never make friends with her or thank her. But I do believe that, far down in her heart, far below all speech and behaviour, she is glad."

"It is impossible," murmured Lucy, and then, remembering the experiences of her own heart, she said: "No—it is just possible."

Youth enwrapped them; the song of Phaethon announced passion requited, love attained. But they were conscious of a love more mysterious than this. The song died away; they heard the river, bearing down the snows of winter into the Mediterranean.

A PASSAGE TO INDIA

Part 1

Mosque

Chapter 1

Except for the Marabar Caves—and they are twenty miles off—the city of Chandrapore presents nothing extraordinary. Edged rather than washed by the river Ganges, it trails for a couple of miles along the bank, scarcely distinguishable from the rubbish it deposits so freely. There are no bathing-steps on the river front, as the Ganges happens not to be holy here; indeed there is no river front, and bazaars shut out the wide and shifting panorama of the stream. The streets are mean, the temples ineffective, and though a few fine houses exist they are hidden away in gardens or down alleys whose filth deters all but the invited guest. Chandrapore was never large or beautiful, but two hundred years ago it lay on the road between Upper India, then imperial, and the sea, and the fine houses date from that period. The zest for decoration stopped in the eighteenth century, nor was it ever democratic. In the bazaars there is no painting and scarcely any carving. The very wood seems made of mud, the inhabitants of mud moving. So abased, so monotonous is everything that meets the eye, that when the Ganges comes down it might be expected to wash the excrescence back into the soil. Houses do fall, people are drowned and left rotting, but the general outline of the town persists, swelling here, shrinking there, like some low but indestructible form of life.

Inland, the prospect alters. There is an oval maidan, and a long sallow hospital. Houses belonging to Eurasians stand on the high ground by the railway station. Beyond the railway—which runs parallel to the river—the land sinks, then rises again rather steeply. On this second rise is laid out the little Civil Station, and viewed hence Chandrapore appears to be a totally different place. It is a city of gardens.

It is no city, but a forest sparsely scattered with huts. It is a tropical pleasance, washed by a noble river. The toddy palms and neem trees and mangoes and peepul that were hidden behind the bazaars now become visible and in their turn hide the bazaars. They rise from the gardens whose ancient tanks nourish them, they burst out of stifling purlieus and unconsidered temples. Seeking light and air, and endowed with more strength than man or his works, they soar above the lower deposit to greet one another with branches and beckoning leaves, and to build a city for the birds. Especially after the rains do they screen what passes below, but at all times, even when scorched or leafless, they glorify the city to the English people who inhabit the rise, so that newcomers cannot believe it to be as meagre as it is described, and have to be driven down to acquire disillusionment. As for the Civil Station itself, it provokes no emotion. It charms not, neither does it repel. It is sensibly planned, with a red-brick Club on its brow, and further back a grocer's and a cemetery, and the bungalows are disposed along roads that intersect at right angles. It has nothing hideous in it, and only the view is beautiful; it shares nothing with the city except the overarching sky.

The sky too has its changes, but they are less marked than those of the vegetation and the river. Clouds map it up at times, but it is normally a dome of blending tints, and the main tint blue. By day the blue will pale down into white where it touches the white of the land, after sunset it has a new circumference—orange, melting upwards into tenderest purple. But the core of blue persists, and so it is by night. Then the stars hang like lamps from the immense vault. The distance between the earth and them is as nothing to the distance behind them; and that further distance, though beyond colour, last freed itself from blue.

The sky settles everything—not only climates and seasons, but when the earth shall be beautiful. By herself she can do little—only feeble outbursts of flowers. But when the sky chooses, glory can rain into the Chandrapore bazaars, or a benediction pass from horizon to horizon. The sky can do this because it is so strong and so enormous. Strength comes from the sun, infused in it daily, size from the prostrate earth. No mountains infringe on the curve. League after league the earth lies flat, heaves a little, is flat again. Only in the south, where a group of fists and fingers are thrust up through the soil, is the endless expanse interrupted. These fists and fingers are the Marabar Hills, containing the extraordinary caves.

Chapter 2

Abandoning his bicycle, which fell before a servant could catch it, the young man sprang up onto the veranda. He was all animation. "Hamidullah, Hamidullah! Am I late?" he cried.

"Do not apologize," said his host. "You are always late."

"Kindly answer my question. Am I late? Has Mahmoud Ali eaten all the food? If so I go elsewhere. Mr Mahmoud Ali, how are you?"

"Thank you, Dr Aziz, I am dying."

"Dying before your dinner? Oh, poor Mahmoud Ali!"

"Hamidullah here is actually dead. He passed away just as you rode up on your bike."

"Yes, that is so," said the other. "Imagine us both as addressing you from another and a happier world."

"Does there happen to be such a thing as a hookah in that happier world of yours?"

"Aziz, don't chatter. We are having a very sad talk."

The hookah had been packed too tight, as was usual in his friend's house, and bubbled sulkily. He coaxed it. Yielding at last, the tobacco jetted up into his lungs and nostrils, driving out the smoke of burning cow-dung that had filled them as he rode through the bazaar. It was delicious. He lay in a trance, sensuous but healthy, through which the talk of the two others did not seem particularly sad—they were discussing as to whether or no it is possible to be friends with an Englishman. Mahmoud Ali argued that it was not, Hamidullah disagreed, but with so many reservations that there was no friction between them. Delicious indeed to lie on the broad veranda with the moon rising in front and the servants preparing dinner behind, and no trouble happening.

"Well, look at my own experience this morning."

"I only contend that it is possible in England," replied Hamidullah, who had been to that country long ago, before the big rush, and had received a cordial welcome at Cambridge.

"It is impossible here. Aziz! The red-nosed boy has again insulted me in court. I do not blame him. He was told that he ought to insult me. Until lately he was quite a nice boy, but the others have got hold of him."

"Yes, they have no chance here, that is my point. They come out intending to be gentlemen, and are told it will not do. Look at Lesley, look at Blakiston, now it is your red-nosed boy, and Fielding will go next. Why, I remember when Turton came out first. It was in another part of the Province. You fellows will not believe me, but I have driven with Turton in his carriage—Turton! Oh yes, we were once quite intimate. He has shown me his stamp collection."

"He would expect you to steal it now. Turton! But red-nosed boy will be far worse than Turton!"

"I do not think so. They all become exactly the same—not worse, not better. I give any Englishman two years, be he Turton or Burton. It is only the difference of a letter. And I give any Englishwoman six months. All are exactly alike. Do you not agree with me?"

"I do not," replied Mahmoud Ali, entering into the bitter fun, and feeling both pain and amusement at each word that was uttered. "For my own part I find such profound differences among our rulers. Red-nose mumbles, Turton talks distinctly, Mrs Turton takes bribes, Mrs Red-nose does not and cannot, because so far there is no Mrs Red-nose."

"Bribes?"

"Did you not know that when they were lent to Central India over a canal scheme some rajah or other gave her a sewing machine in solid gold so that the water should run through his state?"

"And does it?"

"No, that is where Mrs Turton is so skilful. When we poor blacks take bribes, we perform what we are bribed to perform, and the law discovers us in consequence. The English take and do nothing. I admire them."

"We all admire them. Aziz, please pass me the hookah."

"Oh, not yet—hookah is so jolly now."

"You are a very selfish boy." He raised his voice suddenly, and shouted for dinner. Servants shouted back that it was ready. They meant that they wished it was ready, and were so understood, for nobody moved. Then Hamidullah continued, but with changed manner and evident emotion.

"But take my case—the case of young Hugh Bannister. Here is the son of my dear, my dead friends, the Reverend and Mrs Bannister, whose goodness to me in England I shall never forget or describe. They were father and mother to me, I talked to them as I do now. In the vacations their rectory became my home. They entrusted all their children to me—I often carried little Hugh about—I took him up to the funeral of Queen Victoria, and held him in my arms above the crowd."

"Queen Victoria was different," murmured Mahmoud Ali.

"I learn now that this boy is in business as a leather merchant at Cawnpore. Imagine how I long to see him and to pay his fare that this house may be his home. But it is useless. The other Anglo-Indians will have got hold of him long ago. He will probably think that I want something, and I cannot face that from the son of my old friends. Oh, what in this country has gone wrong with everything, Vakil Sahib? I ask you."

Aziz joined in. "Why talk about the English? Brrrr . . . ! Why be either friends with the fellows or not friends? Let us shut them out and be jolly. Queen Victoria and Mrs Bannister were the only exceptions, and they're dead."

"No, no, I do not admit that, I have met others."

"So have I," said Mahmoud Ali, unexpectedly veering. "All ladies are far from alike." Their mood was changed, and they recalled little kindnesses and courtesies. "She said 'Thank you so much' in the most natural way." "She offered me a lozenge when the dust irritated my throat." Hamidullah could remember more important examples of angelic ministration, but the other, who only knew Anglo-India, had to ransack his memory for scraps, and it was not surprising that he should return to "But of course all this is exceptional. The exception does not prove the rule. The average woman is like Mrs Turton, and, Aziz, you know what she is." Aziz did not know, but said he did. He too generalized from his disappointments—it is difficult for members of a subject race to do otherwise. Granted the exceptions, he agreed that all Englishwomen are haughty and venal. The gleam passed from the conversation, whose wintry surface unrolled and expanded interminably.

A servant announced dinner. They ignored him. The elder men had reached their eternal politics, Aziz drifted into the garden. The trees smelt sweet—green-blossomed champak—and scraps of Persian poetry came into his head. Dinner, dinner, dinner . . . but when he returned to the house for it Mahmoud Ali had drifted away in his turn, to speak to his sais. "Come and see my wife a little then," said Hamidullah, and they spent twenty minutes behind the purdah. Hamidullah Begum was a distant aunt of Aziz, and the only female relative he had in Chandrapore, and she had much to say to him on this occasion about a family circumcision that had been celebrated with imperfect pomp. It was difficult to get away, because until they had had their dinner she would not begin hers, and consequently prolonged her remarks in case they should suppose she was impatient. Having censured the circumcision, she bethought her of kindred topics, and asked Aziz when he was going to be married.

Respectful but irritated, he answered, "Once is enough."

"Yes, he has done his duty," said Hamidullah. "Do not tease him so. He carries on his family, two boys and their sister."

"Aunt, they live most comfortably with my wife's mother, where she was living when she died. I can see them whenever I like. They are such very, very small children."

"And he sends them the whole of his salary and lives like a low-grade clerk, and tells no one the reason. What more do you require him to do?"

But this was not Hamidullah Begum's point, and having courteously changed the conversation for a few moments she returned and made it. She said: "What is to become of all our daughters if men refuse to marry? They will marry beneath them, or—" And she began the oft-told tale of a lady of imperial descent who could find no husband in the narrow circle where her pride permitted her to mate, and had lived on unwed, her age now thirty, and would die unwed, for no one would have her now. While the tale was in progress, it convinced the two men, the tragedy seemed a slur on the whole community; better polygamy almost, than that a woman should die without the joys God has intended her to receive. Wedlock, motherhood, power in the house—for what else is she born, and how can the man who has denied them to her stand up to face her creator and his own at the last day? Aziz took his leave saying "Perhaps . . . but later . . ."—his invariable reply to such an appeal.

"You mustn't put off what you think right," said Hamidullah. "That is why India is in such a plight, because we put off things." But seeing that his young relative looked worried he added a few soothing words, and thus wiped out any impression that his wife might have made.

During their absence, Mahmoud Ali had gone off in his carriage, leaving a message that he should be back in five minutes, but they were on no account to wait. They sat down to meat with a distant cousin of the house, Mohammed Latif, who lived on Hamidullah's bounty and who occupied the position neither of a servant nor of an equal. He did not speak unless spoken to, and since no one spoke kept unoffended silence. Now and then he belched, in compliment to the richness of the food. A gentle, happy and dishonest old man; all his life he had never done a stroke of work. So long as someone of his relatives had a house he was sure of a home, and it was unlikely that so large a family would all go bankrupt. His wife led a similar existence some hundreds of miles away—he did not visit her, owing to the expense of the railway ticket. Presently Aziz chaffed him, also the servants, and then began quoting poetry: Persian, Urdu, a little Arabic. His memory was good, and for so young a man he had read largely; the themes he preferred were the decay of Islam and the brevity of love. They listened delighted, for they took the public view of poetry, not the private which obtains in England. It never bored them to hear words, words; they breathed them with the cool night air, never stopping to analyse; the name of the poet, Hafiz, Hali, Iqbal, was sufficient guarantee. India—a hundred Indias—whispered outside beneath the indifferent moon, but for the time India seemed one and their own, and they regained their departed greatness by hearing its departure lamented, they felt young again because reminded that youth must fly. A servant in scarlet interrupted him; he was the chuprassy of the Civil Surgeon, and he handed Aziz a note.

"Old Callendar wants to see me at his bungalow," he said, not rising. "He might have the politeness to say why."

"Some case, I dare say."

"I dare say not, I dare say nothing. He has found out our dinner-hour, that's all, and chooses to interrupt us every time, in order to show his power."

"On the one hand he always does this, on the other it may be a serious case, and you cannot know," said Hamidullah, considerately paving the way towards obedience. "Had you not better clean your teeth after pan?"

"If my teeth are to be cleaned, I don't go at all. I am an Indian, it is an Indian habit to take pan. The Civil Surgeon must put up with it. Mohammed Latif, my bike, please."

The poor relation got up. Slightly immersed in the realms of matter, he laid his hand on the bicycle's saddle, while a servant did the actual wheeling. Between them they took it over a tin-tack. Aziz held his hands under the ewer, dried them, fitted on his green felt hat, and then with unexpected energy whizzed out of Hamidullah's compound.

"Aziz, Aziz, imprudent boy. . . ." But he was far down the bazaar, riding furiously. He had neither light nor bell nor had he a brake, but what use are such adjuncts in a land where the cyclist's only hope is to coast from face to face, and just before he collides with each it vanishes? And the city was fairly empty at this hour. When his tyre went flat, he leapt off and shouted for a tonga.

He did not at first find one, and he had also to dispose of his bicycle at a friend's house. He dallied furthermore to clean his teeth. But at last he was rattling towards the Civil Lines, with a vivid sense of speed. As he entered their arid tidiness, depression suddenly seized him. The roads, named after victorious generals and intersecting at right angles, were symbolic of the net Great Britain had thrown over India. He felt caught in their meshes. When he turned into Major Callendar's compound he could with difficulty restrain himself from getting down from the tonga and approaching the bungalow on foot, and this not because his soul was servile but because his feelings—the sensitive edges of him—feared a gross snub. There had been a "case" last year—an Indian gentleman had driven up to an official's house and been turned back by the servants and told to approach more suitably—only one case among thousands of visits to hundreds of officials, but its fame spread wide. The young man shrank from a repetition of it. He compromised, and stopped the driver just outside the flood of light that fell across the veranda.

The Civil Surgeon was out.

"But the sahib has left me some message?"

The servant returned an indifferent "No". Aziz was in despair. It was a servant whom he had forgotten to tip, and he could do nothing now because there were people in the hall. He was convinced that there was a message, and that the man was withholding it out of revenge. While they argued, the people came out. Both were ladies. Aziz lifted his hat. The first, who was in evening dress, glanced at the Indian and turned instinctively away.

"Mrs Lesley, it *is* a tonga," she cried.

"Ours?" inquired the second, also seeing Aziz, and doing likewise.

"Take the gifts the gods provide, anyhow," she screeched,

and both jumped in. "O tonga-wallah, Club, Club. Why doesn't the fool go?"

"Go, I will pay you tomorrow," said Aziz to the driver, and as they went off he called courteously, "You are most welcome, ladies." They did not reply, being full of their own affairs.

So it had come, the usual thing—just as Mahmoud Ali said. The inevitable snub—his bow ignored, his carriage taken. It might have been worse, for it comforted him somehow that Mesdames Callendar and Lesley should both be fat and weigh the tonga down behind. Beautiful women would have pained him. He turned to the servant, gave him a couple of rupees, and asked again whether there was a message. The man, now very civil, returned the same answer. Major Callendar had driven away half an hour before.

"Saying nothing?"

He had as a matter of fact said, "Damn Aziz"—words that the servant understood, but was too polite to repeat. One can tip too much as well as too little, indeed the coin that buys the exact truth has not yet been minted.

"Then I will write him a letter."

He was offered the use of the house, but was too dignified to enter it. Paper and ink were brought onto the veranda. He began: "Dear Sir,—At your express command I have hastened as a subordinate should—" and then stopped. "Tell him I have called, that is sufficient," he said, tearing the protest up. "Here is my card. Call me a tonga."

"Huzoor, all are at the Club."

"Then telephone for one down to the railway station." And since the man hastened to do this he said, "Enough, enough, I prefer to walk." He commandeered a match and lit a cigarette. These attentions, though purchased, soothed him. They would last as long as he had rupees, which is something. But to shake the dust of Anglo-India off his feet! To escape from the net and be back among manners and gestures that he knew! He began to walk, an unwonted exercise.

He was an athletic little man, daintily put together, but

really very strong. Nevertheless walking fatigued him, as it fatigues everyone in India except the newcomer. There is something hostile in that soil. It either yields, and the foot sinks into a depression, or else it is unexpectedly rigid and sharp, pressing stones or crystals against the tread. A series of these little surprises exhausts; and he was wearing pumps, a poor preparation for any country. At the edge of the Civil Station he turned into a mosque to rest.

He had always liked this mosque. It was gracious, and the arrangement pleased him. The courtyard—entered through a ruined gate—contained an ablution-tank of fresh clear water, which was always in motion, being indeed part of a conduit that supplied the city. The courtyard was paved with broken slabs. The covered part of the mosque was deeper than is usual; its effect was that of an English parish church whose side has been taken out. Where he sat, he looked into three arcades whose darkness was illuminated by a small hanging lamp and by the moon. The front—in full moonlight—had the appearance of marble, and the ninety-nine names of God on the frieze stood out black, as the frieze stood out white against the sky. The contrast between this dualism and the contention of shadows within pleased Aziz, and he tried to symbolize the whole into some truth of religion or love. A mosque by winning his approval let loose his imagination. The temple of another creed, Hindu, Christian or Greek, would have bored him and failed to awaken his sense of beauty. Here was Islam, his own country, more than a Faith, more than a battle-cry, more, much more . . . Islam, an attitude towards life both exquisite and durable, where his body and his thoughts found their home.

His seat was the low wall that bounded the courtyard on the left. The ground fell away beneath him towards the city, visible as a blur of trees, and in the stillness he heard many small sounds. On the right, over in the Club, the English community contributed an amateur orchestra. Elsewhere some Hindus were drumming—he knew they were Hindus, because the rhythm was uncongenial to him—and others were bewailing a corpse—he knew whose, having certified it in the afternoon. There were owls, the Punjab mail . . . and flowers smelt deliciously in the station-master's garden. But the mosque—that alone signified, and he returned to it from the complex appeal of the night, and decked it with meanings the builder had never intended. Some day he too would build a mosque, smaller than this but in perfect taste, so that all who passed by should experience the happiness he felt now. And near it, under a low dome, should be his tomb, with a Persian inscription:

> Alas, without me for thousands of years
> The Rose will blossom and the Spring will bloom,
> But those who have secretly understood my heart—
> They will approach and visit the grave where I lie.

He had seen the quatrain on the tomb of a Deccan king and regarded it as profound philosophy—he always held pathos to be profound. The secret understanding of the heart! He repeated the phrase with tears in his eyes, and as he did so one of the pillars of the mosque seemed to quiver. It swayed in the gloom and detached itself. Belief in ghosts ran in his blood, but he sat firm. Another pillar moved, a third, and then an Englishwoman stepped out into the moonlight. Suddenly he was furiously angry and shouted: "Madam! Madam! Madam!"

"Oh! Oh!" the woman gasped.

"Madam, this is a mosque, you have no right here at all; you should have taken off your shoes; this is a holy place for Moslems."

"I have taken them off."

"You have?"

"I left them at the entrance."

"Then I ask your pardon."

Still startled, the woman moved out, keeping the ablution-tank between them. He called after her, "I am truly sorry for speaking."

"Yes, I was right, was I not? If I remove my shoes, I am allowed?"

"Of course, but so few ladies take the trouble, especially if thinking no one is there to see."

"That makes no difference. God is here."

"Madam!"

"Please let me go."

"Oh, can I do you some service now or at any time?"

"No, thank you, really none—good night."

"May I know your name?"

She was now in the shadow of the gateway, so that he could not see her face, but she saw his, and she said with a change of voice, "Mrs Moore."

"Mrs—" Advancing, he found that she was old. A fabric bigger than the mosque fell to pieces, and he did not know whether he was glad or sorry. She was older than Hamidullah Begum, with a red face and white hair. Her voice had deceived him.

"Mrs Moore, I am afraid I startled you. I shall tell our community—my friends—about you. That God is here—very good, very fine indeed. I think you are newly arrived in India."

"Yes—how did you know?"

"By the way you address me. No, but can I call you a carriage?"

"I have only come from the Club. They are doing a play that I have seen in London, and it was so hot."

"What was the name of the play?"

"*Cousin Kate.*"

"I think you ought not to walk at night alone, Mrs Moore. There are bad characters about and leopards may come across from the Marabar Hills. Snakes also."

She exclaimed; she had forgotten the snakes.

"For example, a six-spot beetle," he continued. "You pick it up, it bites, you die."

"But you walk alone yourself."

"Oh, I am used to it."

"Used to snakes?"

They both laughed. "I'm a doctor," he said. "Snakes don't dare bite me." They sat down side by side in the entrance, and slipped on their evening shoes. "Please may I ask you a question now? Why do you come to India at this time of year, just as the cold weather is ending?"

"I intended to start earlier, but there was an unavoidable delay."

"It will soon be so unhealthy for you! And why ever do you come to Chandrapore?"

"To visit my son. He is the City Magistrate here."

"Oh no, excuse me, that is quite impossible. Our City Magistrate's name is Mr Heaslop. I know him intimately."

"He's my son all the same," she said, smiling.

"But, Mrs Moore, how can he be?"

"I was married twice."

"Yes, now I see, and your first husband died."

"He did, and so did my second husband."

"Then we are in the same box," he said cryptically. "Then is the City Magistrate the entire of your family now?"

"No, there are the younger ones—Ralph and Stella in England."

"And the gentleman here, is he Ralph and Stella's half-brother?"

"Quite right."

"Mrs Moore, this is all extremely strange, because like yourself I have also two sons and a daughter. Is not this the same box with a vengeance?"

"What are their names? Not also Ronny, Ralph and Stella, surely?"

The suggestion delighted him. "No, indeed. How funny it sounds! Their names are quite different and will surprise you. Listen, please. I am about to tell you my children's names. The first is called Ahmed, the second is called Karim, the third—she is the eldest—Jamila. Three children are enough. Do not you agree with me?"

"I do."

They were both silent for a little, thinking of their respective families. She sighed and rose to go.

"Would you care to see over the Minto Hospital one

morning?" he inquired. "I have nothing else to offer at Chandrapore."

"Thank you, I have seen it already, or I should have liked to come with you very much."

"I suppose the Civil Surgeon took you."

"Yes, and Mrs Callendar."

His voice altered. "Ah! A very charming lady."

"Possibly, when one knows her better."

"What? What? You didn't like her?"

"She was certainly intending to be kind, but I did not find her exactly charming."

He burst out with: "She has just taken my tonga without my permission—do you call that being charming?—and Major Callendar interrupts me night after night from where I am dining with my friends and I go at once, breaking up a most pleasant entertainment, and he is not there and not even a message. Is this charming, pray? But what does it matter? I can do nothing and he knows it. I am just a subordinate, my time is of no value, the veranda is good enough for an Indian, yes, yes, let him stand, and Mrs Callendar takes my carriage and cuts me dead. . . ."

She listened.

He was excited partly by his wrongs, but much more by the knowledge that someone sympathized with them. It was this that led him to repeat, exaggerate, contradict. She had proved her sympathy by criticizing her fellow countrywoman to him, but even earlier he had known. The flame that not even beauty can nourish was springing up, and though his words were querulous his heart began to glow secretly. Presently it burst into speech.

"You understand me, you know what I feel. Oh, if others resembled you!"

Rather surprised, she replied: "I don't think I understand people very well. I only know whether I like or dislike them."

"Then you are an Oriental."

She accepted his escort back to the Club, and said at the gate that she wished she was a member, so that she could have asked him in.

"Indians are not allowed into the Chandrapore Club even as guests," he said simply. He did not expatiate on his wrongs now, being happy. As he strolled downhill beneath the lovely moon, and again saw the lovely mosque, he seemed to own the land as much as anyone owned it. What did it matter if a few flabby Hindus had preceded him there, and a few chilly English succeeded?

Chapter 3

The third act of *Cousin Kate* was well advanced by the time Mrs Moore re-entered the Club. Windows were barred, lest the servants should see their memsahibs acting, and the heat was consequently immense. One electric fan revolved like a wounded bird, another was out of order. Disinclined to return to the audience, she went into the billiard-room, where she was greeted by "I want to see the *real* India," and her appropriate life came back with a rush. This was Adela Quested, the queer, cautious girl whom Ronny had commissioned her to bring from England, and Ronny was her son, also cautious, whom Miss Quested would probably though not certainly marry, and she herself was an elderly lady.

"I want to see it too, and I only wish we could. Apparently the Turtons will arrange something for next Tuesday."

"It'll end in an elephant ride, it always does. Look at this evening. *Cousin Kate*! Imagine, *Cousin Kate*! But where have you been off to? Did you succeed in catching the moon in the Ganges?"

The two ladies had happened, the night before, to see the moon's reflection in a distant channel of the stream. The water had drawn it out, so that it had seemed larger than the real moon, and brighter, which had pleased them.

"I went to the mosque, but I did not catch the moon."

"The angle would have altered—she rises later."

"Later and later," yawned Mrs Moore, who was tired after her walk. "Let me think—we don't see the other side of the moon out here, no."

"Come, India's not as bad as all that," said a pleasant voice. "Other side of the earth, if you like, but we stick to the same old moon." Neither of them knew the speaker, nor did they ever see him again. He passed with his friendly word through red-brick pillars into the darkness.

"We aren't even seeing the other side of the world; that's our complaint," said Adela. Mrs Moore agreed; she too was disappointed at the dullness of their new life. They had made such a romantic voyage across the Mediterranean and through the sands of Egypt to the harbour of Bombay, to find only a gridiron of bungalows at the end of it. But she did not take the disappointment as seriously as Miss Quested, for the reason that she was forty years older, and had learned that life never gives us what we want at the moment that we consider appropriate. Adventures do occur, but not punctually. She said again that she hoped that something interesting would be arranged for next Tuesday.

"Have a drink," said another pleasant voice. "Mrs Moore—Miss Quested—have a drink, have two drinks." They knew who it was this time—the Collector, Mr Turton, with whom they had dined. Like themselves, he had found the atmosphere of *Cousin Kate* too hot. Ronny, he told them, was stage-managing in place of Major Callendar, whom some native subordinate or other had let down, and doing it very well; then he turned to Ronny's other merits, and in quiet, decisive tones said much that was flattering. It wasn't that the young man was particularly good at the games or the lingo, or that he had much notion of the Law, but—apparently a large but—Ronny was dignified.

Mrs Moore was surprised to learn this, dignity not being a quality with which any mother credits her son. Miss Quested learned it with anxiety, for she had not decided whether she liked dignified men. She tried indeed to discuss this point with Mr Turton, but he silenced her with a good-humoured motion of his hand, and continued what he had come to say. "The long and the short of it is, Heaslop's a sahib; he's the type we want, he's one of us," and another civilian who was leaning over the billiard-table said, "Hear, hear!" The matter was thus placed beyond doubt, and the Collector passed on, for other duties called him.

Meanwhile the performance ended, and the amateur

orchestra played the National Anthem. Conversation and billiards stopped, faces stiffened. It was the Anthem of the Army of Occupation. It reminded every member of the Club that he or she was British and in exile. It produced a little sentiment and a useful accession of will-power. The meagre tune, the curt series of demands on Jehovah, fused into a prayer unknown in England, and though they perceived neither Royalty nor Deity they did perceive something, they were strengthened to resist another day. Then they poured out, offering one another drinks.

"Adela, have a drink; mother, a drink."

They refused—they were weary of drinks—and Miss Quested, who always said exactly what was in her mind, announced anew that she was desirous of seeing the real India.

Ronny was in high spirits. The request struck him as comic, and he called out to another passer-by: "Fielding! How's one to see the real India?"

"Try seeing Indians," the man answered, and vanished.

"Who was that?"

"Our schoolmaster—Government College."

"As if one could avoid seeing them," sighed Mrs Lesley.

"I've avoided," said Miss Quested. "Excepting my own servant, I've scarcely spoken to an Indian since landing."

"Oh, lucky you."

"But I want to see them."

She became the centre of an amused group of ladies. One said: "Wanting to see Indians! How new that sounds!" Another: "Natives! Why, fancy!" A third, more serious, said: "Let me explain. Natives don't respect one any the more after meeting one, you see."

"That occurs after so many meetings."

But the lady, entirely stupid and friendly, continued: "What I mean is, I was a nurse before my marriage, and came across them a great deal, so I know. I really do know the truth about Indians. A most unsuitable position for any Englishwoman—I was a nurse in a Native State. One's only hope was to hold sternly aloof."

"Even from one's patients?"

"Why, the kindest thing one can do to a native is to let him die," said Mrs Callendar.

"How if he went to heaven?" asked Mrs Moore, with a gentle but crooked smile.

"He can go where he likes as long as he doesn't come near me. They give me the creeps."

"As a matter of fact I have thought about what you were saying about heaven, and that is why I am against missionaries," said the lady who had been a nurse. "I am all for chaplains, but all against missionaries. Let me explain."

But before she could do so the Collector intervened.

"Do you really want to meet the Aryan Brother, Miss Quested? That can be easily fixed up. I didn't realize he'd amuse you." He thought a moment. "You can practically see any type you like. Take your choice. I know the Government people and the landowners, Heaslop here can get hold of the barrister crew, while if you want to specialize on education we can come down on Fielding."

"I'm tired of seeing picturesque figures pass before me as a frieze," the girl explained. "It was wonderful when we landed, but that superficial glamour soon goes."

Her impressions were of no interest to the Collector; he was only concerned to give her a good time. Would she like a Bridge Party? He explained to her what that was—not the game, but a party to bridge the gulf between East and West; the expression was his own invention, and amused all who heard it.

"I only want to meet those Indians whom you come across socially—as your friends."

"Well, we don't come across them socially," he said, laughing. "They're full of all the virtues, but we don't, and it's now eleven-thirty, and too late to go into the reasons."

"Miss Quested, what a name!" remarked Mrs Turton to her husband as they drove away. She had not taken to the new young lady, thinking her ungracious and cranky. She trusted that she hadn't been brought out to marry nice little Heaslop, though it looked like it. Her husband agreed with her in his heart, but he never spoke against an Englishwoman if he could avoid doing so, and he only said that Miss Quested naturally made mistakes. He added: "India does wonders for the judgement, especially during the Hot Weather; it has even done wonders for Fielding." Mrs Turton closed her eyes at this name and remarked that Mr Fielding wasn't pukka, and had better marry Miss Quested, for she wasn't pukka. Then they reached their bungalow, low and enormous, the oldest and most uncomfortable bungalow in the Civil Station, with a sunk soup-plate of a lawn, and they had one drink more, this time of barley-water, and went to bed. Their withdrawal from the Club had broken up the evening, which, like all gatherings, had an official tinge. A community that bows the knee to a Viceroy and believes that the divinity that hedges a king can be transplanted, must feel some reverence for any viceregal substitute. At Chandrapore the Turtons were little gods; soon they would retire to some suburban villa, and die exiled from glory.

"It's decent of the great man," chattered Ronny, much gratified at the civility that had been shown to his guests. "Do you know, he's never given a Bridge Party before? Coming on top of the dinner too! I wish I could have arranged something myself, but when you know the natives better you'll realize it's easier for the Burra Sahib than for me. They know him—they know he can't be fooled—I'm still fresh comparatively. No one can even begin to think of knowing this country until he has been in it twenty years.—Hullo, the mater! Here's your cloak.—Well: for an example of the mistakes one makes. Soon after I came out I asked one of the pleaders to have a smoke with me—only a cigarette, mind. I found afterwards that he had sent touts all over the bazaar to announce the fact—told all the litigants, 'Oh, you'd better come to my Vakil Mahmoud Ali—he's in with the City Magistrate.' Ever since then I've dropped on him in court as hard as I could. It's taught me a lesson, and I hope him."

"Isn't the lesson that you should invite all the pleaders to have a smoke with you?"

"Perhaps, but time's limited and the flesh weak. I prefer my smoke at the Club amongst my own sort, I'm afraid."

"Why not ask the pleaders to the Club?" Miss Quested persisted.

"Not allowed." He was pleasant and patient, and evidently understood why she did not understand. He implied that he had once been as she, though not for long. Going to the veranda, he called firmly to the moon. His sais answered, and without lowering his head he ordered his trap to be brought round.

Mrs Moore, whom the Club had stupefied, woke up outside. She watched the moon, whose radiance stained with primrose the purple of the surrounding sky. In England the moon had seemed dead and alien; here she was caught in the shawl of night together with earth and all the other stars. A sudden sense of unity, of kinship with the heavenly bodies, passed into the old woman and out, like water through a tank, leaving a strange freshness behind. She did not dislike *Cousin Kate* or the National Anthem, but their note had died into a new one, just as cocktails and cigars had died into invisible flowers. When the mosque, long and domeless, gleamed at the turn of the road, she exclaimed, "Oh yes—that's where I got to—that's where I've been."

"Been there when?" asked her son.

"Between the acts."

"But, mother, you can't do that sort of thing."

"Can't mother?" she replied.

"No, really not in this country. It's not done. There's the danger from snakes for one thing. They are apt to lie out in the evening."

"Ah yes, so the young man there said."

"This sounds very romantic," said Miss Quested, who was exceedingly fond of Mrs Moore, and was glad she should have had this little escapade. "You meet a young man in a mosque, and then never let me know!"

"I was going to tell you, Adela, but something changed

the conversation and I forgot. My memory grows deplorable."

"Was he nice?"

She paused, then said emphatically: "Very nice."

"Who was he?" Ronny inquired.

"A doctor. I don't know his name."

"A doctor? I know of no young doctor in Chandrapore. How odd! What was he like?"

"Rather small, with a little moustache and quick eyes. He called out to me when I was in the dark part of the mosque—about my shoes. That was how we began talking. He was afraid I had them on, but I remembered luckily. He told me about his children, and then we walked back to the Club. He knows you well."

"I wish you had pointed him out to me. I can't make out who he is."

"He didn't come into the Club. He said he wasn't allowed to."

Thereupon the truth struck him, and he cried: "Oh, good gracious! Not a Mohammedan? Why ever didn't you tell me you'd been talking to a native? I was going all wrong."

"A Mohammedan! How perfectly magnificent!" exclaimed Miss Quested. "Ronny, isn't that like your mother? While we talk about seeing the real India, she goes and sees it, and then forgets she's seen it."

But Ronny was ruffled. From his mother's description he had thought the doctor might be young Muggins from over the Ganges, and had brought out all the comradely emotions. What a mix-up! Why hadn't she indicated by the tone of her voice that she was talking about an Indian? Scratchy and dictatorial, he began to question her. "He called to you in the mosque, did he? How? Impudently? What was he doing there himself at that time of night?—No, it's not their prayer time."—This in answer to a suggestion of Miss Quested's, who showed the keenest interest. "So he called to you over your shoes. Then it was impudence. It's an old trick. I wish you had had them on."

"I think it was impudence, but I don't know about a trick," said Mrs Moore. "His nerves were all on edge—I could tell from his voice. As soon as I answered he altered."

"You oughtn't to have answered."

"Now look here," said the logical girl, "wouldn't you expect a Mohammedan to answer if you asked him to take off his hat in church?"

"It's different, it's different; you don't understand."

"I know I don't, and I want to. What is the difference, please?"

He wished she wouldn't interfere. His mother did not signify—she was just a globe-trotter, a temporary escort, who could retire to England with what impressions she chose. But Adela, who meditated spending her life in the country, was a more serious matter; it would be tiresome if she started crooked over the native question. Pulling up the mare, he said, "There's your Ganges."

Their attention was diverted. Below them a radiance had suddenly appeared. It belonged neither to water nor moonlight, but stood like a luminous sheaf upon the fields of darkness. He told them that it was where the new sandbank was forming, and that the dark ravelled bit at the top was the sand, and that the dead bodies floated down that way from Benares, or would if the crocodiles let them. "It's not much of a dead body that gets down to Chandrapore."

"Crocodiles down in it too, how terrible!" his mother murmured. The young people glanced at each other and smiled; it amused them when the old lady got these gentle creeps, and harmony was restored between them consequently. She continued: "What a terrible river! What a wonderful river!" and sighed. The radiance was already altering, whether through shifting of the moon or of the sand; soon the bright sheaf would be gone, and a circlet, itself to alter, be burnished upon the streaming void. The women discussed whether they would wait for the change or not, while the silence broke into patches of unquietness and the mare shivered. On her account they did not wait, but drove on to the City Magistrate's bungalow, where Miss

Quested went to bed, and Mrs Moore had a short interview with her son.

He wanted to inquire about the Mohammedan doctor in the mosque. It was his duty to report suspicious characters, and conceivably it was some disreputable hakim who had prowled up from the bazaar. When she told him that it was someone connected with the Minto Hospital, he was relieved, and said that the fellow's name must be Aziz, and that he was quite all right, nothing against him at all.

"Aziz! What a charming name!"

"So you and he had a talk. Did you gather he was well-disposed?"

Ignorant of the force of this question, she replied, "Yes, quite, after the first moment."

"I meant, generally. Did he seem to tolerate us—the brutal conqueror, the sun-dried bureaucrat, that sort of thing?"

"Oh yes, I think so, except the Callendars—he doesn't care for the Callendars at all."

"Oh. So he told you that, did he? The Major will be interested. I wonder what was the aim of the remark."

"Ronny, Ronny! You're never going to pass it on to Major Callendar?"

"Yes, rather. I must, in fact!"

"But, my dear boy—"

"If the Major heard I was disliked by any native subordinate of mine, I should expect him to pass it on to me."

"But, my dear boy—a private conversation!"

"Nothing's private in India. Aziz knew that when he spoke out, so don't you worry. He had some motive in what he said. My personal belief is that the remark wasn't true."

"How not true?"

"He abused the Major in order to impress you."

"I don't know what you mean, dear."

"It's the educated native's latest dodge. They used to cringe, but the younger generation believe in a show of manly independence. They think it will pay better with the itinerant M.P. But whether the native swaggers or cringes there's always something behind every remark he makes, always something, and if nothing else he's trying to increase his izzat—in plain Anglo-Saxon, to score. Of course there are exceptions."

"You never used to judge people like this at home."

"India isn't home," he retorted, rather rudely, but in order to silence her he had been using phrases and arguments that he had picked up from older officials, and he did not feel quite sure of himself. When he said "Of course there are exceptions," he was quoting Mr Turton, while "increasing the izzat" was Major Callendar's own. The phrases worked and were in current use at the Club, but she was rather clever at detecting the first- from the second-hand, and might press him for definite examples.

She only said, "I can't deny that what you say sounds very sensible, but you really must not hand on to Major Callendar anything I have told you about Doctor Aziz."

He felt disloyal to his caste, but he promised, adding, "In return please don't talk about Aziz to Adela."

"Not talk about him? Why?"

"There you go again, mother—I really can't explain everything. I don't want Adela to be worried, that's the fact; she'll begin wondering whether we treat the natives properly, and all that sort of nonsense."

"But she came out to be worried—that's exactly why she's here. She discussed it all on the boat. We had a long talk when we went on shore at Aden. She knows you in play, as she put it, but not in work, and she felt she must come and look round, before she decided—and before you decided. She is very, very fair-minded."

"I know," he said dejectedly.

The note of anxiety in his voice made her feel that he was still a little boy, who must have what he liked, so she promised to do as he wished, and they kissed good night. He had not forbidden her to think about Aziz, however, and she did this when she retired to her room. In the light of her son's comment she reconsidered the scene at the mosque, to see whose impression was correct. Yes, it could be worked into quite an unpleasant scene. The doctor had begun by bullying her, had said Mrs Callendar was nice, and then—finding the ground safe—had changed; he had alternately whined over his grievances and patronized her, had run a dozen ways in a single sentence, had been unreliable, inquisitive, vain. Yes, it was all true, but how false as a summary of the man; the essential life of him had been slain.

Going to hang up her cloak, she found that the tip of the peg was occupied by a small wasp. She had known this wasp or his relatives by day; they were not as English wasps, but had long yellow legs which hung down behind when they flew. Perhaps he mistook the peg for a branch—no Indian animal has any sense of an interior. Bats, rats, birds, insects will as soon nest inside a house as out; it is to them a normal growth of the eternal jungle, which alternately produces houses trees, houses trees. There he clung, asleep, while jackals in the plain bayed their desires and mingled with the percussion of drums.

"Pretty dear," said Mrs Moore to the wasp. He did not wake, but her voice floated out, to swell the night's uneasiness.

Chapter 4

The Collector kept his word. Next day he issued invitation cards to numerous Indian gentlemen in the neighbourhood, stating that he would be at home in the garden of the Club between the hours of five and seven on the following Tuesday, also that Mrs Turton would be glad to receive any ladies of their families who were out of purdah. His action caused much excitement and was discussed in several worlds.

"It is owing to orders from the L.G.," was Mahmoud Ali's explanation. "Turton would never do this unless compelled. Those high officials are different—they sympathize, the Viceroy sympathizes, they would have us treated properly. But they come too seldom and live too far away. Meanwhile—"

"It is easy to sympathize at a distance," said an old gentleman with a beard. "I value more the kind word that is spoken close to my ear. Mr Turton has spoken it, from whatever cause. He speaks, we hear. I do not see why we need discuss it further." Quotations followed from the Koran.

"We have not all your sweet nature, Nawab Bahadur, nor your learning."

"The Lieutenant-Governor may be my very good friend, but I give him no trouble—'How do you do, Nawab Bahadur?' 'Quite well, thank you, Sir Gilbert; how are you?'—and all is over. But I can be a thorn in Mr Turton's flesh, and if he asks me I accept the invitation. I shall come in from Dilkusha specially, though I have to postpone other business."

"You will make yourself chip," suddenly said a little black man.

There was a stir of disapproval. Who was this ill-bred upstart, that he should criticize the leading Mohammedan landowner of the district? Mahmoud Ali, though sharing his opinion, felt bound to oppose it. "Mr Ram Chand!" he said, swaying forward stiffly with his hands on his hips.

"Mr Mahmoud Ali!"

"Mr Ram Chand, the Nawab Bahadur can decide what is cheap without our valuation, I think."

"I do not expect I shall make myself cheap," said the Nawab Bahadur to Mr Ram Chand, speaking very pleasantly, for he was aware that the man had been impolite and he desired to shield him from the consequences. It had passed through his mind to reply, "I expect I shall make myself cheap," but he rejected this as the less courteous alternative. "I do not see why we should make ourselves cheap. I do not see why we should. The invitation is worded very graciously." Feeling that he could not further decrease the social gulf between himself and his auditors, he sent his elegant grandson, who was in attendance on him, to fetch his car. When it came, he repeated all that he had said before, though at greater length, ending up with "Till Tuesday, then, gentlemen all, when I hope we may meet in the flower-gardens of the Club."

This opinion carried great weight. The Nawab Bahadur was a big proprietor and a philanthropist, a man of benevolence and decision. His character among all the communities in the Province stood high. He was a straightforward enemy and a staunch friend, and his hospitality was proverbial. "Give, do not leave; after death who will thank you?" was his favourite remark. He held it a disgrace to die rich. When such a man was prepared to motor twenty-five miles to shake the Collector's hand, the entertainment took another aspect. For he was not like some eminent men, who give out that they will come, and then fail at the last moment, leaving the small fry floundering. If he said he would come, he would come, he would never deceive his supporters. The gentlemen whom he had lectured now urged one another to attend the party, although convinced at heart that his advice was unsound.

He had spoken in the little room near the courts where the

pleaders waited for clients; clients, waiting for pleaders, sat in the dust outside. These had not received a card from Mr Turton. And there were circles even beyond these—people who wore nothing but a loincloth, people who wore not even that, and spent their lives in knocking two sticks together before a scarlet doll—humanity grading and drifting beyond the educated vision, until no earthly invitation can embrace it.

All invitations must proceed from heaven perhaps; perhaps it is futile for men to initiate their own unity, they do but widen the gulfs between them by the attempt. So at all events thought old Mr Graysford and young Mr Sorley, the devoted missionaries who lived out beyond the slaughter-houses, always travelled third on the railways, and never came up to the Club. In our Father's house are many mansions, they taught, and there alone will the incompatible multitudes of mankind be welcomed and soothed. Not one shall be turned away by the servants on that veranda, be he black or white, not one shall be kept standing who approaches with a loving heart. And why should the divine hospitality cease here? Consider, with all reverence, the monkeys. May there not be a mansion for the monkeys also? Old Mr Graysford said No, but young Mr Sorley, who was advanced, said Yes; he saw no reason why monkeys should not have their collateral share of bliss, and he had sympathetic discussions about them with his Hindu friends. And the jackals? Jackals were indeed less to Mr Sorley's mind, but he admitted that the mercy of God, being infinite, may well embrace all mammals. And the wasps? He became uneasy during the descent to wasps, and was apt to change the conversation. And oranges, cactuses, crystals and mud? And the bacteria inside Mr Sorley? No, no, this is going too far. We must exclude someone from our gathering, or we shall be left with nothing.

Chapter 5

The Bridge Party was not a success—at least it was not what Mrs Moore and Miss Quested were accustomed to consider a successful party. They arrived early, since it was given in their honour, but most of the Indian guests had arrived even earlier, and stood massed at the further side of the tennis lawns, doing nothing.

"It is only just five," said Mrs Turton. "My husband will be up from his office in a moment and start the thing. I have no idea what we have to do. It's the first time we've ever given a party like this at the Club. Mr Heaslop, when I'm dead and gone will you give parties like this? It's enough to make the old type of Burra Sahib turn in his grave."

Ronny laughed deferentially. "You wanted something not picturesque and we've provided it," he remarked to Miss Quested. "What do you think of the Aryan Brother in a topi and spats?"

Neither she nor his mother answered. They were gazing rather sadly over the tennis lawn. No, it was not picturesque; the East, abandoning its secular magnificence, was descending into a valley whose further side no man can see.

"The great point to remember is that no one who's here matters; those who matter don't come. Isn't that so, Mrs Turton?"

"Absolutely true," said the great lady, leaning back. She was "saving herself up", as she called it—not for anything that would happen that afternoon or even that week, but for some vague future occasion when a high official might come along and tax her social strength. Most of her public appearances were marked by this air of reserve.

Assured of her approbation, Ronny continued: "The educated Indians will be no good to us if there's a row, it's simply not worth while conciliating them, that's why they don't matter. Most of the people you see are seditious at heart, and the rest'd run squealing. The cultivator—he's another story. The Pathan—he's a man if you like. But these people—don't imagine they're India." He pointed to the dusky line beyond the court, and here and there it flashed a pince-nez or shuffled a shoe, as if aware that he was despising it. European costume had lighted like a leprosy. Few had yielded entirely, but none were untouched. There was a silence when he had finished speaking, on both sides of the court; at least, more ladies joined the English group, but their words seemed to die as soon as uttered. Some kites hovered overhead, impartial, over the kites passed the mass of a vulture, and, with an impartiality exceeding all, the sky, not deeply coloured but translucent, poured light from its whole circumference. It seemed unlikely that the series stopped here. Beyond the sky must not there be something that overarches all the skies, more impartial even than they? Beyond which again. . . .

They spoke of *Cousin Kate.*

They had tried to reproduce their own attitude to life upon the stage, and to dress up as the middle-class English people they actually were. Next year they would do *Quality Street* or *The Yeomen of the Guard.* Save for this annual incursion, they left literature alone. The men had no time for it, the women did nothing that they could not share with the men. Their ignorance of the arts was notable, and they lost no opportunity of proclaiming it to one another; it was the public-school attitude, flourishing more vigorously than it can yet hope to do in England. If Indians were shop, the arts were bad form, and Ronny had repressed his mother when she inquired after his viola; a viola was almost a demerit, and certainly not the sort of instrument one mentioned in public. She noticed now how tolerant and conventional his judgements had become; when they had seen *Cousin Kate* in London together in the past, he had scorned it; now he pretended that it was a good play, in order to hurt nobody's feelings. An "unkind notice" had appeared in the local paper, "the sort of thing no white man could have written", as Mrs Lesley said. The play was praised, to be sure, and so were the stage management and the performance as a whole, but the notice contained the following sentence: "Miss Derek, though she charmingly looked her part, lacked the necessary experience, and occasionally forgot her words." This tiny breath of genuine criticism had given deep offence, not indeed to Miss Derek, who was as hard as nails, but to her friends. Miss Derek did not belong to Chandrapore. She was stopping for a fortnight with the McBrydes, the police people, and she had been so good as to fill up a gap in the cast at the last moment. A nice impression of local hospitality she would carry away with her.

"To work, Mary, to work," cried the Collector, touching his wife on the shoulder with a switch.

Mrs Turton got up awkwardly. "What do you want me to do? Oh, those purdah women! I never thought any would come. Oh dear!"

A little group of Indian ladies had been gathering in a third quarter of the grounds, near a rustic summer-house, in which the more timid of them had already taken refuge. The rest stood with their backs to the company and their faces pressed into a bank of shrubs. At a little distance stood their male relatives, watching the venture. The sight was significant: an island bared by the turning tide, and bound to grow.

"I consider they ought to come over to me."

"Come along, Mary, get it over."

"I refuse to shake hands with any of the men, unless it has to be the Nawab Bahadur."

"Whom have we so far?" He glanced along the line. "H'm! H'm! Much as one expected. We know why he's here, I think—over that contract—and he wants to get the right side of me for Mohurram, and he's the astrologer who wants to dodge the municipal building regulations, and he's that Parsee, and he's—hullo! There he goes—smash into our hollyhocks. Pulled the left rein when he meant the right. All as usual."

"They ought never to have been allowed to drive in; it's so bad for them," said Mrs Turton, who had at last begun her progress to the summer-house, accompanied by Mrs Moore, Miss Quested and a terrier. "Why they come at all I don't know. They hate it as much as we do. Talk to Mrs McBryde. Her husband made her give purdah parties until she struck."

"This isn't a purdah party," corrected Miss Quested.

"Oh, really," was the haughty rejoinder.

"Do kindly tell us who these ladies are," asked Mrs Moore.

"You're superior to them, anyway. Don't forget that. You're superior to everyone in India except one or two of the ranis, and they're on an equality."

Advancing, she shook hands with the group and said a few words of welcome in Urdu. She had learned the lingo, but only to speak to her servants, so she knew none of the politer forms, and of the verbs only the imperative mood. As soon as her speech was over, she inquired of her companions, "Is that what you wanted?"

"Please tell these ladies that I wish we could speak their language, but we have only just come to their country."

"Perhaps we speak yours a little," one of the ladies said.

"Why, fancy, she understands!" said Mrs Turton.

"Eastbourne, Piccadilly, High Park Corner," said another of the ladies.

"Oh yes, they're English-speaking."

"But now we can talk; how delightful!" cried Adela, her face lighting up.

"She knows Paris also," called one of the onlookers.

"They pass Paris on the way, no doubt," said Mrs Turton, as if she was describing the movements of migratory birds. Her manner had grown more distant since she had discovered that some of the group was westernized, and might apply her own standards to her.

"The shorter lady, she is my wife, she is Mrs Bhattacharya," the onlooker explained. "The taller lady, she is my sister, she is Mrs Das."

The shorter and the taller ladies both adjusted their saris, and smiled. There was a curious uncertainty about their gestures, as if they sought for a new formula which neither East nor West could provide. When Mrs Bhattacharya's husband spoke, she turned away from him, but she did not mind seeing the other men. Indeed, all the ladies were uncertain, cowering, recovering, giggling, making tiny gestures of atonement or despair at all that was said, and alternately fondling the terrier or shrinking from him. Miss Quested now had her desired opportunity; friendly Indians were before her, and she tried to make them talk, but she failed, she strove in vain against the echoing walls of their civility. Whatever she said produced a murmur of deprecation, varying into a murmur of concern when she dropped her pocket-handkerchief. She tried doing nothing, to see what that produced, and they too did nothing. Mrs Moore was equally unsuccessful. Mrs Turton waited for them with a detached expression; she had known what nonsense it all was from the first.

When they took their leave, Mrs Moore had an impulse, and said to Mrs Bhattacharya, whose face she liked, "I wonder whether you would allow us to call on you some day."

"When?" she replied, inclining charmingly.

"Whenever is convenient."

"All days are convenient."

"Thursday . . ."

"Most certainly."

"We shall enjoy it greatly, it would be a real pleasure. What about the time?"

"All hours."

"Tell us which you would prefer. We're quite strangers to your country; we don't know when you have visitors," said Miss Quested.

Mrs Bhattacharya seemed not to know either. Her gesture implied that she had known, since Thursdays began, that English ladies would come to see her on one of them, and so always stayed in. Everything pleased her, nothing surprised. She added, "We leave for Calcutta today."

"Oh, do you?" said Adela, not at first seeing the implication. Then she cried, "Oh, but if you do we shall find you gone."

Mrs Bhattacharya did not dispute it. But her husband called from the distance, "Yes, yes, you come to us Thursday."

"But you'll be in Calcutta."

"No, no, we shall not." He said something swiftly to his wife in Bengali. "We expect you Thursday."

"Thursday . . ." the woman echoed.

"You can't have done such a dreadful thing as to put off going for our sake?" exclaimed Mrs Moore.

"No, of course not, we are not such people." He was laughing.

"I believe that you have. Oh, please—it distresses me beyond words."

Everyone was laughing now, but with no suggestion that they had blundered. A shapeless discussion occurred, during which Mrs Turton retired, smiling to herself. The upshot was that they were to come Thursday, but early in the morning, so as to wreck the Bhattacharya plans as little as possible, and Mr Bhattacharya would send his carriage to fetch them, with servants to point out the way. Did he know where they lived? Yes, of course he knew, he knew everything; and he laughed again. They left among a flutter of compliments and smiles, and three ladies, who had hitherto taken no part in the reception, suddenly shot out of the summer-house like exquisitely coloured swallows, and salaamed them.

Meanwhile the Collector had been going his rounds. He made pleasant remarks and a few jokes, which were applauded lustily, but he knew something to the discredit of nearly every one of his guests, and was consequently perfunctory. When they had not cheated, it was bhang, women or worse, and even the desirables wanted to get something out of him. He believed that a Bridge Party did good rather than harm, or he would not have given one, but he was under no illusions, and at the proper moment he retired to the English side of the lawn. The impressions he left behind him were various. Many of the guests, especially the humbler and less anglicized, were genuinely grateful. To be addressed by so high an official was a permanent asset. They did not mind how long they stood, or how little happened, and when seven o'clock struck they had to be turned out. Others were grateful with more intelligence. The Nawab Bahadur, indifferent for himself and for the distinction with which he was greeted, was moved by the mere kindness that must have prompted the invitation. He knew the difficulties. Hamidullah also thought that the Collector had played up well. But others, such as Mahmoud Ali, were cynical; they were firmly convinced that Turton had been made to give the party by his official superiors and was all the time consumed with impotent rage, and they infected some who were inclined to a healthier view. Yet even Mahmoud Ali was glad he had come. Shrines are fascinating, especially when rarely opened, and it amused him to note the ritual of the English Club, and to caricature it afterwards to his friends.

After Mr Turton, the official who did his duty best was Mr Fielding, the Principal of the little Government College. He knew little of the District and less against the inhabitants, so he was in a less cynical state of mind. Athletic and cheerful, he romped about, making numerous mistakes which the parents of his pupils tried to cover up, for he was popular among them. When the moment for refreshments came, he did not move back to the English side, but burned his mouth with gram. He talked to anyone and he ate anything. Amid much that was alien, he learned that the two new ladies from England had been a great success, and that their politeness in wishing to be Mrs Bhattacharya's guests had pleased not only her but all Indians who heard of it. It pleased Mr Fielding also. He scarcely knew the two new ladies, still he decided to tell them what pleasure they had given by their friendliness.

He found the younger of them alone. She was looking through a nick in the cactus hedge at the distant Marabar Hills, which had crept near, as was their custom at sunset; if the sunset had lasted long enough, they would have reached the town, but it was swift, being tropical. He gave her his information, and she was so much pleased and thanked him so heartily that he asked her and the other lady to tea.

"I'd like to come very much indeed, and so would Mrs Moore, I know."

"I'm rather a hermit, you know."

"Much the best thing to be in this place."

"Owing to my work and so on, I don't get up much to the Club."

"I know, I know, and we never get down from it. I envy you being with Indians."

"Do you care to meet one or two?"

"Very, very much indeed; it's what I long for. This party today makes me so angry and miserable. I think my countrymen out here must be mad. Fancy inviting guests and not treating them properly! You and Mr Turton and perhaps Mr McBryde are the only people who showed any common politeness. The rest make me perfectly ashamed, and it's got worse and worse."

It had. The Englishmen had intended to play up better, but had been prevented from doing so by their womenfolk, whom they had to attend, provide with tea, advise about dogs, etc. When tennis began, the barrier grew impenetrable. It had been hoped to have some sets between East and West, but this was forgotten, and the courts were monopolized by the usual Club couples. Fielding resented it too, but did not say so to the girl, for he found something theoretical in her outburst. Did she care about Indian music? he inquired; there was an old professor down at the College who sang.

"Oh, just what we wanted to hear. And do you know Doctor Aziz?"

"I know all about him. I don't know him. Would you like him asked too?"

"Mrs Moore says he is so nice."

"Very well, Miss Quested. Will Thursday suit you?"

"Indeed it will, and that morning we go to this Indian lady's. All the nice things are coming Thursday."

"I won't ask the City Magistrate to bring you. I know he'll be busy at that time."

"Yes, Ronny is always hard-worked," she replied, contemplating the hills. How lovely they suddenly were! But she couldn't touch them. In front, like a shutter, fell a vision of her married life. She and Ronny would look into the Club like this every evening, then drive home to dress; they would see the Lesleys and the Callendars and the Turtons and the Burtons, and invite them and be invited by them, while the true India slid by unnoticed. Colour would remain—the pageant of birds in the early morning, brown bodies, white turbans, idols whose flesh was scarlet or blue—and movement would remain as long as there were crowds in the bazaar and bathers in the tanks. Perched up on the seat of a dogcart, she would see them. But the force that lies behind colour and movement would escape her even more effectually than it did now. She would see India always as a frieze, never as a spirit, and she assumed that it was a spirit of which Mrs Moore had had a glimpse.

And sure enough they did drive away from the Club in a few minutes, and they did dress, and to dinner came Miss Derek and the McBrydes, and the menu was: Julienne soup full of bullety bottled peas, pseudo-cottage bread, fish full of branching bones, pretending to be plaice, more bottled peas with the cutlets, trifle, sardines on toast: the menu of Anglo-India. A dish might be added or subtracted as one rose or fell in the official scale, the peas might rattle less or more, the sardines and the vermouth be imported by a different firm, but the tradition remained: the food of exiles, cooked by servants who did not understand it. Adela thought of the young men and women who had come out before her, P.-and-O.-ful after P.-and-O.-ful, and had been set down to the same food and the same ideas, and been snubbed in the same good-humoured way until they kept to the accredited themes and began to snub others. "I should never get like that," she thought, for she was young herself; all the same, she knew that she had come up against something that was both insidious and tough, and against which she needed allies. She must gather around her at Chandrapore a few people who felt as she did, and she was glad to have met Mr Fielding and the Indian lady with the unpronounceable name. Here at all events was a nucleus; she should know much better where she stood in the course of the next two days.

Miss Derek—she companioned a Maharani in a remote Native State. She was genial and gay and made them all laugh about her leave, which she had taken because she felt she deserved it, not because the Maharani said she might go. Now she wanted to take the Maharajah's motor-car as well; it had gone to a Chiefs' Conference at Delhi, and she had a great scheme for burgling it at the junction as it came back in the train. She was also very funny about the Bridge Party—indeed she regarded the entire peninsula as a comic opera. "If one couldn't see the laughable side of these people one'd be done for," said Miss Derek. Mrs McBryde—it was she who had been the nurse—ceased not to exclaim: "Oh, Nancy, how topping! Oh, Nancy, how killing! I wish I could look at things like that." Mr McBryde did not speak much; he seemed nice.

When the guests had gone, and Adela gone to bed, there was another interview between mother and son. He wanted her advice and support—while resenting interference. "Does Adela talk to you much?" he began. "I'm so driven with work, I don't see her as much as I hoped, but I hope she finds things comfortable."

"Adela and I talk mostly about India. Dear, since you mention it, you're quite right—you ought to be more alone with her than you are."

"Yes, perhaps, but then people'd gossip."

"Well, they must gossip some time! Let them gossip."

"People are so odd out here, and it's not like home—one's always facing the footlights, as the Burra Sahib said. Take a silly little example: when Adela went out to the boundary of the Club compound, and Fielding followed her. I saw Mrs Callendar notice it. They notice everything, until they're perfectly sure you're their sort."

"I don't think Adela'll ever be quite their sort—she's much too individual."

"I know, that's so remarkable about her," he said

thoughtfully. Mrs Moore thought him rather absurd. Accustomed to the privacy of London, she could not realize that India, seemingly so mysterious, contains none, and that consequently the conventions have greater force. "I suppose nothing's on her mind," he continued.

"Ask her, ask her yourself, my dear boy."

"Probably she's heard tales of the heat, but of course I should pack her off to the hills every April—I'm not one to keep a wife grilling in the plains."

"Oh, it wouldn't be the weather."

"There's nothing in India but the weather, my dear mother; it's the alpha and omega of the whole affair."

"Yes, as Mr McBryde was saying, but it's much more the Anglo-Indians themselves who are likely to get on Adela's nerves. She doesn't think they behave pleasantly to Indians, you see."

"What did I tell you?" he exclaimed, losing his gentle manner. "I knew it last week. Oh, how like a woman to worry over a side-issue!"

She forgot about Adela in her surprise. "A side-issue, a side-issue?" she repeated. "How can it be that?"

"We're not out here for the purpose of behaving pleasantly!"

"What do you mean?"

"What I say. We're out here to do justice and keep the peace. Them's my sentiments. India isn't a drawing-room."

"Your sentiments are those of a god," she said quietly, but it was his manner rather than his sentiments that annoyed her.

Trying to recover his temper, he said, "India likes gods."

"And Englishmen like posing as gods."

"There's no point in all this. Here we are, and we're going to stop, and the country's got to put up with us, gods or no gods. Oh, look here," he broke out, rather pathetically, "what do you and Adela want me to do? Go against my class, against all the people I respect and admire out here? Lose such power as I have for doing good in this country, because my behaviour isn't pleasant? You neither of you understand what work is, or you'd never talk such eyewash.

I hate talking like this, but one must occasionally. It's morbidly sensitive to go on as Adela and you do. I noticed you both at the Club today—after the Collector had been at all that trouble to amuse you. I am out here to work, mind, to hold this wretched country by force. I'm not a missionary or a Labour Member or a vague sentimental sympathetic literary man. I'm just a servant of the Government; it's the profession you wanted me to choose myself, and that's that. We're not pleasant in India, and we don't intend to be pleasant. We've something more important to do."

He spoke sincerely. Every day he worked hard in the court trying to decide which of two untrue accounts was the less untrue, trying to dispense justice fearlessly, to protect the weak against the less weak, the incoherent against the plausible, surrounded by lies and flattery. That morning he had convicted a railway clerk of overcharging pilgrims for their tickets, and a Pathan of attempted rape. He expected no gratitude, no recognition for this, and both clerk and Pathan might appeal, bribe their witnesses more effectually in the interval, and get their sentences reversed. It was his duty. But he did expect sympathy from his own people, and except from newcomers he obtained it. He did think he ought not to be worried about Bridge Parties when the day's work was over and he wanted to play tennis with his equals or rest his legs upon a long chair.

He spoke sincerely, but she could have wished with less gusto. How Ronny revelled in the drawbacks of his situation! How he did rub it in that he was not in India to behave pleasantly, and derived positive satisfaction therefrom! He reminded her of his public-school days. The traces of young-man humanitarianism had sloughed off, and he talked like an intelligent and embittered boy. His words without his voice might have impressed her, but when she heard the self-satisfied lilt of them, when she saw the mouth moving so complacently and competently beneath the little red nose, she felt, quite illogically, that this was not the last word on India. One touch of regret—not the canny substitute but the true regret from the heart—would have made him a different man, and the British Empire a different institution.

"I'm going to argue, and indeed dictate," she said, clinking her rings. "The English *are* out here to be pleasant."

"How do you make that out, mother?" he asked, speaking gently again, for he was ashamed of his irritability.

"Because India is part of the earth. And God has put us on the earth in order to be pleasant to each other. God . . . is . . . love." She hesitated, seeing how much he disliked the argument, but something made her go on. "God has put us on earth to love our neighbours and to show it, and He is omnipresent, even in India, to see how we are succeeding."

He looked gloomy, and a little anxious. He knew this religious strain in her, and that it was a symptom of bad health; there had been much of it when his stepfather died. He thought, "She is certainly ageing, and I ought not to be vexed with anything she says."

"The desire to behave pleasantly satisfies God. . . . The sincere if impotent desire wins His blessing. I think everyone fails, but there are so many kinds of failure. Goodwill and more goodwill and more goodwill. Though I speak with the tongues of . . ."

He waited until she had done, and then said gently: "I quite see that. I suppose I ought to get off to my files now, and you'll be going to bed."

"I suppose so, I suppose so." They did not part for a few minutes, but the conversation had become unreal since Christianity had entered it. Ronny approved of religion as long as it endorsed the National Anthem, but he objected when it attempted to influence his life. Then he would say in respectful yet decided tones, "I don't think it does to talk about these things, every fellow has to work out his own religion," and any fellow who heard him muttered, "Hear!"

Mrs Moore felt that she had made a mistake in mentioning God, but she found Him increasingly difficult to avoid as she grew older, and He had been constantly in her thoughts since she entered India, though oddly enough He satisfied her less. She must needs pronounce His name frequently, as the greatest she knew, yet she had never found it less efficacious.

Outside the arch there seemed always an arch, beyond the remotest echo a silence. And she regretted afterwards that she had not kept to the real serious subject that had caused her to visit India—namely the relationship between Ronny and Adela. Would they, or would they not, succeed in becoming engaged to be married?

Chapter 6

Aziz had not gone to the Bridge Party. Immediately after his meeting with Mrs Moore he was diverted to other matters. Several surgical cases came in, and kept him busy. He ceased to be either outcaste or poet, and became the medical student, very gay, and full of details of operations, which he poured into the shrinking ears of his friends. His profession fascinated him at times, but he required it to be exciting, and it was his hand, not his mind, that was scientific. The knife he loved and used skilfully, and he also liked pumping in the latest serums. But the boredom of regime and hygiene repelled him, and after inoculating a man for enteric he would go away and drink unfiltered water himself. "What can you expect from the fellow?" said dour Major Callendar. "No grit, no guts." But in his heart he knew that if Aziz and not he had operated last year on Mrs Graysford's appendix the old lady would probably have lived. And this did not dispose him any better towards his subordinate.

There was a row the morning after the mosque—they were always having rows. The Major, who had been up half the night, wanted damn well to know why Aziz had not come promptly when summoned.

"Sir, excuse me, I did. I mounted my bike, and it bust in front of the Cow Hospital. So I had to find a tonga."

"Bust in front of the Cow Hospital, did it? And how did you come to be there?"

"I beg your pardon?"

"Oh Lord, oh Lord! When I live here"—he kicked the gravel—"and you live there—not ten minutes from me—and the Cow Hospital is right ever so far away the other side of you—*there*—then how did you come to be passing the Cow Hospital on the way to me? Now do some work for a change."

He strode away in a temper, without waiting for the excuse, which as far as it went was a sound one: the Cow Hospital was in a straight line between Hamidullah's house and his own, so Aziz had naturally passed it. He never realized that the educated Indians visited one another constantly, and were weaving, however painfully, a new social fabric. Caste "or something of the sort" would prevent them. He only knew that no one ever told him the truth, although he had been in the country for twenty years.

Aziz watched him go with amusement. When his spirits were up he felt that the English are a comic institution, and he enjoyed being misunderstood by them. But it was an amusement of the emotions and nerves, which an accident or the passage of time might destroy; it was apart from the fundamental gaiety that he reached when he was with those whom he trusted. A disobliging simile involving Mrs Callendar occurred to his fancy. "I must tell that to Mahmoud Ali, it'll make him laugh," he thought. Then he got to work. He was competent and indispensable, and he knew it. The simile passed from his mind while he exercised his professional skill.

During these pleasant and busy days, he heard vaguely that the Collector was giving a party, and that the Nawab Bahadur said everyone ought to go to it. His fellow assistant, Dr Panna Lal, was in ecstasies at the prospect, and was urgent that they should attend it together in his new tumtum. The arrangement suited them both. Aziz was spared the indignity of a bicycle or the expense of hiring, while Dr Panna Lal, who was timid and elderly, secured someone who could manage his horse. He could manage it himself but only just, and he was afraid of the motors and of the unknown turn into the Club grounds. "Disaster may come," he said politely, "but we shall at all events get there safe, even if we do not get back." And with more logic: "It will, I think, create a good impression should two doctors arrive at the same time."

But when the time came Aziz was seized with a revulsion, and determined not to go. For one thing his spell of work, lately concluded, left him independent and healthy. For another, the day chanced to fall on the anniversary of his wife's death. She had died soon after he had fallen in love with her; he had not loved her at first. Touched by Western feeling, he disliked union with a woman whom he had never seen; moreover, when he did see her, she disappointed him, and he begat his first child in mere animality. The change began after its birth. He was won by her love for him, by a loyalty that implied something more than submission, and by her efforts to educate herself against that lifting of the purdah that would come in the next generation if not in theirs. She was intelligent, yet had old-fashioned grace. Gradually he lost the feeling that his relatives had chosen wrongly for him. Sensuous enjoyment—well, even if he had had it, it would have dulled in a year, and he had gained something instead, which seemed to increase the longer they lived together. She became the mother of a son . . . and in giving him a second son she died. Then he realized what he had lost, and that no woman could ever take her place; a friend would come nearer to her than another woman. She had gone, there was no one like her, and what is that uniqueness but love? He amused himself, he forgot her at times; but at other times he felt that she had sent all the beauty and joy of the world into Paradise, and he meditated suicide. Would he meet her beyond the tomb? Is there such a meeting-place? Though orthodox, he did not know. God's unity was indubitable and indubitably announced, but on all other points he wavered like the average Christian; his belief in the life to come would pale to a hope, vanish, reappear, all in a single sentence or a dozen heartbeats, so that the corpuscles of his blood rather than he seemed to decide which opinion he should hold, and for how long. It was so with all his opinions. Nothing stayed, nothing passed that did not return; the circulation was ceaseless and kept him young, and he mourned his wife the more sincerely because he mourned her seldom.

It would have been simpler to tell Dr Lal that he had changed his mind about the party, but until the last minute he did not know that he had changed it; indeed, he didn't change it, it changed itself. Unconquerable aversion welled. Mrs Callendar, Mrs Lesley—no, he couldn't stand them in his sorrow: they would guess it—for he dowered the British matron with strange insight—and would delight in torturing him, they would mock him to their husbands. When he should have been ready, he stood at the post office, writing a telegram to his children, and found on his return that Dr Lal had called for him, and gone on. Well, let him go on, as befitted the coarseness of his nature. For his own part, he would commune with the dead.

And, unlocking a drawer, he took out his wife's photograph. He gazed at it, and tears spouted from his eyes. He thought, "How unhappy I am!" But because he really was unhappy another emotion soon mingled with his self-pity: he desired to remember his wife and could not. Why could he remember people whom he did not love? They were always so vivid to him, whereas the more he looked at this photograph the less he saw. She had eluded him thus, ever since they had carried her to her tomb. He had known that she would pass from his hands and eyes, but had thought she could live in his mind, not realizing that the very fact that we have loved the dead increases their unreality, and that the more passionately we invoke them the further they recede. A piece of brown cardboard and three children—that was all that was left of his wife. It was unbearable, and he thought again, "How unhappy I am!" and became happier. He had breathed for an instant the mortal air that surrounds Orientals and all men, and he drew back from it with a gasp, for he was young. "Never, never shall I get over this," he told himself. "Most certainly my career is a failure, and my sons will be badly brought up." Since it was certain, he strove to avert it, and looked at some notes he had made on a case at the hospital. Perhaps some day a rich person might require this particular operation, and he gain a large sum. The notes interesting him on their own account, he locked the photograph up again. Its moment was over, and he did not think about his wife any more.

After tea his spirits improved, and he went round to see

Hamidullah. Hamidullah had gone to the party, but his pony had not, so Aziz borrowed it, also his friend's riding-breeches and polo mallet. He repaired to the Maidan. It was deserted except at its rim, where some bazaar youths were training. Training for what? They would have found it hard to say, but the word had got into the air. Round they ran, weedy and knock-kneed—the local physique was wretched—with an expression on their faces not so much of determination as of a determination to be determined. "Maharajah, salaam," he called for a joke. The youths stopped and laughed. He advised them not to over-exert themselves. They promised they would not, and ran on.

Riding into the middle, he began to knock the ball about. He could not play, but his pony could, and he set himself to learn, free from all human tension. He forgot the whole damned business of living as he scurried over the brown platter of the Maidan, with the evening wind on his forehead, and the encircling trees soothing his eyes. The ball shot away towards a stray subaltern who was also practising; he hit it back to Aziz and called, "Send it along again."

"All right."

The newcomer had some notion of what to do, but his horse had none, and forces were equal. Concentrated on the ball, they somehow became fond of one another, and smiled when they drew rein to rest. Aziz liked soldiers—they either accepted you or swore at you, which was preferable to the civilian's hauteur—and the subaltern liked anyone who could ride.

"Often play?" he asked.

"Never."

"Let's have another chukker."

As he hit, his horse bucked and off he went, cried "Oh God!" and jumped on again. "Don't you ever fall off?"

"Plenty."

"Not you."

They reined up again, the fire of good fellowship in their eyes. But it cooled with their bodies, for athletics can only raise a temporary glow. Nationality was returning, but before it could exert its poison they parted, saluting each other. "If only they were all like that," each thought.

Now it was sunset. A few of his co-religionists had come to the Maidan, and were praying with their faces towards Mecca. A Brahmany bull walked towards them, and Aziz, though disinclined to pray himself, did not see why they should be bothered with the clumsy and idolatrous animal. He gave it a tap with his polo mallet. As he did so, a voice from the road hailed him: it was Dr Panna Lal, returning in high distress from the Collector's party.

"Dr Aziz, Dr Aziz, where you been? I waited ten full minutes' time at your house, then I went."

"I am so awfully sorry—I was compelled to go to the post office."

One of his own circle would have accepted this as meaning that he had changed his mind, an event too common to merit censure. But Dr Lal, being of low extraction, was not sure whether an insult had not been intended, and he was further annoyed because Aziz had buffeted the Brahmany bull. "Post office? Do you not send your servants?" he said.

"I have so few—my scale is very small."

"Your servant spoke to me. I saw your servant."

"But, Dr Lal, consider. How could I send my servant when you were coming? You come, we go, my house is left alone, my servant comes back perhaps, and all my portable property has been carried away by bad characters in the meantime. Would you have that? The cook is deaf—I can never count on my cook—and the boy is only a little boy. Never, never do I and Hassan leave the house at the same time together. It is my fixed rule." He said all this and much more out of civility, to save Dr Lal's face. It was not offered as truth and should not have been criticized as such. But the other demolished it—an easy and ignoble task. "Even if this so, what prevents leaving a chit saying where you go?" and so on. Aziz detested ill-breeding, and made his pony caper. "Further away, or mine will start out of sympathy," he wailed, revealing the true source of his irritation. "It has been so rough and wild this afternoon. It spoiled some most valuable blossoms in the Club garden, and had to be dragged back by four men. English ladies and gentlemen looking on, and the Collector Sahib himself taking a note. But, Dr Aziz, I'll not take up your valuable time. This will not interest you, who have so many engagements and telegrams. I am just a poor old doctor who thought right to pay my respects when I was asked and where I was asked. Your absence, I may remark, drew commentaries."

"They can damn well comment."

"It is fine to be young. Damn well! Oh, very fine. Damn whom?"

"I go or not as I please."

"Yet you promise me, and then fabricate this tale of a telegram. Go forward, Dapple."

They went, and Aziz had a wild desire to make an enemy for life. He could do it so easily by galloping near them. He did it. Dapple bolted. He thundered back onto the Maidan. The glory of his play with the subaltern remained for a little, he galloped and swooped till he poured with sweat, and until he returned the pony to Hamidullah's stable he felt the equal of any man. Once on his feet, he had creeping fears. Was he in bad odour with the powers that be? Had he offended the Collector by absenting himself? Dr Panna Lal was a person of no importance, yet was it wise to have quarrelled even with him? The complexion of his mind turned from human to political. He thought no longer, "Can I get on with people?" but "Are they stronger than I?" breathing the prevalent miasma.

At his home a chit was awaiting him, bearing the Government stamp. It lay on his table like a high explosive, which at a touch might blow his flimsy bungalow to bits. He was going to be cashiered because he had not turned up at the party. When he opened the note, it proved to be quite different: an invitation from Mr Fielding, the Principal of Government College, asking him to come to tea the day after tomorrow. His spirits revived with violence. They would have revived in any case, for he possessed a soul that could suffer but not stifle, and led a steady life beneath his mutability.

But this invitation gave him particular joy, because Fielding had asked him to tea a month ago, and he had forgotten about it—never answered, never gone, just forgotten. And here came a second invitation, without a rebuke or even an allusion to his slip. Here was true courtesy—the civil deed that shows the good heart—and snatching up his pen he wrote an affectionate reply, and hurried back for news to Hamidullah's. For he had never met the Principal, and believed that the one serious gap in his life was going to be filled. He longed to know everything about the splendid fellow—his salary, preferences, antecedents, how best one might please him. But Hamidullah was still out, and Mahmoud Ali, who was in, would only make silly rude jokes about the party.

Chapter 7

This Mr Fielding had been caught by India late. He was over forty when he entered that oddest portal, the Victoria terminus at Bombay, and—having bribed a European ticket-inspector—took his luggage into the compartment of his first tropical train. The journey remained in his mind as significant. Of his two carriage companions one was a youth, fresh to the East like himself, the other a seasoned Anglo-Indian of his own age. A gulf divided him from either: he had seen too many cities and men to be the first or to become the second. New impressions crowded on him, but they were not the orthodox new impressions; the past conditioned them, and so it was with his mistakes. To regard an Indian as if he were an Italian is not, for instance, a common error, nor perhaps a fatal one, and Fielding often attempted analogies between this peninsula and that other, smaller and more exquisitely shaped, that stretches into the classic waters of the Mediterranean.

His career, though scholastic, was varied, and had included going to the bad and repenting thereafter. By now he was a hard-bitten, good-tempered, intelligent fellow on the verge of middle age, with a belief in education. He did not mind whom he taught: public-school boys, mental defectives and policemen had all come his way, and he had no objection to adding Indians. Through the influence of friends, he was nominated Principal of the little college at Chandrapore, liked it, and assumed he was a success. He did succeed with his pupils, but the gulf between himself and his countrymen, which he had noticed in the train, widened distressingly. He could not at first see what was wrong. He was not unpatriotic, he always got on with Englishmen in England, all his best friends were English, so why was it not the same out here? Outwardly of the large shaggy type, with sprawling limbs and blue eyes, he appeared to inspire confidence until he spoke. Then something in his manner puzzled people and failed to allay the distrust which his profession naturally inspired. There needs must be this evil of brains in India, but woe to him through whom they are increased! The feeling grew that Mr Fielding was a disruptive force, and rightly, for ideas are fatal to caste, and he used ideas by that most potent method—interchange. Neither a missionary nor a student, he was happiest in the give-and-take of a private conversation. The world, he believed, is a globe of men who are trying to reach one another and can best do so by the help of goodwill plus culture and intelligence—a creed ill suited to Chandrapore, but he had come out too late to lose it. He had no racial feeling—not because he was superior to his brother civilians, but because he had matured in a different atmosphere, where the herd-instinct does not flourish. The remark that did him most harm at the Club was a silly aside to the effect that the so-called white races are really pinko-gray. He only said this to be cheery, he did not realize that "white" has no more to do with a colour than "God save the King" with a god, and that it is the height of impropriety to consider what it does connote. The pinko-gray male whom he addressed was subtly scandalized; his sense of insecurity was awoken, and he communicated it to the rest of the herd.

Still, the men tolerated him for the sake of his good heart and strong body; it was their wives who decided that he was not a sahib really. They disliked him. He took no notice of them, and this, which would have passed without comment in feminist England, did him harm in a community where the male is expected to be lively and helpful. Mr Fielding never advised one about dogs or horses, or dined, or paid his midday calls, or decorated trees for one's children at Christmas, and though he came to the Club it was only to get his tennis or billiards, and to go. This was true. He had discovered that it is possible to keep in with Indians and Englishmen, but that he who would also keep in with Englishwomen must drop the Indians. The two wouldn't combine. Useless to blame either party, useless to blame them for blaming one another. It just was so, and one had to choose. Most Englishmen preferred their own kinswomen, who, coming out in increasing numbers, made life on the home pattern yearly more possible. He had found it convenient and pleasant to associate with Indians and he must pay the price. As a rule no Englishwoman entered the College except for official functions, and if he invited Mrs Moore and Miss Quested to tea it was because they were newcomers who would view everything with an equal if superficial eye, and would not turn on a special voice when speaking to his other guests.

The College itself had been slapped down by the Public Works department, but its grounds included an ancient garden and a garden-house, and here he lived for much of the year. He was dressing after a bath when Dr Aziz was announced. Lifting up his voice, he shouted from the bedroom, "Please make yourself at home." The remark was unpremeditated, like most of his actions; it was what he felt inclined to say.

To Aziz it had a very definite meaning. "May I really, Mr Fielding? It's very good of you," he called back; "I like unconventional behaviour so extremely." His spirits flared up, he glanced round the living-room. Some luxury in it, but no order—nothing to intimidate poor Indians. It was also a very beautiful room, opening into the garden through three high arches of wood. "The fact is I have long wanted to meet you," he continued. "I have heard so much about your warm heart from the Nawab Bahadur. But where is one to meet in a wretched hole like Chandrapore?" He came close up to the door. "When I was greener here, I'll tell you what: I used to wish you to fall ill so that we could meet that way." They laughed, and encouraged by his success he began to improvise. "I said to myself, 'How does Mr Fielding look this morning? Perhaps pale. And the Civil Surgeon is pale too, he will not be able to attend upon him when the shivering commences.' I should have been sent for instead. Then we would have had jolly talks, for you are a celebrated student of Persian poetry."

"You know me by sight, then."

"Of course, of course. You know me?"

"I know you very well by name."

"I have been here such a short time, and always in the bazaar. No wonder you have never seen me, and I wonder you know my name. I say, Mr Fielding?"

"Yes?"

"Guess what I look like before you come out. That will be a kind of game."

"You're five feet nine inches high," said Fielding, surmising this much through the ground glass of the bedroom door.

"Jolly good. What next? Have I not a venerable white beard?"

"Blast!"

"Anything wrong?"

"I've stamped on my last collar-stud."

"Take mine, take mine."

"Have you a spare one?"

"Yes, yes, one minute."

"Not if you're wearing it yourself."

"No, no, one in my pocket." Stepping aside, so that his outline might vanish, he wrenched off his collar, and pulled out of his shirt the back stud, a gold stud, which was part of a set that his brother-in-law had brought him from Europe. "Here it is," he cried.

"Come in with it if you don't mind the unconventionality."

"One minute again." Replacing his collar, he prayed that it would not spring up at the back during tea. Fielding's bearer, who was helping him to dress, opened the door for him.

"Many thanks." They shook hands, smiling. He began to look round, as he would have with any old friend. Fielding was not surprised at the rapidity of their intimacy. With so emotional a people it was apt to come at once or never, and he and Aziz, having heard only good of each other, could afford to dispense with preliminaries.

"But I always thought that Englishmen kept their rooms

so tidy. It seems that this is not so. I need not be so ashamed." He sat down gaily on the bed; then, forgetting himself entirely, drew up his legs and folded them under him. "Everything ranged coldly on shelves was what *I* thought.—I say, Mr Fielding, is the stud going to go in?"

"I hae ma doots."

"What's that last sentence, please? Will you teach me some new words and so improve my English?"

Fielding doubted whether "everything ranged coldly on shelves" could be improved. He was often struck by the liveliness with which the younger generation handled a foreign tongue. They altered the idiom, but they could say whatever they wanted to say quickly; there were none of the babuisms ascribed to them up at the Club. But then the Club moved slowly; it still declared that few Mohammedans and no Hindus would eat at an Englishman's table, and that all Indian ladies were in impenetrable purdah. Individually it knew better; as a club it declined to change.

"Let me put in your stud. I see . . . the shirt back's hole is rather small and to rip it wider a pity."

"Why in hell does one wear collars at all?" grumbled Fielding as he bent his neck.

"We wear them to pass the police."

"What's that?"

"If I'm biking in English dress—starch collar, hat with ditch—they take no notice. When I wear a fez, they cry, 'Your lamp's out!' Lord Curzon did not consider this when he urged natives of India to retain their picturesque costumes. —Hooray! Stud's gone in.—Sometimes I shut my eyes and dream I have splendid clothes again and am riding into battle behind Alamgir. Mr Fielding, must not India have been beautiful then, with the Mogul Empire at its height and Alamgir reigning at Delhi upon the Peacock Throne?"

"Two ladies are coming to tea to meet you—I think you know them."

"Meet me? I know no ladies."

"Not Mrs Moore and Miss Quested?"

"Oh yes—I remember." The romance at the mosque had

sunk out of his consciousness as soon as it was over. "An excessively aged lady; but will you please repeat the name of her companion?"

"Miss Quested."

"Just as you wish." He was disappointed that other guests were coming, for he preferred to be alone with his new friend.

"You can talk to Miss Quested about the Peacock Throne if you like—she's artistic, they say."

"Is she a Post-Impressionist?"

"Post-Impressionism, indeed! Come along to tea. This world is getting too much for me altogether."

Aziz was offended. The remark suggested that he, an obscure Indian, had no right to have heard of Post-Impressionism—a privilege reserved for the Ruling Race, that. He said stiffly, "I do not consider Mrs Moore my friend, I only met her accidentally in my mosque," and was adding, "A single meeting is too short to make a friend," but before he could finish the sentence the stiffness vanished from it, because he felt Fielding's fundamental goodwill. His own went out to it, and grappled beneath the shifting tides of emotion which can alone bear the voyager to an anchorage but may also carry him across it onto the rocks. He was safe really—as safe as the shore-dweller who can only understand stability and supposes that every ship must be wrecked, and he had sensations the shore-dweller cannot know. Indeed, he was sensitive rather than responsive. In every remark he found a meaning, but not always the true meaning, and his life, though vivid, was largely a dream. Fielding, for instance, had not meant that Indians are obscure, but that Post-Impressionism is; a gulf divided his remark from Mrs Turton's "Why, they speak English," but to Aziz the two sounded alike. Fielding saw that something had gone wrong, and equally that it had come right, but he didn't fidget, being an optimist where personal relations were concerned, and their talk rattled on as before.

"Besides the ladies I am expecting one of my assistants—Narayan Godbole."

"Oho, the Deccani Brahman!"

"He wants the past back too, but not precisely Alamgir."

"I should think not. Do you know what Deccani Brahmans say? That England conquered India from them—from them, mind, and not from the Moguls. Is not that like their cheek? They have even bribed it to appear in textbooks, for they are so subtle and immensely rich. Professor Godbole must be quite unlike all other Deccani Brahmans from all I can hear say. A most sincere chap."

"Why don't you fellows run a club in Chandrapore, Aziz?"

"Perhaps—some day. . . . Just now I see Mrs Moore and —what's her name—coming."

How fortunate that it was an "unconventional" party, where formalities are ruled out! On this basis Aziz found the English ladies easy to talk to, he treated them like men. Beauty would have troubled him, for it entails rules of its own, but Mrs Moore was so old and Miss Quested so plain that he was spared this anxiety. Adela's angular body and the freckles on her face were terrible defects in his eyes, and he wondered how God could have been so unkind to any female form. His attitude towards her remained entirely straightforward in consequence.

"I want to ask you something, Dr Aziz," she began. "I heard from Mrs Moore how helpful you were to her in the mosque, and how interesting. She learned more about India in those few minutes' talk with you than in the three weeks since we landed."

"Oh, please do not mention a little thing like that. Is there anything else I may tell you about my country?"

"I want you to explain a disappointment we had this morning; it must be some point of Indian etiquette."

"There honestly is none," he replied. "We are by nature a most informal people."

"I am afraid we must have made some blunder and given offence," said Mrs Moore.

"That is even more impossible. But may I know the facts?"

"An Indian lady and gentleman were to send their

carriage for us this morning at nine. It has never come. We waited and waited and waited; we can't think what happened."

"Some misunderstanding," said Fielding, seeing at once that it was the type of incident that had better not be cleared up.

"Oh no, it wasn't that," Miss Quested persisted. "They even gave up going to Calcutta to entertain us. We must have made some stupid blunder, we both feel sure."

"I wouldn't worry about that."

"Exactly what Mr Heaslop tells me," she retorted, reddening a little. "If one doesn't worry, how's one to understand?"

The host was inclined to change the subject, but Aziz took it up warmly, and on learning fragments of the delinquents' name pronounced that they were Hindus.

"Slack Hindus—they have no idea of society; I know them very well because of a doctor at the hospital. Such a slack unpunctual fellow! It is as well you did not go to their house, for it would give you a wrong idea of India. Nothing sanitary. I think for my own part they grew ashamed of their house and that is why they did not send."

"That's a notion," said the other man.

"I do so hate mysteries," Adela announced.

"We English do."

"I dislike them not because I'm English, but from my own personal point of view," she corrected.

"I like mysteries but I rather dislike muddles," said Mrs Moore.

"A mystery is a muddle."

"Oh, do you think so, Mr Fielding?"

"A mystery is only a high-sounding term for a muddle. No advantage in stirring it up, in either case. Aziz and I know well that India's a muddle."

"India's—oh, what an alarming idea!"

"There'll be no muddle when you come to see me," said Aziz, rather out of his depth. "Mrs Moore and everyone—I invite you all—oh, please."

The old lady accepted: she still thought the young doctor

excessively nice; moreover, a new feeling, half languor, half excitement, bade her turn down any fresh path. Miss Quested accepted out of adventure. She also liked Aziz, and believed that when she knew him better he would unlock his country for her. His invitation gratified her, and she asked him for his address.

Aziz thought of his bungalow with horror. It was a detestable shanty near a low bazaar. There was practically only one room in it, and that infested with small black flies. "Oh, but we will talk of something else now," he exclaimed. "I wish I lived here. See this beautiful room! Let us admire it together for a little. See those curves at the bottom of the arches. What delicacy! It is the architecture of Question and Answer. Mrs Moore, you are in India; I am not joking." The room inspired him. It was an audience-hall built in the eighteenth century for some high official, and though of wood had reminded Fielding of the Loggia de' Lanzi at Florence. Little rooms, now Europeanized, clung to it on either side, but the central hall was unpapered and unglassed, and the air of the garden poured in freely. One sat in public—on exhibition, as it were—in full view of the gardeners who were screaming at the birds and of the man who rented the tank for the cultivation of water-chestnut. Fielding let the mango trees too—there was no knowing who might not come in—and his servants sat on his steps night and day to discourage thieves. Beautiful certainly, and the Englishman had not spoilt it, whereas Aziz in an occidental moment would have hung Maude Goodmans on the walls. Yet there was no doubt to whom the room really belonged. . . .

"I am doing justice here. A poor widow who has been robbed comes along and I give her fifty rupees, to another a hundred, and so on and so on. I should like that."

Mrs Moore smiled, thinking of the modern method as exemplified in her son. "Rupees don't last for ever, I'm afraid," she said.

"Mine would. God would give me more when he saw I gave. Always be giving, like the Nawab Bahadur. My father was the same, that is why he died poor." And pointing about the room he peopled it with clerks and officials, all benevolent because they lived long ago. "So we would sit giving for ever—on a carpet instead of chairs, that is the chief change between now and then, but I think we would never punish anyone."

The ladies agreed.

"Poor criminal, give him another chance. It only makes a man worse to go to prison and be corrupted." His face grew very tender—the tenderness of one incapable of administration, and unable to grasp that if the poor criminal is let off he will again rob the poor widow. He was tender to everyone except a few family enemies whom he did not consider human; on these he desired revenge. He was even tender to the English; he knew at the bottom of his heart that they could not help being so cold and odd and circulating like an ice-stream through his land. "We punish no one, no one," he repeated, "and in the evening we will give a great banquet with a nautch, and lovely girls shall shine on every side of the tank with fireworks in their hands, and all shall be feasting and happiness until the next day, when there shall be justice as before—fifty rupees, a hundred, a thousand—till peace comes. Ah, why didn't we live in that time?—But are you admiring Mr Fielding's house? Do look how the pillars are painted blue, and the verandas, pavilions—what do you call them?—that are above us inside are blue also. Look at the carving on the pavilions. Think of the hours it took. Their little roofs are curved to imitate bamboo. So pretty—and the bamboos waving by the tank outside. Mrs Moore! Mrs Moore!"

"Well?" she said, laughing.

"You remember the water by our mosque? It comes down and fills this tank—a skilful arrangement of the Emperors. They stopped here going down into Bengal. They loved water. Wherever they went they created fountains, gardens, hammams. I was telling Mr Fielding I would give anything to serve them."

He was wrong about the water, which no Emperor, however skilful, can cause to gravitate uphill; a depression of some depth together with the whole of Chandrapore lay between the mosque and Fielding's house. Ronny would have pulled him up, Turton would have wanted to pull him up, but restrained himself. Fielding did not even want to pull him up; he had dulled his craving for verbal truth and cared chiefly for truth of mood. As for Miss Quested, she accepted everything Aziz said as true verbally. In her ignorance, she regarded him as "India", and never surmised that his outlook was limited and his method inaccurate, and that no one is India.

He was now much excited, chattering away hard, and even saying damn when he got mixed up in his sentences. He told them of his profession, and of the operations he had witnessed and performed, and he went into details that scared Mrs Moore, though Miss Quested mistook them for proofs of his broad-mindedness; she had heard such talk at home in advanced academic circles, deliberately free. She supposed him to be emancipated as well as reliable and placed him on a pinnacle which he could not retain. He was high enough for the moment, to be sure, but not on any pinnacle. Wings bore him up, and flagging would deposit him.

The arrival of Professor Godbole quieted him somewhat, but it remained his afternoon. The Brahman, polite and enigmatic, did not impede his eloquence, and even applauded it. He took his tea at a little distance from the outcastes, from a low table placed slightly behind him, to which he stretched back, and as it were encountered food by accident; all feigned indifference to Professor Godbole's tea. He was elderly and wizen with a gray moustache and gray-blue eyes, and his complexion was as fair as a European's. He wore a turban that looked like pale purple macaroni, coat, waistcoat, dhoti, socks with clocks. The clocks matched the turban, and his whole appearance suggested harmony—as if he had reconciled the products of East and West, mental as well as physical, and could never be discomposed. The ladies were interested in him, and hoped that he would supplement Dr Aziz by saying something about religion. But he only ate—ate and ate, smiling, never letting his eyes catch sight of his hand.

Leaving the Mogul Emperors, Aziz turned to topics that could distress no one. He described the ripening of the mangoes, and how in his boyhood he used to run out in the rains to a big mango grove belonging to an uncle, and gorge there. "Then back with water streaming over you and perhaps rather a pain inside. But I did not mind. All my friends were paining with me. We have a proverb in Urdu: 'What does unhappiness matter when we are all unhappy together?' which comes in conveniently after mangoes. Miss Quested, do wait for mangoes. Why not settle altogether in India?"

"I'm afraid I can't do that," said Adela. She made the remark without thinking what it meant. To her, as to the three men, it seemed in key with the rest of the conversation, and not for several minutes—indeed, not for half an hour—did she realize that it was an important remark, and ought to have been made in the first place to Ronny.

"Visitors like you are too rare."

"They are indeed," said Professor Godbole. "Such affability is seldom seen. But what can we offer to detain them?"

"Mangoes, mangoes."

They laughed. "Even mangoes can be got in England now," put in Fielding. "They ship them in ice-cold rooms. You can make India in England apparently, just as you can make England in India."

"Frightfully expensive in both cases," said the girl.

"I suppose so."

"And nasty."

But the host wouldn't allow the conversation to take this heavy turn. He turned to the old lady, who looked flustered and put out—he could not imagine why—and asked about her own plans. She replied that she should like to see over the College. Everyone immediately rose, with the exception of Professor Godbole, who was finishing a banana.

"Don't you come too, Adela; you dislike institutions."

"Yes, that is so," said Miss Quested, and sat down again.

Aziz hesitated. His audience was splitting up. The more familiar half was going, but the more attentive remained.

Reflecting that it was an "unconventional" afternoon, he stopped.

Talk went on as before. Could one offer the visitors unripe mangoes in a fool? "I speak now as a doctor: no." Then the old man said: "But I will send you up a few healthy sweets. I will give myself that pleasure."

"Miss Quested, Professor Godbole's sweets are delicious," said Aziz sadly, for he wanted to send sweets too and had no wife to cook them. "They will give you a real Indian treat. Ah, in my poor position I can give you nothing."

"I don't know why you say that, when you have so kindly asked us to your house."

He thought again of his bungalow with horror. Good heavens, the stupid girl had taken him at his word! What was he to do? "Yes, all that is settled," he cried. "I invite you all to see me in the Marabar Caves."

"I shall be delighted."

"Oh, that is a most magnificent entertainment compared to my poor sweets. But has not Miss Quested visited our caves already?"

"No. I've not even heard of them."

"Not heard of them?" both cried. "The Marabar Caves in the Marabar Hills?"

"We hear nothing interesting up at the Club. Only tennis and ridiculous gossip."

The old man was silent, perhaps feeling that it was unseemly of her to criticize her race, perhaps fearing that if he agreed she would report him for disloyalty. But the young man uttered a rapid "I know".

"Then tell me everything you will, or I shall never understand India. Are they the hills I sometimes see in the evening? What are these caves?"

Aziz undertook to explain, but it presently appeared that he had never visited the caves himself—had always been "meaning" to go, but work or private business had prevented him, and they were so far. Professor Godbole chaffed him pleasantly. "My dear young sir, the pot and the kettle! Have you ever heard that useful proverb?"

"Are they large caves?" she asked.

"No, not large."

"Do describe them, Professor Godbole."

"It will be a great honour." He drew up his chair and an expression of tension came over his face. Taking the cigarette-box, she offered to him and to Aziz, and lit up herself. After an impressive pause he said: "There is an entrance in the rock which you enter, and through the entrance is the cave."

"Something like the caves at Elephanta?"

"Oh no, not at all; at Elephanta there are sculptures of Siva and Parvati. There are no sculptures at Marabar."

"They are immensely holy, no doubt," said Aziz, to help on the narrative.

"Oh no, oh no."

"Still, they are ornamented in some way."

"Oh no."

"Well, why are they so famous? We all talk of the famous Marabar Caves. Perhaps that is our empty brag."

"No, I should not quite say that."

"Describe them to this lady, then."

"It will be a great pleasure." He forewent the pleasure, and Aziz realized that he was keeping back something about the caves. He realized because he often suffered from similar inhibitions himself. Sometimes, to the exasperation of Major Callendar, he would pass over the one relevant fact in a position, to dwell on the hundred irrelevant. The Major accused him of disingenuousness, and was roughly right, but only roughly. It was rather that a power he couldn't control capriciously silenced his mind. Godbole's had been silenced now; no doubt not willingly, he was concealing something. Handled subtly, he might regain control and announce that the Marabar Caves were—full of stalactites, perhaps; Aziz led up to this, but they weren't.

The dialogue remained light and friendly, and Adela had no conception of its underdrift. She did not know that the comparatively simple mind of the Mohammedan was encountering Ancient Night. Aziz played a thrilling game. He was handling a human toy that refused to work—he knew that much. If it worked, neither he nor Professor Godbole would be the least advantaged, but the attempt enthralled him and was akin to abstract thought. On he chattered, defeated at every move by an opponent who would not even admit that a move had been made, and further than ever from discovering what, if anything, was extraordinary about the Marabar Caves.

Into this Ronny dropped.

With an annoyance he took no trouble to conceal, he called from the garden: "What's happened to Fielding? Where's my mother?"

"Good evening!" she replied coolly.

"I want you and mother at once. There's to be polo."

"I thought there was to be no polo."

"Everything's altered. Some soldier men have come in. Come along and I'll tell you about it."

"Your mother will return shortly, sir," said Professor Godbole, who had risen with deference. "There is but little to see at our poor college."

Ronny took no notice, but continued to address his remarks to Adela; he had hurried away from his work to take her to see the polo, because he thought it would give her pleasure. He did not mean to be rude to the two men, but the only link he could be conscious of with an Indian was the official, and neither happened to be his subordinate. As private individuals he forgot them.

Unfortunately Aziz was in no mood to be forgotten. He would not give up the secure and intimate note of the last hour. He had not risen with Godbole, and now, offensively friendly, called from his seat, "Come along up and join us, Mr Heaslop; sit down till your mother turns up."

Ronny replied by ordering one of Fielding's servants to fetch his master at once.

"He may not understand that. Allow me—" Aziz repeated the order idiomatically.

Ronny was tempted to retort; he knew the type; he knew all the types, and this was the spoilt westernized. But he was a servant of the Government, it was his job to avoid "incidents", so he said nothing, and ignored the provocation that Aziz continued to offer. Aziz was provocative. Everything he said had an impertinent flavour or jarred. His wings were failing, but he refused to fall without a struggle. He did not mean to be impertinent to Mr Heaslop, who had never done him harm, but here was an Anglo-Indian who must become a man before comfort could be regained. He did not mean to be greasily confidential to Miss Quested, only to enlist her support; nor to be loud and jolly towards Professor Godbole. A strange quartet—he fluttering to the ground, she puzzled by the sudden ugliness, Ronny fuming, the Brahman observing all three, but with downcast eyes and hands folded, as if nothing was noticeable. A scene from a play, thought Fielding, who now saw them from the distance across the garden, grouped among the blue pillars of his beautiful hall.

"Don't trouble to come, mother," Ronny called; "we're just starting." Then he hurried to Fielding, drew him aside and said with pseudo-heartiness, "I say, old man, do excuse me, but I think perhaps you oughtn't to have left Miss Quested alone."

"I'm sorry, what's up?" replied Fielding, also trying to be genial.

"Well . . . I'm the sun-dried bureaucrat, no doubt; still, I don't like to see an English girl left smoking with two Indians."

"She stopped, as she smokes, by her own wish, old man."

"Yes, that's all right in England."

"I really can't see the harm."

"If you can't see, you can't see. . . . Can't you see that fellow's a bounder?"

Aziz, flamboyant, was patronizing Mrs Moore.

"He isn't a bounder," protested Fielding. "His nerves are on edge, that's all."

"What should have upset his precious nerves?"

"I don't know. He was all right when I left."

"Well, it's nothing I've said," said Ronny reassuringly. "I never even spoke to him."

"Oh well, come along now, and take your ladies away; the catastrophe's over."

"Fielding . . . don't think I'm taking it badly, or anything of that sort. . . . I suppose you won't come on to the polo with us? We should all be delighted."

"I'm afraid I can't, thanks all the same. I'm awfully sorry you feel I've been remiss. I didn't mean to be."

So the leave-taking began. Everyone was cross or wretched. It was as if irritation exuded from the very soil. Could one have been so petty on a Scotch moor or an Italian alp? Fielding wondered afterwards. There seemed no reserve of tranquillity to draw upon in India. Either none, or else tranquillity swallowed up everything, as it appeared to do for Professor Godbole. Here was Aziz all shoddy and odious, Mrs Moore and Miss Quested both silly, and he himself and Heaslop both decorous on the surface, but detestable really and detesting each other.

"Goodbye, Mr Fielding, and thank you so much. . . . What lovely college buildings!"

"Goodbye, Mrs Moore."

"Goodbye, Mr Fielding. Such an interesting afternoon. . . ."

"Goodbye, Miss Quested."

"Goodbye, Dr Aziz."

"Goodbye, Mrs Moore."

"Goodbye, Dr Aziz."

"Goodbye, Miss Quested." He pumped her hand up and down to show that he felt at ease. "You'll jolly jolly well not forget those caves, won't you? I'll fix the whole show up in a jiffy."

"Thank you. . . ."

Inspired by the devil to a final effort, he added: "What a shame you leave India so soon! Oh, do reconsider your decision, do stay."

"Goodbye, Professor Godbole," she continued, suddenly agitated. "It's a shame we never heard you sing."

"I may sing now," he replied, and did.

His thin voice rose, and gave out one sound after another. At times there seemed rhythm, at times there was the illusion of a Western melody. But the ear, baffled repeatedly, soon lost any clue, and wandered in a maze of noises, none harsh or unpleasant, none intelligible. It was the song of an unknown bird. Only the servants understood it. They began to whisper to one another. The man who was gathering water-chestnut came naked out of the tank, his lips parted with delight, disclosing his scarlet tongue. The sounds continued and ceased after a few moments as casually as they had begun—apparently halfway through a bar, and upon the subdominant.

"Thanks so much; what was that?" asked Fielding.

"I will explain in detail. It was a religious song. I placed myself in the position of a milkmaiden. I say to Shri Krishna: 'Come! Come to me only.' The God refuses to come. I grow humble and say: 'Do not come to me only. Multiply yourself into a hundred Krishnas, and let one go to each of my hundred companions, but one, O Lord of the Universe, come to me.' He refuses to come. This is repeated several times. The song is composed in a raga appropriate to the present hour, which is the evening."

"But He comes in some other song, I hope?" said Mrs Moore gently.

"Oh no, He refuses to come," repeated Godbole, perhaps not understanding her question. "I say to Him, Come, come, come, come, come, come. He neglects to come."

Ronny's steps had died away, and there was a moment of absolute silence. No ripple disturbed the water, no leaf stirred.

Chapter 8

Although Miss Quested had known Ronny well in England, she felt well advised to visit him before deciding to be his wife. India had developed sides of his character that she had never admired. His self-complacency, his censoriousness, his lack of subtlety, all grew vivid beneath a tropic sky; he seemed more indifferent than of old to what was passing in the minds of his fellows, more certain that he was right about them or that if he was wrong it didn't matter. When proved wrong, he was particularly exasperating; he always managed to suggest that she needn't have bothered to prove it. The point she made was never the relevant point, her arguments conclusive but barren, she was reminded that he had expert knowledge and she none, and that experience would not help her because she could not interpret it. A public school, London University, a year at a crammer's, a particular sequence of posts in a particular province, a fall from a horse and a touch of fever were presented to her as the only training by which Indians and all who reside in their country can be understood; the only training she could comprehend, that is to say, for of course above Ronny there stretched the higher realms of knowledge, inhabited by Callendars and Turtons, who had been not one year in the country but twenty and whose instincts were superhuman. For himself he made no extravagant claims; she wished he would. It was the qualified brag of the callow official, the "I am not perfect, but—" that got on her nerves.

How gross he had been at Mr Fielding's—spoiling the talk and walking off in the middle of the haunting song! As he drove them away in the tum-tum, her irritation became unbearable, and she did not realize that much of it was directed against herself. She longed for an opportunity to fly out at him, and since he felt cross too, and they were both in India, an opportunity soon occurred. They had scarcely left the College grounds before she heard him say to his mother, who was with him on the front seat, "What was that about caves?" and she promptly opened fire.

"Mrs Moore, your delightful doctor has decided on a picnic, instead of a party in his house; we are to meet him out there—you, myself, Mr Fielding, Professor Godbole—exactly the same party."

"Out where?" asked Ronny.

"The Marabar Caves."

"Well, I'm blessed," he murmured after a pause. "Did he descend to any details?"

"He did not. If you had spoken to him, we could have arranged them."

He shook his head, laughing.

"Have I said anything funny?"

"I was only thinking how the worthy doctor's collar climbed up his neck."

"I thought you were discussing the caves."

"So I am. Aziz was exquisitely dressed, from tie-pin to spats, but he had forgotten his back collar-stud, and there you have the Indian all over: inattention to detail; the fundamental slackness that reveals the race. Similarly, to 'meet' in the caves as if they were the clock at Charing Cross, when they're miles from a station and each other."

"Have you been to them?"

"No, but I know all about them, naturally."

"Oh, naturally!"

"Are you too pledged to this expedition, mother?"

"Mother is pledged to nothing," said Mrs Moore, rather unexpectedly. "Certainly not to this polo. Will you drive up to the bungalow first, and drop me there, please? I prefer to rest."

"Drop me too," said Adela. "I don't want to watch polo either, I'm sure."

"Simpler to drop the polo," said Ronny. Tired and disappointed, he quite lost self-control, and added in a loud lecturing voice: "I won't have you messing about with

Indians any more! If you want to go to the Marabar Caves you'll go under British auspices."

"I've never heard of these caves, I don't know what or where they are," said Mrs Moore, "but I really can't have"—she tapped the cushion beside her—"so much quarrelling and tiresomeness!"

The young people were ashamed. They dropped her at the bungalow and drove on together to the polo, feeling it was the least they could do. Their crackling bad humour left them, but the heaviness of their spirit remained; thunderstorms seldom clear the air. Miss Quested was thinking over her own behaviour, and didn't like it at all. Instead of weighing Ronny and herself, and coming to a reasoned conclusion about marriage, she had incidentally, in the course of a talk about mangoes, remarked to mixed company that she didn't mean to stop in India. Which meant that she wouldn't marry Ronny; but what a way to announce it, what a way for a civilized girl to behave! She owed him an explanation, but unfortunately there was nothing to explain. The "thorough talk" so dear to her principles and temperament had been postponed until too late. There seemed no point in being disagreeable to him and formulating her complaints against his character at this hour of the day, which was the evening. . . . The polo took place on the Maidan, near the entrance of Chandrapore city. The sun was already declining and each of the trees held a premonition of night. They walked away from the governing group to a distant seat, and there, feeling that it was his due and her own, she forced out of herself the undigested remark: "We must have a thorough talk, Ronny, I'm afraid."

"My temper's rotten, I must apologize," was his reply. "I didn't mean to order you and mother about, but of course the way those Bengalis let you down this morning annoyed me, and I don't want that sort of thing to keep happening."

"It's nothing to do with them that I . . ."

"No, but Aziz would make some similar muddle over the caves. He meant nothing by the invitation, I could tell by his voice; it's just their way of being pleasant."

"It's something very different, nothing to do with caves, that I wanted to talk over with you." She gazed at the colourless grass. "I've finally decided we are not going to be married, my dear boy."

The news hurt Ronny very much. He had heard Aziz announce that she would not return to the country, but had paid no attention to the remark, for he never dreamt that an Indian could be a channel of communication between two English people. He controlled himself and said gently, "You never said we should marry, my dear girl; you never bound either yourself or me—don't let this upset you."

She felt ashamed. How decent he was! He might force his opinions down her throat, but did not press her to an "engagement", because he believed, like herself, in the sanctity of personal relationships; it was this that had drawn them together at their first meeting, which had occurred among the grand scenery of the English Lakes. Her ordeal was over, but she felt it should have been more painful and longer. Adela will not marry Ronny. It seemed slipping away like a dream. She said: "But let us discuss things; it's all so frightfully important, we mustn't make false steps. I want next to hear your point of view about me—it might help us both."

His manner was unhappy and reserved. "I don't much believe in this discussing—besides, I'm so dead with all the extra work Mohurram's bringing, if you'll excuse me."

"I only want everything to be absolutely clear between us, and to answer any questions you care to put to me on my conduct."

"But I haven't got any questions. You've acted within your rights, you were quite right to come out and have a look at me doing my work, it was an excellent plan, and anyhow it's no use talking further—we should only get up steam." He felt angry and bruised; he was too proud to tempt her back, but he did not consider that she had behaved badly, because where his compatriots were concerned he had a generous mind.

"I suppose then there is nothing else; it's unpardonable of

me to have given you and your mother all this bother," said Miss Quested heavily, and frowned up at the tree beneath which they were sitting. A little green bird was observing her, so brilliant and neat that it might have hopped straight out of a shop. On catching her eye it closed its own, gave a small skip and prepared to go to bed. Some Indian wild bird. "Yes, nothing else," she repeated, feeling that a profound and passionate speech ought to have been delivered by one or both of them. "We've been awfully British over it, but I suppose that's all right."

"As we are British, I suppose it is."

"Anyhow, we've not quarrelled, Ronny."

"Oh, that would have been too absurd. Why should we quarrel?"

"I think we shall keep friends."

"I know we shall."

"Quite so."

As soon as they had exchanged this admission, a wave of relief passed through them both, and then transformed itself into a wave of tenderness, and passed back. They were softened by their own honesty, and began to feel lonely and unwise. Experiences, not character, divided them; they were not dissimilar, as humans go; indeed, when compared with the people who stood nearest to them in point of space they became practically identical. The Bhil who was holding an officer's polo pony, the Eurasian who drove the Nawab Bahadur's car, the Nawab Bahadur himself, the Nawab Bahadur's debauched grandson—none would have examined a difficulty so frankly and coolly. The mere fact of examination caused it to diminish. Of course they were friends, and for ever. "Do you know what the name of that green bird up above us is?" she asked, putting her shoulder rather nearer to his.

"Bee-eater."

"Oh no, Ronny, it has red bars on its wings."

"Parrot," he hazarded.

"Good gracious, no."

The bird in question dived into the dome of the tree. It

was of no importance, yet they would have liked to identify it, it would somehow have solaced their hearts. But nothing in India is identifiable, the mere asking of a question causes it to disappear or to merge in something else.

"McBryde has an illustrated bird-book," he said dejectedly. "I'm no good at all at birds, in fact I'm useless at any information outside my own job. It's a great pity."

"So am I. I'm useless at everything."

"What do I hear?" shouted the Nawab Bahadur at the top of his voice, causing both of them to start. "What most improbable statement have I heard? An English lady useless? No, no, no, no, no." He laughed genially, sure, within limits, of his welcome.

"Hullo, Nawab Bahadur! Been watching the polo again?" said Ronny tepidly.

"I have, sahib, I have."

"How do you do?" said Adela, likewise pulling herself together. She held out her hand. The old gentleman judged from so wanton a gesture that she was new to his country, but he paid little heed. Women who exposed their faces became by that one act so mysterious to him that he took them at the valuation of their menfolk rather than at his own. Perhaps they were not immoral, and anyhow they were not his affair. On seeing the City Magistrate alone with a maiden at twilight, he had borne down on them with hospitable intent. He had a new little car, and wished to place it at their disposal; the City Magistrate would decide whether the offer was acceptable.

Ronny was by this time rather ashamed of his curtness to Aziz and Godbole, and here was an opportunity of showing that he could treat Indians with consideration when they deserved it. So he said to Adela, with the same sad friendliness that he had employed when discussing the bird, "Would half an hour's spin entertain you at all?"

"Oughtn't we to get back to the bungalow?"

"Why?" He gazed at her.

"I think perhaps I ought to see your mother and discuss future plans."

"That's as you like, but there's no hurry, is there?"

"Let me take you to the bungalow, and first the little spin," cried the old man, and hastened to the car.

"He may show you some aspect of the country I can't, and he's a real loyalist. I thought you might care for a bit of a change."

Determined to give him no more trouble, she agreed, but her desire to see India had suddenly decreased. There had been a factitious element in it.

How should they seat themselves in the car? The elegant grandson had to be left behind. The Nawab Bahadur got up in front, for he had no intention of neighbouring an English girl. "Despite my advanced years, I am learning to drive," he said. "Man can learn everything if he will but try." And foreseeing a further difficulty he added: "I do not do the actual steering. I sit and ask my chauffeur questions, and thus learn the reason for everything that is done before I do it myself. By this method serious and I may say ludicrous accidents, such as befell one of my compatriots during that delightful reception at the English Club, are avoided. Our good Panna Lal! I hope, sahib, that great damage was not done to your flowers. Let us have our little spin down the Gangavati road. Half one league onwards!" He fell asleep.

Ronny instructed the chauffeur to take the Marabar road rather than the Gangavati, since the latter was under repair, and settled himself down beside the lady he had lost. The car made a burring noise and rushed along a chaussée that ran upon an embankment above melancholy fields. Trees of a poor quality bordered the road, indeed the whole scene was inferior, and suggested that the countryside was too vast to admit of excellence. In vain did each item in it call out, "Come, come." There was not enough god to go round. The two young people conversed feebly and felt unimportant. When the darkness began, it seemed to well out of the meagre vegetation, entirely covering the fields each side of them before it brimmed over the road. Ronny's face grew dim—an event that always increased her esteem for his character. Her hand touched his, owing to a jolt, and one of the thrills so frequent in the animal kingdom passed between them, and announced that all their difficulties were only a lovers' quarrel. Each was too proud to increase the pressure, but neither withdrew it, and a spurious unity descended on them, as local and temporary as the gleam that inhabits a firefly. It would vanish in a moment, perhaps to reappear, but the darkness is alone durable. And the night that encircled them, absolute as it seemed, was itself only a spurious unity, being modified by the gleams of day that leaked up round the edges of the earth, and by the stars.

They gripped . . . bump, jump, a swerve, two wheels lifted in the air, brakes on, bump with tree at edge of embankment, standstill. An accident. A slight one. Nobody hurt. The Nawab Bahadur awoke. He cried out in Arabic, and violently tugged his beard.

"What's the damage?" inquired Ronny, after the moment's pause that he permitted himself before taking charge of a situation. The Eurasian, inclined to be flustered, rallied to the sound of his voice, and, every inch an Englishman, replied, "You give me five minutes' time, I'll take you any damn anywhere."

"Frightened, Adela?" He released her hand.

"Not a bit."

"I consider not to be frightened the height of folly," cried the Nawab Bahadur quite rudely.

"Well, it's all over now, tears are useless," said Ronny, dismounting. "We had some luck butting that tree."

"All over . . . oh yes, the danger is past, let us smoke cigarettes, let us do anything we please. Oh yes . . . enjoy ourselves—oh my merciful God . . ." His words died into Arabic again.

"Wasn't the bridge. We skidded."

"We didn't skid," said Adela, who had seen the cause of the accident, and thought everyone must have seen it too. "We ran into an animal."

A loud cry broke from the old man; his terror was disproportionate and ridiculous.

"An animal?"

"A large animal rushed up out of the dark on the right and hit us."

"By Jove, she's right," Ronny exclaimed. "The paint's gone."

"By Jove, sir, your lady is right," echoed the Eurasian. Just by the hinges of the door was a dent, and the door opened with difficulty.

"Of course I'm right. I saw its hairy back quite plainly."

"I say, Adela, what was it?"

"I don't know the animals any better than the birds here—too big for a goat."

"Exactly, too big for a goat . . ." said the old man.

Ronny said, "Let's go into this; let's look for its tracks."

"Exactly; you wish to borrow this electric torch."

The English people walked a few steps back into the darkness, united and happy. Thanks to their youth and upbringing, they were not upset by the accident. They traced back the writhing of the tyres to the source of their disturbance. It was just after the exit from a bridge; the animal had probably come up out of the nullah. Steady and smooth ran the marks of the car, ribbons neatly nicked with lozenges; then all went mad. Certainly some external force had impinged, but the road had been used by too many objects for any one track to be legible, and the torch created such high lights and black shadows that they could not interpret what it revealed. Moreover, Adela in her excitement knelt and swept her skirts about, until it was she if anyone who appeared to have attacked the car. The incident was a great relief to them both. They forgot their abortive personal relationship, and felt adventurous as they muddled about in the dust.

"I believe it was a buffalo," she called to their host, who had not accompanied them.

"Exactly."

"Unless it was a hyena."

Ronny approved this last conjecture. Hyenas prowl in nullahs and headlights dazzle them.

"Excellent, a hyena," said the Indian with an angry irony and a gesture at the night. "Mr Harris!"

"Half a mo-ment. Give me ten minutes' time."

"Sahib says hyena."

"Don't worry Mr Harris. He saved us from a nasty smash. Harris, well done!"

"A smash, sahib, that would not have taken place had he obeyed and taken us Gangavati side, instead of Marabar."

"My fault that. I told him to come this way because the road's better. Mr Lesley has made it pukka right up to the hills."

"Ah, now I begin to understand." Seeming to pull himself together, he apologized slowly and elaborately for the accident. Ronny murmured, "Not at all," but apologies were his due, and should have started sooner; because English people are so calm at a crisis, it is not to be assumed that they are unimportant. The Nawab Bahadur had not come out very well.

At that moment a large car approached from the opposite direction. Ronny advanced a few steps down the road, and with authority in his voice and gesture stopped it. It bore the inscription "Mudkul State" across its bonnet. All friskiness and friendliness, Miss Derek sat inside.

"Mr Heaslop, Miss Quested, what are you holding up an innocent female for?"

"We've had a breakdown."

"But how putrid!"

"We ran into a hyena!"

"How absolutely rotten!"

"Can you give us a lift?"

"Yes, indeed."

"Take me too," said the Nawab Bahadur.

"Heh, what about me?" cried Mr Harris.

"Now what's all this? I'm not an omnibus," said Miss Derek with decision. "I've a harmonium and two dogs in here with me as it is. I'll take three of you if one'll sit in front and nurse a pug. No more."

"I will sit in front," said the Nawab Bahadur.

"Then hop in; I've no notion who you are."

"Heh no, what about my dinner? I can't be left alone all

the night." Trying to look and feel like a European, the chauffeur interposed aggressively. He still wore a topi, despite the darkness, and his face, to which the Ruling Race had contributed little beyond bad teeth, peered out of it pathetically, and seemed to say: "What's it all about? Don't worry me so, you blacks and whites. Here I am, stuck in damn India same as you, and you got to fit me in better than this."

"Nussu will bring you out some suitable dinner upon a bicycle," said the Nawab Bahadur, who had regained his usual dignity. "I shall dispatch him with all possible speed. Meanwhile, repair my car."

They sped off, and Mr Harris, after a reproachful glance, squatted down upon his hams. When English and Indians were both present, he grew self-conscious, because he did not know to whom he belonged. For a little he was vexed by opposite currents in his blood, then they blended, and he belonged to no one but himself.

But Miss Derek was in tearing spirits. She had succeeded in stealing the Mudkul car. Her Maharajah would be awfully sick, but she didn't mind; he could sack her if he liked. "I don't believe in these people letting you down," she said. "If I didn't snatch like the devil, I should be nowhere. He doesn't want the car, silly fool! Surely it's to the credit of his State I should be seen about in it at Chandrapore during my leave. He ought to look at it that way. Anyhow he's got to look at it that way. My Maharani's different—my Maharani's a dear. That's her fox-terrier, poor little devil. I fished them both out with the driver. Imagine taking dogs to a Chiefs' Conference! As sensible as taking Chiefs, perhaps." She shrieked with laughter. "The harmonium—the harmonium's my little mistake, I own. They rather had me over the harmonium. I meant it to stop on the train. Oh lor'!"

Ronny laughed with restraint. He did not approve of English people taking service under the Native States, where they obtain a certain amount of influence, but at the expense of the general prestige. The humorous triumphs of a freelance are of no assistance to an administrator, and he told the young lady that she would outdo Indians at their own game if she went on much longer.

"They always sack me before that happens, and then I get another job. The whole of India seethes with maharanis and ranis and begums who clamour for such as me."

"Really. I had no idea."

"How could you have any idea, Mr Heaslop? What should he know about maharanis, Miss Quested? Nothing. At least I should hope not."

"I understand those big people are not particularly interesting," said Adela quietly, disliking the young woman's tone. Her hand touched Ronny's again in the darkness, and to the animal thrill there was now added a coincidence of opinion.

"Ah, there you're wrong. They're priceless."

"I would scarcely call her wrong," broke out the Nawab Bahadur, from his isolation on the front seat, whither they had relegated him. "A Native State, a Hindu State, the wife of a ruler of a Hindu State, may beyond doubt be a most excellent lady, and let it not be for a moment supposed that I suggest anything against the character of Her Highness the Maharani of Mudkul. But I fear she will be uneducated, I fear she will be superstitious. Indeed, how could she be otherwise? What opportunity of education has such a lady had? Oh, superstition is terrible, terrible! Oh, it is the great defect in our Indian character!"—and, as if to point his criticism, the lights of the Civil Station appeared on a rise to the right. He grew more and more voluble. "Oh, it is the duty of each and every citizen to shake superstition off, and though I have little experience of Hindu States, and none of this particular one, namely Mudkul (the Ruler, I fancy, has a salute of but eleven guns)—yet I cannot imagine that they have been as successful as British India, where we see reason and orderliness spreading in every direction, like a most health-giving flood!"

Miss Derek said "Golly!"

Undeterred by the expletive, the old man swept on. His tongue had been loosed and his mind had several points to make. He wanted to endorse Miss Quested's remark that big people are not interesting, because he was bigger himself than many an independent chief; at the same time, he must neither remind nor inform her that he was big, lest she felt she had committed a discourtesy. This was the groundwork of his oration; worked in with it was his gratitude to Miss Derek for the lift, his willingness to hold a repulsive dog in his arms, and his general regret for the trouble he had caused the human race during the evening. Also he wanted to be dropped near the city to get hold of his cleaner, and to see what mischief his grandson was up to. As he wove all these anxieties into a single rope, he suspected that his audience felt no interest, and that the City Magistrate fondled either maiden behind the cover of the harmonium, but good breeding compelled him to continue; it was nothing to him if they were bored, because he did not know what boredom is, and it was nothing to him if they were licentious, because God has created all races to be different. The accident was over, and his life, equably useful, distinguished, happy, ran on as before and expressed itself in streams of well-chosen words.

When this old geyser left them, Ronny made no comment, but talked lightly about polo; Turton had taught him that it is sounder not to discuss a man at once, and he reserved what he had to say on the Nawab's character until later in the evening. His hand, which he had removed to say goodbye, touched Adela's again; she caressed it definitely, he responded, and their firm and mutual pressure surely meant something. They looked at each other when they reached the bungalow, for Mrs Moore was inside it. It was for Miss Quested to speak, and she said nervously, "Ronny, I should like to take back what I said on the Maidan." He assented, and they became engaged to be married in consequence.

Neither had foreseen such a consequence. She had meant to revert to her former condition of important and cultivated uncertainty, but it had passed out of her reach at its appropriate hour. Unlike the green bird or the hairy animal, she was labelled now. She felt humiliated again, for she deprecated labels, and she felt too that there should have been another scene between her lover and herself at this point, something dramatic and lengthy. He was pleased instead of distressed, he was surprised, but he had really nothing to say. What indeed is there to say? To be or not to be married, that was the question, and they had decided it in the affirmative.

"Come along and let's tell the mater all this"—opening the perforated zinc door that protected the bungalow from the swarms of winged creatures. The noise woke the mater up. She had been dreaming of the absent children who were so seldom mentioned, Ralph and Stella, and did not at first grasp what was required of her. She too had become used to thoughtful procrastination, and felt alarmed when it came to an end.

When the announcement was over, he made a gracious and honest remark. "Look here, both of you, see India if you like and as you like—I know I made myself rather ridiculous at Fielding's, but . . . it's different now. I wasn't quite sure of myself."

"My duties here are evidently finished, I don't want to see India now; now for my passage back," was Mrs Moore's thought. She reminded herself of all that a happy marriage means, and of her own happy marriages, one of which had produced Ronny. Adela's parents had also been happily married, and excellent it was to see the incident repeated by the younger generation. On and on! The number of such unions would certainly increase as education spread and ideals grew loftier, and characters firmer. But she was tired by her visit to Government College, her feet ached, Mr Fielding had walked too fast and far, the young people had annoyed her in the tum-tum, and given her to suppose they were breaking with each other, and though it was all right now she could not speak as enthusiastically of wedlock or of anything as she should have done. Ronny was suited, now she must go home and help the others, if they wished. She was past marrying herself, even unhappily; her function was to help others, her reward to be informed that she was sympathetic. Elderly ladies must not expect more than this.

They dined alone. There was much pleasant and affectionate talk about the future. Later on they spoke of passing events, and Ronny reviewed and recounted the day from his own point of view. It was a different day from the women's, because, while they had enjoyed themselves or thought, he had worked. Mohurram was approaching, and as usual the Chandrapore Mohammedans were building paper towers of a size too large to pass under the branches of a certain peepul tree. One knew what happened next; the tower stuck, a Mohammedan climbed up the peepul and cut the branch off, the Hindus protested, there was a religious riot, and Heaven knew what, with perhaps the troops sent for. There had been deputations and Conciliation Committees under the auspices of Turton, and all the normal work of Chandrapore had been hung up. Should the procession take another route, or should the towers be shorter? The Mohammedans offered the former, the Hindus insisted on the latter. The Collector had favoured the Hindus, until he suspected that they had artificially bent the tree nearer the ground. They said it sagged naturally. Measurements, plans, an official visit to the spot. But Ronny had not disliked his day, for it proved that the British were necessary to India; there would certainly have been bloodshed without them. His voice grew complacent again; he was here not to be pleasant but to keep the peace, and now that Adela had promised to be his wife she was sure to understand.

"What does our old gentleman of the car think?" she asked, and her negligent tone was exactly what he desired.

"Our old gentleman is helpful and sound, as he always is over public affairs. You've seen in him our show Indian."

"Have I really?"

"I'm afraid so. Incredible, aren't they, even the best of them? They're all—they all forget their back collar-studs sooner or later. You've had to do with three sets of Indians today, the Bhattacharyas, Aziz, and this chap, and it really isn't a coincidence that they've all let you down."

"I like Aziz, Aziz is my real friend," Mrs Moore interposed.

"When the animal runs into us the Nawab loses his head, deserts his unfortunate chauffeur, intrudes upon Miss Derek . . . no great crimes, no great crimes, but no white man would have done it."

"What animal?"

"Oh, we had a small accident on the Marabar road. Adela thinks it was a hyena."

"An accident?" she cried.

"Nothing; no one hurt. Our excellent host awoke much rattled from his dreams, appeared to think it was our fault, and chanted Exactly, exactly."

Mrs Moore shivered, "A ghost!" But the idea of a ghost scarcely passed her lips. The young people did not take it up, being occupied with their own outlooks, and deprived of support it perished, or was reabsorbed into the part of the mind that seldom speaks.

"Yes, nothing criminal," Ronny summed up, "but there's the native, and there's one of the reasons why we don't admit him to our clubs, and how a decent girl like Miss Derek can take service under natives puzzles me. . . . But I must get on with my work. Krishna!" Krishna was the peon who should have brought the files from his office. He had not turned up, and a terrific row ensued. Ronny stormed, shouted, howled, and only the experienced observer could tell that he was not angry, did not much want the files, and only made a row because it was the custom. Servants, quite understanding, ran slowly in circles, carrying hurricane lamps. Krishna the earth, Krishna the stars replied, until the Englishman was appeased by their echoes, fined the absent peon eight annas, and sat down to his arrears in the next room.

"Will you play patience with your future mother-in-law, dear Adela, or does it seem too tame?"

"I should like to—I don't feel a bit excited—I'm just glad it's settled up at last, but I'm not conscious of vast changes. We are all three the same people still."

"That's much the best feeling to have." She dealt out the first row of "demon".

"I suppose so," said the girl thoughtfully.

"I feared at Mr Fielding's that it might be settled the other way . . . black knave on a red queen. . . ." They chatted gently about the game.

Presently Adela said: "You heard me tell Aziz and Godbole I wasn't stopping in their country. I didn't mean it, so why did I say it? I feel I haven't been—frank enough, attentive enough, or something. It's as if I got everything out of proportion. You have been so very good to me, and I meant to be good when I sailed, but somehow I haven't been. . . . Mrs Moore, if one isn't absolutely honest, what is the use of existing?"

She continued to lay out her cards. The words were obscure, but she understood the uneasiness that produced them. She had experienced it twice herself, during her own engagements—this vague contrition and doubt. All had come right enough afterwards and doubtless would this time—marriage makes most things right enough. "I wouldn't worry," she said. "It's partly the odd surroundings; you and I keep on attending to trifles instead of what's important; we are what the people here call 'new'."

"You mean that my bothers are mixed up with India?"

"India's—" She stopped.

"What made you call it a ghost?"

"Call what a ghost?"

"The animal thing that hit us. Didn't you say 'Oh, a ghost' in passing?"

"I couldn't have been thinking of what I was saying."

"It was probably a hyena, as a matter of fact."

"Ah, very likely."

And they went on with their patience. Down in Chandrapore the Nawab Bahadur waited for his car. He sat behind his town house (a small unfurnished building which he rarely entered) in the midst of the little court that always improvises itself round Indians of position. As if turbans were the natural product of darkness a fresh one would occasionally froth to the front, incline itself towards him, and retire. He was preoccupied, his diction was appropriate to a religious subject.

Nine years previously, when first he had had a car, he had driven it over a drunken man and killed him, and the man had been waiting for him ever since. The Nawab Bahadur was innocent before God and the Law, he had paid double the compensation necessary; but it was no use, the man continued to wait in an unspeakable form, close to the scene of his death. None of the English people knew of this, nor did the chauffeur; it was a racial secret communicable more by blood than speech. He spoke now in horror of the particular circumstances: he had led others into danger, he had risked the lives of two innocent and honoured guests. He repeated: "If I had been killed, what matter? It must happen some time; but they who trusted me—" The company shuddered and invoked the mercy of God. Only Aziz held aloof, because a personal experience restrained him: was it not by despising ghosts that he had come to know Mrs Moore? "You know, Nureddin," he whispered to the grandson—an effeminate youth whom he seldom met, always liked, and invariably forgot—"you know, my dear fellow, we Moslems simply must get rid of these superstitions, or India will never advance. How long must I hear of the savage pig upon the Marabar road?" Nureddin looked down. Aziz continued: "Your grandfather belongs to another generation, and I respect and love the old gentleman, as you know. I say nothing against him, only that it is wrong for us, because we are young. I want you to promise me—Nureddin, are you listening?—not to believe in evil spirits, and if I die (for my health grows very weak) to bring up my three children to disbelieve in them too." Nureddin smiled, and a suitable answer rose to his pretty lips, but before he could make it the car arrived, and his grandfather took him away.

The game of patience up in the Civil Lines went on longer than this. Mrs Moore continued to murmur "Red ten on a black knave," Miss Quested to assist her, and to intersperse among the intricacies of the play details about the hyena, the engagement, the Maharani of Mudkul, the Bhattacharyas, and the day generally, whose rough desiccated surface acquired as it receded a definite outline, as India itself might, could it be viewed from the moon. Presently the players went to bed, but not before other people had woken up elsewhere, people whose emotions they could not share, and whose existence they ignored. Never tranquil, never perfectly dark, the night wore itself away, distinguished from other nights by two or three blasts of wind, which seemed to fall perpendicularly out of the sky and to bounce back into it, hard and compact, leaving no freshness behind them: the Hot Weather was approaching.

Chapter 9

Aziz fell ill as he foretold—slightly ill. Three days later he lay abed in his bungalow, pretending to be very ill. It was a touch of fever, which he would have neglected if there was anything important at the hospital. Now and then he groaned and thought he should die, but did not think so for long, and a very little diverted him. It was Sunday, always an equivocal day in the East, and an excuse for slacking. He could hear church bells as he drowsed, both from the Civil Station and from the missionaries out beyond the slaughterhouse—different bells and rung with different intent, for one set was calling firmly to Anglo-India, and the other feebly to mankind. He did not object to the first set; the other he ignored, knowing their inefficiency. Old Mr Graysford and young Mr Sorley made converts during a famine, because they distributed food; but when times improved they were naturally left alone again, and, though surprised and aggrieved each time this happened, they never learned wisdom. "No Englishman understands us except Mr Fielding," he thought; "but how shall I see him again? If he entered this room the disgrace of it would kill me." He called to Hassan to clear up, but Hassan, who was testing his wages by ringing them on the step of the veranda, found it possible not to hear him; heard and didn't hear, just as Aziz had called and hadn't called. "That's India all over . . . how like us . . . there we are. . . ." He dozed again, and his thoughts wandered over the varied surface of life.

Gradually they steadied upon a certain spot—the Bottomless Pit according to missionaries, but he had never regarded it as more than a dimple. Yes, he did want to spend an evening with some girls, singing and all that, the vague jollity that would culminate in voluptuousness. Yes, that was what he did want. How could it be managed? If Major Callendar had been an Indian, he would have remembered what young men are, and granted two or three days' leave to Calcutta without asking questions. But the Major assumed either that his subordinates were made of ice, or that they repaired to the Chandrapore bazaars—disgusting ideas both. It was only Mr Fielding who—

"Hassan!"

The servant came running.

"Look at those flies, brother"; and he pointed to the horrible mass that hung from the ceiling. The nucleus was a wire which had been inserted as a homage to electricity. Electricity had paid no attention, and a colony of eye-flies had come instead and blackened the coils with their bodies.

"Huzoor, those are flies."

"Good, good, they are, excellent, but why have I called you?"

"To drive them elsewhere," said Hassan, after painful thought.

"Driven elsewhere, they always return."

"Huzoor."

"You must make some arrangement against flies; that is why you are my servant," said Aziz gently.

Hassan would call the little boy to borrow the step-ladder from Mahmoud Ali's house; he would order the cook to light the primus stove and heat water; he would personally ascend the steps with a bucket in his arms, and dip the end of the coil into it.

"Good, very good. Now what have you to do?"

"Kill flies."

"Good. Do it."

Hassan withdrew, the plan almost lodged in his head, and began to look for the little boy. Not finding him, his steps grew slower, and he stole back to his post on the veranda, but did not go on testing his rupees, in case his master heard them clink. On twittered the Sunday bells; the East had returned to the East via the suburbs of England, and had become ridiculous during the detour.

Aziz continued to think about beautiful women.

His mind here was hard and direct, though not brutal. He had learned all he needed concerning his own constitution many years ago, thanks to the social order into which he had been born, and when he came to study medicine he was repelled by the pedantry and fuss with which Europe tabulates the facts of sex. Science seemed to discuss everything from the wrong end. It didn't interpret his experiences when he found them in a German manual, because by being there they ceased to be his experiences. What he had been told by his father or mother or had picked up from servants—it was information of that sort that he found useful, and handed on as occasion offered to others.

But he must not bring any disgrace on his children by some silly escapade. Imagine if it got about that he was not respectable! His professional position too must be considered, whatever Major Callendar thought. Aziz upheld the proprieties, though he did not invest them with any moral halo, and it was here that he chiefly differed from an Englishman. His conventions were social. There is no harm in deceiving society as long as she does not find you out, because it is only when she finds you out that you have harmed her; she is not like a friend or God, who are injured by the mere existence of unfaithfulness. Quite clear about this, he meditated what type of lie he should tell to get away to Calcutta, and had thought of a man there who could be trusted to send him a wire and a letter that he could show to Major Callendar, when the noise of wheels was heard in his compound. Someone had called to inquire. The thought of sympathy increased his fever, and with a sincere groan he wrapped himself in his quilt.

"Aziz, my dear fellow, we are greatly concerned," said Hamidullah's voice. One, two, three, four bumps, as people sat down upon his bed.

"When a doctor falls ill it is a serious matter," said the voice of Mr Syed Mohammed, the assistant engineer.

"When an engineer falls ill, it is equally important," said the voice of Mr Haq, a police inspector.

"Oh yes, we are all jolly important, our salaries prove it."

"Dr Aziz took tea with our Principal last Thursday afternoon," piped Rafi, the engineer's nephew. "Professor Godbole, who also attended, has sickened too, which seems rather a curious thing, sir, does it not?"

Flames of suspicion leapt up in the breast of each man. "Humbug!" exclaimed Hamidullah, in authoritative tones, quenching them.

"Humbug, most certainly," echoed the others, ashamed of themselves. The wicked schoolboy, having failed to start a scandal, lost confidence and stood up with his back to the wall.

"Is Professor Godbole ill?" inquired Aziz, penetrated by the news. "I am sincerely sorry." Intelligent and compassionate, his face peeped out of the bright crimson folds of the quilt. "How do you do, Mr Syed Mohammed, Mr Haq? How very kind of you to inquire after my health! How do you do, Hamidullah? But you bring me bad news. What is wrong with him, the excellent fellow?"

"Why don't you answer, Rafi? You're the great authority," said his uncle.

"Yes, Rafi's the great man," said Hamidullah, rubbing it in. "Rafi is the Sherlock Holmes of Chandrapore. Speak up, Rafi."

Less than the dust, the schoolboy murmured the word "Diarrhoea," but took courage as soon as it had been uttered, for it improved his position. Flames of suspicion shot up again in the breasts of his elders, though in a different direction. Could what was called diarrhoea really be an early case of cholera?

"If this is so, this is a very serious thing; this is scarcely the end of March. Why have I not been informed?" cried Aziz.

"Dr Panna Lal attends him, sir."

"Oh yes, both Hindus; there we have it; they hang together like flies and keep everything dark. Rafi, come here. Sit down. Tell me all the details. Is there vomiting also?"

"Oh yes indeed, sir, and the serious pains."

"That settles it. In twenty-four hours he will be dead."

Everybody looked and felt shocked, but Professor Godbole had diminished his appeal by linking himself with a co-religionist. He moved them less than when he had appeared as a suffering individual. Before long they began to condemn him as a source of infection. "All illness proceeds from Hindus," Mr Haq said. Mr Syed Mohammed had visited religious fairs, at Allahabad and at Ujjain, and described them with biting scorn. At Allahabad there was flowing water, which carried impurities away, but at Ujjain the little river Sipra was banked up, and thousands of bathers deposited their germs in the pool. He spoke with disgust of the hot sun, the cow-dung and marigold flowers, and the encampment of saddhus, some of whom strode stark naked through the streets. Asked what was the name of the chief idol at Ujjain, he replied that he did not know, he had disdained to inquire, he really could not waste his time over such trivialities. His outburst took some time, and in his excitement he fell into Punjabi (he came from that side) and was unintelligible.

Aziz liked to hear his religion praised. It soothed the surface of his mind, and allowed beautiful images to form beneath. When the engineer's noisy tirade was finished, he said, "That is exactly my own view." He held up his hand, palm outward, his eyes began to glow, his heart to fill with tenderness. Issuing still further from his quilt, he recited a poem by Ghalib. It had no connection with anything that had gone before, but it came from his heart and spoke to theirs. They were overwhelmed by its pathos; pathos, they agreed, is the highest quality in art; a poem should touch the hearer with a sense of his own weakness, and should institute some comparison between mankind and flowers. The squalid bedroom grew quiet; the silly intrigues, the gossip, the shallow discontent were stilled, while words accepted as immortal filled the indifferent air. Not as a call to battle, but as a calm assurance came the feeling that India was one; Moslem; always had been; an assurance that lasted until they looked out of the door. Whatever Ghalib had felt, he had anyhow lived in India, and thus consolidated it for them; he had gone with his own tulips and roses, but tulips and roses do not go. And the sister kingdoms of the north—Arabia, Persia, Ferghana, Turkestan—stretched out their hands as he sang, sadly, because all beauty is sad, and greeted ridiculous Chandrapore, where every street and house was divided against itself, and told her that she was a continent and a unity.

Of the company, only Hamidullah had any comprehension of poetry. The minds of the others were inferior and rough. Yet they listened with pleasure, because literature had not been divorced from their civilization. The police inspector, for instance, did not feel that Aziz had degraded himself by reciting, nor break into the cheery guffaw with which an Englishman averts the infection of beauty. He just sat with his mind empty, and when his thoughts, which were mainly ignoble, flowed back into it they had a pleasant freshness. The poem had done no "good" to anyone, but it was a passing reminder, a breath from the divine lips of beauty, a nightingale between two worlds of dust. Less explicit than the call to Krishna, it voiced our loneliness nevertheless, our isolation, our need for the Friend who never comes yet is not entirely disproved. Aziz it left thinking about women again, but in a different way: less definite, more intense. Sometimes poetry had this effect on him, sometimes it only increased his local desires, and he never knew beforehand which effect would ensue; he could discover no rule for this or for anything else in life.

Hamidullah had called in on his way to a worrying Committee of Notables, nationalist in tendency, where Hindus, Moslems, two Sikhs, two Parsees, a Jain, and a Native Christian tried to like one another more than came natural to them. As long as someone abused the English, all went well, but nothing constructive had been achieved, and if the English were to leave India the committee would vanish also. He was glad that Aziz, whom he loved and whose family was connected with his own, took no interest in politics, which ruin the character and career, yet nothing can be achieved without them. He thought of Cambridge—sadly, as of another poem that had ended. How happy he had been there, twenty years ago! Politics had not mattered in Mr and Mrs Bannister's rectory. There, games, work and pleasant society had interwoven, and appeared to be sufficient substructure for a national life. Here all was wire-pulling and fear. Messrs Syed Mohammed and Haq—he couldn't even trust them, although they had come in his carriage, and the schoolboy was a scorpion. Bending down, he said: "Aziz, Aziz, my dear boy, we must be going, we are already late. Get well quickly, for I do not know what our little circle would do without you."

"I shall not forget those affectionate words," replied Aziz.

"Add mine to them," said the engineer.

"Thank you, Mr Syed Mohammed, I will."

"And mine," "And, sir, accept mine," cried the others, stirred each according to his capacity towards goodwill. Little ineffectual unquenchable flames! The company continued to sit on the bed and to chew sugar-cane, which Hassan had run for into the bazaar, and Aziz drank a cup of spiced milk. Presently there was the sound of another carriage. Dr Panna Lal had arrived, driven by horrid Mr Ram Chand. The atmosphere of a sick-room was at once re-established, and the invalid retired under his quilt.

"Gentlemen, you will excuse, I have come to inquire by Major Callendar's orders," said the Hindu, nervous of the den of fanatics into which his curiosity had called him.

"Here he lies," said Hamidullah, indicating the prostrate form.

"Dr Aziz, Dr Aziz, I come to inquire."

Aziz presented an expressionless face to the thermometer.

"Your hand also, please." He took it, gazed at the flies on the ceiling, and finally announced: "Some temperature."

"I think not much," said Ram Chand, desirous of fomenting trouble.

"Some; he should remain in bed," repeated Dr Panna

Lal, and shook the thermometer down, so that its altitude remained for ever unknown. He loathed his young colleague since the disasters with Dapple, and he would have liked to do him a bad turn and report to Major Callendar that he was shamming. But he might want a day in bed himself soon—besides, though Major Callendar always believed the worst of natives, he never believed them when they carried tales about one another. Sympathy seemed the safer course. "How is stomach?" he inquired. "How head?" And catching sight of the empty cup he recommended a milk diet.

"This is a great relief to us, it is very good of you to call, doctor sahib," said Hamidullah, buttering him up a bit.

"It is only my duty."

"We know how busy you are."

"Yes, that is true."

"And how much illness there is in the city."

The doctor suspected a trap in this remark; if he admitted that there was or was not illness, either statement might be used against him. "There is always illness," he replied, "and I am always busy—it is a doctor's nature."

"He has not a minute, he is due double sharp at Government College now," said Ram Chand.

"You attend Professor Godbole there perhaps?"

The doctor looked professional and was silent.

"We hope his diarrhoea is ceasing."

"He progresses, but not from diarrhoea."

"We are in some anxiety over him—he and Dr Aziz are great friends. If you could tell us the name of his complaint we should be grateful to you."

After a cautious pause he said, "Haemorrhoids."

"And so much, my dear Rafi, for your cholera," hooted Aziz, unable to restrain himself.

"Cholera, cholera, what next, what now?" cried the doctor, greatly fussed. "Who spreads such untrue reports about my patients?"

Hamidullah pointed to the culprit.

"I hear cholera, I hear bubonic plague, I hear every species of lie. Where will it end, I ask myself sometimes.

This city is full of misstatements, and the originators of them ought to be discovered and punished authoritatively."

"Rafi, do you hear that? Now why do you stuff us up with all this humbug?"

The schoolboy murmured that another boy had told him, also that the bad English grammar the Government obliged them to use often gave the wrong meaning for words, and so led scholars into mistakes.

"That is no reason you should bring a charge against a doctor," said Ram Chand.

"Exactly, exactly," agreed Hamidullah, anxious to avoid an unpleasantness. Quarrels spread so quickly and so far, and Messrs Syed Mohammed and Haq looked cross, and ready to fly out. "You must apologize properly, Rafi, I can see your uncle wishes it," he said. "You have not yet said that you are sorry for the trouble you have caused this gentleman by your carelessness."

"It is only a boy," said Dr Panna Lal, appeased.

"Even boys must learn," said Ram Chand.

"Your own son failing to pass the lowest standard, I think," said Syed Mohammed suddenly.

"Oh, indeed? Oh yes, perhaps. He has not the advantage of a relative in the Prosperity Printing Press."

"Nor you the advantage of conducting their cases in the courts any longer."

Their voices rose. They attacked one another with obscure allusions and had a silly quarrel. Hamidullah and the doctor tried to make peace between them. In the midst of the din someone said, "I say! Is he ill or isn't he ill?" Mr Fielding had entered unobserved. All rose to their feet, and Hassan, to do an Englishman honour, struck with a sugar-cane at the coil of flies.

Aziz said "Sit down" coldly. What a room! What a meeting! Squalor and ugly talk, the floor strewn with fragments of cane and nuts, and spotted with ink, the pictures crooked upon the dirty walls, no punkah! He hadn't meant to live like this or among these third-rate people. And in his confusion he thought only of the insignificant Rafi, whom he had laughed at, and allowed to be teased. The boy must be sent away happy, or hospitality would have failed, along the whole line.

"It is good of Mr Fielding to condescend to visit our friend," said the police inspector. "We are touched by this great kindness."

"Don't talk to him like that, he doesn't want it, and he doesn't want three chairs; he's not three Englishmen," he flashed. "Rafi, come here. Sit down again. I'm delighted you could come with Mr Hamidullah, my dear boy; it will help me to recover, seeing you."

"Forgive my mistakes," said Rafi, to consolidate himself.

"Well, are you ill, Aziz, or aren't you?" Fielding repeated.

"No doubt Major Callendar has told you that I am shamming."

"Well, are you?" The company laughed, friendly and pleased. "An Englishman at his best," they thought; "so genial."

"Inquire from Dr Panna Lal."

"You're sure I don't tire you by stopping?"

"Why, no! There are six people present in my small room already. Please remain seated, if you will excuse the informality." He turned away and continued to address Rafi, who was terrified at the arrival of his Principal, remembered that he had tried to spread slander about him, and yearned to get away.

"He is ill and he is not ill," said Hamidullah, offering a cigarette. "And I suppose that most of us are in that same case."

Fielding agreed; he and the pleasant sensitive barrister got on well. They were fairly intimate and beginning to trust each other.

"The whole world looks to be dying, still it doesn't die, so we must assume the existence of a beneficent Providence."

"Oh, that is true, how true!" said the policeman, thinking religion had been praised.

"Does Mr Fielding think it's true?"

"Think which true? The world isn't dying. I'm certain of that!"

"No, no—the existence of Providence."

"Well, I don't believe in Providence."

"But how then can you believe in God?" asked Syed Mohammed.

"I don't believe in God."

A tiny movement as of "I told you so!" passed round the company, and Aziz looked up for an instant, scandalized. "Is it correct that most are atheists in England now?" Hamidullah inquired.

"The educated thoughtful people? I should say so, though they don't like the name. The truth is that the West doesn't bother much over belief and disbelief in these days. Fifty years ago, or even when you and I were young, much more fuss was made."

"And does not morality also decline?"

"It depends what you call—yes, yes, I suppose morality does decline."

"Excuse the question, but if this is the case, how is England justified in holding India?"

There they were! Politics again. "It's a question I can't get my mind onto," he replied. "I'm out here personally because I needed a job. I cannot tell you why England is here or whether she ought to be here. It's beyond me."

"Well-qualified Indians also need jobs in the educational."

"I guess they do; I got in first," said Fielding, smiling.

"Then excuse me again—is it fair an Englishman should occupy one when Indians are available? Of course I mean nothing personally. Personally we are delighted you should be here, and we benefit greatly by this frank talk."

There is only one answer to a conversation of this type: "England holds India for her good." Yet Fielding was disinclined to give it. The zeal for honesty had eaten him up. He said: "I'm delighted to be here too—that's my answer, there's my only excuse. I can't tell you anything about fairness. It mayn't have been fair I should have been born.

I take up some other fellow's air, don't I, whenever I breathe? Still, I'm glad it's happened, and I'm glad I'm out here. However big a badmash one is—if one's happy in consequence, that's some justification."

The Indians were bewildered. The line of thought was not alien to them, but the words were too definite and bleak. Unless a sentence paid a few compliments to Justice and Morality in passing, its grammar wounded their ears and paralysed their minds. What they said and what they felt were (except in the case of affection) seldom the same. They had numerous mental conventions, and when these were flouted they found it very difficult to function. Hamidullah bore up best. "And those Englishmen who are not delighted to be in India—have they no excuse?" he asked.

"None. Chuck 'em out."

"It may be difficult to separate them from the rest," he laughed.

"Worse than difficult, wrong," said Mr Ram Chand. "No Indian gentleman approves chucking out as a proper thing. Here we differ from those other nations. We are so spiritual."

"Oh that is true, how true!" said the police inspector.

"Is it true, Mr Haq? I don't consider us spiritual. We can't co-ordinate, we can't co-ordinate, it only comes to that. We can't keep engagements, we can't catch trains. What more than this is the so-called spirituality of India? You and I ought to be at the Committee of Notables, we're not; our friend Dr Lal ought to be with his patients, he isn't. So we go on, and so we shall continue to go, I think, until the end of time."

"It is not the end of time, it is scarcely ten-thirty, ha ha!" cried Dr Panna Lal, who was again in confident mood. "Gentlemen, if I may be allowed to say a few words, what an interesting talk, also thankfulness and gratitude to Mr Fielding in the first place teaches our sons and gives them all the great benefits of his experience and judgement—"

"Dr Lal!"

"Dr Aziz?"

"You sit on my leg."

"I beg pardon, but some might say your leg kicks."

"Come along, we tire the invalid in either case," said Fielding, and they filed out—four Mohammedans, two Hindus and the Englishman. They stood on the veranda while their conveyances were summoned out of various patches of shade.

"Aziz has a high opinion of you, he only did not speak because of his illness."

"I quite understand," said Fielding, who was rather disappointed with his call. The Club comment, "making himself cheap as usual", passed through his mind. He couldn't even get his horse brought up. He had liked Aziz so much at their first meeting, and had hoped for developments.

Chapter 10

The heat had leapt forward in the last hour, the street was deserted as if a catastrophe had cleaned off humanity during the inconclusive talk. Opposite Aziz's bungalow stood a large unfinished house belonging to two brothers, astrologers, and a squirrel hung head downwards on it, pressing its belly against burning scaffolding and twitching a mangy tail. It seemed the only occupant of the house, and the squeaks it gave were in tune with the infinite, no doubt, but not attractive except to other squirrels. More noises came from a dusty tree, where brown birds creaked and floundered about looking for insects; another bird, the invisible coppersmith, had started his "ponk ponk". It matters so little to the majority of living beings what the minority, that calls itself human, desires or decides. Most of the inhabitants of India do not mind how India is governed. Nor are the lower animals of England concerned about England, but in the tropics the indifference is more prominent, the inarticulate world is closer at hand and readier to resume control as soon as men are tired. When the seven gentlemen who had held such various opinions inside the bungalow came out of it, they were aware of a common burden, a vague threat which they called "the bad weather coming". They felt that they could not do their work, or would not be paid enough for doing it. The space between them and their carriages, instead of being empty, was clogged with a medium that pressed against their flesh, the carriage cushions scalded their trousers, their eyes pricked, domes of hot water accumulated under their headgear and poured down their cheeks. Salaaming feebly, they dispersed for the interiors of other bungalows, to recover their self-esteem and the qualities that distinguished them from each other.

All over the city, and over much of India, the same retreat on the part of humanity was beginning, into cellars, up hills, under trees. April, herald of horrors, is at hand. The sun was returning to his kingdom with power but without beauty—that was the sinister feature. If only there had been beauty! His cruelty would have been tolerable then. Through excess of light, he failed to triumph, he also; in his yellowy-white overflow not only matter, but brightness itself lay drowned. He was not the unattainable Friend, either of men or birds or other suns, he was not the eternal promise, the never-withdrawn suggestion that haunts our consciousness; he was merely a creature, like the rest, and so debarred from glory.

Chapter 11

Although the Indians had driven off, and Fielding could see his horse standing in a small shed in the corner of the compound, no one troubled to bring it to him. He started to get it himself, but was stopped by a call from the house. Aziz was sitting up in bed, looking dishevelled and sad. "Here's your home," he said sardonically. "Here's the celebrated hospitality of the East. Look at the flies. Look at the chunam coming off the walls. Isn't it jolly? Now I suppose you want to be off, having seen an oriental interior."

"Anyhow, you want to rest."

"I can rest the whole day, thanks to worthy Dr Lal. Major Callendar's spy, I suppose you know, but this time it didn't work. I am allowed to have a slight temperature."

"Callendar doesn't trust anyone, English or Indian; that's his character, and I wish you weren't under him; but you are, and that's that."

"Before you go, for you are evidently in a great hurry, will you please unlock that drawer? Do you see a piece of brown paper at the top?"

"Yes."

"Open it."

"Who is this?"

"She was my wife. You are the first Englishman she has ever come before. Now put her photograph away."

He was astonished, as a traveller who suddenly sees, between the stones of the desert, flowers. The flowers have been there all the time, but suddenly he sees them. He tried to look at the photograph, but in itself it was just a woman in a sari, facing the world. He muttered, "Really, I don't know why you pay me this great compliment, Aziz, but I do appreciate it."

"Oh, it's nothing, she was not a highly educated woman or even beautiful, but put it away. You would have seen her, so why should you not see her photograph?"

"You would have allowed me to see her?"

"Why not? I believe in the purdah, but I should have told her you were my brother, and she would have seen you. Hamidullah saw her, and several others."

"Did she think they were your brothers?"

"Of course not, but the word exists and is convenient. All men are my brothers, and as soon as one behaves as such he may see my wife."

"And when the whole world behaves as such, there will be no more purdah?"

"It is because you can say and feel such a remark as that, that I show you the photograph," said Aziz gravely. "It is beyond the power of most men. It is because you behave well while I behave badly that I show it you. I never expected you to come back just now when I called you. I thought, 'He has certainly done with me; I have insulted him.' Mr Fielding, no one can ever realize how much kindness we Indians need, we do not even realize it ourselves. But we know when it has been given. We do not forget, though we may seem to. Kindness, more kindness, and even after that more kindness. I assure you it is the only hope." His voice seemed to arise from a dream. Altering it, yet still deep below his normal surface, he said: "We can't build up India except on what we feel. What is the use of all these reforms, and Conciliation Committees for Mohurram, and shall we cut the tazia short or shall we carry it another route, and Councils of Notables and official parties where the English sneer at our skins?"

"It's beginning at the wrong end, isn't it? I know, but institutions and the Government don't." He looked again at the photograph. The lady faced the world at her husband's wish and her own, but how bewildering she found it, the echoing contradictory world!

"Put her away, she is of no importance, she is dead," said Aziz gently. "I showed her to you because I have nothing else to show. You may look round the whole of my bungalow now, and empty everything. I have no other secrets, my three children live away with their grandmamma, and that is all."

Fielding sat down by the bed, flattered at the trust reposed in him, yet rather sad. He felt old. He wished that he too could be carried away on waves of emotion. The next time they met, Aziz might be cautious and standoffish. He realized this, and it made him sad that he should realize it. Kindness, kindness, and more kindness—yes, that he might supply, but was that really all that the queer nation needed? Did it not also demand an occasional intoxication of the blood? What had he done to deserve this outburst of confidence, and what hostage could he give in exchange? He looked back at his own life. What a poor crop of secrets it had produced! There were things in it that he had shown to no one, but they were so uninteresting, it wasn't worth while lifting a purdah on their account. He'd been in love, engaged to be married, lady broke it off, memories of her and thoughts about her had kept him from other women for a time; then indulgence, followed by repentance and equilibrium. Meagre really, except the equilibrium, and Aziz didn't want to have that confided to him—he would have called it "everything ranged coldly on shelves".

"I shall not really be intimate with this fellow," Fielding thought, and then "nor with anyone." That was the corollary. And he had to confess that he really didn't mind, that he was content to help people, and like them as long as they didn't object, and if they objected pass on serenely. Experience can do much, and all that he had learned in England and Europe was an assistance to him, and helped him towards clarity, but clarity prevented him from experiencing something else.

"How did you like the two ladies you met last Thursday?" he asked.

Aziz shook his head distastefully. The question reminded him of his rash remark about the Marabar Caves.

"How do you like Englishwomen generally?"

"Hamidullah liked them in England. Here we never look

at them. Oh no, much too careful. Let's talk of something else."

"Hamidullah's right: they are much nicer in England. There's something that doesn't suit them out here."

Aziz after another silence said, "Why are you not married?"

Fielding was pleased that he had asked. "Because I have more or less come through without it," he replied. "I was thinking of telling you a little about myself some day if I can make it interesting enough. The lady I liked wouldn't marry me—that is the main point, but that's fifteen years ago and now means nothing."

"But you haven't children."

"None."

"Excuse the following question: have you any illegitimate children?"

"No. I'd willingly tell you if I had."

"Then your name will entirely die out."

"It must."

"Well." He shook his head. "This indifference is what the Oriental will never understand."

"I don't care for children."

"Caring has nothing to do with it," he said impatiently.

"I don't feel their absence, I don't want them weeping around my deathbed and being polite about me afterwards, which I believe is the general notion. I'd far rather leave a thought behind me than a child. Other people can have children. No obligation, with England getting so chock-a-block and overrunning India for jobs."

"Why don't you marry Miss Quested?"

"Good God! Why, the girl's a prig."

"Prig, prig? Kindly explain. Isn't that a bad word?"

"Oh, I don't know her, but she struck me as one of the more pathetic products of Western education. She depresses me."

"But prig, Mr Fielding? How's that?"

"She goes on and on as if she's at a lecture—trying ever so hard to understand India and life, and occasionally taking a note."

"I thought her so nice and sincere."

"So she probably is," said Fielding, ashamed of his roughness: any suggestion that he should marry always does produce overstatements on the part of the bachelor, and a mental breeze. "But I can't marry her if I wanted to, for she has just become engaged to the City Magistrate."

"Has she indeed? I am so glad!" he exclaimed with relief, for this exempted him from the Marabar expedition: he would scarcely be expected to entertain regular Anglo-Indians.

"It's the old mother's doing. She was afraid her dear boy would choose for himself, so she brought out the girl on purpose, and flung them together until it happened."

"Mrs Moore did not mention that to me among her plans."

"I may have got it wrong—I'm out of Club gossip. But anyhow they're engaged to be married."

"Yes, you're out of it, my poor chap," he smiled. "No Miss Quested for Mr Fielding. However, she was not beautiful. She has practically no breasts, if you come to think of it."

He smiled too, but found a touch of bad taste in the reference to a lady's breasts.

"For the City Magistrate they shall be sufficient perhaps, and he for her. For you I shall arrange a lady with breasts like mangoes. . . ."

"No, you won't."

"I will not really, and besides your position makes it dangerous for you." His mind had slipped from matrimony to Calcutta. His face grew grave. Fancy if he had persuaded the Principal to accompany him there, and then got him into trouble! And abruptly he took up a new attitude towards his friend, the attitude of the protector who knows the dangers of India and is admonitory. "You can't be too careful in every way, Mr Fielding; whatever you say or do in this damned country there is always some envious fellow on the lookout. You may be surprised to know that there were at least three spies sitting here when you came to inquire. I was really a good deal upset that you talked in that fashion about God. They will certainly report it."

"To whom?"

"That's all very well, but you spoke against morality also, and you said you had come to take other people's jobs. All that was very unwise. This is an awful place for scandal. Why, actually one of your own pupils was listening."

"Thanks for telling me that; yes, I must try and be more careful. If I'm interested, I'm apt to forget myself. Still, it doesn't do real harm."

"But speaking out may get you into trouble."

"It's often done so in the past."

"There, listen to that! But the end of it might be that you lost your job."

"If I do, I do. I shall survive it. I travel light."

"Travel light! You are a most extraordinary race," said Aziz, turning away as if he were going to sleep, and immediately turning back again. "Is it your climate, or what?"

"Plenty of Indians travel light too—saddhus and such. It's one of the things I admire about your country. Any man can travel light until he has a wife or children. That's part of my case against marriage. I'm a holy man minus the holiness. Hand that on to your three spies, and tell them to put it in their pipes."

Aziz was charmed and interested, and turned the new idea over in his mind. So this was why Mr Fielding and a few others were so fearless! They had nothing to lose. But he himself was rooted in society and Islam. He belonged to a tradition which bound him, and he had brought children into the world, the society of the future. Though he lived so vaguely in this flimsy bungalow, nevertheless he was placed, placed.

"I can't be sacked from my job, because my job's Education. I believe in teaching people to be individuals, and to understand other individuals. It's the only thing I do believe in. At Government College, I mix it up with trigonometry, and so on. When I'm a saddhu, I shall mix it up with something else."

He concluded his manifesto, and both were silent. The

eye-flies became worse than ever and danced close up to their pupils, or crawled into their ears. Fielding hit about wildly. The exercise made him hot, and he got up to go.

"You might tell your servant to bring my horse. He doesn't seem to appreciate my Urdu."

"I know. I gave him orders not to. Such are the tricks we play on unfortunate Englishmen. Poor Mr Fielding! But I will release you now. Oh dear! With the exception of yourself and Hamidullah, I have no one to talk to in this place. You like Hamidullah, don't you?"

"Very much."

"Do you promise to come at once to us when you are in trouble?"

"I never can be in trouble."

"There goes a queer chap, I trust he won't come to grief," thought Aziz, left alone. His period of admiration was over, and he reacted towards patronage. It was difficult for him to remain in awe of anyone who played with all his cards on the table. Fielding, he discovered on closer acquaintance, was truly warm-hearted and unconventional, but not what can be called wise. That frankness of speech in the presence of Ram Chand, Rafi and Co. was dangerous and inelegant. It served no useful end.

But they were friends, brothers. That part was settled, their compact had been subscribed by the photograph, they trusted one another, affection had triumphed for once in a way. He dropped off to sleep amid the happier memories of the last two hours—poetry of Ghalib, female grace, good old Hamidullah, good Fielding, his honoured wife and dear boys. He passed into a region where these joys had no enemies but bloomed harmoniously in an eternal garden, or ran down watershoots of ribbed marble, or rose into domes whereunder were inscribed, black against white, the ninety-nine attributes of God.

Part 2

Caves

Chapter 12

The Ganges, though flowing from the foot of Vishnu and through Siva's hair, is not an ancient stream. Geology, looking further than religion, knows of a time when neither the river nor the Himalayas that nourish it existed, and an ocean flowed over the holy places of Hindustan. The mountains rose, their debris silted up the ocean, the gods took their seats on them and contrived the river, and the India we call immemorial came into being. But India is really far older. In the days of the prehistoric ocean the southern part of the peninsula already existed, and the high places of Dravidia have been land since land began, and have seen on the one side the sinking of a continent that joined them to Africa, and on the other the upheaval of the Himalayas from a sea. They are older than anything in the world. No water has ever covered them, and the sun who has watched them for countless aeons may still discern in their outlines forms that were his before our globe was torn from his bosom. If flesh of the sun's flesh is to be touched anywhere, it is here, among the incredible antiquity of these hills.

Yet even they are altering. As Himalayan India rose, this India, the primal, has been depressed, and is slowly re-entering the curve of the earth. It may be that in aeons to come an ocean will flow here too, and cover the sun-born rocks with slime. Meanwhile the plain of the Ganges encroaches on them with something of the sea's action. They are sinking beneath the newer lands. Their main mass is untouched, but at the edge their outposts have been cut off and stand knee-deep, throat-deep, in the advancing soil. There is something unspeakable in these outposts. They are like nothing else in the world, and a glimpse of them makes the breath catch. They rise abruptly, insanely, without the proportion that is kept by the wildest hills elsewhere, they bear no relation to anything dreamt or seen. To call them "uncanny" suggests ghosts, and they are older than all spirit. Hinduism has scratched and plastered a few rocks, but the shrines are unfrequented, as if pilgrims, who generally seek the extraordinary, had here found too much of it. Some saddhus did once settle in a cave, but they were smoked out, and even Buddha, who must have passed this way down to the Bo Tree of Gaya, shunned a renunciation more complete than his own, and has left no legend of struggle or victory in the Marabar.

The caves are readily described. A tunnel eight feet long, five feet high, three feet wide, leads to a circular chamber about twenty feet in diameter. This arrangement occurs again and again throughout the group of hills, and this is all, this is a Marabar cave. Having seen one such cave, having seen two, having seen three, four, fourteen, twenty-four, the visitor returns to Chandrapore uncertain whether he has had an interesting experience or a dull one or any experience at all. He finds it difficult to discuss the caves, or to keep them apart in his mind, for the pattern never varies, and no carving, not even a bees' nest or a bat, distinguishes one from another. Nothing, nothing attaches to them, and their reputation—for they have one—does not depend upon human speech. It is as if the surrounding plain or the passing birds have taken upon themselves to exclaim "Extraordinary!" and the word has taken root in the air, and been inhaled by mankind.

They are dark caves. Even when they open towards the sun, very little light penetrates down the entrance tunnel into the circular chamber. There is little to see, and no eye to see it, until the visitor arrives for his five minutes, and strikes a match. Immediately another flame rises in the depths of the rock and moves towards the surface like an imprisoned spirit; the walls of the circular chamber have been most marvellously polished. The two flames approach and strive to unite, but cannot, because one of them breathes air, the other stone. A mirror inlaid with lovely colours divides the lovers, delicate stars of pink and gray interpose, exquisite nebulae, shadings fainter than the tail of a comet or the midday moon, all the evanescent life of the granite, only here visible. Fists and fingers thrust above the advancing soil —here at last is their skin, finer than any covering acquired by the animals, smoother than windless water, more voluptuous than love. The radiance increases, the flames touch one another, kiss, expire. The cave is dark again, like all the caves.

Only the wall of the circular chamber has been polished thus. The sides of the tunnel are left rough, they impinge as an afterthought upon the internal perfection. An entrance was necessary, so mankind made one. But elsewhere, deeper in the granite, are there certain chambers that have no entrances? Chambers never unsealed since the arrival of the gods? Local report declares that these exceed in number those that can be visited, as the dead exceed the living—four hundred of them, four thousand or million. Nothing is inside them, they were sealed up before the creation of pestilence or treasure; if mankind grew curious and excavated, nothing, nothing would be added to the sum of good or evil. One of them is rumoured within the boulder that swings on the summit of the highest of the hills; a bubble-shaped cave that has neither ceiling nor floor, and mirrors its own darkness in every direction infinitely. If the boulder falls and smashes, the cave will smash too—empty as an Easter egg. The boulder because of its hollowness sways in the wind, and even moves when a crow perches upon it; hence its name and the name of its stupendous pedestal: the Kawa Dol.

Chapter 13

These hills look romantic in certain lights and at suitable distances, and seen of an evening from the upper veranda of the Club they caused Miss Quested to say conversationally to Miss Derek that she should like to have gone, that Dr Aziz at Mr Fielding's had said he would arrange something, and that Indians seem rather forgetful. She was overheard by the servant who offered them vermouths. This servant understood English. And he was not exactly a spy, but he kept his ears open, and Mahmoud Ali did not exactly bribe him, but did encourage him to come and squat with his own servants, and would happen to stroll their way when he was there. As the story travelled, it accreted emotion, and Aziz learned with horror that the ladies were deeply offended with him, and had expected an invitation daily. He thought his facile remark had been forgotten. Endowed with two memories, a temporary and a permanent, he had hitherto relegated the caves to the former. Now he transferred them once for all, and pushed the matter through. They were to be a stupendous replica of the tea-party. He began by securing Fielding and old Godbole, and then commissioned Fielding to approach Mrs Moore and Miss Quested when they were alone—by this device Ronny, their official protector, could be circumvented. Fielding didn't like the job much; he was busy, caves bored him, he foresaw friction and expense, but he would not refuse the first favour his friend had asked from him, and did as required. The ladies accepted. It was a little inconvenient in the present press of their engagements, still, they hoped to manage it after consulting Mr Heaslop. Consulted, Ronny raised no objection, provided Fielding undertook full responsibility for their comfort. He was not enthusiastic about the picnic, but then no more were the ladies—no one was enthusiastic, yet it took place.

Aziz was terribly worried. It was not a long expedition—a train left Chandrapore just before dawn, another would bring them back for tiffin—but he was only a little official still, and feared to acquit himself dishonourably. He had to ask Major Callendar for half a day's leave, and be refused because of his recent malingering; despair; renewed approach of Major Callendar through Fielding, and contemptuous snarling permission. He had to borrow cutlery from Mahmoud Ali without inviting him. Then there was the question of alcohol: Mr Fielding, and perhaps the ladies, were drinkers, so must he provide whiskey-sodas and ports? There was the problem of transport from the wayside station of Marabar to the caves. There was the problem of Professor Godbole and his food, and of Professor Godbole and other people's food—two problems, not one problem. The Professor was not a very strict Hindu—he would take tea, fruit, soda-water and sweets, whoever cooked them, and vegetables and rice if cooked by a Brahman; but not meat, not cakes lest they contained eggs, and he would not allow anyone else to eat beef: a slice of beef upon a distant plate would wreck his happiness. Other people might eat mutton, they might eat ham. But over ham Aziz's own religion raised its voice: he did not fancy other people eating ham. Trouble after trouble encountered him, because he had challenged the spirit of the Indian earth, which tries to keep men in compartments.

At last the moment arrived.

His friends thought him most unwise to mix himself up with English ladies, and warned him to take every precaution against unpunctuality. Consequently he spent the previous night at the station. The servants were huddled on the platform, enjoined not to stray. He himself walked up and down with old Mohammed Latif, who was to act as major-domo. He felt insecure and also unreal. A car drove up, and he hoped Fielding would get out of it, to lend him solidity. But it contained Mrs Moore, Miss Quested and their Goanese servant. He rushed to meet them, suddenly happy. "But you've come after all. Oh how very very kind of you!" he cried. "This is the happiest moment in all my life."

The ladies were civil. It was not the happiest moment in their lives, still, they looked forward to enjoying themselves as soon as the bother of the early start was over. They had not seen him since the expedition was arranged, and they thanked him adequately.

"You don't require tickets—please stop your servant. There are no tickets on the Marabar branch-line; it is its peculiarity. You come to the carriage and rest till Mr Fielding joins us. Did you know you are to travel purdah? Will you like that?"

They replied that they should like it. The train had come in, and a crowd of dependents were swarming over the seats of the carriage like monkeys. Aziz had borrowed servants from his friends, as well as bringing his own three, and quarrels over precedence were resulting. The ladies' servant stood apart, with a sneering expression on his face. They had hired him while they were still globe-trotters, at Bombay. In a hotel or among smart people he was excellent, but as soon as they consorted with anyone whom he thought second-rate he left them to their disgrace.

The night was still dark, but had acquired the temporary look that indicates its end. Perched on the roof of a shed, the station-master's hens began to dream of kites instead of owls. Lamps were put out, in order to save the trouble of putting them out later; the smell of tobacco and the sound of spitting arose from third-class passengers in dark corners; heads were unshrouded, teeth cleaned on the twigs of a tree. So convinced was a junior official that another sun would rise, that he rang a bell with enthusiasm. This upset the servants. They shrieked that the train was starting, and ran to both ends of it to intercede. Much had still to enter the purdah carriage—a box bound with brass, a melon wearing a fez, a towel containing guavas, a step-ladder and a gun. The guests played up all right. They had no race-consciousness—Mrs Moore was too old, Miss Quested too new—and they behaved to Aziz as to any young man who had been kind to them in the country. This moved him deeply. He had expected them to arrive with Mr Fielding, instead of which they trusted themselves to be with him a few moments alone.

"Send back your servant," he suggested. "He is unnecessary. Then we shall all be Moslems together."

"And he is such a horrible servant. Antony, you can go; we don't want you," said the girl impatiently.

"Master told me to come."

"Mistress tells you to go."

"Master says, keep near the ladies all the morning."

"Well, your ladies won't have you." She turned to the host. "Do get rid of him, Dr Aziz!"

"Mohammed Latif!" he called.

The poor relative exchanged fezzes with the melon, and peeped out of the window of the railway carriage, whose confusion he was superintending.

"Here is my cousin, Mr Mohammed Latif. Oh no, don't shake hands. He is an Indian of the old-fashioned sort, he prefers to salaam. There, I told you so. Mohammed Latif, how beautifully you salaam. See, he hasn't understood; he knows no English."

"You spick a lie," said the old man gently.

"I spick a lie! Oh, jolly good. Isn't he a funny old man? We will have great jokes with him later. He does all sorts of little things. He is not nearly as stupid as you think, and awfully poor. It's lucky ours is a large family." He flung an arm round the grubby neck. "But you get inside, make yourselves at home; yes, you lie down." The celebrated oriental confusion appeared at last to be at an end. "Excuse me, now I must meet our other two guests!"

He was getting nervous again, for it was ten minutes to the time. Still, Fielding was an Englishman, and they never do miss trains, and Godbole was a Hindu and did not count, and, soothed by this logic, he grew calmer as the hour of departure approached. Mohammed Latif had bribed Antony not to come. They walked up and down the platform, talking usefully. They agreed that they had overdone the servants, and must leave two or three behind at Marabar station. And Aziz explained that he might be playing one or two practical jokes at the caves—not out of unkindness, but to make the guests laugh. The old man assented with slight sideway motions of the head: he was always willing to be ridiculed, and he bade Aziz not spare him. Elated by his importance, he began an indecent anecdote.

"Tell me another time, brother, when I have more leisure, for now, as I have already explained, we have to give pleasure to non-Moslems. Three will be Europeans, one a Hindu, which must not be forgotten. Every attention must be paid to Professor Godbole, lest he feel that he is inferior to my other guests."

"I will discuss philosophy with him."

"That will be kind of you; but the servants are even more important. We must not convey an impression of disorganization. It can be done, and I expect you to do it. . . ."

A shriek from the purdah carriage. The train had started.

"Merciful God!" cried Mohammed Latif. He flung himself at the train, and leapt onto the footboard of a carriage. Aziz did likewise. It was an easy feat, for a branch-line train is slow to assume special airs. "We're monkeys, don't worry," he called, hanging on to a bar and laughing. Then he howled: "Mr Fielding! Mr Fielding!"

There were Fielding and old Godbole, held up at the level-crossing. Appalling catastrophe! The gates had been closed earlier than usual. They leapt from their tonga; they gesticulated, but what was the good? So near and yet so far! As the train joggled past over the points there was time for agonized words.

"Bad, bad, you have destroyed me."

"Godbole's pujah did it," cried the Englishman.

The Brahman lowered his eyes, ashamed of religion. For it was so: he had miscalculated the length of a prayer.

"Jump on, I must have you," screamed Aziz, beside himself.

"Right, give a hand."

"He's not to, he'll kill himself," Mrs Moore protested. He jumped, he failed, missed his friend's hand, and fell back onto the line. The train rumbled past. He scrambled onto his feet, and bawled after them, "I'm all right, you're all right, don't worry," and then they passed beyond range of his voice.

"Mrs Moore, Miss Quested, our expedition is a ruin." He swung himself along the footboard, almost in tears.

"Get in, get in; you'll kill yourself as well as Mr Fielding. I see no ruin."

"How is that? Oh, explain to me!" he said piteously, like a child.

"We shall be all Moslems together now, as you promised."

She was perfect as always, his dear Mrs Moore. All the love for her he had felt at the mosque welled up again, the fresher for forgetfulness. There was nothing he would not do for her. He would die to make her happy.

"Get in, Dr Aziz, you make us giddy," the other lady called. "If they're so foolish as to miss the train, that's their loss, not ours."

"I am to blame. I am the host."

"Nonsense, go to your carriage. We're going to have a delightful time without them."

Not perfect like Mrs Moore, but very sincere and kind. Wonderful ladies, both of them, and for one precious morning his guests. He felt important and competent. Fielding was a loss personally, being a friend, increasingly dear, yet if Fielding had come he himself would have remained in leading-strings. "Indians are incapable of responsibility," said the officials, and Hamidullah sometimes said so too. He would show those pessimists that they were wrong. Smiling proudly, he glanced outward at the country, which was still invisible except as a dark movement in the darkness; then upwards at the sky, where the stars of the sprawling Scorpion had begun to pale. Then he dived through a window into a second-class carriage.

"Mohammed Latif, by the way, what is in these caves, brother? Why are we all going to see them?"

Such a question was beyond the poor relative's scope. He could only reply that God and the local villagers knew, and that the latter would gladly act as guides.

Chapter 14

Most of life is so dull that there is nothing to be said about it, and the books and talk that would describe it as interesting are obliged to exaggerate, in the hope of justifying their own existence. Inside its cocoon of work or social obligation, the human spirit slumbers for the most part, registering the distinction between pleasure and pain, but not nearly as alert as we pretend. There are periods in the most thrilling day during which nothing happens, and though we continue to exclaim "I do enjoy myself" or "I am horrified" we are insincere. "As far as I feel anything, it is enjoyment, horror"—it's no more than that really, and a perfectly adjusted organism would be silent.

It so happened that Mrs Moore and Miss Quested had felt nothing acutely for a fortnight. Ever since Professor Godbole had sung his queer little song, they had lived more or less inside cocoons, and the difference between them was that the elder lady accepted her own apathy, while the younger resented hers. It was Adela's faith that the whole stream of events is important and interesting, and if she grew bored she blamed herself severely and compelled her lips to utter enthusiasms. This was the only insincerity in a character otherwise sincere, and it was indeed the intellectual protest of her youth. She was particularly vexed now because she was both in India and engaged to be married, which double event should have made every instant sublime.

India was certainly dim this morning, though seen under the auspices of Indians. Her wish had been granted, but too late. She could not get excited over Aziz and his arrangements. She was not the least unhappy or depressed, and the various odd objects that surrounded her—the comic "purdah" carriage, the piles of rugs and bolsters, the rolling melons, the scent of sweet oils, the ladder, the brass-bound box, the sudden irruption of Mahmoud Ali's butler from the lavatory with tea and poached eggs upon a tray—they were all new and amusing, and led her to comment appropriately, but they wouldn't bite into her mind. So she tried to find comfort by reflecting that her main interest would henceforward be Ronny.

"What a nice cheerful servant! What a relief after Antony!"

"They startle one rather. A strange place to make tea in," said Mrs Moore, who had hoped for a nap.

"I want to sack Antony. His behaviour on the platform has decided me."

Mrs Moore thought that Antony's better self would come to the front at Simla. Miss Quested was to be married at Simla; some cousins, with a house looking straight onto Tibet, had invited her.

"Anyhow, we must get a second servant, because at Simla you will be at the hotel, and I don't think Ronny's Baldeo . . ." She loved plans.

"Very well, you get another servant, and I'll keep Antony with me. I am used to his unappetizing ways. He will see me through the Hot Weather."

"I don't believe in the Hot Weather. People like Major Callendar who always talk about it—it's in the hope of making one feel inexperienced and small, like their everlasting 'I've been twenty years in this country'."

"I believe in the Hot Weather, but never did I suppose it would bottle me up as it will." For owing to the sage leisureliness of Ronny and Adela they could not be married till May, and consequently Mrs Moore could not return to England immediately after the wedding, which was what she had hoped to do. By May a barrier of fire would have fallen across India and the adjoining sea, and she would have to remain perched up in the Himalayas waiting for the world to get cooler.

"I won't be bottled up," announced the girl. "I've no patience with these women here who leave their husbands grilling in the plains. Mrs McBryde hasn't stopped down once since she married; she leaves her quite intelligent husband alone half the year, and then's surprised she's out of touch with him."

"She has children, you see."

"Oh yes, that's true," said Miss Quested, disconcerted.

"It is the children who are the first consideration. Until they are grown up, and married off. When that happens one has again the right to live for oneself—in the plains or the hills, as suits."

"Oh yes, you're perfectly right. I never thought it out."

"If one has not become too stupid and old." She handed her empty cup to the servant.

"My idea now is that my cousins shall find me a servant in Simla, at all events to see me through the wedding, after which Ronny means to reorganize his staff entirely. He does it very well for a bachelor; still, when he is married no doubt various changes will have to be made—his old servants won't want to take their orders from me, and I don't blame them."

Mrs Moore pushed up the shutters and looked out. She had brought Ronny and Adela together by their mutual wish, but really she could not advise them further. She felt increasingly (vision or nightmare?) that, though people are important, the relations between them are not, and that in particular too much fuss has been made over marriage; centuries of carnal embracement, yet man is no nearer to understanding man. And today she felt this with such force that it seemed itself a relationship, itself a person, who was trying to take hold of her hand.

"Anything to be seen of the hills?"

"Only various shades of the dark."

"We can't be far from the place where my hyena was." She peered into the timeless twilight. The train crossed a nullah. "Pomper, pomper, pomper," was the sound that the wheels made as they trundled over the bridge, moving very slowly. A hundred yards on came a second nullah, then a third, suggesting the neighbourhood of higher ground. "Perhaps this is mine; anyhow, the road runs parallel with the railway." Her accident was a pleasant memory; she felt in her dry, honest way that it had given her a good shake-up, and taught her Ronny's true worth. Then she went back to her plans; plans had been a passion with her from girlhood. Now and then she paid tribute to the present, said how friendly and intelligent Aziz was, ate a guava, couldn't eat a fried sweet, practised her Urdu on the servant; but her thoughts ever veered to the manageable future, and to the Anglo-Indian life she had decided to endure. And, as she appraised it with its adjuncts of Turtons and Burtons, the train accompanied her sentences, "pomper, pomper", the train half asleep, going nowhere in particular and with no passenger of importance in any of its carriages, the branch-line train, lost on a low embankment between dull fields. Its message—for it had one—avoided her well-equipped mind. Far away behind her, with a shriek that meant business, rushed the Mail, connecting up important towns such as Calcutta and Lahore, where interesting events occur and personalities are developed. She understood that. Unfortunately, India has few important towns. India is the country, fields, fields, then hills, jungle, hills, and more fields. The branch-line stops, the road is only practicable for cars to a point, the bullock-carts lumber down the side-tracks, paths fray out into the cultivation, and disappear near a splash of red paint. How can the mind take hold of such a country? Generations of invaders have tried, but they remain in exile. The important towns they build are only retreats, their quarrels the malaise of men who cannot find their way home. India knows of their trouble. She knows of the whole world's trouble, to its uttermost depth. She calls "Come" through her hundred mouths, through objects ridiculous and august. But come to what? She has never defined. She is not a promise, only an appeal.

"I will fetch you from Simla when it's cool enough. I will unbottle you in fact," continued the reliable girl. "We then see some of the Mogul stuff—how appalling if we let you miss the Taj!—and then I will see you off at Bombay. Your last glimpse of this country really shall be interesting." But

Mrs Moore had fallen asleep, exhausted by the early start. She was in rather low health, and ought not to have attempted the expedition, but had pulled herself together in case the pleasure of the others should suffer. Her dreams were of the same texture, but there it was her other children who were wanting something, Stella and Ralph, and she was explaining to them that she could not be in two families at once. When she awoke, Adela had ceased to plan, and leant out of a window, saying, "They're rather wonderful."

Astonishing even from the rise of the Civil Station, here the Marabar were gods to whom earth is a ghost. Kawa Dol was nearest. It shot up in a single slab, on whose summit one rock was poised—if a mass so great can be called one rock. Behind it, recumbent, were the hills that contained the other caves, isolated each from his neighbour by broad channels of the plain. The assemblage, ten in all, shifted a little as the train crept past them, as if observing its arrival.

"I'd not have missed this for anything," said the girl, exaggerating her enthusiasm. "Look, the sun's rising—this'll be absolutely magnificent—come quickly—look. I wouldn't have missed this for anything. We should never have seen it if we'd stuck to the Turtons and their eternal elephants."

As she spoke, the sky to the left turned angry orange. Colour throbbed and mounted behind a pattern of trees, grew in intensity, was yet brighter, incredibly brighter, strained from without against the globe of the air. They awaited the miracle. But at the supreme moment, when night should have died and day lived, nothing occurred. It was as if virtue had failed in the celestial fount. The hues in the east decayed, the hills seemed dimmer though in fact better lit, and a profound disappointment entered with the morning breeze. Why, when the chamber was prepared, did the bridegroom not enter with trumpets and shawms, as humanity expects? The sun rose without splendour. He was presently observed trailing yellowish behind the trees, or against insipid sky, and touching the bodies already at work in the fields.

"Ah, that must be the false dawn—isn't it caused by dust

in the upper layers of the atmosphere that couldn't fall down during the night? I think Mr McBryde said so. Well, I must admit that England has it as regards sunrises. Do you remember Grasmere?"

"Ah, dearest Grasmere!" Its little lakes and mountains were beloved by them all. Romantic yet manageable, it sprang from a kindlier planet. Here an untidy plain stretched to the knees of the Marabar.

"Good morning, good morning, put on your topis," shouted Aziz from further down the train. "Put on your topis at once, the early sun is highly dangerous for heads. I speak as a doctor."

"Good morning, good morning, put on your own."

"Not for my thick head," he laughed, banging it and holding up pads of his hair.

"Nice creature he is," murmured Adela.

"Listen—Mohammed Latif says 'Good morning' next." Various pointless jests.

"Dr Aziz, what's happened to your hills? The train has forgotten to stop."

"Perhaps it is a circular train and goes back to Chandrapore without a break. Who knows!"

Having wandered off into the plain for a mile, the train slowed up against an elephant. There was a platform too, but it shrivelled into insignificance. An elephant, waving her painted forehead at the morn! "Oh, what a surprise!" called the ladies politely. Aziz said nothing, but he nearly burst with pride and relief. The elephant was the one grand feature of the picnic, and God alone knew what he had gone through to obtain her. Semi-official, she was best approached through the Nawab Bahadur, who was best approached through Nureddin, but he never answered letters, but his mother had great influence with him and was a friend of Hamidullah Begum's, who had been excessively kind and had promised to call on her provided the broken shutter of the purdah carriage came back soon enough from Calcutta. That an elephant should depend from so long and so slender a string filled Aziz with content, and with humorous appreciation of the East, where the friends of friends are a reality, where everything gets done some time, and sooner or later everyone gets his share of happiness. And Mohammed Latif was likewise content, because two of the guests had missed the train, and consequently he could ride on the howdah instead of following in a cart, and the servants were content, because an elephant increased their self-esteem, and they tumbled out the luggage into the dust with shouts and bangs, issuing orders to one another, and convulsed with goodwill.

"It takes an hour to get there, an hour to get back, and two hours for the caves, which we will call three," said Aziz, smiling charmingly. There was suddenly something regal about him. "The train back is at eleven-thirty, and you will be sitting down to your tiffin in Chandrapore with Mr Heaslop at exactly your usual hour, namely one-fifteen. I know everything about you. Four hours—quite a small expedition—and an hour extra for misfortunes, which occur somewhat frequently among my people. My idea is to plan everything without consulting you; but you, Mrs Moore, or, Miss Quested, you are at any moment to make alterations if you wish, even if it means giving up the caves. Do you agree? Then mount this wild animal."

The elephant had knelt, gray and isolated, like another hill. They climbed up the ladder, and he mounted shikar fashion, treading first on the sharp edge of the heel and then into the looped-up tail. When Mohammed Latif followed him, the servant who held the end of the tail let go of it according to previous instructions, so that the poor relative slipped and had to cling to the netting over the buttocks. It was a little piece of court buffoonery, and distressed only the ladies, whom it was intended to divert. Both of them disliked practical jokes. Then the beast rose in two shattering movements, and poised them ten feet above the plain. Immediately below was the scurf of life that an elephant always collects round its feet—villagers, naked babies. The servants flung crockery into tongas. Hassan annexed the stallion intended for Aziz, and defied Mahmoud Ali's man from its altitude. The Brahman who had been hired to cook for Professor Godbole was planted under an acacia tree, to await their return. The train, also hoping to return, wobbled away through the fields, turning its head this way and that like a centipede. And the only other movement to be seen was a movement as of antennae, really the counterpoises of the wells which rose and fell on their pivots of mud all over the plain and dispensed a feeble flow of water. The scene was agreeable rather than not in the mild morning air, but there was little colour in it, and no vitality.

As the elephant moved towards the hills (the pale sun had by this time saluted them to the base, and pencilled shadows down their creases), a new quality occurred, a spiritual silence which invaded more senses than the ear. Life went on as usual, but had no consequences, that is to say, sounds did not echo or thoughts develop. Everything seemed cut off at its root, and therefore infected with illusion. For instance, there were some mounds by the edge of the track, low, serrated, and touched with whitewash. What were these mounds—graves, breasts of the goddess Parvati? The villagers beneath gave both replies. Again, there was a confusion about a snake, which was never cleared up. Miss Quested saw a thin, dark object reared on end at the further side of a watercourse, and said, "A snake!" The villagers agreed, and Aziz explained: yes, a black cobra, very venomous, who had reared himself up to watch the passing of the elephant. But when she looked through Ronny's field-glasses she found it wasn't a snake, but the withered and twisted stump of a toddy-palm. So she said, "It isn't a snake." The villagers contradicted her. She had put the word into their minds, and they refused to abandon it. Aziz admitted that it looked like a tree through the glasses, but insisted that it was a black cobra really, and improvised some rubbish about protective mimicry. Nothing was explained, and yet there was no romance. Films of heat, radiated from the Kawa Dol precipices, increased the confusion. They came at irregular intervals and moved capriciously. A patch of field would jump as if it was being fried, and then lie quiet. As they drew closer the radiation stopped.

The elephant walked straight at the Kawa Dol as if she would knock for admission with her forehead, then swerved, and followed a path round its base. The stones plunged straight into the earth, like cliffs into the sea, and while Miss Quested was remarking on this, and saying that it was striking, the plain quietly disappeared, peeled off, so to speak, and nothing was to be seen on either side but the granite, very dead and quiet. The sky dominated as usual, but seemed unhealthily near, adhering like a ceiling to the summits of the precipices. It was as if the contents of the corridor had never been changed. Occupied by his own munificence, Aziz noticed nothing. His guests noticed a little. They did not feel that it was an attractive place or quite worth visiting, and wished it could have turned into some Mohammedan object, such as a mosque, which their host would have appreciated and explained. His ignorance became evident, and was really rather a drawback. In spite of his gay, confident talk, he had no notion how to treat this particular aspect of India; he was lost in it without Professor Godbole, like themselves.

The corridor narrowed, then widened into a sort of tray. Here, more or less, was their goal. A ruined tank held a little water which would do for the animals, and close above the mud was punched a black hole—the first of the caves. Three hills encircled the tray. Two of them pumped out heat busily, but the third was in shadow, and here they camped.

"A horrid, stuffy place really," murmured Mrs Moore to herself.

"How quick your servants are!" Miss Quested exclaimed. For a cloth had already been laid, with a vase of artificial flowers in its centre, and Mahmoud Ali's butler offered them poached eggs and tea for the second time.

"I thought we would eat this before our caves, and breakfast after."

"Isn't this breakfast?"

"This breakfast? Did you think I should treat you so strangely?" He had been warned that English people never stop eating, and that he had better nourish them every two hours until a solid meal was ready.

"How very well it is all arranged!"

"That you shall tell me when we return to Chandrapore. Whatever disgraces I bring upon myself, you remain my guests." He spoke gravely now. They were dependent on him for a few hours, and he felt grateful to them for placing themselves in such a position. All was well so far: the elephant held a fresh-cut bough to her lips, the tonga shafts stuck up into the air, the kitchen-boy peeled potatoes, Hassan shouted, and Mohammed Latif stood as he ought, with a peeled switch in his hand. The expedition was a success, and it was Indian; an obscure young man had been allowed to show courtesy to visitors from another country, which is what all Indians long to do—even cynics like Mahmoud Ali—but they never have the chance. Hospitality had been achieved, they were "his" guests; his honour was involved in their happiness, and any discomfort they endured would tear his own soul.

Like most Orientals, Aziz overrated hospitality, mistaking it for intimacy, and not seeing that it is tainted with the sense of possession. It was only when Mrs Moore or Fielding was near him that he saw further, and knew that it is more blessed to receive than to give. These two had strange and beautiful effects on him—they were his friends, his for ever, and he theirs for ever; he loved them so much that giving and receiving became one. He loved them even better than the Hamidullahs, because he had surmounted obstacles to meet them, and this stimulates a generous mind. Their images remained somewhere in his soul up to his dying day, permanent additions. He looked at her now as she sat on a deckchair, sipping his tea, and had for a moment a joy that held the seeds of its own decay, for it would lead him to think, "Oh, what more can I do for her?" and so back to the dull round of hospitality. The black bullets of his eyes filled with soft expressive light, and he said, "Do you ever remember our mosque, Mrs Moore?"

"I do. I do," she said, suddenly vital and young.

"And how rough and rude I was, and how good you were."

"And how happy we both were."

"Friendships last longest that begin like that, I think. Shall I ever entertain your other children?"

"Do you know about the others? She will never talk about them to me," said Miss Quested, unintentionally breaking a spell.

"Ralph and Stella, yes, I know everything about them. But we must not forget to visit our caves. One of the dreams of my life is accomplished in having you both here as my guests. You cannot imagine how you have honoured me. I feel like the Emperor Babur."

"Why like him?" she inquired, rising.

"Because my ancestors came down with him from Afghanistan. They joined him at Herat. He also had often no more elephants than one, none sometimes, but he never ceased showing hospitality. When he fought or hunted or ran away, he would always stop for a time among hills, just like us; he would never let go of hospitality and pleasure, and if there was only a little food he would have it arranged nicely, and if only one musical instrument he would compel it to play a beautiful tune. I take him as my ideal. He is the poor gentleman, and he became a great king."

"I thought another Emperor is your favourite—I forget the name—you mentioned him at Mr Fielding's: what my book calls Aurangzebe."

"Alamgir? Oh yes, he was of course the more pious. But Babur—never in his whole life did he betray a friend, so I can only think of him this morning. And you know how he died? He laid down his life for his son. A death far more difficult than battle. They were caught in the heat. They should have gone back to Kabul for the bad weather, but could not for reasons of state, and at Agra Humayun fell sick. Babur walked round the bed three times, and said, 'I have borne it away,' and he did bear it away; the fever left his son and came to him instead, and he died. That is why I prefer Babur to Alamgir. I ought not to do so, but I do. However, I mustn't delay you. I see you are ready to start."

"Not at all," she said, sitting down by Mrs Moore again. "We enjoy talk like this very much." For at last he was talking about what he knew and felt, talking as he had in Fielding's garden-house; he was again the oriental guide whom they appreciated.

"I always enjoy conversing about the Moguls. It is the chief pleasure I know. You see, those first six Emperors were all most wonderful men, and as soon as one of them is mentioned, no matter which, I forget everything else in the world except the other five. You could not find six such kings in all the countries of the earth, not, I mean, coming one after the other—father, son."

"Tell us something about Akbar."

"Ah, you have heard the name of Akbar. Good. Hamidullah—whom you shall meet—will tell you that Akbar is the greatest of all. I say, 'Yes, Akbar is very wonderful, but half a Hindu; he was not a true Moslem,' which makes Hamidullah cry, 'No more was Babur, he drank wine.' But Babur always repented afterwards, which makes the entire difference, and Akbar never repented of the new religion he invented instead of the Holy Koran."

"But wasn't Akbar's new religion very fine? It was to embrace the whole of India."

"Miss Quested, fine but foolish. You keep your religion, I mine. That is the best. Nothing embraces the whole of India, nothing, nothing, and that was Akbar's mistake."

"Oh, do you feel that, Dr Aziz?" she said thoughtfully. "I hope you're not right. There will have to be something universal in this country—I don't say religion, for I'm not religious, but something, or how else are barriers to be broken down?"

She was only recommending the universal brotherhood he sometimes dreamed of, but as soon as it was put into prose it became untrue.

"Take my own case," she continued—it was indeed her own case that had animated her. "I don't know whether you happen to have heard, but I'm going to marry Mr Heaslop."

"On which my heartiest congratulations."

"Mrs Moore, may I put our difficulty to Dr Aziz—I mean our Anglo-Indian one?"

"It is your difficulty, not mine, my dear."

"Ah, that's true. Well, by marrying Mr Heaslop I shall become what is known as an Anglo-Indian."

He held up his hand in protest. "Impossible. Take back such a terrible remark."

"But I shall; it's inevitable. I can't avoid the label. What I do hope to avoid is the mentality. Women like—" She stopped, not quite liking to mention names; she would boldly have said "Mrs Turton and Mrs Callendar" a fortnight ago. "Some women are so—well, ungenerous and snobby about Indians, and I should feel too ashamed for words if I turned like them, but—and here's my difficulty—there's nothing special about me, nothing specially good or strong, which will help me to resist my environment and avoid becoming like them. I've most lamentable defects. That's why I want Akbar's 'universal religion' or the equivalent to keep me decent and sensible. Do you see what I mean?"

Her remarks pleased him, but his mind shut up tight because she had alluded to her marriage. He was not going to be mixed up in that side of things. "You are certain to be happy with any relative of Mrs Moore's," he said with a formal bow.

"Oh, my happiness—that's quite another problem. I want to consult you about this Anglo-Indian difficulty. Can you give me any advice?"

"You are absolutely unlike the others, I assure you. You will never be rude to my people."

"I am told we all get rude after a year."

"Then you are told a lie," he flashed, for she had spoken the truth and it touched him on the raw; it was itself an insult in these particular circumstances. He recovered himself at once and laughed, but her error broke up their conversation—their civilization it had almost been—which scattered like the petals of a desert flower, and left them in the middle of the hills. "Come along," he said, holding out a hand to each. They got up a little reluctantly, and addressed themselves to sightseeing.

The first cave was tolerably convenient. They skirted the puddle of water, and then climbed up over some unattractive stones, the sun crashing on their backs. Bending their heads, they disappeared one by one into the interior of the hills. The small black hole gaped where their varied forms and colours had momentarily functioned. They were sucked in like water down a drain. Bland and bald rose the precipices; bland and glutinous the sky that connected the precipices; solid and white, a Brahmany kite flapped between the rocks with a clumsiness that seemed intentional. Before man, with his itch for the seemly, had been born, the planet must have looked thus. The kite flapped away.... Before birds, perhaps. . . . And then the hole belched, and humanity returned.

A Marabar cave had been horrid as far as Mrs Moore was concerned, for she had nearly fainted in it, and had some difficulty in preventing herself from saying so as soon as she got into the air again. It was natural enough: she had always suffered from faintness, and the cave had become too full, because all their retinue followed them. Crammed with villagers and servants, the circular chamber began to smell. She lost Aziz and Adela in the dark, didn't know who touched her, couldn't breathe, and some vile naked thing struck her face and settled on her mouth like a pad. She tried to regain the entrance tunnel, but an influx of villagers swept her back. She hit her head. For an instant she went mad, hitting and gasping like a fanatic. For not only did the crush and stench alarm her; there was also a terrifying echo.

Professor Godbole had never mentioned an echo; it never impressed him, perhaps. There are some exquisite echoes in India; there is the whisper round the dome at Bijapur; there are the long, solid sentences that voyage through the air at Mandu, and return unbroken to their creator. The echo in a Marabar cave is not like these, it is entirely devoid of distinction. Whatever is said, the same monotonous noise replies, and quivers up and down the walls until it is absorbed into the roof. "Boum" is the sound as far as the human alphabet can express it, or "bou-oum", or "ou-boum"—

utterly dull. Hope, politeness, the blowing of a nose, the squeak of a boot, all produce "boum". Even the striking of a match starts a little worm coiling, which is too small to complete a circle, but is eternally watchful. And if several people talk at once an overlapping howling noise begins, echoes generate echoes, and the cave is stuffed with a snake composed of small snakes, which writhe independently.

After Mrs Moore all the others poured out. She had given the signal for the reflux. Aziz and Adela both emerged smiling and she did not want him to think his treat was a failure, so smiled too. As each person emerged she looked for a villain, but none was there, and she realized that she had been among the mildest individuals, whose only desire was to honour her, and that the naked pad was a poor little baby, astride its mother's hip. Nothing evil had been in the cave, but she had not enjoyed herself; no, she had not enjoyed herself, and she decided not to visit a second one.

"Did you see the reflection of his match—rather pretty?" asked Adela.

"I forget . . ."

"But he says this isn't a good cave, the best are on the Kawa Dol."

"I don't think I shall go on to there. I dislike climbing."

"Very well, let's sit down again in the shade until breakfast's ready."

"Ah, but that'll disappoint him so; he has taken such trouble. You should go on; you don't mind."

"Perhaps I ought to," said the girl, indifferent to what she did, but desirous of being amiable.

The servants etc. were scrambling back to the camp, pursued by grave censures from Mohammed Latif. Aziz came to help the guests over the rocks. He was at the summit of his powers, vigorous and humble, too sure of himself to resent criticism, and he was sincerely pleased when he heard they were altering his plans. "Certainly, Miss Quested, so you and I will go together, and leave Mrs Moore here, and we will not be long, yet we will not hurry, because we know that will be her wish."

"Quite right. I'm sorry not to come too, but I'm a poor walker."

"Dear Mrs Moore, what does anything matter so long as you are my guest? I am very glad you are *not* coming, which sounds strange, but you are treating me with true frankness, as a friend."

"Yes, I am your friend," she said, laying her hand on his sleeve, and thinking, despite her fatigue, how very charming, how very good, he was, and how deeply she desired his happiness. "So may I make another suggestion? Don't let so many people come with you this time. I think you may find it more convenient."

"Exactly, exactly," he cried, and, rushing to the other extreme, forbade all except one guide to accompany Miss Quested and him to the Kawa Dol. "Is that all right?" he inquired.

"Quite right, now enjoy yourselves, and when you come back tell me all about it." And she sank into the deckchair.

If they reached the big pocket of caves, they would be away nearly an hour. She took out her writing-pad and began, "Dear Stella, Dear Ralph," then stopped, and looked at the queer valley and their feeble invasion of it. Even the elephant had become a nobody. Her eye rose from it to the entrance tunnel. No, she did not wish to repeat that experience. The more she thought over it, the more disagreeable and frightening it became. She minded it much more now than at the time. The crush and the smells she could forget, but the echo began in some indescribable way to undermine her hold on life. Coming at a moment when she chanced to be fatigued, it had managed to murmur: "Pathos, piety, courage—they exist, but are identical, and so is filth. Everything exists, nothing has value." If one had spoken vileness in that place, or quoted lofty poetry, the comment would have been the same—"ou-boum". If one had spoken with the tongues of angels and pleaded for all the unhappiness and misunderstanding in the world, past, present, and to come, for all the misery men must undergo whatever their opinion and position, and however much they dodge or bluff—it would amount to the same, the serpent would descend and return to the ceiling. Devils are of the North, and poems can be written about them, but no one could romanticize the Marabar, because it robbed infinity and eternity of their vastness, the only quality that accommodates them to mankind.

She tried to go on with her letter, reminding herself that she was only an elderly woman who had got up too early in the morning and journeyed too far, that the despair creeping over her was merely her despair, her personal weakness, and that even if she got a sunstroke and went mad the rest of the world would go on. But suddenly, at the edge of her mind, Religion appeared, poor little talkative Christianity, and she knew that all its divine words from "Let there be light" to "It is finished" only amounted to "boum". Then she was terrified over an area larger than usual; the universe, never comprehensible to her intellect, offered no repose to her soul, the mood of the last two months took definite form at last, and she realized that she didn't want to write to her children, didn't want to communicate with anyone, not even with God. She sat motionless with horror, and, when old Mohammed Latif came up to her, thought he would notice a difference. For a time she thought, "I am going to be ill," to comfort herself, then she surrendered to the vision. She lost all interest, even in Aziz, and the affectionate and sincere words that she had spoken to him seemed no longer hers but the air's.

Chapter 15

Miss Quested and Aziz and a guide continued the slightly tedious expedition. They did not talk much, for the sun was getting high. The air felt like a warm bath into which hotter water is trickling constantly, the temperature rose and rose, the boulders said, "I am alive," the small stones answered, "I am almost alive." Between the chinks lay the ashes of little plants. They meant to climb to the rocking-stone on the summit, but it was too far, and they contented themselves with the big group of caves. *En route* for these, they encountered several isolated caves, which the guide persuaded them to visit, but really there was nothing to see; they lit a match, admired its reflection in the polish, tested the echo and came out again. Aziz was "pretty sure they should come on some interesting old carvings soon", but only meant he wished there were some carvings. His deeper thoughts were about the breakfast. Symptoms of disorganization had appeared as he left the camp. He ran over the menu: an English breakfast, porridge and mutton chops, but some Indian dishes to cause conversation, and pan afterwards. He had never liked Miss Quested as much as Mrs Moore, and had little to say to her, less than ever now that she would marry a British official.

Nor had Adela much to say to him. If his mind was with the breakfast, hers was mainly with her marriage. Simla next week, get rid of Antony, a view of Tibet, tiresome wedding bells, Agra in October, see Mrs Moore comfortably off from Bombay—the procession passed before her again, blurred by the heat, and then she turned to the more serious business of her life at Chandrapore. There were real difficulties here—Ronny's limitations and her own—but she enjoyed facing difficulties, and decided that if she could control her peevishness (always her weak point), and neither rail against Anglo-India nor succumb to it, their married life ought to be happy and profitable. She mustn't be too theoretical; she would deal with each problem as it came up, and trust to Ronny's common sense and her own. Luckily, each had abundance of common sense and goodwill.

But as she toiled over a rock that resembled an inverted saucer she thought, "What about love?" The rock was nicked by a double row of footholds, and somehow the question was suggested by them. Where had she seen footholds before? Oh yes, they were the pattern traced in the dust by the wheels of the Nawab Bahadur's car. She and Ronny—no, they did not love each other.

"Do I take you too fast?" inquired Aziz, for she had paused, a doubtful expression on her face. The discovery had come so suddenly that she felt like a mountaineer whose rope has broken. Not to love the man one's going to marry! Not to find it out till this moment! Not even to have asked oneself the question until now! Something else to think out. Vexed rather than appalled, she stood still, her eyes on the sparkling rock. There was esteem and animal contact at dusk, but the emotion that links them was absent. Ought she to break her engagement off? She was inclined to think not—it would cause so much trouble to others; besides, she wasn't convinced that love is necessary to a successful union. If love is everything, few marriages would survive the honeymoon. "No, I'm all right, thanks," she said, and, her emotions well under control, resumed the climb, though she felt a bit dashed. Aziz held her hand, the guide adhered to the surface like a lizard and scampered about as if governed by a personal centre of gravity.

"Are you married, Dr Aziz?" she asked, stopping again, and frowning.

"Yes, indeed, do come and see my wife"—for he felt it more artistic to have his wife alive for a moment.

"Thank you," she said absently.

"She is not in Chandrapore just now."

"And have you children?"

"Yes, indeed, three," he replied in firmer tones.

"Are they a great pleasure to you?"

"Why, naturally, I adore them," he laughed.

"I suppose so." What a handsome little Oriental he was, and no doubt his wife and children were beautiful too, for people usually get what they already possess. She did not admire him with any personal warmth, for there was nothing of the vagrant in her blood, but she guessed he might attract women of his own race and rank, and she regretted that neither she nor Ronny had physical charm. It does make a difference in a relationship—beauty, thick hair, a fine skin. Probably this man had several wives—Mohammedans always insist on their full four, according to Mrs Turton. And, having no one else to speak to on that eternal rock, she gave rein to the subject of marriage and said in her honest, decent, inquisitive way: "Have you one wife or more than one?"

The question shocked the young man very much. It challenged a new conviction of his community, and new convictions are more sensitive than old. If she had said, "Do you worship one god or several?" he would not have objected. But to ask an educated Indian Moslem how many wives he has—appalling, hideous! He was in trouble how to conceal his confusion. "One, one in my own particular case," he sputtered, and let go of her hand. Quite a number of caves were at the top of the track, and thinking "Damn the English even at their best" he plunged into one of them to recover his balance. She followed at her leisure, quite unconscious that she had said the wrong thing, and not seeing him she also went into a cave, thinking with half her mind "Sight-seeing bores me" and wondering with the other half about marriage.

Chapter 16

He waited in his cave a minute, and lit a cigarette so that he could remark on rejoining her, "I bolted in to get out of the draught," or something of the sort. When he returned, he found the guide, alone, with his head on one side. He had heard a noise, he said, and then Aziz heard it too: the noise of a motor-car. They were now on the outer shoulder of the Kawa Dol, and by scrambling twenty yards they got a glimpse of the plain. A car was coming towards the hills down the Chandrapore road. But they could not get a good view of it, because the precipitous bastion curved at the top, so that the base was not easily seen, and the car disappeared as it came nearer. No doubt it would stop almost exactly beneath them, at the place where the pukka road degenerated into a path, and the elephant had turned to sidle into the hills.

He ran back, to tell the strange news to his guest.

The guide explained that she had gone into a cave.

"Which cave?"

He indicated the group vaguely.

"You should have kept her in sight, it was your duty," said Aziz severely. "Here are twelve caves at least. How am I to know which contains my guest? Which is the cave I was in myself?"

The same vague gesture. And Aziz, looking again, could not even be sure he had returned to the same group. Caves appeared in every direction—it seemed their original spawning-place—and the orifices were always the same size. He thought, "Merciful heavens, Miss Quested is lost," then pulled himself together, and began to look for her calmly.

"Shout!" he commanded.

When they had done this for a while, the guide explained that to shout is useless, because a Marabar cave can hear no sound but its own. Aziz wiped his head, and sweat began to stream inside his clothes. The place was so confusing; it was partly a terrace, partly a zigzag, and full of grooves that led this way and that like snake-tracks. He tried to go into every one, but he never knew where he had started. Caves got behind caves or confabulated in pairs, and some were at the entrance of a gully.

"Come here!" he called gently, and when the guide was in reach he struck him in the face for a punishment. The man fled, and he was left alone. He thought, "This is the end of my career, my guest is lost." And then he discovered the simple and sufficient explanation of the mystery.

Miss Quested wasn't lost. She had joined the people in the car—friends of hers, no doubt, Mr Heaslop perhaps. He had a sudden glimpse of her, far down the gully—only a glimpse, but there she was, quite plain, framed between rocks, and speaking to another lady. He was so relieved that he did not think her conduct odd. Accustomed to sudden changes of plan, he supposed that she had run down the Kawa Dol impulsively, in the hope of a little drive. He started back alone towards his camp, and almost at once caught sight of something which would have disquieted him very much a moment before: Miss Quested's field-glasses. They were lying at the verge of a cave, halfway down an entrance tunnel. He tried to hang them over his shoulder, but the leather strap had broken, so he put them into his pocket instead. When he had gone a few steps, he thought she might have dropped something else, so he went back to look. But the previous difficulty recurred: he couldn't identify the cave. Down in the plain he heard the car starting; however, he couldn't catch a second glimpse of that. So he scrambled down the valley-face of the hill towards Mrs Moore, and here he was more successful: the colour and confusion of his little camp soon appeared, and in the midst of it he saw an Englishman's topi, and beneath it—oh joy!—smiled not Mr Heaslop, but Fielding.

"Fielding! Oh, I have so wanted you!" he cried, dropping the "Mr" for the first time.

And his friend ran to meet him, all so pleasant and jolly,

no dignity, shouting explanations and apologies about the train. Fielding had come in the newly arrived car—Miss Derek's car—that other lady was Miss Derek. Chatter, chatter, all the servants leaving their cooking to listen. Excellent Miss Derek! She had met Fielding by chance at the post office, said, "Why haven't you gone to the Marabar?" heard how he missed the train, offered to run him there and then. Another nice English lady. Where was she? Left with car and chauffeur while Fielding found camp. Car couldn't get up—no, of course not—hundreds of people must go down to escort Miss Derek and show her the way. The elephant in person. . . .

"Aziz, can I have a drink?"

"Certainly not." He flew to get one.

"Mr Fielding!" called Mrs Moore, from her patch of shade; they had not spoken yet, because his arrival had coincided with the torrent from the hill.

"Good morning again!" he cried, relieved to find all well.

"Mr Fielding, have you seen Miss Quested?"

"But I've only just arrived. Where is she?"

"I do not know."

"Aziz! Where have you put Miss Quested to?"

Aziz, who was returning with a drink in his hand, had to think for a moment. His heart was full of new happiness. The picnic, after a nasty shock or two, had developed into something beyond his dreams, for Fielding had not only come, but brought an uninvited guest. "Oh, she's all right," he said; "she went down to see Miss Derek. Well, here's luck! Chin-chin!"

"Here's luck, but chin-chin I do refuse," laughed Fielding, who detested the phrase. "Here's to India!"

"Here's luck, and here's to England!"

Miss Derek's chauffeur stopped the cavalcade which was starting to escort his mistress up, and informed it that she had gone back with the other young lady to Chandrapore; she had sent him to say so. She was driving herself.

"Oh yes, that's quite likely," said Aziz. "I knew they'd gone for a spin."

"Chandrapore? The man's made a mistake," Fielding exclaimed.

"Oh no, why?" He was disappointed, but made light of it; no doubt the two young ladies were great friends. He would prefer to give breakfast to all four; still, guests must do as they wish, or they become prisoners. He went away cheerfully to inspect the porridge and the ice.

"What's happened?" asked Fielding, who felt at once that something had gone queer. All the way out Miss Derek had chattered about the picnic, called it an unexpected treat, and said that she preferred Indians who didn't invite her to their entertainments to those who did. Mrs Moore sat swinging her foot, and appeared sulky and stupid. She said: "Miss Derek is most unsatisfactory and restless, always in a hurry, always wanting something new; she will do anything in the world except go back to the Indian lady who pays her."

Fielding, who didn't dislike Miss Derek, replied: "She wasn't in a hurry when I left her. There was no question of returning to Chandrapore. It looks to me as if Miss Quested's in the hurry."

"Adela? She's never been in a hurry in her life," said the old lady sharply.

"I say it'll prove to be Miss Quested's wish, in fact I know it is," persisted the schoolmaster. He was annoyed—chiefly with himself. He had begun by missing a train—a sin he was never guilty of—and now that he did arrive it was to upset Aziz's arrangements for the second time. He wanted someone to share the blame, and frowned at Mrs Moore rather magisterially. "Aziz is a charming fellow," he announced.

"I know," she answered, with a yawn.

"He has taken endless trouble to make a success of our picnic."

They knew one another very little, and felt rather awkward at being drawn together by an Indian. The racial problem can take subtle forms. In their case it had induced a sort of jealousy, a mutual suspicion. He tried to goad her enthusiasm; she scarcely spoke. Aziz fetched them to breakfast.

"It is quite natural about Miss Quested," he remarked, for he had been working the incident a little in his mind, to get rid of its roughnesses. "We were having an interesting talk with our guide, then the car was seen, so she decided to go down to her friend." Incurably inaccurate, he already thought that this was what had occurred. He was inaccurate because he was sensitive. He did not like to remember Miss Quested's remark about polygamy, because it was unworthy of a guest, so he put it from his mind, and with it the knowledge that he had bolted into a cave to get away from her. He was inaccurate because he desired to honour her, and—facts being entangled—he had to arrange them in her vicinity, as one tidies the ground after extracting a weed. Before breakfast was over, he had told a good many lies. "She ran to her friend, I to mine," he went on, smiling. "And now I am with my friends and they are with me and each other, which is happiness."

Loving them both, he expected them to love each other. They didn't want to. Fielding thought with hostility, "I knew these women would make trouble," and Mrs Moore thought, "This man, having missed the train, tries to blame us"; but her thoughts were feeble; since her faintness in the cave she was sunk in apathy and cynicism. The wonderful India of her opening weeks, with its cool nights and acceptable hints of infinity, had vanished.

Fielding ran up to see one cave. He wasn't impressed. Then they got on the elephant, and the picnic began to unwind out of the corridor and escaped under the precipice towards the railway station, pursued by stabs of hot air. They came to the place where he had quitted the car. A disagreeable thought now struck him, and he said: "Aziz, exactly where and how did you leave Miss Quested?"

"Up there." He indicated the Kawa Dol cheerfully.

"But how—" A gully, or rather a crease, showed among the rocks at this place; it was scurfy with cactuses. "I suppose the guide helped her."

"Oh, rather, most helpful."

"Is there a path off the top?"

"Millions of paths, my dear fellow."

Fielding could see nothing but the crease. Everywhere else the glaring granite plunged into the earth.

"But you saw them get down safe?"

"Yes, yes, she and Miss Derek, and go off in the car."

"Then the guide came back to you?"

"Exactly. Got a cigarette?"

"I hope she wasn't ill," pursued the Englishman. The crease continued as a nullah across the plain, the water draining off this way towards the Ganges.

"She would have wanted me, if she was ill, to attend her."

"Yes, that sounds sense."

"I see you're worrying, let's talk of other things," he said kindly. "Miss Quested was always to do what she wished, it was our arrangement. I see you are worrying on my account, but really I don't mind, I never notice trifles."

"I do worry on your account. I consider they have been impolite!" said Fielding, lowering his voice. "She had no right to dash away from your party, and Miss Derek had no right to abet her."

So touchy as a rule, Aziz was unassailable. The wings that uplifted him did not falter, because he was a Mogul Emperor who had done his duty. Perched on his elephant, he watched the Marabar Hills recede, and saw again, as provinces of his kingdom, the grim untidy plain, the frantic and feeble movements of the buckets, the white shrines, the shallow graves, the suave sky, the snake that looked like a tree. He had given his guests as good a time as he could, and if they came late or left early that was not his affair. Mrs Moore slept, swaying against the rods of the howdah, Mohammed Latif embraced her with efficiency and respect, and by his own side sat Fielding, whom he began to think of as "Cyril".

"Aziz, have you figured out what this picnic will cost you?"

"Sh! my dear chap, don't mention that part. Hundreds and hundreds of rupees. The completed account will be too awful; my friends' servants have robbed me right and left, and as for an elephant, she apparently eats gold. I can trust you not to repeat this. And M.L.—please employ initials, he listens—is far the worst of all."

"I told you he's no good."

"He is plenty of good for himself; his dishonesty will ruin me."

"Aziz, how monstrous!"

"I am delighted with him really, he has made my guests comfortable; besides, it is my duty to employ him, he is my cousin. If money goes, money comes. If money stays, death comes. Did you ever learn that useful Urdu proverb? Probably not, for I have just invented it."

"My proverbs are: A penny saved is a penny earned; A stitch in time saves nine; Look before you leap; and the British Empire rests on them. You will never kick us out, you know, until you cease employing M.L.s and such."

"Oh, kick you out? Why should I trouble over that dirty job? Leave it to the politicians. . . . No, when I was a student I got excited over your damned countrymen, certainly; but if they'll let me get on with my profession, and not be too rude to me officially, I really don't ask for more."

"But you do; you take them to a picnic."

"This picnic is nothing to do with English or Indian; it is an expedition of friends."

So the cavalcade ended, partly pleasant, partly not; the Brahman cook was picked up, the train arrived, pushing its burning throat over the plain, and the twentieth century took over from the sixteenth. Mrs Moore entered her carriage, the three men went to theirs, adjusted the shutters, turned on the electric fan and tried to get some sleep. In the twilight, all resembled corpses, and the train itself seemed dead though it moved—a coffin from the scientific North which troubled the scenery four times a day. As it left the Marabars, their nasty little cosmos disappeared, and gave place to the Marabars seen from a distance, finite and rather romantic. The train halted once under a pump, to drench the stock of coal in its tender. Then it caught sight of the main line in the distance, took courage, and bumped forward, rounded the Civil Station, surmounted the level-crossing (the rails were scorching now), and clanked to a standstill. Chandrapore, Chandrapore! The expedition was over.

And as it ended, as they sat up in the gloom and prepared to enter ordinary life, suddenly the long-drawn strangeness of the morning snapped. Mr Haq, the Inspector of Police, flung open the door of their carriage and said in shrill tones: "Dr Aziz, it is my highly painful duty to arrest you."

"Hullo, some mistake," said Fielding, at once taking charge of the situation.

"Sir, they are my instructions. I know nothing."

"On what charge do you arrest him?"

"I am under instructions not to say."

"Don't answer me like that. Produce your warrant."

"Sir, excuse me, no warrant is required under these particular circumstances. Refer to Mr McBryde."

"Very well, so we will. Come along, Aziz, old man; nothing to fuss about, some blunder."

"Dr Aziz, will you kindly come? A closed conveyance stands in readiness."

The young man sobbed—his first sound—and tried to escape out of the opposite door onto the line.

"That will compel me to use force," Mr Haq wailed.

"Oh, for God's sake—" cried Fielding, his own nerves breaking under the contagion, and pulled him back before a scandal started, and shook him like a baby. A second later, and he would have been out, whistles blowing, a man-hunt. . . . "Dear fellow, we're coming to McBryde together, and inquire what's gone wrong—he's a decent fellow, it's all unintentional . . . he'll apologize. Never, never act the criminal."

"My children and my name!" he gasped, his wings broken.

"Nothing of the sort. Put your hat straight and take my arm. I'll see you through."

"Ah, thank God, he comes," the Inspector exclaimed.

They emerged into the midday heat, arm in arm. The station was seething. Passengers and porters rushed out of every recess, many Government servants, more police. Ronny escorted Mrs Moore. Mohammed Latif began wailing. And before they could make their way through the chaos Fielding was called off by the authoritative tones of Mr Turton, and Aziz went on to prison alone.

Chapter 17

The Collector had watched the arrest from the interior of the waiting-room, and throwing open its perforated doors of zinc he was now revealed like a god in a shrine. When Fielding entered, the doors clapped to, and were guarded by a servant, while a punkah, to mark the importance of the moment, flapped dirty petticoats over their heads. The Collector could not speak at first. His face was white, fanatical, and rather beautiful—the expression that all English faces were to wear at Chandrapore for many days. Always brave and unselfish, he was now fused by some white and generous heat; he would have killed himself, obviously, if he had thought it right to do so. He spoke at last. "The worst thing in my whole career has happened," he said. "Miss Quested has been insulted in one of the Marabar Caves."

"Oh no, oh no, no," gasped the other, feeling sickish.

"She escaped—by God's grace."

"Oh no, no, but not Aziz . . . not Aziz . . ."

He nodded.

"Absolutely impossible, grotesque."

"I called you to preserve you from the odium that would attach to you if you were seen accompanying him to the Police Station," said Turton, paying no attention to his protest, indeed scarcely hearing it.

He repeated "Oh no" like a fool. He couldn't frame other words. He felt that a mass of madness had arisen and tried to overwhelm them all; it had to be shoved back into its pit somehow, and he didn't know how to do it, because he did not understand madness; he had always gone ahead sensibly and quietly until a difficulty came right. "Who lodges this infamous charge?" he asked, pulling himself together.

"Miss Derek and—the victim herself. . . ." He nearly broke down, unable to repeat the girl's name.

"Miss Quested herself definitely accuses him of—"

He nodded, and turned his face away.

"Then she's mad."

"I cannot pass that last remark," said the Collector, waking up to the knowledge that they differed, and trembling with fury. "You will withdraw it instantly. It is the type of remark you have permitted yourself to make ever since you came to Chandrapore."

"I'm excessively sorry, sir; I certainly withdraw it unconditionally." For the man was half mad himself.

"Pray, Mr Fielding, what induced you to speak to me in such a tone?"

"The news gave me a very great shock, so I must ask you to forgive me. I cannot believe that Dr Aziz is guilty."

He slammed his hand on the table. "That—that is a repetition of your insult in an aggravated form."

"If I may venture to say so, no," said Fielding, also going white, but sticking to his point. "I make no reflection on the good faith of the two ladies, but the charge they are bringing against Aziz rests upon some mistake, and five minutes will clear it up. The man's manner is perfectly natural; besides, I know him to be incapable of infamy."

"It does indeed rest upon a mistake," came the thin, biting voice of the other. "It does indeed. I have had twenty-five years' experience of this country"—he paused, and "twenty-five years" seemed to fill the waiting-room with their staleness and ungenerosity—"and during those twenty-five years I have never known anything but disaster result when English people and Indians attempt to be intimate socially. Intercourse, yes. Courtesy, by all means. Intimacy—never, never. The whole weight of my authority is against it. I have been in charge at Chandrapore for six years, and if everything has gone smoothly, if there has been mutual respect and esteem, it is because both peoples kept to this simple rule. Newcomers set our traditions aside, and in an instant what you see happens, the work of years is undone, and the good name of my District ruined for a generation. I—I—can't see the end of this day's work, Mr Fielding. You, who are imbued with modern ideas—no doubt you can. I wish I had never lived to see its beginning, I know that. It is the end of me. That a lady, that a young lady engaged to my most valued subordinate—that she—an English girl fresh from England—that I should have lived—"

Involved in his own emotions, he broke down. What he had said was both dignified and pathetic, but had it anything to do with Aziz? Nothing at all, if Fielding was right. It is impossible to regard a tragedy from two points of view, and, whereas Turton had decided to avenge the girl, he hoped to save the man. He wanted to get away and talk to McBryde, who had always been friendly to him, was on the whole sensible, and could, anyhow, be trusted to keep cool.

"I came down particularly on your account—while poor Heaslop got his mother away. I regarded it as the most friendly thing I could do. I meant to tell you that there will be an informal meeting at the Club this evening to discuss the situation, but I am doubtful whether you will care to come. Your visits there are always infrequent."

"I shall certainly come, sir, and I am most grateful to you for all the trouble you have taken over me. May I venture to ask—where Miss Quested is?"

He replied with a gesture: she was ill.

"Worse and worse, appalling," he said feelingly.

But the Collector looked at him sternly, because he was keeping his head. He had not gone mad at the phrase "an English girl fresh from England", he had not rallied to the banner of race. He was still after facts, though the herd had decided on emotion. Nothing enrages Anglo-India more than the lantern of reason if it is exhibited for one moment after its extinction is decreed. All over Chandrapore that day the Europeans were putting aside their normal personalities and sinking themselves in their community. Pity, wrath, heroism, filled them, but the power of putting two and two together was annihilated.

Terminating the interview, the Collector walked onto the

platform. The confusion there was revolting. A chuprassy of Ronny's had been told to bring up some trifles belonging to the ladies, and was appropriating for himself various articles to which he had no right; he was a camp-follower of the angry English. Mohammed Latif made no attempt to resist him. Hassan flung off his turban, and wept. All the comforts that had been provided so liberally were rolled about and wasted in the sun. The Collector took in the situation at a glance, and his sense of justice functioned though he was insane with rage. He spoke the necessary word, and the looting stopped. Then he drove off to his bungalow and gave rein to his passions again. When he saw the coolies asleep in the ditches or the shopkeepers rising to salute him on their little platforms, he said to himself: "I know what you're like at last; you shall pay for this, you shall squeal."

Chapter 18

Mr McBryde, the District Superintendent of Police, was the most reflective and best educated of the Chandrapore officials. He had read and thought a good deal, and, owing to a somewhat unhappy marriage, had evolved a complete philosophy of life. There was much of the cynic about him, but nothing of the bully; he never lost his temper or grew rough, and he received Aziz with courtesy, was almost reassuring. "I have to detain you until you get bail," he said, "but no doubt your friends will be applying for it, and of course they will be allowed to visit you, under regulations. I am given certain information, and have to act on it—I'm not your judge." Aziz was led off weeping. Mr McBryde was shocked at his downfall, but no Indian ever surprised him, because he had a theory about climatic zones. The theory ran: "All unfortunate natives are criminals at heart, for the simple reason that they live south of latitude 30. They are not to blame, they have not a dog's chance—we should be like them if we settled here." Born at Karachi, he seemed to contradict his theory, and would sometimes admit as much with a sad, quiet smile.

"Another of them found out," he thought, as he set to work to draft his statement to the Magistrate.

He was interrupted by the arrival of Fielding.

He imparted all he knew without reservations. Miss Derek had herself driven in the Mudkul car about an hour ago, she and Miss Quested both in a terrible state. They had gone straight to his bungalow, where he happened to be, and there and then he had taken down the charge and arranged for the arrest at the railway station.

"What is the charge, precisely?"

"That he followed her into the cave and made insulting

advances. She hit at him with her field-glasses; he pulled at them and the strap broke, and that is how she got away. When we searched him just now, they were in his pocket."

"Oh no, oh no, no; it'll be cleared up in five minutes," he cried again.

"Have a look at them."

The strap had been newly broken, the eye-piece was jammed. The logic of evidence said "Guilty".

"Did she say any more?"

"There was an echo that appears to have frightened her. Did you go into those caves?"

"I saw one of them. There was an echo. Did it get on her nerves?"

"I couldn't worry her overmuch with questions. She'll have plenty to go through in the witness-box. They don't bear thinking about, these next weeks. I wish the Marabar Hills and all they contain were at the bottom of the sea. Evening after evening one saw them from the Club, and they were just a harmless name. . . . Yes, we start already." For a visiting-card was brought: Vakil Mahmoud Ali, legal adviser to the prisoner, asked to be allowed to see him. McBryde sighed, gave permission, and continued: "I heard some more from Miss Derek—she is an old friend of us both and talks freely; well—her account is that you went off to locate the camp, and almost at once she heard stones falling on the Kawa Dol and saw Miss Quested running straight down the face of a precipice. Well. She climbed up a sort of gully to her, and found her practically done for—her helmet off—"

"Was a guide not with her?" interrupted Fielding.

"No. She had got among some cactuses. Miss Derek saved her life coming just then—she was beginning to fling herself about. She helped her down to the car. Miss Quested couldn't stand the Indian driver, cried 'Keep him away'—and it was that that put our friend on the track of what had happened. They made straight for our bungalow, and are there now. That's the story as far as I know it yet. She sent the driver to join you. I think she behaved with great sense."

"I suppose there's no possibility of my seeing Miss Quested?" he asked suddenly.

"I hardly think that would do. Surely."

"I was afraid you'd say that. I should very much like to."

"She is in no state to see anyone. Besides, you don't know her well."

"Hardly at all. . . . But you see I believe she's under some hideous delusion, and that that wretched boy is innocent."

The policeman started in surprise, and a shadow passed over his face, for he could not bear his dispositions to be upset. "I had no idea that was in your mind," he said, and looked for support at the signed deposition, which lay before him.

"Those field-glasses upset me for a minute, but I've thought since: it's impossible that, having attempted to assault her, he would put her glasses into his pocket."

"Quite possible, I'm afraid; when an Indian goes bad, he goes not only very bad, but very queer."

"I don't follow."

"How should you? When you think of crime you think of English crime. The psychology here is different. I dare say you'll tell me next that he was quite normal when he came down from the hill to greet you. No reason he should not be. Read any of the Mutiny records; which, rather than the Bhagavad Gita, should be your bible in this country. Though I'm not sure that the one and the other are not closely connected. Am I not being beastly? But, you see, Fielding, as I've said to you once before, you're a schoolmaster, and consequently you come across these people at their best. That's what puts you wrong. They can be charming as boys. But I know them as they really are, after they have developed into men. Look at this, for instance." He held up Aziz's pocket-case. "I am going through the contents. They are not edifying. Here is a letter from a friend who apparently keeps a brothel."

"I don't want to hear his private letters."

"It'll have to be quoted in court, as bearing on his morals. He was fixing up to see women at Calcutta."

"Oh, that'll do, that'll do."

McBryde stopped, naïvely puzzled. It was obvious to him that any two sahibs ought to pool all they knew about any Indian, and he could not think where the objection came in.

"I dare say you have the right to throw stones at a young man for doing that, but I haven't. I did the same at his age."

So had the Superintendent of Police, but he considered that the conversation had taken a turn that was undesirable. He did not like Fielding's next remark either.

"Miss Quested really cannot be seen? You do know that for a certainty?"

"You have never explained to me what's in your mind here. Why on earth do you want to see her?"

"On the off-chance of her recanting before you send in that report and he's committed for trial, and the whole thing goes to blazes. Old man, don't argue about this, but do of your goodness just ring up your wife or Miss Derek and inquire. It'll cost you nothing."

"It's no use ringing up them," he replied, stretching out for the telephone. "Callendar settles a question like that, of course. You haven't grasped that she's seriously ill."

"He's sure to refuse, it's all he exists for," said the other desperately.

The expected answer came back: the Major would not hear of the patient being troubled.

"I only wanted to ask her whether she is certain, dead certain, that it was Aziz who followed her into the cave."

"Possibly my wife might ask her that much."

"But *I* wanted to ask her. I want someone who believes in him to ask her."

"What difference does that make?"

"She is among people who disbelieve in Indians."

"Well, she tells her own story, doesn't she?"

"I know, but she tells it to you."

McBryde raised his eyebrows, murmuring: "A bit too finespun. Anyhow, Callendar won't hear of you seeing her. I'm sorry to say he gave a bad account just now. He says that she is by no means out of danger."

They were silent. Another card was brought into the office—Hamidullah's. The opposite army was gathering.

"I must put this report through now, Fielding."

"I wish you wouldn't."

"How can I not?"

"I feel that things are rather unsatisfactory as well as most disastrous. We are heading for a most awful smash. I can see your prisoner, I suppose."

He hesitated. "His own people seem in touch with him all right."

"Well, when he's done with them."

"I wouldn't keep you waiting; good heavens, you take precedence of any Indian visitor, of course. I meant, what's the good? Why mix yourself up with pitch?"

"I say he's innocent—"

"Innocence or guilt, why mix yourself up? What's the good?"

"Oh, good, good," he cried, feeling that every earth was being stopped. "One's got to breathe occasionally, at least I have. I mayn't see her, and now I mayn't see him. I promised him to come up here with him to you, but Turton called me off before I could get two steps."

"Sort of all-white thing our Collector would do," he muttered sentimentally. And trying not to sound patronizing he stretched his hand over the table, and said: "We shall all have to hang together, old man, I'm afraid. I'm your junior in years, I know, but very much your senior in service; you don't happen to know this poisonous country as well as I do, and you must take it from me that the general situation is going to be nasty at Chandrapore during the next few weeks, very nasty indeed."

"So I have just told you."

"But at a time like this there's no room for—well—personal views. The man who doesn't toe the line is lost."

"I see what you mean."

"No, you don't see entirely. He not only loses himself, he weakens his friends. If you leave the line, you leave a gap in the line. These jackals"—he pointed at the lawyers' cards—"are looking with all their eyes for a gap."

"Can I visit Aziz?" was his answer.

"No." Now that he knew of Turton's attitude, the policeman had no doubts. "You may see him on a magistrate's order, but on my own responsibility I don't feel justified. It might lead to more complications."

He paused, reflecting that if he had been either ten years younger or ten years longer in India, he would have responded to McBryde's appeal. The bit between his teeth, he then said, "To whom do I apply for an order?"

"City Magistrate."

"That sounds comfortable!"

"Yes, one can't very well worry poor Heaslop."

More "evidence" appeared at this moment—the table-drawer from Aziz's bungalow, borne with triumph in a corporal's arms.

"Photographs of women. Ah!"

"That's his wife," said Fielding, wincing.

"How do you know that?"

"He told me."

McBryde gave a faint, incredulous smile, and started rummaging in the drawer. His face became inquisitive and slightly bestial. "Wife indeed, I know those wives!" he was thinking. Aloud he said: "Well, you must trot off now, old man, and the Lord help us, the Lord help us all. . . ."

As if his prayer had been heard, there was a sudden rackety-dacket on a temple bell.

Chapter 19

Hamidullah was the next stage. He was waiting outside the Superintendent's office, and sprang up respectfully when he saw Fielding. To the Englishman's passionate "It's all a mistake" he answered, "Ah, ah, has some evidence come?"

"It will come," said Fielding, holding his hand.

"Ah yes, Mr Fielding; but when once an Indian has been arrested, we do not know where it will stop." His manner was deferential. "You are very good to greet me in this public fashion. I appreciate it; but, Mr Fielding, nothing convinces a magistrate except evidence. Did Mr McBryde make any remark when my card came in? Do you think my application annoyed him, will prejudice him against my friend at all? If so, I will gladly retire."

"He's not annoyed, and if he was, what does it matter?"

"Ah, it's all very well for you to speak like that, but we have to live in this country."

The leading barrister of Chandrapore, with the dignified manner and Cambridge degree, had been rattled. He too loved Aziz, and knew he was calumniated; but faith did not rule his heart, and he prated of "policy" and "evidence" in a way that saddened the Englishman. Fielding, too, had his anxieties—he didn't like the field-glasses or the discrepancy over the guide—but he relegated them to the edge of his mind, and forbade them to infect its core. Aziz *was* innocent, and all action must be based on that, and the people who said he was guilty were wrong, and it was hopeless to try to propitiate them. At the moment when he was throwing in his lot with Indians, he realized the profundity of the gulf that divided him from them. They always do something disappointing. Aziz had tried to run away from the police,

Mohammed Latif had not checked the pilfering. And now Hamidullah!—instead of raging and denouncing, he temporized. Are Indians cowards? No, but they are bad starters and occasionally jib. Fear is everywhere; the British Raj rests on it; the respect and courtesy Fielding himself enjoyed were unconscious acts of propitiation. He told Hamidullah to cheer up, all would end well; and Hamidullah did cheer up, and became pugnacious and sensible. McBryde's remark, "If you leave the line, you leave a gap in the line," was being illustrated.

"First and foremost, the question of bail . . ."

Application must be made this afternoon. Fielding wanted to stand surety. Hamidullah thought the Nawab Bahadur should be approached.

"Why drag in him, though?"

To drag in everyone was precisely the barrister's aim. He then suggested that the lawyer in charge of the case should be a Hindu; the defence would then make a wider appeal. He mentioned one or two names—men from a distance who would not be intimidated by local conditions—and said he should prefer Amritrao, a Calcutta barrister, who had a high reputation professionally and personally, but who was notoriously anti-British.

Fielding demurred; this seemed to him going to the other extreme. Aziz must be cleared, but with a minimum of racial hatred. Amritrao was loathed at the Club. His retention would be regarded as a political challenge.

"Oh no, we must hit with all our strength. When I saw my friend's private papers carried in just now in the arms of a dirty policeman, I said to myself, 'Amritrao is the man to clear up this.' "

There was a lugubrious pause. The temple bell continued to jangle harshly. The interminable and disastrous day had scarcely reached its afternoon. Continuing their work, the wheels of Dominion now propelled a messenger on a horse from the Superintendent to the Magistrate with an official report of the arrest. "Don't complicate, let the cards play themselves," entreated Fielding, as he watched the man disappear into dust. "We're bound to win, there's nothing else we can do. She will never be able to substantiate the charge."

This comforted Hamidullah, who remarked with complete sincerity, "At a crisis, the English are really unequalled."

"Goodbye, then, my dear Hamidullah (we must drop the 'Mr' now). Give Aziz my love when you see him, and tell him to keep calm, calm, calm. I shall go back to the College now. If you want me, ring me up; if you don't, don't, for I shall be very busy."

"Goodbye, my dear Fielding, and you actually are on our side against your own people?"

"Yes. Definitely."

He regretted taking sides. To slink through India unlabelled was his aim. Henceforward he would be called "anti-British", "seditious"—terms that bored him, and diminished his utility. He foresaw that besides being a tragedy there would be a muddle; already he saw several tiresome little knots, and each time his eye returned to them they were larger. Born in freedom, he was not afraid of muddle, but he recognized its existence.

This section of the day concluded in a queer vague talk with Professor Godbole. The interminable affair of the Russell's viper was again in question. Some weeks before, one of the masters at the College, an unpopular Parsee, had found a Russell's viper nosing round his classroom. Perhaps it had crawled in of itself, but perhaps it had not, and the staff still continued to interview their Principal about it, and to take up his time with their theories. The reptile is so poisonous that he did not like to cut them short, and this they knew. Thus when his mind was bursting with other troubles, and he was debating whether he should compose a letter of appeal to Miss Quested, he was obliged to listen to a speech which lacked both basis and conclusion, and floated through air. At the end of it Godbole said, "May I now take my leave?"—always an indication that he had not come to his point yet. "Now I take my leave, I must tell you how glad I am to hear that after all you succeeded in reaching the Marabar. I feared my unpunctuality had prevented you, but you went (a far pleasanter method) in Miss Derek's car. I hope the expedition was a successful one."

"The news has not reached you yet, I can see."

"Oh yes."

"No; there has been a terrible catastrophe about Aziz."

"Oh yes. That is all round the College."

"Well, the expedition where that occurs can scarcely be called a successful one," said Fielding, with an amazed stare.

"I cannot say. I was not present."

He stared again—a most useless operation, for no eye could see what lay at the bottom of the Brahman's mind, and yet he had a mind and a heart too, and all his friends trusted him, without knowing why. "I am most frightfully cut up," he said.

"So I saw at once on entering your office. I must not detain you, but I have a small private difficulty on which I want your help; I am leaving your service shortly, as you know."

"Yes, alas!"

"And am returning to my birthplace in Central India to take charge of education there. I want to start a high school there on sound English lines, that shall be as like Government College as possible."

"Well?" he sighed, trying to take an interest.

"At present there is only vernacular education at Mau. I shall feel it my duty to change all that. I shall advise His Highness to sanction at least a high school in the capital, and if possible another in each pargana."

Fielding sunk his head on his arms; really, Indians were sometimes unbearable.

"The point—the point on which I desire your help is this: what name should be given to the school?"

"A name? A name for a school?" he said, feeling sickish suddenly, as he had done in the waiting-room.

"Yes, a name, a suitable title, by which it can be called, by which it may be generally known."

"Really—I have no names for schools in my head. I can think of nothing but our poor Aziz. Have you grasped that at the present moment he is in prison?"

"Oh yes. Oh no, I do not expect an answer to my question now. I only meant that when you are at leisure you might think the matter over, and suggest two or three alternative titles for schools. I had thought of the 'Mr Fielding High School', but failing that, the 'King-Emperor George the Fifth'."

"Godbole!"

The old fellow put his hands together, and looked sly and charming.

"Is Aziz innocent or guilty?"

"That is for the court to decide. The verdict will be in strict accordance with the evidence, I make no doubt."

"Yes, yes, but your personal opinion. Here's a man we both like, generally esteemed; he lives here quietly doing his work. Well, what's one to make of it? Would he or would he not do such a thing?"

"Ah, that is rather a different question from your previous one, and also more difficult; I mean difficult in our philosophy. Dr Aziz is a most worthy young man, I have a great regard for him; but I think you are asking me whether the individual can commit good actions or evil actions, and that is rather difficult for us." He spoke without emotion and in short tripping syllables.

"I ask you: did he do it or not? Is that plain? I know he didn't, and from that I start. I mean to get at the true explanation in a couple of days. My last notion is that it's the guide who went round with them. Malice on Miss Quested's part—it couldn't be that, though Hamidullah thinks so. She has certainly had some appalling experience. But you tell me, oh no—because good and evil are the same."

"No, not exactly, please, according to our philosophy. Because nothing can be performed in isolation. All perform a good action, when one is performed, and when an evil action is performed, all perform it. To illustrate my meaning, let me take the case in point as an example. I am informed that an evil action was performed in the Marabar Hills, and that a highly esteemed English lady is now seriously ill in consequence. My answer to that is this: that action was performed by Dr Aziz." He stopped and sucked in his thin cheeks. "It was performed by the guide." He stopped again. "It was performed by you." Now he had an air of daring and of coyness. "It was performed by me." He looked shyly down the sleeve of his own coat. "And by my students. It was even performed by the lady herself. When evil occurs, it expresses the whole of the universe. Similarly when good occurs."

"And similarly when suffering occurs, and so on and so forth, and everything is anything and nothing something," he muttered in his irritation, for he needed the solid ground.

"Excuse me, you are now again changing the basis of our discussion. We were discussing good and evil. Suffering is merely a matter for the individual. If a young lady has sunstroke, that is a matter of no significance to the universe. Oh no, not at all. Oh no, not the least. It is an isolated matter, it only concerns herself. If she thought her head did not ache, she would not be ill, and that would end it. But it is far otherwise in the case of good and evil. They are not what we think them, they are what they are, and each of us has contributed to both."

"You're preaching that evil and good are the same."

"Oh no, excuse me once again. Good and evil are different, as their names imply. But, in my own humble opinion, they are both of them aspects of my Lord. He is present in the one, absent in the other, and the difference between presence and absence is great, as great as my feeble mind can grasp. Yet absence implies presence, absence is not non-existence, and we are therefore entitled to repeat, 'Come, come, come, come.' " And in the same breath, as if to cancel any beauty his words might have contained, he added, "But did you have time to visit any of the interesting Marabar antiquities?"

Fielding was silent, trying to meditate and rest his brain.

"Did you not even see the tank by the usual camping-ground?" he nagged.

"Yes, yes," he answered distractedly, wandering over half a dozen things at once.

"That is good, then you saw the Tank of the Dagger." And he related a legend which might have been acceptable if he had told it at the tea-party a fortnight ago. It concerned a Hindu rajah who had slain his own sister's son, and the dagger with which he performed the deed remained clamped to his hand until in the course of years he came to the Marabar Hills, where he was thirsty and wanted to drink but saw a thirsty cow and ordered the water to be offered to her first, which, when done, "dagger fell from his hand, and to commemorate miracle he built Tank". Professor Godbole's conversations frequently culminated in a cow. Fielding received this one in gloomy silence.

In the afternoon he obtained a permit and saw Aziz, but found him unapproachable through misery. "You deserted me" was the only coherent remark. He went away to write his letter to Miss Quested. Even if it reached her, it would do no good, and probably the McBrydes would withhold it. Miss Quested did pull him up short. She was such a dry, sensible girl, and quite without malice: the last person in Chandrapore wrongfully to accuse an Indian.

Chapter 20

Although Miss Quested had not made herself popular with the English, she brought out all that was fine in their character. For a few hours an exalted emotion gushed forth, which the women felt even more keenly than the men, if not for so long. "What can we do for our sister?" was the only thought of Mesdames Callendar and Lesley, as they drove through the pelting heat to inquire. Mrs Turton was the only visitor admitted to the sick-room. She came out ennobled by an unselfish sorrow. "She is my own darling girl," were the words she spoke, and then, remembering that she had called her "not pukka" and resented her engagement to young Heaslop, she began to cry. No one had ever seen the Collector's wife cry. Capable of tears—yes, but always reserving them for some adequate occasion, and now it had come. Ah, why had they not all been kinder to the stranger, more patient, given her not only hospitality but their hearts? The tender core of the heart that is so seldom used—they employed it for a little, under the stimulus of remorse. If all is over (as Major Callendar implied), well, all is over, and nothing can be done, but they retained some responsibility in her grievous wrong that they couldn't define. If she wasn't one of them, they ought to have made her one, and they could never do that now, she had passed beyond their invitation. "Why don't one think more of other people?" sighed pleasure-loving Miss Derek. These regrets only lasted in their pure form for a few hours. Before sunset, other considerations adulterated them, and the sense of guilt (so strangely connected with our first sight of any suffering) had begun to wear away.

People drove into the Club with studious calm—the jog-trot of country gentlefolk between green hedgerows, for the natives must not suspect that they were agitated. They exchanged the usual drinks, but everything tasted different, and then they looked out at the palisade of cactuses stabbing the purple throat of the sky; they realized that they were thousands of miles from any scenery that they understood. The Club was fuller than usual, and several parents had brought their children into the rooms reserved for adults, which gave the air of the Residency at Lucknow. One young mother—a brainless but most beautiful girl—sat on a low ottoman in the smoking-room with her baby in her arms; her husband was away in the District, and she dared not return to her bungalow in case the "niggers attacked". The wife of a small railway official, she was generally snubbed; but this evening, with her abundant figure and masses of corn-gold hair, she symbolized all that is worth fighting and dying for; more permanent a symbol, perhaps, than poor Adela. "Don't worry, Mrs Blakiston, those drums are only Mohurram," the men would tell her. "Then they've started," she moaned, clasping the infant and rather wishing he would not blow bubbles down his chin at such a moment as this. "No, of course not, and anyhow, they're not coming to the Club." "And they're not coming to the Burra Sahib's bungalow either, my dear, and that's where you and your baby'll sleep tonight," answered Mrs Turton, towering by her side like Pallas Athene, and determining in the future not to be such a snob.

The Collector clapped his hands for silence. He was much calmer than when he had flown out at Fielding. He was indeed always calmer when he addressed several people than in a *tête-à-tête*. "I want to talk specially to the ladies," he said. "Not the least cause for alarm. Keep cool, keep cool. Don't go out more than you can help, don't go into the city, don't talk before your servants. That's all."

"Harry, is there any news from the city?" asked his wife, standing at some distance from him, and also assuming her public-safety voice. The rest were silent during the august colloquy.

"Everything absolutely normal."

"I had gathered as much. Those drums are merely Mohurram, of course."

"Merely the preparations for it—the procession is not till next week."

"Quite so, not till Monday."

"Mr McBryde's down there disguised as a Holy Man," said Mrs Callendar.

"That's exactly the sort of thing that must not be said," he remarked, pointing at her. "Mrs Callendar, be more careful than that, please, in these times."

"I . . . well, I . . ." She was not offended; his severity made her feel safe.

"Any more questions? Necessary questions."

"Is the—where is he—" Mrs Lesley quavered.

"Jail. Bail has been refused."

Fielding spoke next. He wanted to know whether there was an official bulletin about Miss Quested's health, or whether the grave reports were due to gossip. His question produced a bad effect, partly because he had pronounced her name; she, like Aziz, was always referred to by a periphrasis.

"I hope Callendar may be able to let us know how things are going before long."

"I fail to see how that last question can be termed a necessary question," said Mrs Turton.

"Will all ladies leave the smoking-room now, please?" he cried, clapping his hands again. "And remember what I have said. We look to you to help us through a difficult time, and you can help us by behaving as if everything is normal. It is all I ask. Can I rely on you?"

"Yes, indeed, oh indeed," they chorused out of peaked, anxious faces. They moved out, subdued yet elated, Mrs Blakiston in their midst like a sacred flame. His simple words had reminded them that they were an outpost of Empire. By the side of their compassionate love for Adela another sentiment sprang up which was to strangle it in the long run. Its first signs were prosaic and small. Mrs Turton made her loud, hard jokes at bridge, Mrs Lesley began to knit a comforter.

When the smoking-room was clear, the Collector sat on the edge of a table, so that he could dominate without formality. His mind whirled with contradictory impulses. He wanted to avenge Miss Quested and punish Fielding, while remaining scrupulously fair. He wanted to flog every native that he saw, but to do nothing that would lead to a riot or to the necessity for military intervention. The dread of having to call in the troops was vivid to him; soldiers put one thing straight, but leave a dozen others crooked, and they love to humiliate the civilian administration. One soldier was in the room this evening—a stray subaltern from a Gurkha regiment; he was a little drunk, and regarded his presence as providential. The Collector sighed. There seemed nothing for it but the old weary business of compromise and moderation. He longed for the good old days when an Englishman could satisfy his own honour and no questions asked afterwards. Poor young Heaslop had taken a step in this direction by refusing bail, but the Collector couldn't feel this was wise of poor young Heaslop. Not only would the Nawab Bahadur and others be angry, but the Government of India itself also watches—and behind it is that caucus of cranks and cravens, the British Parliament. He had constantly to remind himself that, in the eyes of the law, Aziz was not yet guilty, and the effort fatigued him.

The others, less responsible, could behave naturally. They had started speaking of "women and children"—that phrase that exempts the male from sanity when it has been repeated a few times. Each felt that all he loved best in the world was at stake, demanded revenge, and was filled with a not unpleasing glow, in which the chilly and half-known features of Miss Quested vanished, and were replaced by all that is sweetest and warmest in the private life. "But it's the women and children," they repeated, and the Collector knew he ought to stop them intoxicating themselves, but he hadn't the heart. "They ought to be compelled to give hostages," etc. Many of the said women and children were leaving for the Hill Station in a few days, and the suggestion was made that they should be packed off at once in a special train.

"*And* a jolly suggestion," the subaltern cried. "The Army's got to come in sooner or later." (A special train was in his mind inseparable from troops.) "This would never have happened if Barabas Hill was under military control. Station a bunch of Gurkhas at the entrance of the cave was all that was wanted."

"Mrs Blakiston was saying if only there were a few Tommies," remarked someone.

"English no good," he cried, getting his loyalties mixed. "Native troops for this country. Give me the sporting type of native, give me Gurkhas, give me Rajputs, give me Jats, give me the Punjabi, give me Sikhs, give me Marathas, Bhils, Afridis and Pathans, and really, if it comes to that, I don't mind if you give me the scum of the bazaars. Properly led, mind. I'd lead them anywhere—"

The Collector nodded at him pleasantly, and said to his own people: "Don't start carrying arms about. I want everything to go on precisely as usual, until there's cause for the contrary. Get the womenfolk off to the hills, but do it quietly, and for heaven's sake no more talk of special trains. Never mind what you think or feel. Possibly I have feelings too. One isolated Indian has attempted—is charged with an attempted crime." He flipped his forehead hard with his fingernail, and they all realized that he felt as deeply as they did, and they loved him, and determined not to increase his difficulties. "Act upon that fact until there are more facts," he concluded. "Assume every Indian is an angel."

They murmured, "Right you are, so we will. . . . Angels. . . . Exactly. . . ." From the subaltern: "Exactly what I said. The native's all right if you get him alone. Lesley! Lesley! You remember the one I had a knock with on your maidan last month. Well, he was all right. Any native who plays polo is all right. What you've got to stamp on is these educated classes, and, mind, I do know what I'm talking about this time."

The smoking-room door opened, and let in a feminine buzz. Mrs Turton called out, "She's better," and from both sections of the community a sigh of joy and relief rose. The

Civil Surgeon, who had brought the good news, came in. His cumbrous, pasty face looked ill-tempered. He surveyed the company, saw Fielding crouched below him on an ottoman, and said, "H'm!" Everyone began pressing him for details. "No one's out of danger in this country as long as they have a temperature," was his answer. He appeared to resent his patient's recovery, and no one who knew the old Major and his ways was surprised at this.

"Squat down, Callendar; tell us all about it."

"Take me some time to do that."

"How's the old lady?"

"Temperature."

"My wife heard she was sinking."

"So she may be. I guarantee nothing. I really can't be plagued with questions, Lesley."

"Sorry, old man."

"Heaslop's just behind me."

At the name of Heaslop a fine and beautiful expression was renewed on every face. Miss Quested was only a victim, but young Heaslop was a martyr; he was the recipient of all the evil intended against them by the country they had tried to serve; he was bearing the sahib's cross. And they fretted because they could do nothing for him in return; they felt so craven sitting on softness and attending the course of the law.

"I wish to God I hadn't given my jewel of an assistant leave. I'd cut my tongue out first. To feel I'm responsible, that's what hits me. To refuse, and then give in under pressure. That is what I did, my sons, that is what I did."

Fielding took his pipe from his mouth and looked at it thoughtfully. Thinking him afraid, the other went on: "I understood an Englishman was to accompany the expedition. That is why I gave in."

"No one blames you, my dear Callendar," said the Collector, looking down. "We are all to blame in the sense that we ought to have seen the expedition was insufficiently guaranteed, and stopped it. I knew about it myself; we lent our car this morning to take the ladies to the station. We are all implicated in that sense, but not an atom of blame attaches to you personally."

"I don't feel that. I wish I could. Responsibility is a very awful thing, and I've no use for the man who shirks it." His eyes were directed on Fielding. Those who knew that Fielding had undertaken to accompany and missed the early train were sorry for him; it was what is to be expected when a man mixes himself up with natives; always ends in some indignity. The Collector, who knew more, kept silent, for the official in him still hoped that Fielding would toe the line. The conversation turned to women and children again, and under its cover Major Callendar got hold of the subaltern, and set him on to bait the schoolmaster. Pretending to be more drunk than he really was, he began to make semi-offensive remarks.

"Heard about Miss Quested's servant?" reinforced the Major.

"No, what about him?"

"Heaslop warned Miss Quested's servant last night never to lose sight of her. Prisoner got hold of this and managed to leave him behind. Bribed him. Heaslop has just found out the whole story, with names and sums—a well-known pimp to those people gave the money, Mohammed Latif by name. So much for the servant. What about the Englishman—our friend here? How did they get rid of him? Money again."

Fielding rose to his feet, supported by murmurs and exclamations, for no one yet suspected his integrity.

"Oh, I'm being misunderstood, apologies," said the Major offensively. "I didn't mean they bribed Mr Fielding."

"Then what do you mean?"

"They paid the other Indian to make you late—Godbole. He was saying his prayers. I know those prayers!"

"That's ridiculous . . ." He sat down again, trembling with rage; person after person was being dragged into the mud.

Having shot this bolt, the Major prepared the next. "Heaslop also found out something from his mother. Aziz paid a herd of natives to suffocate her in a cave. That was the end of her, or would have been, only she got out. Nicely planned, wasn't it? Neat. Then he could go on with the girl. He and she and a guide, provided by the same Mohammed Latif. Guide now can't be found. Pretty." His voice broke into a roar. "It's not the time for sitting down. It's the time for action. Call in the troops and clear the bazaars."

The Major's outbursts were always discounted, but he made everyone uneasy on this occasion. The crime was even worse than they had supposed—the unspeakable limit of cynicism, untouched since 1857. Fielding forgot his anger on poor old Godbole's behalf, and became thoughtful; the evil was propagating in every direction, it seemed to have an existence of its own, apart from anything that was done or said by individuals, and he understood better why both Aziz and Hamidullah had been inclined to lie down and die. His adversary saw that he was in trouble, and now ventured to say, "I suppose nothing that's said inside the Club will go outside the Club?" winking the while at Lesley.

"Why should it?" responded Lesley.

"Oh, nothing. I only heard a rumour that a certain member here present has been seeing the prisoner this afternoon. You can't run with the hare and hunt with the hounds, at least not in this country."

"Does anyone here present want to?"

Fielding was determined not to be drawn again. He had something to say, but it should be at his own moment. The attack failed to mature, because the Collector did not support it. Attention shifted from him for a time. Then the buzz of women broke out again. The door had been opened by Ronny.

The young man looked exhausted and tragic, also gentler than usual. He always showed deference to his superiors, but now it came straight from his heart. He seemed to appeal for their protection in the insult that had befallen him, and they, in instinctive homage, rose to their feet. But every human act in the East is tainted with officialism, and while honouring him they condemned Aziz and India. Fielding realized this, and he remained seated. It was an ungracious, a caddish thing to do, perhaps an unsound thing to do, but he felt he had been passive long enough, and that he might be drawn into the wrong current if he did not make a stand. Ronny, who had not seen him, said in husky tones, "Oh, please—please all sit down, I only want to listen to what has been decided."

"Heaslop, I'm telling them I'm against any show of force," said the Collector apologetically. "I don't know whether you will feel as I do, but that is how I am situated. When the verdict is obtained, it will be another matter."

"You are sure to know best; I have no experience, I can't tell."

"How is your mother, old boy?"

"Better, thank you. I wish everyone would sit down."

"Some have never got up," the young soldier said.

"And the Major brings us an excellent report of Miss Quested," Turton went on.

"I do, I do, I'm satisfied."

"You thought badly of her earlier, did you not, Major? That's why I refused bail."

Callendar laughed with friendly inwardness, and said: "Heaslop, Heaslop, next time bail's wanted, ring up the old doctor before giving it; his shoulders are broad, and, speaking in the strictest confidence, don't take the old doctor's opinion too seriously. He's a blithering idiot, we can always leave it at that, but he'll do the little he can towards keeping in quod the—" He broke off with affected politeness. "Oh, but he has one of his friends here."

The subaltern called, "Stand up, you swine."

"Mr Fielding, what has prevented you from standing up?" said the Collector, entering the fray at last. It was the attack for which Fielding had waited, and to which he must reply.

"May I make a statement, sir?"

"Certainly."

Seasoned and self-contained, devoid of the fervours of nationality or youth, the schoolmaster did what was for him a comparatively easy thing. He stood up and said, "I believe Dr Aziz to be innocent."

"You have a right to hold that opinion if you choose, but pray is that any reason why you should insult Mr Heaslop?"

"May I conclude my statement?"

"Certainly."

"I am waiting for the verdict of the courts. If he is guilty I resign from my service, and leave India. I resign from the Club now."

"Hear, hear!" said voices, not entirely hostile, for they liked the fellow for speaking out.

"You have not answered my question. Why did you not stand when Mr Heaslop entered?"

"With all deference, sir, I am not here to answer questions, but to make a personal statement, and I have concluded it."

"May I ask whether you have taken over charge of this District?"

Fielding moved towards the door.

"One moment, Mr Fielding. You are not to go yet, please. Before you leave the Club, from which you do very well to resign, you will express some detestation of the crime, and you will apologize to Mr Heaslop."

"Are you speaking to me officially, sir?"

The Collector, who never spoke otherwise, was so infuriated that he lost his head. He cried: "Leave this room at once, and I deeply regret that I demeaned myself by meeting you at the station. You have sunk to the level of your associates; you are weak, weak, that is what is wrong with you—"

"I want to leave the room, but cannot while this gentleman prevents me," said Fielding lightly; the subaltern had got across his path.

"Let him go," said Ronny, almost in tears.

It was the only appeal that could have saved the situation. Whatever Heaslop wished must be done. There was a slight scuffle at the door, from which Fielding was propelled, a little more quickly than is natural, into the room where the ladies were playing cards. "Fancy if I'd fallen or got angry," he thought. Of course he was a little angry. His peers had never offered him violence or called him weak before, besides, Heaslop had heaped coals of fire on his head. He wished he had not picked the quarrel over poor suffering Heaslop, when there were cleaner issues at hand.

However, there it was, done, muddled through, and to cool himself and regain mental balance he went onto the upper veranda for a moment, where the first object he saw was the Marabar Hills. At this distance and hour they leapt into beauty; they were Monsalvat, Valhalla, the towers of a cathedral, peopled with saints and heroes, and covered with flowers. What miscreant lurked in them, presently to be detected by the activities of the law? Who was the guide, and had he been found yet? What was the "echo" of which the girl complained? He did not know, but presently he would know. Great is information, and she shall prevail. It was the last moment of the light, and as he gazed at the Marabar Hills they seemed to move graciously towards him like a queen, and their charm became the sky's. At the moment they vanished they were everywhere, the cool benediction of the night descended, the stars sparkled, and the whole universe was a hill. Lovely, exquisite moment—but passing the Englishman with averted face and on swift wings. He experienced nothing himself; it was as if someone had told him there was such a moment, and he was obliged to believe. And he felt dubious and discontented suddenly, and wondered whether he was really and truly successful as a human being. After forty years' experience, he had learned to manage his life and make the best of it on advanced European lines, had developed his personality, explored his limitations, controlled his passions—and he had done it all without becoming either pedantic or worldly. A creditable achievement, but as the moment passed he felt he ought to have been working at something else the whole time—he didn't know at what, never would know, never could know, and that was why he felt sad.

Chapter 21

Dismissing his regrets, as inappropriate to the matter in hand, he accomplished the last section of the day by riding off to his new allies. He was glad that he had broken with the Club, for he would have picked up scraps of gossip there, and reported them down in the city, and he was glad to be denied this opportunity. He would miss his billiards, and occasional tennis, and cracks with McBryde, but really that was all, so light did he travel. At the entrance of the bazaars, a tiger made his horse shy—a youth dressed up as a tiger, the body striped brown and yellow, a mask over the face. Mohurram was working up. The city beat a good many drums, but seemed good-tempered. He was invited to inspect a small tazia—a flimsy and frivolous erection, more like a crinoline than the tomb of the grandson of the Prophet, done to death at Kerbela. Excited children were pasting coloured paper over its ribs. The rest of the evening he spent with the Nawab Bahadur, Hamidullah, Mahmoud Ali, and others of the confederacy. The campaign was also working up. A telegram had been sent to the famous Amritrao, and his acceptance received. Application for bail was to be renewed —it could not well be withheld now that Miss Quested was out of danger. The conference was serious and sensible, but marred by a group of itinerant musicians, who were allowed to play in the compound. Each held a large earthenware jar, containing pebbles, and jerked it up and down in time to a doleful chant. Distracted by the noise, he suggested their dismissal, but the Nawab Bahadur vetoed it; he said that musicians, who had walked many miles, might bring good luck.

Late at night, he had an inclination to tell Professor Godbole of the tactical and moral error he had made in being rude to Heaslop, and to hear what he would say. But the old fellow had gone to bed, and slipped off unmolested to his new job in a day or two; he always did possess the knack of slipping off.

Chapter 22

Adela lay for several days in the McBrydes' bungalow. She had been touched by the sun, also hundreds of cactus spines had to be picked out of her flesh. Hour after hour Miss Derek and Mrs McBryde examined her through magnifying glasses, always coming on fresh colonies, tiny hairs that might snap off and be drawn into the blood if they were neglected. She lay passive beneath their fingers, which developed the shock that had begun in the cave. Hitherto she had not much minded whether she was touched or not; her senses were abnormally inert, and the only contact she anticipated was that of mind. Everything now was transferred to the surface of her body, which began to avenge itself, and feed unhealthily. People seemed very much alike, except that some would come close while others kept away. "In space things touch, in time things part," she repeated to herself while the thorns were being extracted—her brain so weak that she could not decide whether the phrase was a philosophy or a pun.

They were kind to her, indeed over-kind, the men too respectful, the women too sympathetic; whereas Mrs Moore, the only visitor she wanted, kept away. No one understood her trouble, or knew why she vibrated between hard common sense and hysteria. She would begin a speech as if nothing particular had happened. "I went into this detestable cave," she would say dryly, "and I remember scratching the wall with my fingernail, to start the usual echo, and then as I was saying there was this shadow, or sort of shadow, down the entrance tunnel, bottling me up. It seemed like an age, but I suppose the whole thing can't have lasted thirty seconds really. I hit at him with the glasses, he pulled me round the cave by the strap, it broke, I escaped, that's all.

He never actually touched me once. It all seems such nonsense." Then her eyes would fill with tears. "Naturally I'm upset, but I shall get over it." And then she would break down entirely, and the women would feel she was one of themselves and cry too, and men in the next room murmur: "Good God, good God!" No one realized that she thought tears vile, a degradation more subtle than anything endured in the Marabar, a negation of her advanced outlook and the natural honesty of her mind. Adela was always trying to "think the incident out", always reminding herself that no harm had been done. There was "the shock", but what is that? For a time her own logic would convince her, then she would hear the echo again, weep, declare she was unworthy of Ronny, and hope her assailant would get the maximum penalty. After one of these bouts, she longed to go out into the bazaars and ask pardon from everyone she met, for she felt in some vague way that she was leaving the world worse than she found it. She felt that it was her crime, until the intellect, reawakening, pointed out to her that she was inaccurate here, and set her again upon her sterile round.

If only she could have seen Mrs Moore! The old lady had not been well either, and was disinclined to come out, Ronny reported. And consequently the echo flourished, raging up and down like a nerve in the faculty of her hearing, and the noise in the cave, so unimportant intellectually, was prolonged over the surface of her life. She had struck the polished wall—for no reason—and before the comment had died away he followed her, and the climax was the falling of her field-glasses. The sound had spouted after her when she escaped, and was going on still like a river that gradually floods the plain. Only Mrs Moore could drive it back to its source and seal the broken reservoir. Evil was loose . . . she could even hear it entering the lives of others. . . . And Adela spent days in this atmosphere of grief and depression. Her friends kept up their spirits by demanding holocausts of natives, but she was too worried and weak to do that.

When the cactus thorns had all been extracted, and her

temperature fallen to normal, Ronny came to fetch her away. He was worn with indignation and suffering, and she wished she could comfort him; but intimacy seemed to caricature itself, and the more they spoke the more wretched and self-conscious they became. Practical talk was the least painful, and he and McBryde now told her one or two things which they had concealed from her during the crisis, by the doctor's orders. She learned for the first time of the Mohurram troubles. There had nearly been a riot. The last day of the festival, the great procession left its official route, and tried to enter the Civil Station, and a telephone had been cut because it interrupted the advance of one of the larger paper towers. McBryde and his police had pulled the thing straight—a fine piece of work. They passed on to another and very painful subject: the trial. She would have to appear in court, identify the prisoner, and submit to cross-examination by an Indian lawyer.

"Can Mrs Moore be with me?" was all she said.

"Certainly, and I shall be there myself," Ronny replied. "The case won't come before me; they've objected to me on personal grounds. It will be at Chandrapore—we thought at one time it would be transferred elsewhere."

"Miss Quested realizes what all that means, though," said McBryde sadly. "The case will come before Das."

Das was Ronny's assistant—own brother to the Mrs Bhattacharya whose carriage had played them false last month. He was courteous and intelligent, and with the evidence before him could only come to one conclusion; but that he should be judge over an English girl had convulsed the station with wrath, and some of the women had sent a telegram about it to Lady Mellanby, the wife of the Lieutenant-Governor.

"I must come before someone."

"That's—that's the way to face it. You have the pluck, Miss Quested." He grew very bitter over the arrangements, and called them "the fruits of democracy". In the old days an Englishwoman would not have had to appear, nor would any Indian have dared to discuss her private affairs. She would have made her deposition, and judgement would have followed. He apologized to her for the condition of the country, with the result that she gave one of her sudden little shoots of tears. Ronny wandered miserably about the room while she cried, treading upon the flowers of the Kashmir carpet that so inevitably covered it or drumming on the brass Benares bowls. "I do this less every day, I shall soon be quite well," she said, blowing her nose and feeling hideous. "What I need is something to do. That is why I keep on with this ridiculous crying."

"It's not ridiculous, we think you wonderful," said the policeman very sincerely. "It only bothers us that we can't help you more. Your stopping here—at such a time—is the greatest honour this house—" He too was overcome with emotion. "By the way, a letter came here for you while you were ill," he continued. "I opened it, which is a strange confession to make. Will you forgive me? The circumstances are peculiar. It is from Fielding."

"Why should he write to me?"

"A most lamentable thing has happened. The defence got hold of him."

"He's a crank, a crank," said Ronny lightly.

"That's your way of putting it, but a man can be a crank without being a cad. Miss Quested had better know how he behaved to you. If you don't tell her, somebody else will." He told her. "He is now the mainstay of the defence, I needn't add. He is the one righteous Englishman in a horde of tyrants. He receives deputations from the bazaar, and they all chew betel-nut and smear one another's hands with scent. It is not easy to enter into the mind of such a man. His students are on strike—out of enthusiasm for him they won't learn their lessons. If it weren't for Fielding one would never have had the Mohurram trouble. He has done a very grave disservice to the whole community. The letter lay here a day or two, waiting till you were well enough, then the situation got so grave that I decided to open it in case it was useful to us."

"Is it?" she said feebly.

"Not at all. He only has the impertinence to suggest you have made a mistake."

"Would that I had!" She glanced through the letter, which was careful and formal in its wording. "Dr Aziz is innocent," she read. Then her voice began to tremble again. "But think of his behaviour to you, Ronny. When you had already to bear so much for my sake! It was shocking of him. My dear, how can I repay you? How can one repay when one has nothing to give? What is the use of personal relationships when everyone brings less and less to them? I feel we ought all to go back into the desert for centuries and try and get good. I want to begin at the beginning. All the things I thought I'd learned are just a hindrance, they're not knowledge at all. I'm not fit for personal relationships. Well, let's go, let's go. Of course Mr Fielding's letter doesn't count; he can think and write what he likes, only he shouldn't have been rude to you when you had so much to bear. That's what matters. . . . I don't want your arm, I'm a magnificent walker, no, don't touch me, please."

Mrs McBryde wished her an affectionate goodbye—a woman with whom she had nothing in common and whose intimacy oppressed her. They would have to meet now, year after year, until one of their husbands was superannuated. Truly Anglo-India had caught her with a vengeance, and perhaps it served her right for having tried to take up a line of her own. Humbled yet repelled, she gave thanks. "Oh, we must help one another, we must take the rough with the smooth," said Mrs McBryde. Miss Derek was there too, still making jokes about her comic Maharajah and Rani. Required as a witness at the trial, she had refused to send back the Mudkul car; they would be frightfully sick. Both Mrs McBryde and Miss Derek kissed her, and called her by her Christian name. Then Ronny drove her back. It was early in the morning, for the day, as the Hot Weather advanced, swelled like a monster at both ends, and left less and less room for the movements of mortals.

As they neared his bungalow, he said: "Mother's looking forward to seeing you, but of course she's old, one mustn't forget that. Old people never take things as one expects, in my opinion." He seemed warning her against approaching disappointment, but she took no notice. Her friendship with Mrs Moore was so deep and real that she felt sure it would last, whatever else happened. "What can I do to make things easier for you? It's you who matter," she sighed.

"Dear old girl to say so."

"Dear old boy." Then she cried: "Ronny, she isn't ill too?"

He reassured her: Major Callendar was not dissatisfied.

"But you'll find her—irritable. We are an irritable family. Well, you'll see for yourself. No doubt my own nerves are out of order, and I expected more from mother when I came in from the office than she felt able to give. She is sure to make a special effort for you; still, I don't want your homecoming to be a disappointing one. Don't expect too much."

The house came in sight. It was a replica of the bungalow she had left. Puffy, red, and curiously severe, Mrs Moore was revealed upon a sofa. She didn't get up when they entered, and the surprise of this roused Adela from her own troubles.

"Here you are both back," was the only greeting.

Adela sat down and took her hand. It withdrew, and she felt that, just as others repelled her, so did she repel Mrs Moore.

"Are you all right? You appeared all right when I left," said Ronny, trying not to speak crossly, but he had instructed her to give the girl a pleasant welcome, and he could not but feel annoyed.

"I am all right," she said heavily. "As a matter of fact I have been looking at my return ticket. It is interchangeable, so I have a much larger choice of boats home than I thought."

"We can go into that later, can't we?"

"Ralph and Stella may be wanting to know when I arrive."

"There is plenty of time for all such plans. How do you think our Adela looks?"

"I am counting on you to help me through; it is such a blessing to be with you again, everyone else is a stranger," said the girl rapidly.

But Mrs Moore showed no inclination to be helpful. A sort of resentment emanated from her. She seemed to say: "Am I to be bothered for ever?" Her Christian tenderness had gone, or had developed into a hardness, a just irritation against the human race; she had taken no interest at the arrest, asked scarcely any questions, and had refused to leave her bed on the awful last night of Mohurram, when an attack was expected on the bungalow.

"I know it's all nothing; I must be sensible, I do try—" Adela continued, working again towards tears. "I shouldn't mind if it had happened anywhere else; at least I really don't know where it did happen."

Ronny supposed that he understood what she meant: she could not identify or describe the particular cave, indeed almost refused to have her mind cleared up about it, and it was recognized that the defence would try to make capital out of this during the trial. He reassured her: the Marabar Caves were notoriously like one another; indeed, in the future they were to be numbered in sequence with white paint.

"Yes, I mean that, at least not exactly; but there is this echo that I keep on hearing."

"Oh, what of the echo?" asked Mrs Moore, paying attention to her for the first time.

"I can't get rid of it."

"I don't suppose you ever will."

Ronny had emphasized to his mother that Adela would arrive in a morbid state, yet she was being positively malicious.

"Mrs Moore, what is this echo?"

"Don't you know?"

"No—what is it? Oh, do say! I felt you would be able to explain it . . . this will comfort me so. . . ."

"If you don't know, you don't know; I can't tell you."

"I think you're rather unkind not to say."

"Say, say, say," said the old lady bitterly. "As if anything can be said! I have spent my life in saying or in listening to sayings; I have listened too much. It is time I was left in peace. Not to die," she added sourly. "No doubt you expect me to die, but when I have seen you and Ronny married, and seen the other two and whether they want to be married —I'll retire then into a cave of my own." She smiled, to bring down her remark into ordinary life and thus add to its bitterness. "Somewhere where no young people will come asking questions and expecting answers. Some shelf."

"Quite so, but meantime a trial is coming on," said her son hotly, "and the notion of most of us is that we'd better pull together and help one another through, instead of being disagreeable. Are you going to talk like that in the witness-box?"

"Why should I be in the witness-box?"

"To confirm certain points in our evidence."

"I have nothing to do with your ludicrous law courts," she said, angry. "I will not be dragged in at all."

"I won't have her dragged in, either; I won't have any more trouble on my account," cried Adela, and again took the hand, which was again withdrawn. "Her evidence is not the least essential."

"I thought she would want to give it. No one blames you, mother, but the fact remains that you dropped off at the first cave, and encouraged Adela to go on with him alone, whereas if you'd been well enough to keep on too nothing would have happened. He planned it, I know. Still, you fell into his trap, just like Fielding and Antony before you. . . . Forgive me for speaking so plainly, but you've no right to take up this high and mighty attitude about law courts. If you're ill, that's different; but you say you're all right and you seem so, in which case I thought you'd want to take your part, I did really."

"I'll not have you worry her, whether she's well or ill," said Adela, leaving the sofa and taking his arm; then dropped it with a sigh and sat down again. But he was pleased she had rallied to him and surveyed his mother patronizingly. He had never felt easy with her. She was by no means the dear old lady outsiders supposed, and India had brought her into the open.

"I shall attend your marriage, but not your trial," she informed them, tapping her knee; she had become very restless, and rather ungraceful. "Then I shall go to England."

"You can't go to England in May, as you agreed."

"I have changed my mind."

"Well, we'd better end this unexpected wrangle," said the young man, striding about. "You appear to want to be left out of everything, and that's enough."

"My body, my miserable body," she sighed. "Why isn't it strong? Oh, why can't I walk away and be gone? Why can't I finish my duties and be gone? Why do I get headaches and puff when I walk? And all the time this to do and that to do and this to do in your way and that to do in her way, and everything sympathy and confusion and bearing one another's burdens. Why can't this be done and that be done in my way and they be done and I at peace? Why has anything to be done, I cannot see. Why all this marriage, marriage? . . . The human race would have become a single person centuries ago if marriage was any use. And all this rubbish about love, love in a church, love in a cave, as if there is the least difference, and I held up from my business over such trifles!"

"What do you want?" he said, exasperated. "Can you state it in simple language? If so, do."

"I want my pack of patience cards."

"Very well, get them."

He found, as he expected, that the poor girl was crying. And, as always, an Indian close outside the window, a mali in this case, picking up sounds. Much upset, he sat silent for a moment, thinking over his mother and her senile intrusions. He wished he had never asked her to visit India, or been under any obligation to her.

"Well, my dear girl, this isn't much of a homecoming," he said at last. "I had no idea she had this up her sleeve."

Adela had stopped crying. An extraordinary expression was on her face, half relief, half horror. She repeated, "Aziz, Aziz."

They all avoided mentioning that name. It had become

synonymous with the Power of Evil. He was "the prisoner", "the person in question", "the defence", and the sound of it now rang out like the first note of a new symphony.

"Aziz . . . have I made a mistake?"

"You're over-tired," he cried, not much surprised.

"Ronny, he's innocent; I made an awful mistake."

"Well, sit down anyhow." He looked round the room, but only two sparrows were chasing one another. She obeyed and took hold of his hand. He stroked it and she smiled, and gasped as if she had risen to the surface of the water, then touched her ear.

"My echo's better."

"That's good. You'll be perfectly well in a few days, but you must save yourself up for the trial. Das is a very good fellow, we shall all be with you."

"But Ronny, dear Ronny, perhaps there oughtn't to be any trial."

"I don't quite know what you're saying, and I don't think you do."

"If Dr Aziz never did it he ought to be let out."

A shiver like impending death passed over Ronny. He said hurriedly, "He was let out—until the Mohurram riot, when he had to be put in again." To divert her, he told her the story, which was held to be amusing. Nureddin had stolen the Nawab Bahadur's car and driven Aziz into a ditch in the dark. Both of them had fallen out, and Nureddin had cut his face open. Their wailing had been drowned by the cries of the faithful, and it was quite a time before they were rescued by the police. Nureddin was taken to the Minto Hospital, Aziz restored to prison, with an additional charge against him of disturbing the public peace. "Half a minute," he remarked when the anecdote was over, and went to the telephone to ask Callendar to look in as soon as he found it convenient, because she hadn't borne the journey well.

When he returned, she was in a nervous crisis, but it took a different form—she clung to him, and sobbed: "Help me to do what I ought. Aziz is good. You heard your mother say so."

"Heard what?"

"He's good; I've been so wrong to accuse him."

"Mother never said so."

"Didn't she?" she asked, quite reasonable, open to every suggestion anyway.

"She never mentioned that name once."

"But, Ronny, I heard her."

"Pure illusion. You can't be quite well, can you, to make up a thing like that."

"I suppose I can't. How amazing of me!"

"I was listening to all she said, as far as it could be listened to; she gets very incoherent."

"When her voice dropped she said it—towards the end, when she talked about love—love—I couldn't follow, but just then she said: 'Dr Aziz never did it.' "

"Those words?"

"The idea more than the words."

"Never, never, my dear girl. Complete illusion. His name was not mentioned by anyone. Look here—you are confusing this with Fielding's letter."

"That's it, that's it," she cried, greatly relieved. "I knew I'd heard his name somewhere. I am so grateful to you for clearing this up—it's the sort of mistake that worries me, and proves I'm neurotic."

"So you won't go saying he's innocent again, will you? For every servant I've got is a spy." He went to the window. The mali had gone, or rather had turned into two small children—impossible they should know English, but he sent them packing. "They all hate us," he explained. "It'll be all right after the verdict, for I will say this for them, they do accept the accomplished fact; but at present they're pouring out money like water to catch us tripping, and a remark like yours is the very thing they look out for. It would enable them to say it was a put-up job on the part of us officials. You see what I mean."

Mrs Moore came back, with the same air of ill-temper, and sat down with a flump by the card-table. To clear the confusion up, Ronny asked her pointblank whether she had mentioned the prisoner. She could not understand the question, and the reason of it had to be explained. She replied: "I never said his name," and began to play patience.

"I thought you said, 'Aziz is an innocent man,' but it was in Mr Fielding's letter."

"Of course he is innocent," she answered indifferently; it was the first time she had expressed an opinion on the point.

"You see, Ronny, I was right," said the girl.

"You were not right, she never said it."

"But she thinks it."

"Who cares what she thinks?"

"Red nine on black ten—" from the card-table.

"She can think, and Fielding too, but there's such a thing as evidence, I suppose."

"I know, but—"

"Is it again my duty to talk?" asked Mrs Moore, looking up. "Apparently, as you keep interrupting me."

"Only if you have anything sensible to say."

"Oh, how tedious . . . trivial . . ." and as when she had scoffed at love, love, love, her mind seemed to move towards them from a great distance and out of darkness. "Oh, why is everything still my duty? When shall I be free from your fuss? Was he in the cave and were you in the cave and on and on . . . and Unto us a son is born, unto us a child is given . . . and am I good and is he bad and are we saved?. . . and ending everything the echo."

"I don't hear it so much," said Adela, moving towards her. "You send it away, you do nothing but good, you are so good."

"I am not good, no, bad." She spoke more calmly and resumed her cards, saying as she turned them up: "A bad old woman, bad, bad, detestable. I used to be good with the children growing up, also I meet this young man in his mosque, I wanted him to be happy. Good, happy, small people. They do not exist, they were a dream. . . . But I will not help you to torture him for what he never did. There are different ways of evil and I prefer mine to yours."

"Have you any evidence in the prisoner's favour?" said

Ronny in the tones of the just official. "If so, it is your bounden duty to go into the witness-box for him instead of for us. No one will stop you."

"One knows people's characters, as you call them," she retorted disdainfully, as if she really knew more than character but could not impart it. "I have heard both English and Indians speak well of him, and I felt it isn't the sort of thing he would do."

"Feeble, mother, feeble."

"Most feeble."

"And most inconsiderate to Adela."

Adela said: "It would be so appalling if I was wrong. I should take my own life."

He turned on her with: "What was I warning you just now? You know you're right, and the whole station knows it."

"Yes, he . . . . This is very, very awful. I'm as certain as ever he followed me . . . only, wouldn't it be possible to withdraw the case? I dread the idea of giving evidence more and more, and you are all so good to women here and you have so much more power than in England—look at Miss Derek's motor-car. Oh, of course it's out of the question, I'm ashamed to have mentioned it; please forgive me."

"That's all right," he said inadequately. "Of course I forgive you, as you call it. But the case has to come before a magistrate now; it really must, the machinery has started."

"She has started the machinery; it will work to its end."

Adela inclined towards tears in consequence of this unkind remark, and Ronny picked up the list of steamship sailings with an excellent notion in his head. His mother ought to leave India at once; she was doing no good to herself or to anyone else there.

Chapter 23

Lady Mellanby, wife to the Lieutenant-Governor of the Province, had been gratified by the appeal addressed to her by the ladies of Chandrapore. She could not do anything—besides, she was sailing for England; but she desired to be informed if she could show sympathy in any other way. Mrs Turton replied that Mr Heaslop's mother was trying to get a passage, but had delayed too long, and all the boats were full; could Lady Mellanby use her influence? Not even Lady Mellanby could expand the dimensions of a P. and O., but she was a very, very nice woman, and she actually wired offering the unknown and obscure old lady accommodation in her own reserved cabin. It was like a gift from heaven; humble and grateful, Ronny could not but reflect that there are compensations for every woe. His name was familiar at Government House owing to poor Adela, and now Mrs Moore would stamp it on Lady Mellanby's imagination, as they journeyed across the Indian Ocean and up the Red Sea. He had a return of tenderness for his mother—as we do for our relatives when they receive conspicuous and unexpected honour. She was not negligible, she could still arrest the attention of a high official's wife.

So Mrs Moore had all she wished; she escaped the trial, the marriage, and the Hot Weather; she would return to England in comfort and distinction, and see her other children. At her son's suggestion, and by her own desire, she departed. But she accepted her good luck without enthusiasm. She had come to that state where the horror of the universe and its smallness are both visible at the same time—the twilight of the double vision in which so many elderly people are involved. If this world is not to our taste, well, at all events there is Heaven, Hell, Annihilation—one or other of those large things, that huge scenic background of stars, fires, blue or black air. All heroic endeavour, and all that is known as art, assumes that there is such a background, just as all practical endeavour, when the world is to our taste, assumes that the world is all. But in the twilight of the double vision a spiritual muddledom is set up for which no high-sounding words can be found; we can neither act nor refrain from action, we can neither ignore nor respect Infinity. Mrs Moore had always inclined to resignation. As soon as she landed in India it seemed to her good, and when she saw the water flowing through the mosque-tank, or the Ganges, or the moon, caught in the shawl of night with all the other stars, it seemed a beautiful goal and an easy one. To be one with the universe! So dignified and simple. But there was always some little duty to be performed first, some new card to be turned up from the diminishing pack and placed, and, while she was pottering about, the Marabar struck its gong.

What had spoken to her in that scoured-out cavity of the granite? What dwelt in the first of the caves? Something very old and very small. Before time, it was before space also. Something snub-nosed, incapable of generosity—the undying worm itself. Since hearing its voice, she had not entertained one large thought, she was actually envious of Adela. All this fuss over a frightened girl! Nothing had happened, "and if it had," she found herself thinking with the cynicism of a withered priestess, "if it had, there are worse evils than love." The unspeakable attempt presented itself to her as love: in a cave, in a church—boum, it amounts to the same. Visions are supposed to entail profundity, but—wait till you get one, dear reader! The abyss also may be petty, the serpent of eternity made of maggots; her constant thought was: "Less attention should be paid to my future daughter-in-law and more to me, there is no sorrow like my sorrow," although when the attention was paid she rejected it irritably.

Her son couldn't escort her to Bombay, for the local situation continued acute, and all officials had to remain at their posts. Antony couldn't come either, in case he never returned to give his evidence. So she travelled with no one who could remind her of the past. This was a relief. The heat had drawn back a little before its next advance, and the journey was not unpleasant. As she left Chandrapore the moon, full again, shone over the Ganges and touched the shrinking channels into threads of silver, then veered and looked into her window. The swift and comfortable mail-train slid with her through the night, and all the next day she was rushing through Central India, through landscapes that were baked and bleached but had not the hopeless melancholy of the plain. She watched the indestructible life of man and his changing faces, and the houses he has built for himself and God, and they appeared to her not in terms of her own trouble but as things to see. There was, for instance, a place called Asirgarh which she passed at sunset and identified on a map—an enormous fortress among wooded hills. No one had ever mentioned Asirgarh to her, but it had huge and noble bastions and to the right of them was a mosque. She forgot it. Ten minutes later, Asirgarh reappeared. The mosque was to the left of the bastions now. The train in its descent through the Vindhyas had described a semicircle round Asirgarh. What could she connect it with except its own name? Nothing; she knew no one who lived there. But it had looked at her twice and seemed to say: "I do not vanish." She woke in the middle of the night with a start, for the train was falling over the western cliff. Moonlit pinnacles rushed up at her like the fringes of a sea; then a brief episode of plain, the real sea, and the soupy dawn of Bombay. "I have not seen the right places," she thought, as she saw embayed in the platforms of the Victoria terminus the end of the rails that had carried her over a continent and could never carry her back. She would never visit Asirgarh or the other untouched places; neither Delhi nor Agra nor the Rajputana cities nor Kashmir, nor the obscurer marvels that had sometimes shone through men's speech: the bilingual rock of Girnar, the statue of Shri Belgola, the ruins of Mandu and Hampi, temples of Khajuraho, gardens of Shalimar. As she drove through the huge city which the West has built and abandoned with a gesture of despair, she longed to stop, though it was only Bombay, and disentangle the hundred Indias that passed each other in its streets. The feet of the horses moved her on, and presently the boat sailed and thousands of cocoanut palms appeared all round the anchorage and climbed the hills to wave her farewell. "So you thought an echo was India; you took the Marabar Caves as final?" they laughed. "What have we in common with them, or they with Asirgarh? Goodbye!" Then the steamer rounded Colaba, the continent swung about, the cliff of the Ghats melted into the haze of a tropic sea. Lady Mellanby turned up and advised her not to stand in the heat; "We are safely out of the frying-pan," said Lady Mellanby, "it will never do to fall into the fire."

Chapter 24

Making sudden changes of gear, the heat accelerated its advance after Mrs Moore's departure, until existence had to be endured and crime punished with the thermometer at a hundred and twelve. Electric fans hummed and spat, water splashed onto screens, ice clinked, and outside these defences, between a grayish sky and a yellowish earth, clouds of dust moved hesitatingly. In Europe life retreats out of the cold, and exquisite fireside myths have resulted—Balder, Persephone—but here the retreat is from the source of life, the treacherous sun, and no poetry adorns it, because disillusionment cannot be beautiful. Men yearn for poetry though they may not confess it; they desire that joy shall be graceful, and sorrow august, and infinity have a form, and India fails to accommodate them. The annual helter-skelter of April, when irritability and lust spread like a canker, is one of her comments on the orderly hopes of humanity. Fish manage better: fish, as the tanks dry, wriggle into the mud and wait for the rains to uncake them. But men try to be harmonious all the year round, and the results are occasionally disastrous. The triumphant machine of civilization may suddenly hitch and be immobilized into a car of stone, and at such moments the destiny of the English seems to resemble their predecessors', who also entered the country with intent to refashion it, but were in the end worked into its pattern and covered with its dust.

Adela, after years of intellectualism, had resumed her morning kneel to Christianity. There seemed no harm in it, it was the shortest and easiest cut to the unseen, and she could tack her troubles onto it. Just as the Hindu clerks asked Lakshmi for an increase in pay, so did she implore Jehovah for a favourable verdict. God who saves the King will surely support the police. Her deity returned a consoling reply, but the touch of her hands on her face started prickly heat, and she seemed to swallow and expectorate the same insipid clot of air that had weighed on her lungs all the night. Also the voice of Mrs Turton disturbed her. "Are you ready, young lady?" it pealed from the next room.

"Half a minute," she murmured. The Turtons had received her after Mrs Moore left. Their kindness was incredible, but it was her position, not her character, that moved them: she was the English girl who had had the terrible experience and for whom too much could not be done. No one, except Ronny, had any idea of what passed in her mind, and he only dimly, for where there is officialism every human relationship suffers. In her sadness she said to him, "I bring you nothing but trouble; I was right on the Maidan, we had better just be friends," but he protested, for the more she suffered the more highly he valued her. Did she love him? This question was somehow draggled up with the Marabar, it had been in her mind as she entered the fatal cave. Was she capable of loving anyone?

"Miss Quested, Adela, what d'ye call yourself, it's half past seven; we ought to think of starting for that court when you feel inclined."

"She's saying her prayers," came the Collector's voice.

"Sorry, my dear; take your time. . . . Was your chota hazri all right?"

"I can't eat; might I have a little brandy?" she asked, deserting Jehovah.

When it was brought, she shuddered, and said she was ready to go.

"Drink it up; not a bad notion, a peg."

"I don't think it'll really help me, Burra Sahib."

"You sent brandy down to the court, didn't you, Mary?"

"I should think I did, champagne too."

"I'll thank you this evening, I'm all to pieces now," said the girl, forming each syllable carefully as if her trouble would diminish if it were accurately defined. She was afraid of reticence, in case something that she herself did not perceive took shape beneath it, and she had rehearsed with Mr McBryde in an odd, mincing way her terrible adventure in the cave, how the man had never actually touched her but dragged her about, and so on. Her aim this morning was to announce, meticulously, that the strain was appalling, and she would probably break down under Mr Amritrao's cross-examination and disgrace her friends. "My echo has come back again badly," she told them.

"How about aspirin?"

"It is not a headache, it is an echo."

Unable to dispel the buzzing in her ears, Major Callendar had diagnosed it as a fancy, which must not be encouraged. So the Turtons changed the subject. The cool little lick of the morning breeze was passing over the earth, dividing night from day; it would fail in ten minutes, but they might profit by it for their drive down into the city.

"I am sure to break down," she repeated.

"You won't," said the Collector, his voice full of tenderness.

"Of course she won't, she's a real sport."

"But, Mrs Turton . . ."

"Yes, my dear child?"

"If I do break down, it is of no consequence. It would matter in some trials, not in this. I put it to myself in the following way: I can really behave as I like, cry, be absurd, I am sure to get my verdict, unless Mr Das is most frightfully unjust."

"You're bound to win," he said calmly, and did not remind her that there was bound to be an appeal. The Nawab Bahadur had financed the defence, and would ruin himself sooner than let an "innocent Moslem perish", and other interests, less reputable, were in the background too. The case might go up from court to court, with consequences that no official could foresee. Under his very eyes, the temper of Chandrapore was altering. As his car turned out of the compound, there was a tap of silly anger on its paint—a pebble thrown by a child. Some larger stones were dropped near the mosque. In the Maidan, a squad of native police on motor-cycles waited to escort them through the bazaars. The Collector was irritated and muttered, "McBryde's an old woman"; but Mrs Turton said, "Really, after Mohurram a show of force will do no harm; it's ridiculous to pretend they don't hate us, do give up that farce." He replied in an odd, sad voice, "I don't hate them, I don't know why," and he didn't hate them; for if he did he would have had to condemn his own career as a bad investment. He retained a contemptuous affection for the pawns he had moved about for so many years, they must be worth his pains. "After all, it's our women who make everything more difficult out here," was his inmost thought, as he caught sight of some obscenities upon a long blank wall, and beneath his chivalry to Miss Quested resentment lurked, waiting its day—perhaps there is a grain of resentment in all chivalry. Some students had gathered in front of the City Magistrate's Court—hysterical boys whom he would have faced if alone, but he told the driver to work round to the rear of the building. The students jeered, and Rafi (hiding behind a comrade that he might not be identified) called out that the English were cowards.

They gained Ronny's private room, where a group of their own sort had collected. None were cowardly, all nervy, for queer reports kept coming in. The sweepers had just struck, and half the commodes of Chandrapore remained desolate in consequence—only half, and sweepers from the District, who felt less strongly about the innocence of Dr Aziz, would arrive in the afternoon, and break the strike, but why should the grotesque incident occur? And a number of Mohammedan ladies had sworn to take no food until the prisoner was acquitted; their death would make little difference, indeed, being invisible, they seemed dead already, nevertheless it was disquieting. A new spirit seemed abroad, a rearrangement, which no one in the stern little band of whites could explain. There was a tendency to see Fielding at the back of it; the idea that he was weak and cranky had been dropped. They abused Fielding vigorously: he had been seen driving up with the two counsels, Amritrao and

Mahmoud Ali; he encouraged the Boy Scout movement for seditious reasons; he received letters with foreign stamps on them, and was probably a Japanese spy. This morning's verdict would break the renegade, but he had done his country and the Empire incalculable disservice. While they denounced him, Miss Quested lay back with her hands on the arms of her chair and her eyes closed, reserving her strength. They noticed her after a time, and felt ashamed of making so much noise.

"Can we do nothing for you?" Miss Derek said.

"I don't think so, Nancy, and I seem able to do nothing for myself."

"But you're strictly forbidden to talk like that; you're wonderful."

"Yes indeed," came the reverent chorus.

"My old Das is all right," said Ronny, starting a new subject in low tones.

"Not one of them's all right," contradicted Major Callendar.

"Das is, really."

"You mean he's more frightened of acquitting than convicting, because if he acquits he'll lose his job," said Lesley with a clever little laugh.

Ronny did mean that, but he cherished "illusions" about his own subordinates (following the finer traditions of his service here), and he liked to maintain that his old Das really did possess moral courage of the public-school brand. He pointed out that—from one point of view—it was good that an Indian was taking the case. Conviction was inevitable; so better let an Indian pronounce it, there would be less fuss in the long run. Interested in the argument, he let Adela become dim in his mind.

"In fact, you disapprove of the appeal I forwarded to Lady Mellanby," said Mrs Turton with considerable heat. "Pray don't apologize, Mr Heaslop; I am accustomed to being in the wrong."

"I didn't mean that . . ."

"All right. I said don't apologize."

"Those swine are always on the lookout for a grievance," said Lesley, to propitiate her.

"Swine, I should think so," the Major echoed. "And what's more, I'll tell you what. What's happened is a damn good thing really, barring of course its application to present company. It'll make them squeal and it's time they did squeal. I've put the fear of God into them at the hospital anyhow. You should see the grandson of our so-called leading loyalist." He tittered brutally as he described poor Nureddin's present appearance. "His beauty's gone, five upper teeth, two lower and a nostril. . . . Old Panna Lal brought him the looking-glass yesterday and he blubbered. . . . I laughed; I laughed, I tell you, and so would you; that used to be one of these buck niggers, I thought, now he's all septic; damn him, blast his soul—er—I believe he was unspeakably immoral—er—" He subsided, nudged in the ribs, but added, "I wish I'd had the cutting up of my late assistant too; nothing's too bad for these people."

"At last some sense is being talked," Mrs Turton cried, much to her husband's discomfort.

"That's what I say; I say there's not such a thing as cruelty after a thing like this."

"Exactly, and remember it afterwards, you men. You're weak, weak, weak. Why, they ought to crawl from here to the caves on their hands and knees whenever an Englishwoman's in sight, they oughtn't to be spoken to, they ought to be spat at, they ought to be ground into the dust, we've been far too kind with our Bridge Parties and the rest."

She paused. Profiting by her wrath, the heat had invaded her. She subsided into a lemon squash, and continued between the sips to murmur, "Weak, weak." And the process was repeated. The issues Miss Quested had raised were so much more important than she was herself that people inevitably forgot her.

Presently the case was called.

Their chairs preceded them into the court, for it was important that they should look dignified. And when the chuprassies had made all ready they filed into the ramshackly room with a condescending air, as if it was a booth at a fair. The Collector made a small official joke as he sat down, at which his entourage smiled, and the Indians, who could not hear what he said, felt that some new cruelty was afoot, otherwise the sahibs would not chuckle.

The court was crowded and of course very hot, and the first person Adela noticed in it was the humblest of all who were present, a person who had no bearing officially upon the trial: the man who pulled the punkah. Almost naked, and splendidly formed, he sat on a raised platform near the back, in the middle of the central gangway, and he caught her attention as she came in, and he seemed to control the proceedings. He had the strength and beauty that sometimes come to flower in Indians of low birth. When that strange race nears the dust and is condemned as untouchable, then nature remembers the physical perfection that she accomplished elsewhere, and throws out a god—not many, but one here and there, to prove to society how little its categories impress her. This man would have been notable anywhere; among the thin-hammed, flat-chested mediocrities of Chandrapore he stood out as divine, yet he was of the city, its garbage had nourished him, he would end on its rubbish-heaps. Pulling the rope towards him, relaxing it rhythmically, sending swirls of air over others, receiving none himself, he seemed apart from human destinies, a male Fate, a winnower of souls. Opposite him, also on a platform, sat the little Assistant Magistrate, cultivated, self-conscious and conscientious. The punkah-wallah was none of these things; he scarcely knew that he existed and did not understand why the court was fuller than usual, indeed he did not know that it was fuller than usual, didn't even know he worked a fan, though he thought he pulled a rope. Something in his aloofness impressed the girl from middle-class England, and rebuked the narrowness of her sufferings. In virtue of what had she collected this roomful of people together? Her particular brand of opinions, and the suburban Jehovah who sanctified them—by what right did they claim so much importance in the world, and assume the title of civilization?

Mrs Moore—she looked round, but Mrs Moore was far away on the sea; it was the kind of question they might have discussed on the voyage out, before the old lady had turned disagreeable and queer.

While thinking of Mrs Moore she heard sounds, which gradually grew more distinct. The epoch-making trial had started, and the Superintendent of Police was opening the case for the prosecution.

Mr McBryde was not at pains to be an interesting speaker; he left eloquence to the defence, who would require it. His attitude was, "Everyone knows the man's guilty, and I am obliged to say so in public before he goes to the Andamans." He made no moral or emotional appeal, and it was only by degrees that the studied negligence of his manner made itself felt, and lashed part of the audience to fury. Laboriously did he describe the genesis of the picnic. The prisoner had met Miss Quested at an entertainment given by the Principal of Government College, and had there conceived his intentions concerning her: prisoner was a man of loose life, as documents found upon him at his arrest would testify, also his fellow assistant, Dr Panna Lal, was in a position to throw light on his character, and Major Callendar himself would speak. Here Mr McBryde paused. He wanted to keep the proceedings as clean as possible, but Oriental Pathology, his favourite theme, lay all around him, and he could not resist it. Taking off his spectacles, as was his habit before enunciating a general truth, he looked into them sadly, and remarked that the darker races are physically attracted by the fairer, but not vice versa—not a matter for bitterness this, not a matter for abuse, but just a fact which any scientific observer will confirm.

"Even when the lady is so uglier than the gentleman?"

The comment fell from nowhere, from the ceiling perhaps. It was the first interruption, and the Magistrate felt bound to censure it. "Turn that man out," he said. One of the native policemen took hold of a man who had said nothing, and turned him out roughly. Mr McBryde resumed his spectacles and proceeded. But the comment had upset Miss Quested. Her body resented being called ugly, and trembled.

"Do you feel faint, Adela?" asked Miss Derek, who tended her with loving indignation.

"I never feel anything else, Nancy. I shall get through, but it's awful, awful."

This led to the first of a series of scenes. Her friends began to fuss around her, and the Major called out: "I must have better arrangements than this made for my patient; why isn't she given a seat on the platform? She gets no air."

Mr Das looked annoyed and said: "I shall be happy to accommodate Miss Quested with a chair up here in view of the particular circumstances of her health." The chuprassies passed up not one chair but several, and the entire party followed Adela onto the platform, Mr Fielding being the only European who remained in the body of the hall.

"That's better," remarked Mrs Turton, as she settled herself.

"Thoroughly desirable change for several reasons," replied the Major.

The Magistrate knew that he ought to censure this remark, but did not dare to. Callendar saw that he was afraid, and called out authoritatively, "Right, McBryde, go ahead now; sorry to have interrupted you."

"Are you all right yourselves?" asked the Superintendent.

"We shall do, we shall do."

"Go on, Mr Das, we are not here to disturb you," said the Collector patronizingly. Indeed, they had not so much disturbed the trial as taken charge of it.

While the prosecution continued, Miss Quested examined the hall—timidly at first, as though it would scorch her eyes. She observed to left and right of the punkah-man many a half-known face. Beneath her were gathered all the wreckage of her silly attempt to see India—the people she had met at the Bridge Party, the man and his wife who hadn't sent their carriage, the old man who would lend his car, various servants, villagers, officials, and the prisoner himself. There he sat—strong, neat little Indian with very black hair, and pliant hands. She viewed him without special emotion. Since they last met, she had elevated him into a principle of evil, but now he seemed to be what he had always been—a slight acquaintance. He was negligible, devoid of significance, dry like a bone, and though he was "guilty" no atmosphere of sin surrounded him. "I suppose he *is* guilty. Can I possibly have made a mistake?" she thought. For this question still occurred to her intellect, though since Mrs Moore's departure it had ceased to trouble her conscience.

Pleader Mahmoud Ali now arose, and asked with ponderous and ill-judged irony whether his client could be accommodated on the platform too: even Indians felt unwell sometimes, though naturally Major Callendar did not think so, being in charge of a Government hospital. "Another example of their exquisite sense of humour," sang Miss Derek. Ronny looked at Mr Das to see how he would handle the difficulty, and Mr Das became agitated, and snubbed Pleader Mahmoud Ali severely.

"Excuse me—" It was the turn of the eminent barrister from Calcutta. He was a fine-looking man, large and bony, with gray closely cropped hair. "We object to the presence of so many European ladies and gentlemen up on the platform," he said in an Oxford voice. "They will have the effect of intimidating our witnesses. Their place is with the rest of the public in the body of the hall. We have no objection to Miss Quested remaining on the platform, since she has been unwell; we shall extend every courtesy to her throughout, despite the scientific truths revealed to us by the District Superintendent of Police; but we do object to the others."

"Oh, cut the cackle and let's have the verdict," the Major growled.

The distinguished visitor gazed at the Magistrate respectfully.

"I agree to that," said Mr Das, hiding his face desperately in some papers. "It was only to Miss Quested that I gave permission to sit up here. Her friends should be so excessively kind as to climb down."

"Well done, Das, quite sound," said Ronny with devastating honesty.

"Climb down, indeed, what incredible impertinence!" Mrs Turton cried.

"Do come quietly, Mary," murmured her husband.

"Hi! My patient can't be left unattended."

"Do you object to the Civil Surgeon remaining, Mr Amritrao?"

"I should object. A platform confers authority."

"Even when it's one foot high; so come along all," said the Collector, trying to laugh.

"Thank you very much, sir," said Mr Das, greatly relieved. "Thank you, Mr Heaslop; thank you, ladies all."

And the party, including Miss Quested, descended from its rash eminence. The news of their humiliation spread quickly, and people jeered outside. Their special chairs followed them. Mahmoud Ali (who was quite silly and useless with hatred) objected even to these; by whose authority had special chairs been introduced, why had the Nawab Bahadur not been given one? etc. People began to talk all over the room, about chairs ordinary and special, strips of carpet, platforms one foot high.

But the little excursion had a good effect on Miss Quested's nerves. She felt easier now that she had seen all the people who were in the room. It was like knowing the worst. She was sure now that she should come through "all right"—that is to say, without spiritual disgrace, and she passed the good news on to Ronny and Mrs Turton. They were too much agitated with the defeat to British prestige to be interested. From where she sat, she could see the renegade Mr Fielding. She had had a better view of him from the platform, and knew that an Indian child perched on his knee. He was watching the proceedings, watching her. When their eyes met, he turned his away, as if direct intercourse was of no interest to him.

The Magistrate was also happier. He had won the battle of the platform, and gained confidence. Intelligent and impartial, he continued to listen to the evidence, and tried to forget that later on he would have to pronounce a verdict in accordance with it. The Superintendent trundled steadily forward; he had expected these outbursts of insolence—they are the natural gestures of an inferior race—and he betrayed no hatred of Aziz, merely an abysmal contempt.

The speech dealt at length with the "prisoner's dupes", as they were called—Fielding, the servant Antony, the Nawab Bahadur. This aspect of the case had always seemed dubious to Miss Quested, and she had asked the police not to develop it. But they were playing for a heavy sentence, and wanted to prove that the assault was premeditated. And in order to illustrate the strategy they produced a plan of the Marabar Hills, showing the route that the party had taken, and the "Tank of the Dagger" where they had camped.

The Magistrate displayed interest in archaeology.

An elevation of a specimen cave was produced; it was lettered "Buddhist Cave".

"Not Buddhist, I think, Jain. . . ."

"In which cave is the offence alleged, the Buddhist or the Jain?" asked Mahmoud Ali, with the air of unmasking a conspiracy.

"All the Marabar caves are Jain."

"Yes, sir; then in which Jain cave?"

"You will have an opportunity of putting such questions later."

Mr McBryde smiled faintly at their fatuity. Indians invariably collapse over some such point as this. He knew that the defence had some wild hope of establishing an alibi, that they had tried (unsuccessfully) to identify the guide, and that Fielding and Hamidullah had gone out to the Kawa Dol and paced and measured all one moonlit night. "Mr Lesley says they're Buddhist, and he ought to know if anyone does. But may I call attention to the shape?" And he described what had occurred there. Then he spoke of Miss Derek's arrival, of the scramble down the gully, of the return of the two ladies to Chandrapore, and of the document Miss Quested signed on her arrival, in which mention was made of the field-glasses. And then came the culminating evidence: the discovery of the field-glasses on the prisoner. "I have nothing to add at present," he concluded, removing his spectacles. "I will now call my witnesses. The facts will speak for themselves. The prisoner is one of those individuals who have led a double life. I dare say his degeneracy gained upon him gradually. He has been very cunning at concealing, as is usual with the type, and pretending to be a respectable member of society, getting a Government position even. He is now entirely vicious and beyond redemption, I am afraid. He behaved most cruelly, most brutally, to another of his guests, another English lady. In order to get rid of her, and leave him free for his crime, he crushed her into a cave among his servants. However, that is by the way."

But his last words brought on another storm, and suddenly a new name, Mrs Moore, burst on the court like a whirlwind. Mahmoud Ali had been enraged, his nerves snapped; he shrieked like a maniac, and asked whether his client was charged with murder as well as rape, and who was this second English lady.

"I don't propose to call her."

"You don't because you can't, you have smuggled her out of the country; she is Mrs Moore, she would have proved his innocence, she was on our side, she was poor Indians' friend."

"You could have called her yourself," cried the Magistrate. "Neither side called her, neither must quote her as evidence."

"She was kept from us until too late—I learn too late—this is English justice, here is your British Raj. Give us back Mrs Moore for five minutes only, and she will save my friend, she will save the name of his sons; don't rule her out, Mr Das; take back those words as you yourself are a father; tell me where they have put her, oh, Mrs Moore. . . ."

"If the point is of any interest, my mother should have reached Aden," said Ronny dryly; he ought not to have intervened, but the onslaught had startled him.

"Imprisoned by you there because she knew the truth." He was almost out of his mind, and could be heard saying above the tumult: " I ruin my career, no matter; we are all to be ruined one by one."

"This is no way to defend your case," counselled the Magistrate.

"I am not defending a case, nor are you trying one. We are both of us slaves."

"Mr Mahmoud Ali, I have already warned you, and unless you sit down I shall exercise my authority."

"Do so; this trial is a farce, I am going." And he handed his papers to Amritrao and left, calling from the door histrionically yet with intense passion, "Aziz, Aziz—farewell for ever." The tumult increased, the invocation of Mrs Moore continued, and people who did not know what the syllables meant repeated them like a charm. They became Indianized into Esmiss Esmoor, they were taken up in the street outside. In vain the Magistrate threatened and expelled. Until the magic exhausted itself, he was powerless.

"Unexpected," remarked Mr Turton.

Ronny furnished the explanation. Before she sailed, his mother had taken to talk about the Marabar in her sleep, especially in the afternoon when servants were on the veranda, and her disjointed remarks on Aziz had doubtless been sold to Mahmoud Ali for a few annas; that kind of thing never ceases in the East.

"I thought they'd try something of the sort. Ingenious." He looked into their wide-open mouths. "They get just like that over their religion," he added calmly. "Start and can't stop. I'm sorry for your old Das, he's not getting much of a show."

"Mr Heaslop, how disgraceful dragging in your dear mother," said Miss Derek, bending forward.

"It's just a trick, and they happened to pull it off. Now one sees why they had Mahmoud Ali—just to make a scene on the chance. It is his speciality." But he disliked it more than he showed. It was revolting to hear his mother travestied into Esmiss Esmoor, a Hindu goddess.

"Esmiss Esmoor
Esmiss Esmoor
Esmiss Esmoor
Esmiss Esmoor. . . ."

"Ronny—"

"Yes, old girl?"

"Isn't it all queer?"

"I'm afraid it's very upsetting for you."

"Not the least. I don't mind it."

"Well, that's good."

She had spoken more naturally and healthily than usual. Bending into the middle of her friends, she said: "Don't worry about me, I'm much better than I was; I don't feel the least faint; I shall be all right, and thank you all, thank you, thank you for your kindness." She had to shout her gratitude, for the chant, Esmiss Esmoor, went on.

Suddenly it stopped. It was as if the prayer had been heard, and the relics exhibited. "I apologize for my colleague," said Mr Amritrao, rather to everyone's surprise. "He is an intimate friend of our client, and his feelings have carried him away."

"Mr Mahmoud Ali will have to apologize in person," the Magistrate said.

"Exactly, sir, he must. But we had just learned that Mrs Moore had important evidence which she desired to give. She was hurried out of the country by her son before she could give it; and this unhinged Mr Mahmoud Ali—coming as it does upon an attempt to intimidate our only other European witness, Mr Fielding. Mr Mahmoud Ali would have said nothing had not Mrs Moore been claimed as a witness by the police." He sat down.

"An extraneous element is being introduced into the case," said the Magistrate. "I must repeat that as a witness Mrs Moore does not exist. Neither you, Mr Amritrao, nor, Mr McBryde, you, have any right to surmise what that lady would have said. She is not here, and consequently she can say nothing."

"Well, I withdraw my reference," said the Superintendent wearily. "I would have done so fifteen minutes ago if I had been given the chance. She is not of the least importance to me."

"I have already withdrawn it for the defence." He added with forensic humour: "Perhaps you can persuade the gentlemen outside to withdraw it too," for the refrain in the street continued.

"I am afraid my powers do not extend so far," said Das, smiling.

So peace was restored, and when Adela came to give her evidence the atmosphere was quieter than it had been since the beginning of the trial. Experts were not surprised. There is no stay in your native. He blazes up over a minor point, and has nothing left for the crisis. What he seeks is a grievance, and this he had found in the supposed abduction of an old lady. He would now be less aggrieved when Aziz was deported.

But the crisis was still to come.

Adela had always meant to tell the truth and nothing but the truth, and she had rehearsed this as a difficult task—difficult, because her disaster in the cave was connected, though by a thread, with another part of her life, her engagement to Ronny. She had thought of love just before she went in, and had innocently asked Aziz what marriage was like, and she supposed that her question had roused evil in him. To recount this would have been incredibly painful, it was the one point she wanted to keep obscure; she was willing to give details that would have distressed other girls, but this story of her private failure she dared not allude to, and she dreaded being examined in public in case something came out. But as soon as she rose to reply, and heard the sound of her own voice, she feared not even that. A new and unknown sensation protected her, like magnificent armour. She didn't think what had happened, or even remember in the ordinary way of memory, but she returned to the Marabar Hills, and spoke from them across a sort of darkness to Mr McBryde. The fatal day recurred, in every detail, but now she was of it and not of it at the same time, and this double relation gave it indescribable splendour. Why had she thought the expedition "dull"? Now the sun rose again, the elephant waited, the pale masses of the rock flowed round her and presented the first cave; she entered, and a match was reflected in the polished walls—all beautiful and significant, though she had been blind to it at the time. Questions were asked, and to each she found the exact reply; yes, she had noticed the "Tank of the Dagger", but not known its name; yes, Mrs Moore had been tired after the first cave and sat in the shadow of a great rock, near the dried-up mud. Smoothly the voice in the distance proceeded, leading along the paths of truth, and the airs from the punkah behind her wafted her on. . . .

". . . the prisoner and the guide took you onto the Kawa Dol, no one else being present?"

"The most wonderfully shaped of those hills. Yes." As she spoke, she created the Kawa Dol, saw the niches up the curve of the stone, and felt the heat strike her face. And something caused her to add: "No one else was present to my knowledge. We appeared to be alone."

"Very well, there is a ledge halfway up the hill, or broken ground rather, with caves scattered near the beginning of a nullah."

"I know where you mean."

"You went alone into one of those caves?"

"That is quite correct."

"And the prisoner followed you."

"Now we've got 'im," from the Major.

She was silent. The court, the place of question, awaited her reply. But she could not give it until Aziz entered the place of answer.

"The prisoner followed you, didn't he?" he repeated in the monotonous tones that they both used; they were employing agreed words throughout, so that this part of the proceedings held no surprises.

"May I have half a minute before I reply to that, Mr McBryde?"

"Certainly."

Her vision was of several caves. She saw herself in one, and she was also outside it, watching its entrance, for Aziz to pass in. She failed to locate him. It was the doubt that had often visited her, but solid and attractive, like the hills. "I am not—" Speech was more difficult than vision. "I am not quite sure."

"I beg your pardon?" said the Superintendent of Police.

"I cannot be sure. . . ."

"I didn't catch that answer." He looked scared, his mouth shut with a snap. "You are on that landing, or whatever we term it, and you have entered a cave. I suggest to you that the prisoner followed you."

She shook her head.

"What do you mean, please?"

"No," she said in a flat, unattractive voice. Slight noises began in various parts of the room, but no one yet understood what was occurring except Fielding. He saw that she was going to have a nervous breakdown and that his friend was saved.

"What is that, what are you saying? Speak up, please." The Magistrate bent forward.

"I'm afraid I have made a mistake."

"What nature of mistake?"

"Dr Aziz never followed me into the cave."

The Superintendent slammed down his papers, then picked them up and said calmly: "Now, Miss Quested, let us go on. I will read you the words of the deposition which you signed two hours later in my bungalow."

"Excuse me, Mr McBryde, you cannot go on. I am speaking to the witness myself. And the public will be silent. If it continues to talk, I will have the court cleared. Miss Quested, address your remarks to me, who am the Magistrate in charge of the case, and realize their extreme gravity. Remember you speak on oath, Miss Quested."

"Dr Aziz never—"

"I stop these proceedings on medical grounds," cried the Major on a word from Turton, and all the English rose from their chairs at once, large white figures behind which the little Magistrate was hidden. The Indians rose too, hundreds of things went on at once, so that afterwards each person gave a different account of the catastrophe.

"You withdraw the charge? Answer me," shrieked the representative of Justice.

Something that she did not understand took hold of the girl and pulled her through. Though the vision was over, and she had returned to the insipidity of the world, she remembered what she had learned. Atonement and confession—they could wait. It was in hard prosaic tones that she said, "I withdraw everything."

"Enough—sit down. Mr McBryde, do you wish to continue in the face of this?"

The Superintendent gazed at his witness as if she was a broken machine, and said, "Are you mad?"

"Don't question her, sir; you have no longer the right."

"Give me time to consider—"

"Sahib, you will have to withdraw; this becomes a scandal," boomed the Nawab Bahadur suddenly from the back of the court.

"He shall not," shouted Mrs Turton against the gathering tumult. "Call the other witnesses; we're none of us safe—" Ronny tried to check her, and she gave him an irritable blow, then screamed insults at Adela.

The Superintendent moved to the support of his friends, saying nonchalantly to the Magistrate as he did so, "Right, I withdraw."

Mr Das rose, nearly dead with the strain. He had controlled the case, just controlled it. He had shown that an Indian can preside. To those who could hear him he said, "The prisoner is released without one stain on his character; the question of costs will be decided elsewhere."

And then the flimsy framework of the court broke up, the shouts of derision and rage culminated, people screamed and cursed, kissed one another, wept passionately. Here were the English, whom their servants protected, there Aziz fainted in Hamidullah's arms. Victory on this side, defeat on that—complete for one moment was the antithesis. Then life returned to its complexities, person after person struggled out of the room to their various purposes, and before long no one remained on the scene of the fantasy but the beautiful naked god. Unaware that anything unusual had occurred, he continued to pull the cord of his punkah, to gaze at the empty dais and the overturned special chairs, and rhythmically to agitate the clouds of descending dust.

Chapter 25

Miss Quested had renounced her own people. Turning from them, she was drawn into a mass of Indians of the shop-keeping class, and carried by them towards the public exit of the court. The faint, indescribable smell of the bazaars invaded her, sweeter than a London slum, yet more disquieting: a tuft of scented cotton wool, wedged in an old man's ear, fragments of pan between his black teeth, odorous powders, oils—the Scented East of tradition, but blended with human sweat, as if a great king had been entangled in ignominy and could not free himself, or as if the heat of the sun had boiled and fried all the glories of the earth into a single mess. They paid no attention to her. They shook hands over her shoulder, shouted through her body—for when the Indian does ignore his rulers he becomes genuinely unaware of their existence. Without part in the universe she had created, she was flung against Mr Fielding.

"What do you want here?"

Knowing him for her enemy, she passed on into the sunlight without speaking.

He called after her, "Where are you going, Miss Quested?"

"I don't know."

"You can't wander about like that. Where's the car you came in?"

"I shall walk."

"What madness . . . there's supposed to be a riot on . . . the police have struck, no one knows what'll happen next. Why don't you keep to your own people?"

"Ought I to join them?" she said, without emotion. She felt emptied, valueless; there was no more virtue in her.

"You can't, it's too late. How are you to get round to the

private entrance now? Come this way with me—quick—I'll put you into my carriage."

"Cyril, Cyril, don't leave me," called the shattered voice of Aziz.

"I'm coming back. . . . This way, and don't argue." He gripped her arm. "Excuse manners, but I don't know anyone's position. Send my carriage back any time tomorrow, if you please."

"But where am I to go in it?"

"Where you like. How should I know your arrangements?"

The victoria was safe in a quiet side-lane, but there were no horses, for the sais, not expecting the trial would end so abruptly, had led them away to visit a friend. She got into it obediently. The man could not leave her, for the confusion increased, and spots of it sounded fanatical. The main road through the bazaars was blocked, and the English were regaining the Civil Station by byways; they were caught like caterpillars, and could have been killed off easily.

"What—what have you been doing?" he cried suddenly. "Playing a game, studying life, or what?"

"Sir, I intend these for you, sir," interrupted a student, running down the lane with a garland of jasmine on his arm.

"I don't want the rubbish; get out."

"Sir, I am a horse, we shall be your horses," another cried as he lifted the shafts of the victoria into the air.

"Fetch my sais, Rafi; there's a good chap."

"No, sir, this is an honour for us."

Fielding wearied of his students. The more they honoured him the less they obeyed. They lassoed him with jasmine and roses, scratched the splash-board against a wall, and recited a poem, the noise of which filled the lane with a crowd.

"Hurry up, sir; we pull you in a procession." And, half affectionate, half impudent, they bundled him in.

"I don't know whether this suits you, but anyhow you're safe," he remarked. The carriage jerked into the main bazaar, where it created some sensation. Miss Quested was so loathed in Chandrapore that her recantation was discredited, and the rumour ran that she had been stricken by the Deity in the middle of her lies. But they cheered when they saw her sitting by the heroic Principal (some addressed her as Mrs Moore!), and they garlanded her to match him. Half gods, half guys, with sausages of flowers round their necks, the pair were dragged in the wake of Aziz's victorious landau. In the applause that greeted them some derision mingled. The English always stick together! That was the criticism. Nor was it unjust. Fielding shared it himself, and knew that if some misunderstanding occurred, and an attack was made on the girl by his allies, he would be obliged to die in her defence. He didn't want to die for her, he wanted to be rejoicing with Aziz.

Where was the procession going? To friends, to enemies, to Aziz's bungalow, to the Collector's bungalow, to the Minto Hospital where the Civil Surgeon would eat dust and the patients (confused with prisoners) be released, to Delhi, Simla. The students thought it was going to Government College. When they reached a turning, they twisted the victoria to the right, ran it by side-lanes down a hill and through a garden gate into the mango plantation, and, as far as Fielding and Miss Quested were concerned, all was peace and quiet. The trees were full of glossy foliage and slim green fruit, the tank slumbered; and beyond it rose the exquisite blue arches of the garden-house. "Sir, we fetch the others; sir, it is a somewhat heavy load for our arms," were heard. Fielding took the refugee to his office, and tried to telephone to McBryde. But this he could not do; the wires had been cut. All his servants had decamped. Once more he was unable to desert her. He assigned her a couple of rooms, provided her with ice and drinks and biscuits, advised her to lie down, and lay down himself—there was nothing else to do. He felt restless and thwarted as he listened to the retreating sounds of the procession, and his joy was rather spoilt by bewilderment. It was a victory, but such a queer one.

At that moment Aziz was crying, "Cyril, Cyril . . ." Crammed into a carriage with the Nawab Bahadur, Hamidullah, Mahmoud Ali, his own little boys, and a heap of flowers, he was not content; he wanted to be surrounded by all who loved him. Victory gave no pleasure, he had suffered too much. From the moment of his arrest he was done for, he had dropped like a wounded animal; he had despaired, not through cowardice, but because he knew that an Englishwoman's word would always outweigh his own. "It is Fate," he said; and, "It is Fate," when he was imprisoned anew after Mohurram. All that existed, in that terrible time, was affection, and affection was all that he felt in the first painful moments of his freedom. "Why isn't Cyril following? Let us turn back." But the procession could not turn back. Like a snake in a drain, it advanced down the narrow bazaar towards the basin of the Maidan, where it would turn about itself, and decide on its prey.

"Forward, forward," shrieked Mahmoud Ali, whose every utterance had become a yell. "Down with the Collector, down with the Superintendent of Police."

"Mr Mahmoud Ali, this is not wise," implored the Nawab Bahadur; he knew that nothing was gained by attacking the English, who had fallen into their own pit and had better be left there; moreover, he had great possessions and deprecated anarchy.

"Cyril, again you desert," cried Aziz.

"Yet some orderly demonstration is necessary," said Hamidullah, "otherwise they will still think we are afraid."

"Down with the Civil Surgeon . . . rescue Nureddin."

"Nureddin?"

"They are torturing him."

"Oh, my God . . ."—for this, too, was a friend.

"They are not. I will not have my grandson made an excuse for an attack on the hospital," the old man protested.

"They are. Callendar boasted so before the trial. I heard through the tatties; he said, 'I have tortured that nigger.' "

"Oh, my God, my God. . . . He called him a nigger, did he?"

"They put pepper instead of antiseptic on the wounds."

"Mr Mahmoud Ali, impossible; a little roughness will not hurt the boy, he needs discipline."

"Pepper. Civil Surgeon said so. They hope to destroy us one by one; they shall fail."

The new injury lashed the crowd to fury. It had been aimless hitherto, and had lacked a grievance. When they reached the Maidan and saw the sallow arcades of the Minto they shambled towards it howling. It was near midday. The earth and sky were insanely ugly, the spirit of evil again strode abroad. The Nawab Bahadur alone struggled against it, and told himself that the rumour must be untrue. He had seen his grandson in the ward only last week. But he too was carried forward over the new precipice. To rescue, to maltreat Major Callendar in revenge, and then was to come the turn of the Civil Station generally.

But disaster was averted, and averted by Dr Panna Lal.

Dr Panna Lal had offered to give evidence for the prosecution in the hope of pleasing the English, also because he hated Aziz. When the case broke down, he was in a very painful position. He saw the crash coming sooner than most people, slipped from the court before Mr Das had finished, and drove Dapple off through the bazaars, in flight from the wrath to come. In the hospital he should be safe, for Major Callendar would protect him. But the Major had not come, and now things were worse than ever, for here was a mob, entirely desirous of his blood, and the orderlies were mutinous and would not help him over the back wall, or rather hoisted him and let him drop back, to the satisfaction of the patients. In agony he cried, "Man can but die the once," and waddled across the compound to meet the invasion, salaaming with one hand and holding up a pale yellow umbrella in the other. "Oh, forgive me," he whined as he approached the victorious landau. "Oh, Dr Aziz, forgive the wicked lies I told." Aziz was silent, the others thickened their throats and threw up their chins in token of scorn. "I was afraid, I was mislaid," the suppliant continued. "I was mislaid here, there and everywhere as regards your character. Oh, forgive the poor old hakim who gave you milk when ill! Oh, Nawab Bahadur, whoever merciful, is it my poor little dispensary you require? Take every cursed bottle." Agitated, but alert, he saw them smile at his indifferent English, and suddenly he started playing the buffoon, flung down his umbrella, trod through it, and struck himself upon the nose. He knew what he was doing, and so did they. There was nothing pathetic or eternal in the degradation of such a man. Of ignoble origin, Dr Panna Lal possessed nothing that could be disgraced, and he wisely decided to make the other Indians feel like kings, because it would put them into better tempers. When he found they wanted Nureddin, he skipped like a goat, he scuttled like a hen to do their bidding, the hospital was saved, and to the end of his life he could not understand why he had not obtained promotion on the morning's work. "Promptness, sir, promptness similar to you," was the argument he employed to Major Callendar when claiming it.

When Nureddin emerged, his face all bandaged, there was a roar of relief as though the Bastille had fallen. It was the crisis of the march, and the Nawab Bahadur managed to get the situation into hand. Embracing the young man publicly, he began a speech about Justice, Courage, Liberty and Prudence, ranged under heads, which cooled the passion of the crowd. He further announced that he should give up his British-conferred title, and live as a private gentleman, plain Mr Zulfiqar, for which reason he was instantly proceeding to his country seat. The landau turned, the crowd accompanied it, the crisis was over. The Marabar Caves had been a terrible strain on the local administration; they altered a good many lives and wrecked several careers, but they did not break up a continent or even dislocate a District.

"We will have rejoicings tonight," the old man said. "Mr Hamidullah, I depute you to bring out our friends Fielding and Amritrao, and to discover whether the latter will require special food. The others will keep with me. We shall not go out to Dilkusha until the cool of the evening, of course. I do not know the feelings of other gentlemen; for my own part, I have a slight headache, and I wish I had thought to ask our good Panna Lal for aspirin."

For the heat was claiming its own. Unable to madden,

it stupefied, and before long most of the Chandrapore combatants were asleep. Those in the Civil Station kept watch a little, fearing an attack, but presently they too entered the world of dreams—that world in which a third of each man's life is spent, and which is thought by some pessimists to be a premonition of eternity.

Chapter 26

Evening approached by the time Fielding and Miss Quested met and had the first of their numerous curious conversations. He had hoped, when he woke up, to find someone had fetched her away, but the College remained isolated from the rest of the universe. She asked whether she could have "a sort of interview", and, when he made no reply, said, "Have you any explanation of my extraordinary behaviour?"

"None," he said curtly. "Why make such a charge if you were going to withdraw it?"

"Why indeed?"

"I ought to feel grateful to you, I suppose, but—"

"I don't expect gratitude. I only thought you might care to hear what I have to say."

"Oh, well," he grumbled, feeling rather schoolboyish. "I don't think a discussion between us is desirable. To put it frankly, I belong to the other side in this ghastly affair."

"Would it not interest you to hear my side?"

"Not much."

"I shouldn't tell you in confidence, of course. So you can hand on all my remarks to your side, for there is one great mercy that has come out of all today's misery: I have no longer any secrets. My echo has gone—I call the buzzing sound in my ears an echo. You see, I have been unwell ever since that expedition to the caves, and possibly before it."

The remark interested him rather; it was what he had sometimes suspected himself. "What kind of illness?" he inquired.

She touched her head at the side, then shook it.

"That was my first thought, the day of the arrest: hallucination."

"Do you think that could be so?" she asked with great humility. "What should have given me an hallucination?"

"One of three things certainly happened in the Marabar," he said, getting drawn into a discussion against his will. "One of four things. Either Aziz is guilty, which is what your friends think; or you invented the charge out of malice, which is what my friends think; or you have had an hallucination. I'm very much inclined"—getting up and striding about—"now that you tell me that you felt unwell before the expedition—it's an important piece of evidence—I believe that you yourself broke the strap of the field-glasses; you were alone in that cave the whole time."

"Perhaps. . . ."

"Can you remember when you first felt out of sorts?"

"When I came to tea with you there, in that garden-house."

"A somewhat unlucky party. Aziz and old Godbole were both ill after it too."

"I was not ill—it is far too vague to mention; it is all mixed up with my private affairs. I enjoyed the singing . . . but just about then a sort of sadness began that I couldn't detect at the time . . . no, nothing as solid as sadness: living at half pressure expresses it best. Half pressure. I remember going on to polo with Mr Heaslop at the Maidan. Various other things happened—it doesn't matter what, but I was under par for all of them. I was certainly in that state when I saw the caves, and you suggest (nothing shocks or hurts me)—you suggest that I had an hallucination there, the sort of thing—though in an awful form—that makes some women think they've had an offer of marriage when none was made."

"You put it honestly, anyhow."

"I was brought up to be honest; the trouble is, it gets me nowhere."

Liking her better, he smiled and said, "It'll get us to heaven."

"Will it?"

"If heaven existed."

"Do you not believe in heaven, Mr Fielding, may I ask?" she said, looking at him shyly.

"I do not. Yet I believe that honesty gets us there."

"How can that be?"

"Let us go back to hallucinations. I was watching you carefully through your evidence this morning, and if I'm right the hallucination (what you call half pressure—quite as good a word) disappeared suddenly."

She tried to remember what she had felt in court, but could not; the vision disappeared whenever she wished to interpret it. "Events presented themselves to me in their logical sequence," was what she said, but it hadn't been that at all.

"My belief—and of course I was listening carefully, in hope you would make some slip—my belief is that poor McBryde exorcised you. As soon as he asked you a straightforward question, you gave a straightforward answer, and broke down."

"Exorcise in that sense. I thought you meant I'd seen a ghost."

"I don't go to that length!"

"People whom I respect very much believe in ghosts," she said rather sharply. "My friend Mrs Moore does."

"She's an old lady."

"I think you need not be impolite to her, as well as to her son."

"I did not intend to be rude. I only meant it is difficult, as we get on in life, to resist the supernatural. I've felt it coming on me myself. I still jog on without it, but what a temptation, at forty-five, to pretend that the dead live again; one's own dead; no one else's matter."

"Because the dead don't live again."

"I fear not."

"So do I."

There was a moment's silence, such as often follows the triumph of rationalism. Then he apologized handsomely enough for his behaviour to Heaslop at the Club.

"What does Dr Aziz say of me?" she asked, after another pause.

"He—he has not been capable of thought in his misery,

naturally he's very bitter," said Fielding, a little awkward, because such remarks as Aziz had made were not merely bitter, they were foul. The underlying notion was, "It disgraces me to have been mentioned in connection with such a hag." It enraged him that he had been accused by a woman who had no personal beauty; sexually, he was a snob. This had puzzled and worried Fielding. Sensuality, as long as it is straightforward, did not repel him, but this derived sensuality—the sort that classes a mistress among motor-cars if she is beautiful, and among eye-flies if she isn't—was alien to his own emotions, and he felt a barrier between himself and Aziz whenever it arose. It was, in a new form, the old, old trouble that eats the heart out of every civilization: snobbery, the desire for possessions, creditable appendages; and it is to escape this rather than the lusts of the flesh that saints retreat into the Himalayas. To change the subject, he said: "But let me conclude my analysis. We are agreed that he is not a villain and that you are not one, and we aren't really sure that it was an hallucination. There's a fourth possibility which we must touch on: was it somebody else?"

"The guide."

"Exactly, the guide. I often think so. Unluckily Aziz hit him on the face, and he got a fright and disappeared. It is most unsatisfactory, and we hadn't the police to help us, the guide was of no interest to them."

"Perhaps it was the guide," she said quietly; the question had lost interest for her suddenly.

"Or could it have been one of that gang of Pathans who have been drifting through the district?"

"Someone who was in another cave, and followed me when the guide was looking away? Possibly."

At that moment Hamidullah joined them, and seemed not too pleased to find them closeted together. Like everyone else in Chandrapore, he could make nothing of Miss Quested's conduct. He had overheard their last remarks. "Hullo, my dear Fielding," he said. "So I run you down at last. Can you come out at once to Dilkusha?"

"At once?"

"I hope to leave in a moment, don't let me interrupt," said Adela.

"The telephone has been broken; Miss Quested can't ring up her friends," he explained.

"A great deal has been broken, more than will ever be mended," said the other. "Still, there should be some way of transporting this lady back to the Civil Lines. The resources of civilization are numerous." He spoke without looking at Miss Quested, and he ignored the slight movement she made towards him with her hand.

Fielding, who thought the meeting might as well be friendly, said, "Miss Quested has been explaining a little about her conduct of this morning."

"Perhaps the age of miracles has returned. One must be prepared for everything, our philosophers say."

"It must have seemed a miracle to the onlookers," said Adela, addressing him nervously. "The fact is that I realized before it was too late that I had made a mistake, and had just enough presence of mind to say so. That is all my extraordinary conduct amounts to."

"All it amounts to, indeed," he retorted, quivering with rage but keeping himself in hand, for he felt she might be setting another trap. "Speaking as a private individual, in a purely informal conversation, I admired your conduct, and I was delighted when our warm-hearted students garlanded you. But, like Mr Fielding, I am surprised; indeed, surprise is too weak a word. I see you drag my best friend into the dirt, damage his health and ruin his prospects in a way you cannot conceive owing to your ignorance of our society and religion, and then suddenly you get up in the witness-box: 'Oh no, Mr McBryde, after all I am not quite sure, you may as well let him go.' Am I mad? I keep asking myself. Is it a dream, and if so when did it start? And without doubt it is a dream that has not yet finished. For I gather you have not done with us yet, and it is now the turn of the poor old guide who conducted you round the caves."

"Not at all, we were only discussing possibilities," interposed Fielding.

"An interesting pastime, but a lengthy one. There are one hundred and seventy million Indians in this notable peninsula, and of course one or other of them entered the cave. Of course some Indian is the culprit, we must never doubt that. And since, my dear Fielding, these possibilities will take you some time"—here he put his arm over the Englishman's shoulder and swayed him to and fro gently—"don't you think you had better come out to the Nawab Bahadur's—or I should say to Mr Zulfiqar's, for that is the name he now requires us to call him by?"

"Gladly, in a minute. . . ."

"I have just settled my movements," said Miss Quested. "I shall go to the Dak Bungalow."

"Not the Turtons'?" said Hamidullah, goggle-eyed. "I thought you were their guest."

The Dak Bungalow of Chandrapore was below the average, and certainly servantless. Fielding, though he continued to sway with Hamidullah, was thinking on independent lines, and said in a moment: "I have a better idea than that, Miss Quested. You must stop here at the College. I shall be away at least two days, and you can have the place entirely to yourself, and make your plans at your convenience."

"I don't agree at all," said Hamidullah, with every symptom of dismay. "The idea is a thoroughly bad one. There may quite well be another demonstration tonight, and suppose an attack is made on the College. You would be held responsible for this lady's safety, my dear fellow."

"They might equally attack the Dak Bungalow."

"Exactly, but the responsibility there ceases to be yours."

"Quite so. I have given trouble enough."

"Do you hear? The lady admits it herself. It's not an attack from our people I fear—you should see their orderly conduct at the hospital; what we must guard against is an attack secretly arranged by the police for the purpose of discrediting you. McBryde keeps plenty of roughs for this purpose, and this would be the very opportunity for him."

"Never mind. She is not going to the Dak Bungalow," said Fielding. He had a natural sympathy for the downtrodden—that was partly why he rallied from Aziz—and had become determined not to leave the poor girl in the lurch. Also, he had a newborn respect for her, consequent on their talk. Although her hard schoolmistressy manner remained, she was no longer examining life, but being examined by it; she had become a real person.

"Then where is she to go? We shall never have done with her!" For Miss Quested had not appealed to Hamidullah. If she had shown emotion in court, broke down, beat her breast, and invoked the name of God, she would have summoned forth his imagination and generosity—he had plenty of both. But while relieving the oriental mind she had chilled it, with the result that he could scarcely believe she was sincere, and indeed from his standpoint she was not. For her behaviour rested on cold justice and honesty; she had felt, while she recanted, no passion of love for those whom she had wronged. Truth is not truth in that exacting land unless there go with it kindness and more kindness and kindness again, unless the Word that was with God also is God. And the girl's sacrifice—so creditable according to Western notions—was rightly rejected, because, though it came from her heart, it did not include her heart. A few garlands from students was all that India ever gave her in return.

"But where is she to have her dinner, where is she to sleep? I say here, here, and if she is hit on the head by roughs, she is hit on the head. That is my contribution. Well, Miss Quested?"

"You are very kind. I should have said yes, I think, but I agree with Mr Hamidullah. I must give no more trouble to you. I believe my best plan is to return to the Turtons, and see if they will allow me to sleep, and if they turn me away I must go to the Dak. The Collector would take me in, I know, but Mrs Turton said this morning that she would never see me again." She spoke without bitterness, or, as Hamidullah thought, without proper pride. Her aim was to cause the minimum of annoyance.

"Far better stop here than expose yourself to insults from that preposterous woman."

"Do you find her preposterous? I used to. I don't now."

"Well, here's our solution," said the barrister, who had terminated his slightly minatory caress and strolled to the window. "Here comes the City Magistrate. He comes in a third-class band-ghari for purposes of disguise, he comes unattended, but here comes the City Magistrate."

"At last," said Adela sharply, which caused Fielding to glance at her.

"He comes, he comes, he comes. I cringe. I tremble."

"Will you ask him what he wants, Mr Fielding?"

"He wants you, of course."

"He may not even know I'm here."

"I'll see him first, if you prefer."

When he had gone, Hamidullah said to her bitingly: "Really, really. Need you have exposed Mr Fielding to this further discomfort? He is far too considerate." She made no reply, and there was complete silence between them until their host returned.

"He has some news for you," he said. "You'll find him on the veranda. He prefers not to come in."

"Does he tell me to come out to him?"

"Whether he tells you or not, you will go, I think," said Hamidullah.

She paused, then said, "Perfectly right," and then said a few words of thanks to the Principal for his kindness to her during the day.

"Thank goodness, that's over," he remarked, not escorting her to the veranda, for he held it unnecessary to see Ronny again.

"It was insulting of him not to come in."

"He couldn't very well after my behaviour to him at the Club. Heaslop doesn't come out badly. Besides, Fate has treated him pretty roughly today. He has had a cable to the effect that his mother's dead, poor old soul."

"Oh, really. Mrs Moore. I'm sorry," said Hamidullah rather indifferently.

"She died at sea."

"The heat, I suppose."

"Presumably."

"May is no month to allow an old lady to travel in."

"Quite so. Heaslop ought never to have let her go, and he knows it. Shall we be off?"

"Let us wait until the happy couple leave the compound clear . . . they really are intolerable dawdling there. Ah well, Fielding, you don't believe in Providence, I remember. I do. This is Heaslop's punishment for abducting our witness in order to stop us establishing our alibi."

"You go rather too far there. The poor old lady's evidence could have had no value, shout and shriek Mahmoud Ali as he will. She couldn't see through the Kawa Dol even if she had wanted to. Only Miss Quested could have saved him."

"She loved Aziz, he says, also India, and he loved her."

"Love is of no value in a witness, as a barrister ought to know. But I see there is about to be an Esmiss Esmoor legend at Chandrapore, my dear Hamidullah, and I will not impede its growth."

The other smiled, and looked at his watch. They both regretted the death, but they were middle-aged men, who had invested their emotions elsewhere, and outbursts of grief could not be expected from them over a slight acquaintance. It's only one's own dead who matter. If for a moment the sense of communion in sorrow came to them, it passed. How indeed is it possible for one human being to be sorry for all the sadness that meets him on the face of the earth, for the pain that is endured not only by men, but by animals and plants, and perhaps by the stones? The soul is tired in a moment, and in fear of losing the little she does understand she retreats to the permanent lines which habit or chance have dictated, and suffers there. Fielding had met the dead woman only two or three times, Hamidullah had seen her in the distance once, and they were far more occupied with the coming gathering at Dilkusha, the "victory" dinner, for which they would be most victoriously late. They agreed not to tell Aziz about Mrs Moore till the morrow, because he was fond of her, and the bad news might spoil his fun.

"Oh, this is unbearable!" muttered Hamidullah. For Miss Quested was back again.

"Mr Fielding, has Ronny told you of this new misfortune?"

He bowed.

"Ah me!" She sat down, and seemed to stiffen into a monument.

"Heaslop is waiting for you, I think."

"I do so long to be alone. She was my best friend, far more to me than to him. I can't bear to be with Ronny . . . I can't explain. . . . Could you do me the very great kindness of letting me stop after all?"

Hamidullah swore violently in the vernacular.

"I should be pleased, but does Mr Heaslop wish it?"

"I didn't ask him, we are too much upset—it's so complex, not like what unhappiness is supposed to be. Each of us ought to be alone, and think. Do come and see Ronny again."

"I think he should come in this time," said Fielding, feeling that this much was due to his own dignity. "Do ask him to come."

She returned with him. He was half miserable, half arrogant—indeed, a strange mix-up—and broke at once into uneven speech. "I came to bring Miss Quested away, but her visit to the Turtons has ended, and there is no other arrangement so far, mine are bachelor quarters now—"

Fielding stopped him courteously. "Say no more, Miss Quested stops here. I only wanted to be assured of your approval. Miss Quested, you had better send for your own servant if he can be found, but I will leave orders with mine to do all they can for you, also I'll let the Scouts know. They have guarded the College ever since it was closed, and may as well go on. I really think you'll be as safe here as anywhere. I shall be back Thursday."

Meanwhile Hamidullah, determined to spare the enemy no incidental pain, had said to Ronny: "We hear, sir, that your mother has died. May we ask where the cable came from?"

"Aden."

"Ah, you were boasting she had reached Aden, in court."

"But she died on leaving Bombay," broke in Adela. "She was dead when they called her name this morning. She must have been buried at sea."

Somehow this stopped Hamidullah, and he desisted from his brutality, which had shocked Fielding more than anyone else. He remained silent while the details of Miss Quested's occupation of the College were arranged, merely remarking to Ronny, "It is clearly to be understood, sir, that neither Mr Fielding nor any of us are responsible for this lady's safety at Government College," to which Ronny agreed. After that, he watched the semi-chivalrous behavings of the three English with quiet amusement; he thought Fielding had been incredibly silly and weak, and he was amazed by the younger people's want of proper pride. When they were driving out to Dilkusha, hours late, he said to Amritrao, who accompanied them: "Mr Amritrao, have you considered what sum Miss Quested ought to pay as compensation?"

"Twenty thousand rupees."

No more was then said, but the remark horrified Fielding. He couldn't bear to think of the queer honest girl losing her money and possibly her young man too. She advanced into his consciousness suddenly. And, fatigued by the merciless and enormous day, he lost his usual sane view of human intercourse, and felt that we exist not in ourselves, but in terms of each other's minds—a notion for which logic offers no support and which had attacked him only once before, the evening after the catastrophe, when from the veranda of the Club he saw the fists and fingers of the Marabar swell until they included the whole night sky.

Chapter 27

"Aziz, are you awake?"

"No, so let us have a talk; let us dream plans for the future."

"I am useless at dreaming."

"Good night then, dear fellow."

The Victory Banquet was over, and the revellers lay on the roof of plain Mr Zulfiqar's mansion, asleep, or gazing through mosquito-nets at the stars. Exactly above their heads hung the constellation of the Lion, the disc of Regulus so large and bright that it resembled a tunnel, and when this fancy was accepted all the other stars seemed tunnels too.

"Are you content with our day's work, Cyril?" the voice on his left continued.

"Are you?"

"Except that I ate too much. 'How is stomach, how head?' —I say, Panna Lal and Callendar'll get the sack."

"There'll be a general move at Chandrapore."

"And you'll get promotion."

"They can't well move me down, whatever their feelings."

"In any case we spend our holidays together, and visit Kashmir, possibly Persia, for I shall have plenty of money. Paid to me on account of the injury sustained by my character," he explained with cynical calm. "While with me you shall never spend a single pie. This is what I have always wished, and as the result of my misfortunes it has come."

"You have won a great victory . . ." began Fielding.

"I know, my dear chap, I know; your voice need not become so solemn and anxious. I know what you are going to say next: Let, oh let Miss Quested off paying, so that the English may say, 'Here is a native who has actually behaved like a gentleman; if it was not for his black face we would almost allow him to join our Club.' The approval of your compatriots no longer interests me, I have become anti-British, and ought to have done so sooner, it would have saved me numerous misfortunes."

"Including knowing me."

"I say, shall we go and pour water onto Mohammed Latif's face? He is so funny when this is done to him asleep."

The remark was not a question but a full stop. Fielding accepted it as such and there was a pause, pleasantly filled by a little wind which managed to brush the top of the house. The banquet, though riotous, had been agreeable, and now the blessings of leisure—unknown to the West, which either works or idles—descended on the motley company. Civilization strays about like a ghost here, revisiting the ruins of empire, and is to be found not in great works of art or mighty deeds, but in the gestures well-bred Indians make when they sit or lie down. Fielding, who had dressed up in native costume, learned from his excessive awkwardness in it that all his motions were makeshifts, whereas when the Nawab Bahadur stretched out his hand for food, or Nureddin applauded a song, something beautiful had been accomplished which needed no development. This restfulness of gesture—it is the Peace that passeth Understanding, after all; it is the social equivalent of Yoga. When the whirring of action ceases, it becomes visible, and reveals a civilization which the West can disturb but will never acquire. The hand stretches out for ever, the lifted knee has the eternity though not the sadness of the grave. Aziz was full of civilization this evening, complete, dignified, rather hard, and it was with diffidence that the other said: "Yes, certainly you must let off Miss Quested easily. She must pay all your costs, that is only fair, but do not treat her like a conquered enemy."

"Is she wealthy? I depute you to find out."

"The sums mentioned at dinner when you all got so excited—they would ruin her, they are perfectly preposterous. Look here . . ."

"I am looking, though it gets a bit dark. I see Cyril Fielding to be a very nice chap indeed and my best friend, but in some ways a fool. You think that by letting Miss Quested off easily I shall make a better reputation for myself and Indians generally. No, no. It will be put down to weakness and the attempt to gain promotion officially. I have decided to have nothing more to do with British India, as a matter of fact. I shall seek service in some Moslem state, such as Hyderabad, Bhopal, where Englishmen cannot insult me any more. Don't counsel me otherwise."

"In the course of a long talk with Miss Quested—"

"I don't want to hear your long talks."

"Be quiet. In the course of a long talk with Miss Quested I have begun to understand her character. It's not an easy one, she being a prig. But she is perfectly genuine and very brave. When she saw she was wrong, she pulled herself up with a jerk and said so. I want you to realize what that means. All her friends around her, the entire British Raj pushing her forward. She stops, sends the whole thing to smithereens. In her place I should have funked it. But she stopped, and almost did she become a national heroine, but my students ran us down a side-street before the crowd caught flame. Do treat her considerately. She really mustn't get the worst of both worlds. I know what all these"—he indicated the shrouded forms on the roof—"will want, but you mustn't listen to them. Be merciful. Act like one of your six Mogul Emperors, or all the six rolled into one."

"Not even Mogul Emperors showed mercy until they received an apology."

"She'll apologize if that's the trouble," he cried, sitting up. "Look, I'll make you an offer. Dictate to me whatever form of words you like, and this time tomorrow I'll bring it back signed. This is not instead of any public apology she may make you in law. It's in addition."

" 'Dear Dr Aziz, I wish you had come into the cave; I am an awful old hag, and it is my last chance.' Will she sign that?"

"Well, good night, good night, it's time to go to sleep, after that."

"Good night, I suppose it is."

"Oh, I wish you wouldn't make that kind of remark," he continued after a pause. "It is the one thing in you I can't put up with."

"I put up with all things in you, so what is to be done?"

"Well, you hurt me by saying it; good night."

There was silence, then dreamily but with deep feeling the voice said: "Cyril, I have had an idea which will satisfy your tender mind: I shall consult Mrs Moore."

Opening his eyes, and beholding thousands of stars, he could not reply, they silenced him.

"Her opinion will solve everything; I can trust her so absolutely. If she advises me to pardon this girl, I shall do so. She will counsel me nothing against my real and true honour, as you might."

"Let us discuss that tomorrow morning."

"Is it not strange? I keep on forgetting she has left India. During the shouting of her name in court I fancied she was present. I had shut my eyes, I confused myself on purpose to deaden the pain. Now this very instant I forgot again. I shall be obliged to write. She is now far away, well on her way towards Ralph and Stella."

"To whom?"

"To those other children."

"I have not heard of other children."

"Just as I have two boys and a girl, so has Mrs Moore. She told me in the mosque."

"I knew her so slightly."

"I have seen her but three times, but I know she is an Oriental."

"You are so fantastic. . . . Miss Quested, you won't treat her generously; while over Mrs Moore there is this elaborate chivalry. Miss Quested anyhow behaved decently this morning, whereas the old lady never did anything for you at all, and it's pure conjecture that she would have come forward in your favour, it only rests on servants' gossip. Your emotions never seem in proportion to their objects, Aziz."

"Is emotion a sack of potatoes, so much the pound, to be

measured out? Am I a machine? I shall be told I can use up my emotions by using them, next."

"I should have thought you could. It sounds common sense. You can't eat your cake and have it, even in the world of the spirit."

"If you are right, there is no point in any friendship; it all comes down to give and take, or give and return, which is disgusting, and we had better all leap over this parapet and kill ourselves. Is anything wrong with you this evening that you grow so materialistic?"

"Your unfairness is worse than my materialism."

"I see. Anything further to complain of?" He was good-tempered and affectionate but a little formidable. Imprisonment had made channels for his character, which would never fluctuate as widely now as in the past. "Because it is far better you put all your difficulties before me, if we are to be friends for ever. You do not like Mrs Moore, and are annoyed because I do; however, you will like her in time."

When a person, really dead, is supposed to be alive, an unhealthiness infects the conversation. Fielding could not stand the tension any longer and blurted out: "I'm sorry to say Mrs Moore's dead."

But Hamidullah, who had been listening to all their talk, and did not want the festive evening spoilt, cried from the adjoining bed: "Aziz, he is trying to pull your leg; don't believe him, the villain."

"I do not believe him," said Aziz; he was inured to practical jokes, even of this type.

Fielding said no more. Facts are facts, and everyone would learn of Mrs Moore's death in the morning. But it struck him that people are not really dead until they are felt to be dead. As long as there is some misunderstanding about them, they possess a sort of immortality. An experience of his own confirmed this. Many years ago he had lost a great friend, a woman, who believed in the Christian heaven, and assured him that after the changes and chances of this mortal life they would meet in it again. Fielding was a blank, frank atheist, but he respected every opinion his friend held; to do this is essential in friendship. And it seemed to him for a time that the dead awaited him, and when the illusion faded it left behind it an emptiness that was almost guilt: "This really is the end," he thought, "and I gave her the final blow." He had tried to kill Mrs Moore this evening, on the roof of the Nawab Bahadur's house; but she still eluded him, and the atmosphere remained tranquil. Presently the moon rose—the exhausted crescent that precedes the sun—and shortly after men and oxen began their interminable labour, and the gracious interlude, which he had tried to curtail, came to its natural conclusion.

Chapter 28

Dead she was—committed to the deep while still on the southward track, for the boats from Bombay cannot point towards Europe until Arabia has been rounded; she was further in the tropics than she ever achieved while on shore, when the sun touched her for the last time and her body was lowered into yet another India—the Indian Ocean. She left behind her sore discomfort, for a death gives a ship a bad name. Who was this Mrs Moore? When Aden was reached, Lady Mellanby cabled, wrote, did all that was kind, but the wife of a Lieutenant-Governor does not bargain for such an experience; and she repeated: "I had only seen the poor creature for a few hours when she was taken ill; really this has been needlessly distressing, it spoils one's homecoming." A ghost followed the ship up the Red Sea, but failed to enter the Mediterranean. Somewhere about Suez there is always a social change: the arrangements of Asia weaken and those of Europe begin to be felt, and during the transition Mrs Moore was shaken off. At Port Said the gray blustery North began. The weather was so cold and bracing that the passengers felt it must have broken in the land they had left, but it became hotter steadily there in accordance with its usual law.

The death took subtler and more lasting shapes in Chandrapore. A legend sprang up that an Englishman had killed his mother for trying to save an Indian's life—and there was just enough truth in this to cause annoyance to the authorities. Sometimes it was a cow that had been killed—or a crocodile with the tusks of a boar had crawled out of the Ganges. Nonsense of this type is more difficult to combat than a solid lie. It hides in rubbish-heaps and moves when no one is looking. At one period two distinct tombs containing Esmiss Esmoor's remains were reported: one by the tannery, the other up near the goods station. Mr McBryde visited them both and saw signs of the beginning of a cult—earthenware saucers and so on. Being an experienced official, he did nothing to irritate it, and after a week or so the rash died down. "There's propaganda behind all this," he said, forgetting that a hundred years ago, when Europeans still made their home in the countryside and appealed to its imagination, they occasionally became local demons after death—not a whole god perhaps, but part of one, adding an epithet or gesture to what already existed, just as the gods contribute to the great gods, and they to the philosophic Brahm.

Ronny reminded himself that his mother had left India at her own wish, but his conscience was not clear. He had behaved badly to her, and he had either to repent (which involved a mental overturn), or to persist in unkindness towards her. He chose the latter course. How tiresome she had been with her patronage of Aziz! What a bad influence upon Adela! And now she still gave trouble with ridiculous "tombs", mixing herself up with natives. She could not help it, of course, but she had attempted similar exasperating expeditions in her lifetime, and he reckoned it against her. The young man had much to worry him—the heat, the local tension, the approaching visit of the Lieutenant-Governor, the problems of Adela—and threading them all together into a grotesque garland were these Indianizations of Mrs Moore. What does happen to one's mother when she dies? Presumably she goes to heaven, anyhow she clears out. Ronny's religion was of the sterilized public-school brand, which never goes bad, even in the tropics. Wherever he entered, mosque, cave or temple, he retained the spiritual outlook of the Fifth Form, and condemned as "weakening" any attempt to understand them. Pulling himself together, he dismissed the mater from his mind. In due time he and his half-brother and -sister would put up a tablet to her in the Northamptonshire church where she had worshipped, recording the dates of her birth and death and the fact that she had been buried at sea. This would be sufficient.

And Adela—she would have to depart too; he hoped she

would have made the suggestion herself ere now. He really could not marry her—it would mean the end of his career. Poor lamentable Adela. . . . She remained at Government College, by Fielding's courtesy—unsuitable and humiliating, but no one would receive her at the Civil Station. He postponed all private talk until the award against her was decided. Aziz was suing her for damages in the sub-judge's court. Then he would ask her to release him. She had killed his love, and it had never been very robust; they would never have achieved betrothal but for the accident to the Nawab Bahadur's car. She belonged to the callow academic period of his life which he had outgrown—Grasmere, serious talks and walks, that sort of thing.

Chapter 29

The visit of the Lieutenant-Governor of the Province formed the next stage in the decomposition of the Marabar. Sir Gilbert, though not an enlightened man, held enlightened opinions. Exempted by a long career in the Secretariat from personal contact with the peoples of India, he was able to speak of them urbanely, and to deplore racial prejudice. He applauded the outcome of the trial, and congratulated Fielding on having taken "the broad, the sensible, the only possible charitable view from the first. Speaking confidentially . . ." he proceeded. Fielding deprecated confidences, but Sir Gilbert insisted on imparting them; the affair had been "mishandled by certain of our friends up the hill" who did not realize that "the hands of the clock move forward, not back", etc. etc. One thing he could guarantee: the Principal would receive a most cordial invitation to rejoin the Club, and he begged, nay commanded, him to accept. He returned to his Himalayan altitudes well satisfied; the amount of money Miss Quested would have to pay, the precise nature of what had happened in the caves—these were local details, and did not concern him.

Fielding found himself drawn more and more into Miss Quested's affairs. The College remained closed and he ate and slept at Hamidullah's, so there was no reason she should not stop on if she wished. In her place he would have cleared out, sooner than submit to Ronny's half-hearted and distracted civilities, but she was waiting for the hour-glass of her sojourn to run through. A house to live in, a garden to walk in during the brief moment of the cool—that was all she asked, and he was able to provide them. Disaster had shown her her limitations, and he realized now what a fine loyal character she was. Her humility was touching. She never repined at getting the worst of both worlds; she regarded it as the due punishment of her stupidity. When he hinted to her that a personal apology to Aziz might be seemly, she said sadly: "Of course. I ought to have thought of it myself; my instincts never help me. Why didn't I rush up to him after the trial? Yes, of course I will write him an apology, but please will you dictate it?" Between them they concocted a letter, sincere, and full of moving phrases, but it was not moving as a letter. "Shall I write another?" she inquired. "Nothing matters if I can undo the harm I have caused. I can do this right, and that right; but when the two are put together they come wrong. That's the defect of my character. I have never realized it until now. I thought that if I was just and asked questions I would come through every difficulty." He replied: "Our letter is a failure for a simple reason which we had better face: you have no real affection for Aziz, or Indians generally." She assented. "The first time I saw you, you were wanting to see India, not Indians, and it occurred to me: Ah, that won't take us far. Indians know whether they are liked or not—they cannot be fooled here. Justice never satisfies them, and that is why the British Empire rests on sand." Then she said: "Do I like anyone, though?" Presumably she liked Heaslop, and he changed the subject, for this side of her life did not concern him.

His Indian friends were, on the other hand, a bit above themselves. Victory, which would have made the English sanctimonious, made them aggressive. They wanted to develop an offensive, and tried to do so by discovering new grievances and wrongs, many of which had no existence. They suffered from the usual disillusion that attends warfare. The aims of battle and the fruits of conquest are never the same; the latter have their value and only the saint rejects them, but their hint of immortality vanishes as soon as they are held in the hand. Although Sir Gilbert had been courteous, almost obsequious, the fabric he represented had in no wise bowed its head. British officialism remained, as all-pervading and as unpleasant as the sun; and what was next to be done against it was not very obvious, even to Mahmoud

Ali. Loud talk and trivial lawlessness were attempted, and behind them continued a genuine but vague desire for education. "Mr Fielding, we must all be educated promptly."

Aziz was friendly and domineering. He wanted Fielding to "give in to the East", as he called it, and live in a condition of affectionate dependence upon it. "You can trust me, Cyril." No question of that, and Fielding had no roots among his own people. Yet he really couldn't become a sort of Mohammed Latif. When they argued about it something racial intruded—not bitterly, but inevitably, like the colour of their skins: coffee-colour versus pinko-gray. And Aziz would conclude: "Can't you see that I'm grateful to you for your help and want to reward you?" And the other would retort: "If you want to reward me, let Miss Quested off paying."

The insensitiveness about Adela displeased him. It would, from every point of view, be right to treat her generously, and one day he had the notion of appealing to the memory of Mrs Moore. Aziz had this high and fantastic estimate of Mrs Moore. Her death had been a real grief to his warm heart; he wept like a child and ordered his three children to weep also. There was no doubt that he respected and loved her. Fielding's first attempt was a failure. The reply was: "I see your trick. I want revenge on them. Why should I be insulted and suffer and the contents of my pockets read and my wife's photograph taken to the police-station? Also I want the money—to educate my little boys, as I explained to her." But he began to weaken, and Fielding was not ashamed to practise a little necromancy. Whenever the question of compensation came up, he introduced the dead woman's name. Just as other propagandists invented her a tomb, so did he raise a questionable image of her in the heart of Aziz, saying nothing that he believed to be untrue, but producing something that was probably far from the truth. Aziz yielded suddenly. He felt it was Mrs Moore's wish that he should spare the woman who was about to marry her son, that it was the only honour he could pay her, and he renounced with a passionate and beautiful outburst the whole of the compensation money, claiming only costs. It was fine of him, and, as he foresaw, it won him no credit with the English. They still believed he was guilty, they believed it to the end of their careers, and retired Anglo-Indians in Tunbridge Wells or Cheltenham still murmur to each other: "That Marabar case which broke down because the poor girl couldn't face giving her evidence—that was another bad case."

When the affair was thus officially ended, Ronny, who was about to be transferred to another part of the Province, approached Fielding with his usual constraint and said: "I wish to thank you for the help you have given Miss Quested. She will not of course trespass on your hospitality further; she has as a matter of fact decided to return to England. I have just arranged about her passage for her. I understand she would like to see you."

"I shall go round at once."

On reaching the College, he found her in some upset. He learned that the engagement had been broken by Ronny. "Far wiser of him," she said pathetically. "I ought to have spoken myself, but I drifted on, wondering what would happen. I would willingly have gone on spoiling his life through inertia—one has nothing to do, one belongs nowhere and becomes a public nuisance without realizing it." In order to reassure him, she added: "I speak only of India. I am not astray in England. I fit in there—no, don't think I shall do harm in England. When I am forced back there, I shall settle down to some career. I have sufficient money left to start myself, and heaps of friends of my own type. I shall be quite all right." Then sighing: "But oh, the trouble I've brought on everyone here. . . . I can never get over it. My carefulness as to whether we should marry or not . . . and in the end Ronny and I part and aren't even sorry. We ought never to have thought of marriage. Weren't you amazed when our engagement was originally announced?"

"Not much. At my age one's seldom amazed," he said, smiling. "Marriage is too absurd in any case. It begins and continues for such very slight reasons. The social business props it up on one side, and the theological business on the other, but neither of them are marriage, are they? I've friends who can't remember why they married, no more can their wives. I suspect that it mostly happens haphazard, though afterwards various noble reasons are invented. About marriage I am cynical."

"I am not. This false start has been all my own fault. I was bringing to Ronny nothing that ought to be brought, that was why he rejected me really. I entered that cave thinking: 'Am I fond of him?' I have not yet told you that, Mr Fielding. I didn't feel justified. Tenderness, respect, personal intercourse—I tried to make them take the place—of—"

"I no longer want love," he said, supplying the word.

"No more do I. My experiences here have cured me. But I want others to want it."

"But to go back to our first talk (for I suppose this is our last one)—when you entered that cave, who did follow you, or did no one follow you? Can you now say? I don't like it left in air."

"Let us call it the guide," she said indifferently. "It will never be known. It's as if I ran my finger along that polished wall in the dark, and cannot get further. I am up against something, and so are you. Mrs Moore—she did know."

"How could she have known what we don't?"

"Telepathy, possibly."

The pert, meagre word fell to the ground. Telepathy? What an explanation! Better withdraw it, and Adela did so. She was at the end of her spiritual tether, and so was he. Were there worlds beyond which they could never touch, or did all that is possible enter their consciousness? They could not tell. They only realized that their outlook was more or less similar, and found in this a satisfaction. Perhaps life is a mystery, not a muddle; they could not tell. Perhaps the hundred Indias which fuss and squabble so tiresomely are one, and the universe they mirror is one. They had not the apparatus for judging.

"Write to me when you get to England."

"I shall, often. You have been excessively kind. Now that I'm going, I realize it. I wish I could do something for you in return, but I see you've all you want."

"I think so," he replied after a pause. "I have never felt more happy and secure out here. I really do get on with Indians, and they do trust me. It's pleasant that I haven't had to resign my job. It's pleasant to be praised by an L.-G. Until the next earthquake I remain as I am."

"Of course this death has been troubling me."

"Aziz was so fond of her too."

"But it has made me remember that we must all die; all these personal relations we try to live by are temporary. I used to feel death selected people, it is a notion one gets from novels, because some of the characters are usually left talking at the end. Now 'death spares no one' begins to be real."

"Don't let it become too real, or you'll die yourself. That is the objection to meditating upon death. We are subdued to what we work in. I have felt the same temptation, and had to sheer off. I want to go on living a bit."

"So do I."

A friendliness, as of dwarfs shaking hands, was in the air. Both man and woman were at the height of their powers—sensible, honest, even subtle. They spoke the same language, and held the same opinions, and the variety of age and sex did not divide them. Yet they were dissatisfied. When they agreed, "I want to go on living a bit," or "I don't believe in God," the words were followed by a curious backwash, as though the universe had displaced itself to fill up a tiny void, or as though they had seen their own gestures from an immense height—dwarfs talking, shaking hands and assuring each other that they stood on the same footing of insight. They did not think they were wrong, because as soon as honest people think they are wrong instability sets up. Not for them was an infinite goal behind the stars, and they never sought it. But wistfulness descended on them now, as on other occasions; the shadow of the shadow of a dream fell over their clear-cut interests, and objects never seen again seemed messages from another world.

"And I do like you so very much, if I may say so," he affirmed.

"I'm glad, for I like you. Let's meet again."

"We will, in England, if I ever take home-leave."

"But I suppose you're not likely to do that yet."

"Quite a chance. I have a scheme on now, as a matter of fact."

"Oh, that would be very nice."

So it petered out. Ten days later Adela went off, by the same route as her dead friend. The final beat up before the monsoon had come. The country was stricken and blurred. Its houses, trees and fields were all modelled out of the same brown paste, and the sea at Bombay slid about like broth against the quays. Her last Indian adventure was with Antony, who followed her onto the boat and tried to blackmail her. She had been Mr Fielding's mistress, Antony said. Perhaps Antony was discontented with his tip. She rang the cabin bell and had him turned out, but his statement created rather a scandal, and people did not speak to her much during the first part of the voyage. Through the Indian Ocean and the Red Sea she was left to herself, and to the dregs of Chandrapore.

With Egypt the atmosphere altered. The clean sands, heaped on each side of the canal, seemed to wipe off everything that was difficult and equivocal, and even Port Said looked pure and charming in the light of a rose-gray morning. She went on shore there with an American missionary, they walked out to the Lesseps statue, they drank the tonic air of the Levant. "To what duties, Miss Quested, are you returning in your own country after your taste of the tropics?" the missionary asked. "Observe, I don't say to what do you turn, but to what do you *re*-turn. Every life ought to contain both a turn and a *re*-turn. This celebrated pioneer" (he pointed to the statue) "will make my question clear. He turns to the East, he *re*-turns to the West. You can see it from the cute position of his hands, one of which holds a string of sausages." The missionary looked at her humorously, in order to cover the emptiness of his mind. He had no idea what he meant by "turn" and "return", but he often used words in pairs, for the sake of moral brightness. "I see," she replied. Suddenly, in the Mediterranean clarity, she had seen. Her first duty on returning to England was to look up those other children of Mrs Moore's, Ralph and Stella; then she would turn to her profession. Mrs Moore had tended to keep the products of her two marriages apart, and Adela had not come across the younger branch so far.

Chapter 30

Another local consequence of the trial was a Hindu–Moslem entente. Loud protestations of amity were exchanged by prominent citizens, and there went with them a genuine desire for a good understanding. Aziz, when he was at the hospital one day, received a visit from rather a sympathetic figure: Mr Das. The magistrate sought two favours from him: a remedy for shingles and a poem for his brother-in-law's new monthly magazine. He accorded both.

"My dear Das, why, when you tried to send me to prison, should I try to send Mr Bhattacharya a poem? Eh? That is naturally entirely a joke. I will write him the best I can, but I thought your magazine was for Hindus."

"It is not for Hindus, but Indians generally," he said timidly.

"There is no such person in existence as the general Indian."

"There was not, but there may be when you have written a poem. You are our hero; the whole city is behind you, irrespective of creed."

"I know, but will it last?"

"I fear not," said Das, who had much mental clearness. "And for that reason, if I may say so, do not introduce too many Persian expressions into the poem, and not too much about the bulbul."

"Half a sec," said Aziz, biting his pencil. He was writing out a prescription. "Here you are. . . . Is not this better than a poem?"

"Happy the man who can compose both."

"You are full of compliments today."

"I know you bear me a grudge for trying that case," said the other, stretching out his hand impulsively. "You are so kind and friendly, but always I detect irony beneath your manner."

"No, no, what nonsense!" protested Aziz. They shook hands, in a half-embrace that typified the entente. Between people of distant climes there is always the possibility of romance, but the various branches of Indians know too much about each other to surmount the unknowable easily. The approach is prosaic. "Excellent," said Aziz, patting a stout shoulder and thinking, "I wish they did not remind me of cow-dung"; Das thought, "Some Moslems are very violent." They smiled wistfully, each spying the thought in the other's heart, and Das, the more articulate, said: "Excuse my mistakes, realize my limitations. Life is not easy as we know it on the earth."

"Oh, well, about this poem—how did you hear I sometimes scribbled?" he asked, much pleased, and a good deal moved—for literature had always been a solace to him, something that the ugliness of facts could not spoil.

"Professor Godbole often mentioned it, before his departure for Mau."

"How did he hear?"

"He too was a poet; do you not divine each other?"

Flattered by the invitation, he got to work that evening. The feel of the pen between his fingers generated bulbuls at once. His poem was again about the decay of Islam and the brevity of love; as sad and sweet as he could contrive, but not nourished by personal experience, and of no interest to these excellent Hindus. Feeling dissatisfied, he rushed to the other extreme, and wrote a satire, which was too libellous to print. He could only express pathos or venom, though most of his life had no concern with either. He loved poetry—science was merely an acquisition, which he laid aside when unobserved, like his European dress—and this evening he longed to compose a new song which should be acclaimed by multitudes and even sung in the fields. In what language shall it be written? And what shall it announce? He vowed to see more of Indians who were not Mohammedans, and never to look backward. It is the only healthy course. Of what help, in this latitude and hour, are the glories of Cordova and Samarkand? They have gone, and while we lament them the English occupy Delhi and exclude us from East Africa. Islam itself, though true, throws cross-lights over the path to freedom. The song of the future must transcend creed.

The poem for Mr Bhattacharya never got written, but it had an effect. It led him towards the vague and bulky figure of a mother-land. He was without natural affection for the land of his birth, but the Marabar Hills drove him to it. Half closing his eyes, he attempted to love India. She must imitate Japan. Not until she is a nation will her sons be treated with respect. He grew harder and less approachable. The English, whom he had laughed at or ignored, persecuted him everywhere; they had even thrown nets over his dreams. "My great mistake has been taking our rulers as a joke," he said to Hamidullah next day; who replied with a sigh: "It is far the wisest way to take them, but not possible in the long run. Sooner or later a disaster such as yours occurs, and reveals their secret thoughts about our character. If God himself descended from heaven into their Club and said you were innocent, they would disbelieve Him. Now you see why Mahmoud Ali and self waste so much time over intrigues and associate with creatures like Ram Chand."

"I cannot endure committees. I shall go right away."

"Where to? Turtons and Burtons, all are the same."

"But not in an Indian state."

"I believe the Politicals are obliged to have better manners. It amounts to no more."

"I do want to get away from British India, even to a poor job. I think I could write poetry there. I wish I had lived in Babur's time and fought and written for him. Gone, gone, and not even any use to say 'Gone, gone,' for it weakens us while we say it. We need a king, Hamidullah; it would make our lives easier. As it is, we must try to appreciate these quaint Hindus. My notion now is to try for some post as doctor in one of their states."

"Oh, that is going much too far."

"It is not going as far as Mr Ram Chand."

"But the money, the money—they will never pay an adequate salary, those savage rajahs."

"I shall never be rich anywhere, it is outside my character."

"If you had been sensible and made Miss Quested pay—"

"I chose not to. Discussion of the past is useless," he said, with sudden sharpness of tone. "I have allowed her to keep her fortune and buy herself a husband in England, for which it will be very necessary. Don't mention the matter again."

"Very well, but your life must continue a poor man's; no holidays in Kashmir for you yet, you must stick to your profession and rise to a highly paid post, not retire to a jungle-state and write poems. Educate your children, read the latest scientific periodicals, compel European doctors to respect you. Accept the consequences of your own actions like a man."

Aziz winked at him slowly and said: "We are not in the law courts. There are many ways of being a man; mine is to express what is deepest in my heart."

"To such a remark there is certainly no reply," said Hamidullah, moved. Recovering himself and smiling, he said: "Have you heard this naughty rumour that Mohammed Latif has got hold of?"

"Which?"

"When Miss Quested stopped in the College, Fielding used to visit her . . . rather too late in the evening, the servants say."

"A pleasant change for her if he did," said Aziz, making a curious face.

"But you understand my meaning?"

The young man winked again and said: "Just! Still, your meaning doesn't help me out of my difficulties. I am determined to leave Chandrapore. The problem is, for where? I am determined to write poetry. The problem is, about what? You give me no assistance." Then, surprising both Hamidullah and himself, he had an explosion of nerves. "But who does give me assistance? No one is my friend. All are traitors, even my own children. I have had enough of friends."

"I was going to suggest we go behind the purdah, but your three treacherous children are there, so you will not want to."

"I am sorry, it is ever since I was in prison my temper is strange; take me, forgive me."

"Nureddin's mother is visiting my wife now. That is all right, I think."

"They come before me separately, but not so far together. You had better prepare them for the united shock of my face."

"No, let us surprise them without warning, far too much nonsense still goes on among our ladies. They pretended at the time of your trial they would give up purdah; indeed, those of them who can write composed a document to that effect, and now it ends in humbug. You know how deeply they all respect Fielding, but not one of them has seen him. My wife says she will, but always when he calls there is some excuse—she is not feeling well, she is ashamed of the room, she has no nice sweets to offer him, only Elephants' Ears, and if I say Elephants' Ears are Mr Fielding's favourite sweet, she replies that he will know how badly hers are made, so she cannot see him on their account. For fifteen years, my dear boy, have I argued with my begum, for fifteen years, and never gained a point, yet the missionaries inform us our women are downtrodden. If you want a subject for a poem, take this: The Indian lady as she is and not as she is supposed to be."

Chapter 31

Aziz had no sense of evidence. The sequence of his emotions decided his beliefs, and led to the tragic coolness between himself and his English friend. They had conquered but were not to be crowned. Fielding was away at a conference, and after the rumour about Miss Quested had been with him undisturbed for a few days he assumed it was true. He had no objection on moral grounds to his friends amusing themselves, and Cyril, being middle-aged, could no longer expect the pick of the female market, and must take his amusement where he could find it. But he resented him making up to this particular woman, whom he still regarded as his enemy; also, why had he not been told? What is friendship without confidences? He himself had told things sometimes regarded as shocking, and the Englishman had listened, tolerant, but surrendering nothing in return.

He met Fielding at the railway station on his return, agreed to dine with him, and then started taxing him by the oblique method, outwardly merry. An avowed European scandal there was—Mr McBryde and Miss Derek. Miss Derek's faithful attachment to Chandrapore was now explained: Mr McBryde had been caught in her room, and his wife was divorcing him. "That pure-minded fellow. However, he will blame the Indian climate. Everything is our fault really. Now, have I not discovered an important piece of news for you, Cyril?"

"Not very," said Fielding, who took little interest in distant sins. "Listen to mine." Aziz's face lit up. "At the conference, it was settled—"

"This evening will do for schoolmastery. I should go straight to the Minto now, the cholera looks bad. We begin to have local cases as well as imported. In fact, the whole of life is somewhat sad. The new Civil Surgeon is the same as the last, but does not yet dare to be. That is all any administrative change amounts to. All my suffering has won nothing for us. But look here, Cyril, while I remember it. There's gossip about you as well as McBryde. They say that you and Miss Quested became also rather too intimate friends. To speak perfectly frankly, they say you and she have been guilty of impropriety."

"They would say that."

"It's all over the town, and may injure your reputation. You know, everyone is by no means your supporter. I have tried all I could to silence such a story."

"Don't bother. Miss Quested has cleared out at last."

"It is those who stop in the country, not those who leave it, whom such a story injures. Imagine my dismay and anxiety. I could scarcely get a wink of sleep. First my name was coupled with her and now it is yours."

"Don't use such exaggerated phrases."

"As what?"

"As dismay and anxiety."

"Have I not lived all my life in India? Do I not know what produces a bad impression here?" His voice shot up rather crossly.

"Yes, but the scale, the scale. You always get the scale wrong, my dear fellow. A pity there is this rumour, but such a very small pity—so small that we may as well talk of something else."

"You mind for Miss Quested's sake, though. I can see from your face."

"As far as I do mind. I travel light."

"Cyril, that boastfulness about travelling light will be your ruin. It is raising up enemies against you on all sides, and makes me feel excessively uneasy."

"What enemies?"

Since Aziz had only himself in mind, he could not reply. Feeling a fool, he became angrier. "I have given you list after list of the people who cannot be trusted in this city. In your position I should have the sense to know I was surrounded by enemies. You observe I speak in a low voice. It is because I see your sais is new. How do I know he isn't a spy?" He lowered his voice: "Every third servant is a spy."

"Now, what is the matter?" he asked, smiling.

"Do you contradict my last remark?"

"It simply doesn't affect me. Spies are as thick as mosquitoes, but it's years before I shall meet the one that kills me. You've something else in your mind."

"I've not; don't be ridiculous."

"You have. You're cross with me about something or other."

Any direct attack threw him out of action. Presently he said: "So you and Madamsell Adela used to amuse one another in the evening, naughty boy."

Those drab and high-minded talks had scarcely made for dalliance. Fielding was so startled at the story being taken seriously, and so disliked being called a naughty boy, that he lost his head and cried: "You little rotter! Well, I'm damned. Amusement indeed. Is it likely at such a time?"

"Oh, I beg your pardon, I'm sure. The licentious oriental imagination was at work," he replied, speaking gaily, but cut to the heart; for hours after his mistake he bled inwardly.

"You see, Aziz, the circumstances . . . also the girl was still engaged to Heaslop, also I never felt . . ."

"Yes, yes; but you didn't contradict what I said, so I thought it was true. Oh dear, East and West. Most misleading. Will you please put your little rotter down at his hospital?"

"You're not offended?"

"Most certainly I am not."

"If you are, this must be cleared up later on."

"It has been," he answered, dignified. "I believe absolutely what you say, and of that there need be no further question."

"But the way I said it must be cleared up. I was unintentionally rude. Unreserved regrets."

"The fault is entirely mine."

Tangles like this still interrupted their intercourse. A pause in the wrong place, an intonation misunderstood, and a whole conversation went awry. Fielding had been startled, not shocked, but how convey the difference? There is always trouble when two people do not think of sex at the same moment, always mutual resentment and surprise, even when the two people are of the same race. He began to recapitulate his feelings about Miss Quested. Aziz cut him short with: "But I believe you, I believe. Mohammed Latif shall be severely punished for inventing this."

"Oh, leave it alone, like all gossip—it's merely one of those half-alive things that try to crowd out real life. Take no notice, it'll vanish, like poor old Mrs Moore's tombs."

"Mohammed Latif has taken to intriguing. We are already much displeased with him. Will it satisfy you if we send him back to his family without a present?"

"We'll discuss M.L. at dinner."

His eyes went clotted and hard. "Dinner. This is most unlucky— I forgot. I have promised to dine with Das."

"Bring Das to me."

"He will have invited other friends."

"You are coming to dinner with me as arranged," said Fielding, looking away. "I don't stand this. You are coming to dinner with me. You come."

They had reached the hospital now. Fielding continued round the Maidan alone. He was annoyed with himself, but counted on dinner to pull things straight. At the post office he saw the Collector. Their vehicles were parked side by side while their servants competed in the interior of the building. "Good morning; so you are back," said Turton icily. "I should be glad if you will put in your appearance at the Club this evening."

"I have accepted re-election, sir. Do you regard it as necessary I should come? I should be glad to be excused; indeed, I have a dinner engagement this evening."

"It is not a question of your feelings, but of the wish of the Lieutenant-Governor. Perhaps you will ask me whether I speak officially. I do. I shall expect you this evening at six. We shall not interfere with your subsequent plans."

He attended the grim little function in due course. The

skeletons of hospitality rattled—"Have a peg, have a drink." He talked for five minutes to Mrs Blakiston, who was the only surviving female. He talked to McBryde, who was defiant about his divorce, conscious that he had sinned as a sahib. He talked to Major Roberts, the new Civil Surgeon; and to young Milner, the new City Magistrate; but the more the Club changed the more it promised to be the same thing. "It is no good," he thought, as he returned past the mosque, "we all build upon sand; and the more modern the country gets, the worse'll be the crash. In the old eighteenth century, when cruelty and injustice raged, an invisible power repaired their ravages. Everything echoes now; there's no stopping the echo. The original sound may be harmless, but the echo is always evil." This reflection about an echo lay at the verge of Fielding's mind. He could never develop it. It belonged to the universe that he had missed or rejected. And the mosque missed it too. Like himself, those shallow arcades provided but a limited asylum. "There is no God but God" doesn't carry us far through the complexities of matter and spirit; it is only a game with words, really, a religious pun, not a religious truth.

He found Aziz overtired and dispirited, and he determined not to allude to their misunderstanding until the end of the evening; it would be more acceptable then. He made a clean breast about the Club—said he had only gone under compulsion, and should never attend again unless the order was renewed. "In other words, probably never; for I am going quite soon to England."

"I thought you might end in England," he said very quietly, then changed the conversation. Rather awkwardly they ate their dinner, then went out to sit in the Mogul garden-house.

"I am only going for a little time. On official business. My service is anxious to get me away from Chandrapore for a bit. It is obliged to value me highly, but does not care for me. The situation is somewhat humorous."

"What is the nature of the business? Will it leave you much spare time?"

"Enough to see my friends."

"I expected you to make such a reply. You are a faithful friend. Shall we now talk about something else?"

"Willingly. What subject?"

"Poetry," he said, with tears in his eyes. "Let us discuss why poetry has lost the power of making men brave. My mother's father was also a poet, and fought against you in the Mutiny. I might equal him if there was another mutiny. As it is, I am a doctor, who has won a case and has three children to support, and whose chief subject of conversation is official plans."

"Let us talk about poetry." He turned his mind to the innocuous subject. "You people are sadly circumstanced. What ever are you to write about? You cannot say 'The rose is faded' for evermore. We know it's faded. Yet you can't have patriotic poetry of the 'India, my India' type, when it's nobody's India."

"I like this conversation. It may lead to something interesting."

"You are quite right in thinking that poetry must touch life. When I knew you first, you used it as an incantation."

"I was a child when you knew me first. Everyone was my friend then. The Friend: a Persian expression for God. But I do not want to be a religious poet either."

"I hoped you would be."

"Why, when you yourself are an atheist?"

"There is something in religion that may not be true, but has not yet been sung."

"Explain in detail."

"Something that the Hindus have perhaps found."

"Let them sing it."

"Hindus are unable to sing."

"Cyril, you sometimes make a sensible remark. That will do for poetry for the present. Let us now return to your English visit."

"We haven't discussed poetry for two seconds," said the other, smiling.

But Aziz was addicted to cameos. He held the tiny

conversation in his hand, and felt it epitomized his problem. For an instant he recalled his wife, and, as happens when a memory is intense, the past became the future, and he saw her with him in a quiet Hindu jungle Native State, far away from foreigners. He said: "I suppose you will visit Miss Quested."

"If I have time. It will be strange seeing her in Hampstead."

"What is Hampstead?"

"An artistic and thoughtful little suburb of London—"

"And there she lives in comfort; you will enjoy seeing her. . . . Dear me, I've got a headache this evening. Perhaps I am going to have cholera. With your permission, I'll leave early."

"When would you like the carriage?"

"Don't trouble—I'll bike."

"But you haven't got your bicycle. My carriage fetched you—let it take you away."

"Sound reasoning," he said, trying to be gay. "I have not got my bicycle. But I am seen too often in your carriage. I am thought to take advantage of your generosity by Mr Ram Chand." He was out of sorts and uneasy. The conversation jumped from topic to topic in a broken-backed fashion. They were affectionate and intimate, but nothing clicked tight.

"Aziz, you have forgiven me the stupid remark I made this morning?"

"When you called me a little rotter?"

"Yes, to my eternal confusion. You know how fond I am of you."

"That is nothing, of course, we all of us make mistakes. In a friendship such as ours a few slips are of no consequence."

But, as he drove off, something depressed him—a dull pain of body or mind, waiting to rise to the surface. When he reached the bungalow he wanted to return and say something very affectionate; instead, he gave the sais a heavy tip, and sat down gloomily on the bed, and Hassan massaged him incompetently. The eye-flies had colonized the top of an almeira; the red stains on the durry were thicker, for Mohammed Latif had slept here during his imprisonment and spat a good deal; the table drawer was scarred where the police had forced it open; everything in Chandrapore was used up, including the air. The trouble rose to the surface now: he was suspicious; he suspected his friend of intending to marry Miss Quested for the sake of her money, and of going to England for that purpose.

"Huzoor?"—for he had muttered.

"Look at those flies on the ceiling. Why have you not drowned them?"

"Huzoor, they return."

"Like all evil things."

To divert the conversation, Hassan related how the kitchen-boy had killed a snake, good, but killed it by cutting it in two, bad, because it becomes two snakes.

"When he breaks a plate, does it become two plates?"

"Glasses and a new teapot will similarly be required, also for myself a coat."

Aziz sighed. Each for himself. One man needs a coat, another a rich wife; each approaches his goal by a clever detour. Fielding had saved the girl a fine of twenty thousand rupees, and now followed her to England. If he desired to marry her all was explained: she would bring him a larger dowry. Aziz did not believe his own suspicions—better if he had, for then he would have denounced and cleared the situation up. Suspicion and belief could in his mind exist side by side. They sprang from different sources, and need never intermingle. Suspicion in the Oriental is a sort of malignant tumour, a mental malady, that makes him self-conscious and unfriendly suddenly; he trusts and mistrusts at the same time in a way the Westerner cannot comprehend. It is his demon, as the Westerner's is hypocrisy. Aziz was seized by it, and his fancy built a satanic castle, of which the foundation had been laid when Fielding and he talked at Dilkusha under the stars. The girl had surely been Cyril's mistress when she stopped in the College—Mohammed Latif was right. But was that all? Perhaps it was Cyril who followed her into the cave. . . . No; impossible. Cyril hadn't been on the Kawa Dol at all. Impossible. Ridiculous. Yet the fancy left him trembling with misery. Such treachery

—if true—would have been the worst in Indian history; nothing so vile, not even the murder of Afzul Khan by Sivaji. He was shaken, as though by a truth, and told Hassan to leave him.

Next day he decided to take his children back to Mussoorie. They had come down for the trial, that he might bid them farewell, and had stayed on at Hamidullah's for the rejoicings. Major Roberts would give him leave, and during his absence Fielding would go off to England. The idea suited both his beliefs and his suspicions. Events would prove which was right, and preserve, in either case, his dignity.

Fielding was conscious of something hostile, and because he was really fond of Aziz his optimism failed him. Travelling light is less easy as soon as affection is involved. Unable to jog forward in the serene hope that all would come right, he wrote an elaborate letter in the rather modern style: "It is on my mind that you think me a prude about women. I had rather you thought anything else of me. If I live impeccably now, it is only because I am well on in the forties—a period of revision. In the eighties I shall revise again. And before the nineties come—I shall be revised! But, alive or dead, I am absolutely devoid of morals. Do kindly grasp this about me." Aziz did not care for the letter at all. It hurt his delicacy. He liked confidences, however gross, but generalizations and comparisons always repelled him. Life is not a scientific manual. He replied coldly, regretting his inability to return from Mussoorie before his friend sailed: "But I must take my poor little holiday while I can. All must be economy henceforward, all hopes of Kashmir have vanished for ever and ever. When you return I shall be slaving away in some new post."

And Fielding went, and in the last gutterings of Chandrapore—heaven and earth both looking like toffee—the Indian's bad fancies were confirmed. His friends encouraged them, for though they had liked the Principal they felt uneasy at his getting to know so much about their private affairs. Mahmoud Ali soon declared that treachery was afoot. Hamidullah murmured, "Certainly of late he no longer addressed us with his former frankness," and warned Aziz "not to expect too much—he and she are, after all, both members of another race." "Where are my twenty thousand rupees?" he thought. He was absolutely indifferent to money—not merely generous with it, but promptly paying his debts when he could remember to do so—yet these rupees haunted his mind, because he had been tricked about them, and allowed them to escape overseas, like so much of the wealth of India. Cyril would marry Miss Quested—he grew certain of it, all the unexplained residue of the Marabar contributing. It was the natural conclusion of the horrible senseless picnic, and before long he persuaded himself that the wedding had actually taken place.

Chapter 32

Egypt was charming—a green strip of carpet and walking up and down it four sorts of animals and one sort of man. Fielding's business took him there for a few days. He re-embarked at Alexandria—bright blue sky, constant wind, clean low coastline, as against the intricacies of Bombay. Crete welcomed him next with the long snowy ridge of its mountains, and then came Venice. As he landed on the Piazzetta a cup of beauty was lifted to his lips, and he drank with a sense of disloyalty. The buildings of Venice, like the mountains of Crete and the fields of Egypt, stood in the right place, whereas in poor India everything was placed wrong. He had forgotten the beauty of form among idol temples and lumpy hills; indeed, without form, how can there be beauty? Form stammered here and there in a mosque, became rigid through nervousness even, but oh, these Italian churches! San Giorgio standing on the island which could scarcely have risen from the waves without it, the Salute holding the entrance of a canal which, but for it, would not be the Grand Canal! In the old undergraduate days he had wrapped himself up in the many-coloured blanket of St Mark's, but something more precious than mosaics and marbles was offered to him now: the harmony between the works of man and the earth that upholds them, the civilization that has escaped muddle, the spirit in a reasonable form, with flesh and blood subsisting. Writing picture-postcards to his Indian friends, he felt that all of them would miss the joys he experienced now, the joys of form, and that this constituted a serious barrier. They would see the sumptuousness of Venice, not its shape, and though Venice was not Europe it was part of the Mediterranean harmony. The Mediterranean is the human norm. When men leave that exquisite lake, whether through the Bosphorus or the Pillars of Hercules, they approach the monstrous and extraordinary; and the southern exit leads to the strangest experience of all. Turning his back on it yet again, he took the train northward, and tender romantic fancies that he thought were dead for ever flowered when he saw the buttercups and daisies of June.

Part 3

Temple

Chapter 33

Some hundreds of miles westward of the Marabar Hills, and two years later in time, Professor Narayan Godbole stands in the presence of God. God is not born yet—that will occur at midnight—but He has also been born centuries ago, nor can He ever be born, because He is the Lord of the Universe, who transcends human processes. He is, was not, is not, was. He and Professor Godbole stood at opposite ends of the same strip of carpet.

"Tukaram, Tukaram,
Thou art my father and mother and everybody.
Tukaram, Tukaram,
Thou art my father and mother and everybody.
Tukaram, Tukaram,
Thou art my father and mother and everybody.
Tukaram, Tukaram,
Thou art my father and mother and everybody.
Tukaram . . ."

This corridor in the palace at Mau opened through other corridors into a courtyard. It was of beautiful hard white stucco, but its pillars and vaulting could scarcely be seen behind coloured rags, iridescent balls, chandeliers of opaque pink glass, and murky photographs framed crookedly. At the end was the small but famous shrine of the dynastic cult, and the God to be born was largely a silver image the size of a teaspoon. Hindus sat on either side of the carpet where they could find room, or overflowed into the adjoining corridors and the courtyard—Hindus, Hindus only, mild-featured men, mostly villagers, for whom anything outside their villages passed in a dream. They were the toiling ryot, whom some call the real India. Mixed with them sat a few tradesmen out of the little town, officials, courtiers, scions of the ruling house. Schoolboys kept inefficient order. The assembly was in a tender, happy state unknown to an English crowd, it seethed like a beneficent potion. When the villagers broke cordon for a glimpse of the silver image, a most beautiful and radiant expression came into their faces, a beauty in which there was nothing personal, for it caused them all to resemble one another during the moment of its indwelling, and only when it was withdrawn did they revert to individual clods. And so with the music. Music there was, but from so many sources that the sum total was untrammelled. The braying banging crooning melted into a single mass which trailed round the palace before joining the thunder. Rain fell at intervals throughout the night.

It was the turn of Professor Godbole's choir. As Minister of Education, he gained this special honour. When the previous group of singers dispersed into the crowd, he pressed forward from the back, already in full voice, that the chain of sacred sounds might be uninterrupted. He was barefoot and in white, he wore a pale blue turban; his gold pince-nez had caught in a jasmine garland, and lay sideways down his nose. He and the six colleagues who supported him clashed their cymbals, hit small drums, droned upon a portable harmonium, and sang:

"Tukaram, Tukaram,
Thou art my father and mother and everybody.
Tukaram, Tukaram,
Thou art my father and mother and everybody.
Tukaram, Tukaram . . ."

They sang not even to the God who confronted them, but to a saint; they did not one thing which the non-Hindu would feel dramatically correct; this approaching triumph of India was a muddle (as we call it), a frustration of reason and form. Where was the God Himself, in whose honour the congregation had gathered? Indistinguishable in the jumble of His own altar, huddled out of sight amid images of inferior descent, smothered under rose-leaves, overhung by oleographs, outblazed by golden tablets representing the Rajah's ancestors, and entirely obscured, when the wind blew, by the tattered foliage of a banana. Hundreds of electric lights had been lit in His honour (worked by an engine whose thumps destroyed the rhythm of the hymn). Yet His face could not be seen. Hundreds of His silver dishes were piled around Him with the minimum of effect. The inscriptions which the poets of the State had composed were hung where they could not be read, or had twitched their drawing-pins out of the stucco, and one of them (composed in English to indicate His universality) consisted, by an unfortunate slip of the draughtsman, of the words, "God si Love."

God si Love. Is this the final message of India?

"Tukaram, Tukaram . . ."

continued the choir, reinforced by a squabble behind the purdah curtain, where two mothers tried to push their children at the same moment to the front. A little girl's leg shot out like an eel. In the courtyard, drenched by the rain, the small Europeanized band stumbled off into a waltz. "Nights of Gladness" they were playing. The singers were not perturbed by this rival, they lived beyond competition. It was long before the tiny fragment of Professor Godbole that attended to outside things decided that his pince-nez was in trouble, and that until it was adjusted he could not choose a new hymn. He laid down one cymbal, with the other he clashed the air, with his free hand he fumbled at the flowers round his neck. A colleague assisted him. Singing into one another's gray moustaches, they disentangled the chain from the tinsel into which it had sunk. Godbole consulted the music-book, said a word to the drummer, who broke rhythm, made a thick little blur of sound, and produced a new rhythm. This was more exciting, the inner images it evoked more definite, and the singers' expressions became fatuous and languid. They loved all men, the whole universe, and scraps of their past, tiny splinters of detail, emerged for a moment to melt into the universal warmth. Thus Godbole, though she was not important to him, remembered an old woman he had met in Chandrapore days. Chance brought her into his mind while it was in this heated state, he did not select her, she happened to occur among the throng of soliciting images, a tiny splinter, and he impelled her by his spiritual force to that place where completeness can be found. Completeness, not reconstruction. His senses grew thinner, he remembered a wasp seen he forgot where, perhaps on a stone. He loved the wasp equally, he impelled it likewise, he was imitating God. And the stone where the wasp clung—could he . . . no, he could not, he had been wrong to attempt the stone, logic and conscious effort had seduced, he came back to the strip of red carpet and discovered that he was dancing upon it. Up and down, a third of the way to the altar and back again, clashing his cymbals, his little legs twinkling, his companions dancing with him and each other. Noise, noise, the Europeanized band louder, incense on the altar, sweat, the blaze of lights, wind in the bananas, noise, thunder, eleven-fifty by his wrist-watch, seen as he threw up his hands and detached the tiny reverberation that was his soul. Louder shouts in the crowd. He danced on. The boys and men who were squatting in the aisles were lifted forcibly and dropped without changing their shapes into the laps of their neighbours. Down the path thus cleared advanced a litter.

It was the aged Ruler of the State, brought against the advice of his physicians to witness the Birth ceremony.

No one greeted the Rajah, nor did he wish it; this was no moment for human glory. Nor could the litter be set down, lest it defiled the temple by becoming a throne. He was lifted out of it while its feet remained in air, and deposited on the carpet close to the altar, his immense beard was straightened, his legs tucked under him, a paper containing red powder was placed in his hand. There he sat, leaning against a pillar, exhausted with illness, his eyes magnified by many unshed tears.

He had not to wait long. In a land where all else was unpunctual, the hour of the Birth was chronometrically observed. Three minutes before it was due, a Brahman brought forth a model of the village of Gokul (the Bethlehem in that nebulous story) and placed it in front of the altar. The model was on a wooden tray about a yard square; it was of clay, and was gaily blue and white with streamers and paint. Here, upon a chair too small for him and with a head too large, sat King Kansa, who is Herod, directing the murder of some Innocents, and in a corner, similarly proportioned, stood the father and mother of the Lord, warned to depart in a dream. The model was not holy, but more than a decoration, for it diverted men from the actual image of the God, and increased their sacred bewilderment. Some of the villagers thought the Birth had occurred, saying with truth that the Lord must have been born, or they could not see Him. But the clock struck midnight, and simultaneously the rending note of the conch broke forth, followed by the trumpeting of elephants; all who had packets of powder threw them at the altar, and in the rosy dust and incense, and clanging and shouts, Infinite Love took upon itself the form of SHRI KRISHNA, and saved the world. All sorrow was annihilated, not only for Indians, but for foreigners, birds, caves, railways, and the stars; all became joy, all laughter; there had never been disease nor doubt, misunderstanding, cruelty, fear. Some jumped in the air, others flung themselves prone and embraced the bare feet of the universal lover; the women behind the purdah slapped and shrieked; the little girl slipped out and danced by herself, her black pigtails flying. Not an orgy of the body; the tradition of that shrine forbade it. But the human spirit had tried by a desperate contortion to ravish the unknown, flinging down science and history in the struggle, yes, beauty herself. Did it succeed? Books written afterwards say "Yes". But how, if there is such an event, can it be remembered afterwards? How can it be expressed in anything but itself? Not only from the unbeliever are mysteries hid, but the adept himself cannot retain them. He may think, if he chooses, that he has been with God, but, as soon as he thinks it, it becomes history, and falls under the rules of time.

A cobra of papier-mâché now appeared on the carpet, also

a wooden cradle swinging from a frame. Professor Godbole approached the latter with a red silk napkin in his arms. The napkin was God, not that it was, and the image remained in the blur of the altar. It was just a napkin, folded into a shape which indicated a baby's. The Professor dandled it and gave it to the Rajah, who, making a great effort, said, "I name this child Shri Krishna," and tumbled it into the cradle. Tears poured from his eyes, because he had seen the Lord's salvation. He was too weak to exhibit the silk baby to his people, his privilege in former years. His attendants lifted him up, a new path was cleared through the crowd, and he was carried away to a less sacred part of the palace. There, in a room accessible to Western science by an outer staircase, his physician, Dr Aziz, awaited him. His Hindu physician, who had accompanied him to the shrine, briefly reported his symptoms. As the ecstasy receded, the invalid grew fretful. The bumping of the steam-engine that worked the dynamo disturbed him, and he asked for what reason it had been introduced into his home. They replied that they would inquire, and administered a sedative.

Down in the sacred corridors, joy had seethed to jollity. It was their duty to play various games to amuse the newly born God, and to simulate His sports with the wanton dairymaids of Brindaban. Butter played a prominent part in these. When the cradle had been removed, the principal nobles of the State gathered together for an innocent frolic. They removed their turbans, and one put a lump of butter on his forehead, and waited for it to slide down his nose into his mouth. Before it could arrive, another stole up behind him, snatched the melting morsel, and swallowed it himself. All laughed exultantly at discovering that the divine sense of humour coincided with their own. "God si love!" There is fun in heaven. God can play practical jokes upon Himself, draw chairs away from beneath His own posteriors, set His own turbans on fire, and steal His own petticoats when He bathes. By sacrificing good taste, this worship achieved what Christianity has shirked: the inclusion of merriment. All spirit as well as all matter must participate in salvation, and if practical jokes are banned the circle is incomplete. Having swallowed the butter, they played another game which chanced to be graceful: the fondling of Shri Krishna under the similitude of a child. A pretty red and gold ball is thrown, and he who catches it chooses a child from the crowd, raises it in his arms, and carries it round to be caressed. All stroke the darling creature for the Creator's sake, and murmur happy words. The child is restored to his parents, the ball thrown on, and another child becomes for a moment the World's Desire. And the Lord bounds hither and thither through the aisles, chance, and the sport of chance, irradiating little mortals with His immortality. . . . When they had played this long enough—and being exempt from boredom they played it again and again, they played it again and again—they took many sticks and hit them together, whack smack, as though they fought the Pandava wars, and threshed and churned with them, and later on they hung from the roof of the temple, in a net, a great black earthenware jar, which was painted here and there with red, and wreathed with dried figs. Now came a rousing sport. Springing up, they struck at the jar with their sticks. It cracked, broke, and a mass of greasy rice and milk poured onto their faces. They ate and smeared one another's mouths, and dived between each other's legs for what had been pashed upon the carpet. This way and that spread the divine mess, until the line of schoolboys, who had somewhat fended off the crowd, broke for their share. The corridors, the courtyard, were filled with benign confusion. Also the flies awoke and claimed their share of God's bounty. There was no quarrelling, owing to the nature of the gift, for blessed is the man who confers it on another, he imitates God. And those "imitations", those "substitutions", continued to flicker through the assembly for many hours, awaking in each man, according to his capacity, an emotion that he would not have had otherwise. No definite image survived; at the Birth it was questionable whether a silver doll or a mud village, or a silk napkin, or an intangible spirit, or a pious resolution, had been born. Perhaps all these things! Perhaps none! Perhaps all birth is an allegory! Still, it was the main event of the religious year. It caused strange thoughts. Covered with grease and dust, Professor Godbole had once more developed the life of his spirit. He had, with increasing vividness, again seen Mrs Moore, and round her faintly clinging forms of trouble. He was a Brahman, she Christian, but it made no difference, it made no difference whether she was a trick of his memory or a telepathic appeal. It was his duty, as it was his desire, to place himself in the position of the God and to love her, and to place himself in her position and to say to the God, "Come, come, come, come." This was all he could do. How inadequate! But each according to his own capacities, and he knew that his own were small. "One old Englishwoman and one little, little wasp," he thought, as he stepped out of the temple into the gray of a pouring wet morning. "It does not seem much, still, it is more than I am myself."

Chapter 34

Dr Aziz left the palace at the same time. As he returned to his house—which stood in a pleasant garden further up the main street of the town—he could see his old patron paddling and capering in the slush ahead. "Hullo!" he called, and it was the wrong remark, for the devotee indicated by circular gestures of his arms that he did not desire to be disturbed. He added, "Sorry," which was right, for Godbole twisted his head till it didn't belong to his body, and said in a strained voice that had no connection with his mind: "He arrived at the European Guest House perhaps—at least possibly."

"Did he? Since when?"

But time was too definite. He waved his arm more dimly and disappeared. Aziz knew who "he" was—Fielding—but he refused to think about him, because it disturbed his life, and he still trusted the floods to prevent him from arriving. A fine little river issued from his garden gate and gave him much hope. It was impossible that anyone could get across from Deora in such weather as this. Fielding's visit was official. He had been transferred from Chandrapore, and sent on a tour through Central India to see what the remoter states were doing with regard to English education. He had married, he had done the expected with Miss Quested, and Aziz had no wish to see him again.

"Dear old Godbole," he thought, and smiled. He had no religious curiosity, and had never discovered the meaning of this annual antic, but he was well assured that Godbole was a dear old man. He had come to Mau through him and remained on his account. Without him he could never have grasped problems so totally different from those of Chandrapore. For here the cleavage was between Brahman and non-Brahman; Moslems and English were quite out of the running, and sometimes not mentioned for days. Since Godbole was a Brahman, Aziz was one also for purposes of intrigue; they would often joke about it together. The fissures in the Indian soil are infinite: Hinduism, so solid from a distance, is riven into sects and clans, which radiate and join, and change their names according to the aspect from which they are approached. Study it for years with the best teachers, and when you raise your head nothing they have told you quite fits. Aziz, the day of his inauguration, had remarked: "I study nothing, I respect"—making an excellent impression. There was now a minimum of prejudice against him. Nominally under a Hindu doctor, he was really chief medicine man to the court. He had to drop inoculation and such Western whims, but even at Chandrapore his profession had been a game, centring round the operating table, and here in the backwoods he let his instruments rust, ran his little hospital at half steam, and caused no undue alarm.

His impulse to escape from the English was sound. They had frightened him permanently, and there are only two reactions against fright: to kick and scream on committees, or to retreat to a remote jungle, where the sahib seldom comes. His old lawyer friends wanted him to stop in British India and help agitate, and might have prevailed but for the treachery of Fielding. The news had not surprised him in the least. A rift had opened between them after the trial, when Cyril had not joined in his procession; those advocacies of the girl had increased it; then came the postcards from Venice, so cold, so unfriendly that all agreed that something was wrong; and finally, after a silence, the expected letter from Hampstead. Mahmoud Ali was with him at the time. "Some news that will surprise you. I am to marry someone whom you know. . . ." He did not read further. "Here it comes, answer for me—" and he threw it to Mahmoud Ali. Subsequent letters he destroyed unopened. It was the end of a foolish experiment. And, though sometimes at the back of his mind he felt that Fielding had made sacrifices for him, it was now all confused with his genuine hatred of the English. "I am an Indian at last," he thought, standing motionless in the rain.

Life passed pleasantly, the climate was healthy so that the children could be with him all the year round, and he had married again—not exactly a marriage, but he liked to regard it as one—and he read his Persian, wrote his poetry, had his horse, and sometimes got some shikar while the good Hindus looked the other way. His poems were all on one topic—oriental womanhood. "The purdah must go," was their burden, "otherwise we shall never be free." And he declared (fantastically) that India would not have been conquered if women as well as men had fought at Plassy. "But we do not show our women to the foreigner"—not explaining how this was to be managed, for he was writing a poem. Bulbuls and roses would still persist, the pathos of defeated Islam remained in his blood and could not be expelled by modernities. Illogical poems—like their writer. Yet they struck a true note: there cannot be a mother-land without new homes. In one poem—the only one funny old Godbole liked—he had skipped over the mother-land (whom he did not truly love) and gone straight to internationality. "Ah, that is bhakti; ah, my young friend, that is different and very good. Ah, India, who seems not to move, will go straight there while the other nations waste their time. May I translate this particular one into Hindi? In fact, it might be rendered into Sanskrit almost, it is so enlightened. Yes, of course, all your other poems are very good too. His Highness was saying to Colonel Maggs last time he came that we are proud of you"—simpering slightly.

Colonel Maggs was the Political Agent for the neighbourhood, and Aziz's dejected opponent. The Criminal Investigation Department kept an eye on Aziz ever since the trial—they had nothing actionable against him, but Indians who have been unfortunate must be watched, and to the end of his life he remained under observation, thanks to Miss Quested's mistake. Colonel Maggs learned with concern that a suspect was coming to Mau, and, adopting a playful manner, rallied the old Rajah for permitting a Moslem doctor to approach his sacred person. A few years ago, the Rajah would have taken the hint, for the Political Agent then had been a formidable figure, descending with all the thunders of Empire when it was most inconvenient, turning the polity inside out, requiring motor-cars and tiger-hunts, trees cut down that impeded the view from the Guest House, cows milked in his presence, and generally arrogating the control of internal affairs. But there had been a change of policy in high quarters. Local thunders were no longer endorsed, and the group of little states that composed the Agency discovered this and began comparing notes, with fruitful result. To see how much, or how little, Colonel Maggs would stand, became an agreeable game at Mau, which was played by all the Departments of State. He had to stand the appointment of Dr Aziz. The Rajah did not take the hint, but replied that Hindus were less exclusive than formerly, thanks to the enlightened commands of the Viceroy, and he felt it his duty to move with the times.

Yes, all had gone well hitherto, but now, when the rest of the State was plunged in its festival, he had a crisis of a very different sort. A note awaited him at his house. There was no doubt that Fielding had arrived overnight, nor much doubt that Godbole knew of his arrival, for the note was addressed to him, and he had read it before sending it on to Aziz, and had written in the margin, "Is not this delightful news, but unfortunately my religious duties prevent me from taking any action." Fielding announced that he had inspected Mudkul (Miss Derek's former preserve), that he had nearly been drowned at Deora, that he had reached Mau according to timetable, and hoped to remain there two days, studying the various educational innovations of his old friend. Nor had he come alone. His wife and her brother accompanied him. And then the note turned into the sort of note that always did arrive from the State Guest House. Wanting something. No eggs. Mosquito nets torn.

When could they pay their respects to His Highness? Was it correct that a torchlight procession would take place? If so, might they view it? They didn't want to give trouble, but if they might stand in a balcony, or if they might go out in a boat. . . . Aziz tore the note up. He had had enough of showing Miss Quested native life. Treacherous hideous harridan! Bad people altogether. He hoped to avoid them, though this might be difficult, for they would certainly be held up for several days at Mau. Down country, the floods were even worse, and the pale gray faces of lakes had appeared in the direction of the Asirgarh railway station.

Chapter 35

Long before he discovered Mau, another young Mohammedan had retired there—a saint. His mother said to him, "Free prisoners." So he took a sword and went up to the fort. He unlocked a door, and the prisoners streamed out and resumed their previous occupations, but the police were too much annoyed and cut off the young man's head. Ignoring its absence, he made his way over the rocks that separate the fort and the town, killing policemen as he went, and he fell outside his mother's house, having accomplished her orders. Consequently there are two shrines to him today—that of the Head above, and that of the Body below—and they are worshipped by the few Mohammedans who live near, and by Hindus also. "There is no God but God"; that symmetrical injunction melts in the mild airs of Mau; it belongs to pilgrimages and universities, not to feudalism and agriculture. When Aziz arrived, and found that even Islam was idolatrous, he grew scornful, and longed to purify the place, like Alamgir. But soon he didn't mind, like Akbar. After all, this saint had freed prisoners, and he himself had lain in prison. The Shrine of the Body lay in his own garden and produced a weekly crop of lamps and flowers, and when he saw them he recalled his sufferings. The Shrine of the Head made a nice short walk for the children. He was off duty the morning after the great pujah, and he told them to come. Jamila held his hand. Ahmed and Karim ran in front, arguing what the body looked like as it came staggering down, and whether they would have been frightened if they met it. He didn't want them to grow up superstitious, so he rebuked them, and they answered Yes father, for they were well brought up, but, like himself, they were impervious to argument, and after a polite pause they continued saying what their natures compelled them to say.

A slim, tall, eight-sided building stood at the top of the slope, among some bushes. This was the Shrine of the Head. It had not been roofed, and was indeed merely a screen. Inside it crouched a humble dome, and inside that, visible through a grille, was a truncated gravestone, swathed in calico. The inner angles of the screen were cumbered with bees' nests, and a gentle shower of broken wings and other aerial oddments kept falling, and had strewn the damp pavement with their flue. Ahmed, apprised by Mohammed Latif of the character of the bee, said, "They will not hurt us, whose lives are chaste," and pushed boldly in; his sister was more cautious. From the shrine they went to a mosque, which, in size and design, resembled a fire-screen; the arcades of Chandrapore had shrunk to a flat piece of ornamental stucco, with protuberances at either end to suggest minarets. The funny little thing didn't even stand straight, for the rock on which it had been put was slipping down the hill. It, and the shrine, were a strange outcome of the protests of Arabia.

They wandered over the old fort, now deserted, and admired the various views. The scenery, according to their standards, was delightful—the sky gray and black, bellyfuls of rain all over it, the earth pocked with pools of water and slimy with mud. A magnificent monsoon—the best for three years, the tanks already full, bumper crops possible. Out towards the river (the route by which the Fieldings had escaped from Deora) the downpour had been enormous, the mails had to be pulled across by ropes. They could just see the break in the forest trees where the gorge came through, and the rocks above that marked the site of the diamond mine, glistening with wet. Close beneath was the suburban residence of the Junior Rani, isolated by floods, and Her Highness, lax about purdah, to be seen paddling with her handmaidens in the garden and waving her sari at the monkeys on the roof. But better not look close beneath, perhaps—nor towards the European Guest House either.

Beyond the Guest House rose another gray-green gloom of hills, covered with temples like little white flames. There were over two hundred gods in that direction alone, who visited each other constantly, and owned numerous cows, and all the betel-leaf industry, besides having shares in the Asirgarh motor-omnibus. Many of them were in the palace at this moment, having the time of their lives; others, too large or proud to travel, had sent symbols to represent them. The air was thick with religion and rain.

Their white shirts fluttering, Ahmed and Karim ran about over the fort, shrieking with joy. Presently they intersected a line of prisoners, who were looking aimlessly at an old bronze gun. "Which of you is to be pardoned?" they asked. For tonight was the procession of the Chief God, when He would leave the palace, escorted by the whole power of the State, and pass by the jail, which stood down in the town now. As He did so, troubling the waters of our civilization, one prisoner would be released, and then He would proceed to the great Mau tank that stretched as far as the Guest House garden, where something else would happen, some final or subsidiary apotheosis, after which He would submit to the experience of sleep. The Aziz family did not grasp as much as this, being Moslem, but the visit to the jail was common knowledge. Smiling, with downcast eyes, the prisoners discussed with the gentry their chances of salvation. Except for the irons on their legs they resembled other men, nor did they feel different. Five of them, who had not yet been brought to trial, could expect no pardon, but all who had been convicted were full of hope. They did not distinguish between the God and the Rajah in their minds, both were too far above them; but the guard was better educated, and ventured to inquire after His Highness's health.

"It always improves," replied the medicine man. As a matter of fact, the Rajah was dead; the ceremony overnight had overtaxed his strength. His death was being concealed lest the glory of the festival were dimmed. The Hindu physician, the Private Secretary and a confidential servant remained with the corpse, while Aziz had assumed the duty of being seen in public, and misleading people. He had liked the Ruler very much, and might not prosper under his successor, yet he could not worry over such problems yet, for he was involved in the illusion he helped to create. The children continued to run about, hunting for a frog to put in Mohammed Latif's bed, the little fools. Hundreds of frogs lived in their own garden, but they must needs catch one up on the fort. They reported two topis below. Fielding and his brother-in-law, instead of resting after their journey, were climbing the slope to the saint's tomb!

"Throw stones?" asked Karim.

"Put powdered glass in their pan?"

"Ahmed, come here for such wickedness." He raised his hand to smite his first-born, but allowed it to be kissed instead. It was sweet to have his sons with him at this moment, and to know they were affectionate and brave. He pointed out that the Englishmen were State guests, so must not be poisoned, and received, as always, gentle yet enthusiastic assent to his words.

The two visitors entered the octagon, but rushed out at once pursued by some bees. Hither and thither they ran, beating their heads; the children shrieked with derision, and out of heaven, as if a plug had been pulled, fell a jolly dollop of rain. Aziz had not meant to greet his former friend, but the incident put him into an excellent temper. He felt compact and strong. He shouted out, "Hullo, gentlemen, are you in trouble?"

The brother-in-law exclaimed; a bee had got him.

"Lie down in a pool of water, my dear sir—here are plenty. Don't come near me. . . . I cannot control them, they are State bees; complain to His Highness of their behaviour." There was no real danger, for the rain was increasing. The swarm retired to the shrine. He went up to the stranger and pulled a couple of stings out of his wrist, remarking, "Come, pull yourself together and be a man."

"How do you do, Aziz, after all this time? I heard you were settled in here," Fielding called to him, but not in friendly tones. "I suppose a couple of stings don't signify."

"Not the least. I'll send an embrocation over to the Guest House. I heard you were settled in there."

"Why have you not answered my letters?" he asked, going straight for the point, but not reaching it, owing to buckets of rain. His companion, new to the country, cried, as the drops drummed on his topi, that the bees were renewing their attack. Fielding checked his antics rather sharply, then said: "Is there a short cut down to our carriage? We must give up our walk. The weather's pestilential."

"Yes. That way."

"Are you not coming down yourself?"

Aziz sketched a comic salaam; like all Indians, he was skilful in the slighter impertinences. "I tremble, I obey," the gesture said, and it was not lost upon Fielding. They walked down a rough path to the road—the two men first; the brother-in-law (boy rather than man) next, in a state over his arm, which hurt; the three Indian children last, noisy and impudent—all six wet through.

"How goes it, Aziz?"

"In my usual health."

"Are you making anything out of your life here?"

"How much do you make out of yours?"

"Who is in charge of the Guest House?" he asked, giving up his slight effort to recapture their intimacy, and growing more official; he was older and sterner.

"His Highness's Private Secretary, probably."

"Where is he, then?"

"I don't know."

"Because not a soul's been near us since we arrived."

"Really."

"I wrote beforehand to the Durbar, and asked if a visit was convenient. I was told it was, and arranged my tour accordingly; but the Guest House servants appear to have no definite instructions, we can't get any eggs, also my wife wants to go out in the boat."

"There are two boats."

"Exactly, and no oars."

"Colonel Maggs broke the oars when here last."

"All four?"

"He is a most powerful man."

"If the weather lifts, we want to see your torchlight procession from the water this evening," he pursued. "I wrote to Godbole about it, but he has taken no notice; it's a place of the dead."

"Perhaps your letter never reached the Minister in question."

"Will there be any objection to English people watching the procession?"

"I know nothing at all about the religion here. I should never think of watching it myself."

"We had a very different reception both at Mudkul and Deora, they were kindness itself at Deora, the Maharajah and Maharani wanted us to see everything."

"You should never have left them."

"Jump in, Ralph"—they had reached the carriage.

"Jump in, Mr Quested, and Mr Fielding."

"Who on earth is Mr Quested?"

"Do I mispronounce that well-known name? Is he not your wife's brother?"

"Who on earth do you suppose I've married?"

"I'm only Ralph Moore," said the boy, blushing, and at that moment there fell another pailful of the rain, and made a mist round their feet. Aziz tried to withdraw, but it was too late.

"Quested? Quested? Don't you know that my wife was Mrs Moore's daughter?"

He trembled, and went purplish gray; he hated the news, hated hearing the name Moore.

"Perhaps this explains your odd attitude?"

"And pray what is wrong with my attitude?"

"The preposterous letter you allowed Mahmoud Ali to write for you."

"This is a very useless conversation, I consider."

"How ever did you make such a mistake?" said Fielding, more friendly than before, but scathing and scornful. "It's almost unbelievable. I should think I wrote you half a dozen times, mentioning my wife by name. Miss Quested! What an extraordinary notion!" From his smile, Aziz guessed that Stella was beautiful. "Miss Quested is our best friend, she introduced us, but . . . what an amazing notion. Aziz, we must thrash this misunderstanding out later on. It is clearly some devilry of Mahmoud Ali's. He knows perfectly well I married Miss Moore. He called her 'Heaslop's sister' in his insolent letter to me."

The name woke furies in him. "So she is, and here is Heaslop's brother, and you his brother-in-law, and good-bye." Shame turned into a rage that brought back his self-respect. "What does it matter to me who you marry? Don't trouble me here at Mau is all I ask. I do not want you, I do not want one of you in my private life, with my dying breath I say it. Yes, yes, I made a foolish blunder; despise me and feel cold. I thought you married my enemy. I never read your letter. Mahmoud Ali deceived me. I thought you'd stolen my money, but"—he clapped his hands together, and his children gathered round him—"it's as if you stole it. I forgive Mahmoud Ali all things, because he loved me." Then pausing, while the rain exploded like pistols, he said, "My heart is for my own people henceforward," and turned away. Cyril followed him through the mud, apologizing, laughing a little, wanting to argue and reconstruct, pointing out with irrefragable logic that he had married, not Heaslop's betrothed, but Heaslop's sister. What difference did it make at this hour of the day? He had built his life on a mistake, but he had built it. Speaking in Urdu, that the children might understand, he said: "Please do not follow us, whom-ever you marry. I wish no Englishman or Englishwoman to be my friend."

He returned to the house excited and happy. It had been an uneasy, uncanny moment when Mrs Moore's name was mentioned, stirring memories. "Esmiss Esmoor . . ."—as though she was coming to help him. She had always been so good, and that youth whom he had scarcely looked at was her son, Ralph Moore, Stella and Ralph, whom he had promised to be kind to, and Stella had married Cyril.

Chapter 36

All the time the palace ceased not to thrum and tum-tum. The revelation was over, but its effect lasted, and its effect was to make men feel that the revelation had not yet come. Hope existed despite fulfilment, as it will be in heaven. Although the God had been born, His procession—loosely supposed by many to be the Birth—had not taken place. In normal years, the middle hours of this day were signalized by performances of great beauty in the private apartments of the Rajah. He owned a consecrated troupe of men and boys, whose duty it was to dance various actions and meditations of his faith before him. Seated at his ease, he could witness the Three Steps by which the Saviour ascended the universe to the discomfiture of Indra, also the death of the dragon, the mountain that turned into an umbrella, and the saddhu who (with comic results) invoked the God before dining. All culminated in the dance of the milkmaidens before Krishna, and in the still greater dance of Krishna before the milkmaidens, when the music and the musicians swirled through the dark blue robes of the actors into their tinsel crowns, and all became one. The Rajah and his guests would then forget that this was a dramatic performance, and would worship the actors. Nothing of the sort could occur today, because death interrupts. It interrupted less here than in Europe, its pathos was less poignant, its irony less cruel. There were two claimants to the throne, unfortunately, who were in the palace now and suspected what had happened, yet they made no trouble, because religion is a living force to the Hindus, and can at certain moments fling down everything that is petty and temporary in their natures. The festival flowed on, wild and sincere, and all men loved each other, and avoided by instinct whatever could cause inconvenience or pain.

Aziz could not understand this, any more than an average Christian could. He was puzzled that Mau should suddenly be purged from suspicion and self-seeking. Although he was an outsider, and excluded from their rites, they were always particularly charming to him at this time; he and his household received small courtesies and presents, just because he was outside. He had nothing to do all day, except to send the embrocation over to the Guest House, and towards sunset he remembered it, and looked round his house for a local palliative, for the dispensary was shut. He found a tin of ointment belonging to Mohammed Latif, who was unwilling it should be removed, for magic words had been spoken over it while it was being boiled down, but Aziz promised that he would bring it back after application to the stings; he wanted an excuse for a ride.

The procession was beginning to form as he passed the palace. A large crowd watched the loading of the State palanquin, the prow of which protruded in the form of a silver dragon's head through the lofty half-opened door. Gods, big and little, were getting aboard. He averted his eyes, for he never knew how much he was supposed to see, and nearly collided with the Minister of Education. "Ah, you might make me late"—meaning that the touch of a non-Hindu would necessitate another bath; the words were spoken without moral heat. "Sorry," said Aziz. The other smiled, and again mentioned the Guest House party, and, when he heard that Fielding's wife was not Miss Quested, after all, remarked: "Ah, no, he married the sister of Mr Heaslop. Ah, exactly, I have known that for over a year"—also without heat. "Why did you not tell me? Your silence plunged me into a pretty pickle." Godbole, who had never been known to tell anyone anything, smiled again, and said in deprecating tones: "Never be angry with me. I am, as far as my limitations permit, your true friend; besides, it is my holy festival." Aziz always felt like a baby in that strange presence, a baby who unexpectedly receives a toy. He smiled also, and turned his horse into a lane, for the crush increased. The Sweepers' Band was arriving. Playing on sieves and other emblems of their profession, they marched straight at the gate of the palace with the air of a victorious army. All other music was silent, for this was ritually the moment of the Despised and Rejected; the God could not issue from His temple until the unclean sweepers played their tune, they were the spot of filth without which the spirit cannot cohere. For an instant the scene was magnificent. The doors were thrown open, and the whole court was seen inside, barefoot and dressed in white robes; in the fairway stood the Ark of the Lord, covered with cloth of gold and flanked by peacock fans and by stiff circular banners of crimson. It was full to the brim with statuettes and flowers. As it rose from the earth on the shoulders of its bearers, the friendly sun of the monsoons shone forth and flooded the world with colour, so that the yellow tigers painted on the palace walls seemed to spring, and pink and gray skeins of cloud to link up the upper sky. The palanquin moved. . . . The lane was full of State elephants, who would follow it, their howdahs empty out of humility. Aziz did not pay attention to these sanctities, for they had no connection with his own; he felt bored, slightly cynical, like his own dear Emperor Babur, who came down from the north and found in Hindustan no good fruit, no fresh water or witty conversation, not even a friend.

The lane led quickly out of the town onto high rocks and jungle. Here he drew rein and examined the great Mau tank, which lay exposed beneath him to its remotest curve. Reflecting the evening clouds, it filled the nether world with an equal splendour, so that earth and sky leant towards one another, about to clash in ecstasy. He spat, cynical again, more cynical than before. For in the centre of the burnished circle a small black blot was advancing—the Guest House boat. Those English had improvised something to take the place of oars, and were proceeding in their work of patrolling India. The sight endeared the Hindus by comparison, and looking back at the milk-white hump of the palace he hoped that they would enjoy carrying their idol about, for at all events it did not pry into other people's lives. This pose of "seeing India" which had seduced him to Miss Quested at

Chandrapore was only a form of ruling India; no sympathy lay behind it; he knew exactly what was going on in the boat as the party gazed at the steps down which the image would presently descend, and debated how near they might row without getting into trouble officially.

He did not give up his ride, for there would be servants at the Guest House whom he could question; a little information never comes amiss. He took the path by the sombre promontory that contained the royal tombs. Like the palace, they were of snowy stucco, and gleamed by their internal light, but their radiance grew ghostly under approaching night. The promontory was covered with lofty trees, and the fruit-bats were unhooking from the boughs and making kissing sounds as they grazed the surface of the tank; hanging upside down all the day, they had grown thirsty. The signs of the contented Indian evening multiplied: frogs on all sides, cow-dung burning eternally; a flock of belated hornbills overhead, looking like winged skeletons as they flapped across the gloaming. There was death in the air, but not sadness; a compromise had been made between destiny and desire, and even the heart of man acquiesced.

The European Guest House stood two hundred feet above the water, on the crest of a rocky and wooded spur that jutted from the jungle. By the time Aziz arrived, the water had paled to a film of mauve-gray, and the boat vanished entirely. A sentry slept in the Guest House porch, lamps burned in the cruciform of the deserted rooms. He went from one room to another, inquisitive and malicious. Two letters lying on the piano rewarded him, and he pounced and read them promptly. He was not ashamed to do this. The sanctity of private correspondence has never been ratified by the East. Moreover, Mr McBryde had read all his letters in the past, and spread their contents. One letter—the more interesting of the two—was from Heaslop to Fielding. It threw light on the mentality of his former friend, and it hardened him further against him. Much of it was about Ralph Moore, who appeared to be almost an imbecile. "Hand on my brother whenever suits you. I write to you because he is sure to make a bad bundobust." Then: "I quite agree—life is too short to cherish grievances, also I'm relieved you feel able to come into line with the Oppressors of India to some extent. We need all the support we can get. I hope that next time Stella comes my way she will bring you with her, when I will make you as comfortable as a bachelor can—it's certainly time we met. My sister's marriage to you coming after my mother's death and my own difficulties did upset me, and I was unreasonable. It is about time we made it up properly, as you say—let us leave it at faults on both sides. Glad about your son and heir. When next any of you write to Adela, do give her some sort of message from me, for I should like to make my peace with her too. You are lucky to be out of British India at the present moment. Incident after incident, all due to propaganda, but we can't lay our hands on the connecting thread. The longer one lives here, the more certain one gets that everything hangs together. My personal opinion is, it's the Jews."

Thus far the red-nosed boy. Aziz was distracted for a moment by blurred sounds coming from over the water; the procession was under way. The second letter was from Miss Quested to Mrs Fielding. It contained one or two interesting touches. The writer hoped that "Ralph will enjoy his India more than I did mine", and appeared to have given him money for this purpose—"my debt which I shall never repay in person". What debt did Miss Quested imagine she owed the country? He did not relish the phrase. Talk of Ralph's health. It was all "Stella and Ralph", even "Cyril" and "Ronny"—all so friendly and sensible, and written in a spirit he could not command. He envied the easy intercourse that is only possible in a nation whose women are free. These five people were making up their little difficulties, and closing their broken ranks against the alien. Even Heaslop was coming in. Hence the strength of England, and in a spurt of temper he hit the piano, and since the notes had swollen and stuck together in groups of threes he produced a remarkable noise.

"Oh, oh, who is that?" said a nervous and respectful voice;

he could not remember where he had heard its tones before. Something moved in the twilight of an adjoining room. He replied, "State doctor, ridden over to inquire, very little English," slipped the letters into his pocket, and to show that he had free entry to the Guest House struck the piano again.

Ralph Moore came into the light.

What a strange-looking youth, tall, prematurely aged, the big blue eyes faded with anxiety, the hair impoverished and tousled! Not a type that is often exported imperially. The doctor in Aziz thought, "Born of too old a mother," the poet found him rather beautiful.

"I was unable to call earlier owing to pressure of work. How are the celebrated bee-stings?" he asked patronizingly.

"I—I was resting, they thought I had better; they throb rather."

His timidity and evident "newness" had complicated effects on the malcontent. Speaking threateningly, he said, "Come here, please, allow me to look." They were practically alone, and he could treat the patient as Callendar had treated Nureddin.

"You said this morning—"

"The best of doctors make mistakes. Come here, please, for the diagnosis under the lamp. I am pressed for time."

"Aough—"

"What is the matter, pray?"

"Your hands are unkind."

He started and glanced down at them. The extraordinary youth was right, and he put them behind his back before replying with outward anger: "What the devil have my hands to do with you? This is a most strange remark. I am a qualified doctor, who will not hurt you."

"I don't mind pain, there is no pain."

"No pain?"

"Not really."

"Excellent news," sneered Aziz.

"But there is cruelty."

"I have brought you some salve, but how to put it on in

your present nervous state becomes a problem," he continued, after a pause.

"Please leave it with me."

"Certainly not. It returns to my dispensary at once." He stretched forward, and the other retreated to the further side of a table. "Now, do you want me to treat your stings, or do you prefer an English doctor? There is one at Asirgarh. Asirgarh is forty miles away, and the Ringnod dam broken. Now you see how you are placed. I think I had better see Mr Fielding about you; this is really great nonsense, your present behaviour."

"They are out in a boat," he replied, glancing about him for support.

Aziz feigned intense surprise. "They have not gone in the direction of Mau, I hope. On a night like this the people become most fanatical." And, as if to confirm him, there was a sob, as though the lips of a giant had parted; the procession was approaching the jail.

"You should not treat us like this," he challenged, and this time Aziz was checked, for the voice, though frightened, was not weak.

"Like what?"

"Dr Aziz, we have done you no harm."

"Aha, you know my name, I see. Yes, I am Aziz. No, of course your great friend Miss Quested did me no harm at the Marabar."

Drowning his last words, all the guns of the State went off. A rocket from the jail garden gave the signal. The prisoner had been released, and was kissing the feet of the singers. Rose-leaves fall from the houses, sacred spices and cocoanut are brought forth. . . . It was the halfway moment; the God had extended His temple, and paused exultantly. Mixed and confused in their passage, the rumours of salvation entered the Guest House. They were startled and moved onto the porch, drawn by the sudden illumination. The bronze gun up on the fort kept flashing, the town was a blur of light, in which the houses seemed dancing, and the palace waving little wings. The water below, the hills and sky above, were not involved as yet; there was still only a little light and song struggling among the shapeless lumps of the universe. The song became audible through much repetition; the choir was repeating and inverting the names of deities.

"Radhakrishna Radhakrishna,
Radhakrishna Radhakrishna,
Krishnaradha Radhakrishna,
Radhakrishna Radhakrishna,"

they sang, and woke the sleeping sentry in the Guest House; he leant upon his iron-tipped spear.

"I must go back now, good night," said Aziz, and held out his hand, completely forgetting that they were not friends, and focusing his heart on something more distant than the caves, something beautiful. His hand was taken, and then he remembered how detestable he had been, and said gently, "Don't you think me unkind any more?"

"No."

"How can you tell, you strange fellow?"

"Not difficult, the one thing I always know."

"Can you always tell whether a stranger is your friend?"

"Yes."

"Then you are an Oriental." He unclasped as he spoke, with a little shudder. Those words—he had said them to Mrs Moore in the mosque at the beginning of the cycle, from which, after so much suffering, he had got free. Never be friends with the English! Mosque, caves, mosque, caves. And here he was starting again. He handed the magic ointment to him. "Take this, think of me when you use it. I shall never want it back. I must give you one little present, and it is all I have got; you are Mrs Moore's son."

"I am that," he murmured to himself; and a part of Aziz's mind that had been hidden seemed to move and force its way to the top.

"But you are Heaslop's brother also, and alas, the two nations cannot be friends."

"I know. Not yet."

"Did your mother speak to you about me?"

"Yes." And with a swerve of voice and body that Aziz did not follow he added: "In her letters, in her letters. She loved you."

"Yes, your mother was my best friend in all the world." He was silent, puzzled by his own great gratitude. What did this eternal goodness of Mrs Moore amount to? To nothing, if brought to the test of thought. She had not borne witness in his favour, nor visited him in the prison, yet she had stolen to the depths of his heart, and he always adored her. "This is our monsoon, the best weather," he said, while the lights of the procession waved as though embroidered on an agitated curtain. "How I wish she could have seen them, our rains. Now is the time when all things are happy, young and old. They are happy out there with their savage noise, though we cannot follow them; the tanks are all full, so they dance, and this is India. I wish you were not with officials, then I would show you my country, but I cannot. Perhaps I will just take you out on the water now, for one short half-hour."

Was the cycle beginning again? His heart was too full to draw back. He must slip out in the darkness, and do this one act of homage to Mrs Moore's son. He knew where the oars were—hidden to deter the visitors from going out—and he brought the second pair, in case they met the other boat; the Fieldings had pushed themselves out with long poles, and might get into difficulties, for the wind was rising.

Once on the water, he became easy. One kind action was with him always a channel for another, and soon the torrent of his hospitality gushed forth and he began doing the honours of Mau and persuading himself that he understood the wild procession, which increased in lights and sounds as the complications of its ritual developed. There was little need to row, for the freshening gale blew them in the direction they desired. Thorns scratched the keel, they ran into an islet and startled some cranes. The strange temporary life of the August flood-water bore them up and seemed as though it would last for ever.

The boat was a rudderless dinghy. Huddled up in the stern, with the spare pair of oars in his arms, the guest asked no questions about details. There was presently a flash of lightning, followed by a second flash—little red scratches on the ponderous sky. "Was that the Rajah?" he asked.

"What—what do you mean?"

"Row back."

"But there's no Rajah—nothing—"

"Row back, you will see what I mean."

Aziz found it hard work against the advancing wind. But he fixed his eyes on the pin of light that marked the Guest House and backed a few strokes.

"There . . ."

Floating in the darkness was a king, who sat under a canopy, in shining royal robes. . . .

"I can't tell you what that is, I'm sure," he whispered. "His Highness is dead. I think we should go back at once."

They were close to the promontory of the tombs, and had looked straight into the chhatri of the Rajah's father through an opening in the trees. That was the explanation. He had heard of the image—made to imitate life at enormous expense—but he had never chanced to see it before, though he frequently rowed on the lake. There was only one spot from which it could be seen, and Ralph had directed him to it. Hastily he pulled away, feeling that his companion was not so much a visitor as a guide. He remarked, "Shall we go back now?"

"There is still the procession."

"I'd rather not go nearer—they have such strange customs, and might hurt you."

"A little nearer."

Aziz obeyed. He knew with his heart that this was Mrs Moore's son, and indeed until his heart was involved he knew nothing. "Radhakrishna Radhakrishna Radhakrishna Radhakrishna Krishnaradha," went the chant, then suddenly changed, and in the interstice he heard, almost certainly, the syllables of salvation that had sounded during his trial at Chandrapore.

"Mr Moore, don't tell anyone that the Rajah is dead. It is a secret still, I am supposed not to say. We pretend he is alive until after the festival, to prevent unhappiness. Do you want to go still nearer?"

"Yes."

He tried to keep the boat out of the glare of the torches that began to star the other shore. Rockets kept going off, also the guns. Suddenly, closer than he had calculated, the palanquin of Krishna appeared from behind a ruined wall, and descended the carven glistening water-steps. On either side of it the singers tumbled, a woman prominent, a wild and beautiful young saint with flowers in her hair. She was praising God without attributes—thus did she apprehend Him. Others praised Him with attributes, seeing Him in this or that organ of the body or manifestation of the sky. Down they rushed to the foreshore and stood in the small waves, and a sacred meal was prepared, of which those who felt worthy partook. Old Godbole detected the boat, which was drifting in on the gale, and he waved his arms—whether in wrath or joy Aziz never discovered. Above stood the secular power of Mau—elephants, artillery, crowds—and high above them a wild tempest started, confined at first to the upper regions of the air. Gusts of wind mixed darkness and light, sheets of rain cut from the north, stopped, cut from the south, began rising from below, and across them struggled the singers, sounding every note but terror, and preparing to throw God away, God Himself (not that God can be thrown), into the storm. Thus was He thrown year after year, and were others thrown—little images of Ganpati, baskets of ten-day corn, tiny tazias after Mohurram—scapegoats, husks, emblems of passage; a passage not easy, not now, not here, not to be apprehended except when it is unattainable: the God to be thrown was an emblem of that.

The village of Gokul reappeared upon its tray. It was the substitute for the silver image, which never left its haze of flowers; on behalf of another symbol, it was to perish. A servitor took it in his hands, and tore off the blue and white streamers. He was naked, broad-shouldered, thin-waisted—the Indian body again triumphant—and it was his hereditary office to close the gates of salvation. He entered the dark waters, pushing the village before him, until the clay dolls slipped off their chairs and began to gutter in the rain, and King Kansa was confounded with the father and mother of the Lord. Dark and solid, the little waves sipped, then a great wave washed and then English voices cried "Take care!"

The boats had collided with each other.

The four outsiders flung out their arms and grappled, and, with oars and poles sticking out, revolved like a mythical monster in the whirlwind. The worshippers howled with wrath or joy, as they drifted forward helplessly against the servitor. Who awaited them, his beautiful dark face expressionless, and as the last morsels melted on his tray it struck them.

The shock was minute, but Stella, nearest to it, shrank into her husband's arms, then reached forward, then flung herself against Aziz, and her motions capsized them. They plunged into the warm, shallow water, and rose struggling into a tornado of noise. The oars, the sacred tray, the letters of Ronny and Adela, broke loose and floated confusedly. Artillery was fired, drums beaten, the elephants trumpeted, and drowning all an immense peal of thunder, unaccompanied by lightning, cracked like a mallet on the dome.

That was the climax, as far as India admits of one. The rain settled in steadily to its job of wetting everybody and everything through, and soon spoiled the cloth of gold on the palanquin and the costly disc-shaped banners. Some of the torches went out, fireworks didn't catch, there began to be less singing, and the tray returned to Professor Godbole, who picked up a fragment of the mud adhering and smeared it on his forehead without much ceremony. Whatever had happened had happened, and while the intruders picked themselves up the crowds of Hindus began a desultory move back into the town. The image went back too, and on the following day underwent a private death of its own, when some curtains of magenta and green were lowered in front of the dynastic shrine. The singing went on even longer . . . ragged edges of religion . . . unsatisfactory and undramatic tangles. . . . "God si love." Looking back at the great blur of the last twenty-four hours, no man could say where was the emotional centre of it, any more than he could locate the heart of a cloud.

Chapter 37

Friends again, yet aware that they would meet no more, Aziz and Fielding went for their last ride in the Mau jungles. The floods had abated and the Rajah was officially dead, so the Guest House party were departing next morning, as decorum required. What with the mourning and the festival, the visit was a failure. Fielding had scarcely seen Godbole, who promised every day to show him over the King-Emperor George Fifth High School, his main objective, but always made some excuse. This afternoon Aziz let out what had happened: the King-Emperor had been converted into a granary, and the Minister of Education did not like to admit this to his former Principal. The school had been opened only last year by the Agent to the Governor-General, and it still flourished on paper; he hoped to start it again before its absence was remarked and to collect its scholars before they produced children of their own. Fielding laughed at the tangle and waste of energy, but he did not travel as lightly as in the past; education was a continuous concern to him because his income and the comfort of his family depended on it. He knew that few Indians think education good in itself, and he deplored this now on the widest grounds. He began to say something heavy on the subject of Native States, but the friendliness of Aziz distracted him. This reconciliation was a success, anyhow. After the funny shipwreck there had been no more nonsense or bitterness, and they went back laughingly to their old relationship as if nothing had happened. Now they rode between jolly bushes and rocks. Presently the ground opened into full sunlight and they saw a grassy slope bright with butterflies, also a cobra, which crawled across doing nothing in particular, and disappeared among some custard-apple trees. There were round white clouds in the sky, and white pools on the earth; the hills in the distance were purple. The scene was as park-like as England, but did not cease being queer. They drew rein, to give the cobra elbow-room, and Aziz produced a letter that he wanted to send to Miss Quested. A charming letter. He wanted to thank his old enemy for her fine behaviour two years back; perfectly plain was it now that she had behaved well. "As I fell into our largest Mau tank under circumstances our other friends will relate, I thought how brave Miss Quested was, and decided to tell her so, despite my imperfect English. Through you I am happy here with my children instead of in a prison, of that I make no doubt. My children shall be taught to speak of you with the greatest affection and respect."

"Miss Quested will be greatly pleased. I am glad you have seen her courage at last."

"I want to do kind actions all round and wipe out the wretched business of the Marabar for ever. I have been so disgracefully hasty, thinking you meant to get hold of my money: as bad a mistake as the cave itself."

"Aziz, I wish you would talk to my wife. She too believes that the Marabar is wiped out."

"How so?"

"I don't know, perhaps she might tell you, she won't tell me. She has ideas I don't share—indeed, when I'm away from her I think them ridiculous. When I'm with her, I suppose because I'm fond of her, I feel different, I feel half deaf and half blind. My wife's after something. You and I and Miss Quested are, roughly speaking, not after anything. We jog on as decently as we can, you a little in front—a laudable little party. But my wife is not with us."

"What are you meaning? Is Stella not faithful to you, Cyril? This fills me with great concern."

Fielding hesitated. He was not quite happy about his marriage. He was passionate physically again—the final flare-up before the clinkers of middle age—and he knew that his wife did not love him as much as he loved her, and he was ashamed of pestering her. But during the visit to Mau the situation had improved. There seemed a link between them at last—

that link outside either participant that is necessary to every relationship. In the language of theology, their union had been blessed. He could assure Aziz that Stella was not only faithful to him, but likely to become more so; and, trying to express what was not clear to himself, he added dully that different people had different points of view. "If you won't talk about the Marabar to Stella, why won't you talk to Ralph? He is a wise boy really. And (same metaphor) he rides a little behind her, though with her."

"Tell him also, I have nothing to say to him, but he is indeed a wise boy and has always one Indian friend. I partly love him because he brought me back to you to say goodbye. For this is goodbye, Cyril, though to think about it will spoil our ride and make us sad."

"No, we won't think about it." He too felt that this was their last free intercourse. All the stupid misunderstandings had been cleared up, but socially they had no meeting-place. He had thrown in his lot with Anglo-India by marrying a countrywoman, and he was acquiring some of its limitations, and already felt surprise at his own past heroism. Would he today defy all his own people for the sake of a stray Indian? Aziz was a memento, a trophy, they were proud of each other, yet they must inevitably part. And, anxious to make what he could of this last afternoon, he forced himself to speak intimately about his wife, the person most dear to him. He said: "From her point of view, Mau has been a success. It calmed her—both of them suffer from restlessness. She found something soothing, some solution of her queer troubles here." After a silence—myriads of kisses around them as the earth drew the water in—he continued: "Do you know anything about this Krishna business?"

"My dear chap, officially they call it Gokul Ashtami. All the State offices are closed, but how else should it concern you and me?"

"Gokul is the village where Krishna was born—well, more or less born, for there's the same hovering between it and another village as between Bethlehem and Nazareth. What I want to discover is its spiritual side, if it has one."

"It is useless discussing Hindus with me. Living with them teaches me no more. When I think I annoy them, I do not. When I think I don't annoy them, I do. Perhaps they will sack me for tumbling onto their doll's-house; on the other hand, perhaps they will double my salary. Time will prove. Why so curious about them?"

"It's difficult to explain. I never really understood or liked them, except an occasional scrap of Godbole. Does the old fellow still say 'Come, come'?"

"Oh, presumably."

Fielding sighed, opened his lips, shut them, then said with a little laugh, "I can't explain, because it isn't in words at all, but why do my wife and her brother like Hinduism, though they take no interest in its forms? They won't talk to me about this. They know I think a certain side of their lives is a mistake, and are shy. That's why I wish you would talk to them, for at all events you're oriental."

Aziz refused to reply. He didn't want to meet Stella and Ralph again, knew they didn't want to meet him, was incurious about their secrets, and felt good old Cyril to be a bit clumsy. Something—not a sight, but a sound—flitted past him, and caused him to reread his letter to Miss Quested. Hadn't he wanted to say something else to her? Taking out his pen, he added: "For my own part, I shall henceforth connect you with the name that is very sacred in my mind, namely Mrs Moore." When he had finished, the mirror of the scenery was shattered, the meadow disintegrated into butterflies. A poem about Mecca—the Caaba of Union—the thorn-bushes where pilgrims die before they have seen the Friend—they flitted next; he thought of his wife; and then the whole semi-mystic, semi-sensuous overturn, so characteristic of his spiritual life, came to end like a landslip and rested in its due place, and he found himself riding in the jungle with his dear Cyril.

"Oh, shut up," he said. "Don't spoil our last hour with foolish questions. Leave Krishna alone, and talk about something sensible."

They did. All the way back to Mau they wrangled about

politics. Each had hardened since Chandrapore, and a good knock-about proved enjoyable. They trusted each other, although they were going to part, perhaps because they were going to part. Fielding had "no further use for politeness," he said, meaning that the British Empire really can't be abolished because it's rude. Aziz retorted, "Very well, and we have no use for you," and glared at him with abstract hate. Fielding said: "Away from us, Indians go to seed at once. Look at the King-Emperor High School! Look at you, forgetting your medicine and going back to charms. Look at your poems."—"Jolly good poems, I'm getting published Bombay side."—"Yes, and what do they say? Free our women and India will be free. Try it, my lad. Free your own lady in the first place, and see who'll wash Ahmed, Karim and Jamila's faces. A nice situation!"

Aziz grew more excited. He rose in his stirrups and pulled at his horse's head in the hope it would rear. Then he should feel in a battle. He cried: "Clear out, all you Turtons and Burtons. We wanted to know you ten years back—now it's too late. If we see you and sit on your committees, it's for political reasons, don't you make any mistake." His horse did rear. "Clear out, clear out, I say. Why are we put to so much suffering? We used to blame you, now we blame ourselves, we grow wiser. Until England is in difficulties we keep silent, but in the next European war—aha, aha! Then is our time." He paused, and the scenery, though it smiled, fell like a gravestone on any human hope. They cantered past a temple to Hanuman—God so loved the world that he took monkey's flesh upon him—and past a Saivite temple, which invited to lust, but under the semblance of eternity, its obscenities bearing no relation to those of our flesh and blood. They splashed through butterflies and frogs; great trees with leaves like plates rose among the brushwood. The divisions of daily life were returning, the shrine had almost shut.

"Who do you want instead of the English? The Japanese?" jeered Fielding, drawing rein.

"No, the Afghans. My own ancestors."

"Oh, your Hindu friends will like that, won't they?"

"It will be arranged—a conference of oriental statesmen."

"It will indeed be arranged."

"Old story of 'We will rob every man and rape every woman from Peshawar to Calcutta', I suppose, which you get some nobody to repeat and then quote every week in the *Pioneer* in order to frighten us into retaining you! We know!" Still he couldn't quite fit in Afghans at Mau, and, finding he was in a corner, made his horse rear again until he remembered that he had, or ought to have, a mother-land. Then he shouted: "India shall be a nation! No foreigners of any sort! Hindu and Moslem and Sikh and all shall be one! Hurrah! Hurrah for India! Hurrah! Hurrah!"

India a nation! What an apotheosis! Last comer to the drab nineteenth-century sisterhood! Waddling in at this hour of the world to take her seat! She, whose only peer was the Holy Roman Empire, she shall rank with Guatemala and Belgium perhaps! Fielding mocked again. And Aziz in an awful rage danced this way and that, not knowing what to do, and cried: "Down with the English anyhow. That's certain. Clear out, you fellows, double quick, I say. We may hate one another, but we hate you most. If I don't make you go, Ahmed will, Karim will, if it's fifty or five hundred years we shall get rid of you, yes, we shall drive every blasted Englishman into the sea, and then"—he rode against him furiously—"and then," he concluded, half kissing him, "you and I shall be friends."

"Why can't we be friends now?" said the other, holding him affectionately. "It's what I want. It's what you want."

But the horses didn't want it—they swerved apart; the earth didn't want it, sending up rocks through which riders must pass single-file; the temples, the tank, the jail, the palace, the birds, the carrion, the Guest House, that came into view as they issued from the gap and saw Mau beneath: they didn't want it, they said in their hundred voices, "No, not yet," and the sky said, "No, not there."

MAURICE

PART ONE

A note on the text

With a small number of exceptions, the 1960 typescript has been faithfully followed, even where it reads a trifle oddly—as when Alec Scudder, batting in a cricket match, is made to "resign" (i.e. retire), or "Whitmannic" is used in place of "Whitmanesque", or some sentences in the Terminal Note need revising in the light of the Sexual Offences Act of 1967. The exceptions are as follows.

1. The surname of one of the characters has, on the author's written instructions, been altered throughout, and one or two contingent changes made.

2. Spelling, punctuation and capitalization have, where no nuance is involved, been regularized in accordance with normal practice today.

3. A number of obvious typing errors (or in some cases possibly slips of the pen) have been corrected.

4. Rather more diffidently, the following readings have been adopted with the aim of correcting what appear to be either typing errors or slips on Forster's part:

Page	*Line*	*Reading Adopted*	*Typescript*
28	35–36	but he held . . . Durham	but held . . . he
31	6	waiting for Durham	watching Durham
34	27	was	is
94	16	coasting (hooting?)	hoosting or boosting
155	32–33	evidently he had	had evidently
169	27	that he should telephone next week	for next week

5. Finally, on page 106, a famous phrase from Sophocles ("Not to be born is best"—*Oedipus Coloneus,* 1224–5) has been inserted where the 1960 typescript has a blank space, and an earlier typescript supplies a slightly inaccurate version of the quotation.

I

Once a term the whole school went for a walk—that is to say the three masters took part as well as all the boys. It was usually a pleasant outing, and everyone looked forward to it, forgot old scores, and behaved with freedom. Lest discipline should suffer, it took place just before the holidays, when leniency does no harm, and indeed it seemed more like a treat at home than school, for Mrs Abrahams, the Principal's wife, would meet them at the tea place with some lady friends, and be hospitable and motherly.

Mr Abrahams was a preparatory schoolmaster of the old-fashioned sort. He cared neither for work nor games, but fed his boys well and saw that they did not misbehave. The rest he left to the parents, and did not speculate how much the parents were leaving to him. Amid mutual compliments the boys passed out into a public school, healthy but backward, to receive upon undefended flesh the first blows of the world. There is much to be said for apathy in education, and Mr Abrahams's pupils did not do badly in the long run, became parents in their turn, and in some cases sent him their sons. Mr Read, the junior assistant, was a master of the same type, only stupider, while Mr Ducie, the senior, acted as a stimulant, and prevented the whole concern from going to sleep. They did not like him much, but knew that he was necessary. Mr Ducie was an able man, orthodox, but not out of touch with the world, nor incapable of seeing both sides of a question. He was unsuitable for parents and the denser boys, but good for the first form, and had even coached pupils into a scholarship. Nor was he a bad organizer. While affecting to hold the reins and to prefer Mr Read, Mr Abrahams really allowed Mr Ducie a free hand and ended by taking him into partnership.

Mr Ducie always had something on his mind. On this

occasion it was Hall, one of the older boys, who was leaving them to go to a public school. He wanted to have a "good talk" with Hall, during the outing. His colleagues objected, since it would leave them more to do, and the Principal remarked that he had already talked to Hall, and that the boy would prefer to take his last walk with his school-fellows. This was probable, but Mr Ducie was never deterred from doing what is right. He smiled and was silent. Mr Read knew what the "good talk" would be, for early in their acquaintance they had touched on a certain theme professionally. Mr Read had disapproved. "Thin ice," he had said. The Principal neither knew nor would have wished to know. Parting from his pupils when they were fourteen, he forgot they had developed into men. They seemed to him a race small but complete, like the New Guinea pygmies, "my boys". And they were even easier to understand than pygmies, because they never married and seldom died. Celibate and immortal, the long procession passed before him, its thickness varying from twenty-five to forty at a time. "I see no use in books on education. Boys began before education was thought of." Mr Ducie would smile, for he was soaked in evolution.

From this to the boys.

"Sir, may I hold your hand.... Sir, you promised me.... Both Mr Abrahams' hands were bagged and all Mr Read's.... Oh sir, did you hear that? He thinks Mr Read has three hands! ... I didn't, I said 'fingers'. Green eye! Green eye!"

"When you have quite finished—!"

"Sir!"

"I'm going to walk with Hall alone."

There were cries of disappointment. The other masters, seeing that it was no good, called the pack off, and marshalled them along the cliff towards the downs. Hall, triumphant, sprang to Mr Ducie's side, and felt too old to take his hand. He was a plump, pretty lad, not in any way remarkable. In this he resembled his father, who had passed in the procession twenty-five years before, vanished into a public school, married, begotten a son and two daughters, and recently died of pneumonia. Mr Hall had been a good citizen, but lethargic. Mr Ducie had informed himself about him before they began the walk.

"Well, Hall, expecting a pi-jaw, eh?"

"I don't know, sir—Mr Abrahams' given me one with 'Those Holy Fields'. Mrs Abrahams' given me sleeve links. The fellows have given me a set of Guatemalas up to two dollars. Look, sir! The ones with the parrot on the pillar on."

"Splendid, splendid! What did Mr Abrahams say? Told you you were a miserable sinner, I hope."

The boy laughed. He did not understand Mr Ducie, but knew that he was meaning to be funny. He felt at ease because it was his last day at school, and even if he did wrong he would not get into a row. Besides, Mr Abrahams had declared him a success. "We are proud of him; he will do us honour at Sunnington": he had seen the beginning of the letter to his mother. And the boys had showered presents on him, declaring he was brave. A great mistake—he wasn't brave: he was afraid of the dark. But no one knew this.

"Well, what did Mr Abrahams say?" repeated Mr Ducie, when they reached the sands. A long talk threatened, and the boy wished he was up on the cliff with his friends, but he knew that wishing is useless when boy meets man.

"Mr Abrahams told me to copy my father, sir."

"Anything else?"

"I am never to do anything I should be ashamed to have mother see me do. No one can go wrong then, and the public school will be very different from this."

"Did Mr Abrahams say how?"

"All kinds of difficulties—more like the world."

"Did he tell you what the world is like?"

"No."

"Did you ask him?"

"No, sir."

"That wasn't very sensible of you, Hall. Clear things up. Mr Abrahams and I are here to answer your questions. What do you suppose the world—the world of grown-up people is like?"

"I can't tell. I'm a boy," he said, very sincerely. "Are they very treacherous, sir?"

Mr Ducie was amused and asked him what examples of treachery he had seen. He replied that grown-up people would not be unkind to boys, but were they not always cheating one another? Losing his schoolboy manner, he began to talk like a child, and became fanciful and amusing. Mr Ducie lay down on the sand to listen to him, lit his pipe and looked up to the sky. The little watering-place where they lived was now far behind, the rest of the school away in front. The day was gray and windless, with little distinction between clouds and sun.

"You live with your mother, don't you?" he interrupted, seeing that the boy had gained confidence.

"Yes, sir."

"Have you any elder brothers?"

"No, sir—only Ada and Kitty."

"Any uncles?"

"No."

"So you don't know many men?"

"Mother keeps a coachman and George in the garden, but of course you mean gentlemen. Mother has three maid-servants to look after the house, but they are so idle that they will not mend Ada's stockings. Ada is my eldest little sister."

"How old are you?"

"Fourteen and three quarters."

"Well, you're an ignorant little beggar." They laughed. After a pause he said, "When I was your age, my father told me something that proved very useful and helped me a good deal." This was untrue: his father had never told him anything. But he needed a prelude to what he was going to say.

"Did he, sir?"

"Shall I tell you what it was?"

"Please, sir."

"I am going to talk to you for a few moments as if I were your father, Maurice! I shall call you by your real name." Then, very simply and kindly, he approached the mystery of sex. He spoke of male and female, created by God in the beginning in order that the earth might be peopled, and of the period when the male and female receive their powers. "You are just becoming a man now, Maurice; that is why I am telling you about this. It is not a thing that your mother can tell you, and you should not mention it to her nor to any lady, and if at your next school boys mention it to you, just shut them up; tell them you know. Have you heard about it before?"

"No, sir."

"Not a word?"

"No, sir."

Still smoking his pipe, Mr Ducie got up, and choosing a smooth piece of sand drew diagrams upon it with his walking-stick. "This will make it easier," he said to the boy, who watched dully: it bore no relation to his experiences. He was attentive, as was natural when he was the only one in the class, and he knew that the subject was serious and related to his own body. But he could not himself relate it; it fell to pieces as soon as Mr Ducie put it together, like an impossible sum. In vain he tried. His torpid brain would not awake. Puberty was there, but not intelligence, and manhood was stealing on him, as it always must, in a trance. Useless to break in upon that trance. Useless to describe it, however scientifically and sympathetically. The boy assents and is dragged back into sleep, not to be enticed there before his hour.

Mr Ducie, whatever his science, was sympathetic. Indeed he was too sympathetic; he attributed cultivated feelings to

Maurice, and did not realize that he must either understand nothing or be overwhelmed. "All this is rather a bother," he said, "but one must get it over, one mustn't make a mystery of it. Then come the great things—Love, Life." He was fluent, having talked to boys in this way before, and he knew the kind of question they would ask. Maurice would not ask: he only said, "I see, I see, I see," and at first Mr Ducie feared he did not see. He examined him. The replies were satisfactory. The boy's memory was good and—so curious a fabric is the human—he even developed a spurious intelligence, a surface flicker to respond to the beaconing glow of the man's. In the end he did ask one or two questions about sex, and they were to the point. Mr Ducie was much pleased. "That's right," he said. "You need never be puzzled or bothered now."

Love and life still remained, and he touched on them as they strolled forward by the colourless sea. He spoke of the ideal man—chaste with asceticism. He sketched the glory of Woman. Engaged to be married himself, he grew more human, and his eyes coloured up behind the strong spectacles; his cheek flushed. To love a noble woman, to protect and serve her—this, he told the little boy, was the crown of life. "You can't understand now, you will some day, and when you do understand it, remember the poor old pedagogue who put you on the track. It all hangs together—all—and God's in his heaven, All's right with the world. Male and female! Ah wonderful!"

"I think I shall not marry," remarked Maurice.

"This day ten years hence—I invite you and your wife to dinner with my wife and me. Will you accept?"

"Oh sir!" He smiled with pleasure.

"It's a bargain, then!" It was at all events a good joke to end with. Maurice was flattered and began to contemplate marriage. But while they were easing off Mr Ducie stopped, and held his cheek as though every tooth ached. He turned and looked at the long expanse of sand behind.

"I never scratched out those infernal diagrams," he said slowly.

At the further end of the bay some people were following them, also by the edge of the sea. Their course would take them by the very spot where Mr Ducie had illustrated sex, and one of them was a lady. He ran back sweating with fear.

"Sir, won't it be all right?" Maurice cried. "The tide'll have covered them by now."

"Good Heavens... thank God... the tide's rising."

And suddenly for an instant of time, the boy despised him. "Liar," he thought. "Liar, coward, he's told me nothing." ... Then darkness rolled up again, the darkness that is primeval but not eternal, and yields to its own painful dawn.

II

Maurice's mother lived near London, in a comfortable villa among some pines. There he and his sisters had been born, and thence his father had gone up to business every day, thither returning. They nearly left when the church was built, but they became accustomed to it, as to everything, and even found it a convenience. Church was the only place Mrs Hall had to go to—the shops delivered. The station was not far either, nor was a tolerable day school for the girls. It was a land of facilities, where nothing had to be striven for, and success was indistinguishable from failure.

Maurice liked his home, and recognized his mother as its presiding genius. Without her there would be no soft chairs or food or easy games, and he was grateful to her for providing so much, and loved her. He liked his sisters also. When he arrived they ran out with cries of joy, took off his greatcoat and dropped it for the servants on the floor of the hall. It was nice to be the centre of attraction and show off about school. His Guatemala stamps were admired—so were "Those Holy Fields" and a Holbein photograph that Mr Ducie had given him. After tea the weather cleared, and Mrs Hall put on her goloshes and walked with him round the grounds. They went kissing one another and conversing aimlessly.

"Morrie . . ."

"Mummie . . . "

"Now I must give my Morrie a lovely time."

"Where's George?"

"Such a splendid report from Mr Abrahams. He says you remind him of your poor father. . . . Now what shall we do these holidays?"

"I like here best."

"Darling boy . . ." She embraced him, more affectionately than ever.

"There is nothing like home, as everyone finds. Yes, tomatoes—" she liked reciting the names of vegetables. "Tomatoes, radishes, broccoli, onions—"

"Tomatoes, broccoli, onions, purple potatoes, white potatoes," droned the little boy.

"Turnip tops—"

"Mother, where's George?"

"He left last week."

"Why did George leave?" he asked.

"He was getting too old. Howell always changes the boy every two years."

"Oh."

"Turnip-tops," she continued, "potatoes again, beetroot —Morrie, how would you like to pay a little visit to grandpapa and Aunt Ida if they ask us? I want you to have a very nice time this holiday, dear—you have been so good, but then Mr Abrahams is such a good man; you see, your father was at his school too, and we are sending you to your father's old public school too—Sunnington—in order that you may grow up like your dear father in every way."

A sob interrupted her.

"Morrie, *darling*—"

The little boy was in tears.

"My pet, what is it?"

"I don't know . . . I don't know . . ."

"Why, Maurice . . ."

He shook his head. She was grieved at her failure to make him happy, and began to cry too. The girls ran out, exclaiming, "Mother, what's wrong with Maurice?"

"Oh, don't," he wailed. "Kitty, get out—"

"He's overtired," said Mrs Hall—her explanation for everything.

"I'm overtired."

"Come to your room, Morrie—Oh my sweet, this is really too dreadful."

"No—I'm all right." He clenched his teeth, and a great mass of sorrow that had overwhelmed him by rising to the surface began to sink. He could feel it going down into his heart until he was conscious of it no longer. "I'm all right." He looked around him fiercely and dried his eyes. "I'll play Halma, I think." Before the pieces were set, he was talking as before; the childish collapse was over.

He beat Ada, who worshipped him, and Kitty, who did not, and then ran into the garden again to see the coachman. "How d'ye do, Howell. How's Mrs Howell? How d'ye do, Mrs Howell," and so on, speaking in a patronizing voice, different from that he used to gentlefolks. Then altering back, "Isn't it a new garden boy?"

"Yes, Master Maurice."

"Was George too old?"

"No, Master Maurice. He wanted to better himself."

"Oh, you mean he gave notice."

"That's right."

"Mother said he was too old and you gave him notice."

"No, Master Maurice."

"My poor woodstacks'll be glad," said Mrs Howell. Maurice and the late garden boy had been used to play about in them.

"They are Mother's woodstacks, not yours," said Maurice and went indoors. The Howells were not offended, though they pretended to be so to one another. They had been servants all their lives, and liked a gentleman to be a snob. "He has quite a way with him already," they told the cook. "More like his father."

The Barrys, who came to dinner, were of the same opinion. Dr Barry was an old friend, or rather neighbour, of the family, and took a moderate interest in them. No one could be deeply interested in the Halls. Kitty he liked—she had hints of grit in her—but the girls were in bed, and he told his wife afterwards that Maurice ought to have been there too. "And stop there all his life. As he will. Like his father. What is the use of such people?"

When Maurice did go to bed, it was reluctantly. That room always frightened him. He had been such a man all the evening, but the old feeling came over him as soon as his mother had kissed him good night. The trouble was the looking-glass. He did not mind seeing his face in it, nor casting a shadow on the ceiling, but he did mind seeing his shadow on the ceiling reflected in the glass. He would arrange the candle so as to avoid the combination, and then dare himself to put it back and be gripped with fear. He knew what it was, it reminded him of nothing horrible. But he was afraid. In the end he would dash out the candle and leap into bed. Total darkness he could bear, but this room had the further defect of being opposite a street lamp. On good nights the light would penetrate the curtains unalarmingly, but sometimes blots like skulls fell over the furniture. His heart beat violently, and he lay in terror, with all his household close at hand.

As he opened his eyes to look whether the blots had grown smaller, he remembered George. Something stirred in the unfathomable depths of his heart. He whispered, "George, George." Who was George? Nobody—just a common servant. Mother and Ada and Kitty were far more important. But he was too little to argue thus. He did not even know that when he yielded to this sorrow he overcame the spectral and fell asleep.

III

Sunnington was the next stage in Maurice's career. He traversed it without attracting attention. He was not good at work, though better than he pretended, nor colossally good at games. If people noticed him they liked him, for he had a bright friendly face and responded to attention; but there were so many boys of his type—they formed the backbone of the school and we cannot notice each vertebra. He did the usual things—was kept in, once caned, rose from form to form on the classical side till he clung precariously to the sixth, and he became a house prefect, and later a school prefect and member of the first fifteen. Though clumsy, he had strength and physical pluck: at cricket he did not do so well. Having been bullied as a new boy, he bullied others when they seemed unhappy or weak, not because he was cruel but because it was the proper thing to do. In a word, he was a mediocre member of a mediocre school, and left a faint and favourable impression behind. "Hall? Wait a minute, which was Hall? Oh yes, I remember; clean run enough."

Beneath it all, he was bewildered. He had lost the precocious clearness of the child which transfigures and explains the universe, offering answers of miraculous insight and beauty. "Out of the mouths of babes and sucklings . . ." But not out of the mouth of the boy of sixteen. Maurice forgot he had ever been sexless, and only realized in maturity how just and clear the sensations of his earliest days must have been. He sank far below them now, for he was descending the Valley of the Shadow of Life. It lies between the lesser mountains and the greater, and without breathing its fogs no one can come through. He groped about in it longer than most boys.

Where all is obscure and unrealized the best similitude is

a dream. Maurice had two dreams at school; they will interpret him.

In the first dream he felt very cross. He was playing football against a nondescript whose existence he resented. He made an effort and the nondescript turned into George, that garden boy. But he had to be careful or it would reappear. George headed down the field towards him, naked and jumping over the woodstacks. "I shall go mad if he turns wrong now," said Maurice, and just as they collared this happened, and a brutal disappointment woke him up. He did not connect it with Mr Ducie's homily, still less with his second dream, but he thought he was going to be ill, and afterwards that it was somehow a punishment for something.

The second dream is more difficult to convey. Nothing happened. He scarcely saw a face, scarcely heard a voice say, "That is your friend," and then it was over, having filled him with beauty and taught him tenderness. He could die for such a friend, he would allow such a friend to die for him; they would make any sacrifice for each other, and count the world nothing, neither death nor distance nor crossness could part them, because "this is my friend." Soon afterwards he was confirmed and tried to persuade himself that the friend must be Christ. But Christ has a mangy beard. Was he a Greek god, such as illustrates the classical dictionary? More probable, but most probably he was just a man. Maurice forbore to define his dream further. He had dragged it as far into life as it would come. He would never meet that man nor hear that voice again, yet they became more real than anything he knew, and would actually—

"Hall! Dreaming again! A hundred lines!"

"Sir—oh! Dative absolute."

"Dreaming again. Too late."

—would actually pull him back to them in broad daylight and drop a curtain. Then he would reimbibe the face and the four words, and would emerge yearning with tenderness and longing to be kind to everyone, because his friend wished it, and to be good that his friend might become more fond of him. Misery was somehow mixed up with all this happiness. It seemed as certain that he hadn't a friend as that he had one, and he would find a lonely place for tears, attributing them to the hundred lines.

Maurice's secret life can be understood now; it was part brutal, part ideal, like his dreams.

As soon as his body developed he became obscene. He supposed some special curse had descended on him, but he could not help it, for even when receiving the Holy Communion filthy thoughts would arise in his mind. The tone of the school was pure—that is to say, just before his arrival there had been a terrific scandal. The black sheep had been expelled, the remainder were drilled hard all day and policed at night, so it was his fortune or misfortune to have little opportunity of exchanging experiences with his school-fellows. He longed for smut, but heard little and contributed less, and his chief indecencies were solitary. Books: the school library was immaculate, but while at his grandfather's he came across an unexpurgated Martial, and stumbled about in it with burning ears. Thoughts: he had a dirty little collection. Acts: he desisted from these after the novelty was over, finding that they brought him more fatigue than pleasure.

All which, if it can be understood, took place in a trance. Maurice had fallen asleep in the Valley of the Shadow, far beneath the peaks of either range, and knew neither this nor that his school-fellows were sleeping likewise.

The other half of his life seemed infinitely remote from obscenity. As he rose in the school he began to make a religion of some other boy. When this boy, whether older or younger than himself, was present, he would laugh loudly, talk absurdly, and be unable to work. He dared not be kind—it was not the thing—still less to express his admiration in words. And the adored one would shake him off before long, and reduce him to sulks. However, he had his revenges. Other boys sometimes worshipped him, and when he realized this he would shake off them. The adoration was mutual on one occasion, both yearning for they knew not what, but the result was the same. They quarrelled in a few days. All that came out of the chaos were the two feelings of beauty and tenderness that he had first felt in a dream. They grew yearly, flourishing like plants that are all leaves and show no sign of flower. Towards the close of his education at Sunnington the growth stopped. A check, a silence, fell upon the complex processes, and very timidly the youth began to look around him.

IV

He was nearly nineteen.

He stood on the platform on Prize Day, reciting a Greek Oration of his own composition. The hall was full of schoolboys and their parents, but Maurice affected to be addressing the Hague Conference, and to be pointing out to it the folly of its ways. "What stupidity is this, O andres Europenaici, to talk of abolishing war? What? Is not Ares the son of Zeus himself? Moreover, war renders you robust by exercising your limbs, not forsooth like those of my opponent." The Greek was vile: Maurice had got the prize on account of the Thought, and barely thus. The examining master had stretched a point in his favour since he was leaving and a respectable chap, and moreover leaving for Cambridge, where prize books on his shelves would help to advertise the school. So he received Grote's *History of Greece* amid tremendous applause. As he returned to his seat, which was next to his mother, he realized that he had again become popular, and wondered how. The clapping continued—it grew to an ovation; Ada and Kitty were pounding away with scarlet faces on the further side. Some of his friends, also leaving, cried "speech". This was irregular and quelled by the authorities, but the Headmaster himself rose and said a few words. Hall was one of them, and they would never cease to feel him so. The words were just. The school clapped not because Maurice was eminent but because he was average. It could celebrate itself in his image. People ran up to him afterwards saying "jolly good, old man", quite sentimentally, and even "it will be bilge in this hole without you." His relations shared in the triumph. On previous visits he had been hateful to them. "Sorry, mater, but you and the kids will have to walk alone" had been his remark after a football match when they had tried to join on to him in his mud and glory: Ada had cried. Now Ada was chatting quite ably to the Captain of the School, and Kitty was being handed cakes, and his mother was listening to his housemaster's wife, on the disappointments of installing hot air. Everyone and everything had suddenly harmonized. Was this the world?

A few yards off he saw Dr Barry, their neighbour from home, who caught his eye and called out in his alarming way, "Congratulations, Maurice, on your triumph. Overwhelming! I drink to it in this cup"—he drained it—"of extremely nasty tea."

Maurice laughed and went up to him, rather guiltily; for his conscience was bad. Dr Barry had asked him to befriend a little nephew, who had entered the school that term, but he had done nothing—it was not the thing. He wished that he had had more courage now that it was too late and he felt a man.

"And what's the next stage in your triumphal career? Cambridge?"

"So they say."

"So they say, do they? And what do you say?"

"I don't know," said the hero good-temperedly.

"And after Cambridge, what? Stock Exchange?"

"I suppose so—my father's old partner talks of letting me in if all goes well."

"And after you're let in by your father's old partner, what? A pretty wife?"

Maurice laughed again.

"Who will present the expectant world with a Maurice the third? After which old age, grandchildren, and finally the daisies. So that's your notion of a career. Well, it isn't mine."

"What's your notion, Doctor?" called Kitty.

"To help the weak and right the wrong, my dear," he replied, looking across at her.

"I'm sure it is all our notions," said the housemaster's wife, and Mrs Hall agreed.

"Oh no, it's not. It isn't consistently mine, or I should be looking after my Dickie instead of lingering on this scene of splendour."

"Do bring dear Dickie to say how d'ye do to me," asked Mrs Hall. "Is his father down here too?"

"Mother!" Kitty whispered.

"Yes. My brother died last year," said Dr Barry. "The incident slipped your memory. War did not render him robust by exercising his limbs, as Maurice supposes. He got a shell in the stomach."

He left them.

"I think Dr Barry gets cynical," remarked Ada. "I think he's jealous." She was right: Dr Barry, who had been a lady killer in his time, did resent the continuance of young men. Poor Maurice encountered him again. He had been saying goodbye to his housemaster's wife, who was a handsome woman, very civil to the older boys. They shook hands warmly. On turning away he heard Dr Barry's "Well, Maurice; a youth irresistible in love as in war," and caught his cynical glance.

"I don't know what you mean, Dr Barry."

"Oh, you young fellows! Butter wouldn't melt in your mouth these days. Don't know what I mean! Prudish of a petticoat! Be frank, man, be frank. You don't take anyone in. The frank mind's the pure mind. I'm a medical man and an old man and I tell you that. Man that is born of woman must go with woman if the human race is to continue."

Maurice stared after the housemaster's wife, underwent a violent repulsion from her, and blushed crimson: he had remembered Mr Ducie's diagrams. A trouble—nothing as beautiful as a sorrow—rose to the surface of his mind, displayed its ungainliness, and sank. Its precise nature he did not ask himself, for his hour was not yet, but the hint was appalling, and, hero though he was, he longed to be a little boy again, and to stroll half awake for ever by the colourless sea. Dr Barry went on lecturing him, and under the cover of a friendly manner said much that gave pain.

V

He chose a college patronized by his chief school friend Chapman and by other old Sunningtonians, and during his first year managed to experience little in University life that was unfamiliar. He belonged to an Old Boys' Club, and they played games together, tea'd and lunched together, kept up their provincialisms and slang, sat elbow to elbow in hall, and walked arm in arm about the streets. Now and then they got drunk and boasted mysteriously about women, but their outlook remained that of the upper fifth, and some of them kept it through life. There was no feud between them and the other undergraduates, but they were too compact to be popular, too mediocre to lead, and they did not care to risk knowing men who had come from other public schools. All this suited Maurice. He was constitutionally lazy. Though none of his difficulties had been solved, none were added, which is something. The hush continued. He was less troubled by carnal thoughts. He stood still in the darkness instead of groping about in it, as if this was the end for which body and soul had been so painfully prepared.

During his second year he underwent a change. He had moved into college and it began to digest him. His days he might spend as before, but when the gates closed on him at night a new process began. Even as a freshman he made the important discovery that grown-up men behave politely to one another unless there is a reason for the contrary. Some third-year people had called on him in his digs. He had expected them to break his plates and insult the photograph of his mother, and when they did not he ceased planning how some day he should break theirs, thus saving time. And the manners of the dons were even more remarkable. Maurice was only waiting for such an atmosphere himself to soften. He did not enjoy being cruel and rude. It was against his nature. But it was necessary at school, or he might have gone under, and he had supposed it would have been even more necessary on the larger battlefield of the University.

Once inside college, his discoveries multiplied. People turned out to be alive. Hitherto he had supposed that they *were* what he *pretended* to be—flat pieces of cardboard stamped with a conventional design—but as he strolled about the courts at night and saw through the windows some men singing and others arguing and others at their books, there came by no process of reason a conviction that they were human beings with feelings akin to his own. He had never lived frankly since Mr Abrahams's school, and despite Dr Barry did not mean to begin; but he saw that while deceiving others he had been deceived, and mistaken them for the empty creatures he wanted them to think he was. No, they too had insides. "But, O Lord, not such an inside as mine." As soon as he thought about other people as real, Maurice became modest and conscious of sin: in all creation there could be no one as vile as himself: no wonder he pretended to be a piece of cardboard; if known as he was, he would be hounded out of the world. God, being altogether too large an order, did not worry him: he could not conceive of any censure being more terrific than, say, Joey Fetherstonhaugh's, who kept in the rooms below, or of any Hell as bitter as Coventry.

Shortly after this discovery he went to lunch with Mr Cornwallis, the Dean.

There were two other guests, Chapman and a B.A. from Trinity, a relative of the Dean's, by name Risley. Risley was dark, tall and affected. He made an exaggerated gesture when introduced, and when he spoke, which was continually, he used strong yet unmanly superlatives. Chapman caught Maurice's eye and distended his nostrils, inviting him to side against the newcomer. Maurice thought he would wait a bit first. His disinclination to give pain was increasing, and besides he was not sure that he loathed Risley, though no doubt he ought to, and in a minute should. So Chapman ventured alone. Finding Risley adored music, he began to run it down, saying, "I don't go in for being superior," and so on.

"I do!"

"Oh, do you! In that case I beg your pardon."

"Come along, Chapman, you are in need of food," called Mr Cornwallis, and promised himself some amusement at lunch.

" 'Spect Mr Risley isn't. I've put him off with my low talk."

They sat down, and Risley turned with a titter to Maurice and said, "I simply *can't* think of any reply to that;" in each of his sentences he accented one word violently. "It is so humiliating. 'No' won't do. 'Yes' won't do. What *is* to be done?"

"What about saying nothing?" said the Dean.

"To say nothing? Horrible. You must be mad."

"Are you always talking, may one ask?" inquired Chapman.

Risley said he was.

"Never get tired of it?"

"Never."

"Ever tire other people?"

"Never."

"Odd that."

"Do not suggest I've tired you. Untrue, untrue, you're beaming."

"It's not at you if I am," said Chapman, who was hot-tempered.

Maurice and the Dean laughed.

"I come to a standstill again. How amazing are the difficulties of conversation."

"You seem to carry on better than most of us can," remarked Maurice. He had not spoken before, and his voice, which was low but very gruff, made Risley shiver.

"Naturally. It is my forte. It is the only thing I care about, conversation."

"Is that serious?"

"Everything I say is serious." And somehow Maurice knew this was true. It had struck him at once that Risley was serious. "And are you serious?"

"Don't ask me."

"Then talk until you become so."

"Rubbish," growled the Dean.

Chapman laughed tempestuously.

"Rubbish?" He questioned Maurice, who, when he grasped the point, was understood to reply that deeds are more important than words.

"What is the difference? Words *are* deeds. Do you mean to say that these five minutes in Cornwallis's rooms have done nothing for you? Will you *ever* forget you have met me, for instance?"

Chapman grunted.

"But he will not, nor will you. And then I am told we ought to be doing something."

The Dean came to the rescue of the two Sunningtonians. He said to his young cousin, "You're unsound about memory. You confuse what's important with what's impressive. No doubt Chapman and Hall always will remember they've met you—"

"And forget this is a cutlet. Quite so."

"But the cutlet does some good to them, and you none."

"Obscurantist!"

"This is just like a book," said Chapman. "Eh, Hall?"

"I mean," said Risley, "oh how clearly I mean that the cutlet influences your subconscious lives, and I your conscious, and so I am not only more impressive than the cutlet but more important. Your Dean here, who dwells in Medieval Darkness and wishes you to do the same, pretends that only the subconscious, only the part of you that can be touched without your knowledge is important, and daily he drops soporific—"

"Oh, shut up," said the Dean.

"But I am a child of light—"

"Oh, shut up." And he turned the conversation on to normal lines. Risley was not egotistic, though he always talked about himself. He did not interrupt. Nor did he feign indifference. Gambolling like a dolphin, he accompanied them whithersoever they went, without hindering their course. He was at play, but seriously. It was as important to him to go to and fro as to them to go forward, and he loved keeping near them. A few months earlier Maurice would have agreed with Chapman, but now he was sure the man had an inside, and he wondered whether he should see more of him. He was pleased when, after lunch was over, Risley waited for him at the bottom of the sairs and said,

"You didn't see. My cousin wasn't being human."

"He's good enough for us; that's all I know," exploded Chapman. "He's absolutely delightful."

"Exactly. Eunuchs are." And he was gone.

"Well, I'm—" exclaimed the other, but with British self-control suppressed the verb. He was deeply shocked. He didn't mind hot stuff in moderation, he told Maurice, but this was too much, it was bad form, ungentlemanly, the fellow could not have been through a public school. Maurice agreed. You could call your cousin a shit if you liked, but not a eunuch. Rotten style! All the same he was amused, and whenever he was hauled in in the future, mischievous and incongruous thoughts would occur to him about the Dean.

VI

All that day and the next Maurice was planning how he could see this queer fish again. The chances were bad. He did not like to call on a senior-year man, and they were at different colleges. Risley, he gathered, was well known at the Union, and he went to the Tuesday debate in the hope of hearing him: perhaps he would be easier to understand in public. He was not attracted to the man in the sense that he wanted him for a friend, but he did feel he might help him—how, he didn't formulate. It was all very obscure, for the mountains still overshadowed Maurice. Risley, surely capering on the summit, might stretch him a helping hand.

Having failed at the Union, he had a reaction. He didn't want anyone's help; he was all right. Besides, none of his friends would stand Risley, and he must stick to his friends. But the reaction soon passed, and he longed to see him more than ever. Since Risley was so odd, might he not be odd too, and break all the undergraduate conventions by calling? One "ought to be human", and it was a human sort of thing to call. Much struck by the discovery, Maurice decided to be Bohemian also, and to enter the room making a witty speech in Risley's own style. "You've bargained for more than you've gained" occurred to him. It didn't sound very good, but Risley had been clever at not letting him feel a fool, so he would fire it off if inspired to nothing better, and leave the rest to luck.

For it had become an adventure. This man who said one ought to "talk, talk" had stirred Maurice incomprehensibly. One night, just before ten o'clock, he slipped into Trinity and waited in the Great Court until the gates were shut behind him. Looking up, he noticed the night. He was indifferent to beauty as a rule, but "what a show of stars!"

he thought. And how the fountain splashed when the chimes died away, and the gates and doors all over Cambridge had been fastened up. Trinity men were around him—all of enormous intellect and culture. Maurice's set had laughed at Trinity, but they could not ignore its disdainful radiance, or deny the superiority it scarcely troubles to affirm. He had come to it without their knowledge, humbly, to ask its help. His witty speech faded in its atmosphere; and his heart beat violently. He was ashamed and afraid.

Risley's rooms were at the end of a short passage; which since it contained no obstacle was unlighted, and visitors slid along the wall until they hit the door. Maurice hit it sooner than he expected—a most awful whack—and exclaimed "Oh damnation" loudly, while the panels quivered.

"Come in," said a voice. Disappointment awaited him. The speaker was a man of his own college, by name Durham. Risley was out.

"Do you want Mr Risley? Hullo, Hall!"

"Hullo! Where's Risley?"

"I don't know."

"Oh, it's nothing. I'll go."

"Are you going back into college?" asked Durham without looking up: he was kneeling over a castle of pianola records on the floor.

"I suppose so, as he isn't here. It wasn't anything particular."

"Wait a sec, and I'll come too. I'm sorting out the Pathetic Symphony."

Maurice examined Risley's room and wondered what would have been said in it, and then sat on the table and looked at Durham. He was a small man—very small—with simple manners and a fair face, which had flushed when Maurice blundered in. In the college he had a reputation for brains and also for exclusiveness. Almost the only thing Maurice had heard about him was that he "went out too much", and this meeting in Trinity confirmed it.

"I can't find the March," he said. "Sorry."

"All right."

"I'm borrowing them to play on Fetherstonhaugh's pianola."

"Under me."

"Have you come into college, Hall?"

"Yes, I'm beginning my second year."

"Oh yes, of course, I'm third."

He spoke without arrogance, and Maurice, forgetting due honour to seniority, said, "You look more like a fresher than a third-year man, I must say."

"I may do, but I feel like an M.A."

Maurice regarded him attentively.

"Risley's an amazing chap," he continued.

Maurice did not reply.

"But all the same a little of him goes a long way."

"Still you don't mind borrowing his things."

He looked up again. "Oughtn't I to?" he asked.

"I'm only ragging, of course," said Maurice, slipping off the table. "Have you found that music yet?"

"No."

"Because I must be going"; he was in no hurry, but his heart, which had never stopped beating quickly, impelled him to say this.

"Oh. All right."

This was not what Maurice had intended. "What is it you want?" he asked, advancing.

"The March out of the Pathétique—"

"That means nothing to me. So you like this style of music."

"I do."

"A good waltz is more my style."

"Mine too," said Durham, meeting his eye. As a rule Maurice shifted, but he held firm on this occasion. Then Durham said, "The other movement may be in that pile over by the window. I must look. I shan't be long."

Maurice said resolutely, "I must go now."

"All right, I'll stop."

Beaten and lonely, Maurice went. The stars blurred, the night had turned towards rain. But while the porter was getting the keys at the gate he heard quick footsteps behind him.

"Got your March?"

"No, I thought I'd come along with you instead."

Maurice walked a few steps in silence, then said, "Here, give me some of those things to carry."

"I've got them safe."

"Give," he said roughly, and jerked the records from under Durham's arm. No other conversation passed. On reaching their own college they went straight to Fetherstonhaugh's room, for there was time to try a little music over before eleven o'clock. Durham sat down at the pianola. Maurice knelt beside him.

"Didn't know you were in the aesthetic push, Hall," said the host.

"I'm not—I want to hear what they're up to."

Durham began, then desisted, saying he would start with the 5/4 instead.

"Why?"

"It's nearer waltzes."

"Oh, never mind that. Play what you like. Don't go shifting—it wastes time."

But he could not get his way this time. When he put his hand on the roller Durham said, "You'll tear it, let go," and fixed the 5/4 instead.

Maurice listened carefully to the music. He rather liked it.

"You ought to be this end," said Fetherstonhaugh, who was working by the fire. "You should get away from the machine as far as you can."

"I think so—Would you mind playing it again if Fetherstonhaugh doesn't mind?"

"Yes, do, Durham. It is a jolly thing."

Durham refused. Maurice saw that he was not pliable. He said, "A movement isn't like a separate piece—you can't repeat it"—an unintelligible excuse, but apparently valid. He played the Largo, which was far from jolly, and then eleven struck and Fetherstonhaugh made them tea. He and Durham were in for the same Tripos, and talked shop, while Maurice listened. His excitement had never ceased. He saw that Durham was not only clever, but had a tranquil and orderly brain. He knew what he wanted to read, where he was weak, and how far the officials could help him. He had neither the blind faith in tutors and lectures that was held by Maurice and his set nor the contempt professed by Fetherstonhaugh. "You can always learn something from an older man, even if he hasn't read the latest Germans." They argued a little about Sophocles, then in low water Durham said it was a pose in "us undergraduates" to ignore him and advised Fetherstonhaugh to re-read the *Ajax* with his eye on the characters rather than the author; he would learn more that way, both about Greek grammar and life.

Maurice regretted all this. He had somehow hoped to find the man unbalanced. Fetherstonhaugh was a great person, both in brain and brawn, and had a trenchant and copious manner. But Durham listened unmoved, shook out the falsities and approved the rest. What hope for Maurice who was nothing but falsities? A stab of anger went through him. Jumping up, he said good night, to regret his haste as soon as he was outside the door. He settled to wait, not on the staircase itself, for this struck him as absurd, but somewhere between its foot and Durham's own room. Going out into the court, he located the latter, even knocking at the door, though he knew the owner was absent, and looking in he studied furniture and pictures in the firelight. Then he took his stand on a sort of bridge in the courtyard. Unfortunately it was not a real bridge: it only spanned a slight depression in the ground, which the architect had tried to utilize in his effect. To stand on it was to feel in a photographic studio, and the parapet was too low to lean upon. Still, with a pipe in his mouth, Maurice looked fairly natural, and hoped it wouldn't rain.

The lights were out, except in Fetherstonhaugh's room. Twelve struck, then a quarter past. For a whole hour he might have been watching for Durham. Presently there was a noise on the staircase and the neat little figure ran out with a gown round its throat and books in its hand. It was the moment for which he had waited, but he found himself strolling away. Durham went to his rooms behind him. The opportunity was passing.

"Good night," he screamed; his voice was going out of gear, and startling them both.

"Who's that? Good night, Hall. Taking a stroll before bed?"

"I generally do. You don't want any more tea, I suppose?"

"Do I? No, perhaps it's a bit late for tea." Rather tepidly he added, "Like some whisky though?"

"Have you a drop?" leaped from Maurice.

"Yes—come in. Here I keep: ground floor."

"Oh, here!" Durham turned on the light. The fire was nearly out now. He told Maurice to sit down and brought up a table with glasses.

"Say when?"

"Thanks—most awfully, most awfully."

"Soda or plain?" he asked, yawning.

"Soda," said Maurice. But it was impossible to stop, for the man was tired and had only invited him out of civility. He drank and returned to his own room, where he provided himself with plenty of tobacco and went into the court again.

It was absolutely quiet now, and absolutely dark. Maurice walked to and fro on the hallowed grass, himself noiseless, his heart glowing. The rest of him fell asleep, bit by bit, and first of all his brain, his weakest organ. His body followed, then his feet carried him upstairs to escape the dawn. But his heart had lit never to be quenched again, and one thing in him at last was real.

Next morning he was calmer. He had a cold for one thing, the rain having soaked him unnoticed, and for another he had overslept to the extent of missing a chapel and two lectures. It was impossible to get his life straight. After lunch he changed for football, and being in good time flung himself on his sofa to sleep till tea. But he was not hungry. Refusing an invitation, he strolled out into the town and, meeting a Turkish bath, had one. It cured his cold, but made him late for another lecture. When Hall came, he felt he could not face the mass of Old Sunningtonians, and, though he had not signed off, absented himself, and dined alone at the Union. He saw Risley there, but with indifference. Then the evening began again, and he found to his surprise that he was very clear-headed, and could do six hours' work in three. He went to bed at his usual time, and woke up healthy and very happy. Some instinct, deep below his consciousness, had advised him to let Durham and his thoughts about Durham have a twenty-four hours' rest.

They began to see a little of one another. Durham asked him to lunch, and Maurice asked him back, but not too soon. A caution alien to his nature was at work. He had always been cautious pettily, but this was on a large scale. He became alert, and all his actions that October term might be described in the language of battle. He would not venture on to difficult ground. He spied out Durham's weaknesses as well as his strength. And above all he exercised and cleaned his powers.

If obliged to ask himself, "What's all this?" he would have replied, "Durham is another of those boys in whom I was interested at school," but he was obliged to ask nothing, and merely went ahead with his mouth and his mind shut. Each day with its contradictions slipped into the abyss, and he knew that he was gaining ground. Nothing else mattered. If he worked well and was nice socially, it was only a by-product, to which he had devoted no care. To ascend, to stretch a hand up the mountainside until a hand catches it, was the end for which he had been born. He forgot the hysteria of his first night and his stranger recovery. They were steps which he kicked behind him. He never even thought of tenderness and emotion; his considerations about Durham remained cold. Durham didn't dislike him, he was sure. That was all he wanted. One thing at a time. He didn't so much as have hopes, for hope distracts, and he had a great deal to see to.

VII

Next term they were intimate at once.

"Hall, I nearly wrote a letter to you in the vac," said Durham, plunging into a conversation.

"That so?"

"But an awful screed. I'd been having a rotten time."

His voice was not very serious, and Maurice said, "What went wrong? Couldn't you keep down the Christmas pudding?"

It presently appeared that the pudding was allegorical; there had been a big family row.

"I don't know what you'll say—I'd rather like your opinion on what happened if it doesn't bore you."

"Not a bit," said Maurice.

"We've had a bust up on the religious question."

At that moment they were interrupted by Chapman.

"I'm sorry, we're fixing something," Maurice told him. Chapman withdrew.

"You needn't have done that, any time would do for my rot," Durham protested. He went on more earnestly.

"Hall, I don't want to worry you with my beliefs, or rather with their absence, but to explain the situation I must just tell you that I'm unorthodox. I'm not a Christian."

Maurice held unorthodoxy to be bad form and had remarked last term in a college debate that if a man had doubts he might have the grace to keep them to himself. But he only said to Durham that it was a difficult question and a wide one.

"I know—it isn't about that. Leave it aside." He looked for a little into the fire. "It is about the way my mother took it. I told her six months ago—in the summer—and she didn't mind. She made some foolish joke, as she does, but that was all. It just passed over. I was thankful, for it had been on my mind for years. I had never believed since I found something that did me better, quite as a kid, and when I came to know Risley and his crew it seemed imperative to speak out. You know what a point they make of that—it's really their main point. So I spoke out. She said, 'Oh yes, you'll be wiser when you are as old as me': the mildest form of the thing conceivable, and I went away rejoicing. Now it's all come up again."

"Why?"

"Why? On account of Christmas. I didn't want to communicate. You're supposed to receive it three times a year—"

"Yes, I know. Holy Communion."

"—and at Christmas it came round. I said I wouldn't. Mother wheedled me in a way quite unlike her, asked me to do it this once to please her—then got cross, said I would damage her reputation as well as my own—we're the local squires and the neighbourhood's uncivilized. But what I couldn't stand was the end. She said I was wicked. I could have honoured her if she had said that six months before, but now! now to drag in holy words like wickedness and goodness in order to make me do what I disbelieved. I told her I have my own communions. 'If I went to them as you and the girls are doing to yours my gods would kill me!' I suppose that was too strong."

Maurice, not well understanding, said, "So did you go?"

"Where?"

"To the church."

Durham sprang up. His face was disgusted. Then he bit his lip and began to smile.

"No, I didn't go to church, Hall. I thought that was plain."

"I'm sorry—I wish you'd sit down. I didn't mean to offend you. I'm rather slow at catching."

Durham squatted on the rug close to Maurice's chair.

"Have you known Chapman long?" he asked after a pause.

"Here and at school, five years."

"Oh." He seemed to reflect. "Give me a cigarette. Put it in my mouth. Thanks." Maurice supposed the talk was over, but after the swirl he went on. "You see—you mentioned you had a mother and two sisters, which is exactly my own allowance, and all through the row I was wondering what you would have done in my position."

"Your mother must be very different to mine."

"What is yours like?"

"She never makes a row about anything."

"Because you've never yet done anything she wouldn't approve, I expect—and never will."

"Oh no, she wouldn't fag herself."

"You can't tell, Hall, especially with women. I'm sick with her. That's my real trouble that I want your help about."

"She'll come round."

"Exactly, my dear chap, but shall I? I must have been pretending to like her. This row has shattered my lie. I did think I had stopped building lies. I despise her character, I am disgusted with her. There, I have told you what no one else in the world knows."

Maurice clenched his fist and hit Durham lightly on the head with it. "Hard luck," he breathed.

"Tell me about your home life."

"There's nothing to tell. We just go on."

"Lucky devils."

"Oh, I don't know. Are you ragging, or was your vac really beastly, Durham?"

"Absolute Hell, misery and Hell."

Maurice's fist unclenched to reform with a handful of hair in its grasp.

"Waou, that hurts!" cried the other joyously.

"What did your sisters say about Holy Communion?"

"One's married a clerg—No, that hurts."

"Absolute Hell, eh?"

"Hall, I never knew you were a fool—" he possessed himself of Maurice's hand— "and the other's engaged to Archibald London, Esquire, of the—Waou! Ee! Shut up, I'm going." He fell between Maurice's knees.

"Well, why don't you go if you're going?"

"Because I can't go."

It was the first time he had dared to play with Durham. Religion and relatives faded into the background, as he rolled him up in the hearth rug and fitted his head into the waste-paper basket. Hearing the noise, Fetherstonhaugh ran up and helped. There was nothing but ragging for many days after that, Durham becoming quite as silly as himself. Wherever they met, which was everywhere, they would butt and spar and embroil their friends. At last Durham got tired. Being the weaker he was hurt sometimes, and his chairs had been broken. Maurice felt the change at once. His coltishness passed, but they had become demonstrative during it. They walked arm in arm or arm around shoulder now. When they sat it was nearly always in the same position—Maurice in a chair, and Durham at his feet, leaning against him. In the world of their friends this attracted no notice. Maurice would stroke Durham's hair.

And their range increased elsewhere. During this Lent term Maurice came out as a theologian. It was not humbug entirely. He believed that he believed, and felt genuine pain when anything he was accustomed to met criticism—the pain that masquerades among the middle classes as Faith. It was not Faith, being inactive. It gave him no support, no wider outlook. It didn't exist till opposition touched it, when it ached like a useless nerve. They all had these nerves at home, and regarded them as divine, though neither the Bible nor the Prayer Book nor the Sacraments nor Christian ethics nor anything spiritual were alive to them. "But how can people?" they exclaimed, when anything was attacked, and subscribed to Defence Societies. Maurice's father was becoming a pillar of Church and

Society when he died, and other things being alike Maurice would have stiffened too.

But other things were not to be alike. He had this overwhelming desire to impress Durham. He wanted to show his friend that he had something besides brute strength, and where his father would have kept canny silence he began to talk, talk. "You think I don't think, but I can tell you I do." Very often Durham made no reply and Maurice would be terrified lest he was losing him. He had heard it said, "Durham's all right as long as you amuse him, then he drops you," and feared lest by exhibiting his orthodoxy he was bringing on what he tried to avoid. But he could not stop. The craving for notice grew overwhelming, so he talked, talked.

One day Durham said, "Hall, why this thusness?"

"Religion means a lot to me," bluffed Maurice. "Because I say so little you think I don't feel. I care a lot."

"In that case come to coffee after hall."

They were just going in. Durham being a scholar had to read grace, and there was cynicism in his accent. During the meal they looked at each other. They sat at different tables, but Maurice had contrived to move his seat so that he could glance at his friend. The phase of bread pellets was over. Durham looked severe this evening and was not speaking to his neighbours. Maurice knew that he was thoughtful and wondered what about.

"You wanted to get it and you're going to," said Durham, sporting the door.

Maurice went cold and then crimson. But Durham's voice, when he next heard it, was attacking his opinions on the Trinity. He thought he minded about the Trinity, yet it seemed unimportant, beside the fires of his terror. He sprawled in an armchair, all the strength out of him, with sweat on his forehead and hands. Durham moved about getting the coffee ready and saying, "I knew you wouldn't like this, but you have brought it on yourself. You can't expect me to bottle myself up indefinitely. I must let out sometimes."

"Go on," said Maurice, clearing his throat.

"I never meant to talk, for I respect people's opinions too much to laugh at them, but it doesn't seem to me that you have any opinions to respect. They're all second-hand tags —no, tenth-hand."

Maurice, who was recovering, remarked that this was pretty strong.

"You're always saying, 'I care a lot.' "

"And what right have you to assume that I don't?"

"You do care a lot about something, Hall, but it obviously isn't the Trinity."

"What is it then?"

"Rugger."

Maurice had another attack. His hand shook and he spilt the coffee on the arm of the chair. "You're a bit unfair," he heard himself saying. "You might at least have the grace to suggest that I care about people."

Durham looked surprised, but said, "You care nothing about the Trinity, any way."

"Oh, damn the Trinity."

He burst with laughter. "Exactly, exactly. We will now pass on to my next point."

"I don't see the use, and I've a rotten head any way—I mean a headache. Nothing's gained by—all this. No doubt I can't prove the thing—I mean the arrangement of Three Gods in One and One in Three. But it means a lot to millions of people, whatever you may say, and we aren't going to give it up. We feel about it very deeply. God is good. That is the main point. Why go off on a side track?"

"Why feel so deeply about a side track?'

"What?"

Durham tidied up his remarks for him.

"Well, the whole show all hangs together."

"So that if the Trinity went wrong it would invalidate the whole show?"

"I don't see that. Not at all."

He was doing badly, but his head really did ache, and when he wiped the sweat off it re-formed.

"No doubt I can't explain well, as I care for nothing but rugger."

Durham came and sat humorously on the edge of his chair.

"Look out—you've gone into the coffee now."

"Blast—so I have."

While he cleaned himself, Maurice unsported and looked out into the court. It seemed years since he had left it. He felt disinclined to be longer alone with Durham and called to some men to join them. A coffee of the usual type ensued, but when they left Maurice felt equally disinclined to leave with them. He flourished the Trinity again. "It's a mystery," he argued.

"It isn't a mystery to me. But I honour anyone to whom it really is."

Maurice felt uncomfortable and looked at his own thick brown hands. Was the Trinity really a mystery to him? Except at his confirmation had he given the institution five minutes thought? The arrival of the other men had cleared his head, and, no longer emotional, he glanced at his mind. It appeared like his hands—serviceable, no doubt, and healthy, and capable of development. But it lacked refinement, it had never touched mysteries, nor a good deal else. It was thick and brown.

"My position's this," he announced after a pause. "I don't believe in the Trinity, I give in there, but on the other hand I was wrong when I said everything hangs together. It doesn't, and because I don't believe in the Trinity it doesn't mean I am not a Christian."

"What do you believe in?" said Durham, unchecked.

"The—the essentials."

"As?"

In a low voice Maurice said, "The Redemption." He had never spoken the words out of church before and thrilled with emotion. But he did not believe in them any more than in the Trinity, and knew that Durham would detect this. The Redemption was the highest card in the suit, but that suit wasn't trumps, and his friend could capture it with some miserable two.

All that Durham said at the time was, "Dante did believe in the Trinity," and going to the shelf found the concluding passage of the *Paradiso.* He read to Maurice about the three rainbow circles that intersect, and between their junctions is enshadowed a human face. Poetry bored Maurice, but towards the close he cried, "Whose face was it?"

"God's, don't you see?"

"But isn't that poem supposed to be a dream?"

Hall was a muddle-headed fellow, and Durham did not try to make sense of this, nor knew that Maurice was thinking of a dream of his own at school, and of the voice that had said, "That is your friend."

"Dante would have called it an awakening, not a dream."

"Then you think that sort of stuff's all right?"

"Belief's always right," replied Durham, putting back the book. "It's all right and it's also unmistakable. Every man has somewhere about him some belief for which he'd die. Only isn't it improbable that your parents and guardians told it to you? If there is one won't it be part of your own flesh and spirit? Show me that. Don't go hawking out tags like 'The Redemption' or 'The Trinity'."

"I've given up the Trinity."

"The Redemption, then."

"You're beastly hard," said Maurice. "I always knew I was stupid, it's no news. The Risley set are more your sort and you had better talk to them."

Durham looked awkward. He was nonplussed for a reply at last, and let Maurice slouch off without protest. Next day they met as usual. It had not been a tiff but a sudden gradient, and they travelled all the quicker after the rise. They talked theology again, Maurice defending the Redemption. He lost. He realized that he had no sense of Christ's existence or of his goodness, and should be positively sorry if there was such a person. His dislike of Christianity grew and became profound. In ten days he gave up communicating, in three weeks he cut out all the chapels he dared. Durham was puzzled by the rapidity. They were both puzzled, and Maurice, although he had lost and yielded all his opinions, had a queer feeling that he was really winning and carrying on a campaign that he had begun last term.

For Durham wasn't bored with him now. Durham couldn't do without him, and would be found at all hours curled up in his room and spoiling to argue. It was so unlike the man, who was reserved and no great dialectician. He gave as his reason for attacking Maurice's opinions that "They are so rotten, Hall, everyone else up here believes respectably." Was this the whole truth? Was there not something else behind his new manner and furious iconoclasm? Maurice thought there was. Outwardly in retreat, he thought that his Faith was a pawn well lost; for in capturing it Durham had exposed his heart.

Towards the end of term they touched upon a yet more delicate subject. They attended the Dean's translation class, and when one of the men was forging quietly ahead Mr Cornwallis observed in a flat toneless voice: "Omit: a reference to the unspeakable vice of the Greeks." Durham observed afterwards that he ought to lose his fellowship for such hypocrisy.

Maurice laughed.

"I regard it as a point of pure scholarship. The Greeks, or most of them, were that way inclined, and to omit it is to omit the mainstay of Athenian society."

"Is that so?"

"You've read the *Symposium*?"

Maurice had not, and did not add that he had explored Martial.

"It's all in there—not meat for babes, of course, but you ought to read it. Read it this vac."

No more was said at the time, but he was free of another subject, and one that he had never mentioned to any living soul. He hadn't known it could be mentioned, and when Durham did so in the middle of the sunlit court a breath of liberty touched him.

VIII

On reaching home he talked about Durham until the fact that he had a friend penetrated into the minds of his family. Ada wondered whether it was brother to a certain Miss Durham—not but what she was an only child—while Mrs Hall confused it with a don named Cumberland. Maurice was deeply wounded. One strong feeling arouses another, and a profound irritation against his womenkind set in. His relations with them hitherto had been trivial but stable, but it seemed iniquitous that anyone should mispronounce the name of the man who was more to him than all the world. Home emasculated everything.

It was the same with his atheism. No one felt as deeply as he expected. With the crudity of youth he drew his mother apart and said that he should always respect her religious prejudices and those of the girls, but that his own conscience permitted him to attend church no longer. She said it was a great misfortune.

"I knew you would be upset. I cannot help it, mother dearest. I am made that way and it is no good arguing."

"Your poor father always went to church."

"I'm not my father."

"Morrie, Morrie, what a thing to say."

"Well, he isn't," said Kitty in her perky way. "Really, mother, come."

"Kitty, dear, you here," cried Mrs Hall, feeling that disapproval was due and unwilling to bestow it on her son. "We were talking about things not suited, and you are perfectly wrong besides, for Maurice is the image of his father—Dr Barry said so."

"Well, Dr Barry doesn't go to church himself," said Maurice, falling into the family habit of talking all over the shop.

"He is a most clever man," said Mrs Hall with finality, "and Mrs Barry's the same."

This slip of their mother's convulsed Ada and Kitty. They would not stop laughing at the idea of Mrs Barry's being a man, and Maurice's atheism was forgotten. He did not communicate on Easter Sunday, and supposed the row would come then, as in Durham's case. But no one took any notice, for the suburbs no longer exact Christianity. This disgusted him; it made him look at society with new eyes. Did society, while professing to be so moral and sensitive, really mind anything?

He wrote often to Durham—long letters trying carefully to express shades of feeling. Durham made little of them and said so. His replies were equally long. Maurice never let them out of his pocket, changing them from suit to suit and even pinning them in his pyjamas when he went to bed. He would wake up and touch them and, watching the reflections from the street lamp, remember how he used to feel afraid as a little boy.

Episode of Gladys Olcott.

Miss Olcott was one of their infrequent guests. She had been good to Mrs Hall and Ada in some hydro, and, receiving an invitation, had followed it up. She was charming—at least the women said so, and male callers told the son of the house he was a lucky dog. He laughed, they laughed, and having ignored her at first he took to paying her attentions.

Now Maurice, though he did not know it, had become an attractive young man. Much exercise had tamed his clumsiness. He was heavy but alert, and his face seemed following the example of his body. Mrs Hall put it down to his moustache—"Maurice's moustache will be the making of him"—a remark more profound than she realized. Certainly the little black line of it did pull his face together, and show up his teeth when he smiled, and his clothes suited him also: by Durham's advice he kept to flannel trousers, even on Sunday.

He turned his smile on Miss Olcott—it seemed the proper thing to do. She responded. He put his muscles at her service by taking her out in his new side-car. He sprawled at her feet. Finding she smoked, he persuaded her to stop behind with him in the dining-room and to look between his eyes. Blue vapour quivered and shredded and built dissolving walls, and Maurice's thoughts voyaged with it, to vanish as soon as a window was opened for fresh air. He saw that she was pleased, and his family, servants and all, intrigued; he determined to go further.

Something went wrong at once. Maurice paid her compliments, said that her hair etc. was ripping. She tried to stop him, but he was insensitive, and did not know that he had annoyed her. He had read that girls always pretended to stop men who complimented them. He haunted her. When she excused herself from riding with him on the last day he played the domineering male. She was his guest, she came, and having taken her to some scenery that he considered romantic he pressed her little hand between his own.

It was not that Miss Olcott objected to having her hand pressed. Others had done it and Maurice could have done it had he guessed how. But she knew something was wrong. His touch revolted her. It was a corpse's. Springing up she cried, "Mr Hall, don't be silly. I mean *don't* be silly. I am not saying it to make you sillier."

"Miss Olcott—Gladys—I'd rather die than offend—" growled the boy, trying to keep it up.

"I must go back by train," she said, crying a little. "I must, I'm awfully sorry." She arrived home before him with a sensible little story about a headache and dust in her eyes, but his family also knew that something had gone wrong.

Except for this episode the vac passed pleasantly. Maurice did some reading, following his friend's advice rather than his tutor's, and he asserted in one or two ways his belief that he was grown up. At his instigation his mother dismissed the Howells who had long paralysed the outdoor department, and set up a motor-car instead of a carriage. Everyone was impressed, including the Howells. He also called upon his father's old partner. He had inherited some business aptitude and some money, and it was settled that when he left Cambridge he should enter the firm as an unauthorized clerk; Hill and Hall, Stock Brokers. Maurice was stepping into the niche that England had prepared for him.

IX

During the previous term he had reached an unusual level mentally, but the vac pulled him back towards public-schoolishness. He was less alert, he again behaved as he supposed he was supposed to behave—a perilous feat for one who is not dowered with imagination. His mind, not obscured totally, was often crossed by clouds, and though Miss Olcott had passed, the insincerity that led him to her remained. His family were the main cause of this. He had yet to realize that they were stronger than he and influenced him incalculably. Three weeks in their company left him untidy, sloppy, victorious in every item, yet defeated on the whole. He came back thinking, and even speaking, like his mother or Ada.

Till Durham arrived he had not noticed the deterioration. Durham had not been well, and came up a few days late. When his face, paler than usual, peered round the door, Maurice had a spasm of despair, and tried to recollect where they stood last term, and to gather up the threads of the campaign. He felt himself slack, and afraid of action. The worst part of him rose to the surface, and urged him to prefer comfort to joy.

"Hullo, old man," he said awkwardly.

Durham slipped in without speaking.

"What's wrong?"

"Nothing;" and Maurice knew that he had lost touch. Last term he would have understood this silent entrance.

"Anyhow, take a pew."

Durham sat upon the floor beyond his reach. It was late afternoon. The sounds of the May term, the scents of the Cambridge year in flower, floated in through the window and said to Maurice, "You are unworthy of us." He knew that he was three parts dead, an alien, a yokel in Athens.

He had no business here, nor with such a friend.

"I say, Durham—"

Durham came nearer. Maurice stretched out a hand and felt the head nestle against it. He forgot what he was going to say. The sounds and scents whispered, "You are we, we are youth." Very gently he stroked the hair and ran his fingers down into it as if to caress the brain.

"I say, Durham, have you been all right?"

"Have you?"

"No."

"You wrote you were."

"I wasn't."

The truth in his own voice made him tremble. "A rotten vac and I never knew it," and wondered how long he should know it. The mist would lower again, he felt sure, and with an unhappy sigh he pulled Durham's head against his knee, as though it was a talisman for clear living. It lay there, and he had accomplished a new tenderness—stroked it steadily from temple to throat. Then, removing both hands, he dropped them on either side of him and sat sighing.

"Hall."

Maurice looked.

"Is there some trouble?"

He caressed and again withdrew. It seemed as certain that he hadn't as that he had a friend.

"Anything to do with that girl?"

"No."

"You wrote you liked her."

"I didn't—don't."

Deeper sighs broke from him. They rattled in his throat, turning to groans. His head fell back, and he forgot the pressure of Durham on his knee, forgot that Durham was watching his turbid agony. He stared at the ceiling with wrinkled mouth and eyes, understanding nothing except that man has been created to feel pain and loneliness without help from heaven.

Now Durham stretched up to him, stroked his hair. They clasped one another. They were lying breast against breast soon, head was on shoulder, but just as their cheeks met someone called "Hall" from the court, and he answered: he always had answered when people called. Both started violently, and Durham sprang to the mantelpiece where he leant his head on his arm. Absurd people came thundering up the stairs. They wanted tea. Maurice pointed to it, then was drawn into their conversation, and scarcely noticed his friend's departure. It had been an ordinary talk, he told himself, but too sentimental, and he cultivated a breeziness against their next meeting.

This took place soon enough. With half a dozen others he was starting for the theatre after hall when Durham called him.

"I knew you read the *Symposium* in the vac," he said in a low voice.

Maurice felt uneasy.

"Then you understand—without me saying more—"

"How do you mean?"

Durham could not wait. People were all around them, but with eyes that had gone intensely blue he whispered, "I love you."

Maurice was scandalized, horrified. He was shocked to the bottom of his suburban soul, and exclaimed, "Oh, rot!" The words, the manner, were out of him before he could recall them. "Durham, you're an Englishman. I'm another. Don't talk nonsense. I'm not offended, because I know you don't mean it, but it's the only subject absolutely beyond the limit as you know, it's the worst crime in the calendar, and you must never mention it again. Durham! a rotten notion really—"

But his friend was gone, gone without a word, flying across the court, the bang of his door heard through the sounds of spring.

X

A slow nature such as Maurice's appears insensitive, for it needs time even to feel. Its instinct is to assume that nothing either for good or evil has happened, and to resist the invader. Once gripped, it feels acutely, and its sensations in love are particularly profound. Given time, it can know and impart ecstasy; given time, it can sink to the heart of Hell. Thus it was that his agony began as a slight regret; sleepless nights and lonely days must intensify it into a frenzy that consumed him. It worked inwards, till it touched the root whence body and soul both spring, the "I" that he had been trained to obscure, and, realized at last, doubled its power and grew superhuman. For it might have been joy. New worlds broke loose in him at this, and he saw from the vastness of the ruin what ecstasy he had lost, what a communion.

They did not speak again for two days. Durham would have made it longer, but most of their friends were now in common, and they were bound to meet. Realizing this, he wrote Maurice an icy note suggesting that it would be a public convenience if they behaved as if nothing had happened. He added, "I shall be obliged if you will not mention my criminal morbidity to anyone. I am sure you will do this from the sensible way in which you took the news." Maurice did not reply, but first put the note with the letters he had received during the vac and afterwards burnt them all.

He supposed the climax of agony had come. But he was fresh to real suffering as to reality of any kind. They had yet to meet. On the second afternoon they found themselves in the same four at tennis and the pain grew excruciating. He could scarcely stand or see; if he returned Durham's service the ball sent a throb up his arm. Then they were made to be partners; once they jostled, Durham winced, but managed to laugh in the old fashion.

Moreover, it proved convenient that he should come back to college in Maurice's side-car. He got in without demur. Maurice, who had not been to bed for two nights, went light-headed, turned the machine into a by-lane, and travelled top speed. There was a wagon in front, full of women. He drove straight at them, but when they screamed stuck on his brakes, and just avoided disaster. Durham made no comment. As he indicated in his note, he only spoke when others were present. All other intercourse was to end.

That evening Maurice went to bed as usual. But as he laid his head on the pillows a flood of tears oozed from it. He was horrified. A man crying! Fetherstonhaugh might hear him. He wept stifled in the sheets, he sprang about kissing, then struck his head against the wall and smashed the crockery. Someone did come up the stairs. He grew quiet at once and did not recommence when the footsteps died away. Lighting a candle, he looked with surprise at his torn pyjamas and trembling limbs. He continued to cry, for he could not stop, but the suicidal point had been passed, and, remaking the bed, he lay down. His gyp was clearing away the ruins when he opened his eyes. It seemed queer to Maurice that a gyp should have been dragged in. He wondered whether the man suspected anything, then slept again. On waking the second time he found letters on the floor—one from old Mr Grace, his grandfather, about the party that was to be given when he came of age, another from a don's wife asking him to lunch ("Mr Durham is coming too, so you won't be shy"), another from Ada with mention of Gladys Olcott. Yet again he fell asleep.

Madness is not for everyone, but Maurice's proved the thunderbolt that dispels the clouds. The storm had been working up not for three days as he supposed, but for six years. It had brewed in the obscurities of being where no eye pierces, his surroundings had thickened it. It had burst and he had not died. The brilliancy of day was around him, he stood upon the mountain range that overshadows youth, he saw.

Most of the day he sat with open eyes, as if looking into the Valley he had left. It was all so plain now. He had lied. He phrased it "been fed upon lies", but lies are the natural food of boyhood, and he had eaten greedily. His first resolve was to be more careful in the future. He would live straight, not because it mattered to anyone now, but for the sake of the game. He would not deceive himself so much. He would not—and this was the test—pretend to care about women when the only sex that attracted him was his own. He loved men and always had loved them. He longed to embrace them and mingle his being with theirs. Now that the man who returned his love had been lost, he admitted this.

XI

After this crisis Maurice became a man. Hitherto—if human beings can be estimated—he had not been worth anyone's affection, but conventional, petty, treacherous to others, because to himself. Now he had the highest gift to offer. The idealism and the brutality than ran through boyhood had joined at last, and twined into love. No one might want such love, but he could not feel ashamed of it, because it was "he", neither body or soul, nor body and soul, but "he" working through both. He still suffered, yet a sense of triumph had come elsewhere. Pain had shown him a niche behind the world's judgements, whither he could withdraw.

There was still much to learn, and years passed before he explored certain abysses in his being—horrible enough they were. But he discovered the method and looked no more at scratches in the sand. He had awoken too late for happiness, but not for strength, and could feel an austere joy, as of a warrior who is homeless but stands fully armed.

As the term went on he decided to speak to Durham. He valued words highly, having so lately discovered them. Why should he suffer and cause his friend suffering, when words might put all right? He heard himself saying, "I really love you as you love me," and Durham replying, "Is that so? Then I forgive you," and to the ardour of youth such a conversation seemed possible, though somehow he did not conceive it as leading to joy. He made several attempts, but partly through his own shyness, partly through Durham's, they failed. If he went round, the door was sported, or else there were people inside; should he enter, Durham left when the other guests did. He invited him to meals—he could never come; he offered to lift him again for tennis, but an excuse was made. Even if they met in the court, Durham would affect to have forgotten something and run past him or away. He was surprised their friends did not notice the change, but few undergraduates are observant—they have too much to discover within themselves and it was a don who remarked that Durham had stopped honeymooning with that Hall person.

He found his opportunity after a debating society to which both belonged. Durham—pleading his Tripos—had sent in his resignation, but had begged that the society might meet in his rooms first, as he wished to take his share of hospitality. This was like him; he hated to be under an obligation to anyone. Maurice went and sat through a tedious evening. When everyone, including the host, surged out into the fresh air, he remained, thinking of the first night he had visited that room, and wondering whether the past cannot return.

Durham entered, and did not at once see who it was. Ignoring him utterly, he proceeded to tidy up for the night.

"You're beastly hard," blurted Maurice, "you don't know what it is to have a mind in a mess, and it makes you very hard."

Durham shook his head as one who refuses to listen. He looked so ill that Maurice had a wild desire to catch hold of him.

"You might give me a chance instead of avoiding me—I only want to discuss."

"We've discussed the whole evening."

"I mean the *Symposium*, like the ancient Greeks."

"Oh Hall, don't be so stupid—you ought to know that to be alone with you hurts me. No, please don't reopen. It's over. It's over." He went into the other room and began to undress. "Forgive this discourtesy, but I simply can't—my nerves are all nohow after three weeks of this."

"So are mine," cried Maurice.

"Poor, poor chap!"

"Durham, I'm in Hell."

"Oh, you'll get out. It's only the Hell of disgust. You've never done anything to be ashamed of, so you don't know what's really Hell."

Maurice gave a cry of pain. It was so unmistakable that Durham, who was about to close the door between them, said, "Very well, I'll discuss if you like. What's the matter? You appear to want to apologize about something. Why? You behave as if I'm annoyed with you. What have you done wrong? You've been thoroughly decent from first to last."

In vain he protested.

"So decent that I mistook your ordinary friendliness. When you were so good to me, above all the afternoon I came up—I thought it was something else. I am more sorry than I can ever say. I had no right to move out of my books and music, which was what I did when I met you. You won't want my apology any more than anything else I could give, but, Hall, I do make it most sincerely. It is a lasting grief to have insulted you."

His voice was feeble but clear, and his face like a sword. Maurice flung useless words about love.

"That's all, I think. Get married quickly and forget."

"Durham, I love you."

He laughed bitterly.

"I do—I have always—"

"Good night, good night."

"I tell you, I do—I came to say it—in your very own way—I have always been like the Greeks and didn't know."

"Expand the statement."

Words deserted him immediately. He could only speak when he was not asked to.

"Hall, don't be grotesque." He raised his hand, for Maurice had exclaimed. "It's like the very decent fellow you are to comfort me, but there are limits; one or two things I can't swallow."

"I'm not grotesque—"

"I shouldn't have said that. So do leave me. I'm thankful

it's into your hands I fell. Most men would have reported me to the Dean or the Police."

"Oh, go to Hell, it's all you're fit for," cried Maurice, rushed into the court and heard once more the bang of the outer door. Furious he stood on the bridge in a night that resembled the first—drizzly with faint stars. He made no allowance for three weeks of torture unlike his own or for the poison which, secreted by one man, acts differently on another. He was enraged not to find his friend as he had left him. Twelve o'clock struck, one, two, and he was still planning what to say when there is nothing to say and the resources of speech are ended.

Then savage, reckless, drenched with the rain, he saw in the first glimmer of dawn the window of Durham's room, and his heart leapt alive and shook him to pieces. It cried "You love and are loved." He looked round the court. It cried "You are strong, he weak and alone," won over his will. Terrified at what he must do, he caught hold of the mullion and sprang.

"Maurice—"

As he alighted his name had been called out of dreams. The violence went out of his heart, and a purity that he had never imagined dwelt there instead. His friend had called him. He stood for a moment entranced, then the new emotion found him words, and laying his hand very gently upon the pillows he answered "Clive!"

PART TWO

XII

Clive had suffered little from bewilderment as a boy. His sincere mind, with its keen sense of right and wrong, had brought him the belief that he was damned instead. Deeply religious, with a living desire to reach God and to please Him, he found himself crossed at an early age by this other desire, obviously from Sodom. He had no doubt as to what it was: his emotion, more compact than Maurice's, was not split into the brutal and the ideal, nor did he waste years in bridging the gulf. He had in him the impulse that destroyed the City of the Plain. It should not ever become carnal, but why had he out of all Christians been punished with it?

At first he thought God must be trying him, and if he did not blaspheme would recompense him like Job. He therefore bowed his head, fasted, and kept away from anyone whom he found himself inclined to like. His sixteenth year was ceaseless torture. He told no one, and finally broke down and had to be removed from school. During the convalescence he found himself falling in love with a cousin who walked by his bath chair, a young married man. It was hopeless, he was damned.

These terrors had visited Maurice, but dimly: to Clive they were definite, continuous, and not more insistent at the Eucharist than elsewhere. He never mistook them, in spite of the rein he kept on grossness. He could control the body; it was the tainted soul that mocked his prayers.

The boy had always been a scholar, awake to the printed word, and the horrors the Bible had evoked for him were to be laid by Plato. Never could he forget his emotion at first reading the *Phaedrus*. He saw there his malady described exquisitely, calmly, as a passion which we can direct, like any other, towards good or bad. Here was no invitation to licence. He could not believe his good fortune at first—thought there must be some misunderstanding and that he and Plato were thinking of different things. Then he saw that the temperate pagan really did comprehend him, and, slipping past the Bible rather than opposing it, was offering a new guide for life. "To make the most of what I have." Not to crush it down, not vainly to wish that it was something else, but to cultivate it in such ways as will not vex either God or Man.

He was obliged however to throw over Christianity. Those who base their conduct upon what they are rather than upon what they ought to be, always must throw it over in the end, and besides, between Clive's temperament and that religion there is a secular feud. No clear-headed man can combine them. The temperament, to quote the legal formula, is "not to be mentioned among Christians", and a legend tells that all who shared it died on the morning of the Nativity. Clive regretted this. He came of a family of lawyers and squires, good and able men for the most part, and he did not wish to depart from their tradition. He wished Christianity would compromise with him a little and searched the Scriptures for support. There was David and Jonathan; there was even the "disciple that Jesus loved". But the Church's interpretation was against him; he could not find any rest for his soul in her without crippling it, and withdrew higher into the classics yearly.

By eighteen he was unusually mature, and so well under control that he could allow himself to be friendly with anyone who attracted him. Harmony had succeeded asceticism. At Cambridge he cultivated tender emotions for other undergraduates, and his life, hitherto gray, became slightly tinged with delicate hues. Cautious and sane, he advanced, nor was there anything petty in his caution. He was ready to go further should he consider it right.

In his second year he met Risley, himself "that way". Clive did not return the confidence which was given rather freely, nor did he like Risley and his set. But he was stimulated. He was glad to know that there were more of his sort about, and their frankness braced him into telling his mother about his agnosticism; it was all he could tell her. Mrs Durham, a worldly woman, made little protest. It was at Christmas the trouble came. Being the only gentry in the parish, the Durhams communicated separately, and to have the whole village looking on while she and her daughters knelt without Clive in the middle of that long footstool cut her with shame and stung her into anger. They quarrelled. He saw her for what she really was—withered, unsympathetic, empty—and in his disillusion found himself thinking vividly of Hall.

Hall: he was only one of several men whom he rather liked. True he, also, had a mother and two sisters, but Clive was too level-headed to pretend this was the only bond between them. He must like Hall more than he realized—must be a little in love with him. And as soon as they met he had a rush of emotion that carried him into intimacy.

The man was bourgeois, unfinished and stupid—the worst of confidants. Yet he told about his home troubles, touched out of all proportion by his dismissal of Chapman. When Hall started teasing he was charmed. Others held off, regarding him as sedate, and he liked being thrown about by a powerful and handsome boy. It was delightful too when Hall stroked his hair: the faces of the two people in the room would fade: he leant back till his cheek brushed the flannel of the trousers and felt the warmth strike through. He was under no illusion on these occasions. He knew what kind of pleasure he was receiving, and received it honestly, certain that it brought no harm to either of them. Hall was a man who only liked women—one could tell that at a glance.

Towards the end of the term he noticed that Hall had acquired a peculiar and beautiful expression. It came only now and then, was subtle and lay far down; he noticed it first when they were squabbling about theology. It was affectionate, kindly, and to that extent a natural expression, but there was mixed in it something that he had not observed in the man, a touch of—impudence? He was not sure, but liked it. It recurred when they met suddenly or had been silent. It beckoned to him across intellect, saying, "This is all very well, you're clever, we know—but come!" It haunted him so that he watched for it while his brain and tongue were busy, and when it came he felt himself replying, "I'll come—I didn't know."

"You can't help yourself now. You must come."

"I don't want to help myself."

"Come then."

He did come. He flung down all the barriers—not at once, for he did not live in a house that can be destroyed in a day. All that term and through letters afterwards he made the path clear. Once certain that Hall loved him, he unloosed his own love. Hitherto it had been dalliance, a passing pleasure for body and mind. How he despised that now. Love was harmonious, immense. He poured into it the dignity as well as the richness of his being, and indeed in that well-tempered soul the two were one. There was nothing humble about Clive. He knew his own worth, and, when he had expected to go through life without love, he had blamed circumstances rather than himself. Hall, though attractive and beautiful, had not condescended. They would meet on an equality next term.

But books meant so much for him he forgot that they were a bewilderment to others, Had he trusted the body there would have been no disaster, but by linking their love to the past he linked it to the present, and roused in his friend's mind the conventions and the fear of the law. He realized nothing of this. What Hall said he must mean. Otherwise why should he say it? Hall loathed him—had said so, "Oh, rot"—the words hurt more than any abuse, and rang in his ears for days. Hall was the healthy normal Englishman, who had never had a glimmer of what was up.

Great was the pain, great the mortification, but worse followed. So deeply had Clive become one with the beloved that he began to loathe himself. His whole philosophy of life broke down, and the sense of sin was reborn in its ruins, and crawled along corridors. Hall had said he was a criminal, and must know. He was damned. He dare never be friends with a young man again, for fear of corrupting him. Had he not lost Hall his faith in Christianity and attempted his purity besides?

During those three weeks Clive altered immensely, and was beyond the reach of argument when Hall—good, blundering creature—came to his room to comfort him, tried this and that without success, and vanished in a gust of temper. "Oh, go to Hell, it's all you're fit for." Never a truer word but hard to accept from the beloved. Clive's defeat increased: his life had been blown to pieces, and he felt no inward strength to rebuild it and clear out evil. His conclusion was "Ridiculous boy! I never loved him. I only had an image I made up in my polluted mind, and may God help me to get rid of it."

But it was this image that visited his sleep, and caused him to whisper its name.

"Maurice . . ."

"Clive . . ."

"Hall!" he gasped, fully awake. Warmth was upon him. "Maurice, Maurice, Maurice. . . . Oh *Maurice*—"

"I know."

"Maurice, I love you."

"I you."

They kissed, scarcely wishing it. Then Maurice vanished as he had come, through the window.

XIII

"I've missed two lectures already," remarked Maurice, who was breakfasting in his pyjamas.

"Cut them all—he'll only gate you."

"Will you come out in the side-car?"

"Yes, but a long way," said Clive, lighting a cigarette. "I can't stick Cambridge in this weather. Let's get right outside it ever so far and bathe. I can work as we go along— Oh damnation!"—for there were steps on the stairs. Joey Fetherstonhaugh looked in and asked one or other of them to play tennis with him that afternoon. Maurice accepted.

"Maurice! What did you do that for, you fool?"

"Cleared him out quickest. Clive, meet me at the garage in twenty minutes, bring your putrid books, and borrow Joey's goggles. I must dress. Bring some lunch too."

"What about horses instead?"

"Too slow."

They met as arranged. Joey's goggles had offered no difficulty, as he had been out. But as they threaded Jesus Lane they were hailed by the Dean.

"Hall, haven't you a lecture?"

"I overslept," called Maurice contemptuously.

"Hall! Hall! Stop when I speak."

Maurice went on. "No good arguing," he observed.

"Not the least."

They swirled across the bridge and into the Ely road. Maurice said, "Now we'll go to Hell." The machine was powerful, he reckless naturally. It leapt forward into the fens and the receding dome of the sky. They became a cloud of dust, a stench, and a roar to the world, but the air they breathed was pure, and all the noise they heard was the long drawn cheer of the wind. They cared for no one, they were outside humanity, and death, had it come, would only have continued their pursuit of a retreating horizon. A tower, a town—it had been Ely—were behind them, in front the same sky, paling at last as though heralding the sea. "Right turn," again, then "left," "right," until all sense of direction was gone. There was a rip, a grate. Maurice took no notice. A noise arose as of a thousand pebbles being shaken together between his legs. No accident occurred, but the machine came to a standstill among the dark black fields. The song of the lark was heard, the trail of dust began to settle behind them. They were alone.

"Let's eat," said Clive.

They ate on a grassy embankment. Above them the waters of a dyke moved imperceptibly, and reflected interminable willow trees. Man who had created the whole landscape was nowhere to be seen. After lunch Clive thought he ought to work. He spread out his books and was asleep in ten minutes. Maurice lay up by the water, smoking. A farmer's cart appeared, and it did occur to him to ask which county they were in. But he said nothing, nor did the farmer appear to notice him. When Clive awoke it was past three. "We shall want some tea soon," was his contribution.

"All right. Can you mend that bloody bike?"

"Oh yes, didn't something jam?" He yawned and walked down to the machine. "No, I can't, Maurice, can you?"

"Rather not."

They laid their cheeks together and began laughing. The smash struck them as extraordinarily funny. Grandpapa's present too! He had given it to Maurice against his coming of age in August. Clive said, "How if we left it and walked?"

"Yes, who'd do it any harm? Leave the coats and things inside it. Likewise Joey's goggles."

"What about my books?"

"Leave 'em too."

"I shan't want them after hall?"

"Oh, I don't know. Tea's more important than hall. It

stands to reason—well what are you giggling at?—that if we follow a dyke long enough we must come to a pub."

"Why, they use it to water their beer!"

Maurice smote him on the ribs, and for ten minutes they played up amongst the trees, too silly for speech. Pensive again, they stood close together, then hid the bicycle behind dog roses, and started. Clive took his notebook away with him, but it did not survive in any useful form, for the dyke they were following branched.

"We must wade this," he said. "We can't go round or we shall never get anywhere. Maurice look—we must keep in a bee line south."

"All right."

It did not matter which of them suggested what that day; the other always agreed. Clive took off his shoes and socks and rolled his trousers up. Then he stepped upon the brown surface of the dyke and vanished. He reappeared swimming.

"All that deep!" he spluttered, climbing out. "Maurice, no idea! Had you?"

Maurice cried "I say, I must bathe properly." He did so, while Clive carried his clothes. The light grew radiant. Presently they came to a farm.

The farmer's wife was inhospitable and ungracious, but they spoke of her afterwards as "absolutely ripping". She did in the end give them tea and allow Clive to dry near her kitchen fire. She "left payment to them", and, when they overpaid her, grumbled. Nothing checked their spirits. They transmuted everything.

"Goodbye, we're greatly obliged," said Clive. "And if any of your men come across the bike: I wish we could describe where we left it better. Anyhow I'll give you my friend's card. Tie it on the bike if they will be so kind, and bring it down to the nearest station. Something of the sort, I don't know. The station master will wire to us."

The station was five miles on. When they reached it the sun was low, and they were not back in Cambridge till after hall. All this last part of the day was perfect. The train, for some unknown reason, was full, and they sat close together, talking quietly under the hubbub, and smiling. When they parted it was in the ordinary way: neither had an impulse to say anything special. The whole day had been ordinary. Yet it had never come before to either of them, nor was it to be repeated.

XIV

The Dean sent Maurice down.

Mr Cornwallis was not a severe official, and the boy had a tolerable record, but he could not overlook so gross a breach of discipline. "And why did you not stop when I called you, Hall?" Hall made no answer, did not even look sorry. He had a smouldering eye, and Mr Cornwallis, though much annoyed, realized that he was confronted with a man. In a dead, bloodless way, he even guessed what had happened.

"Yesterday you cut chapel, four lectures, including my own translation class, and hall. You have done this sort of thing before. It's unnecessary to add impertinence, don't you think? Well? No reply? You will go down and inform your mother of the reason. I shall inform her too. Until you write me a letter of apology, I shall not recommend your re-admission to the college in October. Catch the twelve o'clock."

"All right."

Mr Cornwallis motioned him out.

No punishment was inflicted on Durham. He had been let off all lectures in view of his Tripos, and even if he had been remiss the Dean would not have worried him; the best classical scholar of his year, he had won special treatment. A good thing he would no longer be distracted by Hall. Mr Cornwallis always suspected such friendships. It was not natural that men of different characters and tastes should be intimate, and although undergraduates, unlike schoolboys, are officially normal, the Dons exercised a certain amount of watchfulness, and felt it right to spoil a love affair when they could.

Clive helped him pack, and saw him off. He said little, lest he depressed his friend, who was still in the heroics, but his heart sank. It was his last term, for his mother would not let him stay up a fourth year, which meant that he and Maurice would never meet in Cambridge again. Their love belonged to it, and particularly to their rooms, so that he could not conceive of their meeting anywhere else. He wished that Maurice had not taken up a strong line with the Dean, but it was too late now, and that the side-car had not been lost. He connected that side-car with intensities—the agony of the tennis court, the joy of yesterday. Bound in a single motion, they seemed there closer to one another than elsewhere; the machine took on a life of its own, in which they met and realized the unity preached by Plato. It had gone, and when Maurice's train went also, actually tearing hand from hand, he broke down, and returning to his room wrote passionate sheets of despair.

Maurice received the letter the next morning. It completed what his family had begun, and he had his first explosion of rage against the world.

XV

"I can't apologize, mother—I explained last night there's nothing to apologize about. They had no right to send me down when everyone cuts lectures. It's pure spite, and you can ask anyone—Ada, do try turning on the coffee instead of the salt water."

She sobbed, "Maurice, you've upset mother: how can you be so unkind and brutal?"

"I'm sure I don't mean to be. I don't see I've been unkind. I shall go straight into the business now, like father did, without taking one of their rotten degrees. I see no harm in that."

"You might have kept your poor father out, he never had any unpleasantness," said Mrs Hall. "Oh Morrie, my darling—and we did so look forward to Cambridge."

"All this crying's a mistake," announced Kitty, who aspired to the functions of a tonic. "It only makes Maurice think he's important, which he isn't: he'll write to the Dean as soon as no one wants him to."

"I shan't. It's unsuitable," replied her brother, hard as iron.

"I don't see that."

"Little girls don't see a good deal."

"I'm not so sure!"

He glanced at her. But she only said that she saw a good deal more than some little boys who thought themselves little men. She was merely maundering, and the fear, tinged with respect, that had arisen in him died down. No, he couldn't apologize. He had done nothing wrong and wouldn't say he had, it was the first taste of honesty he had known for years, and honesty is like blood. In his unbending mood the boy thought it would be possible to live without compromise, and ignore all that didn't yield to himself and Clive! Clive's letter had maddened him. No doubt he is stupid—the sensible lover would apologize and get back to comfort his friend—but it was the stupidity of passion, which would rather have nothing than a little.

They continued talking and weeping. At last he rose, said, "I can't eat to this accompaniment," and went into the garden. His mother followed with a tray. Her very softness enraged him, for love develops the athlete. It cost her nothing to muck about with tender words and toast: she only wanted to make him soft too.

She wanted to know whether she had heard rightly, was he refusing to apologize? She wondered what her father would say, and incidentally learnt that the birthday gift was lying beside some East Anglian drove. She grew seriously concerned, for its loss was more intelligible to her than the loss of a degree. The girls minded too. They mourned the bicycle for the rest of the morning, and, though Maurice could always silence them or send them out of earshot, he felt that their pliancy might sap his strength again, as in the Easter vacation.

In the afternoon he had a collapse. He remembered that Clive and he had only been together one day! And they had spent it careering about like fools—instead of in one another's arms! Maurice did not know that they had thus spent it perfectly—he was too young to detect the triviality of contact for contact's sake. Though restrained by his friend, he would have surfeited passion. Later on, when his love took second strength, he realized how well Fate had served him. The one embrace in the darkness, the one long day in the light and the wind, were twin columns, each useless without the other. And all the agony of separation that he went through now, instead of destroying, was to fulfil.

He tried to answer Clive's letter. Already he feared to ring false. In the evening he received another, composed of the words "Maurice! I love you." He answered, "Clive, I love you." Then they wrote every day and for all their care created new images in each other's hearts. Letters distort even more quickly than silence. A terror seized Clive that something was going wrong, and just before his exam he got leave to run down to town. Maurice lunched with him. It was horrible. Both were tired, and they had chosen a restaurant where they could not hear themselves speak. "I haven't enjoyed it," said Clive when he wished goodbye. Maurice felt relieved. He had pretended to himself that he had enjoyed it, and thus increased his misery. They agreed that they would confine themselves to facts in their letters, and only write when anything was urgent. The emotional strain relaxed, and Maurice, nearer to brain fever than he supposed, had several dreamless nights that healed him. But daily life remained a poor business.

His position at home was anomalous: Mrs Hall wished that someone would decide it for her. He looked like a man and had turned out the Howells last Easter; but on the other hand he had been sent down from Cambridge and was not yet twenty-one. What was his place in her house? Instigated by Kitty, she tried to assert herself, but Maurice, after a genuine look of surprise, laid back his ears. Mrs Hall wavered, and, though fond of her son, took the unwise step of appealing to Dr Barry. Maurice was asked to go round one evening to be talked to.

"Well, Maurice, and how goes the career? Not quite as you expected, eh?"

Maurice was still afraid of their neighbour.

"Not quite as your mother expected, which is more to the point."

"Not quite as anyone expected," said Maurice, looking at his hands.

Dr Barry then said, "Oh, it's all for the best. What do you want with a University Degree? It was never intended for the surburban classes. You're not going to be either a parson or a barrister or a pedagogue. And you are not a county gentleman. Sheer waste of time. Get into harness at once. Quite right to insult the Dean. The city's your place. Your mother—" He paused and lit a cigar, the boy had been offered nothing. "Your mother doesn't understand this. Worrying because you don't apologize. For my own part I think these things right themselves. You got into an atmosphere for which you are not suited, and you've very properly taken the first opportunity to get out of it."

"How do you mean, sir?"

"Oh. Not sufficiently clear? I mean that the county gentleman would apologize by instinct if he found he had behaved like a cad. You've a different tradition."

"I think I must be getting home now," said Maurice, not without dignity.

"Yes, I think you must. I didn't invite you to have a pleasant evening, as I hope you have realized."

"You've spoken straight—perhaps some day I shall too. I know I'd like to."

This set the Doctor off, and he cried:

"How dare you bully your mother, Maurice. You ought to be horsewhipped. You young puppy! Swaggering about instead of asking her to forgive you! I know all about it. She came here with tears in her eyes and asked me to speak. She and your sisters are my respected neighbours, and as long as a woman calls me I'm at her service. Don't answer me, sir, don't answer, I want none of your speech, straight or otherwise. You are a disgrace to chivalry. I don't know what the world is coming to. I don't know what the world— I'm disappointed and disgusted with you."

Maurice, outside at last, mopped his forehead. He was ashamed in a way. He knew he had behaved badly to his mother, and all the snob in him had been touched to the raw. But somehow he could not retract, could not alter. Once out of the rut, he seemed out of it for ever. "A disgrace to chivalry." He considered the accusation. If a woman had been in that side-car, if then he had refused to stop at the Dean's bidding, would Dr Barry have required an apology from him? Surely not. He followed out this train of thought with difficulty. His brain was still feeble.

But he was obliged to use it, for so much in current speech and ideas needed translation before he could understand them.

His mother met him, looking ashamed herself; she felt, as he did, that she ought to have done her own scolding. Maurice had grown up, she complained to Kitty; the children went from one; it was all very sad. Kitty asserted her brother was still nothing but a boy, but all these women had a sense of some change in his mouth and eyes and voice since he had faced Dr Barry.

XVI

The Durhams lived in a remote part of England on the Wilts and Somerset border. Though not an old family they had held land for four generations, and its influence had passed into them. Clive's great-great-uncle had been Lord Chief Justice in the reign of George IV, and the nest he had feathered was Penge. The feathers were inclined to blow about now. A hundred years had nibbled into the fortune, which no wealthy bride had replenished, and both house and estate were marked, not indeed with decay, but with the immobility that precedes it.

The house lay among woods. A park, still ridged with the lines of vanished hedges, stretched around, giving light and air and pasture to horses and Alderney cows. Beyond it the trees began, most planted by old Sir Edwin, who had annexed the common lands. There were two entrances to the park, one up by the village, the other on the clayey road that went to the station. There had been no station in the old days, and the approach from it, which was undignified and led by the back premises, typified an afterthought of England's.

Maurice arrived in the evening. He had travelled straight from his grandfather's at Birmingham, where, rather tepidly, he had come of age. Though in disgrace, he had not been mulcted of his presents, but they were given and received without enthusiasm. He had looked forward so much to being twenty-one. Kitty implied that he did not enjoy it because he had gone to the bad. Quite nicely he pinched her ear for this and kissed her, which annoyed her a good deal. "You have no *sense* of things," she said crossly. He smiled.

From Alfriston Gardens, with its cousins and meat teas, the change to Penge was immense. County families, even when intelligent, have something alarming about them, and Maurice approached any seat with awe. True, Clive had met him and was with him in the brougham, but then so was a Mrs Sheepshanks, who had arrived by his train. Mrs Sheepshanks had a maid, following behind with her luggage and his in a cab, and he wondered whether he ought to have brought a servant too. The lodge gate was held by a little girl. Mrs Sheepshanks wished *everyone* curtsied. Clive trod on his foot when she said this, but he wasn't sure whether accidentally. He was sure of nothing. When they approached he mistook the back for the front, and prepared to open the door. Mrs Sheepshanks said, "Oh, but that's complimentary." Besides, there was a butler to open the door.

Tea, very bitter, was awaiting them, and Mrs Durham looked one way while she poured out the other. People stood about, all looking distinguished or there for some distinguished reason. They were doing things or causing others to do them: Miss Durham booked him to canvass tomorrow for Tariff Reform. They agreed politically; but the cry with which she greeted his alliance did not please him. "Mother, Mr Hall *is* sound." Major Western, a cousin also stopping in the house, would ask him about Cambridge. Did Army men mind one being sent down? . . . No, it was worse than the restaurant, for there Clive had been out of his element too.

"Pippa, does Mr Hall know his room?"

"The Blue Room, mamma."

"The one with no fireplace," called Clive. "Show him up." He was seeing off some callers.

Miss Durham passed Maurice on to the butler. They went up a side staircase, Maurice saw the main flight to the right, and wondered whether he was being slighted. His room was small, furnishly cheaply. It had no outlook. As he knelt down to unpack, a feeling of Sunnington came over him, and he determined, while he was at Penge, to work through all his clothes. They shouldn't suppose he was unfashionable; he was as good as anyone. But he had scarcely reached this conclusion when Clive rushed in with the sunlight behind him. "Maurice, I shall kiss you," he said, and did so.

"Where—what's through there?"

"Our study—" He was laughing, his expression wild and radiant.

"Oh, so that's why—"

"Maurice! Maurice! you've actually come. You're here. This place'll never seem the same again, I shall love it at last."

"It's jolly for me coming," said Maurice chokily: the sudden rush of joy made his head swim.

"Go on unpacking. So I arranged it on purpose. We're up this staircase by ourselves. It's as like college as I could manage."

"It's better."

"I really feel it will be."

There was a knock on the passage door. Maurice started, but Clive though still sitting on his shoulder said "Come in!" indifferently. A housemaid entered with hot water.

"Except for meals we need never be in the other part of the house," he continued. "Either here or out of doors. Jolly, eh? I've a piano." He drew him into the study. "Look at the view. You may shoot rabbits out of this window. By the way, if my mother or Pippa tells you at dinner that they want you to do this or that tomorrow, you needn't worry. Say 'yes' to them if you like. You're actually going to ride with me, and they know it. It's only their ritual. On Sunday, when you haven't been to church they'll pretend afterwards you were there."

"But I've no proper riding breeches."

"I can't associate with you in that case," said Clive and bounded off.

When Maurice returned to the drawing-room he felt he had a greater right to be there than anyone. He walked up to Mrs Sheepshanks, opened his mouth before she could open hers, and was encouraging to her. He took his place in the absurd octet that was forming to go in—Clive and Mrs Sheepshanks, Major Western and another woman, another man and Pippa, himself and his hostess. She apologized for the smallness of the party.

"Not at all," said Maurice, and saw Clive glance at him maliciously: he had used the wrong tag. Mrs Durham then put him through his paces, but he did not care a damn whether he satisfied her or not. She had her son's features and seemed equally able, though not equally sincere. He understood why Clive should have come to despise her.

After dinner the men smoked, then joined the ladies. It was a suburban evening, but with a difference; these people had the air of settling something: they either just had arranged or soon would rearrange England. Yet the gate posts, the roads—he had noticed them on the way up—were in bad repair, and the timber wasn't kept properly, the windows stuck, the boards creaked. He was less impressed than he had expected by Penge.

When the ladies retired Clive said, "Maurice, you look sleepy too." Maurice took the hint, and five minutes afterwards they met again in the study, with all the night to talk into. They lit their pipes. It was the first time they had experienced full tranquillity together, and exquisite words would be spoken. They knew this, yet scarcely wanted to begin.

"I'll tell you my latest now," said Clive. "As soon as I got home I had a row with mother and told her I should stop up a fourth year."

Maurice gave a cry.

"What's wrong?"

"I've been sent down."

"But you're coming back in October."

"I'm not. Cornwallis said I must apologize, and I wouldn't—I thought you wouldn't be up, so I didn't care."

"And I settled to stop because I thought you would be up. Comedy of Errors."

Maurice stared gloomily before him.

"Comedy of Errors, not Tragedy. You can apologize now."

"It's too late."

Clive laughed. "Why too late? It makes it simpler. You didn't like to apologize until the term in which your offence was committed had come to an end. 'Dear Mr Cornwallis: Now that the term is over, I venture to write to you.' I'll draft the letter tomorrow."

Maurice pondered and finally exclaimed "Clive, you're a devil."

"I'm a bit of an outlaw, I grant, but it serves these people right. As long as they talk of the unspeakable vice of the Greeks they can't expect fair play. It served my mother right when I slipped up to kiss you before dinner. She would have no mercy if she knew, she wouldn't attempt, wouldn't want to attempt to understand that I feel to you as Pippa to her fiancé, only far more nobly, far more deeply, body and soul, no starved medievalism of course, only a—a particular harmony of body and soul that I don't think women have even guessed. But you know."

"Yes. I'll apologize."

There was a long interval: they discussed the motor bicycle, which had never been heard of again. Clive made coffee.

"Tell me, what made you wake me that night after the Debating Society. Describe."

"I kept on thinking of something to say, and couldn't, so at last I couldn't even think, so I just came."

"Sort of thing you would do."

"Are you ragging?" asked Maurice shyly.

"My God!" There was a silence. "Tell me now about the night I first came up. Why did you make us both so unhappy?"

"I don't know, I say. I can't explain anything. Why did you mislead me with that rotten Plato? I was still in a muddle. A lot of things hadn't joined up in me that since have."

"But hadn't you been getting hold of me for months? Since first you saw me at Risley's, in fact."

"Don't ask me."

"It's a queer business, any way."

"It's that."

Clive laughed delightedly, and wriggled in his chair. "Maurice, the more I think it over the more certain I am that it's you who are the devil."

"Oh, all right."

"I should have gone through life half awake if you'd had the decency to leave me alone. Awake intellectually, yes, and emotionally in a way; but here—" He pointed with his pipe stem to his heart; and both smiled. "Perhaps we woke up one another. I like to think that any way."

"When did you first care about me?"

"Don't ask me," echoed Clive.

"Oh, be a bit serious—well—what was it in me you first cared about?"

"Like really to know?" asked Clive, who was in the mood Maurice adored—half mischievous, half passionate; a mood of supreme affection.

"Yes."

"Well, it was your beauty."

"My what?"

"Beauty. . . . I used to admire that man over the bookcase most."

"I can give points to a picture, I dare say," said Maurice, having glanced at the Michelangelo. "Clive, you're a silly little fool, and since you've brought it up I think you're beautiful, the only beautiful person I've ever seen. I love your voice and everything to do with you, down to your clothes or the room you are sitting in. I adore you."

Clive went crimson. "Sit up straight and let's change the subject," he said, all the folly out of him.

"I didn't mean to annoy you at all—'

"Those things must be said once, or we should never

know they were in each other's hearts. I hadn't guessed, not so much as least. You've done all right, Maurice." He did not change the subject but developed it into another that had interested him recently, the precise influence of Desire upon our aesthetic judgements. "Look at that picture, for instance. I love it because, like the painter himself, I love the subject. I don't judge it with eyes of the normal man. There seem two roads for arriving at Beauty—one is in common, and all the world has reached Michelangelo by it, but the other is private to me and a few more. We come to him by both roads. On the other hand Greuze—his subject matter repels me. I can only get to him down one road. The rest of the world finds two."

Maurice did not interrupt: it was all charming nonsense to him.

"These private roads are perhaps a mistake," concluded Clive. "But as long as the human figure is painted they will be taken. Landscape is the only safe subject—or perhaps something geometric, rhythmical, inhuman absolutely. I wonder whether that is what the Mohammedans were up to and old Moses—I've just thought of this. If you introduce the human figure you at once arouse either disgust or desire. Very faintly sometimes, but it's there. 'Thou shalt not make for thyself any graven image—' because one couldn't possibly make it for all other people too. Maurice, shall we rewrite history? 'The Aesthetic Philosophy of the Decalogue.' I've always thought it remarkable of God not to have damned you or me in it. I used to put it down to him for righteousness, though now I suspect he was merely ill-informed. Still I might make out a case. Shall I choose it for a Fellowship Dissertation?"

"I can't follow, you know," said Maurice, a little ashamed.

And their love scene drew out, having the inestimable gain of a new language. No tradition overawed the boys. No convention settled what was poetic, what absurd. They were concerned with a passion that few English minds have admitted, and so created untrammelled. Something of exquisite beauty arose in the mind of each at last, something unforgettable and eternal, but built of the humblest scraps of speech and from the simplest emotions.

"I say, will you kiss me?" asked Maurice, when the sparrows woke in the eaves above them, and far out in the woods the ringdoves began to coo.

Clive shook his head, and smiling they parted, having established perfection in their lives, at all events for a time.

XVII

It seems strange that Maurice should have won any respect from the Durham family, but they did not dislike him. They only disliked people who wanted to know them well —it was a positive mania—and the rumour that a man wished to enter county society was a sufficient reason for excluding him from it. Inside (region of high interchange and dignified movements that meant nothing) were to be found several who, like Mr Hall, neither loved their fate nor feared it, and would depart without a sigh if necessary. The Durhams felt they were conferring a favour on him by treating him as one of themselves, yet were pleased he should take it as a matter of course, gratitude being mysteriously connected in their minds with ill breeding.

Wanting only his food and his friend, Maurice did not observe he was a success, and was surprised when the old lady claimed him for a talk towards the end of his visit. She had questioned him about his family and discovered the nakedness thereof, but this time her manner was deferential: she wanted his opinion of Clive.

"Mr Hall, we wish you to help us: Clive thinks so much of you. Do you consider it wise for him to stop up a fourth year at Cambridge?"

Maurice was wanting to wonder which horse he should ride in the afternoon: he only half attended, which gave an appearance of profundity.

"After the deplorable exhibition he has made of himself in the Tripos—is it wise?"

"He means to," said Maurice.

Mrs Durham nodded. "There you have gone to the root of the matter. Clive means to. Well, he is his own master. This place is his. Did he tell you?"

"No."

"Oh, Penge is his absolutely, under my husband's will. I must move to the dower house as soon as he marries—"

Maurice started; she looked at him and saw that he had coloured. "So there *is* some girl," she thought. Neglecting the point for a moment, she returned to Cambridge, and observed how little a fourth year would profit a "yokel"—she used the word with gay assurance—and how desirable it was that Clive should take his place in the countryside. There was the game, there were his tenants, there were finally politics. "His father represented the division, as you doubtless know."

"No."

"What does he talk to you about?" she laughed. "Anyhow, my husband was a member for seven years, and though a Lib is in now, one knows that cannot last. All our old friends are looking to him. But he must take his place, he must fit himself, and what on earth is the good of all this—I forget what—advanced work. He ought to spend the year travelling instead. He must go to America and if possible the Colonies. It has become absolutely indispensable."

"He speaks of travelling after Cambridge. He wants me to go."

"I trust you will—but not Greece, Mr Hall. That is travelling for play. Do dissuade him from Italy and Greece."

"I'd prefer America myself."

"Naturally—anyone sensible would; but he's a student—a dreamer—Pippa says he writes verse. Have you seen any?"

Maurice had seen a poem to himself. Conscious that life grew daily more amazing, he said nothing. Was he the same man who eight months back had been puzzled by Risley? What had deepened his vision? Section after section the armies of humanity were coming alive. Alive, but slightly absurd; they misunderstood *him* so utterly: they exposed their weakness when they thought themselves most acute. He could not help smiling.

"You evidently have..." Then suddenly: "Mr Hall, is there anyone? Some Newnham girl? Pippa declares there is."

"Pippa had better ask then," Maurice replied.

Mrs Durham was impressed. He had met one impertinence with another. Who would have expected such skill in a young man? He seemed even indifferent to his victory, and was smiling to one of the other guests, who approached over the lawn to tea. In the tones that she reserved for an equal she said, "Impress on him about America anyhow. He needs reality. I noticed that last year."

Maurice duly impressed, when they were riding through the glades alone.

"I thought you were going down," was Clive's comment. "Like them. They wouldn't look at Joey." Clive was in full reaction against his family, he hated the worldliness that they combined with complete ignorance of the World. "These children will be a nuisance," he remarked during a canter.

"What children?"

"Mine! The need of an heir for Penge. My mother calls it marriage, but that was all she was thinking of."

Maurice was silent. It had not occurred to him before that neither he nor his friend would leave life behind them.

"I shall be worried eternally. They've always some girl staying in the house as it is."

"Just go on growing old—"

"Eh, boy?"

"Nothing," said Maurice, and reined up. An immense sadness—he believed himself beyond such irritants—had risen up in his soul. He and the beloved would vanish utterly—would continue neither in Heaven nor on Earth. They had won past the conventions, but Nature still faced them, saying with even voice, "Very well, you are thus; I blame none of my children. But you must go the way of all sterility." The thought that he was sterile weighed on the young man with a sudden shame. His mother or Mrs Durham might lack mind or heart, but they had done visible work; they had handed on the torch their sons would tread out.

He had meant not to trouble Clive, but out it all came as soon as they lay down in the fern. Clive did not agree. "Why children?" he asked. "Why always children? For love to end where it begins is far more beautiful, and Nature knows it."

"Yes, but if everyone—"

Clive pulled him back into themselves. He murmured something about Eternity in an hour: Maurice did not understand, but the voice soothed him.

XVIII

During the next two years Maurice and Clive had as much happiness as men under that star can expect. They were affectionate and consistent by nature, and, thanks to Clive, extremely sensible. Clive knew that ecstasy cannot last, but can carve a channel for something lasting, and he contrived a relation that proved permanent. If Maurice made love it was Clive who preserved it, and caused its rivers to water the garden. He could not bear that one drop should be wasted, either in bitterness or in sentimentality, and as time went on they abstained from avowals ("we have said everything") and almost from caresses. Their happiness was to be together; they radiated something of their calm amongst others, and could take their place in society.

Clive had expanded in this direction ever since he had understood Greek. The love that Socrates bore Phaedo now lay within his reach, love passionate but temperate, such as only finer natures can understand, and he found in Maurice a nature that was not indeed fine, but charmingly willing. He led the beloved up a narrow and beautiful path, high above either abyss. It went on until the final darkness—he could see no other terror—and when that descended they would at all events have lived more fully than either saint or sensualist, and would have extracted to their utmost the nobility and sweetness of the world. He educated Maurice, or rather his spirit educated Maurice's spirit, for they themselves became equal. Neither thought "Am I led; am I leading?" Love had caught him out of triviality and Maurice out of bewilderment in order that two imperfect souls might touch perfection.

So they proceeded outwardly like other men. Society received them, as she receives thousands like them. Behind Society slumbered the Law. They had their last year at

Cambridge together, they travelled in Italy. Then the prison house closed, but on both of them. Clive was working for the bar, Maurice harnessed to an office. They were together still.

XIX

By this time their families had become acquainted. "They will never get on," they had agreed. "They belong to different sections of society." But, perhaps out of perversity, the families did get on, and Clive and Maurice found amusement in seeing them together. Both were misogynists, Clive especially. In the grip of their temperaments, they had not developed the imagination to do duty instead, and during their love women had become as remote as horses or cats; all that the creatures did seemed silly. When Kitty asked to hold Pippa's baby, when Mrs Durham and Mrs Hall visited the Royal Academy in unison, they saw a misfit in nature rather than in society, and gave wild explanations. There was nothing strange really: they themselves were sufficient cause. Their passion for each other was the strongest force in either family, and drew everything after it as a hidden current draws a boat. Mrs Hall and Mrs Durham came together because their sons were friends; "and now," said Mrs Hall, "we are friends too."

Maurice was present the day their "friendship" began. The matrons met in Pippa's London house. Pippa had married a Mr London, a coincidence that made a great impression on Kitty, who hoped she would not think of it and laugh during tea. Ada, as too silly for a first visit, had been left at home by Maurice's advice. Nothing happened. Then Pippa and her mother motored out to return the civility. He was in town but again nothing seemed to have happened, except that Pippa had praised Kitty's brains to Ada and Ada's beauty to Kitty, thus offending both girls, and Mrs Hall had warned Mrs Durham against installing hot air at Penge. Then they met again, and as far as he could see it was always like this; nothing, nothing, and still nothing.

Mrs Durham had of course her motives. She was looking out wives for Clive, and put down the Hall girls on her list. She had a theory one ought to cross breeds a bit, and Ada, though suburban, was healthy. No doubt the girl was a fool, but Mrs Durham did not propose to retire to the dower house in practice, whatever she might do in theory, and believed she could best manage Clive through his wife. Kitty had fewer qualifications. She was less foolish, less beautiful, and less rich. Ada would inherit the whole of her grandfather's fortune which was considerable, and had always inherited his good humour. Mrs Durham met old Mr Grace once, and rather liked him.

Had she supposed the Halls were also planning she would have drawn back. Like Maurice they held her by their indifference. Mrs Hall was too idle to scheme, the girls too innocent. Mrs Durham regarded Ada as a favourable line and invited her to Penge. Only Pippa, into whose mind a breath of modernity had blown, began to think her brother's coldness odd. "Clive, *are* you going to marry?" she asked suddenly. But his reply, "No, do tell mother," dispelled her suspicions: it is the sort of reply a man who is going to marry would make.

No one worried Maurice. He had established his power at home, and his mother began to speak of him in the tones she had reserved for her husband. He was not only the son of the house, but more of a personage than had been expected. He kept the servants in order, understood the car, subscribed to this and not to that, tabooed certain of the girls' acquaintances. By twenty-three he was a promising suburban tyrant, whose rule was the stronger because it was fairly just and mild. Kitty protested, but she had no backing and no experience. In the end she had to say she was sorry and to receive a kiss. She was no match for this good-humoured and slightly hostile young man, and she failed to establish the advantage that his escapade at Cambridge had given her.

Maurice's habits became regular. He ate a large breakfast and caught the 8.36 to town. In the train he read the *Daily Telegraph*. He worked till 1.0, lunched lightly, and worked again through the afternoon. Returning home, he had some exercise and a large dinner, and in the evening he read the evening paper, or laid down the law, or played billiards or bridge.

But every Wednesday he slept at Clive's little flat in town. Weekends were also inviolable. They said at home, "You must never interfere with Maurice's Wednesdays or with his weekends. He would be most annoyed."

XX

Clive got through his bar exams successfully, but just before he was called he had a slight touch of influenza with fever. Maurice came to see him as he was recovering, caught it, and went to bed himself. Thus they saw little of one another for several weeks, and when they did meet Clive was still white and nervy. He came down to the Halls', preferring their house to Pippa's, and hoping that the good food and quiet would set him up. He ate little, and when he spoke his theme was the futility of all things.

"I'm a barrister because I may enter public life," he said in reply to a question of Ada's. "But why should I enter public life? Who wants me?"

"Your mother says the county does."

"If the county wants anyone it wants a Radical. But I've talked to more people than my mother, and they're weary of us leisured classes coasting round in motor-cars and asking for something to do. All this solemn to and fro between great houses—it's a game without gaiety. You don't find it played outside England. (Maurice, I'm going to Greece.) No one wants us, or anything except a comfortable home."

"But to give a comfortable home's what public life is," shrilled Kitty.

"Is, or ought to be?"

"Well, it's all the same."

"Is and ought to be are not the same," said her mother, proud of grasping the distinction. "You ought to be not interrupting Mr Durham, whereas you—"

"—is," supplied Ada, and the family laugh made Clive jump.

"We are and we ought to be," concluded Mrs Hall. "Very different."

"Not always," contradicted Clive.

"Not always, remember that, Kitty," she echoed, vaguely admonitory: on other occasions he had not minded her. Kitty cried back to her first assertion. Ada was saying anything, Maurice nothing. He was eating away placidly, too used to such table talk to see that it worried his friend. Between the courses he told an anecdote. All were silent to listen to him. He spoke slowly, stupidly, without attending to his words or taking the trouble to be interesting. Suddenly Clive cut in with "I say—I'm going to faint," and fell off his chair.

"Get a pillow, Kitty: Ada, eau de Cologne," said their brother. He loosened Clive's collar. "Mother, fan him; no; fan him..."

"Silly it is," murmured Clive.

As he spoke, Maurice kissed him.

"I'm all right now."

The girls and a servant came running in.

"I can walk," he said, the colour returning to his face.

"Certainly not," cried Mrs Hall. "Maurice'll carry you—Mr Durham, put your arms round Maurice."

"Come along, old man. The doctor: somebody telephone." He picked up his friend, who was so weak that he began to cry.

"Maurice—I'm a fool."

"Be a fool," said Maurice, and carried him upstairs, undressed him, and put him to bed. Mrs Hall knocked, and going out to her he said quickly, "Mother, you needn't tell the others I kissed Durham."

"Oh, certainly not."

"He wouldn't like it. I was rather upset and did it without thinking. As you know, we are great friends, relations almost."

It sufficed. She liked to have little secrets with her son; it reminded her of the time when she had been so much to him. Ada joined them with a hot water bottle, which he took in to the patient.

"The doctor'll see me like this," Clive sobbed.

"I hope he will."

"Why?"

Maurice lit a cigarette, and sat on the edge of the bed. "We want him to see you at your worst. Why did Pippa let you travel?"

"I was supposed to be well."

"Hell take you."

"Can we come in?" called Ada through the door.

"No. Send the doctor alone."

"He's here," cried Kitty in the distance. A man, little older than themselves, was announced.

"Hullo, Jowitt," said Maurice, rising. "Just cure me this chap. He's had influenza, and is supposed to be well. Result he's fainted, and can't stop crying."

"We know all about that," remarked Mr Jowitt, and stuck a thermometer into Clive's mouth. "Been working hard?"

"Yes, and now wants to go to Greece."

"So he shall. You clear out now. I'll see you downstairs."

Maurice obeyed, convinced that Clive was seriously ill. Jowitt followed in about ten minutes, and told Mrs Hall it was nothing much—a bad relapse. He wrote prescriptions, and said he would send in a nurse. Maurice followed him into the garden, and, laying a hand on his arm, said, "Now tell me how ill he is. This isn't a relapse. It's something more. Please tell me the truth."

"*He's* all right," said the other; somewhat annoyed, for he piqued himself on telling the truth. "I thought you realized that. He's stopped the hysteria and is getting off to sleep. It's just an ordinary relapse. He will have to be more careful this time than the other, that's all."

"And how long will these ordinary relapses, as you call them, go on? At any moment may he have this appalling pain?"

"He's only a bit uncomfortable—caught a chill in the car, he thinks."

"Jowitt, you don't tell me. A grown man doesn't cry, unless he's gone pretty far."

"That is only the weakness."

"Oh, give it your own name," said Maurice, removing his hand. "Besides, I'm keeping you."

"Not a bit, my young friend, I'm here to answer any difficulties."

"Well, if it's so slight, why are you sending in a nurse?"

"To amuse him. I understand he's well off."

"And can't we amuse him?"

"No, because of the infection. You were there when I told your mother none of you ought to go into the room."

"I thought you meant my sisters."

"You equally—more, for you've already caught it from him once."

"I won't have a nurse."

"Mrs Hall has telephoned to the Institute."

"Why is everything done in such a damned hurry?" said Maurice, raising his voice. "I shall nurse him myself."

"Have you wheeling the baby next."

"I beg your pardon?"

Jowitt went off laughing.

In tones that admitted no argument Maurice told his mother he should sleep in the patient's room. He would not have a bed taken in, lest Clive woke up, but lay down on the floor with his head on a foot-stool, and read by the rays of a candle lamp. Before long Clive stirred and said feebly, "Oh damnation, oh damnation."

"Want anything?" Maurice called.

"My inside's all wrong."

Maurice lifted him out of bed and put him on the night stool. When relief had come he lifted him back.

"I can walk: you mustn't do this sort of thing."

"You'd do it for me."

He carried the stool down the passage and cleaned it. Now that Clive was undignified and weak, he loved him as never before.

"You mustn't," repeated Clive, when he came back. "It's too filthy."

"Doesn't worry me," said Maurice, lying down. "Get off to sleep again."

"The doctor told me he'd send a nurse."

"What do you want with a nurse? It's only a touch of diarrhoea. You can keep on all night as far as I'm concerned. Honestly it doesn't worry me—I don't say this to please you. It just doesn't."

"I can't possibly—your office—"

"Look here, Clive, would you rather have a trained nurse or me? One's coming tonight, but I left word she was to be sent away again, because I'd rather chuck the office and look after you myself, and thought you'd rather."

Clive was silent so long that Maurice thought him asleep. At last he sighed, "I suppose I'd better have the nurse."

"Right: she will make you more comfortable than I can. Perhaps you're right."

Clive made no reply.

Ada had volunteered to sit up in the room below, and, according to arrangement, Maurice tapped three times, and while waiting for her studied Clive's blurred and sweaty face. It was useless the doctor talking: his friend was in agony. He longed to embrace him, but remembered this had brought on the hysteria, and besides, Clive was restrained, fastidious almost. As Ada did not come he went downstairs, and found that she had fallen asleep. She lay, the picture of health, in a big leather chair, with her hands dropped on either side and her feet stretched out. Her bosom rose and fell, her heavy black hair served as a cushion to her face, and between her lips he saw teeth and a scarlet tongue. "Wake up," he cried irritably.

Ada woke.

"How do you expect to hear the front door when the nurse comes?"

"How is poor Mr Durham?"

"Very ill; dangerously ill."

"Oh Maurice! Maurice!"

"The nurse is to stop. I called you, but you never came. Go off to bed now, as you can't even help that much."

"Mother said I must sit up, because the nurse mustn't be let in by a man—it wouldn't look well."

"I can't think how you have time to think of such rubbish," said Maurice.

"We must keep the house a good name."

He was silent, then laughed in the way the girls disliked. At the bottom of their hearts they disliked him entirely, but were too confused mentally to know this. His laugh was the only grievance they avowed.

"Nurses are not nice. No nice girl would be a nurse. If they are you may be sure they do not come from nice homes, or they would stop at home."

"Ada, how long were you at school?" asked her brother, as he helped himself to a drink.

"I call going to school stopping at home."

He set down his glass with a clank, and left her. Clive's eyes were open, but he did not speak or seem to know that Maurice had returned, nor did the coming of the nurse arouse him.

XXI

It was plain in a few days that nothing serious was amiss with the visitor. The attack, despite its dramatic start, was less serious than its predecessor, and soon allowed his removal to Penge. His appearance and spirits remained poor, but that must be expected after influenza, and no one except Maurice felt the least uneasiness.

Maurice thought seldom about disease and death, but when he did it was with strong disapproval. They could not be allowed to spoil his life or his friend's, and he brought all his youth and health to bear on Clive. He was with him constantly, going down uninvited to Penge for weekends or for a few days' holiday, and trying by example rather than precept to cheer him up. Clive did not respond. He could rouse himself in company, and even affect interest in a right of way question that had arisen between the Durhams and the British Public, but when they were alone he relapsed into gloom, would not speak, or spoke in a half serious, half joking way that tells of mental exhaustion. He determined to go to Greece. That was the only point on which he held firm. He would go, though the month would be September, and he alone. "It must be done," he said. "It is a vow. Every barbarian must give the Acropolis its chance once."

Maurice had no use for Greece. His interest in the classics had been slight and obscene, and had vanished when he loved Clive. The stories of Harmodius and Aristogeiton, of Phaedrus, of the Theban Band were well enough for those whose hearts were empty, but no substitute for life. That Clive should occasionally prefer them puzzled him. In Italy, which he liked well enough in spite of the food and the frescoes, he had refused to cross to the yet holier land beyond the Adriatic. "It sounds out of repair" was his argument. "A heap of old stones without any paint on. At all events this"—he indicated the library of Siena Cathedral—"you may say what you like, but it is in working order." Clive, in his amusement, jumped up and down upon the Piccolomini tiles, and the custodian laughed too instead of scolding them. Italy had been very jolly—as much as one wants in the way of sight-seeing surely—but in these latter days Greece had cropped up again. Maurice hated the very word, and by a curious inversion connected it with morbidity and death. Whenever he wanted to plan, to play tennis, to talk nonsense, Greece intervened. Clive saw his antipathy, and took to teasing him about it, not very kindly.

For Clive wasn't kind: it was to Maurice the most serious of all the symptoms. He would make slightly malicious remarks, and use his intimate knowledge to wound. He failed: i.e., his knowledge was incomplete, or he would have known the impossibility of vexing athletic love. If Maurice sometimes parried outwardly it was because he felt it human to respond: he always had been put off Christ turning the other cheek. Inwardly nothing vexed him. The desire for union was too strong to admit resentment. And sometimes, quite cheerfully, he would conduct a parallel conversation, hitting out at Clive at times in acknowledgement of his presence, but going his own way towards light, in hope that the beloved would follow.

Their last conversation took place on these lines. It was the evening before Clive's departure, and he had the whole of the Hall family to dine with him at the Savoy, as a return for their kindness to him, and had sandwiched them out between some other friends. "We shall know what it is if you fall *this* time," cried Ada, nodding at the champagne. "Your health!" he replied. "And the health of all ladies. Come, Maurice!" It pleased him to be slightly old-fashioned. Healths were drunk, and only Maurice detected the underlying bitterness.

After the banquet he said to Maurice, "Are you sleeping

at home?"

"No."

"I thought you might want to see your people home."

"Not he, Mr Durham," said his mother. "Nothing I can do or say can make him miss a Wednesday. Maurice is a regular old bachelor."

"My flat's upside down with packing," remarked Clive. "I leave by the morning train, and go straight through to Marseilles."

Maurice took no notice, and came. They stood yawning at each other, while the lift descended for them, then sped upwards, climbed another stage on their feet, and went down a passage that recalled the approach to Risley's rooms at Trinity. The flat, small, dark and silent, lay at the end. It was, as Clive said, littered with rubbish, but his housekeeper, who slept out, had made up Maurice's bed as usual, and had arranged drinks.

"Yet again," remarked Clive.

Maurice liked alcohol, and had a good head.

"I'm going to bed. I see you've found what you wanted."

"Take care of yourself. Don't overdo the ruins. By the way—" He took a phial out of his pocket. "I knew you'd forget this. Chlorodyne."

"Chlorodyne! Your contribution!"

He nodded.

"Chlorodyne for Greece. . . . Ada has been telling me that you thought I was going to die. Why on earth do you worry about my health? There's no fear. I shan't ever have so clean and clear an experience as death."

"I know I shall die some time and I don't want to, nor you to. If either of us goes, nothing's left for both. I don't know if you call that clean and clear?"

"Yes, I do."

"Then I'd rather be dirty," said Maurice, after a pause. Clive shivered.

"Don't you agree?"

"Oh, you're getting like everyone else. You will have a

theory. We can't go quietly ahead, we must always be formulating, though every formula breaks down. 'Dirt at all costs' is to be yours. I say there are cases when one gets too dirty. Then Lethe, if there is such a river, will wash it away. But there may not be such a river. The Greeks assumed little enough, yet too much perhaps. There may be no forgetfulness beyond the grave. This wretched equipment may continue. In other words, beyond the grave there may be Hell."

"Oh, balls."

Clive generally enjoyed his metaphysics. But this time he went on. "To forget everything—even happiness. Happiness! A casual tickling of someone or something against onself—that's all. Would that we had never been lovers! For then, Maurice, you and I should have lain still and been quiet. We should have slept, then had we been at rest with kings and counsellors of the earth, which built desolate places for themselves—"

"What on earth are you talking about?"

"—or as an hidden untimely birth, we had not been: as infants which never saw light. But as it is—Well, don't look so serious."

"Don't try to be funny then," said Maurice. "I never did think anything of your speeches."

"Words conceal thought. That theory?"

"They make a silly noise. I don't care about your thoughts either."

"Then what do you care about in me?"

Maurice smiled: as soon as this question was asked, he felt happy, and refused to answer it.

"My beauty?" said Clive cynically. "These somewhat faded charms. My hair is falling out. Are you aware?"

"Bald as an egg by thirty."

"As an addled egg. Perhaps you like me for my mind. During and after my illness I must have been a delightful companion."

Maurice looked at him with tenderness. He was studying

him, as in the earliest days of their acquaintance. Only then it was to find out what he was like, now what had gone wrong with him. Something was wrong. The diseases still simmered, vexing the brain, and causing it to be gloomy and perverse, and Maurice did not resent this: he hoped to succeed where the doctor had failed. He knew his own strength. Presently he would put it forth as love, and heal his friend, but for the moment he investigated.

"I expect you do like me for my mind—for its feebleness. You always knew I was inferior. You're wonderfully considerate—give me plenty of rope and never snub me as you did your family at dinner."

It was as if he wanted to pick a quarrel.

"Now and then you call me to heel—" He pinched him, pretending to be playful. Maurice started. "What is wrong now? Tired?"

"I'm off to bed."

"I.e., you're tired. Why can't you answer a question? I didn't say 'tired of me', though I might have."

"Have you ordered your taxi for the nine o'clock?"

"No, nor got my ticket. I shan't go to Greece at all. Perhaps it'll be as intolerable as England."

"Well, good night, old man." He went, deeply concerned, to his room. Why would everyone declare Clive was fit to travel? Clive even knew he wasn't himself. So methodical as a rule, he had put off taking his ticket till the last moment. He might still not go, but to express the hope was to defeat it. Maurice undressed, and catching sight of himself in the glass, thought, "A mercy I'm fit." He saw a well-trained serviceable body and a face that contradicted it no longer. Virility had harmonized them and shaded either with dark hair. Slipping on his pyjamas, he sprang into bed, concerned, yet profoundly happy, because he was strong enough to live for two. Clive had helped him. Clive would help him again when the pendulum swung, meanwhile he must help Clive, and all through life they would alternate thus: as he dozed off he had a further vision of love, that was not far from the ultimate.

There was a knock at the wall that divided their rooms.

"What is it?" he called; then, "Come in!" for Clive was now at the door.

"Can I come into your bed?"

"Come along," said Maurice, making room.

"I'm cold and miserable generally. I can't sleep. I don't know why."

Maurice did not misunderstand him. He knew and shared his opinions on this point. They lay side by side without touching. Presently Clive said, "It's no better here. I shall go." Maurice was not sorry, for he could not get to sleep either, though for a different reason, and he was afraid Clive might hear the drumming of his heart, and guess what it was.

XXII

Clive sat in the theatre of Dionysus. The stage was empty, as it had been for many centuries, the auditorium empty; the sun had set though the Acropolis behind still radiated heat. He saw barren plains running down to the sea, Salamiss, Aegina, mountains, all blended in a violet evening. Here dwelt his gods—Pallas Athene in the first place: he might if he chose imagine her shrine untouched, and her statue catching the last of the glow. She understood all men, though motherless and a virgin. He had been coming to thank her for years because she had lifted him out of the mire.

But he saw only dying light and a dead land. He uttered no prayer, believed in no deity, and knew that the past was devoid of meaning like the present, and a refuge for cowards.

Well, he had written to Maurice at last. His letter was journeying down to the sea. Where one sterility touched another, it would embark and voyage past Sunium and Cythera, would land and embark, would land again. Maurice would get it as he was starting for his work. "Against my will I have become normal. I cannot help it." The words had been written.

He descended the theatre wearily. Who could help anything? Not only in sex, but in all things men have moved blindly, have evolved out of slime to dissolve into it when this accident of consequences is over. *μὴ φῦναι τὸν ἅπαντα νικᾷ λόγον*, sighed the actors in this very place two thousand years before. Even that remark, though further from vanity than most, was vain.

XXIII

Dear Clive,

Please come back on receiving this. I have looked out your connections, and you can reach England on Tuesday week if you start at once. I am very anxious about you on account of your letter, as it shows how ill you are. I have waited to hear from you for a fortnight and now comes two sentences, which I suppose mean that you cannot love anyone of your own sex any longer. We will see whether this is so as soon as you arrive!

I called upon Pippa yesterday. She was full of the lawsuit, and thinks your mother made a mistake in closing the path. Your mother has told the village she is not closing it against them. I called to get news of you, but Pippa had not heard either. You will be amused to hear that I have been learning some classical music lately—also golf. I get on as well as can be expected at Hill and Hall's. My mother has gone to Birmingham after changing backwards and forwards for a week. Now you have all the news. Wire on getting this, and again on reaching Dover.

Maurice.

Clive received this letter and shook his head. He was going with some hotel acquaintances up Pentelicus, and tore it to pieces on the top of the mountain. He had stopped loving Maurice and should have to say so plainly.

XXIV

He stopped a week more at Athens, lest by any possibility he was wrong. The change had been so shocking that sometimes he thought Maurice was right, and that it was the finish of his illness. It humiliated him, for he had understood his soul, or, as he said, himself, ever since he was fifteen. But the body is deeper than the soul and its secrets inscrutable. There had been no warning—just a blind alteration of the life spirit, just an announcement, "You who loved men, will henceforward love women. Understand or not, it's the same to me." Whereupon he collapsed. He tried to clothe the change with reason, and understand it, in order that he might feel less humiliated: but it was of the nature of death or birth, and he failed.

It came during illness—possibly through illness. During the first attack, when he was severed from ordinary life and feverish, it seized an opportunity that it would have taken some time or other. He noticed how charming his nurse was and enjoyed obeying her. When he went a drive his eye rested on women. Little details, a hat, the way a skirt is held, scent, laughter, the delicate walk across mud—blended into a charming whole, and it pleased him to find that the women often answered his eye with equal pleasure. Men had never responded—they did not assume he admired them, and were either unconscious or puzzled. But women took admiration for granted. They might be offended or coy, but they understood, and welcomed him into a world of delicious interchange. All through the drive Clive was radiant. How happy normal people made their lives! On how little had he existed for twenty-four years! He chatted to his nurse, and felt her his for ever. He noticed the statues, the advertisements, the daily papers. Passing a cinema palace, he went in. The film was unbearable artistically, but the man who made it, the men and the women who looked on—they knew, and he was one of them.

In no case could the exaltation have lasted. He was like one whose ears have been syringed; for the first few hours he hears super-normal sounds, which vanish when he adjusts himself to the human tradition. He had not gained a sense, but rearranged one, and life would not have appeared as a holiday for long. It saddened at once, for on his return Maurice was waiting for him, and a seizure resulted: like a fit, it struck at him from behind the brain. He murmured that he was too tired to talk, and escaped, and Maurice's illness gave him a further reprieve, during which he persuaded himself that their relations had not altered, and that he might without disloyalty contemplate women. He wrote affectionately and accepted the invitation to recruit, without misgivings.

He said he caught cold in the car; but in his heart he believed that the cause of his relapse was spiritual: to be with Maurice or anyone connected with him was suddenly revolting. The heat at dinner! The voices of the Halls! Their laughter! Maurice's anecdote! It mixed with the food—was the food. Unable to distinguish matter from spirit, he fainted.

But when he opened his eyes it was to the knowledge that love had died, so that he wept when his friend kissed him. Each kindness increased his suffering, until he asked the nurse to forbid Mr Hall to enter the room. Then he recovered and could fly to Penge, where he loved him as much as ever until he turned up. He noticed the devotion, the heroism even, but his friend bored him. He longed for him to go back to town, and actually said so, so near the surface had the rock risen. Maurice shook his head and stopped.

Clive did not give in to the life spirit without a struggle. He believed in the intellect and tried to think himself back into the old state. He averted his eyes from women, and when that failed adopted childish and violent expedients. The one was this visit to Greece, the other—he could not recall it without disgust. Not until all emotion had ebbed would it have been possible. He regretted it deeply, for Maurice now inspired him with a physical dislike that made the future more difficult, and he wished to keep friends with his old lover, and to help him through the approaching catastrophe. It was all so complicated. When love flies it is remembered not as love but as something else. Blessed are the uneducated, who forget it entirely, and are never conscious of folly or pruriency in the past, of long aimless conversations.

XXV

Clive did not wire, nor start at once. Though desirous to be kind and training himself to think reasonably of Maurice, he refused to obey orders as of old. He returned to England at his leisure. He did wire from Folkestone to Maurice's office, and expected to be met at Charing Cross, and when he was not he took a train on to the suburbs, in order to explain as quickly as possible. His attitude was sympathetic and calm.

It was an October evening; the falling leaves, the mist, the hoot of an owl, filled him with pleasing melancholy. Greece had been clear but dead. He liked the atmosphere of the North, whose gospel is not truth, but compromise. He and his friend would arrange something that should include women. Sadder and older, but without a crisis, they would slip into a relation, as evening into night. He liked the night also. It had graciousness and repose. It was not absolutely dark. Just as he was about to lose his way up from the station, he saw another street lamp, and then past that another. There were chains in every direction, one of which he followed to his goal.

Kitty heard his voice, and came from the drawing-room to welcome him. He had always cared for Kitty least of the family—she was not a true woman, as he called it now—and she brought the news that Maurice was away for the night on business. "Mother and Ada are in church," she added. "They have had to walk because Maurice would take the car."

"Where has he gone?"

"Don't ask me. He leaves his address with the servants. We know even less about Maurice than when you were last here, if you think that possible. He has become a most mysterious person." She gave him tea, humming a tune.

Her lack of sense and of charm produced a not unwelcome reaction in her brother's favour. She continued to complain of him in the cowed fashion that she had inherited from Mrs Hall.

"It's only five minutes to church," remarked Clive.

"Yes, they would have been in to receive you if he had let us know. He keeps everything so secret, and then laughs at girls."

"It was I who did not let him know."

"What's Greece like?"

He told her. She was as bored as her brother would have been, and had not his gift of listening beneath words. Clive remembered how often he had held forth to Maurice and felt at the end an access of intimacy. There was a good deal to be saved out of the wreck of that passion. Maurice was big, and so sensible when once he understood.

Kitty proceeded, sketching her own affairs in a slightly clever way. She had asked to go to an Institute to acquire Domestic Economy, and her mother would have allowed her, but Maurice had put his foot down when he heard that the fees were three guineas a week. Kitty's grievances were mainly financial: she wanted an allowance. Ada had one. Ada, as heiress-apparent, had to "learn the value of money. But I am not to learn anything." Clive decided that he would tell his friend to treat the girl better; once before he had interfered, and Maurice, charming to the core, had made him feel he could say anything.

A deep voice interrupted them; the churchgoers were back. Ada came in, dressed in a jersey, tam o'shanter, and grey skirt; the autumn mist had left a delicate bloom upon her hair. Her cheeks were rosy, her eyes bright; she greeted him with obvious pleasure, and though her exclamations were the same as Kitty's they produced a different effect. "Why didn't you let us know?" she cried. "There will be nothing but the pie. We would have given you a real English dinner."

He said he must return to town in a few minutes but

Mrs Hall insisted he should sleep. He was glad to do this. The house now filled with tender memories, especially when Ada spoke. He had forgotten she was so different from Kitty.

"I thought you were Maurice," he said to her. "Your voices are wonderfully alike."

"It's because I have a cold," she said, laughing.

"No, they are alike," said Mrs Hall. "Ada has Maurice's voice, his nose, by which of course I mean the mouth too, and his good spirits and good health. Three things, I often think of it. Kitty on the other hand has his brain."

All laughed. The three women were evidently fond of one another. Clive saw relations that he had not guessed, for they were expanding in the absence of their man. Plants live by the sun, yet a few of them flower at night-fall, and the Halls reminded him of the evening primroses that starred a deserted alley at Penge. When talking to her mother and sister, even Kitty had beauty, and he determined to rebuke Maurice about her; not unkindly, for Maurice was beautiful too, and bulked largely in this new vision.

The girls had been incited by Dr Barry to join an ambulance class, and after dinner Clive submitted his body to be bound. Ada tied up his scalp, Kitty his ankle, while Mrs Hall, happy and careless, repeated "Well, Mr Durham, this is a better illness than the last anyhow."

"Mrs Hall, I wish you would call me by my Christian name."

"Indeed I will. But Ada and Kitty—not you."

"I wish Ada and Kitty would too."

"Clive, then!" said Kitty.

"Kitty, then!"

"Clive."

"Ada—that's better." But he was blushing. "I hate formalities."

"So do I," came the chorus. "I care nothing for anyone's opinion—never did," and fixed him with candid eyes.

"Maurice on the other hand," from Mrs Hall, "is very particular."

"Maurice is a rip really—Waow, you're hurting my head."

"Waow, waow," Ada imitated.

There was a ring at the telephone.

"He has had your wire from the office," announced Kitty "He wants to know whether you're here."

"Say I am."

"He's coming back tonight, then. Now he wants to talk to you."

Clive took the receiver, but only a burr arrived. They had been disconnected. They could not ring Maurice up a they did not know where he was, and Clive felt relieved, for the approach of reality alarmed him. He was so happy being bandaged: his friend would arrive soon enough Now Ada bent over him. He saw features that he knew with a light behind that glorified them. He turned from the dark hair and eyes to the unshadowed mouth or to the curves of the body, and found in her the exact need of his transition. He had seen more seductive women, but none that promised such peace. She was the compromise between memory and desire, she was the quiet evening that Greece had never known. No argument touched her, because she was tenderness, who reconciles present with past. He had not supposed there was such a creature except in Heaven and he did not believe in Heaven. Now much had become possible suddenly. He lay looking into her eyes, where some of his hope lay reflected. He knew that he might make her love him, and the knowledge lit him with temperate fire. It was charming—he desired no more yet, and his only anxiety was lest Maurice should arrive, for a memory should remain a memory. Whenever the others ran out of the room to see whether that noise was the car, he kept her with him, and soon she understood that he wished this, and stopped without his command.

"If you knew what it is to be in England!" he said suddenly.

"Is Greece not nice?"

"Horrible."

She was distressed and Clive also sighed. Their eyes met.

"I'm so sorry, Clive."

"Oh, it's all over."

"What exactly was it—"

"Ada, it was this. While in Greece I had to reconstruct my life from the bottom. Not an easy task, but I think I've done it."

"We often talked of you. Maurice said you would like Greece."

"Maurice doesn't know—no one knows as much as you! I've told you more than anyone. Can you keep a secret?"

"Of course."

Clive was nonplussed. The conversation had become impossible. But Ada never expected continuity. To be alone with Clive, whom she innocently admired, was enough. She told him how thankful she was he had returned. He agreed, with vehemence. "Especially to return here."

"The car!" Kitty shrieked.

"Don't go!" he repeated, catching her hand.

"I must—Maurice—"

"Bother Maurice." He held her. There was a tumult in the hall. "Where's he gone?" his friend was roaring. "Where've you put him?"

"Ada, take me a walk tomorrow. See more of me.... That's settled."

Her brother burst in. Seeing the bandages, he thought there had been an accident, then laughed at his mistake. "Come out of that, Clive. Why did you let them? I say, he looks well. You look well. Good man. Come and have a drink. I'll unpick you. No, girls, not you." Clive followed him, but, turning, had an imperceptible nod from Ada.

Maurice looked like an immense animal in his fur coat.

He slipped it off as soon as they were alone, and came up smiling. "So you don't love me?" he challenged.

"All that must be tomorrow," said Clive, averting his eyes.

"Quite so. Have a drink."

"Maurice, I don't want a row."

"I do."

He waved the glass aside. The storm must burst. "But you mustn't talk to me like this," he continued. "It increases my difficulties."

"I want a row and I'll have it." He came in his oldest manner and thrust a hand into Clive's hair. "Sit down. Now why did you write me that letter?"

Clive did not reply. He was looking with growing dismay into the face he had once loved. The horror of masculinity had returned, and he wondered what would happen if Maurice tried to embrace him.

"Why? Eh? Now you're fit again, tell me."

"Go off my chair, and I will." Then he began one of the speeches he had prepared. It was scientific and impersonal, as this would wound Maurice least. "I have become normal—like other men, I don't know how, any more than I know how I was born. It is outside reason, it is against my wish. Ask any questions you like. I have come down here to answer them, for I couldn't go into details in my letter. But I wrote the letter because it was true."

"True, you say?"

"Was and is the truth."

"You say that you care for women only, not men?"

"I care for men, in the real sense, Maurice, and always shall."

"All that presently."

He too was impersonal, but he had not got off the chair. His fingers remained on Clive's head, touching the bandages, his mood had changed from gaiety to quiet concern. He was neither angry nor afraid, he only wanted to heal, and Clive, in the midst of repulsion, realized what a triumph of love was ruining, and how feeble or how ironical must be the power that governs Man.

"Who made you change?"

He disliked the form of the question. "No one. It was a change in me merely physical." He began to relate his experiences.

"Evidently the nurse," said Maurice thoughtfully. "I wish you had told me before. . . . I knew something had gone wrong and thought of several things, but not this. One oughtn't to keep secrets, or they get worse. One ought to talk, talk, talk—provided one has someone to talk to, as you and I have. If you'd have told me, you would have been right by now."

"Why?"

"Because I should have made you right."

"How?"

"You'll see," he said smiling.

"It's not the least good—I've changed."

"Can the leopard change his spots? Clive, you're in a muddle. It's part of your general health. I'm not anxious now, because you're well otherwise, you even look happy, and the rest must follow. I see you were afraid to tell me, lest it gave me pain, but we've got past sparing each other. You ought to have told me. What else am I here for? You can't trust anyone else. You and I are outlaws. All this"—he pointed to the middle-class comfort of the room—"would be taken from us if people knew."

He groaned. "But I've changed, I've changed."

We can only interpret by our experiences. Maurice could understand muddle, not change. "You only think you've changed," he said, smiling. "I used to think I had when Miss Olcott was here, but it all went when I returned to you."

"I know my own mind," said Clive, getting warm and freeing himself from the chair. "I was never like you."

"You are now. Do you remember how I pretended—"

"Of course I remember. Don't be childish."

"We love each other, and know it. Then what else—"

"Oh, for God's sake, Maurice, hold your tongue. If I love anyone it's Ada." He added, "I take her at random as an example."

But an example was the one thing Maurice could realize. "Ada?" he said, with a change of tone.

"Only to prove to you the sort of thing."

"You scarcely know Ada."

"Nor did I know my nurse or the other women I've mentioned. As I said before, it's no special person, only a tendency."

"Who was in when you arrived?"

"Kitty."

"But it's Ada, not Kitty."

"Yes, but I don't mean—Oh, don't be stupid!"

"What do you mean?"

"Anyhow, you understand, now," said Clive, trying to keep impersonal, and turning to the comforting words with which his discourse should have concluded. "I've changed. Now I want you to understand too that the change won't spoil anything in our friendship that is real. I like you enormously—more than any man I've ever met" (he did not feel this as he said it) "I most enormously respect and admire you. It's character, not passion, that is the real bond."

"Did you say something to Ada just before I came in? Didn't you hear my car come up? Why did Kitty and my mother come out and not you? You must have heard my noise. You knew I flung up my work for you. You never talked to me down the telephone. You didn't write or come back from Greece. How much did you see of her when you were here before?"

"Look here, old man, I can't be cross-questioned."

"You said you could."

"Not about your sister."

"Why not?"

"You must shut up, I say. Come back to what I was saying about character—the real tie between human beings. You can't build a house on the sand, and passion's sand. We want bed rock . . ."

"Ada!" he called, suddenly deliberate.

Clive shouted in horror. "What for?"

"Ada! Ada!"

He rushed at the door and locked it. "Maurice, it mustn't end like this—not a row," he implored. But as Maurice approached he pulled out the key and clenched it, for chivalry had awoken at last. "You can't drag in a woman," he breathed; "I won't have it."

"Give that up."

"I mustn't. Don't make it worse. No—no."

Maurice bore down on him. He escaped: they dodged round the big chair, arguing for the key in whispers.

They touched with hostility, then parted for ever, the key falling between them.

"Clive, did I hurt you?"

"No."

"My darling, I didn't mean to."

"I'm all right."

They looked at one another for a moment before beginning new lives. "What an ending," he sobbed, "what an ending."

"I do rather love her," said Clive, very pale.

"What's going to happen?" said Maurice, sitting down and wiping his mouth. "Arrange . . . I'm done for."

Since Ada was in the passage Clive went out to her: to Woman was his first duty. Having appeased her with vague words, he returned to the smoking-room, but the door was now locked between them. He heard Maurice turn out the electric light and sit down with a thud.

"Don't be an ass anyway," he called nervously. There was no reply. Clive scarcely knew what to do. At any rate he could not stop in the house. Asserting a man's prerogative, he announced that he must sleep in town after all, in which the women acquiesced. He left the darkness within for that without: the leaves fell as he went to the station, the owls hooted, the mist enveloped him. It was so late that the lamps had been extinguished in the suburban roads, and total night without compromise weighed on him, as on his friend. He too suffered and exclaimed, "What an ending!" but he was promised a dawn. The love of women would rise as certainly as the sun, scorching up immaturity and ushering the full human day, and even in his pain he knew this. He would not marry Ada—she had been transitional—but some goddess of the new universe that had opened to him in London, someone utterly unlike Maurice Hall.

PART THREE

XXVI

For three years Maurice had been so fit and happy that he went on automatically for a day longer. He woke with the feeling that it must be all right soon. Clive would come back, apologizing or not as he chose, and he would apologize to Clive. Clive must love him, because his whole life was dependent on love and here it was going on as usual. How could he sleep and rest if he had no friend? When he returned from town to find no news, he remained for a little calm, and allowed his family to speculate on Clive's departure. But he began to watch Ada. She looked sad—even their mother noticed it. Shading his eyes, he watched her. Save for her, he would have dismissed the scene as "one of Clive's long speeches", but she came into that speech as an example. He wondered why she was sad.

"I say—" he called when they were alone; he had no idea what he was going to say, though a sudden blackness should have warned him. She replied, but he could not hear her voice. "What's wrong with you?" he asked, trembling.

"Nothing."

"There is—I can see it. You can't take me in."

"Oh no—really, Maurice, nothing."

"Why did—what did he say?"

"Nothing."

"Who said nothing?" he yelled, crashing both fists on the table. He had caught her.

"Nothing—only Clive."

The name on her lips opened Hell. He suffered hideously and before he could stop himself had spoken words that neither ever forgot. He accused his sister of corrupting his friend. He let her suppose that Clive had complained of her conduct and gone back to town on that account. Her gentle nature was so outraged that she could not defend herself, but sobbed and sobbed, and implored him not to speak to her mother, just as if she were guilty. He assented: jealousy had maddened him.

"But when you see him—Mr Durham—tell him I didn't mean—say there's no one whom I'd rather—"

"—go wrong with," he supplied: not till later did he understand his own blackguardism.

Hiding her face, Ada collapsed.

"I shall not tell him. I shall never see Durham again to tell. You've the satisfaction of breaking up that friendship."

She sobbed, "I don't mind that—you've always been so unkind to us, always." He drew up at last. Kitty had said that sort of thing to him, but never Ada. He saw that beneath their obsequious surface his sisters disliked him: he had not even succeeded at home. Muttering "It's not my fault," he left her.

A refined nature would have behaved better and perhaps have suffered less. Maurice was not intellectual, nor religious, nor had he that strange solace of self-pity that is granted to some. Except on one point his temperament was normal, and he behaved as would the average man who after two years of happiness had been betrayed by his wife. It was nothing to him that Nature had caught up this dropped stitch in order to continue her pattern. While he had love he had kept reason. Now he saw Clive's change as treachery and Ada as its cause, and returned in a few hours to the abyss where he had wandered as a boy.

After this explosion his career went forward. He caught the usual train to town, to earn and spend money in the old manner; he read the old papers and discussed strikes and the divorce laws with his friends. At first he was proud of his self-control: did not he hold Clive's reputation in the hollow of his hand? But he grew more bitter, he wished that he had shouted while he had the strength and smashed down this front of lies. What if he too were involved? His family, his position in society—they had been nothing to him for years. He was an outlaw in disguise. Perhaps among those who took to the greenwood in old time there had been two men like himself—two. At times he entertained the dream. Two men can defy the world.

Yes: the heart of his agony would be loneliness. He took time to realize this, being slow. The incestuous jealousy, the mortification, the rage at his past obtuseness—these might pass, and having done much harm they did pass. Memories of Clive might pass. But the loneliness remained. He would wake and gasp "I've no one!" or "Oh Christ, what a world!" Clive took to visiting him in dreams. He knew there was no one, but Clive, smiling in his sweet way, said "I'm genuine this time," to torture him. Once he had a dream about the dream of the face and the voice, a dream about it, no nearer. Also old dreams of the other sort, that tried to disintegrate him. Days followed nights. An immense silence, as of death, encircled the young man, and as he was going up to town one morning it struck him that he really was dead. What was the use of money-grubbing, eating and playing games? That was all he did or had ever done.

"Life's a damn poor show," he exclaimed, crumpling up the *Daily Telegraph*.

The other occupants of the carriage who liked him began to laugh.

"I'd jump out of the window for twopence."

Having spoken, he began to contemplate suicide. There was nothing to deter him. He had no initial fear of death, and no sense of a world beyond it, nor did he mind disgracing his family. He knew that loneliness was poisoning him, so that he grew viler as well as more unhappy. Under these circumstances might he not cease? He began to compare ways and means, and would have shot himself but for an unexpected event. This event was the illness and death of his grandfather, which induced a new state of mind.

Meanwhile, he had received letters from Clive, but they

always contained the sentence, "We had better not meet just yet." He grasped the situation now—his friend would do anything for him except be with him; it had been thus ever since the first illness, and on these lines he was offered friendship in the future. Maurice did not cease to love, but his heart had been broken; he never had wild thoughts of winning Clive back. What he grasped he grasped with a firmness that the refined might envy, and suffered up to the hilt.

He answered these letters, oddly sincere. He still wrote what was true, and confided that he was unbearably lonely and should blow out his brains before the year ended. But he wrote without emotion. It was more a tribute to their heroic past, and accepted by Durham as such. His replies were unemotional also, and it was plain that, however much help he was given and however hard he tried, he could no longer penetrate into Maurice's mind.

XXVII

Maurice's grandfather was an example of the growth that may come with old age. Throughout life he had been the ordinary business man—hard and touchy—but he retired not too late, and with surprising results. He took to "reading", and though the direct effects were grotesque, a softness was generated that transformed his character. The opinions of others—once to be contradicted or ignored—appeared worthy of note, and their desires worth humouring. Ida, his unmarried daughter, who kept house for him, had dreaded the time "when my father will have nothing to do", and herself impervious, did not realize that he had changed until he was about to leave her.

The old gentleman employed his leisure in evolving a new religion—or rather a new cosmogony, for it did not contradict chapel. The chief point was that God lives inside the sun, whose bright envelope consists of the spirits of the blessed. Sunspots reveal God to men, so that when they occurred Mr Grace spent hours at his telescope, noting the interior darkness. The incarnation was a sort of sunspot.

He was glad to discuss his discovery with anyone, but did not proselytize, remarking that each must settle for himself: Clive Durham, with whom he had once had a long talk, knew as much about his opinions as anyone. They were those of the practical man who tries to think spiritually—absurd and materialistic, but first hand. Mr Grace had rejected the tasteful accounts of the unseen that are handed out by the churches, and for that reason the hellenist had got on with him.

Now he was dying. A past of questionable honesty had faded, and he looked forward to joining those he loved and to be joined in due season by those whom he left behind. He summoned his late employees—men without illusions, but they "humoured the old hypocrite". He summoned his family, whom he had always treated well. His last days were very beautiful. To inquire into the causes of beauty were to inquire too closely, and only a cynic would dispel the blended Sorrow and Peace that perfumed Alfriston Gardens while a dear old man lay dying.

The relations came separately, in parties of two and three. All, except Maurice, were impressed. There was no intrigue, as Mr Grace had been open about his will, and each knew what to expect. Ada, as the favourite grandchild, shared the fortune with her aunt. The rest had legacies. Maurice did not propose to receive his. He did nothing to force Death on, but it waited to meet him at the right moment, probably when he returned.

But the sight of a fellow-traveller disconcerted him. His grandfather was getting ready for a journey to the sun, and, garrulous with illness, poured out to him one December afternoon. "Maurice, you read the papers. You've seen the new theory—" It was that a meteor swarm impinged on the rings of Saturn, and chipped pieces off them that fell into the sun. Now Mr Grace located the wicked in the outer planets of our system, and since he disbelieved in eternal damnation had been troubled how to extricate them. The new theory explained this. They were chipped off and reabsorbed into the good! Courteous and grave, the young man listened until a fear seized him that this tosh might be true. The fear was momentary, yet started one of those rearrangements that affect the whole character. It left him with the conviction that his grandfather was convinced. One more human being had come alive. He had accomplished an act of creation, and as he did so Death turned her head away. "It's a great thing to believe as you do," he said very sadly. "Since Cambridge I believe in nothing—except in a sort of darkness."

"Ah, when I was your age—and now I see a bright light—no electric light can compare to it."

"When you were my age, grandfather, what?"

But Mr Grace did not answer questions. He said, "Brighter than magnesium wire—the light within," then drew a stupid parallel between God, dark inside the glowing sun, and the soul, invisible inside the visible body. "The power within—the soul: let it out, but not yet, not till the evening." He paused. "Maurice, be good to your mother; to your sisters; to your wife and children; to your clerks, as I have." He paused again and Maurice grunted, but not disrespectfully. He was caught by the phrase, "not till the evening, do not let it out till the evening." The old man rambled ahead. One ought to be good—kind—brave: all the old advice. Yet it was sincere. It came from a living heart.

"Why?" he interrupted. "Grandpapa, why?"

"The light within—"

"I haven't one." He laughed lest emotion should master him. "Such light as I had went out six weeks ago. I don't want to be good or kind or brave. If I go on living I shall be—not those things: the reverse of them. I don't want that either; I don't want anything."

"The light within—"

Maurice had neared confidences, but they would not have been listened to. His grandfather didn't, couldn't understand. He was only to get "the light within—be kind", yet the phrase continued the rearrangement that had begun inside him. Why *should* one be kind and good? For someone's sake—for the sake of Clive or God or the sun? But he had no one. No one except his mother mattered and she only a little. He was practically alone, and why should he go on living? There was really no reason, yet he had a dreary feeling he should, because he had not got Death either; she, like Love, had glanced at him for a minute, then turned away, and left him to "play the game". And he might have to play as long as his grandfather, and retire as absurdly.

XXVIII

His change, then, cannot be described as a conversion. There was nothing edifying about it. When he came home and examined the pistol he would never use, he was seized with disgust; when he greeted his mother no unfathomable love for her welled up. He lived on, miserable and misunderstood, as before, and increasingly lonely. One cannot write those words too often: Maurice's loneliness: it increased.

But a change there had been. He set himself to acquire new habits, and in particular those minor arts of life that he had neglected when with Clive. Punctuality, courtesy, patriotism, chivalry even—here were a few. He practised a severe self-discipline. It was necessary not only to acquire the art, but to know when to apply it, and gently to modify his behaviour. At first he could do little. He had taken up a line to which his family and the world were accustomed, and any deviation worried them. This came out very strongly in a conversation with Ada.

Ada had become engaged to his old chum Chapman, and his hideous rivalry with her could end. Even after his grandfather's death he had feared she might marry Clive, and gone hot with jealousy. Clive would marry someone. But the thought of him with Ada remained maddening, and he could scarcely have behaved properly unless it had been removed.

The match was excellent, and having approved of it publicly he took her aside, and said, "Ada, I behaved so badly to you, dear, after Clive's visit. I want to say so now and ask you to forgive me. It's given a lot of pain since. I'm very sorry."

She looked surprised and not quite pleased; he saw that she still disliked him. She muttered, "That's all over—I love Arthur now."

"I wish I had not gone mad that evening, but I happened to be very much worried about something. Clive never said what I let you think he said either. He never blamed you."

"I don't care whether he did. It doesn't signify."

Her brother's apologies were so rare that she seized the opportunity to trample on him. "When did you last see him?"—Kitty had suggested they had quarrelled.

"Not for some time."

"Those weekends and Wednesdays seem to have quite stopped."

"I wish you happiness. Old Chappie's a good fellow. For two people who are in love to marry strikes me as very jolly."

"It's very kind of you to wish me happiness, Maurice, I'm sure. I hope I shall have it whether I am wished it or not." (This was described to Chapman afterwards as a "repartee".) "I'm sure I wish you the same sort of thing you've been wishing me all along equally." Her face reddened. She had suffered a good deal, and was by no means indifferent to Clive, whose withdrawal had hurt her.

Maurice guessed as much and looked gloomily at her. Then he changed the subject, and, being without memory, she recovered her temper. But she could not forgive her brother: indeed it was not right that one of her temperament should, since he had insulted her centrally, and marred the dawning of a love.

Similar difficulties arose with Kitty. She also was on his conscience, but was displeased when he made amends. He offered to pay her fees at the Domestic Institute whereon her soul had been so long set, and, though she accepted, it was ungraciously, and with the remark, "I expect I'm too old now to properly learn anything." She and Ada incited each other to thwart him in little things. Mrs Hall was shocked at first and rebuked them, but finding her son too indifferent to protect himself, she grew indifferent too. She was fond of him, but would not fight for him any more than she would fight against him when he was rude to the Dean. And so it happened that he was considered less in the house, and during the winter rather lost the position he had won at Cambridge. It began to be "Oh, Maurice won't mind—he can walk—sleep on the camp bed—smoke without a fire." He raised no objection—this was the sort of thing he now lived for—but he noted the subtle change and how it coincided with the coming of loneliness.

The world was likewise puzzled. He joined the Territorials—hitherto he had held off on the ground that the country can only be saved by conscription. He supported the social work even of the Church. He gave up Saturday golf in order to play football with the youths of the College Settlement in South London, and his Wednesday evenings in order to teach arithmetic and boxing to them. The railway carriage felt a little suspicious. Hall had turned serious, what! He cut down his expenses that he might subscribe more largely to charities—to preventive charities: he would not give a halfpenny to rescue work. What with all this and what with his stockbroking, he managed to keep on the go.

Yet he was doing a fine thing—proving on how little the soul can exist. Fed neither by Heaven nor by Earth he was going forward, a lamp that would have blown out, were materialism true. He hadn't a God, he hadn't a lover—the two usual incentives to virtue. But on he struggled with his back to ease, because dignity demanded it. There was no one to watch him, nor did he watch himself, but struggles like his are the supreme achievements of humanity, and surpass any legends about Heaven.

No reward awaited him. This work, like much that had gone before, was to fall ruining. But he did not fall with it, and the muscles it had developed remained for another use.

XXIX

The crash came on a Sunday in spring—exquisite weather. They sat round the breakfast table, in mourning because of Grandpa, but otherwise worldly. Besides his mother and sisters, there was impossible Aunt Ida, who lived with them now, and a Miss Tonks, a friend whom Kitty had made at the Domestic Institute, and who indeed seemed its only tangible product. Between Ada and himself stood an empty chair.

"Oh, Mr Durham's engaged to be married," cried Mrs Hall, who was reading a letter. "How friendly of his mother to tell me. Penge, a county estate," she explained to Miss Tonks.

"That won't impress Violet, mother. She's a socialist."

"Am I, Kitty? Good news."

"You mean bad news, Miss Tonks," said Aunt Ida.

"Mother, who toom?"

"You will say 'Who toom' as a joke too often."

"Oh mother, get on, who is she?" asked Ada, having stifled a regret.

"Lady Anne Woods. You can read the letter for yourselves. He met her in Greece. Lady Anne Woods. Daughter of Sir H. Woods."

There was an outcry amongst the well-informed. It was subsequently found that Mrs Durham's sentence ran, "I will now tell you the name of the lady: Anne Woods: daughter of Sir H. Woods." But even then it was remarkable, and owing to Greece romantic.

"Maurice!" said his aunt across the hubbub.

"Hullo!"

"That boy's late."

Leaning back in his chair he shouted "Dickie!" at the ceiling: they were putting up Dr Barry's young nephew for the weekend, to oblige.

"He doesn't even sleep above, so that's no good," said Kitty.

"I'll go up."

He smoked half a cigarette in the garden and returned. The news had nearly upset him after all. It had come so brutally, and—what hurt him as much—no one behaved as if it were his concern. Nor was it. Mrs Durham and his mother were the principals now. Their friendship had survived the heroic.

He was thinking, "Clive might have written: for the sake of the past he might", when his aunt interrupted him. "That boy's never come," she complained.

He rose with a smile. "My fault. I forgot."

"Forgot!" Everyone concentrated on him. "Forgot when you went out specially? Oh Morrie, you are a funny boy." He left the room, pursued by humorous scorn, and almost forgot again. "In there's my work," he thought, and a deadly lassitude fell on him.

He went upstairs with the tread of an older man, and drew breath at the top. He stretched his arms wide. The morning was exquisite—made for others: for them the leaves rustled and the sun poured into the house. He banged at Dickie Barry's door, and, as that seemed no use, opened it.

The boy, who had been to a dance the night before, remained asleep. He lay with his limbs uncovered. He lay unashamed, embraced and penetrated by the sun. The lips were parted, the down on the upper was touched with gold, the hair broken into countless glories, the body was a delicate amber. To anyone he would have seemed beautiful, and to Maurice who reached him by two paths he became the World's desire.

"It's past nine," he said as soon as he could speak.

Dickie groaned and pulled up the bedclothes to his chin.

"Breakfast—wake up."

"How long have you been here?" he asked, opening his eyes, which were all of him that was now visible, and gazing into Maurice's.

"A little," he said, after a pause.

"I'm awfully sorry."

"You can be as late as you like—it's only I didn't want you to miss the jolly day."

Downstairs they were revelling in snobbery. Kitty asked him whether he had known about Miss Woods. He answered "Yes"—a lie that marked an epoch. Then his aunt's voice arrived, was that boy never coming?

"I told him not to hurry," said Maurice, trembling all over.

"Maurice, you're not very practical, dear," said Mrs Hall.

"He's on a visit."

Auntie remarked that the first duty of a visitor was to conform to the rules of the house. Hitherto he had never opposed her, but now he said, "The rule of this house is that everyone does what they like."

"Breakfast is at half past eight."

"For those who like. Those who are sleepy like breakfast at nine or ten."

"No house could go on, Maurice. No servants would stop, as you will find."

"I'd rather servants went than my guests were treated like schoolboys."

"A schoolboy! Haw! He *is* one!"

"Mr Barry's now at Woolwich," said Maurice shortly.

Aunt Ida snorted, but Miss Tonks shot him a glance of respect. The others had not listened, intent on poor Mrs Durham, who would now only have the dower house. The loss of his temper left him very happy. In a few minutes Dickie joined them, and he rose to greet his god. The boy's hair was now flat from the bath, and his graceful body hidden beneath clothes, but he remained extraordinarily beautiful. There was a freshness about him—he might have arrived with the flowers—and he gave the impression of modesty and of good will. When he apologized to Mrs Hall, the note of his voice made Maurice shiver. And this was the child he wouldn't protect at Sunnington! This the guest whose arrival last night he had felt rather a bore.

So strong was the passion, while it lasted, that he believed the crisis of his life had come. He broke all engagements, as in the old days. After breakfast he saw Dickie to his uncle's, got arm in arm with him, and exacted a promise for tea. It was kept. Maurice abandoned himself to joy. His blood heated. He would not attend to the talk, yet even this advantaged him, for when he said "What?" Dickie came over to the sofa. He passed an arm round him.... The entrance of Aunt Ida may have averted disaster, yet he thought he saw response in the candid eyes.

They met once more—at midnight. Maurice was not happy now, for during the hours of waiting his emotion had become physical.

"I'd a latch key," said Dickie, surprised at finding his host up.

"I know."

There was a pause. Both uneasy, they were glancing at each other and afraid to meet a glance.

"Is it a cold night out?"

"No."

"Can I get you anything before I go up?"

"No, thanks."

Maurice went to the switches and turned on the landing light. Then he turned out the lights in the hall and sprang after Dickie, overtaking him noiselessly.

"This is my room," he whispered. "I mean generally. They've turned me out for you." He added, "I sleep here alone." He was conscious that words were escaping him. Having removed Dickie's overcoat he stood holding it, saying nothing. The house was so quiet that they could hear the women breathing in the other rooms.

The boy said nothing either. The varieties of development are endless, and it so happened that he understood the situation perfectly. If Hall insisted, he would not kick up a row, but he had rather not: he felt like that about it.

"I'm above," panted Maurice, not daring. "In the attic over this—if you want anything—all night alone. I always am."

Dickie's impulse was to bolt the door after him, but he dismissed it as unsoldierly, and awoke to the ringing of the breakfast bell, with the sun on his face and his mind washed clean.

XXX

This episode burst Maurice's life to pieces. Interpreting it by the past, he mistook Dickie for a second Clive, but three years are not lived in a day, and the fires died down as quickly as they had risen, leaving some suspicious ashes behind them. Dickie left on the Monday, and by Friday his image had faded. A client then came into the office, a lively and handsome young Frenchman, who implored Monsieur 'All not to swindle him. While they chaffed, a familiar feeling arose, but this time he smelt attendant odours from the abyss. "No, people like me must keep our noses to the grindstone, I'm afraid," he replied, in answer to the Frenchman's prayer to lunch with him, and his voice was so British that it produced shouts of laughter and a pantomime.

When the fellow had gone he faced the truth. His feeling for Dickie required a very primitive name. He would have sentimentalized once and called it adoration, but the habit of honesty had grown strong. What a stoat he had been! Poor little Dickie! He saw the boy leaping from his embrace, to smash through the window and break his limbs, or yelling like a maniac until help came. He saw the police—

"Lust." He said the word out loud.

Lust is negligible when absent. In the calm of his office Maurice expected to subdue it, now that he had found its name. His mind, ever practical, wasted no time in theological despair, but advanced to the grindstone. He had been forewarned, and therefore forearmed, and had only to keep away from boys and young men to ensure success. Yes, from other young men. Certain obscurities of the last six months became clear. For example, a pupil at the Settlement—He wrinkled his nose, as one who needs no further proof.

The feeling that can impel a gentleman towards a person of lower class stands self-condemned.

He did not know what lay ahead. He was entering into a state that would only end with impotence or death. Clive had postponed it. Clive had influenced him, as always. It had been understood between them that their love, though including the body, should not gratify it, and the understanding had proceeded—no words were used—from Clive. He had been nearest to words on the first evening at Penge, when he refused Maurice's kiss, or on the last afternoon there, when they lay amid deep fern. Then had been framed the rule that brought the golden age, and would have sufficed till death. But to Maurice, despite his content, there had been something hypnotic about it. It had expressed Clive, not him, but now that he was alone he cracked hideously, as once at school. And it was not Clive who would heal him. That influence, even if exerted, would have failed, for a relation such as theirs cannot break without transforming both men for ever.

But he could not realize all this. The ethereal past had blinded him, and the highest happiness he could dream was a return to it. As he sat in his office working, he could not see the vast curve of his life, still less the ghost of his father sitting opposite. Mr Hall senior had neither fought nor thought; there had never been any occasion; he had supported society and moved without a crisis from illicit to licit love. Now, looking across at his son, he is touched with envy, the only pain that survives in the world of shades. For he sees the flesh educating the spirit, as his has never been educated, and developing the sluggish heart and the slack mind against their will.

Presently Maurice was called to the telephone. He raised it to his ear, and, after six months' silence, heard the voice of his only friend.

"Hullo," he began, "hullo, you will have heard my news, Maurice."

"Yes, but you didn't write, so I didn't."

"Quite so."

"Where are you now?"

"Off to a restaurant. We want you to come round there. Will you?"

"I'm afraid I can't. I've just refused one invitation to lunch."

"Are you too busy to talk a little?"

"Oh no."

Clive resumed, evidently relieved by the atmosphere. "My young woman's with me. Presently she'll talk too."

"Oh, all right. Tell me all your plans."

"The wedding's next month."

"Best of luck."

Neither could think of anything to say.

"Now for Anne."

"I'm Anne Woods," said a girl's voice.

"My name's Hall."

"What?"

"Maurice Christopher Hall."

"Mine's Anne Clare Wilbraham Woods, but I can't think of anything to say."

"No more can I."

"You're the eighth friend of Clive I've talked to in this way this morning."

"The eighth?"

"I can't hear."

"I said the eighth."

"Oh yes, now I'll give Clive a turn. Goodbye."

Clive resumed. "By the way, can you come down to Penge next week? It's short notice, but later all will be chaos."

"I'm afraid I can't do that very well. Mr Hill's getting married too, so that I'm more or less busy here."

"What, your old partner?"

"Yes, and after him Ada to Chapman."

"So I heard. How about August? Not September, that's almost certainly the by-election. But come in August and see us through that awful Park v. Village cricket match."

"Thanks, I probably could. You had better write nearer the time."

"Oh, of course. By the way, Anne has a hundred pounds in her pocket. Will you invest it for her?"

"Certainly. What does she fancy?"

"You'd better choose. She's not allowed to fancy more than four per cent."

Maurice quoted a few securities.

"I'd like the last one," said Anne's voice. "I didn't catch its name."

"You'll see it on the Contract Note. What's your address, please?"

She informed him.

"All right. Send the cheque when you hear from us. Perhaps I'd better ring off and buy at once."

He did so. Their intercourse was to run on these lines. However pleasant Clive and his wife were to him, he always felt that they stood at the other end of the telephone wire. After lunch he chose their wedding present. His instinct was to give a thumper, but since he was only eighth on the list of the bridegroom's friends, this would seem out of place. While paying three guineas he caught sight of himself in the glass behind the counter. What a solid young citizen he looked—quiet, honourable, prosperous without vulgarity. On such does England rely. Was it conceivable that on Sunday last he had nearly assaulted a boy?

XXXI

As the spring wore away, he decided to consult a doctor. The decision—most alien to his temperament—was forced on him by a hideous experience in the train. He had been brooding in an ill-conditioned way, and his expression aroused the suspicions and the hopes of the only other person in the carriage. This person, stout and greasy-faced, made a lascivious sign, and, off his guard, Maurice responded. Next moment both rose to their feet. The other man smiled, whereupon Maurice knocked him down. Which was hard on the man, who was elderly and whose nose streamed with blood over the cushions, and the harder because he was now consumed with fear and thought Maurice would pull the alarm cord. He spluttered apologies, offered money. Maurice stood over him, black-browed, and saw in this disgusting and dishonourable old age his own.

He loathed the idea of a doctor, but he had failed to kill lust single-handed. As crude as in his boyhood, it was many times as strong, and raged in his empty soul. He might "keep away from young men", as he had naïvely resolved, but he could not keep away from their images, and hourly committed sin in his heart. Any punishment was preferable, for he assumed a doctor would punish him. He could undergo any course of treatment on the chance of being cured, and even if he wasn't he would be occupied and have fewer minutes for brooding.

Whom should he consult? Young Jowitt was the only doctor he knew well, and the day after that railway journey he managed to remark to him in casual tones, "I say, in your rounds here, do you come across unspeakables of the Oscar Wilde sort?" But Jowitt replied, "No, that's in the asylum work, thank God," which was discouraging, and perhaps it might be better to consult someone whom he should never see again. He thought of specialists, but did not know whether there were any for his disease, nor whether they would keep faith if he confided in them. On all other subjects he could command advice, but on this, which touched him daily, civilization was silent.

In the end he braved a visit to Dr Barry. He knew he should have a bad time, but the old man, though a bully and a tease, was absolutely trustworthy, and had been better disposed to him since his civilities to Dickie. They were in no sense friends, which made it easier, and he went so seldom to the house that it would make little difference were he forbidden it for ever.

He went on a cold evening in May. Spring had turned into a mockery, and a wretched summer was expected also. It was exactly three years since he had come here under balmy skies, to receive his lecture about Cambridge, and his heart beat quicker, remembering how severe the old man had been then. He found him in an agreeable mood, playing bridge with his daughter and wife, and urgent that Maurice should make a fourth in their party.

"I'm afraid I want to speak to you, sir," he said with an emotion so intense that he felt he should never accomplish the real words at all.

"Well, speak away."

"I mean professionally."

"Lord, man, I've retired from practice for the last six years. You go to Jericho or Jowitt. Sit down, Maurice. Glad to see you, shouldn't have guessed you were dying. Polly! Whisky for this fading flower."

Maurice remained standing, then turned away so oddly that Dr Barry followed him into the hall and said, "Hi, Maurice, can I seriously do anything for you?"

"I should think you can!"

"I've not even a consulting-room."

"It's an illness too awfully intimate for Jowitt—I'd rather come to you—you're the only doctor alive I dare tell.

Once before I said to you I hoped I'd learn to speak out. It's about that."

"A secret trouble, eh? Well, come along."

They went into the dining-room, which was still strewn with dessert. The Venus de Medici in bronze stood on the mantelpiece, copies of Greuze hung on the walls. Maurice tried to speak and failed, poured out some water, failed again, and broke into a fit of sobbing.

"Take your time," said the old man quite kindly, "and remember of course that this is professional. Nothing you say will ever reach your mother's ears."

The ugliness of the interview overcame him. It was like being back in the train. He wept at the hideousness into which he had been forced, he who had meant to tell no one but Clive. Unable to say the right words, he muttered, "It's about women—"

Dr Barry leapt to a conclusion—indeed he had been there ever since they spoke in the hall. He had had a touch of trouble himself when young, which made him sympathetic about it. "We'll soon fix that up," he said.

Maurice stopped his tears before more than a few had issued, and felt the rest piled in an agonizing bar across his brain. "Oh, fix me for God's sake," he said, and sank into a chair, arms hanging. "I'm close on done for."

"Ah, women! How well I remember when you spouted on the platform at school . . . the year my poor brother died it was . . . you gaped at some master's wife . . . he's a lot to learn and life's a hard school, I remember thinking. Only women can teach us and there are bad women as well as good. Dear, dear!" He cleared his throat. "Well, boy, don't be afraid of me. Only tell me the truth, and I'll get you well. When did you catch the beastly thing? At the Varsity?"

Maurice did not understand. Then his brow went damp. "It's nothing as filthy as that," he said explosively. "In my own rotten way I've kept clean."

Dr Barry seemed offended. He locked the door, saying

"Impotent, eh? Let's have a look," rather contemptuously.

Maurice stripped, throwing the garments from him in a rage. He had been insulted as he had insulted Ada.

"You're all right," was the verdict.

"What d'ye mean, sir, by all right?"

"What I say. You're a clean man. Nothing to worry about here."

He sat down by the fire, and, dulled though he was to impressions, Dr Barry noted the pose. It wasn't artistic, yet it could have been called superb. He sat in his usual position, and his body as well as his face seemed gazing indomitably at the flames. He wasn't going to knuckle under—somehow he gave that impression. He might be slow and clumsy, but if once he got what he wanted he would hold to it till Heaven and Earth blushed crimson.

"You're all right," repeated the other. "You can marry tomorrow if you like, and if you take an old man's advice you will. Cover up now, it's so draughty. What put all this into your head?"

"So you've never guessed," he said, with a touch of scorn in his terror. "I'm an unspeakable of the Oscar Wilde sort." His eyes closed, and driving clenched fists against them he sat motionless, having appealed to Caesar.

At last judgement came. He could scarcely believe his ears. It was "Rubbish, rubbish!" He had expected many things, but not this; for if his words were rubbish his life was a dream.

"Dr Barry, I can't have explained—"

"Now listen to me, Maurice, never let that evil hallucination, that temptation from the devil, occur to you again."

The voice impressed him, and was not Science speaking?

"Who put that lie into your head? You whom I see and know to be a decent fellow! We'll never mention it again. No—I'll not discuss. I'll not discuss. The worst thing I could do for you is to discuss it."

"I want advice," said Maurice, struggling against the

overwhelming manner. "It's not rubbish to me, but my life."

"Rubbish," came the voice authoritatively.

"I've been like this ever since I can remember without knowing why. What is it? Am I diseased? If I am, I want to be cured, I can't put up with the loneliness any more, the last six months specially. Anything you tell me, I'll do. That's all. You must help me."

He fell back into his original position, gazing body and soul into the fire.

"Come! Dress yourself."

"I'm sorry," he murmured, and obeyed. Then Dr Barry unlocked the door and called, "Polly! Whisky!" The consultation was over.

XXXII

Dr Barry had given the best advice he could. He had read no scientific works on Maurice's subject. None had existed when he walked the hospitals, and any published since were in German, and therefore suspect. Averse to it by temperament, he endorsed the verdict of society gladly; that is to say, his verdict was theological. He held that only the most depraved could glance at Sodom, and so, when a man of good antecedents and physique confessed the tendency, "Rubbish, rubbish!" was his natural reply. He was quite sincere. He believed that Maurice had heard some remark by chance, which had generated morbid thoughts, and that the contemptuous silence of a medical man would at once dispel them.

And Maurice went away not unimpressed. Dr Barry was a great name at home. He had twice saved Kitty and had attended Mr Hall through his last illness, and he was so honest and independent and never said what he did not feel. He had been their ultimate authority for nearly twenty years—seldom appealed to, but known to exist and to judge righteousness, and now that he pronounced "rubbish", Maurice wondered whether it might not be rubbish, though every fibre in him protested. He hated Dr Barry's mind; to tolerate prostitution struck him as beastly. Yet he respected it and went away inclined for another argument with destiny.

He was the more inclined for a reason that he could not tell to the doctor. Clive had turned towards women soon after he reached the age of twenty-four. He himself would be twenty-four in August. Was it possible that he would turn also . . . and now that he came to think, few men married before twenty-four. Maurice had the Englishman's inability to conceive variety. His troubles had taught him that other people are alive, but not yet that they are different, and he attempted to regard Clive's development as a forerunner of his own.

It would be jolly certainly to be married, and at one with society and the law. Dr Barry, meeting him on another day, said, "Maurice, you get the right girl—there'll be no more trouble then." Gladys Olcott recurred to him. Of course he was not a crude undergraduate now. He had suffered and explored himself, and knew he was abnormal. But hopelessly so? Suppose he met a woman who was sympathetic in other ways? He wanted children. He was capable of begetting children—Dr Barry had said so. Was marriage impossible after all? The topic was in the air at home, owing to Ada, and his mother would often suggest that he should find someone for Kitty and Kitty someone for him. Her detachment was amazing. The words, "marriage," "love," "a family" had lost all meaning to her during widowhood. A concert ticket sent by Miss Tonks to Kitty revealed possibilities. Kitty could not use it, and offered it round the table. Maurice said he should like to go. She reminded him that it was his Club night, but he said he would cut that. He went, and it happened to be the symphony of Tchaikovsky Clive had taught him to like. He enjoyed the piercing and the tearing and the soothing—the music did not mean more to him than that—and they induced a warm feeling of gratitude towards Miss Tonks. Unfortunately, after the concert he met Risley.

"Symphonie Pathique," said Risley gaily.

"Symphony Pathetic," corrected the Philistine.

"Symphonie Incestueuse et Pathique." And he informed his young friend that Tchaikovsky had fallen in love with his own nephew, and dedicated his masterpiece to him. "I come to see all respectable London flock. Isn't it *supreme*!"

"Queer things you know," said Maurice stuffily. It was odd that when he had a confidant he didn't want one. But he got a life of Tchaikovsky out of the library at once. The episode of the composer's marriage conveys little to the normal reader, who vaguely assumes incompatibility, but it thrilled Maurice. He knew what the disaster meant and how near Dr Barry had dragged him to it. Reading on, he made the acquaintance of "Bob", the wonderful nephew to whom Tchaikovsky turns after the breakdown, and in whom is his spiritual and musical resurrection. The book blew off the gathering dust and he respected it as the one literary work that had ever helped him. But it only helped him backwards. He was where he had been in the train, having gained nothing except the belief that doctors are fools.

Now every avenue seemed blocked, and in his despair he turned to the practices he had abandoned as a boy, and found they did bring him a degraded kind of peace, did still the physical urge into which all his sensations were contracting, and enable him to do his work. He was an average man, and could have won an average fight, but Nature had pitted him against the extraordinary, which only saints can subdue unaided, and he began to lose ground. Shortly before his visit to Penge a new hope dawned, faint and unlovely. It was hypnotism. Mr Cornwallis, Risley told him, had been hypnotized. A doctor had said, "Come, come, you are no eunuch!" and lo! he had ceased to be one. Maurice procured the doctor's address. but did not suppose anything would come of it: one interview with the science sufficed him, and he always felt Risley knew too much; his voice when he gave the address was friendly but slightly amused.

XXXIII

Now that Clive Durham was safe from intimacy, he looked forward to helping his friend, who must have had a pretty rough time since they parted in the smoking-room. Their correspondence had ceased several months ago. Maurice's last had been written after Birmingham, and announced he should not kill himself. Clive had never supposed he would, and was glad the melodrama was over. When they talked down the telephone he heard a man whom he might respect at the other end of it—a fellow who sounded willing to let bygones be bygones and passion acquaintanceship. There was no affectation of ease; poor Maurice sounded shy, a bit huffy even, exactly the condition Clive deemed natural, and felt he could ameliorate.

He was anxious to do what he could. Though the quality of the past escaped him he remembered its proportions, and acknowledged that Maurice had once lifted him out of aestheticism into the sun and wind of love. But for Maurice he would never have developed into being worthy of Anne. His friend had helped him through three barren years, and he would be ungrateful indeed if he did not help his friend. Clive did not like gratitude. He would rather have helped out of pure friendliness. But he had to use the only tool he had, and if all went well, if Maurice kept unemotional, if he remained at the end of a telephone, if he was sound as regarded Anne, if he was not bitter, or too serious or too rough—then they might be friends again, though by a different route and in a different manner. Maurice had admirable qualities—he knew this, and the time might be returning when he would feel it also.

Such thoughts as the above occurred to Clive rarely and feebly. The centre of his life was Anne. Would Anne get on with his mother? Would Anne like Penge, she who had been brought up in Sussex, near the sea? Would she regret the lack of religious opportunities there? And the presence of politics? Besotted with love, he gave her his body and soul, he poured out at her feet all that an earlier passion had taught him, and could only remember with an effort for whom that passion had been.

In the first glow of his engagement, when she was the whole world to him, the Acropolis included, he thought of confessing to her about Maurice. She had confessed a peccadillo to him. But loyalty to his friend withheld him, and he was glad afterwards, for, immortal as Anne proved, she was not Pallas Athene, and there were many points on which he could not touch. Their own union became the chief of these. When he arrived in her room after marriage, she did not know what he wanted. Despite an elaborate education, no one had told her about sex. Clive was as considerate as possible, but he scared her terribly, and left feeling she hated him. She did not. She welcomed him on future nights. But it was always without a word. They united in a world that bore no reference to the daily, and this secrecy drew after it much else of their lives. So much could never be mentioned. He never saw her naked, nor she him. They ignored the reproductive and the digestive functions. So there would never be any question of this episode of his immaturity.

It was unmentionable. It didn't stand between him and her. She stood between him and it, and on second thoughts he was glad, for though not disgraceful it had been sentimental and deserved oblivion.

Secrecy suited him, at least he adopted it without regret. He had never itched to call a spade a spade, and though he valued the body the actual deed of sex seemed to him unimaginative, and best veiled in night. Between men it is inexcusable, between man and woman it may be practised since nature and society approve, but never discussed nor vaunted. His ideal of marriage was temperate and graceful, like all his ideals, and he found a fit helpmate in Anne, who had refinement herself, and admired it in others. They loved each other tenderly. Beautiful conventions received them—while beyond the barrier Maurice wandered, the wrong words on his lips and the wrong desires in his heart, and his arms full of air.

XXXIV

Maurice took a week's holiday in August and reached Penge according to invitation three days before the Park v. Village cricket match. He arrived in an odd and bitter mood. He had been thinking over Risley's hypnotist, and grew much inclined to consult him. It was such a nuisance. For instance, as he drove up through the park he saw a gamekeeper dallying with two of the maids, and felt a pang of envy. The girls were damned ugly, which the man wasn't: somehow this made it worse, and he stared at the trio, feeling cruel and respectable; the girls broke away giggling, the man returned the stare furtively and then thought it safer to touch his cap; he had spoilt that little game. But they would meet again when he had passed, and all over the world girls would meet men, to kiss them and be kissed; might it not be better to alter his temperament and toe the line? He would decide after his visit—for against hope he was still hoping for something from Clive.

"Clive's out," said the young hostess. "He sends you his love or something, and will be in to dinner. Archie London will look after you, but I don't believe you want looking after."

Maurice smiled and accepted some tea. The drawing-room had its old air. Groups of people stood about with the air of arranging something, and though Clive's mother no longer presided she remained in residence, owing to the dower house drains. The sense of dilapidation had increased. Through pouring rain he had noticed gate posts crooked, trees stifling, and indoors some bright wedding presents showed as patches on a threadbare garment. Miss Woods had brought no money to Penge. She was accomplished and delightful, but she belonged to the same class as the Durhams, and every year England grew less inclined to pay her highly.

"Clive's canvassing," she continued, "there'll be a by-election in the autumn. He has at last induced them to induce him to stand;" she had the aristocratic knack of anticipating criticism. "But seriously, it will be a wonderful thing for the poor if he gets in. He is their truest friend, if only they knew it."

Maurice nodded. He felt disposed to discuss social problems. "They want drilling a bit," he said.

"Yes, they need a leader," said a gentle but distinguished voice, "and until they find one they will suffer." Anne introduced the new rector, Mr Borenius. He was her own importation. Clive did not mind whom he appointed if the man was a gentleman and devoted himself to the village. Mr Borenius fulfilled both conditions, and as he was High Church might strike a balance against the outgoing incumbent, who had been Low.

"Oh Mr Borenius, how interesting!" the old lady cried from across the room. "But I suppose in your opinion we all want a leader. I quite agree." She darted her eyes hither and thither. "All of you want a leader, I repeat." And Mr Borenius's eyes followed hers, perhaps looking for something he did not find, for he soon took leave.

"He can't have anything to do at the Rectory," said Anne thoughtfully, "but he always is like that. He comes up to scold Clive about the housing, and won't stop to dinner. You see, he's so sensitive; he worries about the poor."

"I've had to do with the poor too," said Maurice, taking a piece of cake, "but I can't worry over them. One must give them a leg up for the sake of the country generally, that's all. They haven't our feelings. They don't suffer as we should in their place."

Anne looked disapproval, but she felt she had entrusted her hundred pounds to the right sort of stockbroker.

"Caddies and a college mission in the slums is all I know. Still, I've learned a little. The poor don't want pity. They only really like me when I've got the gloves on and am knocking them about."

"Oh, you teach them boxing."

"Yes, and play football . . . they're rotten sportsmen."

"I suppose they are. Mr Borenius says they want love," said Anne after a pause.

"I've no doubt they do, but they won't get it."

"Mr Hall!"

Maurice wiped his moustache and smiled.

"You're *horrible*."

"I didn't think. I suppose that does sound so."

"But do you like being horrible?"

"One gets used to anything," he said, suddenly turning, for the door had blown open behind.

"Well, good gracious me, I scold Clive for being cynical, but you outdo him."

"I get used to being horrible, as you call it, as the poor do to their slums. It's only a question of time." He was speaking rather freely; a biting recklessness had come to him since his arrival. Clive hadn't bothered to be in to receive him. Very well! "After you've banged about a bit you get used to your particular hole. Everyone yapping at the start like a lot of puppies, Waou! Waou!" His unexpected imitation made her laugh. "At last you learn that everyone's far too busy to listen to you, so you stop yapping. That's a fact."

"A man's view," she said, nodding her head. "I'll never let Clive hold it. I believe in sympathy . . . in bearing one another's burdens. No doubt I'm unfashionable. Are you a disciple of Nietzsche?"

"Ask me another!"

Anne liked this Mr Hall, whom Clive had warned her she might find unresponsive. So he was in a way, but evidently he had personality. She understood why her husband had found him a good travelling companion in Italy. "Now why don't you like the poor?" she asked suddenly.

"I don't dislike them. I just don't think about them except when I'm obliged. These slums, syndicalism, all the rest of it, are a public menace, and one has to do one's little bit against them. But not for love. Your Mr Borenius won't face facts."

She was silent, then asked him how old he was.

"Twenty-four tomorrow."

"Well, you're very hard for your age."

"Just now you said I was horrible. You're letting me off very easily, Mrs Durham!"

"Anyhow, you're set, which is worse."

She saw him frown, and, fearing she had been impertinent, turned the talk on to Clive. She had expected Clive to be back by now, she said, and it was the more disappointing because tomorrow Clive would have to be really away. The agent, who knew the constituency, was showing him round. Mr Hall must be forgiving, and he must help them in the cricket match.

"It rather depends upon some other plans.... I might have to..."

She glanced at his face with a sudden curiosity, then said, "Wouldn't you like to see your room?—Archie, take Mr Hall to the Russet Room."

"Thanks.... Is there a post out?"

"Not this evening, but you can wire. Wire you'll stop.... Or oughtn't I to interfere?"

"I may have to wire—I'm not quite sure. Thanks frightfully." Then he followed Mr London to the Russet Room, thinking "Clive might have ... for the sake of the past he might have been here to greet me. He ought to have known how wretched I should feel." He didn't care for Clive, but he could suffer from him. The rain poured out of a leaden sky on to the park, the woods were silent. As twilight fell, he entered a new circle of torment.

He stopped up in the room till dinner, fighting with ghosts he had loved. If this new doctor could alter his being, was it not his duty to go, though body and soul would be violated? With the world as it is, one must marry or decay. He was not yet free of Clive and never would be until something greater intervened.

"Is Mr Durham back?" he inquired, when the housemaid brought hot water.

"Yes, sir."

"Just in?"

"No. About half an hour, sir."

She drew the curtains and hid the sight but not the sound of the rain. Meanwhile Maurice scribbled a wire. " 'Lasker Jones, 6 Wigmore Place, W.,' " he read. " 'Please make appointment Thursday. Hall. C/o Durham, Penge, Wiltshire.' "

"Yes, sir."

"Thanks so much," he said deferentially, and grimaced as soon as he was alone. There was now a complete break between his public and private actions. In the drawing-room he greeted Clive without a tremor. They shook hands warmly, Clive saying, "You look awfully fit. Do you know whom you are going to take in?" and introducing him to a girl. Clive had become quite the squire. All his grievances against society had passed since his marriage. Agreeing politically, they had plenty to talk about.

On his side, Clive was pleased with his visitor. Anne had reported him as "rough, but very nice"—a satisfactory condition. There was a coarseness of fibre about him, but that didn't matter now: that horrible scene about Ada could be forgotten. Maurice also got on well with Archie London—important, for Archie bored Anne and was the sort of man who could fix on to someone. Clive assigned them to each other, for the visit.

In the drawing-room they talked politics again, convinced every one of them that radicals are untruthful, and socialists mad. The rain poured down with a monotony nothing could disturb. In the lulls of conversation its whisper entered the room, and towards the end of the evening there was "tap, tap" on the lid of the piano.

"The family ghost again," said Mrs Durham with a

bright smile.

"There's the sweetest hole in the ceiling," cried Anne. "Clive, can't we leave it?"

"We shall have to," he remarked, ringing the bell. "Let's shift our pianoforte though. It won't stand much more."

"How about a saucer?" said Mr London. "Clive, how about a saucer? Once the rain came through the ceiling of the club. I rang the bell and the servant brought a saucer."

"I ring the bell and the servant brings nothing," said Clive, pealing again. "Yes, we'll have a saucer, Archie, but we must move the piano too. Anne's dear little hole may grow in the night. There's only a lean-to roof over this part of the room."

"Poor Penge!" said his mother. All had risen to their feet, and were gazing at the leak, Anne began to probe the piano's entrails with blotting paper. The evening had broken up, and they were well content to make fun about the rain, which had sent them this hint of its presence.

"Bring a basin, will you," said Clive, when the bell was answered, "and a duster, and get one of the men to help shift the piano and take up the carpet in the bay. The rain's come through again."

"We had to ring twice, ring twice," remarked his mother.

"Le delai s'explique," she added, for when the parlourmaid returned it was with the keeper as well as the valet. "C'est toujours comme ça quand—we have our little idylls below stairs too, you know."

"You men, what do you want to do tomorrow?" said Clive to his guests. "I must go canvassing. Don't come too. It's beyond words dull. Like to take out a gun or what?"

"Very nice," said Maurice and Archie.

"Scudder, do you hear?"

"Le bonhomme est distrait," said his mother. The piano had rucked up a rug, and the servants, not liking to raise their voices before gentlefolk, misunderstood one another's orders, and whispered "What?"

"Scudder, the gentlemen'll shoot tomorrow—I'm sure I don't know what, but come round at ten. Shall we turn in now?"

"Early to bed's the rule here, as you know, Mr Hall," said Anne. Then she wished the three servants good night and led the way upstairs. Maurice lingered to choose a book. Might Lecky's *History of Rationalism* fill a gap? The rain dripped into the basin, the men muttered over the carpet in the bay, and, kneeling, seemed to celebrate some obsequy.

"Damnation, isn't there anything, anything?"

"—ish, he's not talking to us," said the valet to the gamekeeper.

Lecky it was, but his mind proved unequal, and after a few minutes he threw it on the bed and brooded over the telegram. In the dreariness of Penge his purpose grew stronger. Life had proved a blind alley, with a muck heap at the end of it, and he must cut back and start again. One could be absolutely transformed, Risley implied, provided one didn't care a damn for the past. Farewell, beauty and warmth. They ended in muck and must go. Drawing the curtains, he gazed long into the rain, and sighed, and struck his own face, and bit his own lips.

XXXV

The next day was even drearier and the only thing to be said in its favour was that it had the unreality of a nightmare. Archie London chattered, the rain dribbled, and in the sacred name of sport they were urged after rabbits over the Penge estate. Sometimes they shot the rabbits, sometimes missed them, sometimes they tried ferrets and nets. The rabbits needed keeping down and perhaps that was why the entertainment had been forced on them: there was a prudent strain in Clive. They returned to lunch, and Maurice had a thrill: his telegram had arrived from Mr Lasker Jones, granting him an appointment for tomorrow. But the thrill soon passed, Archie thought they had better go after the bunnies again, and he was too depressed to refuse. The rain was now less, on the other hand the mist was thicker, the mud stickier, and towards tea time they lost a ferret. The keeper made out this was their fault, Archie knew better, and explained the matter to Maurice in the smoking-room with the aid of diagrams. Dinner arrived at eight, so did the politicians, and after dinner the drawing-room ceiling dripped into basins and saucers. Then in the Russet Room, the same weather, the same despair, and the fact that now Clive sat on his bed talking intimately did not make any difference. The talk might have moved him had it come earlier, but he had been so pained by the inhospitality, he had spent so lonely and so imbecile a day, that he could respond to the past no longer. His thoughts were all with Mr Lasker Jones, and he wanted to be alone to compose a written statement about his case.

Clive felt the visit had been a failure, but, as he remarked, "Politics can't wait, and you happen to coincide with the rush." He was vexed too at forgetting that today was Maurice's birthday—and was urgent that their guest should stop over the match. Maurice said he was frightfully sorry, but now couldn't, as he had this urgent and unexpected engagement in town.

"Can't you come back after keeping it? We're shocking hosts, but it's such a pleasure having you. Do treat the house as an hotel—go your way, and we'll go ours."

"The fact is I'm hoping to get married," said Maurice, the words flying from him as if they had independent life.

"I'm awfully glad," said Clive, dropping his eyes. "Maurice, I'm awfully glad. It's the greatest thing in the world, perhaps the only one—"

"I know." He was wondering why he had spoken. His sentence flew out into the rain; he was always conscious of the rain and the decaying roofs at Penge.

"I shan't bother you with talk, but I must just say that Anne guessed it. Women are extraordinary. She declared all along that you had something up your sleeve. I laughed, but now I shall have to give in." His eyes rose. "Oh Maurice, I'm so glad. It's very good of you to tell me—it's what I've always wished for you."

"I know you have."

There was a silence. Clive's old manner had come back. He was generous, charming.

"It's wonderful, isn't it?—the—I'm so glad. I wish I could think of something else to say. Do you mind if I just tell Anne?"

"Not a bit. Tell everyone," cried Maurice, with a brutality that passed unnoticed. "The more the better." He courted external pressure. "If the girl I want won't, there's others."

Clive smiled a little at this, but was too pleased to be squeamish. He was pleased partly for Maurice, but also because it rounded off his own position. He hated queerness, Cambridge, the Blue Room, certain glades in the park were—not tainted, there had been nothing disgraceful—but rendered subtly ridiculous. Quite lately he had turned up a poem written during Maurice's first visit to Penge, which might have hailed from the land through the looking-glass, so fatuous it was, so perverse. "Shade from the old hellenic ships." Had he addressed the sturdy undergraduate thus? And the knowledge that Maurice had equally outgrown such sentimentality purified it, and from him also words burst as if they had been alive.

"I've thought more often of you than you imagine, Maurice my dear. As I said last autumn, I care for you in the real sense, and always shall. We were young idiots, weren't we?—but one can get something even out of idiocy. Development. No, more than that, intimacy. You and I know and trust one another just because we were once idiots. Marriage has made no difference. Oh, that's jolly, I do think—"

"You give me your blessing then?"

"I should think so!"

"Thanks."

Clive's eyes softened. He wanted to convey something warmer than development. Dare he borrow a gesture from the past?

"Think of me all tomorrow," said Maurice, "and as for Anne—she may think of me too."

So gracious a reference decided him to kiss the fellow very gently on his big brown hand.

Maurice shuddered.

"You don't mind?"

"Oh no."

"Maurice dear, I wanted just to show I hadn't forgotten the past. I quite agree—don't let's mention it ever again, but I wanted to show just this once."

"All right."

"Aren't you thankful it's ended properly?"

"How properly?"

"Instead of that muddle last year."

"Oh with you."

"Quits, and I'll go."

Maurice applied his lips to the starched cuff of a dress

shirt. Having functioned, he withdrew, leaving Clive more friendly than ever, and insistent he should return to Penge as soon as circumstances allowed this. Clive stopped talking late while the water gurgled over the dormer. When he had gone Maurice drew the curtains and fell on his knees, leaning his chin upon the window sill and allowing the drops to sprinkle his hair.

"Come!" he cried suddenly, surprising himself. Whom had he called? He had been thinking of nothing and the word had leapt out. As quickly as possible he shut out the air and the darkness, and re-enclosed his body in the Russet Room. Then he wrote his statement. It took some time, and, though far from imaginative, he went to bed with the jumps. He was convinced that someone had looked over his shoulder while he wrote. He wasn't alone. Or again, that he hadn't personally written. Since coming to Penge he seemed a bundle of voices, not Maurice, and now he could almost hear them quarrelling inside him. But none of them belonged to Clive: he had got that far.

XXXVI

Archie London was also returning to town, and very early next morning they stood in the hall together waiting for the brougham, while the man who had taken them after rabbits waited outside for a tip.

"Tell him to boil his head," said Maurice crossly. "I offered him five bob and he wouldn't take it. Damned cheek!"

Mr London was scandalized. What were servants coming to? Was it to be nothing but gold? If so, one might as well shut up shop, and say so. He began a story about his wife's monthly nurse. Pippa had treated that woman more than an equal, but what can you expect with half educated people? Half an education is worse than none.

"Hear, hear," said Maurice, yawning.

All the same, Mr London wondered whether noblesse didn't oblige.

"Oh, try if you want to."

He stretched a hand into the rain.

"Hall, he took it all right, you know."

"Did he, the devil?" said Maurice. "Why didn't he take mine? I suppose you gave more."

With shame Mr London confessed this was so. He had increased the tip through fear of a snub. The fellow was the limit evidently, yet he couldn't think it was good taste in Hall to take the matter up. When servants are rude one should merely ignore it.

But Maurice was cross, tired, and worried about his appointment in town, and he felt the episode part of the ungraciousness of Penge. It was in the spirit of revenge that he strolled to the door, and said in his familiar yet alarming way, "Hullo! So five shillings aren't good enough! So you'll only take gold!" He was interrupted by Anne, who had come to see them off.

"Best of luck," she said to Maurice with a very sweet expression, then paused, as if inviting confidences. None came, but she added, "I'm so glad you're not horrible."

"Are you?"

"Men like to be thought horrible. Clive does. Don't you, Clive? Mr Hall, men are very funny creatures." She took hold of her necklace and smiled. "Very funny. Best of luck." By now she was delighted with Maurice. His situation, and the way he took it, struck her as appropriately masculine. "Now a woman in love," she explained to Clive on the doorstep, as they watched their guests start: "now a woman in love never bluffs—I wish I knew the girl's name."

Interfering with the house-servants, the keeper carried out Maurice's case to the brougham, evidently ashamed. "Stick it in then," said Maurice coldly. Amid wavings from Anne, Clive and Mrs Durham, they started, and London recommenced the story of Pippa's monthly nurse.

"How about a little air?" suggested the victim. He opened the window and looked at the dripping park. The stupidity of so much rain! What did it *want* to rain for? The indifference of the universe to man! Descending into woods, the brougham toiled along feebly. It seemed impossible that it should ever reach the station, or Pippa's misfortune cease.

Not far from the lodge there was a nasty little climb, and the road, always in bad condition, was edged with dog roses that scratched the paint. Blossom after blossom crept past them, draggled by the ungenial year: some had cankered, others would never unfold: here and there beauty triumphed, but desperately, flickering in a world of gloom. Maurice looked into one after another, and though he did not care for flowers the failure irritated him. Scarcely anything was perfect. On one spray every flower was lopsided, the next swarmed with caterpillars, or bulged with galls. The indifference of nature! And her incompetence! He leant out of the window to see whether she couldn't bring it off once, and stared straight into the bright brown eyes of a young man.

"God, why there's that keeper chap again!"

"Couldn't be, couldn't have got here. We left him up at the house."

"He could have if he'd run."

"Why should he have run?"

"That's true, why should he have?" said Maurice, then lifted the flap at the back of the brougham and peered through it into the rose bushes, which a haze already concealed.

"Was it?"

"I couldn't see." His companion resumed the narrative at once, and talked almost without ceasing until they parted at Waterloo.

In the taxi Maurice read over his statement, and its frankness alarmed him. He, who could not trust Jowitt, was putting himself into the hands of a quack; despite Risley's assurances, he connected hypnotism with séances and blackmail, and had often growled at it from behind the *Daily Telegraph*; had he not better retire?

But the house seemed all right. When the door opened, the little Lasker Joneses were playing on the stairs—charming children, who mistook him for "Uncle Peter", and clung to his hands; and when he was shut into the waiting room with *Punch* the sense of the normal grew stronger. He went to his fate calmly. He wanted a woman to secure him socially and diminish his lust and bear children. He never thought of that woman as a positive joy—at the worst, Dickie had been that—for during the long struggle he had forgotten what Love is, and sought not happiness at the hands of Mr Lasker Jones, but repose.

That gentleman further relieved him by coming up to his idea of what an advanced scientific man ought to be. Sallow and expressionless, he sat in a large pictureless room before a roll-top desk. "Mr Hall?" he said, and offered a bloodless hand. His accent was slightly American. "Well, Mr Hall, and what's the trouble?" Maurice became detached too. It was as if they met to discuss a third party. "It's all down here," he said, producing the statement. "I've consulted one doctor and he could do nothing. I don't know whether you can."

The statement was read.

"I'm not wrong in coming to you, I hope?"

"Not at all, Mr Hall. Seventy-five per cent of my patients are of your type. Is that statement recent?"

"I wrote it last night."

"And accurate?"

"Well, names and places are a bit changed, naturally."

Mr Lasker Jones did not seem to think it natural. He asked several questions about "Mr Cumberland", Maurice's pseudonym for Clive, and wished to know whether they had ever united: on his lips it was curiously inoffensive. He neither praised nor blamed nor pitied: he paid no attention to a sudden outburst of Maurice's against society. And though Maurice yearned for sympathy—he had not had a word of it for a year—he was glad none came, for it might have shattered his purpose.

He asked, "What's the name of my trouble? Has it one?"

"Congenital homosexuality."

"Congenital how much? Well, can anything be done?"

"Oh, certainly, if you consent."

"The fact is I've an old-fashioned prejudice against hypnotism."

"I'm afraid you may possibly retain that prejudice after trying, Mr Hall. I cannot promise a cure. I spoke to you of my other patients—seventy-five per cent—but in only fifty per cent have I been successful."

The confession gave Maurice confidence, no quack would have made it. "We may as well have a shot," he said, smiling. "What must I do?"

"Merely remain where you are. I will experiment to see how deeply the tendency is rooted. You will return (if you wish) for regular treatment later. Mr Hall! I shall try to send you into a trance, and if I succeed I shall make suggestions to you which will (we hope) remain, and become part of your normal state when you wake. You are not to resist me."

"All right, go ahead."

Then Mr Lasker Jones left his desk and sat in an impersonal way on the arm of Maurice's chair. Maurice felt he was going to have a tooth out. For a little time nothing happened, but presently his eye caught a spot of light on the fire irons, and the rest of the room went dim. He could see whatever he was looking at, but little else, and he could hear the doctor's voice and his own. Evidently he was going into a trance, and the achievement gave him a feeling of pride.

"You're not quite off yet, I think."

"No, I'm not."

He made some more passes. "How about now?"

"I'm nearer off now."

"Quite?"

Maurice agreed, but did not feel sure. "Now that you're quite off, how do you like my consulting-room?"

"It's a nice room."

"Not too dark?"

"Rather dark."

"You can see the picture though, can't you?"

Maurice then saw a picture on the opposite wall, yet he knew that there was none.

"Have a look at it, Mr Hall. Come nearer. Take care of that crack in the carpet though."

"How broad is the crack?"

"You can jump it."

Maurice immediately located a crack, and jumped, but he was not convinced of the necessity.

"Admirable—now what do you suppose this picture is of, whom is it of—?"

"Whom is it of—"

"Edna May."

"Mr Edna May."

"No, Mr Hall, Miss Edna May."

"It's Mr Edna May."

"Isn't she beautiful?"

"I want to go home to my mother." Both laughed at this remark, the doctor leading.

"Miss Edna May is not only beautiful, she is attractive."

"She doesn't attract me," said Maurice pettishly.

"Oh Mr Hall, what an ungallant remark. Look at her lovely hair."

"I like short hair best."

"Why?"

"Because I can stroke it—" and he began to cry. He came to himself in the chair. Tears were wet on his cheeks, but he felt as usual, and started talking at once.

"I say, I had a dream when you woke me up. I'd better tell it you. I thought I saw a face and heard someone say, 'That's your friend.' Is that all right? I often feel it—I can't explain—sort of walking towards me through sleep, though it never gets up to me, that dream."

"Did it get near now?"

"Jolly near. Is that a bad sign?"

"No, oh no—you're open to suggestion, you're open—I made you see a picture on the wall."

Maurice nodded: he had quite forgotten. There was a pause, during which he produced two guineas, and asked for a second appointment. It was arranged that he should telephone next week, and in the interval Mr Lasker Jones wanted him to remain where he was in the country, quietly.

Maurice could not doubt that Clive and Anne would welcome him, nor that their influence would be suitable. Penge was an emetic. It helped him to get rid of the old poisonous life that had seemed so sweet, it cured him of tenderness and humanity. Yes, he'd go back, he said: he would wire to his friends and catch the afternoon express.

"Mr Hall, take exercise in moderation. A little tennis, or

stroll about with a gun."

Maurice lingered to say, "On second thoughts perhaps I won't go back."

"Why so?"

"Well, it seems rather foolish to make that long journey twice in a day."

"You prefer then to stop in your own home?"

"Yes—no—no, all right, I will go back to Penge."

XXXVII

On his return he was amused to find that the young people were just off for twenty-four hours' electioneering. He now cared less for Clive than Clive for him. That kiss had disillusioned. It was such a trivial prudish kiss, and alas! so typical. The less you had the more it was supposed to be—that was Clive's teaching. Not only was the half greater than the whole—at Cambridge Maurice would just accept this—but now he was offered the quarter and told it was greater than the half. Did the fellow suppose he was made of paper?

Clive explained how he wouldn't be going had Maurice held out hopes of returning, and how he would be back for the match any way. Anne whispered, "Was the luck good?" Maurice replied "So-so", whereupon she covered him with her wing and offered to invite his young lady down to Penge. "Mr Hall, is she very charming? I am convinced she has bright brown eyes." But Clive called her off, and Maurice was left to an evening with Mrs Durham and Mr Borenius.

Unusual restlessness was on him. It recalled the initial night at Cambridge, when he had been to Risley's rooms. The rain had stopped during his dash to town. He wanted to walk about in the evening and watch the sun set and listen to the dripping trees. Ghostly but perfect, the evening primroses were expanding in the shrubbery, and stirred him by their odours. Clive had shown him evening primroses in the past, but had never told him they smelt. He liked being out of doors, among the robins and bats, stealing hither and thither bare-headed, till the gong should summon him to dress for yet another meal, and the curtains of the Russet Room close. No, he wasn't the same; a rearrangement of his being had begun as surely as at

Birmingham, when death had looked away, and to Mr Lasker Jones be all credit! Deeper than conscious effort there was a change, which might land him with luck in the arms of Miss Tonks.

As he wandered about, the man whom he had reprimanded in the morning came up, touched his cap, and inquired whether he would shoot tomorrow. Obviously he wouldn't, since it was the cricket match, but the question had been asked in order to pave the way for an apology. "I'm sure I'm very sorry I failed to give you and Mr London full satisfaction, sir," was its form. Maurice, vindictive no longer, said, "That's all right, Scudder." Scudder was an importation—part of the larger life that had come into Penge with politics and Anne; he was smarter than old Mr Ayres the head keeper, and knew it. He implied that he hadn't taken the five shillings because it was too much; he didn't say why he had taken the ten! He added, "Glad to see you down again so soon, sir," which struck Maurice as subtly unsuitable, so he repeated, "That's all right, Scudder," and went in.

It was a dinner-jacket evening—not tails, because they would only be three—and though he had respected such niceties for years he found them suddenly ridiculous. What did clothes matter as long as you got your food, and the other people were good sorts—which they wouldn't be? And as he touched the carapace of his dress shirt a sense of ignominy came over him, and he felt he had no right to criticize anyone who lived in the open air. How dry Mrs Durham seemed—she was Clive with the sap perished. And Mr Borenius—how dry! Though to do Mr Borenius justice he contained surprises. Contemptuous of all parsons, Maurice had paid little attention to this one, and was startled when he came out strong after dessert. He had assumed that as rector of the parish he would be helping Clive in the election. But "I vote for no one who is not a communicant, as Mr Durham understands."

"The Rads are attacking your church, you know," was

all he could think of.

"That is why I do not vote for the Radical candidate. He is a Christian, so naturally I should have done."

"Bit particular, sir, if I may say so. Clive will do all the things you want done. You may be lucky he isn't an atheist. There are a certain amount of those about, you know!"

He smiled in response, saying, "The atheist is nearer the Kingdom of Heaven than the hellenist. 'Unless ye become as little children'—and what is the atheist but a child?"

Maurice looked at his hands, but before he could frame a reply the valet came in to ask whether he had any orders for the keeper.

"I saw him before dinner, Simcox. Nothing, thanks. Tomorrow's the match. I did tell him."

"Yes, but he wonders whether you'd care to go down to the pond between the innings for a bathe, sir, now that the weather has altered. He has just bailed out the boat."

"Very good of him."

"If that's Mr Scudder may I speak to him?" asked Mr Borenius.

"Will you tell him, Simcox? Also tell him I shan't be bathing." When the valet had gone he said, "Would you rather speak to him here? Have him in as far as I'm concerned."

"Thank you, Mr Hall, but I'll go out. He'll prefer the kitchen."

"He'll prefer it no doubt. There are fair young females in the kitchen."

"Ah! Ah!" He had the air of one to whom sex occurs for the first time. "You don't happen to know whether he has anyone in view matrimonally, do you?"

"'Fraid I don't ... saw him kissing two girls at once on my arrival if that's any help."

"It sometimes happens that those men get confidential out shooting. The open air, the sense of companionship—"

"They don't get confidential with me. Archie London

and I got rather fed up with him yesterday as a matter of fact. Too anxious to boss the show. We found him a bit of a swine."

"Excuse the inquiry."

"What's there to excuse?" said Maurice, annoyed with the rector for alluding so smugly to the open air.

"Speaking frankly, I should be glad to see that particular young man settled with a helpmate before he sails." Smiling gently, he added "And all young men."

"What's he sailing for?"

"He is to emigrate." And intoning "to emigrate" in a particular irritating way, he repaired to the kitchen.

Maurice strolled for five minutes in the shrubbery. Food and wine had heated him, and he thought with some inconsequence that even old Chapman had sown some wild oats. He alone—Clive admonishing—combined advanced thought with the conduct of a Sunday scholar. He wasn't Methuselah—he'd a right to a fling. Oh those jolly scents, those bushes where you could hide, that sky as black as the bushes! They were turning away from him. Indoors was his place and there he'd moulder, a respectable pillar of society who has never had the chance to misbehave. The alley that he was pacing opened through a swing gate into the park, but the damp grass there might dull his pumps, so he felt bound to return. As he did so he struck against corduroys, and was held for a moment by both elbows; it had been Scudder escaping from Mr Borenius. Released, he continued his dreamings. Yesterday's shoot, which at the time had made little impression on him, began faintly to glow, and he realized that even during its boredom he had been alive. He felt back from it to the incidents of his arrival, such as the piano-moving: then forwards to the incidents of today, beginning with the five shillings' tip and ending with now. And when he reached "now", it was as if an electric current passed through the chain of insignificant events so that he dropped it and let it smash back into darkness. "Damnation, what a night," he resumed while puffs of air touched him and one another. Then the swing gate in the distance, which had been tinkling for a little, seemed to slam against freedom, and he went indoors.

"Oh Mr Hall!" cried the old lady. "How exquisite is your coiffure."

"My coiffure?" He found that his head was all yellow with evening primrose pollen.

"Oh, don't brush it off. I like it on your black hair. Mr Borenius, is he not quite bacchanalian?"

The clergyman raised sightless eyes. He had been interrupted in the middle of a serious talk. "But Mrs Durham," he persisted. "I understood so distinctly from you that all your servants had been confirmed."

"I thought so, Mr Borenius, I did think so."

"Yet I go into the kitchen, and straight away I discover Simcox, Scudder and Mrs Wetherall. For Simcox and Mrs Wetherall I can make arrangements. Scudder is the serious case, because I have not time to prepare him properly before he sails, even if the bishop could be prevailed upon."

Mrs Durham tried to be grave, but Maurice, whom she rather liked, was laughing. She suggested that Mr Borenius should give Scudder a note to some clergyman abroad—there was bound to be one.

"Yes, but will he present it? He shows no hostility to the Church, but will he be bothered? Had I only been told which of your servants had been confirmed and which had not, this crisis would not have arisen."

"Servants are so inconsiderate," said the old lady. "They tell me nothing. Why, Scudder sprung his notice on Clive in just the same way. His brother invites him. So off he goes. Now Mr Hall, let's have your advice over this crisis: what would you do?"

"Our young friend condemns the entire Church, militant and triumphant."

Maurice roused himself. If the parson hadn't looked so damned ugly he wouldn't have bothered, but he couldn't stand that squinny face sneering at youth. Scudder cleaned a gun, carried a suitcase, baled out a boat, emigrated—did something anyway, while gentlefolk squatted on chairs finding fault with his soul. If he did cadge for tips it was natural, and if he didn't, if his apology was genuine—why then he was a fine fellow. He'd speak anyhow. "How do you know he'll communicate if he's confirmed?" he said. "I don't communicate." Mrs Durham hummed a tune; this was going too far.

"But you were given the opportunity. The priest did what he could for you. He has not done what he could for Scudder and consequently the Church is to blame. That is why I make so much of a point which must appear very trivial to you."

"I'm awfully stupid, but I think I see: you want to make sure that he and not the Church shall be to blame in the future. Well, sir, that may be your idea of religion but it isn't mine and it wasn't Christ's."

It was as smart a speech as he had ever made; since the hypnotism his brain had known moments of unusual power. But Mr Borenius was unassailable. He replied pleasantly, "The unbeliever has always such a very clear idea as to what Belief ought to be, I wish I had half his certainty." Then he arose and went, and Maurice walked him through the short cut through the kitchen garden. Against the wall leant the subject of their deliberations, no doubt awaiting one of the maids; he appeared to be haunting the premises this evening. Maurice would have seen nothing, so thick now was the darkness; it was Mr Borenius who exacted a low "Good night, sir" for them both. A delicate scent of fruit perfumed the air; it had further to be feared that the young man had stolen an apricot. Scents were everywhere that night, despite the cold, and Maurice returned via the shrubbery, that he might inhale the evening primroses.

Again he heard the cautious "Good night, sir", and feeling friendly to the reprobate replied, "Good night, Scudder, they tell me you're emigrating."

"That's my idea, sir," came the voice.

"Well, good luck to you."

"Thank you, sir, it seems rather strange."

"Canada or Australia, I suppose."

"No, sir, the Argentine."

"Ah, ah, a fine country."

"Have you visited it, yourself, sir?"

"Rather not, England for me," said Maurice, strolling on and again colliding with corduroys. Dull talk, unimportant meeting, yet they harmonized with the darkness, the quietness of the hour, they suited him, and as he walked away he was followed by a sense of well-being which lasted until he reached the house. Through its window he could see Mrs Durham all relaxed and ugly. Her face clicked into position as he entered, so did his own, and they exchanged a few affected remarks about his day in town, before parting for bed.

He had taken to sleeping badly during the past year, and knew as soon as he lay down that this would be a night of physical labour. The events of the last twelve hours had excited him, and clashed against one another in his mind. Now it was the early start, now the journey with London, the interview, the return; and at the back of all lurked a fear that he had not said something at that interview that he ought to have said, that he had missed out something vital from his confession to the doctor. Yet what was it? He had drawn up the statement yesterday in this very room, and been satisfied at the time. He began to worry—which Mr Lasker Jones had forbidden him to do, because the introspective are more difficult to heal: he was supposed to lie fallow to the suggestions sown during the trance, and never wonder whether they would germinate or not. But he could not help worrying, and Penge, instead of numbing, seemed more stimulating than most places. How vivid, if complex, were its impressions, how the tangle of flowers and fruit wreathed his brain! Objects he had never seen, such as rain water baled from a boat, he could see tonight, though curtained in tightly. Ah to get out to them! Ah for darkness—not the darkness of a house which coops up a man among furniture, but the darkness where he can be free! Vain wish! He had paid a doctor two guineas to draw the curtains tighter, and presently, in the brown cube of such a room, Miss Tonks would lie prisoned beside him. And, as the yeast of the trance continued to work, Maurice had the illusion of a portrait that changed, now at his will, now against it, from male to female, and came leaping down the football-field where he bathed.... He moaned, half asleep. There was something better in life than this rubbish, if only he could get to it—love—nobility—big spaces where passion clasped peace, spaces no science could reach, but they existed for ever, full of woods some of them, and arched with majestic sky and a friend....

He really was asleep when he sprang up and flung wide the curtains with a cry of "Come!" The action awoke him; what had he done that for? A mist covered the grass of the park, and the tree trunks rose out of it like the channel marks in the estuary near his old private school. It was jolly cold. He shivered and clenched his fists. The moon had risen. Below him was the drawing-room, and the men who were repairing the tiles on the roof of the bay had left their ladder resting against his window sill. What had they done that for? He shook the ladder and glanced into the woods, but the wish to go into them vanished as soon as he could go. What use was it? He was too old for fun in the damp.

But as he returned to his bed a little noise sounded, a noise so intimate that it might have arisen inside his own body. He seemed to crackle and burn and saw the ladder's top quivering against the moonlit air. The head and the shoulders of a man rose up, paused, a gun was leant against the window sill very carefully, and someone he scarcely knew moved towards him and knelt beside him and whisered, "Sir, was you calling out for me? ... Sir, I know.... I know," and touched him.

PART FOUR

XXXVIII

"Had I best be going now, sir?"

Abominably shy, Maurice pretended not to hear.

"We mustn't fall asleep though, awkward if anyone came in," he continued, with a pleasant blurred laugh that made Maurice feel friendly but at the same time diffident and sad. He managed to reply, "You mustn't call me Sir," and the laugh sounded again, as if brushing aside such problems. There seemed to be charm and insight, yet his discomfort increased.

"May I ask your name?" he said awkwardly.

"I'm Scudder."

"I know you're Scudder—I meant your other name."

"Only Alec just."

"Jolly name to have."

"It's only my name."

"I'm called Maurice."

"I saw you when you first drove up, Mr Hall, wasn't it Tuesday, I did think you looked at me angry and gentle both together."

"Who were those people with you?" said Maurice, after a pause.

"Oh that wor only Mill, that wor Milly's cousin. Then do you remember the piano got wet the same evening, and you had great trouble to suit yourself over a book, didn't read it, did you either."

"How ever did you know I didn't read my book?"

"Saw you leaning out of the window instead. I saw you the next night too. I was out on the lawn."

"Do you mean you were out in all that infernal rain?"

"Yes ... watching ... oh, that's nothing, you've got to watch, haven't you ... see, I've not much longer in this country, that's how I kep putting it."

"How beastly I was to you this morning!"

"Oh that's nothing—Excuse the question but is that door locked?"

"I'll lock it." As he did so, the feeling of awkwardness returned. Whither was he tending, from Clive into what companionship?

Presently they fell asleep.

They slept separate at first, as if proximity harassed them, but towards morning a movement began, and they woke deep in each other's arms. "Had I best be going now?" he repeated, but Maurice, through whose earlier night had threaded the dream "Something is a little wrong and had better be," was resting utterly at last, and murmured "No, no."

"Sir, the church has gone four, you'll have to release me."

"Maurice, I'm Maurice."

"But the church has—"

"Damn the church."

He said, "I've the cricket pitch to help roll for the match," but did not move, and seemed in the faint gray light to be smiling proudly. "I have the young birds too—the boat's done—Mr London and Mr Fetherstonhaugh dived splack into the water lilies—they told me all young gentlemen can dive—I never learned to. It seems more natural like not to let the head get under the water. I call that drowning before your day."

"I was taught I'd be ill if I didn't wet my hair."

"Well, you was taught what wasn't the case."

"I expect so—it's a piece with all else I was taught. A master I used to trust as a kid taught me it. I can still remember walking on the beach with him ... oh dear! And the tide came up, all beastly gray..." He shook himself fully awake, as he felt his companion slip from him. "Don't, why did you?"

"There's the cricket—"

"No, there's not the cricket— You're going abroad."

"Well, we'll find another opportunity before I do."

"If you'll stop, I'll tell you my dream. I dreamt of an old grandfather of mine. He was a queer card. I wonder what you'd have made of him. He used to think dead people went to the sun, but he treated his own employees badly."

"I dreamt the Reverend Borenius was trying to drown me, and now really I must go, I can't talk about dreams, don't you see, or I'll catch it from Mr Ayres."

"Did you ever dream you'd a friend, Alec? Nothing else but just 'my friend', he trying to help you and you him. A friend," he repeated, sentimental suddenly. "Someone to last your whole life and you his. I suppose such a thing can't really happen outside sleep."

But the moment for speech had passed. Class was calling, the crack in the floor must reopen at sunrise. When he reached the window Maurice called "Scudder", and he turned like a well-trained dog.

"Alec, you're a dear fellow and we've been very happy."

"You get some sleep, there's no hurry in your case," he said kindly, and took up the gun that had guarded them through the night. The tips of the ladder quivered against the dawn as he descended, then were motionless. There was a tiny crackle from the gravel, a tiny clink from the fence that divided garden and park: then all was as if nothing had been, and silence absolute filled the Russet Room, broken after a time by the sounds of a new day.

XXXIX

Having unlocked the door, Maurice dashed back into bed.

"Curtains drawn, sir, nice sir, nice day for the match," said Simcox entering in some excitement with the tea. He looked at the head of black hair that was all the visitor showed. No answer came, and, disappointed of the morning chat Mr Hall had hitherto accorded, he gathered up the dinner-jacket and its appurtenances, and took them away to brush.

Simcox and Scudder; two servants. Maurice sat up and drank a cup of tea. He would have to give Scudder some handsome present now, indeed he would like to, but what should it be? What could one give a man in that position? Not a motor-bike. Then he remembered that he was emigrating, which made the problem easier. But the anxious look remained on his face, for he was wondering whether Simcox had been surprised at finding the door locked. Also had he meant anything by "Curtains drawn, sir"? Voices sounded under his window. He tried to drowse again, but the acts of other men had impinged.

"Now what will you wear, sir, I wonder?" inquired Simcox, returning. "You'll put on your cricketing flannels straight away perhaps; that rather than the tweed."

"All right."

"College blazer with them, sir?"

"No—never mind."

"Very good, sir." He straightened out a pair of socks and continued meditatively: "Oh, they've moved that ladder at last, I see. About time." Maurice then saw that the tips against the sky had disappeared. "I could have sworn it was here when I brought in your tea, sir. Still, one can never be certain."

"No, one can't," agreed Maurice, speaking with difficulty

and with the sense that he had lost his bearings. He felt relief when Simcox had left, but it was overshadowed by the thought of Mrs Durham and the breakfast table, and by the problem of a suitable present for his late companion. It couldn't be a cheque, lest suspicions were aroused when it was cashed. As he dressed, the trickle of discomfort gathered force. Though not a dandy, he had the suburban gentleman's usual show of toilet appliances, and they all seemed alien. Then the gong boomed, and just as he was going down to breakfast he saw a flake of mud close to the window sill. Scudder had been careful, but not careful enough. He was headachy and faint when, clothed all in white, he at last descended to take his place in society.

Letters—a pile of them, and all subtly annoying. Ada, most civil. Kitty, saying his mother looked done up. Aunt Ida—a postcard—wanting to know whether the chauffeur was supposed to obey orders, or had one misunderstood?, business fatuities, circulars about the College Mission, the Territorial training, the Golf Club, and the Property Defence Association. He bowed humorously over them to his hostess. When she scarcely responded, he went hot round his mouth. It was only that Mrs Durham's own letters worried her. But he did not know this, and was carried out further by the current. Each human being seemed new, and terrified him: he spoke to a race whose nature and numbers were unknown, and whose very food tasted poisonous.

After breakfast Simcox returned to the charge. "Sir, in Mr Durham's absence the servants feel—we should be so honoured if you would captain us against the Village in the forthcoming 'Park versus Village' match."

"I'm not a cricketer, Simcox. Who's your best bat?"

"We have no one better than the under gamekeeper."

"Then make the under gamekeeper captain."

Simcox lingered to say, "Things always go better under a gentleman."

"Tell him to put me to field deep—and I won't bat first:

about eighth if he likes—not first. You might tell him, as I shan't come down till it's time." He closed his eyes, feeling sickish. He had created something whose nature he ignored. Had he been theologically minded, he would have named it remorse, but he kept a free soul, despite confusion.

Maurice hated cricket. It demanded a snickety neatness he could not supply; and, though he had often done it for Clive's sake, he disliked playing with his social inferiors. Footer was different—he could give and take there—but in cricket he might be bowled or punished by some lout, and he felt it unsuitable. Hearing his side had won the toss, he did not go down for half an hour. Mrs Durham and one or two friends already sat in the shed. They were all very quiet. Maurice squatted at their feet, and watched the game. It was exactly like other years. The rest of his side were servants and had gathered a dozen yards away round old Mr Ayres, who was scoring: old Mr Ayres always scored.

"The captain has put himself in first," said a lady. "A gentleman would never have done that. Little points interest me."

Maurice said, "The captain's our best man, apparently."

She yawned and presently criticized: she'd an instinct that man was conceited. Her voice fell idly into the summer air. He was emigrating, said Mrs Durham—the more energetic did—which turned them to politics and Clive. His chin on his knees, Maurice brooded. A storm of distaste was working up inside him, and he did not know against what to direct it. Whether the ladies spoke, whether Alec blocked Mr Borenius's lobs, whether the villagers clapped or didn't clap, he felt unspeakably oppressed: he had swallowed an unknown drug: he had disturbed his life to its foundations, and couldn't tell what would crumble.

When he went out to bat, it was a new over, so that Alec received first ball. His style changed. Abandoning caution, he swiped the ball into the fern. Lifting his eyes, he met Maurice's and smiled. Lost ball. Next time he hit a boundary. He was untrained, but had the cricketing build, and the game took on some semblance of reality. Maurice played up too. His mind had cleared, and he felt that they were against the whole world, that not only Mr Borenius and the field but the audience in the shed and all England were closing round the wickets. They played for the sake of each other and of their fragile relationship—if one fell the other would follow. They intended no harm to the world, but so long as it attacked they must punish, they must stand wary, then hit with full strength, they must show that when two are gathered together majorities shall not triumph. And as the game proceeded it connected with the night, and interpreted it. Clive ended it easily enough. When he came to the ground they were no longer the leading force; people turned their heads, the game languished, and ceased. Alec resigned. It was only fit and proper that the squire should bat at once. Without looking at Maurice, he receded. He too was in white flannels, and their looseness made him look like a gentleman or anyone else. He stood in front of the shed with dignity, and when Clive had done talking offered his bat, which Clive took as a matter of course: then flung himself down by old Ayres.

Maurice met his friend, overwhelmed with spurious tenderness.

"Clive.... Oh my dear, are you back? Aren't you fagged frightfully?"

"Meetings till midnight—another this afternoon—must bat a minute to please these people."

"What! Leaving me again? How frightfully rotten."

"You may well say so, but I really do come back this evening, then your visit really does begin. I've a hundred things to ask you, Maurice."

"Now, gentlemen," said a voice; it was the socialist schoolmaster, out at long stop.

"We stand rebuked," said Clive, but didn't hurry himself. "Anne's cried off the afternoon meeting, so you'll have her for company. Oh look, they've actually mended her dear little hole in the roof of the drawing-room. Maurice! No, I can't remember what I was going to say. Let us join the Olympic Games."

Maurice went out first ball. "Wait for me," called Clive, but he went straight for the house, for he felt sure that the breakdown was coming. As he passed the servants, the majority of them rose to their feet, and applauded him frantically, and the fact that Scudder didn't alarmed him. Was it meant for impertinence? The wrinkled forehead—the mouth—possibly a cruel mouth; head a trifle too small—why was the shirt open at the throat like that? And in the hall of Penge he met Anne.

"Mr Hall, the meeting didn't go." Then she saw his face, which was green-white, cried, "Oh, but you're not well."

"I know," he said, trembling.

Men hate to be fussed, so she only replied, "I'm frightfully sorry, I'll send some ice to your room."

'You've been so kind to me always—"

"Look here, what about a doctor?"

"Never another doctor," he cried frantically.

"We want to be kind to you—naturally. When one's happy oneself one wants the same happiness for others."

"Nothing's the same."

"Mr Hall—!"

"Nothing's the same for anyone. That's why life's this Hell, if you do a thing you're damned, and if you don't you're damned—" he paused, and continued, "Sun too hot—should like a little ice."

She ran for it, and released he flew up to the Russet Room. It brought home to him the precise facts of the situation, and he was violently sick.

XL

He felt better at once, but realized that he must leave Penge. He changed into the serge, packed, and was soon downstairs again with a neat little story. "The sun caught me," he told Anne, "but I'd rather a worrying letter too, and I think I'd better be in town."

"Much, much better," she cried, all sympathy.

"Yes, much better," echoed Clive, who was up from the match. "We'd hoped you'd put it right yesterday, Maurice, but we quite understand, and if you must go you must go."

And old Mrs Durham had also accrued. There was to be a laughing open secret about this girl in town, who had almost accepted his offer of marriage but not quite. It didn't matter how ill he looked or how queerly he behaved, he was officially a lover, and they interpreted everything to their satisfaction and found him delightful.

Clive motored him to the station, since their ways lay together that far. The drive skirted the cricket field before entering the woods. Scudder was fielding now, looking reckless and graceful. He was close to them, and stamped one foot, as though summoning something. That was the final vision, and whether of a devil or a comrade Maurice had no idea. Oh, the situation was disgusting—of that he was certain, and indeed never wavered till the end of his life. But to be certain of a situation is not to be certain of a human being. Once away from Penge he would see clearly perhaps; at all events there was Mr Lasker Jones.

"What sort of man is that keeper of yours who captained us?" he asked Clive, having tried the sentence over to himself first, to be sure it didn't sound odd.

"He's leaving this month," said Clive under the impression that he was giving a reply. Fortunately they were passing the kennels at that moment, and he added, "We shall miss him as regards the dogs, anyhow."

"But not in other ways?"

"I expect we shall do worse. One always does. Hard-working anyhow, and decidedly intelligent, whereas the man I've coming in his place—"; and, glad that Maurice should be interested he sketched the economy of Penge.

"Straight?" He trembled as he asked this supreme question.

"Scudder? A little too smart to be straight. However, Anne would say I'm being unfair. You can't expect our standard of honesty in servants, any more than you can expect loyalty or gratitude."

"I could never run a job like Penge," resumed Maurice after a pause. "I should never know what type of servant to select. Take Scudder for instance. What class of home does he come from? I haven't the slightest idea."

"Wasn't his father the butcher at Osmington? Yes. I think so."

Maurice flung his hat on the floor of the car with all his force. "This is about the limit," he thought, and buried both hands in his hair.

"Head rotten again?"

"Putrid."

Clive kept sympathetic silence, which neither broke until they parted; all the way Maurice sat crouched with the palms of his hands against his eyes. His whole life he had known things but not known them—it was the great defect in his character. He had known it was unsafe to return to Penge, lest some folly leapt out of the woods at him, yet he had returned. He had throbbed when Anne said, "Has she bright brown eyes?" He had known in a way it was wiser not to lean out of his bedroom window again and again into the night and call "Come!" His interior spirit was as sensitive to promptings as most men's, but he could not interpret them. Not till the crisis had come was he clear. And this tangle, so different from Cambridge, resembled it so far that too late he could trace the entanglement. Risley's room had its counterpart in the wild rose and the evening primroses of yesterday, the side-car dash through the fens foreshadowed his innings at cricket.

But Cambridge had left him a hero, Penge a traitor. He had abused his host's confidence and defiled his house in his absence, he had insulted Mrs Durham and Anne. And when he reached home there came a worse blow; he had also sinned against his family. Hitherto they had never counted. Fools to be kind to. They were fools still, but he dare not approach them. Between those commonplace women and himself stretched a gulf that hallowed them. Their chatter, their squabble about precedence, their complaints of the chauffeur, seemed word of a greater wrong. When his mother said "Morrie, now for a nice talk" his heart stopped. They strolled round the garden, as they had done ten years ago, and she murmured the names of vegetables. Then he had looked up to her, now down; now he knew very well what he wanted with the garden boy. And now Kitty, always a message-bearer, rushed out of the house, and in her hand she held a telegram.

Maurice trembled with anger and fear. "Come back, waiting tonight at boathouse, Penge, Alec": a nice message to be handed in through the local post-office! Presumably one of the house-servants had supplied his address, for the telegram was fully directed. A nice situation! It contained every promise of blackmail, at the best it was incredible insolence. Of course he shouldn't answer, nor could there be any question now of giving Scudder a present. He had gone outside his class, and it served him right.

But all that night his body yearned for Alec's, despite him. He called it lustful, a word easily uttered, and opposed to it his work, his family, his friends, his position in society. In that coalition must surely be included his will. For if the will can overleap class, civilization as we have made it will go to pieces. But his body would not be convinced. Chance had mated it too perfectly. Neither argument nor threat could silence it, so in the morning, feeling exhausted and ashamed, he telephoned to Mr Lasker Jones and made a second appointment. Before he was due to go to it a letter came. It arrived at breakfast and he read it under his mother's eyes. It was phrased as follows.

Mr Maurice. Dear Sir. I waited both nights in the boathouse. I said the boathouse as the ladder as taken away and the woods is to damp to lie down. So please come to "the boathouse" tomorrow night or next, pretend to the other gentlemen you want a stroll, easily managed, then come down to the boathouse. Dear Sir, let me share with you once before leaving Old England if it is not asking to much. I have key, will let you in. I leave per Ss Normannia Aug 29. I since cricket match do long to talk with one of my arms round you, then place both arms round you and share with you, the above now seems sweeter to me than words can say. I am perfectly aware I am only a servant that never presume on your loving kindness to take liberties or in any other way.

Yours respectfully,
A. Scudder.
(gamekeeper to C. Durham Esq.)

Maurice, was you taken ill that you left, as the indoors servants say? I hope you feel all as usual by this time. Mind and write if you can't come, for I get no sleep waiting night after night, so come without fail to "Boathouse Penge" tomorrow night, or failing the after.

Well, what did this mean? The sentence Maurice pounced on to the neglect of all others was "I have the key." Yes, he had, and there was a duplicate, kept up at the house, with which an accomplice, probably Simcox— In this light he interpreted the whole letter. His mother and aunt, the coffee he was drinking, the college cups on the sideboard, all said in their different ways, "If you go you are ruined, if you reply your letter will be used to put pressure upon you. You are in a nasty position but you have this advantage: he hasn't a scrap of your handwriting, and he's leaving England in ten days' time. Lie low, and hope for the best." He made a wry face. Butchers' sons and the rest of them may pretend to be innocent and affectionate, but they read the Police Court News, they know.... If he heard again, he must consult a reliable solicitor, just as he was going to Lasker Jones for the emotional fiasco. He had been very foolish, but if he played his cards carefully for the next ten days he ought to get through.

XLI

"Mornin', doctor. Think you can polish me off this time?" he began, very flippant in his manner; then flung himself down in the chair, half closed his eyes and said, "Well, go ahead." He was in a fury to be cured. The knowledge of this interview had helped him to bear up against the vampire. Once normal, he could settle him. He longed for the trance, wherein his personality would melt and be subtly reformed. At the least he gained five minutes' oblivion, while the will of the doctor strove to penetrate his own.

"I will go ahead in one moment, Mr Hall. First tell me how you have been?"

"Oh, as usual. Fresh air and exercise, as you told me. All serene."

"Have you frequented female society with any pleasure?"

"Some ladies were at Penge. I only stayed one night there. The day after you saw me, Friday, I returned to London—that's to say home."

"You had intended to stop longer with your friends, I think."

"I think I did."

Lasker Jones then sat down on the side of his chair. "Let yourself go now," he said quietly.

"Rather."

He repeated the passes. Maurice looked at the fire irons as before.

"Mr Hall, are you going into a trance?"

There was a long silence, broken by Maurice saying gravely, "I'm not quite sure."

They tried again.

"Is the room at all dark, Mr Hall?"

Maurice said, "A bit," in the hope that it would become so. And it did darken a little.

"What do you see?"

"Well, if it's dark I can't be expected to see."

"What did you see last time?"

"A picture."

"Quite so, and what else?"

"What else?"

"What else? A cr— a cr—"

"Crack in the floor."

"And then?"

Maurice changed his position and said, "I stepped over it."

"And then?"

He was silent.

"And then?" the persuasive voice repeated.

"I hear you all right," said Maurice. "The bother is I've not gone off. I went just a little muzzy at the start, but now I'm as wide awake as you are. You might have another shot."

They tried again, with no success.

"What in Hell can have happened? You could bowl me out last week first ball. What's your explanation?"

"You should not resist me."

"Damn it all, I don't."

"You are less suggestible than you were."

"I don't know what that may mean, not being an expert in the jargon, but I swear from the bottom of my heart I want to be healed. I want to be like other men, not this outcast whom nobody wants—"

They tried again.

"Then am I one of your twenty-five per cent failures?"

"I could do a little with you last week, but we do have these sudden disappointments."

"Sudden disappointment, am I? Well, don't be beat, don't give up," he guffawed, affectedly bluff.

"I do not propose to give up, Mr Hall."

Again they failed.

"And what's to happen to me?" said Maurice, with a sudden drop in his voice. He spoke in despair, but Mr Lasker Jones had an answer to every question. "I'm afraid I can only advise you to live in some country that has adopted the Code Napoleon," he said.

"I don't understand."

"France or Italy, for instance. There homosexuality is no longer criminal."

"You mean that a Frenchman could share with a friend and yet not go to prison?"

"Share? Do you mean unite? If both are of age and avoid public indecency, certainly."

"Will the law ever be that in England?"

"I doubt it. England has always been disinclined to accept human nature."

Maurice understood. He was an Englishman himself, and only his troubles had kept him awake. He smiled sadly. "It comes to this then: there always have been people like me and always will be, and generally they have been persecuted."

"That is so, Mr Hall; or, as psychiatry prefers to put it, there has been, is, and always will be every conceivable type of person. And you must remember that your type was once put to death in England."

"Was it really? On the other hand, they could get away. England wasn't all built over and policed. Men of my sort could take to the greenwood."

"Is that so? I was not aware."

"Oh, it's only my own notion," said Maurice, laying the fee down. "It strikes me there may have been more about the Greeks—Theban Band—and the rest of it. Well, this wasn't unlike. I don't see how they could have kept together otherwise—especially when they came from such different classes."

"An interesting theory."

Words flying out of him again, he said, "I've not been

straight with you."

"Indeed, Mr Hall."

What a comfort the man was! Science is better than sympathy, if only it is science.

"Since I was last here I went wrong with a—he's nothing but a gamekeeper. I don't know what to do."

"I can scarcely advise you on such a point."

"I know you can't. But you might tell me whether he's pulling me away from sleep. I half wondered."

"No one can be pulled against his will, Mr Hall."

"I'd a notion he'd stopped me going into the trance, and I wished—that seems silly—that I hadn't happened to have a letter from him in my pocket—read it as I've told you so much. I feel simply walking on a volcano. He's an uneducated man; he's got me in his power. In court would he have a case?"

"I am no lawyer," came the unvarying voice, "but I do not think this letter can be construed as containing a menace. It's a matter on which you should consult your solicitor, not me."

"I'm sorry, but it's been a relief. I wonder if you'd be awfully kind—hynotize me once more. I feel I might go off now I've told you. I'd hoped to get cured without giving myself away. Are there such things as men getting anyone in their power through dreams?"

"I will try on condition your confession is this time exhaustive. Otherwise you waste both my time and your own."

It was exhaustive. He spared neither his lover nor himself. When all was detailed, the perfection of the night appeared as a transient grossness, such as his father had indulged in thirty years before.

"Sit down once again."

Maurice heard a slight noise and swerved.

"It is my children playing overhead."

"I get half to believe in spooks."

"It is merely the children."

Silence returned. The afternoon sunshine fell yellow

through the window upon the roll-top desk. This time Maurice fixed his attention on that. Before recommencing, the doctor took Alec's letter, and solemnly burnt it to ashes before his eyes.

Nothing happened.

XLII

By pleasuring the body Maurice had confirmed—that very word was used in the final verdict—he had confirmed his spirit in its perversion, and cut himself off from the congregation of normal man. In his irritation he stammered; "What I want to know is—what I can't tell you nor you me—how did a country lad like that know so much about me? Why did he thunder up that special night when I was weakest? I'd never let him touch me with my friend in the house, because, damn it all, I'm more or less a gentleman—public school, varsity and so on—I can't even now believe that it was with him." Regretting he had not possessed Clive in the hour of their passion, he left, left his last shelter, while the doctor said perfunctorily. "Fresh air and exercise may do wonders yet." The doctor wanted to get on to his next patient, and he did not care for Maurice's type. He was not shocked like Dr Barry, but he was bored, and never thought of the young invert again.

On the doorstep something rejoined Maurice—his old self perhaps, for as he walked along a voice spoke out of his mortification, and its accents recalled Cambridge; a reckless youthful voice that girded at him for being a fool. "You've done for yourself this time," it seemed to say, and when he stopped outside the park, because the King and Queen were passing, he despised them at the moment he bared his head. It was as if the barrier that kept him from his fellows had taken another aspect. He was not afraid or ashamed any more. After all, the forests and the night were on his side, not theirs; they, not he, were inside a ring fence. He had acted wrongly, and was still being punished—but wrongly because he had tried to get the best of both worlds. "But I must belong to my class, that's fixed," he persisted.

"Very well," said his old self. "Now go home, and

tomorrow morning mind you catch the 8.36 up to the office, for your holiday is over, remember, and mind you never turn your head, as I may, towards Sherwood."

"I'm not a poet, I'm not that kind of an ass—"

The King and Queen vanished into their palace, the sun fell behind the park trees, which melted into one huge creature that had fingers and fists of green.

"The life of the earth, Maurice? Don't you belong to that?"

"Well, what do you call the 'life of the earth'—it ought to be the same as my daily life—the same as society. One ought to be built on the other, as Clive once said."

"Quite so. Most unfortunate, that facts pay no attention to Clive."

"Anyhow, I must stick to my class."

"Night is coming—be quick then—take a taxi—be quick like your father, before doors close."

Hailing one, he caught the 6.20. Another letter from Scudder awaited him on the leather tray in the hall. He knew the writing at once, the "Mr M. Hall" instead of "Esq.", the stamps plastered crooked. He was frightened and annoyed, yet not so much as he would have been in the morning, for though science despaired of him he despaired less of himself. After all, is not a real Hell better than a manufactured Heaven? He was not sorry that he had eluded the manipulations of Mr Lasker Jones. He put the letter into the pocket of his dinner-jacket, where it tugged unread, while he played cards, and heard how the chauffeur had given notice; one didn't know what servants were coming to: to his suggestion that servants might be flesh and blood like ourselves his aunt opposed a loud "They aren't". At bedtime he kissed his mother and Kitty without the fear of defiling them; their short-lived sanctity was over, and all that they did and said had resumed insignificance. It was with no feeling of treason that he locked his door, and gazed for five minutes into the suburban night. He heard owls, the ring of a distant tram and his heart sounding louder than either. The letter was beastly long. The blood began pounding over his body as he unfolded it, but his head kept cool, and he managed to read it as a whole, not merely sentence by sentence.

Mr Hall, Mr Borenius has just spoke to me. Sir, you do not treat me fairly. I am sailing next week, per s.s. Normannia. I wrote you I am going, it is not fair you never write to me. I come of a respectable family, I don't think it fair to treat me like a dog. My father is a respectable tradesman. I am going to be on my own in the Argentine. You say, "Alec, you are a dear fellow"; but you do not write. *I know about you and Mr Durham*. Why do you say "call me Maurice", and then treat me so unfairly? Mr Hall, I am coming to London Tuesday. If you do not want me at your home say where in London, you had better see me – I would make you sorry for it. Sir, nothing of note has occurred since you left Penge. Cricket seems over, some of the great trees as lost some of their leaves, which is very early. Has Mr Borenius spoken to you about certain girls? I can't help being rather rough, it is some men's nature, but you should not treat me like a dog. It was before you came. It is natural to want a girl, you cannot go against human nature. Mr Borenius found out about the girls through the new communion class. He has just spoken to me. I have never come like that to a gentleman before. Were you annoyed at being disturbed so early? Sir, it was your fault, your head was on me. I had my work, I was Mr Durham's servant, not yours. I am not your servant, I will not be treated as your servant, and I don't care if the world knows it. I will show respect *where it's due only*, that is to say to gentleman who are gentleman. Simcox says, "Mr Hall says to put him in about eighth." I put you in fifth, but I was captain, and you have no right to treat me unfairly on that account.

Yours respectfully, A. Scudder.

P.S. *I know something*.

This last was the outstanding point, yet Maurice could brood over the letter as a whole. There was evidently some unsavoury gossip in the under-world about himself and Clive, but what did it matter now? What did it matter if they had been spied on in the Blue Room, or among the ferns, and been misinterpreted? He was concerned with the present. Why should Scudder have mentioned such gossip? What was he up to? Why had he flung out these words, some foul, many stupid, some gracious? While actually reading the letter, Maurice might feel it carrion he must toss on to his solicitor, but when he laid it down and took up his pipe, it seemed the sort of letter he might have written himself. Muddle-headed? How about muddle-headed? If so, it was in his own line! He didn't want such a letter, he didn't know what it wanted—half a dozen things possibly—but he couldn't well be cold and hard over it as Clive had been to him over the original *Symposium* business, and argue, "Here's a certain statement, I shall keep you to it." He replied, "A.S. Yes. Meet me Tuesday 5.0 p.m. entrance of British Museum. B.M. a large building. Anyone will tell you which. M.C.H." That struck him as best. Both were outcasts, and if it came to a scrap must have it without benefit of society. As for the rendezvous, he chose it because they were unlikely to be disturbed there by anyone whom he knew. Poor B.M., solemn and chaste! The young man smiled, and his face became mischievous and happy. He smiled also at the thought that Clive hadn't quite kept out of the mud after all, and though the face now hardened into lines less pleasing, it proved him an athlete, who had emerged from a year of suffering uninjured.

His new vigour persisted next morning, when he returned to work. Before his failure with Lasker Jones he had looked forward to work as a privilege of which he was almost unworthy. It was to have rehabilitated him, so that he could hold up his head at home. But now it too crumbled, and again he wanted to laugh, and wondered why he had been taken in so long. The clientele of Messrs Hill and Hall was drawn from the middle-middle classes, whose highest desire seemed shelter—continuous shelter—not a lair in the darkness to be reached against fear, but shelter everywhere and always, until the existence of earth and sky is forgotten, shelter from poverty and disease and violence and impoliteness; and consequently from joy; God slipped this retribution in. He saw from their faces, as from the faces of his clerks and his partners, that they had never known real joy. Society had catered for them too completely. They had never struggled, and only a struggle twists sentimentality and lust together into love. Maurice would have been a good lover. He could have given and taken serious pleasure. But in these men the strands were untwisted; they were either fatuous or obscene, and in his present mood he despised the latter least. They would come to him and ask for a safe six per cent security. He would reply, "You can't combine high interest with safety —it isn't to be done;" and in the end they would say, "How would it be if I invested most of my money at four per cent, and play about with an odd hundred?" Even so did they speculate in a little vice—not in too much, lest it disorganized domesticity, but in enough to show that their virtue was sham. And until yesterday he had cringed to them.

Why should he serve such men? He began discussing the ethics of his profession, like a clever undergraduate, but the railway carriage did not take him seriously. "Young Hall's all right," remained the verdict. "He'll never lose a single client, not he." And they diagnosed a cynicism not unseemly in a business man. "All the time he's investing steadily, you bet. Remember that slum talk of his in the spring?"

XLIII

The rain was coming down in its old fashion, tapping on a million roofs and occasionally effecting an entry. It beat down the smoke, and caused the fumes of petrol and the smell of wet clothes to linger mixed on the streets of London. In the great forecourt of the Museum it could fall uninterruptedly, plumb onto the draggled doves and the helmets of the police. So dark was the afternoon that some of the lights had been turned on inside, and the great building suggested a tomb, miraculously illuminated by spirits of the dead.

Alec arrived first, dressed no longer in corduroys but in a new blue suit and bowler hat—part of his outfit for the Argentine. He sprang, as he had boasted, of a respectable family—publicans, small tradesmen—and it was only by accident that he had appeared as an untamed son of the woods. Indeed, he liked the woods and the fresh air and water, he liked them better than anything and he liked to protect or destroy life, but woods contain no "openings", and young men who want to get on must leave them. He was determined in a blind way to get on now. Fate had placed a snare in his hands, and he meant to set it. He tramped over the courtyard, then took the steps in a series of springs; having won the shelter of the portico he stood motionless, except for the flicker of his eyes. These sudden changes of pace were typical of the man, who always advanced as a skirmisher, was always "on the spot" as Clive had phrased it in the written testimonial; "during the five months A. Scudder was in my service I found him prompt and assiduous": qualities that he proposed to display now. When the victim drove up he became half cruel, half frightened. Gentlemen he knew, mates he knew; what class of creature was Mr Hall who said "Call me Maurice"?

Narrowing his eyes to slits, he stood as though waiting for orders outside the front porch at Penge.

Maurice approached the most dangerous day of his life without any plan at all, yet something kept rippling in his mind like muscles beneath a healthy skin. He was not supported by pride but he did feel fit, anxious to play the game, and, as an Englishman should, hoped that his opponent felt fit too. He wanted to be decent, he wasn't afraid. When he saw Alec's face glowing through the dirty air his own tingled slightly, and he determined not to strike until he was struck.

"Here you are," he said, raising a pair of gloves to his hat. "This rain's the limit. Let's have a talk inside."

"Where you wish."

Maurice looked at him with some friendliness, and they entered the building. As they did so, Alec raised his head and sneezed like a lion.

"Got a chill? It's the weather."

"What's all this place?" he asked.

"Old things belonging to the nation." They paused in the corridor of Roman emperors. "Yes, it's bad weather. There've only been two fine days. And one fine night," he added mischievously, surprising himself.

But Alec didn't catch on. It wasn't the opening he wanted. He was waiting for signs of fear, that the menial in him might strike. He pretended not to understand the allusion, and sneezed again. The roar echoed down vestibules, and his face, convulsed and distorted, took a sudden appearance of hunger.

"I'm glad you wrote to me the second time. I liked both your letters. I'm not offended—you've never done anything wrong. It's all your mistake about cricket and the rest. I'll tell you straight out I enjoyed being with you, if that's the trouble. Is it? I want you to tell me. I just don't know."

"What's here? *That's* no mistake." He touched his breast pocket, meaningly. "Your writing. And you and the squire —*that's* no mistake—some may wish as it was one."

"Don't drag in that," said Maurice, but without indignation, and it struck him as odd that he had none, and that even the Clive of Cambridge had lost sanctity.

"Mr Hall—you reckernize it wouldn't very well suit you if certain things came out, I suppose."

Maurice found himself trying to get underneath the words.

He continued, feeling his way to a grip. "What's more, I've always been a respectable young fellow until you called me into your room to amuse yourself. It don't hardly seem fair that a gentleman should drag you down. At least that's how my brother sees it." He faltered as he spoke these last words. "My brother's waiting outside now as a matter of fact. He wanted to come and speak to you hisself, he's been scolding me shocking, but I said, 'No Fred no, Mr Hall's a gentleman and can be trusted to behave like one, so you leave 'im to me,' I said, 'and Mr Durham, he's a gentleman too, always was and always will be.' "

"With regard to Mr Durham," said Maurice, feeling inclined to speak on this point: "It's quite correct that I cared for him and he for me once, but he changed, and now he doesn't care any more for me nor I for him. It's the end."

"End o' what?"

"Of our friendship."

"Mr Hall, have you heard what I was saying?"

"I hear everything you say," said Maurice thoughtfully, and continued in exactly the same tone: "Scudder, why do you think it's 'natural' to care both for women and men? You wrote so in your letter. It isn't natural for me. I have really got to think that 'natural' only means oneself."

The man seemed interested. "Couldn't you get a kid of your own, then?" he asked, roughening.

"I've been to two doctors about it. Neither were any good."

"So you can't?"

"No, I can't."

"Want one?" he asked, as if hostile.

"It's not much use wanting."

"I could marry tomorrow if I like," he bragged. While speaking, he caught sight of a winged Assyrian bull, and his expression altered into naïve wonder. "He's big enough, isn't he," he remarked. "They must have owned wonderful machinery to make a thing like that."

"I expect so," said Maurice, also impressed by the bull. "I couldn't tell you. Here seems to be another one."

"A pair, so to speak. Would these have been ornaments?"

"This one has five legs."

"So's mine. A curious idea." Standing each by his monster, they looked at each other, and smiled. Then his face hardened again and he said, "Won't do, Mr Hall. I see your game, but you don't fool me twice, and you'll do better to have a friendly talk with me rather than wait for Fred, I can tell you. You've had your fun and you've got to pay up." He looked handsome as he threatened—including the pupils of his eyes, which were evil. Maurice gazed into them gently but keenly. And nothing resulted from the outburst at all. It fell away like a flake of mud. Murmuring something about "leaving you to think this over", he sat down on a bench. Maurice joined him there shortly. And it was thus for nearly twenty minutes: they kept wandering from room to room as if in search of something. They would peer at a goddess or vase, then move at a single impulse, and their unison was the stranger because on the surface they were at war. Alec recommenced his hints—horrible, reptilian—but somehow they did not pollute the intervening silences, and Maurice failed to get afraid or angry, and only regretted that any human being should have got into such a mess. When he chose to reply their eyes met, and his smile was sometimes reflected on the lips of his foe. The belief grew that the actual situation was a blind—a practical joke almost—and concealed something real, that either desired. Serious and good-tempered, he continued to hold his own, and if he made no offensive it was because his blood wasn't warm. To set it moving, a shock from without was required, and chance administered this.

He was bending over a model of the Acropolis with his forehead a little wrinkled and his lips murmuring, "I see, I see, I see." A gentleman near overheard him, started, peered through strong spectacles, and said "Surely! I may forget faces but never a voice. Surely! You are one of our old boys." It was Mr Ducie.

Maurice did not reply. Alec sidled up closer to participate.

"Surely you were at Mr Abrahams' school. Now wait! Wait! Don't tell me your name. I want to remember it. I will remember it. You're not Sanday, you're not Gibbs. I know. I know. It's Wimbleby."

How like Mr Ducie to get the facts just wrong! To his own name Maurice would have responded, but he now had the inclination to lie; he was tired of their endless inaccuracy, he had suffered too much from it. He replied, "No, my name's Scudder." The correction flew out as the first that occurred to him. It lay ripe to be used, and as he uttered it he knew why. But at the instant of enlightenment Alec himself spoke. "It isn't," he said to Mr Ducie, "and I've a serious charge to bring against this gentleman."

"Yes, awfully serious," remarked Maurice, and rested his hand on Alec's shoulder, so that the fingers touched the back of the neck, doing this merely because he wished to do it, not for another reason.

Mr Ducie did not take notice. An unsuspicious man, he assumed some uncouth joke. The dark gentlemanly fellow couldn't be Wimbleby if he said he wasn't. He said, "I'm extremely sorry, sir, it's so seldom I make a mistake," and then, determined to show he was not an old fool, he addressed the silent pair on the subject of the British Museum—not merely a collection of relics but a place round which one could take—er—the less fortunate, quite so—a stimulating place—it raised questions even in the minds of boys—which one answered—no doubt inadequately; until a patient voice said, "Ben, we are waiting," and Mr Ducie rejoined his wife. As he did so Alec jerked away and muttered, "That's all right. . . . I won't trouble you now."

"Where are you going with your serious charge?" said Maurice, suddenly formidable.

"Couldn't say." He looked back, his colouring stood out against the heroes, perfect but bloodless, who had never known bewilderment or infamy. "Don't you worry—I'll never harm you now, you've too much pluck."

"Pluck be damned," said Maurice, with a plunge into anger.

"It'll all go no further—" He struck his own mouth. "I don't know what came over me, Mr Hall; *I* don't want to harm you, I never did."

"You blackmailed me."

"No, sir, no . . ."

"You did."

"Maurice, listen, I only . . ."

"Maurice am I?"

"You called me Alec. . . . I'm as good as you."

"I don't find you are!" There was a pause; before the storm; then he burst out: "By God, if you'd split on me to Mr Ducie, I'd have broken you. It might have cost me hundreds, but I've got them, and the police always back my sort against yours. You don't know. We'd have got you into quod, for blackmail, after which—I'd have blown out my brains."

"Killed yourself? Death?"

"I should have known by that time that I loved you. Too late ... everything's always too late." The rows of old statues tottered, and he heard himself add, "I don't mean anything, but come outside, we can't talk here." They left the enormous and overheated building, they passed the library, supposed catholic, seeking darkness and rain. On the portico Maurice stopped and said bitterly, "I forgot. Your brother?"

"He's down at father's—doesn't know a word—I was but threatening—"

"—for blackmail."

"Could you but understand..." He pulled out Maurice's note. "Take it if you like.... I don't want it ... never did.... I suppose this is the end."

Assuredly it wasn't that. Unable to part yet ignorant of what could next come, they strode raging through the last glimmering of the sordid day; night, ever one in her quality, came finally, and Maurice recovered his self-control and could look at the new material that passion had gained for him. In a deserted square, against railings that encircled some trees, they came to a halt, and he began to discuss their crisis.

But as he grew calm the other grew fierce. It was as if Mr Ducie had established some infuriating inequality between them, so that one struck as soon as his fellow tired of striking. Alec said savagely, "It rained harder than this in the boathouse, it was yet colder. Why did you not come?"

"Muddle."

"I beg your pardon?"

"You've to learn I'm always in a muddle. I didn't come or write because I wanted to get away from you without wanting. You won't understand. You kept dragging me back and I got awfully frightened. I felt you when I tried to get some sleep at the doctor's. You came hard at me. I knew something was evil but couldn't tell what, so kept pretending it was you."

"What was it?"

"The—situation."

"I don't follow this. Why did you not come to the boathouse?"

"My fear—and your trouble has been fear too. Ever since the cricket match you've let yourself get afraid of me. That's why we've been trying to down one another so and are still."

"I wouldn't take a penny from you, I wouldn't hurt your little finger," he growled, and rattled the bars that kept him from the trees.

"But you're still trying hard to hurt me in my mind."

"Why do you go and say you love me?"

"Why do you call me Maurice?"

"Oh let's give over talking. Here—" and he held out his hand. Maurice took it, and they knew at that moment the greatest triumph ordinary man can win. Physical love means reaction, being panic in essence, and Maurice saw now how natural it was that their primitive abandonment at Penge should have led to peril. They knew too little about each other—and too much. Hence fear. Hence cruelty. And he rejoiced because he had understood Alec's infamy through his own—glimpsing, not for the first time, the genius who hides in man's tormented soul. Not as a hero, but as a comrade, had he stood up to the bluster, and found childishness behind it, and behind that something else.

Presently the other spoke. Spasms of remorse and apology broke him; he was as one who throws off a poison. Then, gathering health, he began to tell his friend everything, no longer ashamed. He spoke of his relations.... He too was embedded in class. No one knew he was in London—Penge thought he was at his father's, his father at Penge—it had been difficult, very. Now he ought to go home—see his brother with whom he returned to the Argentine: his brother connected with trade, and his brother's wife; and he mingled some brag, as those whose education is not literary must. He came of a respectable family, he repeated, he bowed down to no man, not he, he was as good as any gentleman. But while he bragged his arm was gaining Maurice's. They deserved such a caress—the feeling was strange. Words died away, abruptly to recommence. It was Alec who ventured them.

"Stop with me."

Maurice swerved and their muscles clipped. By now they

were in love with one another consciously.

"Sleep the night with me. I know a place."

"I can't, I've an engagement," said Maurice, his heart beating violently. A formal dinner party awaited him of the sort that brought work to his firm and that he couldn't possibly cut. He had almost forgotten its existence. "I have to leave you now and get changed. But look here: Alec; be reasonable. Meet me another evening instead—any day."

"Can't come to London again—father or Mr Ayres will be passing remarks."

"What does it matter if they do?"

"What's your engagement matter?"

They were silent again. Then Maurice said in affectionate yet dejected tones, "All right. To Hell with it," and they passed on together in the rain.

XLIV

"Alec, wake up."

An arm twitched.

"Time we talked plans."

He snuggled closer, more awake than he pretended, warm, sinewy, happy. Happiness overwhelmed Maurice too. He moved, felt the answering grip, and forgot what he wanted to say. Light drifted in upon them from the outside world where it was still raining. A strange hotel, a casual refuge protected them from their enemies a little longer.

"Time to get up, boy. It's morning."

"Git up then."

"How can I the way you hold me!"

"Aren't yer a fidget, I'll learn you to fidget." He wasn't deferential any more. The British Museum had cured that. This was 'oliday, London with Maurice, all troubles over, and he wanted to drowse and waste time, and tease and make love.

Maurice wanted the same, what's pleasanter, but the oncoming future distracted him, the gathering light made cosiness unreal. Something had to be said and settled. O for the night that was ending, for the sleep and the wakefulness, the toughness and tenderness mixed, the sweet temper, the safety in darkness. Would such a night ever return?

"You all right, Maurice?"—for he had sighed. "You comfortable? Rest your head on me more, the way you like more . . . that's it more, and Don't You Worry. You're With Me. Don't Worry."

Yes, he was in luck, no doubt of it. Scudder had proved honest and kind. He was lovely to be with, a treasure, a charmer, a find in a thousand, the longed-for dream. But was he brave?

"Nice you and me like this ..." the lips so close now that it was scarcely speech. "Who'd have thought.... First time I ever seed you I thought, 'Wish I and that one ...' just like that ... 'wouldn't I and him ...' and it is so."

"Yes, and that's why we've got to fight."

"Who wants to fight?" He sounded annoyed. "There's bin enough fighting."

"All the world's against us. We've got to pull ourselves together and make plans, while we can."

"What d'you want to go and say a thing like that for, and spoil it all?"

"Because it has to be said. We can't allow things to go wrong and hurt us again the way they did down at Penge."

Alec suddenly scrubbed at him with the sun-roughened back of a hand and said, "That hurt, didn't it, or oughter. That's how *I* fight." It did hurt a little, and stealing into the foolery was a sort of resentment. "Don't talk to me about Penge," he went on. "Oo! Mah! Penge where I was always a servant and Scudder do this and Scudder do that and the old lady, what do you think she once said? She said, 'Oh would you most kindly of your goodness post this letter for me, what's your name?' What's yer name! Every day for six months I come up to Clive's bloody front porch door for orders, and his mother don't know my name. She's a bitch. I said to 'er, 'What's yer name? Fuck yer name.' I nearly did too. Wish I 'ad too. Maurice, you wouldn't believe how servants get spoken to. It's too shocking for words. That Archie London you're so set on is just as bad, and so are you, so are you. 'Haw my man' and all that. You've no idea how you nearly missed getting me. Near as nothing I never climbed that ladder when you called, he don't want me really, and I went flaming mad when you didn't turn up at the boathouse as I ordered. Too grand! We'll see. Boathouse was a place I always fancied. I'd go down for a smoke before I'd ever heard of you, unlock it easy, got the key on me still as a matter of fact ... boathouse, looking over the pond from the boathouse, very quiet, now and then a fish jump and cushions the way I arrange them."

He was silent, having chattered himself out. He had begun rough and gay and somehow factitious, then his voice had died away into sadness as though truth had risen to the surface of the water and was unbearable.

"We'll meet in your boathouse yet," Maurice said.

"No, we won't." He pushed him away, then heaved, pulled him close, put forth violence, and embraced as if the world was ending. "You'll remember that anyway." He got out and looked down out of the grayness, his arms hanging empty. It was as if he wished to be remembered thus. "I could easy have killed you."

"Or I you."

"Where's my clothes and that gone?" He seemed dazed. "It's so late. I h'aint got a razor even, I didn't reckon staying the night.... I ought—I got to catch a train at once or Fred'll be thinking things."

"Let him."

"My goodness if Fred seed you and me just now."

"Well, he didn't."

"Well, he might have—what I mean is, tomorrow's Thursday isn't it, Friday's the packing, Saturday the *Normannia* sails from Southampton, so it's goodbye to Old England."

"You mean that you and I shan't meet again after now."

"That's right. You've got it quite correct."

And if it wasn't still raining! Wet morning after yesterday's downpour, wet on the roofs and the Museum, at home and on the greenwood. Controlling himself and choosing his words very carefully, Maurice said, "This is just what I want to talk about. Why don't we arrange so as we do meet again?"

"How do you mean?"

"Why don't you stay on in England?"

Alec whizzed round, terrified. Half naked, he seemed also half human. "Stay?" he snarled. "Miss my boat, are you daft? Of all the bloody rubbish I ever heard. Ordering me about again, eh, you would."

"It's a chance in a thousand we've met, we'll never have the chance again and you know it. Stay with me. We love each other."

"I dessay, but that's no excuse to act silly. Stay with you and how and where? What'd your Ma say if she saw me all rough and ugly the way I am?"

"She never will see you. I shan't live at my home."

"Where will you live?"

"With you."

"Oh, will you? No thank you. My people wouldn't take to you one bit and I don't blame them. And how'd you run your job, I'd like to know?"

"I shall chuck it."

"Your job in the city what gives you your money and position? You can't chuck a job."

"You can when you mean to," said Maurice gently. "You can do anything once you know what it is." He gazed at the grayish light that was becoming yellowish. Nothing surprised him in this talk. What he could not conjecture was its outcome. "I shall get work with you," he brought out: the moment to announce this had now come.

"What work?"

"We'll find out."

"Find out and starve out."

"No. There'll be enough money to keep us while we have a look round. I'm not a fool, nor are you. We won't be starving. I've thought out that much, while I was awake in the night and you weren't."

There was a pause. Alec went on more politely: "Wouldn't work, Maurice. Ruin of us both, can't you see, you same as myself."

"I don't know. Might be. Mightn't. 'Class.' I don't know. I know what we do today. We clear out of here and get a decent breakfast and we go down to Penge or whatever you want and see that Fred of yours. You tell him you've changed your mind about emigrating and are taking a job with Mr Hall instead. I'll come with you. I don't care. I'll see anyone, face anything. If they want to guess, let them. I'm fed up. Tell Fred to cancel your ticket, I'll repay for it and that's our start of getting free. Then we'll do the next thing. It's a risk, so's everything else, and we'll only live once."

Alec laughed cynically and continued to dress. His manner resembled yesterday's, though he didn't blackmail. "Yours is the talk of someone who's never had to earn his living," he said. "You sort of trap me with I love you or whatever it is and then offer to spoil my career. Do you realize I've got a definite job awaiting me in the Argentine? Same as you've got here. Pity the *Normannia*'s leaving Saturday, still facts is facts isn't it, all my kit bought as well as my ticket and Fred and wife expecting me."

Maurice saw through the brassiness to the misery behind it, but this time what was the use of insight? No amount of insight would prevent the *Normannia* from sailing. He had lost. Suffering was certain for him, though it might soon end for Alec; when he got out to his new life he would forget his escapade with a gentleman and in time he would marry. Shrewd working-class youngster who knew where his interests lay, he had already crammed his graceful body into his hideous blue suit. His face stuck out of it red, his hands brown. He plastered his hair flat. "Well, I'm off," he said, and as if that wasn't enough said, "Pity we ever met really if you come to think of it."

"That's all right too," said Maurice, looking away from him as he unbolted the door.

"You paid for this room in advance, didn't you, so they won't stop me downstairs? I don't want no unpleasantness to finish with."

"That's all right too." He heard the door shut and he was alone. He waited for the beloved to return. Inevitable that wait. Then his eyes began to smart, and he knew from experience what was coming. Presently he could control himself. He got up and went out, did some telephoning and explanations, placated his mother, apologized to his host, got himself shaved and trimmed up, and attended the office as usual. Masses of work awaited him. Nothing had changed in his life. Nothing remained in it. He was back with his loneliness as it had been before Clive, as it was after Clive, and would now be for ever. He had failed, and that wasn't the saddest: he had seen Alec fail. In a way they were one person. Love had failed. Love was an emotion through which you occasionally enjoyed yourself. It could not do things.

XLV

When the Saturday came he went down to Southampton to see the *Normannia* off.

It was a fantastic decision, useless, undignified, risky, and he had not the least intention of going when he left home. But when he reached London the hunger that tormented him nightly came into the open and demanded its prey, he forgot everything except Alec's face and body, and took the only means of seeing them. He did not want to speak to his lover or to hear his voice or to touch him—all that part was over—only to recapture his image before it vanished for ever. Poor wretched Alec! Who could blame him, how could he have acted differently? But oh, the wretchedness it was causing them both.

He got down to the boat in a dream, and awoke there to a new sort of discomfort: Alec was nowhere in sight, the stewards were busy, and it was some time before they brought him to Mr Scudder, an unattractive middle-aged man, a tradesman, a cad—brother Fred: with him was a bearded elder—presumably the butcher from Osmington. Alec's main charm was the fresh colouring that surged against the cliff of his hair: Fred, facially the same, was sandy and foxlike, and greasiness had replaced the sun's caress. Fred thought highly of himself, as did Alec, but his was the conceit that comes with commercial success and despises manual labour. He did not like having a brother who had chanced to grow up rough, and he thought that Mr Hall, of whom he had never heard, was out to patronize. This made him insolent. "Licky's not aboard yet, but his kit is," he said. "Interested to see his kit?" The father said, "Plenty of time yet," and looked at his watch. The mother said with compressed lips, "He won't be late. When Licky says a thing Licky means it." Fred said, "He can be late if he likes. If I lose his company I can bear it, but he needn't expect me to help him again. What he's cost me..."

"This is where Alec belongs," Maurice reflected. "These people will make him happier than I could have." He filled a pipe with the tobacco that he had smoked for the last six years, and watched Romance wither. Alec was not a hero or god, but a man embedded in society like himself, for whom sea and woodland and the freshening breeze and the sun were preparing no apotheosis. They ought not to have spent that night together in the hotel. It had now raised hopes that were too high. They should have parted with that handshake in the rain.

A morbid fascination kept him among the Scudders, listening to their vulgarity, and tracing the gestures of his friend in theirs. He tried to be pleasant and ingratiate himself, and failed, for his self-confidence had gone. As he brooded a quiet voice said, "Good afternoon, Mr Hall." He could not reply. The surprise was too complete. It was Mr Borenius. And both of them remembered that initial silence of his, and his frightened gaze, and the quick movement with which he removed his pipe from his lips, as if smoking were forbidden by the clergy.

Mr Borenius introduced himself gently to the company; he had come to see his young parishioner off, since the distance was not great from Penge. They discussed which route Alec would arrive by—there seemed some uncertainty—and Maurice tried to slip off, for the situation had become equivocal. But Mr Borenius checked him. "Going on deck?" he inquired; "I too. I too." They returned to the air and sunlight; the shallows of Southampton Water stretched golden around them, edged by the New Forest. To Maurice the beauty of the evening seemed ominous of disaster.

"Now this is very kind of you," said the clergyman, beginning at once. He spoke as one social worker to another, but Maurice thought there was a veil over his voice. He tried to reply—two or three normal sentences would save him—but no words would come, and his underlip trembled like an unhappy boy's. "And the more kind because if I remember rightly you disapprove of young Scudder. You told me when we dined at Penge that he was 'a bit of a swine'—an expression that, as applied to a fellow creature, struck me. I could hardly believe my eyes when I saw you among his friends down here. Believe me, Mr Hall, he will value the attention though he may not appear to. Men like that are more impressionable than the outsider supposes. For good and for evil."

Maurice tried to stop him by saying, "Well ... what about you?"

"I? Why have *I* come? You will only laugh. I have come to bring him a letter of introduction to an Anglican priest at Buenos Aires in the hope that he will get confirmed after landing. Absurd, is it not? But being neither a hellenist nor an atheist I hold that conduct is dependent on faith, and that if a man is a 'bit of a swine' the cause is to be found in some misapprehension of God. Where there is heresy, immorality will sooner or later ensue. But you—how came you to know so precisely when his boat sailed?"

"It ... it was advertised." The trembling spread all over his body, and his clothes stuck to him. He seemed to be back at school, defenceless. He was certain that the rector had guessed, or rather that a wave of recognition had passed. A man of the world would have suspected nothing—Mr Ducie hadn't—but this man had a special sense, being spiritual, and could scent out invisible emotions. Asceticism and piety have their practical side. They can generate insight, as Maurice realized too late. He had assumed at Penge that a white-faced parson in a cassock could never have conceived of masculine love, but he knew now that there is no secret of humanity which, from a wrong angle, orthodoxy has not viewed, that religion is far more acute than science, and if it only added judgement to insight would be the greatest thing in the world. Destitute of the religious sense himself, he had never yet encountered it in another, and the shock was terrific. He feared and hated Mr Borenius, he wanted to kill him.

And Alec—when he arrived, he would be flung into the trap too; they were small people, who could take no risk—far smaller, for instance, than Clive and Anne—and Mr Borenius knew this, and would punish them by the only means in his power.

The voice continued; it had paused for a moment in case the victim chose to reply.

"Yes. To speak frankly, I am far from easy about young Scudder. When he left Penge last Tuesday to go to his parents as he told me, though he never reached them till Wednesday—I had a most unsatisfactory interview with him. He was hard. He resisted me. When I spoke of Confirmation he sneered. The fact being—I could not mention this to you if it weren't for your charitable interest in him—the fact being that he has been guilty of sensuality." There was a pause. "With women. In time, Mr Hall, one gets to recognize that sneer, that hardness, for fornication extends far beyond the actual deed. Were it a deed only, I for one would not hold it anathema. But when the nations went a whoring they invariably ended by denying God, I think, and until all sexual irregularities and not some of them are penal the Church will never reconquer England. I have reason to believe that he spent that missing night in London. But surely—that must be his train."

He went below, and Maurice, utterly to pieces, followed him. He heard voices, but did not understand them; one of them might have been Alec's for all it mattered to him. "This too has gone wrong" began flitting through his brain, like a bat that returns at twilight. He was back in the smoking-room at home with Clive, who said, "I don't love you any more; I'm sorry," and he felt that his life would revolve in cycles of a year, always to the same eclipse. "Like the sun ... it takes a year ..." He thought his grandfather was speaking to him; then the haze cleared, and it was

Alec's mother. "It's not like Licky," she gibbered, and vanished.

Like whom? Bells were ringing, a whistle blew. Maurice ran up on deck; his faculties had returned, and he could see with extraordinary distinctness the masses of men sorting themselves, those to stop in England, those to go, and he knew that Alec was stopping. The afternoon had broken into glory. White clouds sailed over the golden waters and woods. In the midst of the pageant Fred Scudder was raving because his unreliable brother had missed the last train, and the women were protesting while they were hustled up the gangways, and Mr Borenius and old Scudder were lamenting to the officials. How negligible they had all become, beside the beautiful weather and fresh air.

Maurice went ashore, drunk with excitement and happiness. He watched the steamer move, and suddenly she reminded him of the Viking's funeral that had thrilled him as a boy. The parallel was false, yet she was heroic, she was carrying away death. She warped out from the quay, Fred yapping, she swung into the channel to the sound of cheers, she was off at last, a sacrifice, a splendour, leaving smoke that thinned into the sunset, and ripples that died against the wooded shores. For a long time he gazed after her, then turned to England. His journey was nearly over. He was bound for his new home. He had brought out the man in Alec, and now it was Alec's turn to bring out the hero in him. He knew what the call was, and what his answer must be. They must live outside class, without relations or money; they must work and stick to each other till death. But England belonged to them. That, besides companionship, was their reward. Her air and sky were theirs, not the timorous millions' who own stuffy little boxes, but never their own souls.

He faced Mr Borenius, who had lost all grasp of events. Alec had completely routed him. Mr Borenius assumed that love between two men must be ignoble, and so could not interpret what had happened. He became an ordinary person at once, his irony vanished. In a straightforward and rather silly way he discussed what could have befallen young Scudder and then repaired to visit friends in Southampton. Maurice called after him "Mr Borenius do look at the sky—its gone all on fire", but the rector had no use for the sky when on fire, and disappeared.

In his excitement he felt that Alec was close to him. He wasn't, couldn't be, he was elsewhere in the splendour and had to be found, and without a moment's hesitation he set out for Boathouse, Penge. Those words had got into his blood, they were part of Alec's yearnings and blackmailings, and of his own promise in that last desperate embrace. They were all he had to go by. He left Southampton as he had come to it—instinctively—and he felt that not merely things wouldn't go wrong this time but that they daren't, and that the universe had been put in its place. A little local train did its duty, a gorgeous horizon still glowed, and inflamed cloudlets which flared when the main glory faded, and there was even enough light for him to walk up from the station at Penge through quiet fields.

He entered the estate at its lower end, through a gap in the hedge, and it struck him once more how derelict it was, how unfit to set standards or control the future. Night was approaching, a bird called, animals scuttled, he hurried on until he saw the pond glimmering, and black against it the trysting place, and heard the water sipping.

He was here, or almost here. Still confident, he lifted up his voice and called Alec.

There was no answer.

He called again.

Silence and the advancing night. He had miscalculated.

"Likely enough," he thought, and instantly took himself in hand. Whatever happened he must not collapse. He had done that enough over Clive, and to no effect, and to collapse in this graying wilderness might mean going mad. To be strong, to keep calm and to trust—they were still the one hope. But the sudden disappointment revealed to him how exhausted he was physically. He had been on the run ever since early morning, ravaged by every sort of emotion, and he was ready to drop. In a little while he would decide what next should be done, but now his head was splitting, every bit of him ached or was useless and he must rest.

The boathouse offered itself conveniently for that purpose. He went in and found his lover asleep. Alec lay upon piled up cushions, just visible in the last dying of the day. When he woke he did not seem excited or disturbed and fondled Maurice's arm between his hands before he spoke. "So you got the wire," he said.

"What wire?"

"The wire I sent off this morning to your house, telling you . . ." He yawned, "Excuse me, I'm a bit tired, one thing and another . . . telling you to come here without fail." And since Maurice did not speak, indeed could not, he added, "And now we shan't be parted no more, and that's finished."

XLVI

Dissatisfied with his printed appeal to the electors—it struck him as too patronizing for these times—Clive was trying to alter the proofs when Simcox announced, "Mr Hall." The hour was extremely late, and the night dark; all traces of a magnificent sunset had disappeared from the sky. He could see nothing from the porch though he heard abundant noises; his friend, who had refused to come in, was kicking up the gravel, and throwing pebbles against the shrubs and walls.

"Hullo Maurice, come in. Why this thusness?" He asked, a little annoyed, and not troubling to smile since his face was in shadow. "Good to see you back, hope you're better. Unluckily I'm a bit occupied, but the Russet Room's not. Come in and sleep here as before. So glad to see you."

"I've only a few minutes, Clive."

"Look here man, that's fantastic." He advanced into the darkness hospitably, still holding his proof sheets. "Anne'll be furious with me if you don't stay. It's awfully nice you turning up like this. Excuse me if I work at unimportancies for a bit now." Then he detected a core of blackness in the surrounding gloom, and, suddenly uneasy, exclaimed, "I hope nothing's wrong."

"Pretty well everything . . . what you'd call."

Now Clive put politics aside, for he knew that it must be the love affair, and he prepared to sympathize, though he wished the appeal had come when he was less busy. His sense of proportion supported him. He led the way to the deserted alley behind the laurels, where evening primroses gleamed, and embossed with faint yellow the walls of night. Here they would be most solitary. Feeling for a bench, he reclined full length on it, put his hands behind his head, and said, "I'm at your service, but my advice is sleep the night here, and consult Anne in the morning."

"I don't want your advice."

"Well, as you like of course there, but you've been so friendly in telling us about your hopes, and where a woman is in question I would always consult another woman, particularly where she has Anne's almost uncanny insight."

The blossoms opposite disappeared and reappeared, and again Clive felt that his friend, swaying to and fro in front of them, was essential night. A voice said, "It's miles worse for you than that; I'm in love with your gamekeeper"—a remark so unexpected and meaningless to him that he said "Mrs Ayres?" and sat up stupidly.

"No. Scudder."

"Look out," cried Clive, with a glance at darkness. Reassured, he said stiffly, "What a grotesque announcement."

"Most grotesque," the voice echoed, "but I felt after all I owe you I ought to come and tell you about Alec."

Clive had only grasped the minimum. He supposed "Scudder" was a *façon de parler*, as one might say "Ganymede", for intimacy with any social inferior was unthinkable to him. As it was, he felt depressed, and offended, for he had assumed Maurice was normal during the last fortnight, and so encouraged Anne's intimacy. "We did anything we could," he said, "and if you want to repay what you 'owe' us, as you call it, you won't dally with morbid thoughts. I'm so disappointed to hear you talk of yourself like that. You gave me to understand that the land through the looking-glass was behind you at last, when we thrashed out the subject that night in the Russet Room."

"When you brought yourself to kiss my hand," added Maurice, with deliberate bitterness.

"Don't allude to that," he flashed, not for the first and last time, and for a moment causing the outlaw to love him. Then he relapsed into intellectualism. "Maurice—oh, I'm more sorry for you than I can possibly say, and I do, do beg you to resist the return of this obsession. It'll leave you for good if you do. Occupation, fresh air, your friends. . . ."

"As I said before, I'm not here to get advice, nor to talk about thoughts and ideas either. I'm flesh and blood, if you'll condescend to such low things—"

"Yes, quite right; I'm a frightful theorist, I know."

"—and'll mention Alec by his name."

It recalled to both of them the situation of a year back, but it was Clive who winced at the example now. "If Alec is Scudder, he is in point of fact no longer in my service or even in England. He sailed for Buenos Aires this very day. Go on though. I'm reconciled to reopening the subject if I can be of the least help."

Maurice blew out his cheeks, and began picking the flowerets off a tall stalk. They vanished one after another, like candles that the night has extinguished. "I have shared with Alec," he said after deep thought.

"Shared what?"

"All I have. Which includes my body."

Clive sprang up with a whimper of disgust. He wanted to smite the monster, and flee, but he was civilized, and wanted it feebly. After all, they were Cambridge men . . . pillars of society both; he must not show violence. And he did not; he remained quiet and helpful to the very end. But his thin sour disapproval, his dogmatism, the stupidity of his heart, revolted Maurice, who could only have respected hatred.

"I put it offensively," he went on, " but I must make sure you understand. Alec slept with me in the Russet Room that night when you and Anne were away."

"Maurice—oh, good God!"

"Also in town. Also—" here he stopped.

Even in his nausea Clive turned to a generalization—it was part of the mental vagueness induced by his marriage. "But surely—the sole excuse for any relationship between men is that it remain purely platonic."

"I don't know. I've come to tell you what I did." Yes, that was the reason of his visit. It was the closing of a book that would never be read again, and better close such a book than leave it lying about to get dirtied. The volume of their past must be restored to its shelf, and here, here was the place, amid darkness and perishing flowers. He owed it to Alec also. He could suffer no mixing of the old in the new. All compromise was perilous, because furtive, and, having finished his confession, he must disappear from the world that had brought him up. "I must tell you too what he did," he went on, trying to keep down his joy. "He's sacrificed his career for my sake ... without a guarantee I'll give up anything for him ... and I shouldn't have earlier. ... I'm always slow at seeing. I don't know whether that's platonic of him or not, but it's what he did."

"How sacrifice?"

"I've just been to see him off—he wasn't there—"

"Scudder missed his boat?" cried the squire with indignation. "These people are impossible." Then he stopped, faced by the future. "Maurice, Maurice," he said with some tenderness. "Maurice, quo vadis? You're going mad. You've lost all sense of— May I ask whether you intend—'

"No, you may not ask," interrupted the other. "You belong to the past. I'll tell you everything up to this moment—not a word beyond."

"Maurice, Maurice, I care a little bit for you, you know, or I wouldn't stand what you have told me."

Maurice opened his hand. Luminous petals appeared in it. "You care for me a little bit, I do think," he admitted, "but I can't hang all my life on a little bit. You don't. You hang yours on Anne. You don't worry whether your relation with her is platonic or not, you only know it's big enough to hang a life on. I can't hang mine on to the five minutes you spare me from her and politics. You'll do anything for me except see me. That's been it for this whole year of Hell. You'll make me free of the house, and take endless bother to marry me off, because that puts me off your hands. You do care a little for me, I know"—for Clive had protested—"but nothing to speak of, and you don't love me. I was yours once till death if you'd cared to keep me, but I'm someone else's now—I can't hang about whining for ever—and he's mine in a way that shocks you, but why don't you stop being shocked, and attend to your own happiness?"

"Who taught you to talk like this?" Clive gasped.

"You, if anyone."

"I? It's appalling you should attribute such thoughts to me," pursued Clive. Had he corrupted an inferior's intellect? He could not realize that he and Maurice were alike descended from the Clive of two years ago, the one by respectability, the other by rebellion, nor that they must differentiate further. It was a cesspool, and one breath from it at the election would ruin him. But he must not shrink from his duty. He must rescue his old friend. A feeling of heroism stole over him; and he began to wonder how Scudder could be silenced and whether he would prove extortionate. It was too late to discuss ways and means now, so he invited Maurice to dine with him the following week in his club up in town.

A laugh answered. He had always liked his friend's laugh, and at such a moment the soft rumble of it reassured him: it suggested happiness and security. "That's right," he said, and went so far as to stretch his hand into a bush of laurels. "That's better than making me a long set speech, which convinces neither yourself nor me." His last words were "Next Wednesday, say at 7.45. Dinner-jacket's enough, as you know."

They were his last words, because Maurice had disappeared thereabouts, leaving no trace of his presence except a little pile of the petals of the evening primrose, which mourned from the ground like an expiring fire. To the end of his life Clive was not sure of the exact moment of departure, and with the approach of old age he grew uncertain whether the moment had yet occurred. The Blue Room would glimmer, ferns undulate. Out of some external Cambridge his friend began beckoning to him, clothed in the sun, and shaking out the scents and sounds of the May Term.

But at the time he was merely offended at a discourtesy, and compared it with similar lapses in the past. He did not realize that this was the end, without twilight or compromise, that he should never cross Maurice's track again, nor speak to those who had seen him. He waited for a little in the alley, then returned to the house, to correct his proofs and to devise some method of concealing the truth from Anne.

TERMINAL NOTE

Terminal note

In its original form, which it still almost retains, *Maurice* dates from 1913. It was the direct result of a visit to Edward Carpenter at Milthorpe. Carpenter had a prestige which cannot be understood today. He was a rebel appropriate to his age. He was sentimental and a little sacramental, for he had begun life as a clergyman. He was a socialist who ignored industrialism and a simple-lifer with an independent income and a Whitmannic poet whose nobility exceeded his strength and, finally, he was a believer in the Love of Comrades, whom he sometimes called Uranians. It was this last aspect of him that attracted me in my loneliness. For a short time he seemed to hold the key to every trouble. I approached him through Lowes Dickinson, and as one approaches a saviour.

It must have been on my second or third visit to the shrine that the spark was kindled and he and his comrade George Merrill combined to make a profound impression on me and to touch a creative spring. George Merrill also touched my backside—gently and just above the buttocks. I believe he touched most people's. The sensation was unusual and I still remember it, as I remember the position of a long vanished tooth. It was as much psychological as physical. It seemed to go straight through the small of my back into my ideas, without involving my thoughts. If it really did this, it would have acted in strict accordance with Carpenter's yogified mysticism, and would prove that at that precise moment I had conceived.

I then returned to Harrogate, where my mother was taking a cure, and immediately began to write *Maurice*. No other of my books has started off in this way. The general plan, the three characters, the happy ending for two of them, all rushed into my pen. And the whole thing went through without a hitch. It was finished in 1914. The friends, men and women, to whom I showed it liked it. But they were carefully picked. It has not so far had to face the critics or the public, and I have myself been too much involved in it, and for too long, to judge.

A happy ending was imperative. I shouldn't have bothered to write otherwise. I was determined that in fiction anyway two men should fall in love and remain in it for the ever and ever that fiction allows, and in this sense Maurice and Alec still roam the greenwood. I dedicated it "To a Happier Year" and not altogether vainly. Happiness is its keynote—which by the way has had an unexpected result: it has made the book more difficult to publish. Unless the Wolfenden Report becomes law, it will probably have to remain in manuscript. If it ended unhappily, with a lad dangling from a noose or with a suicide pact, all would be well, for there is no pornography or seduction of minors. But the lovers get away unpunished and consequently recommend crime. Mr Borenius is too incompetent to catch them, and the only penalty society exacts is an exile they gladly embrace.

Notes on the three men

In Maurice I tried to create a character who was completely unlike myself or what I supposed myself to be: someone handsome, healthy, bodily attractive, mentally torpid, not a bad business man and rather a snob. Into this mixture I dropped an ingredient that puzzles him, wakes him up, torments him and finally saves him. His surroundings exasperate him by their very normality: mother, two sisters, a comfortable home, a respectable job gradually turn out to be Hell; he must either smash them or be smashed, there is no third course. The working out of such a character, the setting of traps for him which he sometimes eluded, sometimes fell into, and finally did smash, proved a welcome task.

If Maurice is Suburbia, Clive is Cambridge. Knowing

the university, or one corner of it, pretty well, I produced him without difficulty and got some initial hints for him from a slight academic acquaintance. The calm, the superiority of outlook, the clarity and the intelligence, the assured moral standards, the blondness and delicacy that did not mean frailty, the blend of lawyer and squire, all lay in the direction of that acquaintance, though it was I who gave Clive his "hellenic" temperament and flung him into Maurice's affectionate arms. Once there, he took charge, he laid down the lines on which the unusual relationship should proceed. He believed in platonic restraint and induced Maurice to acquiesce, which does not seem to me at all unlikely. Maurice at this stage is humble and inexperienced and adoring, he is the soul released from prison, and if asked by his deliverer to remain chaste he obeys. Consequently the relationship lasts for three years—precarious, idealistic and peculiarly English: what Italian boy would have put up with it?—still it lasts until Clive ends it by turning to women and sending Maurice back to prison. Henceforward Clive deteriorates, and so perhaps does my treatment of him. He has annoyed me. I may nag at him over much, stress his aridity and political pretensions and the thinning of his hair, nothing he or his wife or his mother does is ever right. This works well enough for Maurice, for it accelerates his descent into Hell and toughens him there for the final reckless climb. But it may be unfair on Clive who intends no evil and who feels the last flick of my whip in the final chapter, when he discovers that his old Cambridge friend has relapsed inside Penge itself, and with a gamekeeper.

Alec starts as an emanation from Milthorpe, he is the touch on the backside. But he has no further connection with the methodical George Merrill and in many ways he is a premonition. As I worked at him, I got to know him better, partly through personal experiences, and some of them were useful. He became less of a comrade and more of a person, he became livelier and heavier and demanded more room, and the additions to the novel (there were scarcely any cancellations in it) are all due to him. Not much can be premised about him. He is senior in date to the prickly gamekeepers of D. H. Lawrence, and had not the advantage of their disquisitions, nor, though he might have met my own Stephen Wonham, would they have had more in common than a mug of beer. What was his life before Maurice arrived? Clive's earlier life is easily recalled, but Alec's, when I tried to evoke it, turned into a survey and had to be scrapped. He certainly objected to nothing—one knows that much. No more, once they met, did Maurice, and Lytton Strachey, an early reader, thought this would prove their undoing. He wrote me a delightful and disquieting letter and said that the relationship of the two rested upon curiosity and lust and would only last six weeks. Shades of Edward Carpenter!—whose name Lytton always greeted with a series of little squeaks. Carpenter believed that Uranians remained loyal to each other for ever. And in my experience though loyalty cannot be counted on it can always be hoped for and be worked towards and may flourish in the most unlikely soil. Both the suburban youth and the countrified one are capable of loyalty. Risley, the clever Trinity undergraduate, wasn't, and Risley, as Lytton gleefully detected, was based upon Lytton.

The later additions to the novel necessitated by Alec are two, or rather they fall into two groups.

In the first place he has to be led up to. He must loom upon the reader gradually. He has to be developed from the masculine blur past which Maurice drives into Penge, through the croucher beside the piano and the rejecter of a tip and the haunter of shrubberies and the stealer of apricots into the sharer who gives and takes love. He must loom out of nothing until he is everything. This requires careful handling. If the reader knows too much of what's coming he may be bored. If he knows too little he may be puzzled. Take the half-dozen sentences the two exchange in the dark garden when Mr Borenius has left them and avowal begins to hover. These sentences can reveal less or more, according to the way they are drafted. Have I drafted them appropriately? Or take Alec, when he hears the wild lone cry on his rounds: should he respond at once or—as I have finally decided—should he hesitate until it is repeated? The art called for in these problems is not of a high order, not as high as Henry James thinks, still it has to be employed if the final embrace is to be felt.

In the second place Alec has to be led down from. He has taken a risk and they have loved. What guarantee is there that such love will last? None. So their characters, their attitudes towards each other, the tests through which they are put must suggest that it may last, and the final section of the book had to be much longer than originally planned. The British Museum chapter had to be extended and a whole new chapter inserted after it—the chapter of their passionate and distracted second night, where Maurice comes further into the open and Alec daren't. In the original draft I had only implied all this. Similarly, after Southampton, when Alec too had risked all, I hadn't brought them to their final reunion. All this had to be written out, so that they might be ascribed the fullest possible knowledge of each other. Not until some dangers and some threats had been surmounted could the curtain prepare to fall.

The chapter after their reunion, where Maurice ticks off Clive, is the only possible end to the book. I did not always think so, nor did others, and I was encouraged to write an epilogue. It took the form of Kitty encountering two woodcutters some years later and gave universal dissatisfaction. Epilogues are for Tolstoy. Mine partly failed because the novel's action-date is about 1912, and "some years later" would plunge it into the transformed England of the First World War.

The book certainly dates and a friend has recently remarked that for readers today it can only have a period interest. I wouldn't go as far as that, but it certainly dates—

not only because of its endless anachronisms—its half-sovereign tips, pianola-records, norfolk jackets, Police Court News, Hague Conferences, Libs and Rads and Terriers, uninformed doctors and undergraduates walking arm in arm, but for a more vital reason: it belongs to an England where it was still possible to get lost. It belongs to the last moment of the greenwood. *The Longest Journey* belongs there too, and has similarities of atmosphere. Our greenwood ended catastrophically and inevitably. Two great wars demanded and bequeathed regimentation which the public services adopted and extended, science lent her aid, and the wildness of our island, never extensive, was stamped upon and built over and patrolled in no time. There is no forest or fell to escape to today, no cave in which to curl up, no deserted valley for those who wish neither to reform nor corrupt society but to be left alone. People do still escape, one can see them any night at it in the films. But they are gangsters not outlaws, they can dodge civilization because they are part of it.

September 1960